"Space operas are galaxy-spanning tales of battling star-ships, exploding planets . . . and questions on the nature of good and evil and the evolution of man. Making co-herent stories from this material is a rare talent. . . . PETER HAMILTON HAS JOINED THIS RARE BREED IN A BIG WAY."

—*Denver Post*

"A SPACE OPERA THAT IS BIG, BOISTEROUS, AND HAS SOMETHING FOR EVERYONE. . . . Hamilton's universe will not fit into a single volume. There are just too many heroes to love, villains to hate, and worlds to explore. . . . His imagination knows no bounds!"

—*Science Fiction Weekly*

"HAMILTON'S WORK ENCOMPASSES A BROAD SWEEP OF PHILOSOPHICAL AND MORALISTIC THEMES. . . . The depth and clarity of the future Hamilton envisions is as complex and involving as they come."

—*Publishers Weekly* (starred review)

"HAMILTON HAS CRAFTED HIS FUTURE HISTORY WITH GREAT CARE . . . A SOON-TO-BE CLASSIC SCIENCE FICTION MILIEU."

—*SF Site*

ALSO BY PETER F. HAMILTON

THE NIGHT'S DAWN TRILOGY

THE REALITY DYSFUNCTION
PART 1: EMERGENCE

THE REALITY DYSFUNCTION
PART 2: EXPANSION

THE NEUTRONIUM ALCHEMIST
PART 1: CONSOLIDATION

THE NEUTRONIUM ALCHEMIST
PART 2: CONFLICT

PETER F. HAMILTON

THE
NAKED GOD

PART 1: FLIGHT

ASPECT®

WARNER BOOKS

A Time Warner Company

WARNER BOOKS EDITION

Copyright © 2000 by Peter F. Hamilton
All rights reserved. No part of this book may be reproduced in any form or by any electronic or mechanical means, including information storage and retrieval systems, without permission in writing from the publisher, except by a reviewer who may quote brief passages in a review.

Cover design by Don Puckey/Carol Russo
Cover illustration by Jim Burns

Aspect® name and logo are registered trademarks of Warner Books, Inc.

Warner Books, Inc.,
1271 Avenue of the Americas,
New York, NY 10020

Visit our Web site at
www.twbookmark.com

 A Time Warner Company

Printed in the United States of America

Originally published in hardcover by Warner Books.
First Paperback Printing: November 2000

10 9 8 7 6 5 4 3 2 1

FINALLY, SOME WELL-DESERVED ACKNOWLEDGMENTS

The NIGHT'S DAWN trilogy took me six and a half years to write, during which I was given support, drinks, love, parties, bad jokes, sympathy, friendship, and exotic e-mails by the following:

> John F. Hamilton
> Kate Fell
> Simon Spanton-Walker
> Jane Spanton-Walker
> Kate Farquhar-Tompson
> Christine Manby
> Antony Harwood
> Carys Thomas
> James Lovegrove
> Lou Pitman
> Peter Lavery
> Betsy Mitchell
> Jim Burns
> Dave Garnett
> Jane Adams
> Graham Joyce

Thanks, chaps.
Peter F. Hamilton
Rutland, April 1999

PRINCIPAL CHARACTERS

SHIPS

LADY MACBETH

Joshua Calvert	Captain
Liol Calvert	Fusion specialist
Ashly Hanson	Pilot
Sarha Mitcham	Systems specialist
Dahybi Yadev	Node specialist
Beaulieu	Cosmonik
Peter Adul	Mission specialist
Alkad Mzu	Mission specialist
Oski Katsura	Mission specialist
Samuel	Edenist Intelligence agent

OENONE

Syrinx	Captain
Ruben	Fusion systems
Oxley	Pilot
Cacus	Life support
Edwin	Toroid systems
Serina	Toroid systems
Tyla	Cargo officer
Kempster Getchell	Mission specialist
Renato Vella	Mission specialist
Parker Higgens	Mission specialist
Monica Foulkes	ESA agent

VILLENEUVE'S REVENGE

André Duchamp	Captain
Kingsley Pryor	Capone's agent

Murphy Hewlett ....Confederation marine lieutenant
Amr al-Sahhaf.....................................Captain, staff officer

MONTEREY
Jezzibella...Mood Fantasy artist
Al Capone...Possessor
Kiera Salter..........................Possessor of Marie Skibbow
Leroy Octavius...................................Jezzibella's manager
Libby.....................Jezzibella's dermal technologist
Avram Harwood III.........................Mayor of San Angeles
Emmet Mordden............................Organization lieutenant
Silvano Richmann ....Organization lieutenant
Mickey Pileggi...............................Organization lieutenant
Patricia Mangano.........................Organization lieutenant
Webster Pryor...Hostage
Luigi Balsamo..............ex-Commander, Organization fleet
Cameron Leung ....Hellhawk Zahan
Bernhard Allsop...Possessor
Hudson Proctor........................Possessor, Kiera's deputy
Soi Yin..Hellhawk
Etchells.......................................Hellhawk Stryla

PLANETS

NORFOLK
Luca Comar............................Grant Kavanagh's possessor
Susannah ....Marjorie Kavanagh's possessor
Carmitha ....Romany
Bruce Spanton ....Marauder
Johan ....Mr Butterworth's possessor
Marcella Rye.........................Colsterworth council officer
Véronique ....Olive Fenchurch's possessor

OMBEY
Ralph Hiltch...............................General, Liberation army

Haile .... Jupiter's Kiint
Nang .... Haile's parent
Lieria .... Haile's parent

EARTH

Louise Kavanagh .... Ralfugee
Genevieve Kavanagh .... Refugee
Fletcher Christian .... Possessor
Quinn Dexter .... Messiah of the Light Bringer
Banneth .... High Magus, Edmonton sect
Andy Behoo .... Seller
Ivanov Robson .... Private detective
Brent Roi .... Detective, Halo Police
Courtney .... Edmonton sect activist
Billy-Joe .... Edmonton sect acolyte

OTHERS

CONFEDERATION

Olton Haaker .... Assembly President
Jeeta Anwar .... Chief presidential aide
Mae Ortlieb .... Presidential science aide
Cayeaux .... Edenist ambassador
Sir Maurice Hall .... Kulu Kingdom ambassador

ENDISTS

Wing-Tsit Chong .... Edenist's Founder
Athene .... Syrinx's mother

MOSDVA

Quantook-LOU .... Distributor of resources

TYRATHCA

Barham-PWM .... Breeder electronics regulator

THE
NAKED GOD

PART 1: FLIGHT

1

Jay Hilton was sound asleep when every electrophorescent strip in the paediatric ward sprang up to full intensity. The simple dream of her mother broke apart like a stained-glass statue shattered by a powerful gust of sharp white light; colourful splinters tumbling off into the glare.

Jay blinked heavily against the rush of light, raising her head in confusion. The familiar scenery of the ward hardened around her. She felt so tired. It certainly wasn't morning yet. A huge yawn forced her mouth open. All around her the other children were waking up in bleary-eyed mystification. Holo-morph stickers began reacting to the light, translucent cartoon images rising up to perform their mischievous antics. Animatic dolls cooed sympathetically as children clutched at them for reassurance. Then the doors at the far end of the ward slid open, and the nurses came hurrying in.

One look at the brittle smiles on their faces was all Jay needed. Something was badly wrong. Her heart shivered. Surely not the possessed? Not here?

The nurses began ushering children out of their beds, and along the central aisle towards the doors. Complaints and questions were firmly ignored.

"It's a fire drill," the senior staff nurse called out. "Come along, quickly, now. I want you out of here and into the lifts. Pronto. Pronto." He clapped his hands loudly.

Jay shoved the thin duvet back, and scuttled down off the bed. Her long cotton nightie was tangled round her knees, which took a moment to straighten. She was about to join the others charging along the aisle when she caught the flickers of motion and light outside the window. Every morning since she'd arrived, Jay had sat in front of that window, gazing solemnly out at Mirchusko and its giddy green cloudscape. She'd never seen speckles of light swarming out there before.

Danger.

The silent mental word was spoken so quickly Jay almost didn't catch it. Though the feel of Haile was unmistakable. She looked round, expecting to see the Kiint ambling down the aisle towards her. But there was only the rank of flustered nurses propelling children along.

Knowing full well she wasn't doing what she was supposed to, Jay padded over to the big window, and pressed her nose against it. A slim band of tiny blue-white stars had looped itself round Tranquillity. They were all moving, contracting around the habitat. She could see now that they weren't really stars, they were lengthening. Flames. Brilliant, tiny flames. Hundreds of them.

My friend. My friend. Lifeloss anguish.

Now that was definitely Haile, and intimating plenty of distress. Jay took a step back from the window, seeing misty grey swirls where her face and hands had pressed against it. "What's the matter?" she asked the empty air.

A cascade of new flames burst into existence outside the habitat. Expanding knots blossoming seemingly at random across space. Jay gasped at the sight. There were thousands of them, interlacing and expanding. It was so pretty.

Friend. Friend.

Evacuation procedure initiated.

Jay frowned. The second mental voice came as a faint echo. She thought it was one of the adult Kiint, possibly Lieria. Jay had only encountered Haile's parents a few times. They were awfully intimidating, though they'd been nice enough to her.

Designation. Two.

No. The adult responded forcefully. **Forbidden.**

Designation.

You may not, child. Sorrow felt for all human suffering. But obedience required.

No. Friend. My friend. Designation. Two. Confirmed.

Jay had never felt Haile so determined before. It was kind of scary. "Please?" she asked nervously. "What's happening?"

A torrent of light burst through the window. It was as if a sun had risen over Mirchusko's horizon. All of space was alive with brilliant efflorescences.

The adult Kiint said: **Evacuation enacted.**

Designated.

Jay felt a wash of guilty triumph rushing out from her friend. She wanted to reach out and comfort Haile, who she knew from the adult's reaction was in Big Trouble over something. Instead, she concentrated on forming a beaming smile at the heart of her own mind, hoping Haile would pick it up. Then the air around her was crawling as if she was caught in a breeze.

"Jay!" one of the nurses called. "Come along sweetie, you . . ."

The light around Jay was fading fast, along with the sounds of the ward. She could just hear the nurse's gasp of astonishment. The breeze abruptly turned into a small gale, whipping her nightie around and making her bristly hair stand on end. Some kind of grey fog was forming around her, a perfectly spherical bubble of the stuff, with her at the centre. Except she couldn't feel any dampness in the air. It darkened rapidly, reducing the ward to weak spectral outlines. Then the boundary expanded at a speed so frightening that Jay screamed. The boundary vanished, and with it any sign of the ward. She was alone in space devoid of stars. And falling.

Jay put her hands to her head and screamed again, as hard as she possibly could. It didn't put a stop to any of the horror. She paused to suck down a huge breath. That was when the boundary reappeared out on the edge of nowhere. Hurtling towards her so fast from every direction that she knew the impact would squash her flat. She jammed her eyes shut. "MUMMY!"

Something like a stiff feather tickled the soles of her feet, and she was abruptly standing on solid ground. Jay windmilled her arms for balance, pitching forward. She landed hard on some kind of cool floor, her eyes still tight shut. The air she gulped down was warmer than it had been in the ward, and a lot more humid. Funny smell. Rosy light was playing over her eyelids.

Still crouched on all fours, Jay risked a quick peep as she gathered herself to scream again. The sight which greeted her was so incredible that the breath stalled in her throat. "Oh gosh," was all she eventually managed to squeak.

Joshua initiated the ZTT jump with little enthusiasm. His downcast mood was one which he shared with all the *Lady Mac*'s crew and passengers—at least, those who weren't in zero-tau. To have achieved so much, only to have their final triumph snatched away.

Except . . . Once the initial shock of discovering that Tranquillity had vanished from its orbit had subsided, he wasn't frightened. Not for Ione, or his child. Tranquillity hadn't been destroyed, there was at least that comfort. Which logically meant the habitat had been possessed and snatched out of the universe.

He didn't believe it.

But his intuition was hardly infallible. Perhaps he simply didn't want to believe it. Tranquillity was home. The emotional investment he had in the habitat and its precious contents was enormous. Tell anyone that everything they ever treasured has been erased, and the reaction is always the same. Whatever. His vacillation made him as miserable as the rest of the ship, just for a different reason.

"Jump confirmed," he said. "Samuel, you're on."

Lady Mac had jumped into one of Trafalgar's designated emergence zones, a hundred thousand kilometres above Avon. Her transponder was already blaring out her flight authority codes. Somehow Joshua didn't think that would quite be enough. Not when you barged in unexpected on the Confederation's primary military base in the middle of a crisis like this one.

"I've got distortion fields focusing on us," Dahybi said drolly. "Five of them, I think."

The flight computer alerted Joshua that targeting radars were locking on to the hull. When he accessed the sensors rising out of their recesses, he found three voidhawks and two frigates on interception courses. Trafalgar's strategic defence command was directing a barrage of questions at him. He glanced over at the Edenist as he started to datavise a response. Samuel was lying prone on his acceleration couch, eyes closed as he conversed with other Edenists in the asteroid.

Sarha grinned round phlegmatically. "How many medals do you think they'll give us apiece?"

"Uh oh," Liol grunted. "However many it is, we might be getting them posthumously. I think one of the frigates has just realised our antimatter drive is ever so slightly highly radioactive."

"Great," she grumbled.

Monica Foulkes didn't like the sound of that; as far as the Confederation Navy was aware, it was only Organization ships who were using antimatter. She hadn't wanted to take Mzu back to Tranquillity, and she certainly hadn't wanted to wind up at Trafalgar. But in the discussion which followed their discovery of Tranquillity's disappearance, she didn't exactly have the casting vote. The original agreement between herself and Samuel had just about disintegrated when they rendezvoused with the *Beezling*.

Then Calvert had insisted on the First Admiral being the final arbitrator of what was to be done with Mzu, Adul, and himself. Samuel had agreed. And she couldn't produce any rational argument against it. Silently, she acknowledged that maybe the only true defence against more Alchemists being built was a unified embargo covenant between the major powers. After all, such an agreement almost worked for antimatter.

Not that such angst counted for much right now. Like ninety per cent of her mission to date, the critical deciding factor was outside her control. All she could do was stick close to Mzu, and make sure the prime requirement of technology transfer wasn't violated. Though by allowing it to be deployed against the Organization, she'd probably screwed that up too. Her debrief was shaping up to be a bitch.

Monica frowned over at Samuel, who was still silent, his brow creased up in concentration. She added a little prayer of her own to all the unheard babble of communication whirling around *Lady Mac* for the Navy to exercise some enlightenment and tolerance.

Trafalgar's strategic defence command told Joshua to

old his altitude, but refused to grant any approach vector until his status was established. The Navy's emergence zone patrol ships approached to within a cautious hundred kilometres, and took up a three-dimensional diamond observation formation. Targeting radars remained locked on.

Admiral Lalwani herself talked to Samuel, unable to restrain her incredulity as he explained what had happened. Given that the *Lady Macbeth* contained not only Mzu and others who understood the Alchemist's principals, but a quantity of antimatter as well, the final decision on allowing the ship to dock belonged to the First Admiral himself. It took twenty minutes to arrive, but Joshua eventually received a flight vector from strategic defence command. They were allocated a docking bay in the asteroid's northern spaceport.

"And Joshua," Samuel said earnestly. "Don't deviate from it. Please."

Joshua winked, knowing it was being seen by the hundreds of Edenists who were borrowing the agent's eyes to monitor *Lady Mac*'s bridge. "What, Lagrange Calvert, fly off line?"

The flight to Trafalgar took eighty minutes. The number of antimatter technology specialists waiting for them in the docking bay was almost as great as the number of marines. On top of that were a large complement of uniformed CNIS officers.

They weren't stormed, exactly. No personal weapons were actually taken out of their holsters. Though once the airlock tube was sealed and pressurized, *Lady Mac*'s crew had little to do except hand over the powerdown codes to a Navy maintenance team. Zero-tau pods were opened, and the various bewildered occupants Joshua had accumulated during his pursuit of the Alchemist were ushered off the ship. After a *very* thorough body scan, the polite, steel-

faced CNIS officers escorted everyone to a secure barrac▌
deep inside the asteroid. Joshua wound up in a suite th▌
would have done a four-star hotel credit. Ashly and Li▌
were sharing it with him.

"Well now," Liol said as the door closed behind the▌
"Guilty of carrying antimatter, flung in prison by secret p▌
lice who've never heard of civil rights, and after we'▌
dead, Al Capone is going to invite us to have a quiet word▌
He opened the cherrywood cocktail bar and smiled at th▌
impressive selection of bottles inside. "It can't get ar
worse."

"You forgot Tranquillity being vanquished," Ash▌
chided. Liol waved a bottle in apology.

Joshua slumped down into a soft black leather chair i▌
the middle of the lounge. "It might not get worse for yo▌
Just remember, I know what the Alchemist does, and hov▌
They can't afford to let me go."

"You might know what it does," Ashly said. "But wi▌
respect, Captain, I don't think you would be much help t
anyone seeking the technical details necessary to constru▌
another."

"One hint is all it takes," Joshua muttered. "One carele▌
comment that'll point researchers in the right direction."

"Stop worrying, Josh. The Confederation passed th▌
point a long time ago. Besides, the Navy owes us big-tim▌
and the Edenists, and the Kulu Kingdom. We pulled the▌
arses out of the fire. You'll fly *Lady Mac* again."

"Know what I'd do if I was the First Admiral? Put m▌
into a zero-tau pod for the rest of time."

"I won't let them do that to my little brother."

Joshua put his hands behind his head, and smiled up ▌
Liol. "The second thing I'd do, would be to put you in th▌
pod next to mine."

*

Planets sparkled in the twilight sky. Jay could see at least fifteen of them strung out along a curving line. The nearest one appeared a bit smaller than Earth's moon. She thought that was just because it was a long way off. In every other respect it was similar to any of the Confederation's terra-compatible planets, with deep blue oceans and emerald continents, the whole globe wrapped in thick tatters of white cloud. The only difference was the lights; cities larger than some of Earth's old nations gleamed with magisterial splendour. Entire weather patterns of cloud smeared across the nightside diffused the urban radiance, soaking the oceans in a perpetual pearl gloaming.

Jay sat back on her heels, staring up delightedly at the magical sky. A high wall ringed the area she was in. She guessed that the line of planets extended beyond those she could see, but the wall blocked her view of the horizon. A star with a necklace of inhabited planets! Thousands would be needed to make up such a circle. None of Jay's didactic memories about solar systems mentioned one with so many planets, not even if you counted gas-giant moons.

Friend Jay. Safe. Gleefulness at survival.

Jay blinked, and lowered her gaze. Haile was trying to run towards her. As always when the baby Kiint got over-excited her legs lost most of their coordination. She came very close to tripping with every other step. The sight of her lolloping about chaotically made Jay smile. It faded as she began to take in the scene behind her friend.

She was in some kind of circular arena two hundred metres across, with an ebony marble-like floor. The wall surrounding it was thirty metres high, sealed with a transparent dome. There were horizontal gashes at regular intervals along the vertical surface, windows into brightly lit rooms that seemed to be furnished with large cubes of primary colours. Adult Kiint were moving round inside, although an awful lot of them had stopped what they were doing to look directly at her.

Haile thundered up; half-formed tractamorphic tentacles waving round excitedly. Jay grabbed on to a couple of them, feeling them palpitate wildly inside her fingers.

"Haile! Was that you who did this?"

Two adult Kiint were walking across the arena floor towards her. Jay recognized them as Nang and Lieria. Beyond them, a black star erupted out of thin air. In less than a heartbeat it had expanded to a sphere fifteen metres in diameter, its lower quarter merging with the floor. The surface immediately dissolved to reveal another adult Kiint. Jay stared at the process in fascination. A ZTT jump, but without a starship. She focused hard on her primer-level didactic memory of the Kiint.

I did, Haile confessed. Her tractamorphic flesh writhed in agitation, so Jay just squeezed tighter, offering reassurance. **Only us were designated to evacuate the all around at lifeloss moment. I included you in designation, against parental proscription. Much shame. Puzzlement.** Haile turned her head to face her parents. **Query lifeloss act approval? Many nice friends in the all around.**

We do not approve.

Jay flicked a nervous gaze at the two adults, and pressed herself closer against Haile. Nang formshifted his tractamorphic appendage into a flat tentacle, which he laid across his daughter's back. The juvenile Kiint visibly calmed at the gesture of affection. Jay thought there was a mental exchange of some kind involved, too, sensing a hint of compassion and serenity.

Why did we not help? Haile asked.

We must never interfere in the primary events of other species during their evolution towards Omega comprehension. You must learn and obey this law

above all else. However, it does not prevent us from grieving at their tragedy.

Jay felt the last bit was included for her benefit. "Don't be angry with Haile," she said solemnly. "I would have done the same for her. And I didn't want to die."

Lieria reached out a tentacle tip, and touched Jay's shoulder. **I thank you for the friendship you have shown Haile. In our hearts we are glad you are with us, for you will be completely safe here. I am sorry we could not do more for your friends. But our law cannot be broken.**

A sudden sensation of bleak horror threatened to engulf Jay. "Did Tranquillity really get blown up?" she wailed.

We do not know. It was under a concerted attack when we left. However, Ione Saldana may have surrendered. There is a high possibility the habitat and its population survived.

"We left," Jay whispered wondrously to herself. There were eight adult Kiint standing on the arena floor now, all the researchers from Tranquillity's Laymil project. "Where are we?" She glanced up at the dusky sky again, and that awesome constellation.

This is our home star system. You are the first true human to visit.

"But . . ." Flashes of didactic memory tumbled through her brain. She looked up at those enticing, bright planets again. "This isn't Jobis."

Nang and Lieria looked at each other in what was almost an awkward pause.

No, Jobis is just one of our science mission outposts. It is not in this galaxy.

Jay burst into tears.

Right from the start of the possession crisis the Jovian Consensus had acknowledged that it was a prime target. Its colossal industrial facilities were inevitably destined to produce a torrent of munitions, bolstering the reserve stocks of Adamist navies which thanks to budgetary considerations were not all they should be. The response of the Yosemite Consensus to the Capone Organization had already shown what Edenism was capable of achieving along those lines, and that was with a mere thirty habitats. Jupiter had the resources of four thousand two hundred and fifty at its disposal.

Requests for materiel support started almost as soon as Trafalgar issued its first warning about the nature of the threat which the Confederation was facing. Ambassadors requested and pleaded and called in every favour they thought Edenism owed them to secure a place in production schedules. Payment for the weapons involved loan agreements and fuseodollar transfers on a scale which could have purchased entire stage-four star systems.

On top of that, it was Edenism which was providing the critical support for the Mortonridge Liberation in the form of serjeant constructs to act as foot soldiers. It was the one utterly pivotal psychological campaign waged against the possessed, proving to the Confederation at large that they could be beaten.

Fortunately, the practical aspects of assaulting one or more habitats were extremely difficult. Jupiter already had a superb Strategic Defence network; and among the possessed only the Organization had a fleet which could hope to mount any sort of large-scale offensive, and the distance between Earth and New California almost certainly precluded that. However, the possibility of a lone ship carrying antimatter on a fanatical suicide flight was a strong one. And then there was the remote possibility that Capone would acquire the Alchemist and use it against them. Although Consensus didn't know how the doomsday device worked, a ship certainly had to jump in to deploy it, which in theory gave the Edenists an interception window to destroy the device before it was deployed.

Preparations to solidify their defences had begun immediately. Fully one third of the armaments coming out of the industrial stations were incorporated into a massively expanded SD architecture. The 550,000-km orbital band containing the habitats was the most heavily protected, with the number of SD platforms doubled, and seeded with seven hundred thousand combat wasps to act as mines. A further million combat wasps were arranged in concentric shells around the massive planet out to the orbit of Callisto. Flotillas of multi-spectrum sensor satellites were dispersed among them, searching for any anomaly, however small, which pricked the potent energy storms churning through space around the gas-giant.

Over fifteen thousand heavily armed patrol voidhawks complemented the static defences; circling the volatile cloudscape in elliptical, high-inclination orbits, ready to interdict any remotely suspicious incoming molecule. The fact that so many voidhawks had been taken off civil cargo flights was actually causing a tiny rise in the price of He_3, the first for over two hundred and sixty years.

Consensus considered the economic repercussions to be a worthwhile trade for the security such invulnerable defences provided. No ship, robot, or inert kinetic projectile could get within three million kilometres of Jupiter unless specifically permitted to do so.

Even a lone maniac would acknowledge an attempted attack would be the ultimate in futility.

The gravity fluctuation which appeared five hundred and sixty thousand kilometres above Jupiter's equator was detected instantaneously. It registered as an inordinately pow-

erful twist of space-time in the distortion fields of the closest three hundred voidhawks. The intensity was so great
that the gravitonic detectors in local SD sensor array had to
be hurriedly recalibrated in order to acquire an accurate fix.
Visually it appeared as a ruby star, the gravity field lensing
Jupiter's light in every direction. Surrounding dust motes
and solar wind particles were sucked in, a cascade of pico-
meteorites fizzing brilliant yellow.

Consensus went to condition-one alert status. The sheer
strength of the space warp ruled out any conventional starship emergence. And the location was provocatively close
to the habitats, a hundred thousand kilometres from the
nearest designated emergence zone. Affinity commands
from Consensus were loaded into the combat wasps drifting
inertly among the habitats. Three thousand fusion drives
flared briefly, aligning the lethal drones on their new target.
The patrol voidhawks formed a sub-Consensus of their
own, designating approach vectors and swallow manoeuvres to englobe the invader.

The warp area expanded out to several hundred metres,
alarming individual Edenists, though Consensus itself absorbed the fact calmly. It was already far larger than any
conceivable voidhawk or blackhawk wormhole terminus.
Then it began to flatten out into a perfectly circular two-
dimensional fissure in space-time, and the real expansion
sequence began. Within five seconds it was over eleven
kilometres in diameter. Consensus quickly and concisely
reformed its response pattern. Approaching voidhawks performed frantic fifteen-gee parabolas, curving clear then
swallowing away. An extra eight thousand combat wasps
burst into life, hurtling in towards the Herculean alien men-
ace.

After another three seconds the fissure reached twenty
kilometres in diameter, and stabilized. One side collapsed

inwards, exposing the wormhole's throat. Three small specks zoomed out of the centre. *Oenone* and the other two voidhawks screamed their identity into the general affinity band, and implored: **HOLD YOUR FIRE!**

For the first time in its five hundred and twenty-one year history, the Jovian Consensus experienced the emotion of shock. Even then, its response wasn't entirely blunted. Specialist perceptual thought routines confirmed the three voidhawks remained unpossessed. A five-second lockdown was loaded into the combat wasps.

What is happening? Consensus demanded.

Syrinx simply couldn't resist it. **We have a visitor,** she replied gleefully. Her entire crew was laughing cheerfully around her on the bridge.

The counter-rotating spaceport was the first part to emerge from the gigantic wormhole terminus. A silver-white disk four and a half kilometres in diameter, docking bay lights glittering like small towns huddled at the base of metal valleys, red and green strobes winking bright around the rim. Its slender spindle slid up after it, appearing to pull the dark rust-red polyp endcap along.

That was when the other starships began to rampage out of the terminus; voidhawks, blackhawks, and Confederation Navy vessels streaking off in all directions. Jupiter's SD sensors and patrol voidhawk distortion fields tracked them urgently. Consensus fired guidance updates at the incoming combat wasps, determinedly vectoring them away from the unruly incursion.

The habitat's main cylinder started to coast up out of the terminus, a prodigious seventeen kilometres in diameter. After the first thirty-two kilometres were clear, its central band of starscrapers emerged, hundreds of thousands of windows agleam with the radiance of lazy afternoon sunlight. Their bases just cleared the rim of the wormhole.

There were no more starships to come after that, only the rest of the cylinder. When the emergence was complete, the wormhole irised shut and space returned to its natural state. The flotilla of patrol voidhawks thronging round detected a capacious distortion field folding back into the broad collar of polyp around the base of the habitat's southern endcap that formed the bed of its circumfluous sea.

Consensus directed a phenomenally restrained burst of curiosity at the newcomer.

Greetings, chorused Tranquillity and Ione Saldana. There was a distinct timbre of smugness in the hail.

Dariat did the one thing which he had never expected to do again. He opened his eyes and looked around. His own eyes in his own body; fat unpleasant thing that it was, clad in his usual grubby toga.

The sight which greeted him was familiar: one of Valisk's innumerable shallow valleys out among the pink grass plains. If he wasn't completely mistaken, it was the same patch of ground Anastasia's tribe had occupied the day she died.

"This is the final afterlife?" he asked aloud.

It couldn't be. There was an elusive memory, the same befuddlement as a dream leaves upon waking. Of a sundering, of being torn out of . . .

He had fused with Rubra, the two of them becoming one, vanquishing the foe by shunting Valisk to a realm, or dimension, or state, that the two of them grasped was intrinsically adverse to the possessing souls. Perhaps they had even created the new location by simply willing it to be. And then time went awry.

He gave his surroundings a more considered examination. It was Valisk, all right. The circumfluous sea was about four kilometres away, its clusters of atolls easily recognizable. When he turned the other way, he could see a fat black scar running down two-thirds of the northern endcap.

The light tube was dimmer than it should be, even accounting for the loss of some plasma. It proffered a kind of twilight, but grey rather than the magnificent golden sunset Dariat had experienced every day of his life. The grass plain echoed that malaised atmosphere, it was uneasily torpid. Its resident insects had curled up into dormancy; birds and rodents slunk back reticently to their nests, even the flowers had shrugged off their natural gloss.

Dariat bent down to pick an enervated poppy. And his chubby hand passed clean through the stem. He stared at it in astonishment, for the first time seeing that he was faintly translucent.

Shock finally liberated comprehension. A location hostile to possessors, one which would exorcise them from their enslaved hosts, denying them their energistic power. That was the destination he and Rubra had committed the habitat to.

"Oh, Thoale, you utter bastard. I'm a ghost."

For nearly ten hours the lift capsule had skimmed down the tower linking Supra-Brazil asteroid with the Govcentral state after which it was named, a smooth, silent ride. The only clue to how fast the lift capsules travelled (three thousand kilometres per hour) would come when they passed each other. But as they clung to rails on the exterior of the tower, and the only windows gave a direct view outward, such events remained out of sight to their passengers. Deliberately so; watching another capsule hurtling towards you at a combined speed of six thousand kilometres per hour was considered an absolute psychological no-go zone by the tower operators.

Just before it entered the upper fringes of the atmosphere,

the lift capsule decelerated to subsonic velocity. It reached the stratosphere as dawn broke over South America. On Earth that was no longer an invigorating sight; all the passengers saw was an unbroken murky-grey cloud layer which covered most of the continent and a third of the South Atlantic. Only when the lift capsule was ten kilometres above the frothing upper layer could Quinn see the army of individual streamers from which the gigantic cyclone was composed, flowing around each other at perilous velocities. The seething mass was as compressed as any gas-giant storm band, but infinity drabber.

They descended into the slashing tendrils of cirrus, and the windows immediately reverberated from the barrage of fist-sized raindrops. There was nothing else to see after that, just formless smears of grey. A minute before they reached the ground station, the windows went black as the lift capsule entered the sheath which guarded the bottom of the tower from the worst violence of the planet's rabid weather.

Digits on the Royale Class lounge's touchdown counter reached zero, an event marked by only the slightest tremble as latch clamps closed round the base of the lift capsule. The magnetic rail disengaged, and a transporter rolled it clear of the tower, leaving the reception berth clear for the next capsule. Airlock hatches popped open, revealing long extendable corridors leading into the arrivals complex where treble the usual numbers of customs, immigration, and security officers waited to scan the passengers. Quinn sighed in mild resignation. He'd quite enjoyed the trip down, mellowing out with all the facilities the Royale Class lounge could provide. A welcome period of contemplation, assisted by the Norfolk Tears he'd been drinking.

He had arrived at Earth with one goal: conquest. Now at least he had some notions how to go about subduing the planet for his Lord. The kind of exponential brute force approach the possessed had used up to now just wasn't an option on Earth. The arcologies were too isolated for that. It was curious, but the more Quinn thought about it, the more he realized that Earth was a representation of the Confederation in miniature. Its vast population centres kept separate by an amok nature almost as lethal as the interstellar void. Seeds of his revolution would have to be planted very carefully indeed. If Govcentral security ever suspected an outbreak of possession, the arcology in question would be quarantined. And Quinn knew that even with his energistic powers there would be nothing he could do to escape once the vac-trains had been shut down.

Most of the other passengers had disembarked, and the chief stewardess was glancing in Quinn's direction. He rose up from his deep leather seat, stretching the tiredness from his limbs. There was absolutely no way he'd ever get past the immigration desk, let alone security.

He walked towards the airlock hatch, and summoned the energistic power, mentally moulding it into the now familiar pattern. It crawled over his body, needle spears of static penetrating every cell. A swift groan was the only indication he showed of the grotesquery he experienced passing through the gateway into the ghost realm. His heart stopped, his breathing ceased, and the world about him lost its glimmer of substance. The solidity of walls and floors was still present, but ephemeral. Irrelevant if he really pressed.

The chief stewardess watched the last passenger step into the airlock, and turned back to the bar. Secured below the counter were several bottles of the complimentary Norfolk Tears and other expensive spirits and liqueurs which her team had opened. They were careful never to leave much, at

most a third, before opening a new bottle. But a third of
these drinks was an expensive commodity.

She began inventorying all these bottles as empty in her
stock control block. The team would split them later, filling
their personal flasks, and take them home. As long as they
didn't get too greedy the company supervisor would let it
pass. Her block's datavise turned to nonsense. She gave it
an annoyed glare, and automatically rapped it against the
bar. That was when the lights started to flicker. Puzzled
now, she frowned up at the ceiling. Electrical systems were
failing all over the lounge. The AV pillar projection behind
the bar had crashed into rainbow squiggles, the airlock
hatch activators were whining loudly, though the hatch itself wasn't moving.

"What—?" she grumbled. Power loss was just about impossible in the lift capsules. Every component had multiple
redundancy backups. She was about to call the lift capsule's
operations officer when the lights steadied, and her stock
control block came back on line. "Bloody typical," she
grunted. It still bothered her badly. If things could go wrong
on the ground, they could certainly go wrong half way up
the tower.

She gave the waiting bottles a forlorn glance, knowing
she was giving them up if she logged an official powerdown incident report. The company inspectorate authority
would swarm all over the lift capsule. She carefully erased
the inventory file she'd started, and datavised the lounge
processor for a channel to the operations officer.

The call never got placed. Instead she received a priority
datavise from the arrivals complex security office ordering
her to remain exactly where she was. Outside, an alarm
siren started its high-pitched urgent wailing. The sound
made her jump, in eleven years of riding the tower she'd
only ever heard it during practice drills.

The siren's clamour sounded muffled to Quinn. He'd watched the airlock lights quiver, and sensed the delicate electronic patterns of nearby processors storm wildly as he pushed himself through the gateway. There was nothing he could do about it. It took all of his concentration to marshal his energistic power into the correct pattern. Now it seemed that pattern had an above-average giveaway effect on nearby electronics—though nothing had happened when he'd slipped out of the ghost realm into the Royale Class lounge at the start of the descent. Of course, he wasn't exerting himself then, quite the opposite, he'd actually been reining in the power.

Ah well, something to remember.

Thick security doors were rumbling across the end of the corridor, trapping stragglers among the passengers. Quinn walked past them, and reached the door. It put up a token resistance as he pushed himself through, as if it were nothing more than a vertical sheet of water.

The arrivals complex on the other side was made up from a series of grandiose multi-level reception halls, stitched together by wave stairs and open-shaft lifts. It could cope with seventy passenger lift capsules disembarking at once; a capacity which had been operating at barely twenty-five per cent since the start of the crisis. As Quinn made his way out from the sealed admission chamber at the end of the corridor, his first impression was that the air-conditioning grilles were pumping out adrenaline gas.

Down below on the main concourse, a huge flock of people was running for cover. They didn't know where they were going, the exits were all closed, but they knew where they didn't want to be, and that was anywhere near a lift capsule that was crammed full of possessed. They were damn sure there was no other reason for a security alert of such magnitude.

Up on Quinn's level, badly hyped security guards in bulky kinetic armour were racing for the admission chamber. Officers were screaming orders. All the passengers from the lift capsule were being rounded up at gunpoint and being made to assume the position. Anyone who protested was given a sharp jab with a shock rod. Three stunned bodies were already sprawled on the floor, twitching helplessly. It encouraged healthy cooperation among the remainder.

Quinn went over to the rank of guards who were forming a semicircle around the door to the admission chamber. Eighteen of the stubby rifles were lined up on it. He walked round one guard to get a closer look at the weapon. The guard shivered slightly, as if a chilly breeze was finding its way through the joint overlaps of her armour. Her weapon was some kind of machine pistol. Quinn knew enough about munitions to recognise it as employing chemical bullets. There were several grenades hanging from her belt.

Even though God's Brother had granted him a much greater energistic strength than the average possessed, he would be very hard pressed to defend himself against all eighteen of them firing at him. Earth was obviously taking the threat of possession very seriously indeed.

A new group of people had arrived to move methodically among the whimpering passengers. They weren't in uniforms, just ordinary blue business suits, but the security officers deferred to them. Quinn could sense their thoughts, very calm and focused in comparison to everyone else. Intelligence operatives, most likely.

Quinn decided not to wait and find out. He retreated from the semicircle of guards as an officer was ordering them to open the admission chamber door. The wave stair down to the main concourse had been switched off; so he climbed the frozen steps of silicon two at a time.

People huddled round the barricaded exits felt his passage as a swift ripple of cool air, gone almost as it started. On the plaza outside, more squads of security guards were setting up; two groups were busy mounting heavy-calibre Bradfield rifles on tripods. Quinn shook his head in a kind of bemused admiration, then carefully walked round them. The long row of lifts down to the vac-train station was still working, though there were few people left on the arrivals complex storey to use them. He hopped in to one with a group of frightened-looking business executives just back from a trip to Cavius city on the moon.

The lift took them a kilometre and a half straight down, opening into a circular chamber three hundred metres across. The station's floor was divided up by concentric rows of turnstiles, channelling passengers into the cluster of wave stairs occupying the centre. Information columns of jet-black glass formed a picket line around the outside, knots of fluorescent icons twirling around them like electronic fish. Lines of holographic symbols slithered through the air overhead, weaving sinuously around each other as they guided passengers to the wave stair which led down to their platform.

Quinn sauntered idly round the outside of the information columns for a while, watching the contortions of the holograms overhead. The bustling crowd (all averting their eyes from each other), the confined walls and ceiling, wheezing air conditioners pouring out gritty air, small mechanoids being kicked as they attempted to clean up rubbish—he welcomed them all back into his life. Even though he was going to destroy this world and despoil its people, for a brief interlude it remained the old home. His satisfaction came to a cold halt; the name EDMONTON, in vibrant red letters, trickled over his head, riding along a curving convey of translucent blue arrowheads towards one of the wave stairs. The vac-train was departing in eleven minutes.

It was so tempting. Banneth, at last. To see that face stricken with fear, then suffering—for a long *long* time, the suffering—before the final ignominy of empty-headed imbecility. There were so many stages of torment to inflict on Banneth, so much he wanted to do to her now he had the power; intricate, malicious applications of pain, psychological as well as physical. But the needs of God's Brother came first, even before the near-sexual urgings of his own serpent beast. Quinn turned away from the glowing invitation in disgust, and went to find a vac-train which would take him direct to New York.

People were starting to congregate around the windows of the bars and fast-food outlets which made up the perimeter wall of the station. Kids stared with intrigued expressions at the images coming at them from newschannel AV projectors, while adults achieved the blank-faced otherwhereness which showed they were receiving sensevises. As he passed a pasta stall, Quinn caught a brief glimpse of the image inside a holoscreen above the sweating cook. Jupiter's cloudscape formed an effervescent ginger backdrop to a habitat; dozens of spaceships were swirling round it in what could almost be read as a state of high excitement.

It wasn't relevant to him, so he walked on.

Ione had gone straight to De Beauvoir palace after Tranquillity emerged above Jupiter, coordinating the habitat's maintenance crews and making a public sensevise to reassure people and tell them what to do. The formal reception room was a more appropriate setting for such a broadcast than her private apartment. Now with the immediate crisis over, she was snuggled back in the big chair behind her desk and using Tranquillity's sensitive cells to observe the last of the voidhawks assigned to implement the aid response settle on its docking ledge pedestal. A procession of vehicles trundled over the polyp towards it, cargo flatbed lorries and heavy-lift trucks eager to unload the large fusion generator clamped awkwardly in the voidhawk's cargo cradles.

The generator had come from one of the industrial stations of the nearest Edenist habitat, Lycoris; hurriedly ferried over by Consensus as soon as Tranquillity's status was established. There were currently fifteen technical crews working on similar generators around the docking ledge, powering them up and wiring them in to the habitat's power grid.

When she sank her mentality deeper into the neural strata and the autonomic monitor routines which operated there, Ione could feel the electricity flowing back into the starscrapers through the organic conductors, their mechanical systems gradually coming back on line. The habitat's girdling city had been in emergency powerdown mode since the swallow manoeuvre, along with other non-essential functions. Grandfather Michael's precautions hadn't been perfect after all. She grinned to herself; pretty damn good, though. And even without the Jovian Consensus on hand to help with all its resources, they had the smaller fusion generators in the non-rotating spaceport.

We would have been okay.

Of course we would, Tranquillity said. It managed a mildly chastising tone, surprised at her doubt.

Obviously, nobody had fully thought through the implications of the swallow manoeuvre for Tranquillity. When it entered the wormhole, the hundreds of induction cables radiating out from the endcap rims had been sliced off, eliminating nearly all of the habitat's natural energy generation capability. It would take their extrusion glands several months to grow new ones out to full length.

By which time they might have to move again.

Let's not worry about that right now, Tranquillity said. **We're in the safest orbit in the Confederation; even I was surprised by the amount of fire-power Consensus has amassed here to protect itself. Be content.**

I wasn't complaining.

Nor are our inhabitants.

Ione felt her attention being focused inside the shell.

It was party time in Tranquillity. The whole population had come up out of the starscrapers to wait in the parkland around the lobbies until the electricity was restored. Elderly plutocrats sat on the grass next to students, waitresses shared the queue to the toilets with corporate presidents, Laymil project researchers mingled with society vacuum-heads. Everybody had grabbed a bottle on the way out of their apartment, and the galaxy's biggest mass picnic had erupted spontaneously. Dawn was now five hours late, but the moonlight silver light-tube only enhanced the ambience. People drank, and ran stim programs, and laughed with their neighbour as they told and retold their personal tale of combat-wasp-swarms-I-have-seen-hurtling-towards-me. They thanked God but principally Ione Saldana for rescuing them, and declared their undying love for her, that goddamn beautiful, brilliant, canny, gorgeous girl in whose habitat they were blessed to live. And, hey, Capone; how does it feel, loser? Your almighty Confederation-challenging fleet screwed by a single non-military habitat; everything you could throw at us, and we beat you. Still happy you came back to the wonders of this century?

The residents from the two starscrapers closest to De Beauvoir palace walked over the vales and round the spinnies to pay their respects and voice their gratitude. A huge crowd was singing and chanting outside the gates, calling, pleading for their heroine to appear.

Ione slid the focus over them, smiling when she saw Dominique and Clement in the throng, as well as a wildly drunk Kempster Getchell. There were others she knew, too, directors and managers of multistellar companies and finance institutions, all swept along with tide of emotion. Red-faced, exhilarated, and calling her name with hoarse throats. She let the focus float back to Clement.

Invite him in, Tranquillity urged warmly.

Maybe.

Survival of dangerous events is a sexual trigger for humans. You should indulge your instincts. He will make you happy, and you deserve that more than anything.

Romantically put.

Romance has nothing to do with this. Enjoy the release he will bring.

What about you? You performed the swallow manoeuvre.

When you are happy, I am happy.

She laughed out loud. "Oh what the hell, why not."

That is good. But I think you will have to make a public appearance first. This crowd is good-natured, but quite determined to thank you.

Yes. She sobered. **But there is one last official duty.**

Indeed. Tranquillity's tone matched her disposition.

Ione felt the mental conversation widen to incorporate the Jovian Consensus. Armira, the Kiint ambassador to Jupiter, was formally invited to converse with them.

Our swallow manoeuvre has produced an unexpected event, Ione said. **We are hopeful that you can clarify it for us.**

Armira injected a sensation of stately amusement into the affinity band. **I would suggest, Ione Saldana and Tran-**

quillity, that your entire swallow manoeuvre was an unexpected event.

It certainly surprised the Kiint we were host to, she said. They all left, very suddenly.

I see. Armira's thoughts hardened, denying them any hint of his emotional content.

Tranquillity replayed the memory it had from the time of the attack, showing all the Kiint vanishing inside event horizons.

What you have seen demonstrated is an old ability, Armira responded dispassionately. We developed the emergency exodus facility during the era when we were engaged in interstellar travel. It is merely a sophisticated application of your distortion field systems. My colleagues helping with your Laymil research project would have used it instinctively when they believed they were threatened.

We're sure they would, Consensus said. And who can blame them? That's not the point. The fact that you have this ability is most enlightening to us. We have always regarded as somewhat fanciful your claim that your race's interest in star travel is now over. Although the fact that you had no starships added undeniable weight to the argument. Now we have seen your personal teleport ability, the original claim is exposed as a complete fallacy.

We do not have the same level of interest in travelling to different worlds that you do, Armira said.

Of course not. Our starships are principally concerned with commercial and colonization flights, and an unfortunate amount of military activity. Your technological level would preclude anything as simple as commercial activity. We also believe that you are peaceful, although you must have considerable knowledge of advanced weapons. That leaves colonization and exploration.

A correct analysis.

Are you still conducting these activities?

To some degree.

Why did you not tell us this, why have you hidden your true abilities behind a claim of mysticism and disinterest?

You know the answer to that, Armira said. Humans discovered the Jiciro race three hundred years ago; yet you have still not initiated contact and revealed yourselves to them. Their technology and culture is at a very primitive level, and you know what will happen if they are exposed to the Confederation. All that they have will be supplanted by what they will interpret as futuristic items of convenience, they will cease to develop anything for themselves. Who knows what achievements would be lost to the universe?

That argument does not pertain here, Consensus said. The Jiciro do not know what the stars are, nor that solid matter is composed of atoms. We do. We acknowledge that our technology is inferior to yours. But equally you know that one day we will achieve your current level. You are denying us knowledge we already know exists, and you have done so twice, in this field and in your understanding of the beyond. This is not an act of fellowship; we have opened ourselves to you in honesty and friendship, we have not hidden our flaws from you; yet you have clearly not reciprocated. Our conclusion is that you are simply studying us. We would now like to know why. As sentient entities we have that right.

Study is a pejorative term. We learn of you, as you do us. Admittedly that process is imbalanced, but given our respective natures, that is inevitable. As to bestowing our technology; that would be interference of the grandest order. If you want something, achieve it for yourselves.

Same argument you gave us concerning the beyond, Ione remarked testily.

Of course, Armira said. Tell me, Ione Saldana, what would your reaction have been if a xenoc race announced that you had an immortal soul, and proved it, and then went on to demonstrate that the beyond awaited, though as Laton said, only for some? Would you have greeted such a revelation with thanks?

No, I don't suppose I would.

We know that our introduction to the concept of the beyond was accidental, Consensus said. Something happened on Lalonde which allowed the souls to come back and possess the living. Something extraneous. This calamity has been inflicted upon us. Surely such circumstances permit you to intervene?

There was a long pause. We will not intervene in this case, Armira said. For two reasons. Whatever happened on Lalonde happened because you went there. There is more to travelling between stars and exploring the universe than the physical act.

You are saying we must accept responsibly for our actions.

Yes, inevitably.

Very well, with reservations we accept that judgement. Though, please appreciate, we do not like it. What is the second reason?

Understand, there is a faction among my people who have argued that we should intervene in your favour. The possibility was rejected because what we have learned of you so far indicates that your race will come through this time successfully. Edenists especially have the social maturity to face that which follows.

I'm not an Edenist, Ione said. What about me, and all the other Adamists, the majority of our race? Are you going to stand back as we perish and fall into the beyond? Does the survival of an elite few, the sophisticates and the intellectuals, justify discarding the rest? Humans have never practised eugenics, we regard it as an abomination, and rightly so. If that's the price of racial improvement, we're not willing to pay it.

If I am any judge, you too will triumph, Ione Saldana.

Nice to know. But what about all the others?

Fate will determine what happens. I can say no more other than to restate our official response: the answer lies within yourselves.

That is not much of a comfort, Consensus remarked.

I understand your frustration. My one piece of advice is that you should not share what you have learned about my race with the Adamists. Believing we have a solution, and that piety alone will extract it from us, would weaken their incentive to find that answer.

We will consider your suggestion, Consensus said. But Edenism will not voluntarily face the rest of eternity without our cousins. Ultimately, we are one race, however diverse.

I acknowledge your integrity.

I have a final question, Ione said. Where is Jay Hilton? She was taken from Tranquillity at the same time as your researchers. Why?

Armira's thoughts softened, shading as close to embarrassment as Ione had ever known a Kiint to come. That was an error, the ambassador said. And I apologise unreservedly for it. However, you should know the error was made in good faith. A young Kiint included Jay

Hilton in the emergency exodus against parental guidance. She was simply trying to save her friend.

Haile! Ione laughed delightedly. You wicked girl.

I believe she has been severely reprimanded for the incident.

I hope not, Ione said indignantly. She's only a baby.

Quite.

Well, you can bring Jay back now; Tranquillity isn't as vulnerable as you thought.

I apologise again, but Jay Hilton cannot be returned to you at this time.

Why not?

In effect, she has seen too much. I assure you that she is perfectly safe, and we will of course return her to you immediately once your current situation is resolved.

The walls of the prison cell were made from some kind of dull-grey composite, not quite cool enough to be metal, but just as hard. Louise had touched them once before sinking down onto the single cot and hugging her legs, knees tucked up under her chin. The gravity was about half that of Norfolk, better than Phobos, at least; though the air was cooler than it had been on the *Jamrana*. She spent some time wondering about Endron, the old systems specialist from the *Far Realm*, thinking he might have betrayed them and alerted High York's authorities, then decided it really didn't matter. Her one worry now was that she'd been separated from Gen; her sister would be very frightened by what was happening.

And I got her into this mess. Mother will kill me.

Except Mother was in no position to do anything. Louise hugged herself tighter, fighting the way her lips kept trembling.

The door slid open, and two female police officers

stepped in. Louise assumed they were police, they wore pale blue uniforms with Govcentral's bronze emblem on their shoulders, depicting a world where continents shaped as hands gripped together.

"Okay, Kavanagh," said the one with sergeant stripes. "Let's go."

Louise straightened her legs, looking cautiously from one to the other. "Where?"

"Interview."

"I'd just shove you out the bloody airlock, it's up to me," said the other. "Trying to sneak one of those bastards in here. Bitch."

"Leave it," the sergeant ordered.

"I wasn't . . . ." Louise started. She pursed her lips helplessly. It was so complicated, and heaven only knew how many laws she'd broken on the way to High York.

They marched her down a short corridor and into another room. It made her think of hospitals. White walls, everything clean, a table in the middle that was more like a laboratory bench, cheap waiting room chairs, various processor blocks in a tall rack in one corner, more lying on the table. Brent Roi was sitting behind the table; he'd taken off the customs uniform he'd worn to greet the *Jamrana*, now he was in the same blue suit as the officers escorting her. He waved her into the chair facing him.

Louise sat, hunching her shoulders exactly the way she was always scolding Gen for doing. She waited for a minute with downcast eyes, then glanced up. Brent Roi was giving her a level stare.

"You're not a possessed," he said. "The tests prove that."

Louise pulled nervously at the black one-piece overall she'd been given, the memory of those tests vivid in her mind. Seven armed guards had been pointing their machine guns at her as the technicians ordered her to strip. They'd put her inside sensor loops, pressed hand-held scanners against her, taken samples. It was a million times worse than any medical examination. Afterwards, the only thing she'd been allowed to keep was the medical nanonic package round her wrist.

"That's good," she said in a tiny voice.

"So how did he blackmail you?"

"Who?"

"The possessed guy calling himself Fletcher Christian."

"Um. He didn't blackmail me, he was looking after us."

"So you rolled over and let him fuck you in return for protection against the other possessed?"

"No."

Brent Roi shrugged. "He preferred your little sister?"

"No! Fletcher is a decent man. You shouldn't say such things."

"Then what the hell are you doing here, Louise? Why did you try and infiltrate a possessed into the O'Neill Halo?"

"I wasn't. It's not like that. We came here to warn you."

"Warn who?"

"Earth. Govcentral. There's somebody coming here. Somebody terrible."

"Yeah?" Brent Roi raised a sceptical eyebrow. "Who's that then?"

"He's called Quinn Dexter. I've met him, he's worse than any normal possessed. Much worse."

"In what way?"

"More powerful. And he's full of hate. Fletcher says there's something wrong about him, he's different somehow."

"Ah, the expert on possession. Well, if anyone is going to know, it'll be him."

Louise frowned, unsure why the official was being so difficult. "We came here to warn you," she insisted. "Dexter said he was coming to Earth. He wants revenge on someone called Banneth. You have to guard all the spaceports, and make sure he doesn't get down to the surface. It would be a disaster. He'll start the possession down there."

"And why do you care?"

"I told you. I've met him. I know what he's like."

"Worse than ordinary possessed; yet you seemed to have survived. How did you manage that, Louise?"

"We were helped."

"By Fletcher?"

"No . . . I don't know who it was."

"All right, so you escaped this fate worse than death, and you came here to warn us."

"Yes."

"How did you get off Norfolk, Louise?"

"I bought tickets on a starship."

"I see. And you took Fletcher Christian with you. Were you worried there were possessed among the starship crew?"

"No. That was one place I was sure there wouldn't be any possessed."

"So although you knew there were no possessed on board, you still took Christian with you as protection. Was that your idea, or his?"

"I . . . It . . . He was with us. He'd been with us since we left home."

"Where is home, Louise?"

"Cricklade manor. But Dexter came and possessed everyone. That's when we fled to Norwich."

"Ah yes, Norfolk's capital. So you brought Christian with you to Norwich. Then when that started to fall to the possessed, you thought you'd better get offplanet, right?"

"Yes."

"Did you know Christian was a possessed when you bought the tickets?"

"Yes, of course."

"And when you bought them, did you also know Dexter wanted to come to Earth?"

"No, that was after."

"So was it dear old samaritan Fletcher Christian who suggested coming here to warn us?"

"Yes."

"And you agreed to help him?"

"Yes."

"So where were you going to go originally, before Fletcher Christian made you change your mind and come here?"

"Tranquillity."

Brent Roi nodded in apparent fascination. "That's a rather strange place for a young lady from Norfolk's landowner class to go. What made you chose that habitat?"

"My fiancé lives there. If anyone can protect us, he can."

"And who is your fiancé, Louise?"

She smiled sheepishly. "Joshua Calvert."

"Joshua Cal . . . You mean *Lagrange* Calvert?"

"No, Joshua."

"The captain of the *Lady Macbeth*?"

"Yes. Do you know him?"

"Let's say, the name rings a bell." He sat back and folded his arms, regarding Louise with a strangely mystified expression.

"Can I see Genevieve now?" she asked timidly. No one had actually said she was under arrest yet. She felt a lot more confident now the policeman had actually listened to her story.

"In a little while, possibly. We just have to review the information you've provided us with."

"You do believe me about Quinn Dexter, don't you? You must make sure he doesn't get down to Earth."

"Oh, I assure you, we will do everything we can to make sure he doesn't get through our security procedures."

"Thank you." She glanced awkwardly at the two female officers standing on either side of her chair. "What's going to happen to Fletcher?"

"I don't know, Louise, that's not my department. But I imagine they'll attempt to flush him out of the body he's stolen."

"Oh." She stared at the floor.

"Do you think they're wrong to try that, Louise?"

"No. I suppose not." The words were troubling to speak; the truth, but not what was right. None of what had happened was right.

"Good." Brent Roi signalled her escort. "We'll talk again in a little while." When the door closed behind her, he couldn't help a grimace of pure disbelief.

"What do you think?" his supervisor datavised.

"I have never heard someone sprout quite so much bullshit in a single interview before," Brent Roi replied. "Either she's a retard, or we're up against a new type of possessed infiltration."

"She's not a retard."

"Then what the hell is she? Nobody is that dumb, it's not possible."

"I don't believe she's dumb, either. Our problem is, we're so used to dealing with horrendous complexities of subterfuge, we never recognise the simple truth when we see it."

"Oh come on, you don't actually believe that story?"

"She is, as you said, from the Norfolk landowner class; that doesn't exactly prepare her for the role of galactic master criminal. And she is travelling with her sister."

"That's just cover."

"Brent, you are depressingly cynical."

"Yes, sir." He held on to his exasperation, it never made the slightest impression on his supervisor. The anonymous entity who had guided the last twenty years of his life lacked many ordinary human responses. There were times when Brent Roi wondered if he was actually dealing with a xenoc. Not that there was much he could do about that now; whatever branch of whatever agency the supervisor belonged to, it was undoubtedly a considerable power within Govcentral. His own smooth, accelerated promotion through the Halo police force was proof of that.

"There are factors of Miss Kavanagh's story which my colleagues and I find uniquely interesting."

"Which factors?" Brent asked.

"You know better than that."

"All right. What do you want me to do with her?"

"Endron has confirmed the Phobos events to the Martian police, however we must establish exactly what happened to Kavanagh on Norfolk. Initiate a direct memory retrieval procedure."

Over the last five hundred years, the whole concept of Downtown had acquired a new-ish and distinctly literal meaning in New York; naturally enough, so did Uptown. One thing, though, would never change; the arcology still jealously guarded its right to boast the tallest individual building on the planet. While the odd couple of decades per century might see the title stolen away by upstart rivals in Europe or Asia, the trophy always came home eventually.

The arcology now sprawled across more than four thousand square kilometres, housing (officially) three hundred million people. With New Manhattan at the epicentre, fifteen crystalline domes, twenty kilometres in diameter, were clumped together in a semicircle along the eastern seaboard, sheltering entire districts of ordinary skyscrapers (defined as buildings under one kilometre high) from the pummelling heat and winds. Where the domes intersected, gigantic conical megatowers soared up into the contused sky. More than anything, these colossi conformed to the old concept of "arcology" as a single city-in-a-building. They had apartments, shopping malls, factories, offices, design bureaus, stadiums, universities, parks, police stations, council chambers, hospitals, restaurants, bars, and spaces for every other human activity of the Twenty-seventh Century. Thousands of their inhabitants were born, lived, and died inside them without ever once leaving.

At five and a half kilometres tall, the Reagan was the current global champion, its kilometre-wide base resting on the bedrock where the town of Ridgewood had stood in the times before the armada storms. An apartment on any of its upper fifty floors cost fifteen million fuseodollars apiece, and the last one was sold twelve years before they were built. Their occupants, the new breed of Uptowners, enjoyed a view as spectacular as it was possible to have on Earth. Although impenetrably dense cloud swathed the arcology for a minimum of two days out of every seven; when it was clear the hot air was very clear indeed. Far below them, under the transparent hexagonal sheets which comprised the roof of the domes, the tide of life ebbed and flowed for their amusement. By day, an exotic hustle as kaleidoscope rivers of vehicles flowed along the elevated 3D web of roads and rails; by night, a shimmering tapestry of neon pixels.

Surrounding the Reagan, streets and skyscrapers fanned out in a radial of deep carbon-concrete canyons, like buttress roots climbing up to support the main tower. The lower levels of these canyons were badly cluttered, where the skyscraper bases were twice as broad as their peaks, and the elevated roads formed a complex intersecting grid for the first hundred and fifty metres above the ground. High expressways throwing off curving slip roads at each junction down to the local traffic lanes; broad freight-only flyovers shaking from the eighty-tonne autotrucks grumbling along them twenty-four hours a day, winding like snakes into tunnels which led to sub-basement loading yards; metro transit carriages gliding along a mesh of rails so labyrinthine that only an AI could run the network. Rents were cheap near the ground, where there was little light but plenty of noise, and the heavy air gusting between dirty vertical walls had been breathed a hundred times before. Entropy in the arcology meant a downward drift. Everything that was worn-out, obsolete, demode, economically redundant—down it came to settle on the ground, where it could descend no further. People as well as objects.

Limpet-like structures proliferated among the crisscross of road support girders bridging the gap between the skyscrapers, shanty igloos woven from salvaged plastic and carbotanium composite, multiplying over the decades until they clotted into their own light-killing roof. Under them, leeched to the streets themselves, were the market stalls and fast-food counters; a souk economy of fifth-hand cast-offs and date-expired sachets shuffled from family to family in an eternal round robin. Crime here was petty and incestuous, gangs ruled their turf, pushers ruled the gangs. Police made token patrols in the day, and went off-shift as the unseen sun sank below the rim of the domes above.

This was Downtown. It was everywhere, but always beneath the feet of ordinary citizens, invisible. Quinn adored it. The people who dwelt here were almost in the ghost realm already; nothing they did ever affected the real world. He walked up out of the subway onto a gloomy street jammed with canopied stalls and wheel-less vans, all with their skirt of goods guarded by vigilant owners. Graffiti struggled with patches of pale mould for space on the sky-scraper walls. There were few windows, and those were merely armoured slits revealing little of the mangy shops and bars inside. Metallic thunder from the roads above was as permanent as the air which carried it.

Several looks were quickly thrown Quinn's way before eyes were averted for fear of association. He smiled to himself as he strode confidently among the stalls. As if his attitude wasn't enough to mark him out as an interloper, he had clothed himself in his jet-black priest robe again.

It was the simplest way. He wanted to find the sect, but he'd never been to New York before. Everybody in Downtown knew about the sect, this was their prime recruiting ground. There would be a coven close by, there always was. He just needed someone who knew the location.

Sure enough, he hadn't got seventy metres from the subway when they saw him. A pair of waster kids busy laughing as they pissed on the woman they'd just beaten unconscious. Her two-year-old kid lay on the sidewalk bawling as blood and urine pooled round its feet. The victim's bag had been ripped apart, scattering its pitiful contents on the ground around her. They put Quinn in mind of Jackson Gael; late-adolescence, with pumped bodies, their muscle shape defined by some exercise but mostly tailored-hormones. One of them wore a T-shirt with the slogan: CHEMICAL WARFARE MACHINE. The other was more body-proud, favouring a naked torso.

He was the one who saw Quinn first, grunted in amazement, and nudged his partner. They sealed their flies and sauntered over.

Quinn slowly pushed his hood down. Hyper-sensitive to trouble, the street was de-populating rapidly. Pedestrians, already nervous from the mugging, slipped away behind the forest of support pillars. Market stall shutters were slammed down.

The two waster kids stopped in front of Quinn, who grinned in welcome. "I haven't had sex for ages," Quinn said. He looked straight at the one wearing the T-shirt. "So I think I'll fuck you first tonight."

The waster kid snarled, and threw a punch with all the strength his inflated muscles could manage. Quinn remained perfectly still. The fist struck his jaw, just to the left of his chin. There was a crunch which could easily be heard above the traffic's clamour. The waster kid bellowed, first in shock, then in agony. His whole body shook as he slowly pulled his hand back. Every knuckle was broken, as if he had punched solid stone. He cradled it with frightened tenderness, whimpering.

"I'd like to say take me to your leader," Quinn said, as if he hadn't even noticed the punch. "But organising yourselves takes brains. So I guess I'm out of luck."

The second waster kid had paled, shaking his head and taking a couple of steps backward.

"Don't run," Quinn said, his voice sharp.

The waster kid paused for a second, then turned and bolted. His jeans burst into flames. He screamed, stumbling to a halt, and flailing wildly at the burning fabric. His hands ignited. The shock silenced him for a second as he held them up disbelievingly in front of his face. Then he screamed again, and kept on screaming, staggering about drunkenly. He crashed into one of the flimsy stalls which crumpled, folding about him. The fire was burning deeper into his flesh now, spreading along his arms, and up onto his torso. His screaming became weaker as he bucked about in the smouldering wreckage.

The T-shirted kid raced over to him. But all he could do

was look down in a horror of indecision as the flames grew hotter.

"For Christ's sake," he wailed at Quinn. "Stop it. Stop it!"

Quinn laughed. "Your first lesson is that God's Brother cannot be stopped."

The body was motionless and silent now, a black glistening husk at the centre of the flames. Quinn put a hand on the shoulder of the sobbing waster kid at his side. "It hurts you, doesn't it? Watching this?"

"Hurts! Hurts? You bastard." Even with a face screwed up from pain and rage, he didn't dare try to twist free from Quinn's hand.

"I have a question," Quinn said. "And I've chosen you to answer it for me." His hand moved down, caressing the waster kid's chest before it reached his crotch. He tightened his fingers round the kid's balls, aroused by the fear he was inflicting.

"Yes, God, yes. Anything," the kid snivelled. His eyes were closed, denying what he could of this nightmare.

"Where is the nearest coven of the Light Bringer sect?"

Even with the pain and dread scrambling his thoughts, the waster kid managed to stammer: "This dome, district seventeen, eighty-thirty street. They got a centre somewhere along there."

"Good. You see, you've learnt obedience, already. That's very smart of you. I'm almost impressed. Now there's only one lesson left."

The waster kid quailed. "What?"

"To love me."

The coven's headquarters had chewed its way, maggot-fashion, into the corner of the Hauck skyscraper on eighty-thirty street. What had once been a simple lattice of cube rooms, arranged by mathematics rather than art, was now a jumbled warren of darkened chambers. Acolytes had knocked holes in some walls, nailed up barricades in the corridors, pulled down ceilings, sealed off stairwells; drones shaping their nest to the design of the magus. From the outside it looked the same, a row of typically shabby Downtown shops along the street, selling goods cheaper than anywhere else—they could afford to, everything was stolen by the acolytes. But above the shops, the slim windows were blacked out, and according to the building management processors, the rooms unoccupied, and therefore not liable to pay rent.

Inside, the coven members buzzed about industriously twenty-four hours a day. Looked at from a strictly corporate viewpoint, which was how magus Garth always regarded his coven, it was quite a prosperous operation. Ordinary acolytes, the real sewer-bottom shit of the human race, were sent out boosting from the upper levels; bringing back a constant supply of consumer goodies that were either used by the sect or sold off in the coven-front shops and affiliated street market stalls. Sergeant acolytes were deployed primarily as enforcers to keep the others in line, but also to run a more sophisticated distribution net among the dome's lower-middle classes; competing (violently) with ordinary pushers out in the bars and clubs. Senior acolytes, the ones who actually had a working brain cell, were given didactic memory courses and employed running the pirate factory equipment, bootlegging MF albums, black sensevise programs, and AV activant software; as well as synthesizing an impressive pharmacopoeia of drugs, hormones, and proscribed viral vectors.

In addition to these varied retail enterprises, the coven still engaged in the more traditional activities of crime syndicates. Although sensevise technology had essentially eliminated a lot of prostitution outside of Downtown, that still left protection rackets, extortion, clean water theft, blackmail, kidnapping, data theft, game-rigging, civic-service fraud, power theft, embezzlement, and vehicle theft, among others.

The coven performed all of them with gusto, if not finesse. Magus Garth was satisfied with their work. They hadn't missed their monthly target in over three years, making the required financial offering to New York's high magus over in dome two. His only worry was that the High Magus could realize how lucrative the coven was, and demand a higher offering. Increased payments would cut into Garth's personal profits, the eight per cent he'd been skimming every month for the last five years.

There were times when Garth wondered why nobody had noticed. But then, looking at sergeant acolyte Wener, maybe he shouldn't be all that surprised. Wener was in his thirties, a big man, but rounded rather than wedge-shaped like most of the acolytes. He had a thick beard, dark hair sprouting from his face in almost simian proportions. His head was in keeping with the rest of his body, though Garth suspected the bone thickness would be a lot greater than average. An overhanging forehead and jutting chin gave him a permanently sullen, resentful expression—appropriately enough. You couldn't geneer that quality, it was a demonstration that the incest taboo was finally starting to lose force among Downtown residents. Fifteen years in the sect, and Wener was as far up the hierarchy as he'd ever get.

"They got Tod, and Jay-Dee," Wener said. He smiled at the memory. "Tod went down swinging. Hit a couple of cops before they shot him with a fucking nervejam. They started kicking him then. I got out."

"How come they spotted you?" Garth asked. He'd sent Wener and five others out to steam a mall. Simple enough, two of you bang into a civilian, cut a bag strap, slice trouser pocket fabric. Any protest: you get crushed by a circle of aggressive faces and tough young bodies looking for an excuse to hurt you as bad as they can.

Wener shifted some flesh around on top of his shoulders, his way of shrugging. "Dunno. Cops maybe saw what was going down."

"Ah, fuck it." Garth knew. They'd hit a streak and stayed too long, allowed the mall patrols to realize what was happening. "Did Tod and Jay-Dee have anything on them?"

"Credit disks."

"Shit." That was it. The cops would send them straight down to the Justice Hall, walk them past a judge whose assistant's assistant would access the case file and slap them with an Involuntary Transportation sentence. Two more loyal followers lost to some asshole colony. Though Garth had heard that the quarantine was even affecting colony starship flights. Ivet holding pens at every orbital tower station were getting heavily overcrowded, the news companies were hot with rumours of riots.

Wener was shoving his hands in his pockets, pulling out credit disks and other civilian crap: fleks, jewellery, palm-sized blocks . . . "I got this. The steam wasn't a total zero." He spilt the haul on Garth's desk, and gave the magus a hopeful look.

"Okay, Wener. But you've got to be more careful in the future. Fuck it, God's Brother doesn't like failure."

"Yes, magus."

"All right, get the hell out of my sight before I give you to Hot Spot for a night."

Wener lumbered out of the sanctum, and closed the door. Garth datavised the room's management processor to turn up the lights. Candles and shadowy gloom were the sect's habitual trappings. When acolytes were summoned before him, the study conformed to that: a sombre cave lit by a few spluttering red candles in iron candelabrums, its walls invisible.

Powerful beams shone down out of the ceiling, revealing a richly furnished den; drinks cabinet filled with a good selection of bottles, an extensive AV and sensevise flek library, new-marque Kulu Corporation desktop processor (genuine—not a bootleg), some of the weirder art stuff that was impossible to fence. A homage to his own greed, and devoutness. If you see something you want: take it.

"Kerry!" he yelled.

She came in from his private apartment, butt naked. He hadn't allowed her to wear clothes since the day her brother brought her in. Best-looking girl the coven had acquired in ages. A few tweaks with cosmetic adaptation packages, pandering to his personal tastes, and she was visual perfection.

"Get my fifth invocation robes," he told her. "Hurry up. I've got the initiation in ten minutes."

She bobbed her head apprehensively, and retreated back into the apartment. Garth started picking up the junk Wener had left, reading the flek labels, datavising the blocks for a menu. A gentle gust of cool air wafted across his face. The candles flickered. It broke his concentration for a moment. Air conditioner screwed up again.

There was nothing of any interest among Wener's haul, no blackmail levers; some of the fleks were company files, but a quick check found no commercially sensitive items. He was indifferent about that. Data was the other offering the coven made to the High Magus, and that on a weekly basis. A gift that never brought any return, other than the invisible umbrella of political protection the sect extended to its senior members. So Garth played along, considering it his insurance premium. The reports were more than a simple summary of what was happening inside the coven; the High Magus insisted on knowing what action was going down on the street, every street.

Years of being out on the street at the hard edge had taught Garth the value of good intelligence, but this was like a fetish with the High Magus.

Kerry returned with his robes. The fifth invocation set were appropriately flamboyant, black and purple, embroidered with scarlet pentagrams and nonsense runes. But they were a symbol of authority, and the sect was very strict about internal discipline. Kerry helped him into them, then hung a gold chain with an inverted cross round his neck. When he looked into a mirror he was satisfied with what he saw. The body might be sagging slightly these days, but he used weapon implants rather than straight physical violence to assert himself now; while the shaven skull and eyes recessed by cosmetic adaptation packages gave him a suitably ominous appearance.

The temple was at the centre of the headquarters, a cavity three stories high. Straight rows of severed steel reinforcement struts poking out of the walls showed where the floors and ceilings used to be. A broad pentagon containing an inverted cross was painted across the rear wall. It was illuminated from below by a triple row of skull candles, great gobs of wax in upturned craniums. Stars, demons, and runes formed a constellation around it, although they were fading under layers of soot. The altar was a long carbon-concrete slab, ripped from the sidewalk outside, and mounted on jagged pillars of carbotanium. Impressively solid, if nothing else. There was a black brazier on top of it, lithe blue flames slithering out of the trash bricks it was filled with, sending up a plume of sweet-stinking smoke. A pair of tall serpent-shaped candle sticks flanked it. Ten iron hoops, sunk into the carbon concrete, trailed lengths of chain which ended in manacles.

Just over half of the coven's acolytes were waiting obediently when Garth arrived. Standing in rows, wearing their grey robes, with coloured belts denoting seniority. Garth would have preferred more. But they were stretched pretty thin right now. A turf dispute with a gang operating out of ninety-ten street had resulted in several clashes. The gang lord was doubtless thinking it would all be settled with a boundary agreement. Garth was going to cure him of that illusion. God's Brother did not negotiate. Acolytes had the gang under observation, building up a picture of their entire operation. It wasn't something the gang understood or could ever emulate, they didn't have the discipline or the drive. Their only motivation was to claw in enough money to pay for their own stim fixes.

That was what made the sect different; serving God's Brother so rewarding.

In another week Garth would unlock the weapons stash and launch a raid. The High Magus had already arranged for him to take delivery of sequestration nanonics; that would be the fate of the gang's leadership, turned into biological mechanoids. Any attractive youths would be used as bluesense meat after the acolytes had enjoyed their victory orgy. And, inevitably, there would be a sacrifice.

The acolytes bowed to Garth, who went to stand in front of the altar. Five initiates were shackled to it. Three boys and a two girls, lured in by the promises and the treachery of friends. One of the boys stood defiantly straight, determined to show he could take whatever the initiation threw at him so he could claim his place, the other two were just surly and subdued. Garth had ordered one of the girls to be tranked after he'd spoken to her earlier. She'd virtually been abducted by an acolyte angry at losing her to an outside rival, and was likely to go into a mental melt-down if she wasn't eased in to her new life; she had strong ambitions to better herself and rise out of Downtown.

Garth held up his arms, and made the sign of the inverted cross. "With flesh we bond in the night," he intoned.

The acolytes started a low, mournful chanting, swaying softly in unison.

"Pain we love," Garth told them. "Pain frees the serpent beast. Pain shows us what we are. Your servants, Lord."

He was almost in a trance state as he spoke the words, he'd said them so many times before. So many initiations. The coven had a high turnover, arrests, stim burnouts, fights. But never drop outs.

Indoctrination and discipline helped, but his main weapon of control was belief. Belief in your own vileness, and knowing there was no shame in it. Wanting things to get worse, to destroy and hurt and ruin. The easy way forward . . . once you give in to your true self, your serpent beast. All that started right here, with the ceremony.

It was a deliberate release of sex and violence, an empowerment of the most base instincts, permitting little resistance. So easy to join, so natural to immerse yourself in the frenzy around you. Indulge the need to belong, to be the same as your brethren family. An act which gave the existing acolytes that fraternity.

As to the initiates, they passed through the eye of the needle. Fear kept them in place at first, fear of knowing how exquisitely ugly the sect really was, how they would be dealt with if they disobeyed or attempted to leave. Then the cycle would turn, and there would be another initiation. Only this time it would be them showing their devotion to God's Brother, revelling in the unchaining of their serpent beast. Doing as they had been done by, and enraptured by the accomplishment.

Whoever had designed the ritual, Garth thought, had really understood basic conditioning psychology. Such elemental barbarism was the only possible way to exert any kind of control over a Downtown savage. And there was no other sort of resident here.

"In darkness we see You, Lord," Garth recited. "In darkness we live. In darkness we wait for the true Night that You will bring us. Into that Night we will follow You." He lowered his arms.

"We will follow You," the acolytes echoed. Their rustling voices had become hot with expectation.

"When You light the true path of salvation at the end of the world, we will follow You."

"We will follow You."

"When Your legions fall upon the angels of the false lord, we will follow You."

"We will follow You."

"When the time . . ."

"That time is now," a single clear voice announced.

The acolytes grunted in surprise, while Garth spluttered to a halt, more astonished than outraged at the interruption. They all knew how important he considered the sect's ceremonies, how intolerant of sacrilege. Only true believers can inspire belief in others.

"Who said that?" he demanded.

A figure walked forward from the back of the temple, clad in a midnight-black robe. The opening at the front of the hood seemed to absorb all light, there was no hint of the head it contained. "I am your new messiah, and I have come among you to bring our Lord's Night to this planet."

Garth tried to use his retinal implants to see into the hood, but they couldn't detect any light in there, even infrared was useless. Then his neural nanonics reported innumerable program crashes. He yelled: "Shit!" and thrust his left hand out at the robed figure, index finger extended. The fire command to his microdart launcher never arrived.

"Join with me," Quinn ordered. "Or I will find more worthy owners for your bodies."

One of the acolytes launched herself at Quinn, booted foot swinging for his kneecap. Two others were right behind her, fists drawn back.

Quinn raised an arm, his sleeve falling to reveal an albino hand with grizzled claw fingers. Three thin streamers of white fire lashed out from the talons, searingly bright in the gloomy, smoke-heavy air. They struck his attackers, who were flung backwards as if they'd been hit by a shotgun blast.

Garth grabbed one of the serpent candlesticks, and swung it wildly, aiming to smash it down on Quinn's head. Not even a possessed would be able to survive a mashed brain, the invading soul would be forced out. Air thickened around the candlestick, slowing its momentum until it halted ten centimetres above the apex of Quinn's hood. The serpent's head, which held the candle, hissed and closed its mouth, biting the rod of wax in half.

"Swamp him!" Garth shouted. "He can't defeat all of us. Sacrifice yourself, for God's Brother."

A few of the acolytes edged closer to Quinn, but most stayed where they were. The candlestick began to glow along its entire length. Pain stabbed into Garth's hands. He could hear his skin sizzling. Squirts of greasy smoke puffed out. But he couldn't let go; his fingers wouldn't move. He saw them blister and blacken; bubbling juices ran down his wrists.

"Kill him," he cried. "Kill. Kill." His burning hands made him scream out in agony.

Quinn leant towards him. "Why?" he asked. "This is the

time of God's Brother. He sent me here to lead you. Obey me."

Garth fell to his knees, arms shaking, charred hands still clenched round the gleaming candlestick. "You're a possessed."

"I was a possessed. I returned. My belief in Him freed me."

"You'll possess all of us," the magus hissed.

"Some of you. But that is what the sect prays for. An army of the damned; loyal followers of our darkest Lord." He turned to the acolytes and held up his hands. For the first time his face was visible within, pale and deadly intent. "The waiting is over. I have come, and I bring you victory for eternity. No more pathetic squabbling over black stimulants, no more wasting your life mugging geriatric farts. His true work waits to be done. I know how to bring Night to this planet. Kneel before me, become true warriors of darkness, and together we will rain stone upon this land until it bleeds and dies."

Garth screamed again. All that was left now of his fingers were black bones soldered to the candlestick. "Kill him, shitbrains!" he roared. "Smash the fucker into bedrock, curse you." But through eyes blurred with tears he could see the acolytes slowly sinking to the floor in front of Quinn. It was like a wave effect, spreading across the temple. Wener was the closest to Quinn, his simple face alive with admiration and excitement. "I'm with you," the lumbering acolyte yelled. "Let me kill people for you. I want to kill everyone, kill the whole world. I hate them. I hate them real bad."

Garth groaned in mortification. They believed him! Believed the shit was a real messenger from God's Brother.

Quinn closed his eyes and smiled in joy as he gloried in their adulation. Finally, he was back among his own. "We will show the Light Bringer we are the worthy ones," he promised them. "I will guide you over an ocean of blood to His Empire. And from there we will hear the false lord weeping at the end of the universe."

The acolytes cheered and laughed rapturously. This was what they craved; no more of the magus's tactical restraint, at last they could unleash violence and horror without end, begin the war against the light, their promised destiny.

Quinn turned and glanced down at magus Garth. "You: fuckbrain. Grovel, lick the shit off my feet, and I'll allow you to join the crusade as a whore for the soldiers."

The candlestick clattered to the ground, with the roast remains of Garth's hands still attached. He bared his teeth at the deranged possessor standing over him. "I serve my Lord alone. You can go to hell."

"Been there," Quinn said urbanely. "Done that. Come back." His hand descended on Garth's head as if in anointment. "But you will be of use to me. Your body, anyway." His needle-sharp talons pierced the skin.

The magus discovered that the pain of losing his hands was merely the overture to a very long and quite excruciating symphony.

2

It was designated Bureau Seven, which somewhat inevitably for a government organization was acronymed down to B7. To anyone with Govcentral alpha-rated clearance, it was listed as one of the hundreds of bland committees which made up the management hierarchy of the Govcentral Internal Security Directorate. Officially its function was Policy Integration and Resource Allocation, a vital coordination role. The more senior GISD Bureaus produced their requirements for information and actions, and it was B7's job to make sure none of the new objectives clashed with current operations before they designated local arcology offices with carrying out the project and assigned funds. If there was any anomaly to be found with B7, it was that such an important and sensitive responsibility did not have a political appointee assigned to run it. Certainly the chiefs of Bureaus 1 through 6 changed with every new administration, reflecting fresh political priorities; and several hundred minor posts among the lower Bureaus were also up for grabs as a loyalty reward to the new President's retinue. Again, no junior positions were available in B7.

So B7 carried on as it always had, isolated and insular. In

fact, just how insular would have come as a great shock to any outsider who investigated the nature of its members—that is, a shock in the brief period left to them before being quietly terminated.

Although the antithesis of democracy themselves, they did take the job of guarding the republic of Earth extremely seriously. Possession was the one threat which actually had the potential not just to overthrow but actually eliminate Govcentral, a prospect which hadn't arisen for nearly four hundred and fifty years, since the population pressures of the Great Dispersal.

Possession, therefore, was the reason why a full meeting of all sixteen members had been convened for the first time in twelve years. Their sensenviron conference had a standard format, a white infinity-walled room with an oval table in the centre seating their generated representations. There was no seniority among them, each had his or her separate area of responsibility, the majority of which were designated purely on geographical terms, although there were supervisors for GISD's divisions dealing in military intelligence.

An omnidirectional projection hung over the table, showing a warehouse on Norfolk which was burning with unnatural ferocity. Several museum-piece fire engines were racing towards it, along with men in khaki uniforms.

"It would appear the Kavanagh girl is telling the truth," said the Central American supervisor.

"I never doubted it," Western Europe replied.

"She's certainly not possessed," said Military Intelligence. "Not now, anyway. But she'd still have those memories if she had been."

"If she'd been possessed, she would have admitted it," Western Europe said indolently. "You're building in complications for us."

"Do you want a full personality debrief to confirm her authenticity?" Southern Africa asked.

"I don't think we should," Western Europe said. He absorbed the mildly polite expressions of surprise the representations around the table were directing at him.

"Care to share with us?" Southern Pacific asked archly.

Western Europe looked at the Military Intelligence supervisor. "I believe we have crossover from the *Mount's Delta*?"

Military Intelligence gave a perfunctory nod. "Yes. We confirmed that the starship was carrying two people when it docked at Supra-Brazil. One of them slaughtered the other in an extravagantly gory fashion right after docking was completed, the body was literally exploded. All that we can tell you about the victim is that he was male. We still don't know who he was, there's certainly no correlating DNA profile stored in our memory cores. I've requested that all governments we're in contact with run a search through their records, but I don't hold out much hope."

"Why not?" Southern Pacific asked.

"The *Mount's Delta* came from Nyvan; he was probably one of their citizens. None of their nations remain intact."

"Not relevant, anyway," said Western Europe.

"Agreed," Military Intelligence said. "Once we'd stripped down the *Mount's Delta*, we ran extremely thorough forensic tests on the life support capsule and its environmental systems. Analysis on the faecal residue left in the waste cycle mechanism identified the other occupant's DNA for us. And this is where the story gets interesting, because we have a very positive match on his DNA." Military Intelligence datavised the sensevise's controlling processor, and the image above the table changed. Now it showed an image taken from Louise Kavanagh's brain a few minutes before the warehouse was fired; a young man with a pale, stern face, dressed in a jet-black robe. The viewing angle was such that he looked down on the members of B7 with a derisory sneer. "Quinn Dexter. He was an Ivet shipped to Lalonde last year, sentenced for resisting arrest, the police thought he was running an illegal package into Edmonton. He was as it happens. Sequestration nanonics."

"Oh Christ," Central America muttered.

"The Kavanagh girl confirms he was on Norfolk, and both she and Fletcher Christian strongly suspect he was the one who took over the frigate *Tantu*. Following that, the *Tantu* made one unsuccessful attempt to penetrate Earth defences, and immediately withdrew, damaging itself in the process."

Western Europe datavised the sensenviron management processor, and the image above the table changed again. "Dexter got to Nyvan. One of the surviving asteroids confirmed that the *Tantu* docked at Jesup asteroid. That's when their real troubles started. Ships from Jesup planted the nukes in the abandoned asteroids." He pointed at the image of Nyvan which had replaced Dexter. It was a world like nothing previously seen in the galaxy, as if a ball of lava had congealed in space, a crinkled black surface crust riddled with contorted fissures of radiant red light. The two atmospheric aspects were in constant conflict, supernatural and supernature boiling against each other with harrowing aggression.

"Dexter was there on Lalonde at incident one, according to Laton and our Edenist friends," Western Europe said remorselessly. "He was on Norfolk, which we now recognize as the major distribution source of infection. He was at Nyvan which has elevated the crisis to a completely new stage; as far as we can tell one which has proved as hostile to the possessed as it is to the ordinary population. And now we are certain he arrived here at Supra-Brazil." He looked directly at the South America supervisor.

"There was an alert at the Brazil tower station fifteen hours after the *Mount's Delta* arrived," South America said tonelessly. "Just after its descent, one of the lift capsules suffered exactly the kind of electronic glitches known to be inflicted by the possessed. We had the entire arrivals complex sealed and surrounded within ninety seconds. Nothing. No sign of any possessed."

"But you think he's here?" East Europe pressed.

South America smiled without humour. "We know he is. After the alert, we hauled in everyone who came down on the lift capsule, passengers and crew. This is what we got from several neural nanonics memory cells." Nyvan faded away to show a slightly fuzzy two-dimensional picture, indicating a low-grade recording. The figure in the Royale Class lounge wearing a blue-silk suit, and slumped comfortably in a deep chair was undoubtedly Dexter.

"Merciful Allah," North Pacific exclaimed. "We'll have to shut down the vac-trains. It's our one advantage. I don't care how good he is at eluding our sensors, the little shit can't walk a thousand kilometres along a vacuum tunnel. Isolate the bastard, and hit him with an SD platform strike."

"I believe even we would have trouble shutting down the vac-trains," South Pacific said significantly. "Not without questions being asked."

"I don't mean we should issue the order," North Pacific snapped. "Feed the information up to B3, and make the President's office authorize it."

"If the public find out there's a possessed on Earth, there will be absolute pandemonium," North Africa said. "Even we would have trouble retaining control over the arcologies."

"Better than being possessed," North America said. "Because that's what he'll do to the arcology populations if we don't stop him. Even we would be in danger."

"I think his objective is more complex than that," Western Europe said. "We know what he did to Nyvan, I think we can assume he wants to do the same thing here."

"Not a chance," Military Intelligence said. "Even if he could sneak around up in the Halo, which I doubt, he'd never acquire enough nukes to split an asteroid open. You can't remove one of those beauts from storage without anyone knowing."

"Maybe, but there's something else. Kavanagh and Fletcher Christian both say that Dexter is here to hunt down Banneth and have his revenge on her. I checked Dexter's file; he used to be a sect member in Edmonton. Banneth was his magus."

"So what?" asked North Pacific. "You know what those crazy brute sect members do to each other when the lights go off. I'm not surprised he wants to beat the crap out of Banneth."

"You're missing the point," Western Europe said patiently. "Why would the soul possessing Quinn Dexter's body care about Dexter's old magus?" He looked questioningly round the table. "We're dealing with something new, here, something different. An ordinary person who has somehow gained the same powers of the possessed, if not superior ones. His goals are not going to be the same as theirs, this craving they have to flee the universe."

North America caught it first. "Shit. He used to be a sect member."

"And presumably remains so," Western Europe agreed. "He was still performing their ceremony on Lalonde; that was incident one, after all. Dexter is a true believer in the Light Bringer teachings."

"You think he's come back to find his God?"

"It's not a god he worships, it's the devil. But no, he's not here to find him. My people ran a psychological profile simulation; what they got indicates he's come back to prepare the way for his Lord, the Light Bringer, who glories in war and chaos. He'll try to unleash as much mayhem and destruction on both us and the possessed as it's possible to do. Nyvan was just the warm up. The real game is going to be played out down here."

"Well that settles it then," North Pacific said. "We have to close the vac-trains. It'll mean losing an entire arcology to him; but we can save the rest."

"Don't be so melodramatic," Western Europe said. "Dexter is a problem; a novel one, granted. He's different, and more powerful than all the others B7 has faced over the centuries. But that's what we are here for, ultimately, to solve problems which would defeat conventional government action. We simply have to locate a weakness and use it."

"An invisible megalomaniac as powerful as a minor god has a weakness?" North Pacific said. "Allah preserve us, I should like to hear what it is."

"The Kavanagh girl has escaped him twice. Both times it was due to the intervention of an unknown possessed. We have an ally."

"On Norfolk! Which has bloody vanished."

"Nevertheless, Dexter does not command total support from the possessed. He is not invincible. And we have what should be a decisive advantage over him."

"Which is?"

"We know about him. He knows nothing about us. That can be exploited to trap him."

"Ah yes," the Halo supervisor said contentedly. "Now I understand the reluctance for a personality debrief on the Kavanagh girl."

"Well I don't," South America declared querulously.

"Personality debrief requires a much more invasive procedure," Western Europe said. "At the moment Kavanagh is not aware of what has happened to her. That means we can use her ignorance to get very close to Dexter."

"Close to . . ." South Pacific trailed off. "My God, you want to use her as a lightning conductor."

"Exactly. At the moment we have one chance for proximity, and that's Banneth. Unfortunately there is only a limited degree of preparation we can make with her. The possessed, and therefore presumably Dexter, can sense the emotional content of the minds around them. We have to proceed with extreme caution if he is to be lured into a termination option. If he learns someone is hunting him, we could lose several arcologies, if not more. Moving the Kavanagh girl back into the game doubles our chances of engineering an encounter with him."

"That's goddamn risky," North America said.

"No, I like it," Halo said. "It has subtlety; that's more us than closing down the vac-trains and using SD fire to incinerate entire arcology domes."

"Oh heaven preserve we should let our standard of style drop when the whole fucking world is about to go down the can," South Pacific groused.

"Does anyone have a substantial objection?" Western Europe enquired.

"Your operation," North Pacific said hotly. "Your responsibility."

"Responsibility?" Australia chided lightly.

There were several smiles around the table as North Pacific glowered.

"Naturally I accept the consequences," Western Europe purred volubly.

"You're always such an arrogant little shit when you're this age, aren't you?" North Pacific said.

Western Europe just laughed.

The three Confederation Navy marines were polite, insistent, and resolutely uncommunicative. They escorted Joshua the entire length of Trafalgar. Which, he thought, was a hopeful sign; he was being taken away from the CNIS section. A day and a half of interviews with sourfaced CNIS investigators, cooperating like a good citizen. None of his questions answered in return. Certainly no access to a lawyer—one of the investigators had given him a filthy look when he half-jokingly asked for legal aid. Net processors wouldn't respond to his datavises. He didn't know where the rest of his crew was. Didn't know what was happening to *Lady Mac*. And could make a pretty good guess what kind of report Monica and Samuel were concocting.

From the tube carriage station a lift took them up to a floor which was plainly officer country. A wide corridor, good carpet, discrete lighting, holograms of famous Naval events (few he recognized), intent men and women looping from office to office, none of them under the rank of senior lieutenant. Joshua was led into a reception room with two captains sitting at desks. One of them stood, and saluted the marines. "We'll take him from here."

"What is this?" Joshua asked. It definitely wasn't a firing squad on the other side of the ornate double doors in front of him, and hopefully not a courtroom either.

"The First Admiral will see you now," the captain said.

"Er," Joshua said lamely. "Okay, then."

The large circular office had a window overlooking the asteroid's biosphere. It was night outside, the solartubes reduced to a misty oyster glimmer revealing little of the landscape. Big holoscreens on the walls were flashing up external sensor images of Avon and the asteroid's spaceports. Joshua looked for *Lady Mac* among the docking bays, but couldn't find her.

The captain beside him saluted. "Captain Calvert, sir."

Joshua locked eyes with the man sitting behind the big teak desk in front of him, receiving a mildly intrigued gaze from Samual Aleksandrovich.

"So," the First Admiral said. "Lagrange Calvert. You fly some very tight manoeuvres, Captain."

Joshua narrowed his eyes, unsure just how much irony was being applied here. "I just do what comes naturally."

"Indeed you do. I accessed that section of your file, also." The First Admiral smiled at some internal joke, and waved a hand. "Please sit down, Captain."

A blue-steel chair swelled up out of the floor in front of the desk. Alkad Mzu was sitting in the one next to it, body held rigid, staring ahead. On the other side of her, Monica and Samuel had relaxed back into their own chairs. The First Admiral introduced the demure Edenist woman beside them as Admiral Lalwani, the CNIS chief. Joshua responded with a very nervous twitch of greeting.

"I think I had better start by saying the Confederation Navy would like to thank you for your part in the Nyvan affair, and solving the Alchemist problem for us," the First Admiral said. "I do not like to dwell on the consequences had the Capone Organization acquired it."

"I'm not under arrest?"

"No."

Joshua let out a hefty breath of relief. "Jesus!" He grinned at Monica, who responded with a laconic smile.

"Er, so can I go now?" he asked without much hope.

"Not quite," Lalwani said. "You're one of the few people who knows how the Alchemist works," she told him.

Joshua did his best not to glance at Mzu. "A very brief description."

"Of the principals," Mzu said.

"And I believe you told Samuel and agent Foulkes that you would submit to internal exile in Tranquillity so no one else could obtain the information," Lalwani said.

"Did I? No."

Monica pantomimed deep thought. "Your exact words were: I'll stay in Tranquillity if we survive this, but I have to know."

"And you said you'd stay there with me," Joshua snapped back. He scowled at her. "Ever heard of Hiroshima?"

"The first time an atomic bomb was used on Earth," Lalwani said.

"Yeah. At the time the only real secret about an atom bomb was the fact that it was possible to build one that worked. Once it got used, that secret was out."

"The relevance being?"

"Anyone who visits the location where we deployed Alchemist and sees the result, is going to be able to figure out those precious principals of yours. After that, it's just a question of engineering. Besides, the possessed won't build another. They're not geared around that kind of action."

"Capone's Organization might be able to," Monica said. "They certainly thought they could, remember? They wanted Mzu at any price, incarnate or just her soul. And who's going to know where the Alchemist was used unless you and your crew tell them?"

"Jesus, what do you people want from me?"

"Very little," said the First Admiral. "I think we've established to everyone's satisfaction that you're trustworthy." He grinned at Joshua's sour expression. "Despite what that may do to your reputation. So I'm just going to ask you to agree to a few ground rules. You do not discuss the Alchemist with anyone. And I mean anyone."

"Easy enough."

"For the duration of our current crisis you do not put yourself in a position where you will encounter the possessed."

"I've already encountered them twice, I don't intend to do it again."

"That effectively means you will not fly anywhere outside the Sol system. Once you get home, you stay there."

"Right." Joshua frowned. "You want me to go to Sol?"

"Yes. You will take Dr Mzu and the *Beezling* survivors there. As you pointed out with your Hiroshima analogy, we cannot push the information genie back into the lamp, but we can certainly initiate damage limitation. The relevant governments have agreed that Dr Mzu can be returned to a neutral nation, where she will not communicate any details of the Alchemist to anyone. The doctor has consented to that."

"They'll get it eventually," Joshua said softly. "No matter what agreements they sign, governments will try to build Alchemists."

"No doubt," Samual Aleksandrovich said. "But such problems are for the future. And that is going to be a very different place to today, is it not, Captain?"

"If we solve today, then, yeah. It'll be different. Even today is different than yesterday."

"So. Lagrange Calvert has become a philosopher?"

"Haven't we all, knowing what we do now?"

The First Admiral nodded reluctantly. "Perhaps it's not such a bad thing. Somebody has to find a solution. The more there are of us searching, the quicker it will be revealed."

"That's a lot of faith you have there, Admiral."

"Of course. If I didn't have faith in the human race, I would have no right to sit in this chair."

Joshua gave him a strong look. The First Admiral wasn't quite what he'd envisaged, the gung-ho military archetype. That made him more confident for the future. Slightly. "Okay, so where do you want me to take the doc in the Sol system, exactly?"

Samual Aleksandrovich smiled broadly. "Ah yes, this is one piece of news I shall enjoy imparting."

Friend Jay, please cry not.

Haile's voice was no stronger than the memory of a dream. Jay had closed up her mind as tight as her eyelids. She just lay on the floor, all curled up, sobbing at . . . everything. Ever since that terrible day on Lalonde when the Ivets went mad, she and Mummy had been torn further and further apart. First the cramped house on the savannah. Then Tranquillity, where she'd heard rumours of the possessed taking Lalonde out of the universe—even though the paediatric ward staff had been careful about allowing the refugee kids access to any news. Now this, flying like an angel to another galaxy. Where she'd never get back from. And she'd never see Mummy ever again. Everyone she knew was either dead, or about to be possessed. She wailed louder, so much it hurt her throat.

The back of her head was full of warm whispers, pushing to be let in.

Jay, please restrain yourself.

She is developing cyclic trauma psychosis.

We should impose a thalamic regulator routine.

Humans respond better to chemical suppressers.

Certainty?

Ambiguous context.

Referral to Corpus.

Tractamorphic flesh was slithering round her, rubbing gently. She shook at the touch of it.

Then there was a sharp regular clicking sound, *tac tac tac*, like heels on the cool hard floor. Human heels.

"What in seven heavens' name do you lot think you're doing?" a woman's voice asked sharply. "Give the poor dear some air, for goodness sake. Come on, get back. Right back. Move out the way." There followed the distinctive sound of a human hand being slapped against a Kiint hide.

Jay stopped crying.

"Move! You too, you little terror."

That causes painfulness, Haile protested.

"Then learn to move quicker."

Jay smeared some of the tears from her eyes, and peered up just in time to see someone's finger and thumb pinching the crater ridge of skin around Haile's ear, hauling her aside. The baby Kiint's legs were getting all twisted round as she skittled hurriedly out of the way.

The owner of the hand smiled down at Jay. "Well well, sweetie, haven't you just caused a stir? And whatever are all these tears for? I suppose you had a bit of shock when they jumped you here. Don't blame you. That stupid leaping through the darkness stunt used to give me the chronic heebie-jeebies every time. I'll take a Model-T over that any day. Now there was a really gracious method of transport. Would you like a hanky, wipe your face a bit?"

"Uh," Jay said. She'd never seen a woman quite so old before; her brown Mediterranean skin was deeply wrinkled, and her back curved slightly, giving her shoulders a permanent hunch. The dress she wore had come straight out from a history text, lemon-yellow cotton printed with tiny white flowers, complemented by a wide belt and lace collar and cuffs. Thin snow-white hair had been permed into a neat beret; and a double loop of large pearls round her neck chittered softly with every movement. It was as if she'd turned age into a statement of pride. But her green eyes were vividly alert.

A frilly lace handkerchief was pulled from her sleeve, and proffered to Jay.

"Thank you," Jay gulped. She took the hanky, and blew into it heavily. The huge adult Kiint had all backed off, standing several paces behind the small woman, keeping close together in a mutual support group. Haile was pressed against Lieria, who had formshifted a tractamorphic arm to stroke her daughter soothingly.

"So now, sweetie, why don't you start by telling me your name."

"Jay Hilton."

"Jay." The woman's jowls bobbled, as if she was sucking on a particularly hard mint. "That's nice. Well, Jay, I'm Tracy Dean."

"Hello. Um, you are real, aren't you?"

Tracy laughed. "Oh yes, sweetie, I'm genuine flesh and blood, all right. And before you ask why I'm here, this is my home now. But we'll save the explanations until tomorrow. Because they're very long and complicated, and you're tired and upset. You need to get some sleep now."

"I don't want to sleep," Jay stammered. "Everybody in Tranquillity's dead, and I'm here. And I want Mummy. And she's gone."

"Oh, Jay, no, sweetie." Tracy knelt beside the little girl, and hugged her tight. Jay was sniffling again, ready to burst into tears. "Nobody's dead. Tranquillity swallowed away clean before any of the combat wasps reached it. These silly oafs got it all wrong and panicked. Aren't they stupid?"

"Tranquillity's alive?"

"Yes."

"And Ione, and Father Horst, and everybody?"

"Yes, all safe and sound. Tranquillity is orbiting Jupiter right this minute. That surprised everybody, let me tell you."

"But . . . how did it do that?"

"We're not quite sure yet, but it must have an awful lot of energy patterning cells tucked away somewhere inside it." She gave Jay a sly grin, and winked. "Tricky people, those Saldanas. And very clever with it, thankfully."

Jay managed an experimental smile.

"That's better. Now, let's see about finding you that bed for the night." Tracy rose to her feet, holding Jay's hand.

Jay used her free hand to wipe the handkerchief across her face as she scrambled to her feet. "Oh right." Actually, she thought that talk of explanations sounded quite fascinating now. There was so much about this place she wanted to know. It would be worth staying awake for.

You now have betterness, query? Haile asked anxiously.

Jay nodded enthusiastically at her friend. "Much better."

That is good.

I will assume complete Jay Hilton guardian responsibility now.

Jay cocked her head to give Tracy Dean a sideways look. How could she use the Kiint mental voice?

Confirm, Nang said. The words Jay could hear in her head speeded up then, becoming a half-imagined birdsong, but suffused with feeling.

We will venture wide together, Haile said. **See new things. There is muchness here to see.**

"Tomorrow, maybe," Tracy said. "We have to get Jay settled in here first."

Jay shrugged at her friend.

"Now then, Jay, we're going to jump out of here. It'll be

the same as before, but this time you know it's happening, and I'll be with you the whole time. All right?"

"Couldn't we just walk, or use a groundcar, or something?"

Tracy smiled sympathetically. "Not really, sweetie." She pointed up at the planets arching over the dark sky. "My home is on one of those."

"Oh. But I will be seeing Haile while I'm here, won't I?" Jay raised her hand and waved at her friend. Haile formshifted the tip on one of her tractamorphic arms into a human hand, and wriggled the fingers.

We will build the castles of sand again.

"Close your eyes," Tracy said. "It's easier that way." Her arm went round Jay's shoulder. "Are you ready?"

This time it wasn't so bad. There was that quick breeze ruffling her nightie again, and despite having her eyes shut her stomach was telling her very urgently that she was falling again. A squeak crept out of her lips in spite of her best efforts.

"It's all right sweetie, we're here now. You can open your eyes again."

The breeze had vanished, its departure signalling a whole symphony of fresh sound. Hot sunlight tingled her skin; when she breathed in she could taste salt.

Jay opened her eyes. There was a beach in front of her, one which made the little cove on Tranquillity seem quite pallid by comparison. The powder-fine sand was snow-white, stretching out on either side of her for as far as she could see. Wonderfully clear turquoise water lapped against it, languid waves rolling in from a reef several hundred metres out. A beautiful three-masted yacht of some golden wood was anchored half-way between the shore and the reef, undeniably human in design.

Jay grinned at it, then shielded her eyes with a hand and

looked round. She was standing on a circle of the same ebony material as before, but this time there was no encircling wall or watching Kiint. The only artefact was a bright orange cylinder, as tall as she was, standing next to the edge. Scatterings of sand were drifting onto the circle.

Behind her, a thick barricade of trees and bushes lined the rear of the beach. Long creeper tendrils had slithered out of them over the hard-packed sand, knitting together in a tough lacework that sprouted blue and pink palm-sized flowers. The only noise was the waves and some kind of honking in the distance, almost like a flock of geese. When she searched the cloudless sky, she could see several birds flapping and gliding about in the distance. The arch of planets was a line of silver disks twinkling away into the horizon.

"Where are we now?" Jay asked.

"Home." Tracy's face managed to produce even more wrinkles as she sniffed distastefully. "Not that anywhere is really home after spending two thousand years swanning loyally round Earth and the Confederation planets."

Jay stared at her in astonishment. "You're two thousand years old?"

"That's right, sweetie. Why, don't I look it?"

Jay blushed. "Well . . ."

Tracy laughed, and took hold of her hand. "Come along, let's find you that bed. I'll think I'll put you in my guest quarters. That'll be simplest. Never thought I'd ever get to use them."

They walked off the ebony circle. Up ahead of them, Jay could see some figures lazing on the beach, while others were swimming in the sea. Their strokes were slow and controlled. She realized they were all as old as Tracy. Now Jay was paying attention, she could make out several chalets lurking in the vegetation behind the beach. They were strung out on either side of a white stone building with a red tile roof and a sizeable, well-manicured garden; it looked like some terribly exclusive clubhouse. Still more old people were sitting at iron tables on the lawns, reading, playing what looked like a board game, or just staring out to sea. Mauve-coloured globes, the size of a head, were floating through the air, moving sleekly from table to table. If they found an empty glass or plate they would absorb it straight through their surface. In many cases they would extrude a replacement; the new glasses were full, and the plates piled with sandwiches or biscuit-type snacks.

Jay walked along obediently at Tracy's side, her head swivelling about as she took in the amazing new sights. As they approached the big building, people looked their way and smiled encouragingly, nodding, waving.

"Why are they doing that?" Jay asked. All the excitement and fright had worn off now she knew she was safe, leaving her very tired.

Tracy chuckled. "Having you here is the biggest event that's happened to this place for a long time. Probably ever."

Tracy led her towards one of the chalets; a simple wooden structure with a veranda running along the front, on which stood big clay pots full of colourful plants. Jay could only think of the pretty little houses of the Juliffe villages on the day she and her mother had started sailing upriver to Aberdale. She sighed at the recollection. The universe had become very strange since then.

Tracy patted her gently. "Almost there, sweetie." They started up the steps to the veranda.

"Hi there," a man's voice called brightly.

Tracy groaned impatiently. "Richard, leave her alone. The poor little dear's dead on her feet."

A young man in scarlet shorts and a white T-shirt was

jogging barefoot across the sands towards them. He was tall with an athletic figure, his long blond hair tied back into a ponytail by a flamboyant leather lace. He pouted at the rebuke, then winked playfully at Jay. "Oh, come on, Trace; just paying my respects to a fellow escapee. Hello, Jay, my name's Richard Keaton." He gave a bow, and stuck his hand out.

Jay smiled uncertainly at him, and put out her own hand. He shook it formally. His whole attitude put her in mind of Joshua Calvert, which was comforting. "Did you jump out of Tranquillity as well?" she asked.

"Heavens, no, nothing like that. I was on Nyvan when someone tried to drop a dirty great lump of metal on me. Thought it best I slipped away when no one was looking."

"Oh."

"I know everything is real weird for you right now, so I just wanted you to have this." He produced a doll resembling some kind of animal, a flattish humanoid figure made from badly worn out brown-gold velvet; its mouth and nose were just lines of black stitching, and its eyes were amber glass. One semicircular ear had been torn off, allowing tufts of yellowing stuffing to peek out of the gash.

Jay gave the battered old thing a suspicious look, it wasn't anything like the animatic dolls back in Tranquillity's paediatric ward. In fact, it looked even more primitive than any toy on Lalonde. Which was pretty hard to believe. "Thank you," she said awkwardly as he proffered it. "What is it?"

"This is Prince Dell, my old Teddy Bear. Which dates me. But friends like this were all the rage on Earth when I was young. He's the ancestor of all those animatic dolls you kids have these days. If you hold him close at night he keeps troubles away from your dreams. But you have to keep cuddling him tight for him to be able to do that properly. Something to do with earth magic and contact; funny stuff like that. He used to sleep with me until I was a lot older than you. I thought he might be able to help you tonight."

He sounded so serious and hopeful that Jay took the bear from him and examined it closely. Prince Dell really was very tatty, but she could just picture him in the embrace of a sleeping boy with blond hair. The boy was smiling blissfully.

"All right," she said. "I'll hold on to him tonight. Thank you very much." It seemed a bit silly, but it was kind of him to be so considerate.

Richard Keaton smiled gladly. "That's good. The Prince hasn't had much to do for a long time. He'll be happy to have a new friend. Make sure you treat him nicely, he's a bit delicate now, poor thing."

"I will," Jay promised. "Are you really old, as well?"

"Older than most people you've ever met, but nothing like as antique as good old Trace, here."

"Huh," Tracy sniffed critically. "If you're quite finished."

Richard rolled his eyes for Jay's benefit. "Sweet dreams, Jay. I'll see you tomorrow, we've got lots to talk about."

"Richard," Tracy asked reluctantly. "Did Calvert do it?"

A huge smile flashed over his face. "Oh yeah. He did it. The Alchemist is neutralized. Just as well, it was a brute of a weapon."

"Typical. If they'd just devote ten per cent of their military budget and all that ingenuity into developing their social conditions."

"Preaching to the converted!"

"Are you talking about Joshua?" Jay asked. "What's he done?"

"Something very good," Richard said.

"Amazingly," Tracy muttered dryly.

"But . . ."

"Tomorrow, sweetie," Tracy said firmly. "Along with everything else. I promise. Right now, you're going to bed. Enough delaying tactics."

Richard waved, and walked away. Jay held Prince Dell against her tummy as Tracy's hand pressed into her back, propelling her up the steps and into the chalet. She glanced down at the ancient bear again. His dull glass eyes stared right back at her, it was an incredibly melancholic expression.

The first hellhawk came flashing out of its wormhole terminus twelve thousand kilometres from Monterey asteroid. New California's gravitonic detector warning satellites immediately datavised an alert to the naval tactical operations centre. The high pitched audio alarm startled Emmet Mordden, who was the duty officer in the large chamber. At the time he was sitting with his feet up on the commander's console, reading through a four-hundred-sheet hard copy guide of a Quantumsoft accountancy program in preparation for his next upgrade to the Treasury computers. With most of the Organization fleet away at Tranquillity, and the planet reasonably stable right now, it was a quiet duty, just right to catch up on his technical work.

Emmet's feet hit the floor as the AI responsible for threat analysis squirted a mass of symbols and vectors up on one of the huge wall-mounted holoscreens. In front of him, the equally surprised SD network operators scrambled to interpret what was happening. There weren't many of them among the eight rows of consoles in the centre, nothing like the full complement which the Organization had needed at the height of the Edenist harassment campaign. Right now, spaceflight traffic was at a minimum, and the contingent of

Valisk hellhawks on planetary defence duty had done a superb job of clearing Edenist stealth mines and spy globes from space around the planet.

"What is it?" Emmet asked automatically; by which time another three wormholes had opened. The precariously-stacked pile of hard copy avalanched off his console as he determinedly cleared his keyboard ready to respond.

The AI had acquired X-ray laser lock on for the first four targets, and was requesting fire authority. Another ten wormholes were opening. Jull von Holger, who acted as the go-between for the Valisk hellhawks and the operations centre, leapt to his feet, shouting: "Don't shoot!" He waved his arms frantically. "They're ours! They're our hellhawks."

Emmet hesitated, his fingers hovering over the keys. According to his console displays, over eighty wormholes had now opened to disgorge bitek starships. "What the fuck do they think they're doing busting in on us like that? Why aren't they with the fleet?" Suspicion flowered among his thoughts; and he didn't care that von Holger could sense it. Hellhawks were dangerously powerful craft, and with the fleet away they could make real trouble. He'd never really trusted Kiera Salter.

Jull von Holger's face went through a wild panoply of emotion-derived contortions as he conducted fast affinity conversations with the unexpected arrivals. "They're not from the fleet. They've come here directly from Valisk." He halted for a moment, shocked. "It's gone. Valisk has gone. We lost to that little prat Dariat."

"Holy shit," Hudson Proctor gasped.

Kiera stuck her head round the bathroom door as the beautician tried to wrap her sopping wet hair in a huge fluffy purple towel. The Quayle suite in the Monterey

Hilton was a temple to opulence and personal luxury. As Rubra had denied everyone access to the Valisk starscrapers, along with their apartment bathrooms, Kiera had simply groomed herself with energistic power alone. She had forgotten what it was to sprawl in a Jacuzzi with a selector that could blend in any of a dozen exotic salts. And as for having her hair styled properly rather than forcing it into shape . . .

"What?" she snapped in annoyance; though the beacon-bright dismay in her associate's mind tempered any real fury at being interrupted.

"The hellhawks are here," he said. "All of them. They've come from Valisk. It's . . ." He flinched in trepidation. Delivering bad news to Kiera was always a desperately negative career move. Just because she had the kind of teenage-sweetheart looks which could (and had) suckered in non-possessed kids from right across the Confederation didn't mean her behaviour matched. Quite the opposite—she took a perverse enjoyment from that, too. "Bonney chased after Dariat, apparently. There was a big fight in one of the starscrapers. Plenty of our people got flung back into the beyond. Then she forced him to ally with Rubra, or something."

"What happened?"

"They, er—Valisk's gone. The two of them took the habitat out of the universe."

Kiera stared at him, little wisps of steam starting to lick out of her hair. She'd always bitterly regretted that Marie Skibbow didn't have some kind of affinity faculty; its absence had always put at her at a slight disadvantage in Valisk. But she'd coped, the entire worldlet and its formidable starships had belonged to her. She'd been a power to contend with. Even Capone had sought out her help. Now—

Kiera gave the non-possessed beautician girl a blank-eyed glance. "Get lost."

"Ma'am." The girl curtseyed, and almost sprinted for the suite's double doors on the other side of the lounge.

Kiera allowed herself a muted scream of fury when the doors closed. "That fucking Dariat! I knew it! I fucking knew he was a disaster waiting to happen."

"We're still in charge of the hellhawks," Hudson Proctor said. "That gives us a big chunk of Capone's action; and the Organization is in charge of a couple of star systems, with more on the way. It's not such a loss. If we'd been inside the habitat it would be one hell of a lot worse."

"If I'd been inside, it would never have happened," she snapped back. Her hair was abruptly dry, and her robe blurred, running like hot wax until it became a sharp mauve business suit. "Control," she murmured almost to herself. "That's the key here."

Hudson Proctor could sense her focusing on him, both her eyes and her mind.

"Are you with me?" she asked. "Or are you going to ask good old Al if you can sign on as one of his lieutenants?"

"Why would I do that?"

"Because if I can't keep control of the hellhawks, I'm nothing to the Organization." She smiled thinly. "You and I would have to start right back at the beginning again. With the hellhawks obeying us, we'll still be players."

He glanced out of the big window, searching space for a sight of the bitek starships. "We've got no hold on them any more," he said dejectedly. "Without the affinity-capable bodies stored in Valisk, there's no way they'll do as they're ordered. And there aren't any more of Rubra's family left for us to replace them with. We've lost."

Kiera shook her head impatiently. Considering she'd co-opted the ex-general to her council for his ability to think tactically, he was doing a remarkably poor job of it. But then, maybe a politician's instinct was naturally quicker at finding an opponent's weakness. "There's one thing left which they can't do for themselves."

"And that is?"

"Eat. The only sources of their nutrient fluid which they'll be able to use are on Organization-held asteroids. Without food, even bitek organisms will wither and die. And we know our energistic power can't magic up genuine food."

"Then Capone will control them."

"No." Kiera could sense his anxiety at the prospect of losing his status, and knew she could rely on him. She closed her eyes, focusing on assignments for the small number of her people she'd brought with her to Monterey. "Which is the most reliable hellhawk we've got on planetary defence?"

"Reliable?"

"Loyal, idiot. To me."

"That'll probably be Etchells in the *Stryla*. He's a regular little Nazi, always complaining hellhawks never see enough battle action. Doesn't get on too well with the others, either."

"Perfect. Call him back to Monterey's docking ledges and go on board. I want you to visit every Organization asteroid in this system with a nutrient fluid production system. And blow it to shit."

Hudson gave her an astounded look, trepidation replacing the earlier anxiety. "The asteroids?"

"No, shithead! Just the production systems. You don't even have to dock, just use an X-ray laser. That'll leave Monterey as their only supply point." She smiled happily. "The Organization has enough to do right now without the burden of maintaining all that complicated machinery. I think I'll go down there right now with our experts, and relieve them."

It wasn't dawn which arose over the wolds, inasmuch as there was no sun to slide above the horizon any more, but none the less the darkened sky grew radiant in homage to Norfolk's lost diurnal rhythm. Luca Comar felt it developing because he was a part of making it happen. By coming to this place he had freed himself from the clamour of the souls lost within the beyond, their tormented screams and angry pleas. In exchange he had gained an awareness of community.

Born at the tail end of the Twenty-first Century he'd grown up in the Amsterdam arcology. It was a time when people still clung to the hope that the planet could be healed, their superb technology employed to turn the clock back to the nevertime of halcyon pastoral days. In his youth, Luca dreamed of the land returned to immense parkland vistas with proud white and gold cities straddling the horizon. A child brought up by some of the last hippies on Earth, his formative years were spent loving the knowledge that togetherness was all. Then he turned eighteen, and for the first time in his existence reality had bitten, and bitten hard; he had to get a job, and an apartment, and pay taxes. Not nice. He resented it until the day his body died.

So now he had stolen a new body, and with the strange powers that theft had bestowed, he'd joined with the others of this planet to create their own Gaia. Unity of life was a pervasive, shroud-like presence wrapping itself around the planet, replacing the regimented order of the universe as their provider. Because the new inhabitants of Norfolk wished there to be a dawn, there was one. And as they equally desired night, so the light was banished. He contributed a little of himself to this Gaia, some of his wishes, some of his strength, a constant avowal of thanks to this new phase of his existence.

Luca sat on the edge of the huge bed in the master bedroom to watch the light strengthen outside Cricklade; a silver warmth shining down from the sky, its uniformity leaving few shadows. With it came the sense of anticipation, a new day to be treasured because of the opportunity it might bring.

A dull dawn, bland and boring, just as the days have become. We used to have two suns, and revelled in the contrast of colours they brought, the battle of shadows. They had energy and majesty, they inspired. But this, this . . .

The woman on the bed beside Luca stretched and rolled over, resting her chin in her hand and smiling up at him. "Morning," she purred.

He grinned back. Lucy was good company, sharing a lot of his enthusiasms, as well as a wicked sense of humour. A tall woman, great figure, thick chestnut hair worn long, barely into her mid-twenties. He never asked how much of her appearance was hers, and how much belonged to her host. The age of your host had swiftly become taboo. He liked to think himself modern enough so that bedding a ninety-year-old wouldn't bother him, age and looks being different concepts here. He still didn't ask, though. The solid image was good enough.

An image so close to Marjorie it verges on the idolatrous. Did this Lucy see that in my heart?

Luca yawned widely. "I'd better get going. We have to inspect the mill this morning, and I need to know how much seed corn we've actually got left in the silos over in the estate's western farms. I don't believe what the residents are telling me. It doesn't correspond with what Grant knows."

Lucy pulled a dour face. "One week in heaven, and the four horsemen are already giving us the eye."

"Alas, this is not heaven, I'm afraid."

"And don't I know it. Fancy having to work for a living when you're dead. God, the indignity."

"The wages of sin, lady. We did have one hell of a party to start with, after all."

She flopped back down on the bed, tongue poised tautly on her upper lip. "Sure did. You know I was quite repressed back when I was alive first time around. Sexually, that is."

"Hallelujah, it's a miracle cure."

She gave a husky chuckle, then sobered. "I'm supposed to be helping out in the kitchen today. Cooking the workers lunch, then taking it out to the fields for them. Bugger, it's like some kind of Amish festival. And how come we're reverting to gender stereotypes?"

"What do you mean?"

"It's us girls that are doing all the cooking."

"Not all of you."

"The majority. You should work out a better rota for us."

"Why me?"

"You seem to be taking charge around here. Quite the little baron."

"Okay, I designate you to draw up a proper equitable rota." He stuck his tongue out at her. "You should be good at secretarial work."

The pillow hit him on the side of his head, nearly knocking him off the bed. He caught the next one, and put it out of her reach. "I didn't do it deliberately," he said seriously. "People tell me what they can do, and I shove them at the first matching job. We need to get a list of occupations and skills sorted out."

She moaned. "Bureaucracy in heaven, that's worse than sexism."

"Just think yourself lucky we haven't got round to introducing taxes yet." He started searching round for his trousers. Luckily, the Manor had entire wardrobes of Grant Kavanagh's high-quality clothes. They weren't quite Luca's style, but at least they fitted perfectly. And the outdoor gear was hard-wearing, too. It saved him from having to dream up new stuff. That was harder here, in this realm. Imagined items took a long time to form, but when they did, they had more substance, and persevered longer. Concentrate hard enough and long enough on changing something, and the change would become permanent, requiring no more attention.

But that was inert objects: clothes, stone, wood, even chunks of machinery (not electronics), they could all be fashioned by the mind. Which was fortunate; Norfolk's low-technology infrastructure could be repaired with relative ease. Physical appearance, too, could be governed by a wish, flesh gradually morphing into a new form—inevitably firmer and younger. The majority of possessed were intent on reverting to their original features. As seen through a rose-tinted mirror, Luca suspected. Having quite so many beautiful people emerge in one place together was statistically implausible.

Not that vanity was their real problem. The one intractable difficulty of this new life was food. Energistic power simply could not conjure any into existence; no matter how creative or insistent you were. Oh, you could cover a plate with a mountain of caviar; but cancel the illusion and the glistening black mass would relapse into a pile of leaves, or whatever raw material you were trying to bend to your will.

Irony or mockery, Luca couldn't quite decide what their deliverance had led them to. But whichever it was, eternity tilling the fields was better than eternity in the beyond. He finished dressing, and gave Lucy an expectant, slightly chiding look.

"All right," she grumbled. "I'm getting up. I'll pull my communal weight."

He kissed her. "Catch you later."

Lucy waited until the door shut behind him, then pulled the sheets back over her head.

Most of the manor's residents were already awake and bustling about. Luca said a dozen good-mornings as he made his way downstairs. As he walked along the grand corridors, the state of the building gradually registered. Windows left ajar, allowing the nightly sprinkling of rain to stain the carpets and furniture; open doors showed him glimpses of rooms with clothes strewn everywhere, remnants of meals on plates, grey mould growing out of mugs, sheets unwashed since the start of Norfolk's possession. It wasn't apathy, exactly, more like teenage carelessness—the belief that mum will always be around to clean up after you.

Bloody squalor junkies. Wouldn't have happened in my day, by damn.

There were over thirty people having their breakfast in Cricklade's dining hall, which now served as the community's canteen. The big chamber was three stories high, with a wooden ceiling supported by skilfully carved rafters. Cascade chandeliers hung on strong chains; their light globes were inoperative, but they bounced plenty of the sky's ambient light around the hall, illuminating the elaborate Earthwoodland frescos painted between every window. A thick blue and cream coloured Chinese carpet silenced Luca's boots as he walked over to the counter and helped himself to scrambled egg from an iron baking dish.

The plate he used was chipped, the silver cutlery was tarnished, and the polish on the huge central table was scuffed and scratched. He nodded to his companions as he sat, holding back any criticism. Focus on priorities, he told him-

self. Things were up and running at a basic level, that's
what counts. The food was plain but adequate; not rationed
exactly, but carefully controlled. They were all reverting to
a more civilized state of behaviour.

For a while after Quinn left, Cricklade's new residents
had joyfully discarded the sect's loathsome teachings which
the monster had imposed, and dived into a continual orgy of
sex and overconsumption. It was a reaction to the beyond;
deliberately immersing themselves in complete sensory-
glut. Nothing mattered except feeling, and taste, and smell.
Luca had eaten and drunk his way through the manor's extensive cuisine supplies, shagged countless girls with su-
permodel looks, flung himself into ludicrously dangerous
games, persecuted and hounded the non-possessed. Then,
with painful slowness, the morning after had finally
dawned, bringing the burden of responsibility and even a
degree of decency.

It was the day when the bathroom shower nozzle squirted
raw sewage over him that Luca started to gather up like-
minded people and set about restoring the estate to working
order. Pure hedonistic anarchy, it turned out, was not a sustainable environment.

Luca saw Susannah emerge from the door leading to the
kitchen. His every movement suddenly became very cautious. She was carrying a fresh bowl of steaming tomatoes,
which she plonked down on the self-service counter.

As he had applied himself to getting the farming side of
the estate functional again, so she had taken on the manor
itself. She was making a good job of providing meals and
keeping the place rolling along (even though it wasn't
maintained as it had been in the old days). Appropriately
enough, for Susannah was possessing Marjorie Kavanagh's
body. Naturally, there had been little room for physical improvement; she'd discarded about a decade, and shortened

her extravagant landowner hair considerably, but the essential figure and features remained the same.

She picked up an empty bowl and walked back to the kitchen. Their eyes met, and she gave him a slightly confused smile before she disappeared back through the door.

Luca swallowed the mush of egg in his mouth before he choked on it. There had been so much he wanted to cram into that moment. So much to say. And their troubled thoughts had resonated together. She knew what he knew, and he knew . . .

Ridiculous!

Hardly. She belongs with us.

Ridiculous because Susannah had found someone: Austin. They were happy together. And I have Lucy. For convenience. For sex. Not for love.

Luca forked up the last of his eggs, and washed them down with some tea. Impatience boiled through him. I need to be out there, get those damn slackers cracking.

He found Johan sitting at the other end of the table, with the single slice of toast and glass of orange which was his whole meal. "You ready yet?" he asked curtly.

Johan's rounded face registered an ancient expression of suffering, creasing up into lines so ingrained they must have been there since birth. There was a glint of sweat on his brow. "Yes, sir; I'm fit for another day."

Luca could have mouthed the ritual reply in tandem. Johan was possessing Mr Butterworth. The physical transformation from a lumbering, chubby sixty-year-old to virile twenty-something youth was almost complete, though some of the old estate manager's original characteristics seemed to defy modification.

"Come on then, let's be going."

He strode out of the hall, directing sharp glances at several of the men around the table as he went. Johan was al-

ready rising to his feet to scurry after Luca. Those who had
received the visual warning crammed food in their mouths
and stood hurriedly, anxious not to be left behind.

Luca had a dozen of them follow him into the stables,
where they started to saddle up their horses. The estate's
rugged farm ranger vehicles were still functional, but nobody was using them right now. The electricity grid had
been damaged during the wild times, and only a couple of
possessed in Stoke County owned up to having the knowledge to repair it. Progress was slow; the small amount of
power coming from the geothermal cables was reserved for
tractors.

It took Luca a couple of minutes to saddle up his horse;
buckles and straps fastened into place without needing to
think—Grant's knowledge. Then he led the piebald mare
out into the courtyard, past the burnt out ruins of the other
stable block. Most of the horses Louise had set free during
the fire had come back; they still had over half of the
manor's superb herd left.

He had to ride slower than he liked, allowing the others
to keep up. But the freedom of the wolds made up for it. All
as it should be. Almost.

Individual farms huddled in the lee of the shallow valleys, stolid stone houses seeking protection against Norfolk's arctic winters; they were scattered about the estate
almost at random. Their fields had all been ploughed now,
and the tractors were out drilling the second crop. Luca had
gone round the storage warehouses himself, selecting the
stock of barley, wheat, maize, oats, a dozen varieties of
beans, vegetables. Some fields had already started to
sprout, dusting the rich dark soil with a gossamer haze of
luxuriant emerald. It was going to be a good yield, the
nightly rain they conjured up would ensure that.

He was thankful that most of the disruption to the estate

had been superficial. It just needed a firm guiding hand to get everything back on track.

As they approached Colsterworth, the farms were closer together, fields forming a continual quilt. Luca led his team round the outskirts. The streets were busy, clotted by the town's residents as they strove for activity and normality. Nearly all of them recognized Luca as he rode past. His influence wasn't quite so great here, though it was his objectives which had been adopted. The town had elected itself a council of sorts, who acknowledged Luca had the right goals in restarting the county's basic infrastructure. A majority of the townsfolk went along with the council, repairing the water pump house and the sewage treatment plant, clearing the burnt carriages and carts from the streets, even attempting to repair the telephone system. But the council's real power came from food distribution, over which it had a monopoly, loyalists mounting a round the clock guard on the warehouses.

Luca spurred his horse over the canal bridge, a wood and iron arch in the Victorian tradition. The structure was another of the council's repair projects, lengths of genuine fresh timber had been dovetailed into the original seasoned planking; energistic power had been utilised to reform the iron girders that had been smashed and twisted (somehow they couldn't quite match the blue paint colour, so the new sections were clearly visible).

The Moulin de Hurley was on the other bank, a big mill house which supplied nearly a quarter of Kesteven island with flour. It had dark-red brick walls cut by tall iron-rimmed windows; one end was built over a small stream, which churned excitedly out of a brick arch before emptying into the canal at the end of the wharf. A series of tree-lined reservoir ponds were staggered up the gentle curve of the valley which rose away behind the building.

There was a team appointed by the council to help him waiting by the Moulin's gates. Their leader, Marcella Rye, was standing right underneath the metal archway supporting an ornate letter K. Which gave Luca a warm sensation of contentment. After all, he owned the mill. No! The Kavanaghs. The Kavanaghs owned it. Used to own it.

Luca greeted Marcella enthusiastically, hoping the flush of bonhomie would prevent her from sensing his agitation at the lapse. "I think it'll be relatively easy to get this up and running again," he said expansively. "The water powers the large grinder mechanism, and there's a geothermal cable to run the smaller machines. It should still be producing electricity."

"Glad to hear it. The storage sheds were ransacked, of course," she pointed at a cluster of large outbuildings. Their big wooden doors had been wrenched open; splintered and scorched, they now hung at a precarious angle. "But once the food was gone, nobody bothered with the place."

"Fine, as long as there's no . . ." Luca broke off, sensing the whirl of alarm in Johan's thoughts. He turned just in time to see the man stumble, his legs giving way to pitch him onto his knees. "What's—?"

Johan's youthful outline was wavering as he pressed his fists against his forehead; his whole face was contorted in an agony of concentration.

Luca knelt beside him. "Shit, what is it?"

"Nothing," Johan hissed. "Nothing. I'm okay, just dizzy that's all." Sweat was glistening all over his face and hands. "Heat from the ride got to me. I'll be fine." He clambered to his feet, wheezing heavily.

Luca gave him a confused glance, not understanding at all. How could anyone be ill in a realm in which a single thought had the power of creation? Johan must be severely hung over; a body wasn't flawlessly obedient to the mind's wishes here. They still had to eat, after all. But his deputy didn't normally go in for heroic benders.

Marcella was frowning at them, uncertain. Johan gave a forced *I'm fine* nod. "We'd best go in," he said.

Nobody had been in the mill since the day Quinn Dexter had arrived in town. It was cool inside; the power was off, and the tall smoked-glass windows filtered the daylight down to a listless pearl. Luca led the party along the dispenser line. Large, boxy stainless steel machines stood silent above curving conveyer belts.

"Initial grinding is done at the far end," he lectured. "Then these machines blend and refine the flour, and bag it. We used to produce twelve different types in here: plain, self-raising, granary, savoury, strong white—you name it. Sent them all over the island."

"Very homely," Marcella drawled.

Luca let it ride. "I can release new stocks of grain from the estate warehouses. But—" He went over to one of the hulking machines, and tugged a five pound bag from the feed mechanism below the hopper nozzle; it was made of thick paper, with the Moulin's red and green water wheel logo printed on the front. "Our first problem is going to be finding a new stock of these to package the flour in. They used to come from a company in Boston."

"So? Just think them up."

Luca wondered how she'd wound up with this assignment. Refused to sleep with the council leader? "Even if we only produce white flour for the bakeries, and package it in sacks, you're looking at a couple of hundred a day," he explained patiently. "Then you need flour for pastry and cakes, which people will want to bake at home. That's several thousand bags a day. They'd all have to be thought up individually."

"All right, so what do you suggest?"

"Actually, we were hoping you might like to come up with a solution. After all, we're supplying the expertise to get the mill going again, and providing you with grain."

"Gee, thanks."

"No thanks needed. This isn't a Communist society, we're not giving it away. You'll have to pay for it."

"It's as much ours as it is yours." Her voice had risen until it was almost an indignant squeal.

"Possession is nine-tenths of the law." He grinned mirthlessly. "Ask your host." His mind detected his people were sharing his amusement; even Johan's thoughts were lighter. The townies were highly uncomfortable with the facts being presented.

Marcella regarded him with blatant mistrust. "How do you propose we pay?"

"Some kind of ledger, I suppose. Work owed to us. After all, we're the ones growing the food for you."

"And we're running the mill for you, and transporting the stuff all over the county."

"Good. That's a start then isn't it? I'm sure there'll be other useful industries in Colsterworth, too. Our tractors and field machinery will need spares. Now all we need is a decent exchange rate."

"I'm going to have to go back to the council with this."

"Naturally." Luca had reached the wall separating the dispenser line from the chamber housing the main grinder. There were several large electrical distribution boxes forming their own mosaic over the bricks. Each one had an amber light glowing brightly on the front. He started pressing the trip buttons in a confident sequence. The broad tube lights overhead flickered as they came alight, sending down a blue-white radiance almost brighter than the sky outside. Luca smiled in satisfaction at his mental prowess. The circuitry for governing this old island was mapped out in his mind now, percolating up from his host.

His modest feeling of contentment faded, absorbed by a new body of emotion slipping over his perceptual horizon. Around him, the others were reacting in the same fashion. All of them turned instinctively to face the same outer wall, as if trying to stare through the bricks. A group of people were approaching Colsterworth. Dark thoughts sliding through Norfolk's atmosphere of the mind like threatening storm clouds.

"I think we'd better go take a look," Luca said. There were no dissenters.

They used the railway to get about over the island, adapting one of the utilitarian commuter trains which had trundled between the island's towns. A steam-powered ironclad fortress now clanked and hissed its way along the rails, hauling a couple of Orient Express carriages behind it. Several sets of what looked like twin recoilless ack-ack guns had been mounted at both ends of the train, while the barrel of a big tank cannon pointed along the top of the boiler, emerging from the combination turret/driver's cabin.

Just outside Colsterworth, where the rail went over the canal before it got to the station, Luca and Marcella stood side by side on the embankment at the head of their combined teams. More people were emerging from the town, bolstering their numbers. Antibodies responding to an incursive virus, Luca thought. And they were right to do so. People here were made to wear their hearts on their sleeves, visible to everyone else. It saved a lot of bullshitting around. Plain for all to see, those coming down the track were set on just one thing.

The train let out a long annoyed whistle, sending a fountain of steam rocketing up into the sky. Metallic screeches and janglings came pouring out of the engine when its riders realized how committed the townie blockaders were. Its pistons pounded away, reversing the wheel spin.

Luca and Marcella stood their ground as it howled forwards. A thought-smile flashed between them, and they stared down at the tracks, concentrating. The rails just in front of their feet creaked once, then split cleanly. Bolts holding them to the timber sleepers shot into the air, and the rails started to curl up, rolling into huge spirals. Flame spewed out of the train's wheels. The riders had to exert a lot of energistic strength to halt its momentum. It stopped a couple of yards short of the coils. Billows of angry steam jetted out of valves all along the underside, water splattered down onto the tracks. A thick iron door banged open on the side of the driver's cabin. Bruce Spanton jumped down.

He was dressed in anti-hero black leathers, impenetrable sunglasses pressed tight against his face. Heavy boots crunched on the gravel chippings of the embankment as he stalked towards the huddled townsfolk. A holster with a gold-plated Uzi slapped his leg with every step.

"Hello," Luca muttered, "Somebody watched way too many bad cable movies when they were younger."

Marcella subdued a grin as the ersatz Bad Guy halted in front of them.

"You," Bruce Spanton growled. "You're in my way, friend. You must feel lucky to try a move like that."

"What do you boys want here?" Luca asked wearily. The bad vibes emanating from Spanton and the others in the train weren't entirely forged. Not everyone on Norfolk had calmed down after returning from the beyond.

"Me and the guys, just passing through," Spanton said challengingly. "No law against that, here, is there?"

"No law, but plenty of wishes," Luca said. "This county

doesn't want you. I'm sure you'll respect that majority opinion."

"Tough shit. You got us. What you gonna do, call the cops?"

A big silver Western sheriff's badge mushroomed on the front of Marcella's tunic. "I am the police in Colsterworth."

"Listen," Bruce Spanton said. "We're just here to check out the town. Have us a bit of fun. Stock up on some food, grab some Norfolk Tears. Then tomorrow we'll be gone. We don't want no trouble; it's not as if we want to stay here. Crappy dump like this, not our scene. Know what I mean?"

"And how are you going to pay for your food?" Marcella asked. Luca did his best not to turn and frown at her.

"Pay for it?" Spanton yelled in astonishment. "What the fuck are you scoring, sister? We don't pay for anything any more. That got left behind along with all the rest of the lawyers and shit we had to put up with back there."

"It doesn't work like that," Luca said. "It's our food. Not yours."

"It's not yours, shithead. It belongs to everyone."

"We've got it. You don't. It's ours. That simple enough for you?"

"Fuck you. We've got to eat. We've got a right to eat."

"I remember you now," Luca said. "You were one of Dexter's people. Real devout arse licker. Do you miss him?"

Bruce Spanton stabbed a finger at Luca. "I'm going to remember you, shithead. And you're going to wish I fucking hadn't."

"Learn the rules when you go abroad," Luca said forcefully. "And then live by them. Now either you climb back on your pathetic little cartoon mean machine and leave. Or, you stay and find yourself a useful job, and earn a living like everybody else. Because we're not in the business of supporting worthless parasite scum like you."

"Get a jo . . ." disbelief and rage made Bruce Spanton splutter to a halt. "What the hell is this?"

"For you, exactly that: Hell. Now get out of our county before we run you out." Luca heard several cheers from behind him.

The sound made Bruce Spanton look up. He glanced round the crowd, sensing their mood, the belligerence and resentment focusing on him. "You fuckers are crazy. You know that? Crazy! We've just escaped from all this shit. And you're trying to bring it back."

"All we're doing is building ourselves a life as best we can," Luca said. "Join in, or fuck off."

"Oh we'll be back," Bruce Spanton said, tight lipped. "You'll see. And people will join us, not you. Know why? Because it's easier." He stomped off back to the train.

Marcella grinned at his back. "We won. We showed the bastards, eh? Not such a bad combination, you and me. We won't be seeing them again."

"This is a small island on a small planet," Luca said, more troubled than he wanted to be by Spanton's parting shot.

3

Sinon's serjeant body had been divested of its last medical package just five hours before the *Catalpa* flew out of its wormhole terminus above Ombey. The voidhawk's crew toroid was overcrowded, carrying thirty-five of the hulking serjeants and their five-strong biomedical supervisory team in addition to the usual crew. Heavy dull-rust coloured bodies stood almost shoulder to shoulder as they performed lumbering callisthenics all around the central corridor, discovering for themselves the parameters of their new physiques.

There was no fatigue in the fashion of a genuinely human body, the tiredness and tingling aches. Instead blood sugar depletion and muscle tissue stress registered as mental warning tones within the neural array housing the controlling personality. Sinon thought they must be similar to a neural nanonic display, but grey and characterless rather than the full-spectrum iconographic programs which Adamists enjoyed. Interpreting them was simple enough, thankfully.

He was actually quite satisfied with the body he now possessed (even though it was unable to smile at that particular irony for him). The deep scars of the serjeant's assembly surgery were almost healed. What minimal restriction they imposed on his movements would be gone within a few more days. Even his sensorium was up to the standard of an Edenist body. Michael Saldana certainly hadn't skimped on the design of the bitek construct's genetic sequence.

Acclimatisation to his new circumstances had twinned a growing confidence throughout the flight. A psychological boost similar to a patient recovering from his injuries as more and more of the medical packages became redundant. In this case shared with all the other serjeant personalities who were going through identical emotional uplifts, the general affinity band merging their emerging gratification into synergistic optimism.

Despite a total lack of hormonal glands, Sinon was hot for the Mortonridge Liberation campaign to begin. He asked the *Catalpa* to share the view provided by its sensor blisters as the wormhole terminus closed behind them. The external image surged into his mind; featuring Ombey as a silver and blue crescent a hundred and twenty thousand kilometres ahead. Several settled asteroids swung along high orbits, grubby brown specks muffled by a fluctuating swirl of silver stardust as their industrial stations deflected spears of raw sunlight. Larger, more regular motes of light swarmed around *Catalpa*, its cousins emerging from their termini and accelerating in towards the planet.

This particular squadron was comprised of just over three hundred of the bitek starships. It wasn't even the first to arrive at the Kingdom principality today. The Royal Navy's strategic defence centre on Guyana had combined its flight management operations and sensors with civil traffic control to guide the torrent of arriving starships into parking orbits.

The voidhawks headed down towards the planet, merging into a long line as they spiralled into alignment over the equator. They shared the five hundred kilometre orbit with their cousins and Adamist starships from every star system officially allied to the Kingdom. Military and civil transports unloaded their cargo pods into fleets of flyers and spaceplanes; Confederation Navy assault cruisers had brought an entire battalion of marines, and even the voidhawks were eager to see the huge Kulu Royal Navy Aquilae-class starships.

After reaching low orbit, the *Catalpa* had to wait a further eight hours before its spaceplane received clearance to ferry the first batch of serjeants down to Fort Forward. Sinon was on it as the night-shadowed ocean fled past underneath the glowing fuselage. Their little craft had aerobraked down to mach five when Xingu's western coastline rose over the horizon ahead. The red cloud was just visible to the sensors, a slice of curving red light, as if the fissure between land and sky had been rendered in gleaming neon. Then their altitude dropped, and it sank away.

They must know we're here, Choma said. **With ten thousand spaceship flights hyperbooming across the ocean every day, they'll hear us arriving if nothing else.** In the Twenty-fifth Century, Choma had been an astroengineering export manager based at Jupiter. Although he'd readily admitted to the other serjeant personalities that his personal knowledge-base of obsolete deep space startracker sensors was not very relevant to the Liberation, his main interest was strategy games, combined with the odd bit of role-playing. For himself and his fellow quirky enthusiasts, the kind of simulation arenas available to Edenists through perceptual reality environments were anathema. They wanted authentic mud, forests, rock faces, redoubts, heavy backpacks, heat, costumes, horse riding, marches, aching joints, flagons of ale, making love in the long grass, and songs around the campsite. To the amusement of the other inhabitants, they would take over vast tracts of habitat parkland for their contests; it was quite a faddish activity at the time. All of which made Choma the closest thing Sinon's squad had to an experienced soldier.

A lot of the old strategy game players had come out of the multiplicity to animate serjeant bodies. Slightly surprisingly, very few ex-intelligence agency operatives had joined them, the people whose genuine field operations experience would really have been valuable.

Very likely, Sinon agreed. **Dariat demonstrated his perceptive ability to the Kohistan Consensus; no doubt the combined faculty of the Mortonridge possessed will provide them with some foreknowledge.**

That and the ring of starships overhead. The convoys aren't exactly unobtrusive.

But they are obscured by the red cloud.

Don't count on it.

Does that worry you? Sinon asked.

Not really. Surprise was never going to be our strategic high-ground. Best we could hope for is the scale of the Liberation being a nasty shock to Ekelund and her troops.

I wish I had experience of the combat situations we will be facing rather than theoretical memories.

I expect that experience is going to be one thing you'll be collecting plenty of, in a very short timespan.

The *Catalpa*'s spaceplane landed at Fort Forward's new spaceport, racing along one of the three prefabricated runways laid out in parallel. Another was touching down forty-five seconds behind it; that managed to spark a Judeo of concern in Sinon's mind. Even with an AI in charge of slotting the traffic together, margins were being stretched. Ion field flyers were landing and launching vertically from pads on the other side of the spaceport's control tower at a much faster rate than the runways could handle spaceplanes.

For the moment, the spaceport's principal concern was to offload cargo and send it on to Fort Forward. The hangars were frantically busy, heavy-lift mechanoids and humans combining to keep the flow of pods going; any delay here would have a knock on effect right back up to orbit. Nearly all of the Liberation's ground vehicles were assigned to carry cargo. Passenger vehicles were still up in orbit.

Sinon and the others were given a static charge test by Royal Marines as they got to the bottom of the spaceplane's stairs. That it was perfunctory was understandable, but Sinon was satisfied to see they did test everybody. As soon as they were cleared the spaceplane taxied away, joining a queue of similar craft waiting to take off. Another one rolled into place, extending its airstair. The Marine squad moved forward again.

An Edenist liaison officer they never even saw told them that they were going to have to get to Fort Forward on foot. They were part of a long line of serjeants and marines marching along a road of freshly unrolled micro-mesh composite next to the new six-lane motorway. After they got underway, Sinon realized that it wasn't only Confederation Marines who made up the human contingent of the Liberation's ground forces. He walked over to a boosted mercenary taller than himself. The mercenary's brown skin had exactly the same texture as leather, long buttress ropes of muscle were clumped round the neck, supporting a nearly-globular skull armoured with silicolithium like an all-over helmet. In place of a nose and mouth, there was an oval cage grill at the front, and the saucer eyes were set very wide apart, giving little overlap, normal apart from the blue-green irises, which appeared to be multifaceted.

When Sinon asked, she said her name was Elana Duncan. "Excuse me for inquiring," he said. "But what exactly are you doing here?"

"I'm a volunteer," Elana Duncan replied with an overtly feminine voice. "We're part of the occupation force. You guys take the ground from those bastards, we'll hold on to it for you. That's the plan. Listen up, I know you Edenists don't approve of my kind. But there aren't enough marines to secure the whole of Mortonridge, so you've got to use us. That, and I had some friends on Lalonde."

"I don't disapprove. If anything I'm rather glad there's someone here who has actually been under fire before. I wish I had."

"Yeah? Now, see, that's what I don't get. You're cannon fodder, and you know you're cannon fodder. But it doesn't bother you. Me, I know I'm taking a gamble, that's a life-choice I made a long time ago."

"It doesn't bother me, because I'm not human, just a very sophisticated bitek automaton. I don't have a brain, just a collection of processors."

"But you got a personality, dontcha?"

"This is only an edited copy of me."

"Ha. You must be very confident about that. A life is a life, after all." She broke off, and tipped her head back, neck muscles flexing like heavy deltoids. "Now there's a sight which makes all this worthwhile. You can't beat those old warships for blunt spectacle."

A CK500-090 Thunderbird spaceplane was coming in to land. The giant delta-wing craft was at least twice the size of any of the civil cargo spaceplane using the runways. Air thundered turbulently in its wake as it slipped round to line up on its approach path, large sections of the trailing edges bending with slow agility to alter the wing camber. Then a bewildering number of hatches were sliding open all across its fuselage belly; twelve sets of undercarriage bogies dropped down. The Thunderbird hit the runway with a roar louder than a sonic boom. Chemical rockets in the nose fired to slow it, dirty ablation smoke was pouring out of all ninety-six brake drums.

"God damn," Elana Duncan murmured. "I never thought I'd ever see an operation like this, never mind be a part of it. A real live land army on the move. I'm centuries after my time, you know, I belong back in the Nineteen and Twentieth Centuries, marching on Moscow with Napoleon, or struggling across Spain. I was born for war, Sinon."

"That's stupid. You know you have a soul now. You shouldn't be risking it like this. You have invented a crusade for yourself to follow rather than achieve anything as an individual. That is wrong."

"It's my soul, and in a way I'm no different to Edenists."

Sinon felt a rush of real surprise. "How so?"

"I'm perfectly adjusted to what I am. The fact that my goals are different to those of your society doesn't matter. You know what I think? Edenists don't get caught in the beyond because you're cool enough under pressure to figure your way out. Well, me too, pal. Laton said there was a way out. I believe him. The Kiint found it. Just knowing that it's possible is my ticket to exit. I'll be happy searching because I know it's not pointless, I won't suffer like those dumbasses that wound up trapped. They're losers, they gave up. Not me. That's why I'm signed up on this mad Liberation idea, it's just part of getting ready for the big battle. Good training, is all."

She gave his shoulder an avuncular pat with a hand whose fingers had been replaced by three big claws, and marched off.

That's an excess of fatalism, Choma remarked. **What a strange psychology.**

She is content, Sinon answered. **I wish her well in that.**

*

A large quantity of love had been invested in constructing
the farmhouse. Even the Kulu aristocracy with their expensive showy buildings employed modern materials in their
fabric. And Mortonridge was a designated rapid growth
area, with government subsidies to help develop the farms.
A resolutely middle-class province. Their buildings were
substantial, but cheap: assembled from combinations of
carbon concrete, uniform-strength pulpwood planks, bricks
made from grains of clay cemented by geneered bacteria,
spongesteel structural girders, bonded silicon glass. For all
their standardisation, such basic components afforded a
wealth of diversity to architects.

But this was unmistakable and original. Beautifully
crude. A house of stone, quarried with an industrial fission
blade from a local outcrop; large cubes making the walls
thick enough to repel the equatorial heat and keep the
rooms cool without air conditioning. The floor and roof
beams were harandrid timbers, sturdy lengths dovetailed
and pegged together as only a master carpenter could manage. Inside, they'd been left uncovered, the gaps between
filled with reed and plaster, then whitewashed. It was as
historic as any of the illusions favoured by the possessed,
not that anyone could mistake something so solid for an
ephemeral aspiration.

There was a barn attached at the end, also stone, forming
one side of the farmyard. Its big wooden doors were
swinging open in the breeze the day the Karmic Crusader
pulled up outside. Stephanie Ash had been tired and fed up
by the time they pulled off the main road and drove along
the unmarked dirt track. Investigating it had been Moyo's
idea.

"The road must lead somewhere," he insisted. "This land

was settled recently. Nothing's had time to fall into disuse yet."

She hadn't bothered to argue with him. They'd driven a long way down the M6 after handing the children over, a journey which meant having to pass back through Annette Ekelund's army. This time they'd been pointedly ignored by the troops billeted in Chainbridge. After that they'd zig-zagged from coast to coast looking for a refuge, somewhere self-sufficient where they could rest up and wait for the grand events beyond Mortonridge to play themselves out. But the towns in the northern section of the peninsular were still occupied, though there was a steady drift out to farms. They were unwelcome there; the possessed were learning to guard their food stocks. Every unoccupied farm they'd visited had been ransacked for food and livestock. It was a monotonous trend, and finding a functional power supply to recharge the Karmic Crusader was becoming more diffi-cult.

After the joy and accomplishment of evacuating the chil-dren, the comedown to excluded refugee status was hard. Stephanie hadn't exactly lost faith, but the narrow road was no different to any of the dozens they'd driven down the last few days. Hope rebutted unfailingly each time.

The road took the bus through a small forest of aborigi-nal trees, then dipped into a shallow, lightly-wooded valley which meandered extravagantly. A stream bubbled along the lush grassy floor, its speed revealing they were actually travelling up at quite an angle. After four kilometres, the valley ended by opening out into a nearly circular basin. It was so regular, Stephanie suspected it was an ancient im-pact crater. A lacework of silver brooks threaded their way down the sides, feeding a lake at the centre, which was the origin of the valley's stream. The farmhouse stood above the shore, separated from the rippling water by a neatly trimmed lawn. Behind it, someone had converted the north-facing walls of the basin into stepped terraces, making a perfect sun-trap. The levels were cultivated with dozens of terrestrial fruit and vegetable plants; from citrus tree groves to lettuce, avocados to rhubarb. Almost all the aboriginal vegetation had been removed; even the south side looked as if it was covered in terrestrial grass. Goats and sheep were wandering around grazing peacefully.

They all piled out of the Karmic Crusader, smiling like entranced children.

"There's nobody here," Rana said. "Can you sense it? This whole place is empty."

"Oh goodness," Tina exclaimed nervously. She took the last step off the bus's stairs, her scarlet stilettos sinking awkwardly into the road's loose-packed gravel surface. "Do you really think so? This is simply paradise. It's just what we all deserve after everything we've done for others. I couldn't bear us being thrown out by someone else claiming they were here first. It would be excruciating."

"There are no vehicles left," McPhee grunted. "The owners probably received the Kingdom's warning and cleared out before Ekelund's people arrived in these parts."

"Lucky for them," Rana said.

"More so for us," Moyo said. "It's absolutely bloody perfect."

"I think the irrigation system is screwed," McPhee said. He was shielding his eyes with a hand as he squinted up at the terraces. "There, see? There must be channels to divert the brooks so that each level receives a decent supply. But it's spilling over like a waterfall. The plants will drown."

"No they won't," Franklin Quigly said. "It's not broken. The power's off, and there's no one here to manage it. That's all. We could get it fixed inside of a day. That's if we're staying."

They all turned to look at Stephanie. She was amused rather than gratified by the compliment. "Oh I think so." She smiled at her ragged little band. "We're not going to find anywhere better."

They spent the rest of the day wandering round the farmhouse and the terraces. The basin was an intensive-cultivation market garden; there were no cereal crops on any of the terraces. There were signs of a hurried departure all through the building, drawers pulled out, clothes spilled on the shiny floorboards, a tap left running, two old suitcases abandoned half-packed in one of the bedrooms. But there was a lot of basic foodstuffs left in the pantry, flour, jams, jellied fruit, eggs, whole cheeses; a big freezer was filled with fish and joints of meat. Whoever the farm belonged to, they didn't believe in modern sachets and readymade meals.

Tina took one look inside the kitchen with its simple array of shining copper pots and pans, and sniffed with emphatic disapproval. "You can take the worship of all things rustic too far, you know."

"It's appropriate to what we are now," Stephanie told her. "The consumer convenience society cannot exist in our universe."

"Well just don't expect me to give up silk stockings, darling."

Moyo, Rana, and McPhee scrambled up to the top of the basin to a small building they assumed was a pumphouse for the irrigation system. Stephanie and the rest started clearing out the farmhouse. By the third day, they'd got the terrace irrigation equipment working again. Not perfectly, their presence still glitched some of the management processors; but there was a manual back-up control panel in the pumphouse. Even the clouds' gloomy claret illumination had grudgingly brightened as they established themselves and began exterting their influence. It wasn't the pure sunlight which shone upon towns and larger groups of possessed, but the plants gleefully absorbed the increased rain of photons, and perked up accordingly.

A week later Stephanie had every right to be content as she walked out into the relatively cool air of early morning. The right, but not the reality. She opened the iron-framed French doors which led out to the lawn, and stepped barefoot onto the dewy grass.

As usual the red clouds tossed through the sky above, their massive braids strumming the air until it groaned in protest. This time, though, a more subtler resonance was carried by the rancorous vapour. It couldn't be heard, it merely preyed on the mind like a troublesome dream.

She walked down to the shore of the lake, her head turning slowly from side to side as she scanned the sky, questing for some kind of hint. Anything. The nettling sensation had been building for many days now. Whatever the origin, it was too far away for her senses to distinguish, skulking below the horizon like a malevolent moon.

"So you like feel the cosmic blues sounding out, too?" Cochrane said ruefully.

Stephanie jumped, she hadn't noticed him approach. The bells on the ancient hippy's velvet flares were silent as he trod lightly over the grass. An exceptionally large reefer hung from the corner of his mouth. It smelt different than usual, not nearly as sweet.

He caught her puzzlement, and his beard parted to show a smug grin. Fingers with many rings plucked the brown tube from his mouth, and held it vertically. "Guess what I found growing on some forgotten terrace? This Mr Taxpaying Johnny Appleseed we've taken over from here wasn't quite as straight as his fellow Rotarians believed. Know what this is? Only like genuine nicotiana. And as illegal as hell around these parts. Man but it feels good, first real drag I've had in centuries."

Stephanie smiled indulgently as he stuck it back in his mouth. Indulgent was all you could be with Cochrane. Moyo was coming out of the farmhouse, his mind darkened with concern.

"You know it's here, too, don't you?" she asked sadly. "This must be what Ekelund meant when she told me the Saldana Princess was preparing."

"And Lieutenant Anver," Moyo muttered.

"The earth can feel war's coming, that blood's going to be spilt. How very . . . biblical; bad vibes in the aether. I'd so hoped Ekelund was wrong, that she was just trying to justify maintaining her army by claiming phantom enemies were waiting on the other side of the hill."

"No way," Cochrane said. "The bad dude cavalry's like mounting up. They'll charge us soon, guns blazing."

"Why us?" Stephanie asked. "Why this planet? We said we wouldn't threaten them. We promised, and we kept it."

Moyo put his arm round her. "Being here is a threat to them."

"But it's so stupid. I just want to be left alone, I want time to come to terms with what's happened. That's all. We've got this beautiful farm, and we're making it work without hurting anybody. It's good here. We can support ourselves, and have enough time left over to think. That doesn't make us a threat or a danger to the Confederation. If we were allowed to carry on we might be able to make some progress towards an answer for this mess."

"I wish we could be left alone," Moyo told her sadly. "I wish they'd listen to us. But they won't. I know what it'll be like out there now. Common sense and reason won't matter. Forcing us out of Mortonridge is a political goal. Once the Saldanas and other Confederation leaders have declared it, they won't be able to pull back. We're in the path of a proverbial irresistible force."

"Perhaps if I went back up to the firebreak and spoke to them. They know me. They might listen."

Alarm at what she was saying made Moyo tighten his grip around her. "No. I don't want you doing anything crazy like that. Besides, they wouldn't listen. Not them. They'd smile politely for a while, then shove you into zero-tau. I couldn't stand that, I've only just found you."

She rested her head against him, quietly thankful for his devotion. He'd been there for her since the very first day. More than a lover, a constant source of strength.

"You can't go," Cochrane said. "Not you. These cats would like fall apart without you to guide them. We need you here, man. You're our den mother."

"But we won't last long if we stay here, and the Princess sends her army to find us."

"A little more time is better than the big zippo. And who knows what our karma's got mapped out for us before the jackbooks kick our door down."

"You're not normally the optimist," Stephanie teased.

"Face it babe, I'm not normally alive. That kinda warps your outlook, dig? You gotta have faith these days, man. Some cool happening will come along to like blow our minds away."

"Groovy," Moyo deadpanned.

"All right, you win," Stephanie assured them. "No noble sacrifices on my part. I'll stay here."

"Maybe they'll never come," Moyo said. "Maybe Ekelund will defeat them."

"Not a chance," Stephanie said. "She's good, and she's mean, which is everything it takes. But she's not that good. Just stop and feel the weight of them building up out there.

Ekelund will cause them a whole load of grief when the invasion starts, but she won't stop them."

"What will you do then, when they reach the farm? Will you fight?"

"I don't think so. I might lash out, that's human nature. But fight? No. What about you? You said you would, once."

"That was back when I thought it might do some good. I suppose I've grown up since then."

"But it's still not fair," she complained bitterly. "I adore this taste of life. I think going back to the beyond will be worse now. Next time, we'll know that is doesn't have to be permanent, even though it probably will be. It would have been far better if we'd been spared knowing. Why is the universe persecuting us like this?"

"It's karma, man," Cochrane said. "Bad karma."

"I thought karma was paying for your actions. I never hurt anyone badly enough for this."

"Original sin," Moyo said. "Nasty concept."

"You're wrong," she said. "Both of you. If I know anything now, it's that our religions are lies. Horrid, dirty lies. I don't believe in God, or destiny, not any more. There has to be a natural explanation for all this, a cosmological reason." She sank into Moyo's embrace, too tired even for anger. "But I'm not smart enough to work it out. I don't think any of us are. We're just going to have to wait until someone clever finds it for us. Damn, I hate that. Why can't I be good at the big things?"

Moyo kissed her brow. "There are forty kids on the other side of the firebreak who are mighty glad you achieved what you did. I wouldn't call that a small thing."

Cochrane blew a smoke ring in the direction of the oppressive presence beyond the firebreak. "Anyhow, nobody's served us an eviction order on these bodies yet. The evil Kingdom's warlords have got to like catch us first. I'm going to make chasing after me tragically expensive to the taxpayers. That always pisses them off bigtime."

We really should be doing this in a perceptual reality, Sinon moaned. **I mean: actual physical training. It's barbaric. I'm amazed Ralph Hiltch hasn't assigned us a crusty old drill sergeant to knock us into shape. We've got the right scenario.**

That morning, the serjeants had been driven out to a training ground ten kilometres east of Fort Forward, a rugged stretch of land with clumps of trees and mock-up buildings. It was one of twenty-five new training zones, their basic facilities thrown up as quickly as Fort Forward itself. Royal Marine engineers were busy constructing another ten.

Choma half-ignored Sinon's diatribe, concentrating on the bungalow in front of them. The rest of the squad were spread out round the dilapidated building in a semicircle, learning to cling to whatever cover was available. Stupid really, he thought, considering the possessed can sense us from hundreds of metres. But it added to the feeling of authenticity. The point which Sinon was missing.

Suddenly, one of the small bushes fifty metres away shimmered silver, and metamorphosed into a green-skinned hominoid with bug-eyes. Balls of white light shot away from his pointing hand. The two serjeants swivelled smoothly, lining their machine guns up on the apparition.

Ours, they told the rest of the squad. Sinon squeezed the trigger down with his right index finger, while his left hand twisted the gun's side grip, selecting the fire rate. The small chemical projectile cases reverberated loudly as they fired, smothering all other sounds. Ripples of static shivered over the end of the barrel as the pellets hammered into their target.

The static gun was the weapon which the Kingdom had developed to arm the serjeants for the Liberation. A simple enough derivative of an ordinary machine gun, the principal modification was to the bullet. Inert kinetic tips had been replaced by spherical pellets which carried a static charge. Their shape reduced their velocity from ordinary bullets (and their accuracy), though they could still inflict a lethal amount of damage on a human target, while their electrical discharge played havoc with the energistic ability of a possessed. Every pellet carried the same level of charge, but the variable rate of fire would allow the serjeants to cope with the different strengths of the individual possessed they encountered; and as the gun's mechanism was mechanical, the possessed couldn't glitch it—in theory.

It took three seconds of concentrated fire on the green monster before it stopped flinging white light back at Sinon and Choma. The image collapsed into an ordinary human male, who pitched forward. A holographic projector lens glinted in the bush behind it

You were too slow to respond to the target's strength, their supervisor told them, **in a genuine combat situation his white fire would have disabled the pair of you. And, Sinon . . .**

Yes?

Work on improving your aim, that entire first burst you fired was wide.

Acknowledged, Sinon informed the supervisor curtly. He adopted singular engagement mode to talk to Choma. **Wide shooting, indeed! I was simply bringing the gun round onto the target. Approaching fire can be a large psychological inhibitor.**

Certainly can, Choma replied with strict neutrality. He was scanning the land ahead, alert for new dangers. It would be just like the training ground controllers to hit them immediately again.

I think I am beginning to comprehend the gun's parameters, Sinon declared. My thought routines are assimilating its handling characteristics at an autonomic level.

Choma risked a mildly exasperated glance at his squad mate. That's the whole point of this training. We can hardly accept a tutorial thought routine from a habitat, now can we? The Consensus didn't even know about static guns when we left Saturn. Besides, I always said the best lessons are the ones you learn the hard way.

You and your atavistic Olympiad philosophy. No wonder it fell out of fashion by the time I was born.

But you're getting the hang of it, aren't you?

I suppose so.

Good. Now come on, we'd better advance to the building or we'll wind up on latrine duty.

At least the serjeant's lips and throat allowed Sinon to sigh plaintively. Very well.

Princess Kirsten had switched her retinal implants to full resolution so that she could watched the squads advancing over various sections of the training ground. There was a old saying running loose in her mind, as if one file was continually leaking from a memory cell: I don't know about the enemy, but by God they frighten me. This was the first time she'd ever encountered the big bitek constructs outside of a sensevise. Their size and mien combined to make them both impressive and imposing; she was now rather glad Ralph Hiltch had the courage to suggest using them. At the time she'd been only too happy deferring the final choice to Allie. The family does so lack the bravery to make really important decisions, thank God he still has the guts. It was the same even when we were kids, we all waited for his pronouncement. This is the first time.

Several hundred of the dark figures were currently crawling, slithering, and in some cases running through the undergrowth, bushes, and long grass while colourful holographic images popped into existence to waylay them. The sound of gunfire rattled through the air; it was a noise she was becoming very familiar with.

"They're making good progress," Ralph Hiltch said. He was standing beside the Princess on the roof of the training ground's management centre, which gave them an uninterrupted view over the rumpled section of land which the Liberation army had annexed. Their respective entourages were arranged behind them, officers and cabinet ministers forming an edgy phalanx. "It only takes two sessions on average to train up a serjeant. The support troops need a little longer. Don't get me wrong, those marines are excellent troops; I don't just mean the Kingdom's, our allies have sent their best, and the mercs are formidable at the best of times. It's just that they're all way too reliant on their neural nanonic programs for fire control and tactics, so we really discourage their usage. If a possessed does break through the front line, that's the first piece of equipment that's going to glitch."

"How many serjeants are ready?" Kirsten asked.

"About two hundred and eighty thousand. We're training them up at the rate of thirty thousand a day. And there's another five training grounds opening each day. I'd like the rate increased, but even with the Confederation Navy brigades, I've only got a limited number of engineering corps; I have to balance their assignments. Completing the accommodation sections of Fort Forward is my priority."

"It would appear as though you have everything under control."

"Simple enough, we just tell the AI what we want, and it designates for us. This is the first time in history a land army commander doesn't have to worry unduly about logistics."

"Providing a possessed doesn't get near the AI."

"Unlikely, ma'am; believe me, unlikely. And even that's in our contingency file."

"Good, I'd hate us to become overconfident. So when do you think you'll be able to begin the Liberation?"

"Ideally, I'd like to wait another three weeks." He acknowledged the Princess's raised eyebrow with a grudging smile. They'd spent the best part of two hours that morning under the gaze of rover reporters, inspecting the tremendous flow of materiel and personnel surging through Fort Forward's spaceport. To most people it looked as if they already had the military resources to invade a couple of planets. "Our greatest stretch is going to be the opening assault. We have to ring the entire peninsula, and it's got to be one very solid noose, we can't risk anything less. That'll have to be achieved with inexperienced troops and untested equipment. The more time spent preparing, the greater chance we have for success."

"I'm aware of that, Ralph. But you were talking about balance a moment ago." She glanced back at Leonard DeVille, who responded with a reluctant twitch. "Expectations are running rather high, and not just here on Ombey. We've demanded and received a colossal amount of support from our political allies and the Confederation Navy. I don't need to remind you what the King said."

"No ma'am." His last meeting with Alastair II, the time when he'd received his commission needed no file. The King had been adamant about the factors at play, the cost of external support, and the public weight of anticipation and belief.

Success. That was what everyone wanted, and expected him to deliver, on many fronts. And I have to give them that. This was all my idea. And my fault.

Unlike the Princess, Ralph didn't have the luxury of glancing round his people for signs of support. He could well imagine Janne Palmer's opinion—she'd be right too.

"We can begin preliminary deployment in another three days," he said. "That way we'll be able to start the actual Liberation in eight days' time."

"All right, Ralph. You have another eight days' grace. No more."

"Yes ma'am. Thank you."

"Have you actually managed to test one of the static guns on a possessed yet?"

"I'm afraid not, ma'am, no."

"Isn't that taking a bit of a chance? Surely you need to know their effectiveness, if any?"

"They'll either work, or not; and we don't want to give Ekelund's people any advance warning just in case they can devise a counter. We'll know if they're any use within seconds of our first encounter. If they don't, then the ground troops will revert to ordinary light arms. I just hope to God they don't have to, we'll inflict a hell of a lot of damage on the bodies we're trying to recover. But the theory's perfect, and the machinery's all so beautifully simple as well. Cathal and Dean dreamed up the concept. It should have been obvious from the start. I should have come up with it."

"I think you've worked enough miracles, Ralph. All the family wants from you now is a mundane little victory."

He nodded his thanks, and stared out over the training ground again. It was changeover time, hundreds of grubby-red serjeants were on the move, along with a good number of ordinary troops. Though ordinary was a relative term when referring to the boosted mercenaries.

"One question," Leonard DeVille said; he sounded apologetic, if not terribly sincere about it. "I know this isn't quite what you want to hear right now, Ralph. But you have allocated room for the rover reporters to observe the action during the assault, haven't you? The AI does know that's a requirement?"

Ralph grinned. This time he gave Palmer a direct look before locking eyes with the Home Office Minister. The Princess was diplomatically focused on the returning serjeants.

"Oh yes. We're putting them right in the front line for you. You'll get sensevises every bit as hot as the one Kelly Tirrel produced on Lalonde. This is going to be one very public war."

Chainbridge was different now. When Annette Ekelund had first arrived here, she'd transformed it into a simple headquarters and garrison town. Close enough to the firebreak to deploy her irregulars if the Kingdom sent any of its threatened "punishment" squads over to snatch possessed. Far enough away so that it was outside the range of any inquisitive sensors—incidentally making it reasonably safe from SD fire. So she'd gathered her followers to her, and allowed them their illusion of freedom. A genuine rabble army, with a licence to carouse and cavort for ninety per cent of the time, with just a few of her orders to follow the morning after. Something to do, something vaguely exciting and heroic-seeming, gave them a sense of identity and purpose. For that, they stayed together.

It made them into a unit for her, however unwieldy and unreliable. That was when Chainbridge resembled a provincial town under occupation by foreign troops with unlimited expense accounts. Not a bad analogy. There were parties and dances every evening, and other people began to hang around, if for no other reason than the army made damn sure they had full access to Mortonridge's dwindling food supplies. It was a happy town kept in good order, Annette even established the hub of Mortonridge's downgraded communication net in the old town hall, which was commandeered as her command post. The net allowed her to retain a certain degree of control over the peninsula, keeping her in touch with the councils she'd left in charge of the towns her forces had taken over. There wasn't much she could do to enforce her rule, short of complete overkill and send in a brigade of her troops, but in the main she'd created a small society which worked. That was before any of the inhabitants really believed that the Kingdom would break its word and invade with the express intention of ripping body from usurping soul.

Now Chainbridge's parties had ended. The few inhabited buildings had lost their ornate appearance in favour of a bleakly oppressive, fortress-like solidity. Non-combatants, the good-timers and hangers on, had left, drifting away into the countryside. The town was preparing for war.

From her office window in the town hall, she could look down on the large cobbled square below. The fountains were off, their basins dry and duned by clumps of litter. Vehicles were parked in neat ranks under the rows of leghorn trees that circled the outer edge of the square. They were mostly manual-drive cars and four-wheel drive farm rovers, as per her instructions. None of them wore any kind of illusory image. Engineers were working on several of them, readying them for the coming ordeal.

Annette came back to the long table where her ten senior officers were sitting. Delvan and Milne had taken the chairs on either side of hers; the two people she relied on the most. Delvan claimed to have been an officer in the First World War; while Milne had been an engineer's mate during

Earth's steamship era, which made him a wizard with all things mechanical, though he freely admitted to knowing very little about electronics. Beyond them, sat Soi Hon, who was a veteran of early-Twenty-first Century bush wars, an ecological agitator, he called himself. Annette gathered his battles hadn't been fought along national lines, but rather corporate ones. Whatever he wanted to describe himself as, his tactical know-how in the situation they faced was invaluable. The rest of them were just divisional commanders, gaining the loyalty of their troops through personality or reputation. Just how much loyalty, was a moot point.

"What are today's figures?" Annette asked.

"Nearly forty deserted last night," Delvan said. "Little shits. In my day they would have been shot for that kind of cowardice."

"Fortunately, we're not in your day," Soi Hon said. "When I fought the desecrators who stole my land I had legions of the people who did what they had to because our cause was just. We needed no military police and prisons to enforce the orders of our commanders then, nor do we here. If in their hearts people do not want to fight, then forcing them will not make them good soldiers."

"God is on the side of the big battalions," Delvan sneered. "Owning your claptrap nobility doesn't guarantee victory."

"We are not going to win." Soi Hon smiled peacefully. "You do understand that, don't you?"

"We'll have a damn good try, and to hell with your defeatist talk. I'm surprised you didn't leave with the rest of them."

"I think that'll do," Annette said. "Delvan, you know Soi Hon is right, you've felt what the Kingdom is gathering to fling against us. The King would never commit his forces against us unless he was convinced of the outcome. And he has the backing of the Edenists, who even more than he, won't engage in a foolhardy venture. This is a showpiece war; they intend to demonstrate to the Confederation's general public that we are beatable. They cannot afford to lose, no matter what it costs them."

"So what the hell do you want us to do, then?" Delvan asked.

"Make that cost exorbitant," Soi Hon said. "Such people always assign a value to everything in monetary terms. We might not be able to defeat them on Mortonridge, but we can certainly prevent any further Liberation campaigns after this one."

"Their troops will have reporters with them," Annette said. "They'll want to showcase their triumphs. This war will be fought on two fronts, the physical one here, and the emotional one broadcast by the media across the Confederation. That is the important one, the one we have to win. Those reporters must be shown the terrifying price of opposing us. I believe Milne has been making some preparations."

"Not doing so bad on that front, lass," Milne said. He sucked on a big clay pipe for emphasis, every inch the solid reliable NCO. "I've been training up a few lads, teaching them tricks of trade, like. We can't use electrical circuits, of course, not our type. So we've gone back to basics. I've come up with a nice little mix of chemicals for an explosive; we're shoving it into booby traps as fast as we can make 'em."

"What kind of booby traps?" Delvan asked.

"Anti-personnel mines, ground vehicle snares, primed buildings, spiked pits; that kind of thing. Soi's been showing us what he used to rig up when he was fighting. Right tricky stuff, it is, too. All with mechanical triggers, so their sensors won't pick them up, even if they can get them working under the red cloud. I'd say we're due to give Hiltch's boys a load of grief once they cross the firebreak. We've also rigged bridges to blow, as well as the major junction flyovers along the M6. That ought to slow the buggers down."

"All very good," Delvan said. "But with respect, I don't think a few scraps of rubble will make much difference to their transport. I remember the tanks we used to have, great big brutes, they were. But by heaven they could crunch across almost every surface; and the engineers have had seven centuries to improve on that."

"Ruining the road junctions might not make a huge impact, but it will certainly have some effect," Soi Hon said impassively. "We know how large this Liberation army is, even in these times that makes it unwieldy. They will use the M6, if not for front line troops, then certainly for their supplies and auxiliaries. If we delay them even by an hour a day, we add to the cost. Slowing them down will also give us time to respond and retaliate. It is a good tactic."

"Okay, I'm not arguing with you. But these booby traps and blown bridges are a passive response. Come on man, what've you got that'll allow us to attack them?"

"My lads have found quite a few light engineering factories and the like in Chainbridge," Milne said. "The machine tools still work if you switch 'em to manual. Right now, I've got 'em churning out parts for a high velocity hunting rifle. I don't know what the hell that sparky machine gun is that the souls have seen Hiltch's boys practising with. But I reckon my rifle's got an easy twice the range of 'em."

"They'll be wearing armour," Delvan warned.

"Aye, I know that. But Soi's told me about kinetic enhanced impact bullets. Our armourers are doing their best to produce them, you'll have a decent stock in another few

days. We'll be able to inflict a lot of damage with them, you
see if we don't."

"Thanks, Milne," Annette said. "You've done a great job,
considering what you've had to work with, and what we're
facing."

Milne cocked his pipe at her. "We'll put up a good account of ourselves, lass, no worries."

"I'm sure." She gazed round at the rest of her commanders. There was a good range of emotions distributed
among them, from clear nerves to stupid over-confidence.
"Now we know roughly what our own capabilities are, we
need to start working out how we're going to deploy. Delvan, you're probably the best strategist we have . . ."

"Butt-headed traditionalist," Soi Hon muttered sotto
voce.

Annette raised a warning eyebrow and the old guerrilla
made a conciliatory shrug. "What is Hiltch likely to do?"
she asked.

"Two things," Delvan said, ignoring Soi. "Firstly, their
initial assault is going to be a lulu. He'll throw everything
he's got at us, on as many fronts as he can afford to open.
We'll be facing massive troop incursions, this wretched
space warship bombardment, aircraft carpet bombing, artillery. The aim is to demoralise us right from the start,
make it quite clear from the scale of the Liberation that
we'll lose, drumming it home in a fashion we can't possibly
ignore. I'd recommend that we actually pull back a little
way from the borders of the peninsula; don't give him an
easy target. Leave it to Milne's booby traps to snarl up his
timetable, and stall any immediate visible success he wants
to lay on for the reporters."

"Okay, I can cope with that. What's his second likely objective?"

"His target missions. If he's got any sense, he'll go for

our population centres first. Our power declines with our numbers, which will make his mopping up operation a damn sight easier."

"Population centres," Annette exclaimed in annoyance. "What population centres? People are deserting the towns in droves. The councils are reporting we're now down to less than half the numbers we had in urban areas when we took over Mortonridge. They're like our deserters, heading for the hills. Right now we're spread over this land thinner than a pigeon's fart."

"It's not the hills they're after," Soi said, his soft tone a rebuke. "It's the farms. Which was only to be expected. You are well aware of the food situation across the peninsula. Had your efforts been directed at developing our civil infrastructure instead of our military base, it would be a different story."

"Is that a criticism?"

His gentle laugh was infuriating, mockingly superior. "A plea for industrialisation, from me? Please! I regard the land and the people as integral. Nature provides us with our true state. It is our towns and cities with their machines and hunger, which have birthed the corruption that has contaminated human society for millennia. The defence of people who chose to live with the land is paramount."

"Okay, thanks for the party manifesto. But it doesn't alter what I said. We haven't got that many population centres to lure Hiltch's forces into ambush."

"We will have. I suspect Delvan is correct when he says Hiltch will want to open with a grand gesture. That should work in our favour. As always when a land is invaded, its people pull together. They'll see that as individuals they can offer no resistance to the Liberation forces, and they'll flee their isolation in search of group sanctuary. We will gather ourselves together as a people again. Then the battle will be joined in full."

Annette's growing smile was a physical demonstration of the satisfaction spreading through her thoughts. "Remember Stephanie Ash, what I told her about having to decide whose side she was on? That self-righteous cow just stood there smiling politely the whole time, knowing her world view was the real thing and that I'd come round to her way of thinking in the end. Looks like I'll have the last laugh after all—even if it is only a short one. Damn, I'm going to enjoy that almost as much as I am bollixing up my dear old friend Ralph's campaign."

"You really think we'll be able to start recruiting into the regiments again?" Delvan asked Soi Hon.

"Can you think of nothing but your own position and power? It is not the regiments which will inflict the worst casualties, but the united people. Group ten of us together, and the destructive potential of our energistic power is an order of magnitude greater than any artillery the Liberation forces can bring to bear."

"Which is less than one per cent of the lowest powered maser on a Strategic Defence platform, and that's before we get into the heavy duty systems like their X-ray lasers," Annette said, tired of their bickering. "It's not our numbers which matter, but our ability to communicate and organise. That's what we have to safeguard until the last of us is shoved into zero-tau."

"I agree," Delvan said. "The whole war is going to be an extremely fluid situation from the start. Lightning strikes, hit the bastards and run, are what we should be planning for."

"Exactly, that's where I expect you two to combine for me. Your overall strategy, Delvan, combined with Soi's tactics. It's a lethal alliance, the equivalent of the Kingdom and the Edenists."

"An inspired comparison," Soi chuckled.

"My pleasure. All right, let's start looking at the map, and see who we're going to send where."

It was Emmet Mordden, again, who was on duty in the operations centre when the Organization fleet started to emerge above New California. The hellhawks were first, their wormholes opening more or less in the official emergence zone, a hundred thousand kilometres above Monterey. That gave them some warning that the Adamist craft were en route. Emmet quickly called in five more operatives to monitor their rag-tag arrival. They certainly aimed for the emergence zone, but with possessed officers on board aiming and hitting were increasingly separate concepts. Event horizons started to inflate across a vast section of space around the planet; the only thing regular about them was the timing. One every twenty seconds.

The big flight trajectory holoscreens ringing the centre had to change perspective several times, clicking down through their magnification to encompass space right out to Requa, New California's fourth moonlet. Black icons started to erupt across the screen as if it was being struck by dirty rain.

The AI began to absorb the swarm of information datavised in from the SD sensor platforms, and started plotting the starships' erratic trajectories. Multiple vector lines sprang up on every console display. The operators studied them urgently, opening communication circuits to verify the ships were still under Organization control. Emmet got so carried along by the pandemonium of the first few minutes it took a while before he began to realize something was badly wrong with the whole episode. Firstly, they were too early, Admiral Kolhammer's task force couldn't possibly have arrived at Tranquillity yet. Secondly, there were too many ships. Even if the ambush had been a massive success, some ships would have been lost. Of all Capone's lieutenants, he had the most pragmatic view of just how effective the fleet ships were.

Those two ugly facts were just beginning to register, when he sensed the dismay bubbling up among Jull von Holger's thoughts, as the hellhawk liaison man communicated with his colleagues.

"What the hell is it?" Emmet demanded. "Why are they back here? Did they lose, chicken out, or what?"

Jull von Holger shook his head in bewilderment, most reluctant to be the messenger of bad news. "No. No, they didn't lose. Their target . . . Tranquillity jumped away."

Emmet frowned at him.

"Look, just call Luigi, okay. I don't understand it myself."

Emmet gave him a long dissatisfied look, then turned to his own console. He ordered it to find the *Salvatore*'s transponder, and open a channel to the flagship. "What's going on?" he asked when a fuzzy picture of Luigi Balsamo appeared in the corner of his display.

"She tricked us," Luigi shouted angrily. "That Saldana bitch ran away. Christ knows how she managed it, but the whole thing vanished down a wormhole. Nobody told us a habitat could do that. You never warned us, did you? You're supposed to be the Organization's technical whiz kid. Why the fuck didn't you say something?"

"About what? What do you mean it went down a wormhole? What went down a wormhole?"

"Why don't you *listen*, shitbrain? The habitat! The habitat vanished in front of us!"

Emmet stared at the image, refusing to believe what he'd heard. "I'm calling Al," he said eventually.

It was the first time Luigi had ever been intimidated by the big double doors of the Nixon suite. There were a couple of soldiers on duty outside, wearing their standard fawn-brown double-breasted suits, big square-jawed guys with a dark rasp of stubble, glossy Thompson machine guns held prominently. He could sense several people milling about inside, their familiar thoughts dull and unhappy as they waited for him. He thought of all the punishments and reprimands he'd attended in his own capacity as one of the Organization's elite lieutenants. The omens weren't good.

One of the soldiers opened the doors, a superior in-the-know grin on his face. He didn't say anything, just made a mocking gesture of welcome. Luigi resisted the urge to smash his face to pulp, and walked in.

"What the fuck happened?" Al bellowed.

Luigi glanced round at the semicircle of erstwhile friends as the doors closed behind him. Patricia was there, as was Silvano, Jezzibella, Emmet, Mickey, and that little bitch Kiera. All of them going with the tide that was sweeping him away to drown.

"We were given some very bad information." He looked pointedly at Patricia. "Perez sold us a dummy. And you bought it."

"He didn't," she snapped. "He possessed one of the First Admiral's top aids in Trafalgar. Kolhammer was heading straight for Tranquillity."

"And we would have got him, too. If somebody had just warned me. I mean, Jesus H Christ, an entire goddamn habitat flitting off. Do you have any idea how big that thing was?"

"Who cares?" Al said. "The habitat wasn't your main target. You were there to blow up Kolhammer's ships."

"The only way we could do that was if we'd captured the habitat first," Luigi said angrily. "Don't try blaming all this on me. I did everything you asked."

"Who the fuck else am I going to blame?" Al asked. "You were there, it was your responsibility."

"Nobody has ever heard of a habitat that can do that before," Luigi ground out. "Nobody." He shoved an accusatory finger at Jezzibella. "Right?"

For whatever reason, Jezzibella had assumed her impish adolescent girl persona, red ribbons tying her hair into ponytails, a white blouse and grey pleated skirt not really covering her body. She pouted, a gesture which was almost obscenely provocative. It was an act which various judges had been asked to ban when she performed it live on tour. "Right. But I'm hardly an expert on energy patterning systems, now am I?"

"Christ almighty. Emmet?" It was almost a plea.

"It is unprecedented," Emmet said with some sympathy.

"And you." Luigi glared at Kiera. "You lived in a habitat. You knew all about how they work, why didn't you tell us?" The attack didn't quite kick up the response he expected. A flash of icy anger twisted Kiera's thoughts, while Al simply sneered scornfully.

"Valisk was not capable of performing a swallow manoeuvre," she said. "As far as we know, only Tranquillity has that ability. Certainly none of the Edenist habitats can. I don't know about the other three independent habitats."

"Didn't stop Valisk from vanishing, though, did it," Al muttered snidely.

Silvano gave an over-loud laugh, while Jezzibella smiled demurely at Kiera's discomfort. Luigi looked from one to the other in puzzlement. "Okay, so are we agreed? It was a shitty situation, sure. But there was nothing I could do about it. That Saldana girl took everyone by surprise."

"You were the fleet's commander," Al said. "I gave you that job because I thought you were smart, man, that you had some flare and imagination. A guy with a few qualities, know what I mean? If all I want is some putz who expects a slap on the back every time he does what he's told I would have given the job to Bernhard Alsop. I expected more from you, Luigi, a lot more."

"Like what? I mean, come on here, tell me, Al, just what the hell would you have done?"

"Stopped it from flying out. Don't you get it, Luigi? You were my man on the ground. I was goddamn depending on you to bring the Organization through this okay. Instead, I'm left with shit all over my face. Once you saw what was happening you should have zeroed the place."

"Christ, why won't any of you *listen*? I was fucking trying to zero it, Al. That's what spooked Saldana; that's what made her scoot the hell out of there. I'd got nearly five thousand of those war rockets chasing after her faster than a coyote with a hornet up its ass, and she got clean away. There was *nothing* we could do. We were damn lucky to cut free ourselves. The explosions from all those war rockets did some damage, too, we were . . ."

"Wooha there," Al held up a hand. "What explosions? You just said the combat wasps never touched Tranquillity."

"Yeah, but most of them detonated when they hit the wormhole entrance. I don't understand none too well; the technical boys, they say it's like a solid barrier, but it's made out of nothing. Beats me. Anyway, the first ones started to go off, and . . . hell, you know how powerful antimatter is, they set off the others. The whole lot went off like a string of goddamn firecrackers."

"All of them? Five thousand antimatter-powered combat wasps?"

"That's right. Like I said, we were lucky to get out alive."

"Sure you were." Al's voice had dropped to a dangerous monotone. "You're alive, and I'm out one planet which we postponed invading, I'm down a Confederation Navy task force you were supposed to ambush, and I've also got to replace five thousand combat wasps fuelled up by the goddamn rarest substance in the whole fucking universe. Jeez, I'm real glad you're back. Seeing you here smiling away in once piece makes me feel absolutely fucking peachy. You piece of *shit*! Do you have any idea how badly you've screwed up?"

"It wasn't my fault!"

"Oh absolutely. You're right. No way are you to blame for this. And you know what? I bet I know who it was. Yeah. Yeah, now I think about it, I know. It was me. That's right, me. I'm to blame. I'm the asshole here. I made the biggest fucking mistake of my life when I put you in charge."

"Yeah? Well I didn't hear you whining none when I came back from Arnstat. Remember that day? I delivered a whole fucking planet on a fucking plate for you, Al. You gave me the keys for the city back then. Parties, girls, you even made Avvy track down a genuine copy of the Clark Gable *Gone with the Wind* for me. Nothing. Nothing was too much trouble. I was loyal to you, then, and I'm loyal to you now. I don't deserve any of this. All you lost was a few lousy rockets and some fancy fuel. I put my life on the line for you, Al. And we all know how goddamn precious that is now, don't we? Well, do *you* know what? I don't deserve to be treated like this. It ain't right."

Al scowled, looking round the other lieutenants. They all kept their faces blank, of course, but their minds were boiling. Annoyance and doubt were the predominant emotions. He guessed his own mind would show the same. He was fucking furious with Luigi, it was the first defeat the Organization had been dealt, the news boys would crow about it clear over the Confederation. His image would take a terrible battering, and as Jez always said: image was everything in the modern world. The aura of the Organization's invincibility would be hit badly. Yet at the same time, Luigi was right, he had done his best, right from the start when they'd all walked into City Hall in the ballsiest escapade this side of the Trojan horse.

"By rights, I ought to fucking fry you, Luigi," Al said darkly. "We've been set back weeks thanks to what happened at Tranquillity. I've got to find another planet to invade, I've got to wait until we've built up a decent new stock of antimatter, the reporters will hang me out to dry, everyone's confidence is busted. But I'm not going to. And the only reason I'm not going to is because you came back here like a man. You ain't afraid to admit you made a mistake."

There was a new flash of anger in Luigi's mind at that. Al waited, mildly intrigued, but it was never voiced. He materialised a Havana, and took a comfortable drag before saying: "So I'll make you an offer. You can stay with the Organization, but I'm going to bust you right back down to the bottom of the ladder again. You're a private zero class, Luigi. I know the other guys'll go hard on you for a while, but you stay loyal, you keep your nose clean, and you can work your way back up again. I can't be no fairer than that."

Luigi gawped at Al, struggling with disbelief at what he'd just heard while a strangled choke growled up from his throat. His mind was telegraphing the notion of outright rebellion. Al fixed him with *the look,* all humour eradicated. "You won't like the alternative."

"All right, Al," Luigi said slowly. "I can live with that. But I'm telling you, I'll be back in charge of the fleet inside of six months."

Al guffawed, and clapped Luigi's arm. "That's my boy. I knew I made the right decision with you." Luigi managed a brief smile, and turned to walk out of the room. Al slumped his shoulders when the doors shut. "Guess that's one guy we've lost for good."

Jezzibella rubbed his arm in sympathy. "You did the right thing, baby. It was honourable. He did fuck up something chronic."

"I wouldn't have been so generous," Kiera said. "You shouldn't show so much kindness. People will see it as a weakness."

"You're dealing with people, not mechanoids," Jezzibella said blankly. "You have to make allowances for the odd mistake. If you shoot every waiter who spills a cup of coffee over your skirt, you wind up with a self service bar."

Kiera smiled condescendingly at her. "What you'll actually wind up with is a group of highly efficient waiters who can do the job effectively."

"You mean, like the way your team handled things on Valisk?"

"All teams need an effective leader."

Al was tempted to let them go for it—nothing like a good catfight. But one bust-up among his senior lieutenants was enough for today. So instead, he said: "Speaking of which, Kiera, are the hellhawks going to keep flying for me?"

"Of course they will, Al. I've been busy setting up my new flight coordination office in one of the docking ledge departure lounges. Close to the action, as it were. They'll do what I tell them to."

"Uh huh." He didn't like the implications of that sweetly spoken assurance any more than the unpleasant note of victory rippling through her mind. And judging by the sudden suspicion colouring Jez's thoughts, neither did she.

It was one of those absurd left right, left right sideways shuffles that seemingly automatically occurs when two people try to get out of each other's way simultaneously which finally blew Beth's temper. She'd come out of the washroom at one end of the *Mindori*'s life support module to find Jed standing outside waiting to use it. He immediately dropped his head so he didn't have to look at her and danced to one side. A move she instinctively matched. They dodged about for a couple of seconds.

The next thing Jed knew was a hand grasping his collar, and hauling him into the washroom. Bright mock sunbeams poured through the smoked-glass portholes, producing large white ovals on the polished wood floor. Archaic brass plumbing gleamed and sparkled all around the small compartment. Jed's knee banged painfully on the rim of the enamel bath as Beth smoothly slewed his weight round like some kind of ice skater act. The door slammed shut, the lock *snicked* and he was shoved flat against the wall. "Listen ball-brain," she snarled "I was not shagging him. Okay?"

He risked a sneer, praying she wasn't still carrying the nervejam stick. "Yeah? So what were you doing in bed with him?"

"Sleeping." She saw the new expression of derision forming on his face, and twisted his sweatshirt fabric just a fraction tighter. "Sleeping," she repeated forcefully. "Jeeze, mate, the guy's brain is totally zonked. It took a time to get him quietened down, that's all. I dozed off. Big deal. If you hadn't stormed out so bloody fast you would have seen I still had all my clobber on."

"That's it?"

"What the hell do you expect? The pair of us were working our way through a kama sutra recording? Is that what you think of me? That I'm going to leap into bed with the first geriatric I meet?"

Jed knew his answer to that question was going to be critical, and possibly close to fatal if he got it wrong. "No," he insisted, willing himself to believe it totally. Voice only would never be good enough. He often suspected Beth had some kind of advanced telepathic ability. "I don't think that of you at all. Um . . . you've got more class that that. I always said so."

"Hummm." Her grip on his sweatshirt loosened slightly. "You mean you were always miffed I didn't let you shag me."

"That's not it!" he protested.

"Really?"

Jed thought that jibe was best ignored in its entirety. "What do you make of this delay?" he asked.

"Bit odd. I don't understand why we didn't dock with Valisk before we went on another rendezvous. I mean, we were already there in the Srinagar system, least that's what I thought."

"Yeah. I didn't see Valisk, though, just some gas giant. Then the ship swallowed away again. I thought I was going to die. We were *there*."

"Choi-Ho and Maxim said this new rendezvous was major-league important when I asked them. They clammed up pretty smart when I asked them where it was, though. You think that's important?"

"Course it's important. Question is, why?"

"We might have to dodge some navy patrols to make the new rendezvous. That'll be risky."

"So why not tell us?"

"There's a lot of kids on board. Could be they don't want to worry them."

"Makes sense."

"But you don't reckon?"

"Dunno. It's funny, you know. We busted our balls to get a flight. Everything we had got left behind, our families, friends, everything. But I didn't have any doubts. Now we're as good as there . . . I don't know, it's just such a big thing. Maybe I'm a bit scared. What about you?"

Beth gave him a careful look, unsure just how much she should reveal. He really had invested a lot in the ideal of Valisk and all it promised. "Jed, I know Gerald's a bit flaky, but he told me something."

"A bit flaky."

"Jed! He said Kiera is actually called Marie, that she's his daughter. He reckons that Valisk is no different to any other place the possessed have taken over."

"Crap," he said angrily. "That's total crap. Look, Beth. We know Kiera is a possessor, she's never hidden that. But she's only borrowing that girl's body. She said things like that won't matter after Valisk leaves the universe. She can take on her own form again."

"Yes, but, Jed . . . His daughter."

"Just a weird coincidence, that's all. Mind, it explains why the old fart is so crazy."

She nodded reluctantly. "Maybe. But then again it wouldn't do any harm to start thinking the unthinkable, would it?"

He took hold of both her arms, just above the elbows. "We'll be all right," he said intently. "You've accessed

Kiera's recording enough times. You know she's telling us the truth. This is like wedding night nerves."

She gave his hands a curious glance; normally she would have instantly shaken free from such a grip. But this flight was not an ordinary time. "Yeah. Thanks, mate." She gave him a timid smile.

Jed returned an equally uncertain flutter. He started to slowly lean forward, bringing his face down towards hers. Her lips parted slightly. He closed his eyes. Then a finger was resting on his chin.

"Not here," Beth said. "Not in a dunny."

Beth actually let him hold her hand as they walked along the life support module's central corridor. Somehow it didn't seem to matter so much now. Back on Koblat it would have meant everyone knowing: Beth and Jed, Jed and Beth. The boys would have smiled and whooped and given Jed the thumbs up. "Well done mate. Scored with an ice maiden, nice one. So what does she look like with her kit off? Are they big tits? Is she any good at it? Has she gone down on you yet?" While the girls would have clustered round her and asked if he'd said he loved her. Does he devote enough time to you? Are you going to apply for an apartment together?

It was a horrendous cycle spinning around her, a compendium of everything she hated about Koblat. The loss of any purpose to life. Surrendering to the company and signing on as another of its cheaply produced multi-function biological tools. She knew several girls on her corridor level who were grandmothers at twenty-eight.

Their weakness had given her the strength to strive for at least the hope of something more, to resist almost intolerable peer pressure. Star of her education stream, exceptionally receptive to each didactic memory she received.

Applying for every college scholarship and exchange programme she could locate in the asteroid's memory cores. Enduring the jeers and whispers. But it had been hard hard hard. Then along came Kiera, who offered a way out from all that awful pressure. A life that was different and kind. And Beth had believed, because Kiera was the same sort of age, and empowered, and taking control of her own destiny. And because . . . it was easy. For the first time ever.

They stopped outside the cabin she'd been sharing with Gerald, and Jed kissed her before she could turn the handle. Not a very good kiss, he almost missed her lips, and definitely no tongue like there was in all the low-rated blue sensevise recordings she'd accessed. His anxious expression almost made her laugh, as if he was expecting her to deck him one. Which, she admitted, she probably would have done three weeks ago if he'd come on fresh with her. She got the door open, and they stumbled inside, not bothering with the lights. Jed kissed her again. A better attempt, this time. When he finished, she asked: "Will you think of her?"

"Who?" he asked in confusion.

"You know, her, Kiera. Will you think of her when you're doing it with me?"

"No!" Although there was enough of a quaver in his voice to reveal the truth. To her, if no one else. She knew him well enough, growing up together for ten years. It was almost too close.

He had become—not obsessed, that wasn't strong enough—captivated by Kiera and that exquisite beguiling beauty of hers. In dismay Beth knew it wouldn't be her face he saw when he closed his eyes in ecstasy, not her body he would feel below his fingers. For some reason, despite the humiliation, she didn't really care. After all, she had her own reasons for this. She twined a forearm behind his head, and pulled him down to kiss her again. The lights came on.

Beth gasped in surprise, and twisted to look at the bunk, expecting to see Gerald there. It was empty, the blankets rumpled.

There was a melodic chime from the dresser, and the small mirror above it shimmered with colour. A man's face appeared on it; he was middle aged, with a Mediterranean complexion and a long chin which pulled his lips downwards, making him appear permanently unhappy.

"Sorry to interrupt," he said. "But I think you'll find what I have to say quite important."

Jed had stiffened the second he appeared, quickly pulling his hands away from Beth. She tried not to show how annoyed she was by that; she'd just made *the* decision—what did he have to be guilty about?

"Who are you?" she asked.

"Rocio Condra; I am the soul possessing this hellhawk."

"Oh brother," she murmured. Jed managed to blush even deeper.

"I was listening to your conversation in the washroom. I believe we can help each other."

Beth smiled weakly. "If you're powerful enough to do that, how can we possibly help you? You can do anything."

"My energistic power gives me a great deal of influence over the local environment, I agree. But there are some things which remain beyond me. Listening to you, for example, I had to use a bitek processor; there's one in every section of the *Mindori*'s life support module."

"If you've heard everything we've talked about, then you know about Gerald and Marie," Beth said.

"Indeed. That is why I chose you to make my offer to. You already know everything is not what it seems."

Jed peered at Rocio's image. "What offer?"

"The end requirements haven't yet been finalized. However, if all goes well, I expect I shall require you to perform some physical tasks for me. Nothing too difficult. Just venture into a few places I obviously cannot reach."

"Such as?"

"That is not yet apparent. We will have to advance this partnership one step at a time. As a gesture of goodwill, I am prepared to impart some information to you. If, based on what you hear, you then wish to continue with this relationship, we can move forward together."

Beth gave Jed a puzzled glance, not surprised to find he was equally mystified. "Go on," she said. "We'll listen."

"I am about to swallow into the New California system. We will probably dock at Monterey asteroid, the headquarters of the Capone Organization."

"No way!" Jed cried.

"There never was a new rendezvous, was there?" Beth asked, somehow unsurprised by the revelation.

"No," Rocio said. "We did not dock at Valisk because it is no longer in this universe. There was a battle for control between different factions of possessed inside. The victors subsequently removed it."

Jed took a couple of paces backwards, and sank down onto the bunk. His face was fragile with dismay. "Gone?"

"I'm afraid so. And I am genuinely sorry. I know how much hope you had for your future there. Unfortunately, that hope was extremely misplaced."

"How?" Beth asked through clenched teeth.

"There never was any Deadnight, not really. Kiera Salter simply wanted fresh bodies to possess so that she could expand the habitat's population base. Had you disembarked there, you would have been tortured until you surrendered yourselves to possession."

"Oh Jeeze," Beth whispered. "And Monterey? What's going to happen to us at Monterey?"

"Much the same, I expect. The Organization does retain

professional non-possessed who have specialist fields of expertise. Are you highly qualified in any subject?"

"Us?" Beth barked in consternation. "You've gotta be bloody joking, mate. The only thing we know how to do proper is mess up. Every bloody time." She was afraid she was going to start crying.

"I see," Rocio said. "Well, in return for your help, I am prepared to hide you on board when we dock at Monterey."

"What sort of help?" Jed asked.

Beth wheeled round to glare at him. "Does it bloody matter! *Yes* we'll help. As much as you want."

Rocio's image gave a dry smile. "As I said, my requirements will not be fully established until I have analysed the local situation. It may be that I don't require you to do anything. For the moment, I shall simply hold you in reserve."

"Why?" Beth asked. "You're part of them. You're a possessor. What do you want us for?"

"Because I am not part of them. We are not all the same. I was being coerced into helping Kiera. Now I must find out what has happened to the other hellhawks, and decide what to do next. In order to do that, I must keep every conceivable option open. Having allies who are in no position to betray me will provide an excellent advantage."

"All right," Beth said. "What do we have to do?"

"I will swallow into the New California system in another thirty minutes. Even if Kiera and the other hellhawks have left there, the passengers will have to be disembarked. For now, the pair of you must be hidden. I believe I have a place which will put you outside the perception range of Choi-Ho and Maxim Payne."

"What perception range?" Jed asked.

"All possessed are able to sense the thoughts of other people. The range varies between individuals, of course."

"You mean they know what I'm thinking?" he hooted.

"No. But they are aware of your presence, and with that your emotions. However, such perception through solid matter is difficult; I believe the fluid in some of my tanks will shield you. We just have to get you at the centre of a suitably large cluster."

"There had better be room for five of us in this nest of yours," Beth said sprightly.

"I only require two people."

"Tough, mate. You get yourself a bargain package with us. Gerald and the girls come too."

"I don't need them."

She gave his image a cold smile. "Must have been dead a long time, huh? To forget what it's like to have other people, friends, responsibilities. What? You think we'd leave them behind for Capone. A couple of kids? Come on!"

"The Organization is unlikely to possess the girls. They pride themselves in being altruistic and charitable."

"Good for them. But it doesn't make any difference. You get all five of us, or none at all."

"That's right," Jed said, coming up to stand beside her. "Gari's my sister. I'm not leaving her with Capone."

Rocio sighed heavily. "Very well. But only those three. If you have a flock of second cousins on board, they will have to take their chances with the Organization."

"No second cousins. What do you want us to do?"

It took a lot of nerve to saunter idly into the *Mindori*'s main lounge with a bland expression on his face, knowing what he did. Jed felt he carried it off rather well; his visits to the Blue Fountain in search of sympathetic starship crews had provided a good rehearsal for brazening out awkward moments. There was a big press of Deadnight kids in the lounge, more than usual as the extended flight finally approached its end. All of them gazing eagerly out of the big forward-looking window at the silver-on-black starfield.

Jed let his eyes flick round quickly, confirming Choi-Ho and Maxim Payne weren't anywhere about. Rocio had assured him they were both in their cabin, but he didn't entirely trust everything the hellhawk's soul said.

In this instance, Rocio hadn't lied. The two possessed were nowhere to be seen. Jed walked confidently across the lounge to one of the fitted cupboards on the far side. Its narrow slatted doors were made from rosewood, with small brass handles moulded to resemble rose buds. As he put his hand round the cool metal, it turned to black plastic below his fingers. A narrow display panel appeared briefly to one side, framing a block of grey alphanumerics which flickered too fast to be read. He waited until he heard a discreet *click* then pulled gently. The door opened a fraction, and he moved closer, covering his actions.

Rocio had told him the bitek processor blocks were on the third shelf from the top. The thin gap allowed him to confirm the slim rectangular units were waiting there. It was obviously some kind of general equipment storage cupboard; he could see tool kits, and test blocks, and sensor modules, as well as several devices he couldn't fathom at all. A rack on the fourth shelf contained five compact laser pistols.

He froze.

It was probably Rocio's final assessment of his suitability. If he could turn his back on the weapons he would be resolute enough to be of use to the hellhawk. If he knew anything about this nebulous deal, whatever help Rocio wanted, it would not be small, not when the exchange price was his own life. But a weapon would offer some security, however feeble. And Beth had her nervejam stick.

Knowing his heated thoughts would be betraying his

guilt to Rocio in a way no clandestine visual observation ever could, Jed reached calmly for a pistol, then slid his hand smoothly up to one of the processor blocks. He tucked both of them neatly into his inside jacket pocket, and shut the cupboard door again. The electronic lock vanished instantly beneath a slick ripple of wood grain which lapped over it.

Walking back out of the lounge was the worst part. Some little part of Jed's brain was yelling at him to warn them. All of a sudden, he hated them. Sweetly trusting kids, their eyes happy and shining as they gawped out at the enchanting vista of interstellar space. All that hope suffusing unseen, yet cloying, into the air as they waited for the window to reveal their own special nirvana waiting for them at the end of the next wormhole.

Fools! Blind, stupid, and ridiculously ingenuous. The hatred clarified then. He was looking at multiple reflections of himself.

Beth got Gerald to come along with her, which he did unquestioningly. Jed brought Gari and Navar, who were intensely curious, twittering together as they walked down the length of the corridor. Their curiosity turned to hardedged scepticism as Jed knocked softly on the washroom door.

"You told us this was important," Navar said accusingly.

"It is," he assured her. Something in his tone stalled the scornful sniff she was preparing as a retort.

Beth unlocked the washroom door and slid it open. Jed checked the corridor to make sure no one was watching. With only fifteen minutes to go until the swallow manoeuvre, all the other Deadnights were crowding round the observation ports in the forward cabins. The two girls gave Gerald a confused look as they all crowded into the confined space of the cabin. In turn, Gerald barely noticed them. Jed took the bitek processor block from his pocket. One surface shimmered with a moiré holographic pattern, then cleared to show Rocio's face.

"Well done, Jed," he said. "Bluffing it out is often the best option."

"Yeah, all right, now what?"

"Who's that?" Navar asked.

"We'll explain later," Beth said. "Right now, we've got to get into position ready for when the ship docks." She said it to the girls, although she was actually studying Gerald intently. He was in one of his passive moods, unperturbed by what was happening. She just prayed he stayed that way while they were hidden away.

"Aren't we getting off at Valisk?" Gari asked her big brother in a forlorn voice.

"No, doll, sorry. We're not even docking with Valisk."

"Why not?"

"Guess we got lied to." The bitter sorrow in his voice silenced her.

"You will need to clear the floor," Rocio instructed.

Beth and the two girls climbed into the bath, while Gerald sat on the toilet lid. Jed pressed himself back against the door. The floorboards faded away; rich honey colour bleaching to a sanitary grey-green, resilient texture becoming the uncompromising hardness of silicolithium composite. Some residual evidence of the wood illusion remained, little ridges where the planks had lain, dark flecks in the surface a pallid mimicry of the grain pattern. In the centre of the floor was an inspection hatch, with recessed metal locking clips at each corner.

"Turn the clips ninety degrees clockwise, then pull them up," Rocio said.

Jed knelt down and did as he was told. When the clips

were free, the hatch rose ten centimetres with a swift hiss of air. He swung it aside. There was a narrow metal crawl way below it, bordered by foam-insulated pipes and bundled cables. Beth activated the lightstick she'd brought along, and held it over the hatch. There was a horizontal T-junction a couple of metres down.

"You will go first, Beth," Rocio said, "and light the way. I will supply directions. Jed, you must close the hatch behind you."

Reluctantly, with the girls pouting and scowling, they all climbed down into the crawl way. Jed tugged the hatch back into place after him, nearly catching his fingers as it guillotined shut. When it was in place, the washroom floor silently and fastidiously sealed over with elegant floorboards again.

4

Dariat wandered along the valley, not really paying much attention to anything. Only the memories pulled at him, bittersweet recollections guiding him towards the sacred places he hadn't dared visit in the flesh for thirty years, not even when he'd roamed through Valisk to avoid Bonney and Kiera.

The wide pool, apparently carved into the grey-brown polyp-rock by the stream's enthusiastic flow, nature at its most pleasing. Where tufts of soft pink grass lined the edges, strains of violet and amber moss sprawled over the scattering of boulders, and long fronds of water reeds swayed lazily in the current.

The flat expanse of land between the slope of the valley and an ox-bow loop in the stream. An animal track wound through it, curving round invisible obstacles as it led down to a shallow beach where the herds could drink. Apart from that it was untouched, the pink grass which currently dominated the plains was thick and lush here, its tiny mushroom-shaped spoor fringes poised on the verge of ripeness. Nobody had camped here for years, despite its eminent suitability. None of the Starbridge tribes had ever returned. Not after . . .

Here. He walked to one side of the empty tract, the taller stalks of grass swishing straight through his translucent legs. Yes, this was the place. Anastasia's tepee had been pitched here. A sturdy, colourful contraption. Strong enough to take her weight when she tied the rope round her neck. Was the pink grass slightly thinner here? A rough circle where the pyre had been. Her tribe sending her and her few belongings on their way to the Realms (every possession except one, the Thoale stones, which he had kept safe these thirty years). Her body dispersed in fire and smoke, freeing the soul from any final ties with the physical universe.

How had they *known*? Those simple, backward people. Yet their lives contained such astonishing truth. They more than anyone would be prepared for the beyond. Anastasia wouldn't have suffered in the same way as the lost souls he'd encountered during his own fleeting time there. Not her.

Dariat sat on the grass, his toga crumpling around chubby limbs, though never really chafing. If any of her essence had indeed lingered here, it was long gone now. So now what? He looked up at the light tube, which had become even dimmer than before. The air was cooler, too, nothing like Valisk's usual balmy medium. He was rather surprised that phenomenon registered. How could a ghost sense temperature? But then most aspects of his present state were a mystery.

Dariat?

He shook his head. Hearing things. Just to be certain, he looked around. Nobody, alive or spectral, was in sight. An interesting point though. Would I be able to see another ghost?

Dariat. You are there. We feel you. Answer us.

The voice was like affinity, but much softer. A whisper into the back of his mind. Oh great, a ghost being haunted by another ghost. Thank you again, Thoale. That could only ever happen to me.

Who is this? he asked.

We are Valisk now. Part of us is you.

What is this? What are you?

We are the habitat personality, the combination of yourself and Rubra.

That's crazy. You cannot be me.

But we are. Your memories and personality fused to Rubra's within the neural strata. Remember? The change to us, to the neural strata's thought routines, was corporeal and permanent. We remain intact. You, however, were a possessing soul, you were torn out by the habitat's shift to this realm.

A realm hostile to the possessed, he said rancorously.

Exactly.

Don't I know it. I'm a ghost. That's what the shift did to me. A bloody ghost.

How intriguing. We cannot see you.

I'm in the valley.

Ah.

Dariat could feel the understanding within the personality. It knew which valley he meant. A true affinity.

Can we have access to your sensorium, please. It will allow us to analyse the situation properly.

He couldn't think of a reasonable objection, even though the idea sat uncomfortably. After thirty years of self-imposed mental isolation, sharing came hard. Even with an entity that claimed to be derived from himself.

Very well, he griped. He allowed the affinity link to

widen, showing the personality the world through his eyes—or at least what he imagined to be his eyes.

As requested, he looked at his own body for the personality, walked about, demonstrated how he had no material presence.

Yet you persist in interpreting yourself as having human form, the personality said. **How strange.**

Force of habit, I guess.

More likely to be subconscious reassurance. The pattern is your basic foundation, the origin of quintessential identity. Retention of that is probably critical to your continuation as a valid entity. In other words, you're very set in your ways. But then we know that already, don't we.

I don't believe I'm that self-destructive. So if you wouldn't mind cancelling the insults for a few decades.

As you wish. After all, we do know how to cut the deepest.

Dariat could almost laugh at the impression of déjà vu which the exchange conjured up. He and Rubra had spent days of this same verbal fencing while he was possessing Horgan's body. **Was there a reason you wanted to talk to me? Or did you just want to say hello?**

This realm is not hostile to souls alone. It is also affecting our viability right down to the atomic level. Large sections of the neural strata have ceased to function, nor are such areas static, they flow through the strata at random, requiring persistent monitoring. Such failures threaten even our homogenised presence. We have to run constant storage replication routines to ensure our core identity is not erased.

That's tough, but unless the failure occurs everywhere simultaneously, you'll be safe.

As may be. But the overall efficiency of our cells is

much reduced. The sensitive cell clusters cannot perceive as clearly as before; organ capability is degrading to alarming levels. Muscle membrane response is sluggish. Electrical generation is almost zero. All principal mechanical and electrical systems have shut down. The communication net and most processors are malfunctioning. If this situation continues, we will not be able to retain a working biosphere for more than ten days, a fortnight at most.

I hate to sound negative at a time like this, but what do you expect me to do about it?

The remaining population must be organized to assist us. There are holding procedures which can be enacted to prevent further deterioration.

Physical ones. You'll have to ask the living, not me.

We are attempting to. However, those who have been de-possessed are currently in an extremely disorientated state. Even those we have affinity contact with are unresponsive. As well as undergoing severe psychological trauma, their physiological condition has deteriorated.

So?

There are nearly three hundred of our relatives still in zero-tau. Your idea, remember? Kiera was holding them ready as an incentive for the hellhawk possessors. If they were to be taken out, we would have a functional work force ready to help, one that has a good proportion of qualified technicians among it.

Good idea . . . Wait, how come their zero-tau pods are working when everything else has failed?

The zero-tau systems are self-contained and made from military-grade components, they are also located in the deep caverns. We assumed that combination affords them some protection from whatever is affecting us.

If all you've got to do is flick one switch, why not just use a servitor?

Their physiological situation is even worse than the humans. All the animals in the habitat seem to be suffering from a strong form of sleeping sickness. Our affinity instructions cannot rouse them.

Does that include all the xenoc species?

Yes. Their biochemistry is essentially similar to terrestrial creatures. If our cells are affected, so are theirs.

Okay. Any idea what the problem is? Something like the energistic glitch which the possessed gave out?

Unlikely. It is probably a fundamental property of this realm. We are speculating that the quantum values of this continuum are substantially different from our universe. After all, we did select it to have a detrimental effect on the energy pattern which is a possessing soul. Consequently, we must assume that mass-energy properties here have been altered, that is bound to affect atomic characteristics. But until we can run a full analysis on our quantum state, we cannot offer further speculation.

Ever considered that the devil simply doesn't allow electricity in this particular part of hell?

Your thought is our thought. We prefer to concentrate on the rational. That allows us to construct a hypothesis which will ultimately allow us to salvage this shitty situation.

Yeah, I can live with that. So what is it that you want me to do?

See if you can talk to someone called Tolton. He will switch off the zero-tau pods for us.

Why? Who is he?

A street poet, so he claims. He was one of the inhabitants we managed to keep out of Bonney's clutches.

Does he have affinity?

No. But legend has it that humans can see ghosts.

Shit, you're grasping at straws.

You have an alternative?

Ghosts can get tired. This unwelcome discovery made itself quite clear as Dariat trudged over the grassland towards the ring of starscraper lobbies in the middle of the habitat. But then if you have imaginary muscles, they are put under quite a strain carrying your imaginary body across long distances, especially when that body had Dariat's bulk.

This is bloody unfair, he declared to the personality. When souls come back from the beyond, they all see themselves as physically perfect twenty-five-year-olds.

That's simple vanity.

I wish I was vain.

Valisk's parkland was also becoming less attractive. Now he had hiked out of the valley, the vivid pink grass which cloaked the southern half of the cylinder was grading down to a musky-grey, an effect he equated to a city smog wrapping itself round the landscape. It couldn't be blamed entirely on the diminished illumination; the slim core of plasma in the axial light tube was still a valiant neon blue. Instead it seemed to be part of the overall lack of vitality which was such an obvious feature of this realm. The xenoc plant appeared to be past its peak, as if its spore fringes had already ripened and now it was heading back into dormancy.

None of the insects which usually chirped and flittered among the plains had roused themselves. A few times, he came across field mice and their xenoc analogues, who were sleeping fitfully. They'd just curled up where they were, not making any attempt to return to their nests or warrens.

Ordinary chemical reactions must still be working, he suggested. **If they weren't, then everything would be dead.**

Yes. Although from what we're seeing and experiencing, they must also be inhibited to some degree.

Dariat trudged on. The spiral-springs of grass made the going hard, causing resistance as his legs passed through them. It was though he was walking along a stream bed where the water was coming half-way up his shins. As his complaints became crabbier, the personality guided him towards one of the narrow animal tracks.

After half an hour of easier walking, and pondering his circumstances, he said: **You told me that your electrical generation was almost zero.**

Yes.

But not absolute?

No.

So the habitat must be in some kind of magnetic field if the induction cables are producing a current.

Logically, yes.

But?

Some induction cables are producing a current, the majority are not. And those that are, do so sporadically. Buggered if we can work out what's going on, boy. Besides, we can't locate any magnetic field outside. There's nothing we can see that could be producing one.

What is out there?

Very little.

Dariat felt the personality gathering the erratic images from clusters of sensitive cells speckling the external polyp shell, and formatting them into a coherent visualisation for him. The amount of concentration it took for the personality to fulfil what used to be a profoundly simple task surprised and worried him.

There were no planets. No moons. No stars. No galaxies. Only a murky void.

The eeriest impression he received from the expanded affinity bond was the way Valisk appeared to be in flight. Certainly he was aware of movement of some kind, though it was purely subliminal, impossible to define. The huge cylinder appeared to be gliding through a nebula. Not one recognizable from their universe. This was composed from extraordinarily subtle layers of ebony mist, shifting so slowly they were immensely difficult to distinguish. Had he been seeing it with his own eyes, he would have put it down to overstressed retinas. But there were discernible strands of the smoky substance out there; sparser than atmospheric cloud, denser than whorls of interstellar gas.

Abruptly, a fracture of hoary light shimmered far behind the hub of Valisk's southern endcap, a luminous serpent slithering around the insubstantial billows. Rough tatters of gritty vapour detonated into emerald and turquoise phosphorescence as it twirled past them. The phenomenon was gone inside a second.

Was that lightning? Dariat asked in astonishment.

We have no idea. However, we can't detect any static charge building on our shell. So it probably wasn't electrically based.

Have you seen it before?

That was the third time.

Bloody hell. How far away was it?

That is impossible to determine. We are trying to correlate parallax data from the external sensitive cells. Unfortunately, lack of distinct identifiable reference points within the cloud formations is hampering our endeavour.

You're beginning to sound like an Edenist. Take a guess.

We believe we can see about two hundred kilometres altogether.

Shit. That's all?

Yes.

Anything could be out there, behind that stuff.

You're beginning to catch on, boy.

Can you tell if we're moving? I got the impression we were. But it could just be the way that cloud stuff is shifting round out there.

We have the same notion, but that's all it ever can be. Without a valid reference point, it is impossible to tell. Certainly we're not under acceleration, which would eliminate the possibility we're falling through a gravity field . . . if this realm has gravity, of course.

Okay, how about searching round with a radar? Have you tried that? There are plenty of arrays in the counter-rotating spaceport.

The spaceport has radar, it also has several Adamist starships, and over a hundred remote maintenance drones which could be adapted into sensor probes. None of which are functioning right now, boy. We really do need to bring our relatives out of zero-tau.

Yeah yeah. I'm getting there as quick as I can. You know what, I don't think fusing with my thought routines has made that big an impression on you, has it?

According to the personality, Tolton was in the parkland outside the Gonchraov starscraper lobby. Dariat didn't get there on the first attempt. He encountered the other ghosts before he arrived.

The pink grassland gradually gave way to terrestrial grass and trees a couple of kilometres from the starscraper lobbies. It was a lush manicured jungle which boiled round the habitat's midsection, with gravel tracks winding round the thicker clumps of trees and vines. Big stone slabs formed primitive bridges over the rambling brooks, their support boulders grasped by thick coils of flowering creepers. Petals were drooping sadly as Dariat walked over them. As he drew closer to the lobby, he started to encounter the first of the servitor animal corpses, most of them torn by burnt scars, the impact of white fire. Then he noticed the decaying remains of several of their human victims lying in the undergrowth.

Dariat found the sight inordinately depressing. A nasty reminder of the relentless struggle which Rubra and Kiera had fought for dominance of the habitat. "And who won?" he asked morbidly.

He cleared another of the Neolithic bridges. The trees were thinning out now, becoming more ornate and taller as jungle gave way to parkland. There were flashes of movement in front of him coupled with murmurs of conversation, which made him suddenly self-conscious. Was he going to have to jump up and down waving his arms and shouting to get the living to notice him?

Just as he was psyching himself up for the dismaying inevitable, the little group caught sight of him. There were three men and two women. Their clothes should have clued him in. The eldest man was wearing a very long, foppish coat of yellow velvet with ruffled lace down the front; one of the women had forced her large fleshy frame into a black leather dominatrix uniform, complete with whip; her mousy middle-aged companion was in a baggy woollen overcoat, so deliberately dowdy it was a human stealth covering; of the remaining two men, one was barely out of his teens, a black youth with panther muscles shown off by a slim red waistcoat; while the other was in his thirties, covered by a baggy mechanics overall. They made a highly improbable combination, even for Valisk's residents.

Dariat stopped in surprise and with some gratification, raising a hand in moderate greeting. "Hello there. Glad you can see me. My name's Dariat."

They stared at him, already unhappy expressions displaced by belligerent suspicion.

"You the one Bonney had everyone chasing?" the black guy asked.

Dariat grinned modestly. "That's me."

"Motherfucker. You did this to us!" he screamed. "I had a body. I had my life back. You fucked that. You fucked me. You ruined everything. Everything! You brought us here, you and that shit living in the walls."

Comprehension dawned for Dariat. He could see the faint outlines of branches through the man. "You're a ghost," he exclaimed.

"All of us are," the dominatrix said. "Thanks to you."

"Oh shit," he whispered in consternation.

There are other ghosts? the personality asked. The affinity band was awash with interest.

What does it bloody look like!

The dominatrix took a step towards him; her whip flicked out, cracking loudly. She grinned viciously. "I haven't had a chance to use this properly for a long time, dearie. That's a shame, because I know how to use it real bad."

"Gonna get you plenty of chance to catch up now," the black guy purred to her.

Dariat stood his ground shakily. "You can't blame me for this. I'm one of you."

"Yeah," said the mechanic. "And this time you can't get away." He drew a heavy spanner from his leg pocket.

They must all be here, the personality said. **All the possessing souls.**

Just great.

"Can we hurt him?" the mousy woman asked.

"Let's find out," the dominatrix replied.

"Wait!" Dariat implored. "We need to work together to get the habitat out of this place. Don't you understand? It's collapsing around us, everything's breaking down. We'll be trapped here."

The black guy bared his teeth wide. "We needed you to work with us to beat the habitat back in the real universe."

Dariat flinched. He turned and ran. They gave chase immediately. That they'd catch him was never in doubt. He was appallingly overweight, and he'd just finished a nine kilometre hike. The whip slashed against the back of his left calf. He wailed, not just from the sharp sting, but from the fact it could sting.

They whooped and cheered behind him, delighted by the knowledge they could inflict injury, pain. Dariat staggered over the end of the bridge, and took a few unsteady steps towards the thicker part of jungle. The whip struck him again, flaying his shoulder and cheek, accompanied by the dominatrix's gleeful laugh. Then the lean black guy caught up with him, and jumped high, kicking him in the small of the back.

Dariat went flying, landing flat on his stomach, arms and legs spread wide. Not a single blade of grass even bent as he struck the ground; his bloated body seemed to be lying on a median height of stalks, while longer stems poked straight through him.

The beating began. Feet kicked savagely into his flanks, his legs, neck. The whip whistled down again and again, landing on his spine each time. Then the mechanic stood on his shoulders, and brought the spanner down on his skull. The battering became rhythmic, horrifyingly relentless. Dariat cried out at every terrifying impact. There was pain, in abundance there was pain, but no blood, nor damage, nor bruising or broken bones. The blaze of hurt had its origin in a concussion of hatred and fury. Each blow reinforcing, emphasising how much they wanted him ruined.

His cries grew fainter, though they were just as insistent, and tainted with increasing anguish. The spanner, and the whip, and the boots, and the fists began to sink into him, puncturing his intangible boundary. He was sinking deeper into the grass, the hammering propelling his belly into the soil. Coldness swept into him, a wave racing on ahead of the solid surface with which he was merging. His shape was lacking definition now, its outline becoming less substantial. Even his thoughts began to lose their intensity.

Nothing could stop them. Nothing he said. Nothing he begged. Nothing he could pay. None of his prayers. Nothing. He had to endure it all. Not knowing what the outcome would be; terrifyingly, not knowing what it could be.

They let him be, eventually. After how much time not one of them knew. As much as it took to satisfy their hunger for vengeance. To dull the enjoyment of sadism. To experiment with the novel methods of brutality available to ghosts. There wasn't much of his presence left when they finished. A gauzy patch of pearl luminescence loitering amid the grass, the back of his toga barely bobbing above the surface of the soil. Limbs and head were buried.

Laughing, they walked away.

Amid the coldness, darkness, and apathy, a few strands of thought clung together. A weak filigree of suffering and woe. Everything he was. Very little, really.

Tolton had a brief knowledge of scenes like this. Second-hand knowledge, old and stale, memories of tales told to him by the denizens of the lowest floors of the starscrapers. Tales of covert combat operations, of squads that had been hit by superior firepower, waiting to be evac-ed out of the front line. Their bloody, battered casualties wound up in places like this, a field hospital triage. It was the latest development in the saga of the habitat population's misfortunes. Lately, studying the parkland had become a form of instant archaeology. Evolving stages of residence were laid out in concentric circles, plain to see.

In the beginning was the starscraper lobby, a pleasing rotunda of stone and glass, blending into the superbly maintained parkland. Then with the arrival of possession, the lobby had been smashed up during one of the innumerable firefights between Kiera's followers and Rubra, and a shanty town had sprung up in a ring around it. Tiny Tudor cottages had stood next to Arabian tents, which were pitched alongside shiny Winnebagoes; the richness of imagination on display was splendid. That was before Valisk departed the universe.

After that, the illusion of solidity had melted away like pillars of salt in the rain, exposing rickety shacks assembled from scraps of plastic and metal. They leant together precariously, one stacked against another to provide a highly dubious stability. The narrow strips of grass between were reduced to slippery runnels of mud, often used as open sewers.

So now the survivors of Valisk's latest change in fortune had moved again, repelled from the hovels of their erstwhile possessors, they were simply sprawling uncaringly across the surrounding grass. They lacked the energy and willpower to do anything else. Some lay on their backs, some had curled up, some were sitting against trees, some stumbled about aimlessly. That wasn't so bad, Tolton thought, after what they'd been through a period of stupefaction was understandable. It was the sound which was getting to him. Wails of distress and muffled sobbing min-

gling together to poison the air with harrowing dismay. Five
thousand people having a bad dream in unison.

And just like a bad dream, you couldn't wake them from
it. To begin with, when he'd emerged from his hiding place,
he'd moved from one to another. Offering words of sympathy, a comforting arm around the shoulder. He'd persisted
valiantly for a couple of hours like that, before finally acknowledging how quite pathetically pointless it all was.
Somehow, they would have to get over the psychological
trauma by themselves.

It wasn't going to be easy, not with the ghosts as an ever-
present reminder of their ordeal. The ex-possessors were
still slinking furtively through the outlying trees of the
nearby jungle. For whatever reason, once they'd been expelled from their host bodies, they wouldn't leave. Immediately after Valisk's strange transformation they had clung
longingly to their victims, following them with perverted
devotion as they crawled about shaking and vomiting in reaction to their release. Then as people had gradually started
to recover their wits and take notice, the anger had surfaced. It was that massive deluge of communal hatred
which had forced the ghosts to retreat, rather than the
shouts of abuse and threats of vengeance.

They'd fled into the refuge of the jungle around the parkland, almost bewildered by the response they'd spawned.
But they hadn't gone far. Tolton could see them thronging
out there amid the funereal trees, their eerie pale radiance
casting diaphanous shadows which twisted fluidly amid the
branches and trunks.

But the ghosts never went any further than the trees. It
was as if the greater depths of the darkling habitat frightened them, too. That was the aspect of this whole affair
which worried Tolton the most.

His own wanderings were almost as aimless as anyone in

the throws of recovery. Like them, he didn't relish the idea of venturing through the shanty town, he also considered it prudent not to fraternise with the ghosts. Though somewhere at the back of his mind was some ancient piece of folklore about ghosts never actually killing anybody. Whichever pre-history warlock came up with that prophecy had obviously never encountered these particular ghosts.

So he kept moving, avoiding eye-contact, searching for . . . well, he'd know what when he saw it. Ironically, the thing he missed most was Rubra, and the wealth of knowledge which came with that contact. But the processor block he'd used to stay in touch with the habitat personality had crashed as soon as the change happened. Since then he'd tried using several other blocks. None of them worked, at most he got a trickle of static. He didn't have enough (any, actually) technical knowledge to understand why.

Nor did he understand the change which the habitat had undergone, only the result, the mass exorcism. He assumed it had been imposed by some friendly ally. Except Valisk didn't have any allies. And Rubra had never dropped any hint that this might happen, not in all the weeks he'd kept Tolton hidden from the possessed. There was nothing for it but to keep moving for the delusion of purpose it bestowed, and wait for developments. Whatever they might be.

"Please." The woman's voice was little more than a whisper, but it was focused enough to make Tolton hesitate and try to see who was speaking.

"Please, I need some help. Please." The speaker was in her late middle-age, huddled up against a tree. He walked over to her, avoiding a couple of people who were stretched out, almost comatose, on the grass.

Details were difficult in this leaden twilight. She was wrapped in a large tartan blanket, clutching it to her chest like a shawl. Long unkempt hair partially obscured her face, glossy titian roots contrasted sharply with the dirty faded chestnut of the tresses. The features glimpsed through the tangle were delicate, a pert button nose and long cheekbones, implausibly artistic eyebrows. Her skin seemed very tight, almost stretched, as if to emphasise the curves.

"What's wrong?" Tolton asked gently, cursing himself for the stupidity of the question. As he knelt beside her, the light tube's meagre nimbus glimmered on the tears dribbling down her cheeks.

"I hurt," she said. "Now she's gone, I hurt so badly."

"It'll go. I promise, time will wash it away."

"She slept with hundreds of men," the woman cried wretchedly. "Hundreds. Women, too. I felt the heat in her, she loved it, all of it. That slut, that utter slut. She made my body do things with those animals. Awful, vile things. Things no decent person would ever do."

He tried to take one of her hands, but she snatched it away, turning from him. "It wasn't you," he said. "You didn't do any of those things."

"How can you say that? It was done to me. I felt it all, every minute of it. This is my body. Mine! My flesh and blood. She took that from me. She soiled me, ruined me. I'm so corrupt I'm not even human any more."

"I'm sorry, really I am. But you have to learn not to think like that. If you do, you're letting her win. You've got to put that behind you. It's over, and you've won. She's been exorcised, she's nothing but a neurotic wisp of light. That's all she'll ever be now. I'd call that a victory, wouldn't you?"

"But I hurt," she persisted. Her voice dropped to a confessional tone. "How can I forget when I hurt?"

"Look, there are treatments, memory suppressers, all sorts of cures. Just as soon as we get the power turned back on, you can . . ."

"Not my mind! Not just that." She had begun to plead. "It's my body, my body which hurts."

Tolton started to get a very bad feeling about where the conversation was heading. The woman was shaking persistently, and he was sure some of the moisture glistening on her face had to be perspiration. He flicked an edgy glance back at her unnatural roots. "Where, exactly, does it hurt?"

"My face," she mumbled. "My face aches. It's not me anymore. I couldn't see me when she looked in a mirror."

"They all did that, all imagined themselves to look ridiculously young and pretty. It's an illusion, that's all."

"No. It became real. I'm not me, not now. She even took my identity away from me. And . . ." her voice started trembling. "My shape. She stole my body, and still that wasn't enough. Look, look what she's done to me."

Moving so slowly that Tolton wanted to do it for her, she drew the folds of the blanket apart. For the first time, he actually wished there was less light. To begin with it looked as though someone had badly bungled a cosmetic package adaptation. Her breasts were grossly misshapen. Then he realized that was caused by large bulbs of flesh clinging to the upper surface like skin-coloured leeches. Each one almost doubled the size of the breast, the weight pulling them down heavily. The natural tissue was almost squashed from view.

The worst part of it was, they obviously weren't grafts or implants; whatever the tissue was, it had swollen out of the natural mammary gland. Below them, her abdomen was held anorexically flat by a broad oval slab of unyielding skin. It was as though she'd developed a thick callous across the whole area, fake musculature marked out by faint translucent lines.

"See?" the woman asked, staring down at her exposed chest in abject misery. "Bigger breasts and a flat belly. She really wanted bigger breasts. That was her wish. They'd be more useful to her, more fun, more spectacular. And she could make wishes come true."

"God preserve us," Tolton murmured in horror. He didn't know much about human illnesses, but there were some scraps of relevant information flashing up out of his childhood's basic medical didactic memories. Cancer tumours. Almost a lost disease. Geneering had made human bodies massively resistant to the ancient bane. And for the few isolated instances when it did occur, medical nanonics could penetrate and eradicate the sick cells within hours.

"I used to be a nurse," the woman said, as she ashamedly covered herself with the blanket again. "They're runaways. My breasts are the largest growths, but I must have the same kind of malignant eruptions at every change she instituted."

"What can I do?" he asked hoarsely.

"I need medical nanonic packages. Do you know how to program them?"

"No. I don't even have neural nanonics. I'm a poet, that's all."

"Then, please, find me some. My neural nanonics aren't working either, but a processor block might do instead."

"I . . . Yes, of course." It would mean a trip into the lifeless, lightless starscraper to find some, but his discomfort at that prospect was nothing compared to her suffering. Somehow, he managed to keep a neutral expression on his face as he stood up, even though he was pretty certain a medical nanonic package wouldn't work in this weird environment. But it might, it just might. And if that slender chance existed, then he would bring one for her, no matter what.

He cast round the dismal sight of people strewn about, holding themselves and moaning. The really terrifying doubt engulfed him then. Suppose the anguish wasn't all psychological? Every possessed he'd seen had changed their appearance to some degree. Suppose every change had born a malignancy, even a small one.

"Oh fucking hell, Rubra. Where are you? We need help."

As always, there was no warning when the cell door opened. Louise wasn't even sure when it had swung back. She was curled up on the bunk, dozing, only semi-aware of her surroundings. Quite how long she'd been in this state, she didn't know. Somehow, her time sense had got all fouled up. She remembered the interview with Brent Roi, his sarcasm and unconcealed contempt. Then she'd come back here. Then . . . She'd come back here hours ago. Well, a long time had passed . . . She thought.

I must have fallen asleep.

Which was hard to believe; the colossal worry of the situation had kept her mind feverishly active.

The usual two female police officers appeared in the doorway. Louise blinked up at their wavering outlines, and tried to right herself. Bright lights flashed painfully behind her eyes; she had to clamp her mouth shut against the sudden burst of nausea.

What is wrong with me?

"Woo there, steady on." One of the police officers was sitting on the bed beside her, holding her up.

Louise shook uncontrollably, cold sweat beading on her skin. Her reaction calmed slightly, though it was still terribly hard to concentrate.

"One minute," the woman said. "Let me reprogram your medical package. Try to take some deeper breaths, okay?"

That was simple enough. She gulped down some air, her chest juddering. Another couple of breaths. Her rogue body seemed to be calming. "Wha . . . What?" she panted.

"Anxiety attack," said the policewoman. "We see a lot of them in here. That and worse things."

Louise nodded urgently, an attempt to convince herself that's all it was. No big deal. Nothing badly amiss. The baby's fine—the medical package would insure that. Just stay calm.

"Okay. I'm okay now. Thank you." She proffered a small smile at the police officer, only to be greeted with blank-faced indifference.

"Let's go, then," said the officer standing by the door.

Louise girded herself, and slowly stood on slightly unsteady legs. "Where are we going?"

"Parole Office." She sounded disgusted.

"Where's Genevieve? Where's my sister?"

"Don't know. Don't care. Come on."

Louise was almost shoved out into the corridor. She was improving by the minute, although the headache lingered longer than anything else. A small patch of skin at the back of her skull tingled, as if she'd been stung. Her fingers stroked it absently. Anxiety attack? She hadn't known there was such a thing before. But given everything she currently had to think about, such a malaise was more than likely.

They got into a lift which had to be heading down. The gravity field had risen to almost normal when they got out. This part of the asteroid was different to the cells and interview rooms she'd been kept in until now. Definitely government offices, the standardized furniture and eternally polite personnel with their never-smiling faces were evidence of that. She took a little cheer from the fact these corridors and glimpsed rooms weren't as crushingly bleak as the upper level. Her status had changed for the better. Slightly.

The police officers showed her into a room with a narrow window looking out over High York's biosphere cavern.

Not much to see, it was dawn, or dusk, Louise didn't know which. The grassland and trees soaking up the gold-orange light were a brighter, more welcoming green than the cavern in Phobos. Two curving settees had been set up facing each other in the middle of the floor, bracketing an oval table. Genevieve slouched on one of them, hands stuffed into the pockets of her shipsuit, feet swinging just off the floor, looking out of the window. Her expression was a mongrel cross between sullen resentment and utter boredom.

"Gen." Louise's voice nearly cracked.

Genevieve raced across the room and thudded into her. They hugged each other tightly. "They wouldn't tell me where you were!" Genevive protested loudly. "They wouldn't let me see you. They wouldn't say what was happening."

Louise stroked her sister's hair. "I'm here now."

"It's been forever. Days!"

"No, no. It just seems like that."

"Days," Genevieve insisted.

Louise managed a slightly uncertain smile; wanting for herself the reassurance she was attempting to project. "Have they been questioning you?"

"Yes," Genevieve mumbled morosely. "They kept on and on about what happened in Norwich. I told them a hundred times."

"Me too."

"Everybody must be really stupid on Earth. They don't understand anything unless you've explained it five times."

Louise wanted to laugh at the childish derision in Gen's voice, pitched just perfectly to infuriate any adult.

"And they took my games block away. That's stealing, that is."

"I haven't seen any of my stuff either."

"The food's horrid. I suppose they're too thick to cook it properly. And I haven't had any clean clothes."

"Well, I'll see what I can do."

Brent Roi hurried into the room, and dismissed the two waiting police officers with a casual wave. "Okay, ladies, take a seat."

Louise flashed him a resentful look.

"Please?" he entreated without noticeable sincerity.

Holding hands, the sisters sat on the settee opposite him. "Are we under arrest?" Louise asked.

"No."

"Then you believe what I told you?"

"To my amazement, I find sections of your story contain the odd nugget of truth."

Louise frowned. This attitude was completely different to the one he'd shown her during the interview. Not that he was repenting, more like he'd been proved right instead of her.

"So you'll watch out for Quinn Dexter?"

"Most assuredly."

Genevieve shuddered. "I hate him."

"That's all that truly matters," Louise said. "He must never be allowed to get down to Earth. If you believe me, then I've won."

Brent Roi shifted uncomfortably. "Okay, we've been trying to decide what to do with the pair of you. Which I can tell you is not an easy thing, given what you were attempting. You thought you were doing the right thing, bringing Christian here. But believe me, from the legal side of things, you are about as wrong as it's possible to be. The Halo police commissioner has spent two days being advised by some of our best legal experts on what the hell to do with you, which hasn't improved his temper any. Ordinarily we'd just walk you past a warm judge and fly you off to a penal colony. There'd be no problem obtaining a guilty verdict." He gazed at Genevieve. "Not even your age would get you off."

Genevieve pushed her shoulders up against her neck, and glowered at him.

"However, there are mitigating circumstances, and these are strange times. Lucky for you, that gives the Halo police force a large amount of discretion right now."

"So?" Louise asked calmly. For whatever reason she wasn't afraid; if they were due to face a trial none of this would be happening.

"So. Pretty obviously: we don't want you up here after what you've done; plus you don't have the basic technical knowledge necessary to live in an asteroid settlement, which makes you a liability. Unfortunately, there's an interstellar quarantine in force right now, which means we can't send you off to Tranquillity where your fiancé can take care of you. That just leaves us with one option: Earth. You have money, you can afford to stay there for the duration of the crisis."

Louise glanced at Genevieve, who squashed her lips together with a dismissive lack of interest.

"I'm not going to object," Louise said.

"I couldn't care less if you did," Brent Roi told her. "You have no say in this at all. As well as deporting you, I am officially issuing you with a police caution. You have engaged in an illegal act with the potential of endangering High York, and this will be entered into Govcentral's criminal data memory store with a suspended action designation. Should you at any time in the future be found committing another criminal act of any nature within Govcentral's domain this case will be reactivated and used in your prosecution. Is that clear?"

"Yes," Louise whispered.

"You cause us one more problem, and they'll throw you out of the arcology and lock the door behind you."

"What about Fletcher?" Genevieve asked.

"What about him?" Brent Roi said.

"Is he coming down to Earth with us?"

"No, Gen," Louise said. "He's not." She tried to keep the sorrow from her voice. Fletcher had helped her and Gen through so much, she still couldn't think of him as a possessor, one of the enemy. The last image she had was of him being led out of the big airlock chamber where they'd been detained. A smile of forlorn encouragement on his face, directed at her. Even in defeat, he didn't lose his nobility.

"Your big sister's right," Brent Roi told Genevieve. "Stop thinking about Fletcher."

"Have you killed him?"

"Tough to do. He's already dead."

"Have you?"

"At the moment he's being very cooperative. He's telling us about the beyond, and helping the physics team understand the nature of his energistic power. Once we've learned all we can, then he'll be put into zero-tau. End of story."

"Can we see him before we go?" Louise asked.

"No."

The two female police officers escorted Louise and Genevieve directly up to the counter-rotating spaceport. They were given a standard class berth on the *Scher*, an inter-orbit passenger ship. The interstellar quarantine hadn't yet bitten into the prodigious Earth, Halo, Moon economic triad; outsystem exports made up barely fifteen per cent of their trade. Civil flights between the three were running close to their usual levels.

They arrived at the departure lounge twelve minutes before the ship was scheduled to leave. The police returned their luggage and passports, with Earth immigration clearance loaded in; they also got their processor blocks back. Finally, they handed Louise her Jovian Bank credit disk.

Louise had her suspicions that the whole procedure was deliberately being rushed to keep them off-balance and complacent. Not that she knew how to kick up a fuss. But there was probably some part of their treatment which a good lawyer could find fault with. She didn't really care. *Scher*'s life support capsule had the same lengthy cylindrical layout as the *Jamrana*, except that every deck was full of chairs. A sour stewardess showed them brusquely to their seats, strapped them in, and left to chase other passengers.

"I wanted to change," Genevieve complained. She was pulling dubiously at her shipsuit. "I haven't washed for ages. It's all clammy."

"We'll be able to change when we get to the tower station, I expect."

"Which tower station? Where are we going?"

"I don't know." Louise glanced at the stewardess, who was chiding an elderly woman's attempts to fasten her seat straps. "I think we'll just have to wait and find out."

"Then what? What do we do when we get there?"

"I'm not sure. Let me think for a minute, all right?"

Louise squirmed her shoulders, letting her muscles relax. Freefall always made her body tense up as it tried to assume more natural gravity-evolved postures. Thankfully, the cabin chairs were almost flat, preventing her from getting stomach twinges.

What to do next hadn't bothered her much while she'd been in custody. Convincing Brent Roi about Dexter was her only concern. Now that had been accomplished, or seemed to be. She still couldn't quite believe he had taken

her warnings particularly seriously; they'd been released
far too quickly for that. Dismissed, almost.

The authorities had Fletcher in custody, and he was cooperating with them about possession. That was their true
prize, she thought. They were confident their security procedures would spot Dexter. She wasn't. Not at all. And
she'd made one solemn promise to Fletcher, which covered
exactly this situation.

If I can't help him physically, at least I can honour my
promise. If our positions were reversed, he would. Banneth,
I said I'd find and warn Banneth. Yes. And I will. The sudden resolution did a lot to warm her again.

Then she was aware of a strangely rhythmic buzzing
sound, and blinked her eyes open. Genevieve had activated
her processor block; its AV projector lens was shining a
conical fan of light directly on her face. Frayed serpents of
pastel colour stroked her cheeks and nose, glistening on a
mouth parted in an enraptured smile. Her fingers skated
with fast dextrous motions over the block's surface, sketching eccentric ideograms.

I'm really going to have to do something about this obsession, Louise thought, it can't be healthy.

The stewardess was shouting at a man cradling a crying
child. Tackling Gen was probably best delayed until they
reached Earth.

It wasn't rugged determination, or even victorious self-
confidence which brought him back. Instead, came the slow,
dreadful comprehension that this awful limbo wouldn't end
if he did nothing.

Dariat's thoughts hung amid vast clusters of soil molecules, membranous twists of nebula dust webbing the space
between stars, insipid, enervated. Completely unable to
evaporate, to fade away into blissful non-existence. Instead,

they hummed with chilly misery as they conducted pain-soaked memories round and around on a never ending circuit, humiliation and fear undimmed by time and repetition.

Worse than the beyond. At least in the beyond, there were other souls, memories you could raid to bring an echo of sensation. Here there was only yourself; a soul buried alive. Nothing to comfort you but your own life. Screaming from the pain of the blows which battered him down might have stopped, but the internal scream of self-loathing could never cease. Not incarcerated here. He didn't want to go back, not to the dimly sensed light and air above, the vicious brutality of the ghosts waiting there. Every time he emerged, they would pummel him down again. That was what all of them wanted. He would go through the same suffering again and again. Yet he couldn't stay here, either.

Dariat moved. He thought of himself, visualised pushing his bulky body up through the soil, as if he was doing some kind of appalling fitness-fad exercise. It wasn't anything like that easy. Imagination couldn't power him as before. Something had happened to him, weakening him. The vitality he owned, even as a ghost, had been leeched out by the matter with which he was entwined.

Fantasy muscles trembled as he strained. Finally, along his back, sensation was returning in a paltry trickle. A warmth, but not on his skin. Inside, just below the surface.

It inspired greed, a hunger for more. Nothing else mattered, the warmth was revitalising, a font of life. It leant to his strength, and he began to rise faster through the soil, sucking in more warmth as he went. Soon, his face cleared the ground, and he was moving at an almost normal speed. Extricating himself from the soil meant discovering just how cold he was. Dariat stood up, teeth chattering, arms crossed over his chest, hugging tight as his hands tried to rub some heat into icy flesh. Only his feet were warm, though that was a relative term.

The grass around his sandals was a sickly yellow-brown, dead and drooping. Each blade was covered in a delicate sprinkle of hoarfrost. They made up a roughly oval patch about two metres long. Body-shaped, in fact. He stared at it, completely bewildered.

Damn, I'm cold!

Dariat? That you, boy?

Yes, it's me. One question—he didn't really want to ask, but had to know. **How long was I . . . out for?**

It's been seventeen hours.

Seventeen years was a figure he could have believed in quite easily. **Is that all?**

Yes. What happened?

They beat me into the ground. Literally. It was . . . Bad. Real bad.

Then why didn't you come out earlier?

You won't understand.

Did you kill the grass?

I don't know. I suppose so.

How? We thought you didn't interact with solid matter.

Don't ask me. There was a kind of warmth as I came out. Or maybe it was just hatred which killed the grass, concentrated hatred. That's what they were giving off; Thoale be damned, but they hated me. I'm cold now. He scanned round, searching through the tree trunks for any sign of the other ghosts. After a moment, he walked away from the patch of dead grass, spooked by the place. The opposite of consecrated ground.

Movement felt good, it was making his legs warm up. When he glanced down, he saw a line of frosted footsteps in the grass trailing back to the burial patch. But he was definitely getting warmer. He started walking again, a meagre lick of heat seeping up from his legs to his torso. It would take a long time to dispel the chill, but he was sure it would happen eventually.

The starscraper is the other way, the personality said.

I know. That's why I'm going back to the valley. I'll be safe there.

For a while.

I'm not risking another encounter.

You have to. Look, forewarned is forearmed. Just take it carefully. If you see any ghosts waiting ahead of you, go around them.

I'm not doing it.

You have to. Our internal status is still decaying. We must have those descendants out of zero-tau. What good will a dead habitat do you? You know they're the only chance of salvation any of us have. You know that. You just showed us how bad entombment here is; that could become permanent if we don't get clear.

Shit! He stopped, standing with his fists clenched. Tendrils of frost slithered out from under his soles to wilt the grass.

It's common sense, Dariat. You won't be giving in to Rubra just by agreeing.

That's not—

Ha. Remember what we are.

All right! Bastards. Where's Tolton?

Tolton had found the lightstick in an emergency equipment locker in the starscraper's lobby. It gave out a lustreless purple-tinged glow, and that emerged at a pitiful percentage of its designated output wattage. But after forty minutes, his eyes had acclimatised well. Navigating down through the interior of the starscraper posed few physical problems.

Resolution, however, was a different matter. In his other hand he carried a fire axe from the same locker as the lightstick, it hardly inspired confidence.

Beyond the bubble of radiance which enveloped him, it was very dark indeed. And silent with it. No light shone in through any of the windows; there wasn't even a dripping tap to break the monotony of his timorous footsteps. Three times since he'd been down here, the electrophorescent cells had burst into life. Some arcane random surge of power sending shoals of photons skidding along the vestibules and stairwells. The first time it happened, he'd been petrified. The zips of light appeared from nowhere, racing towards him at high speed. By the time he yelled out and started to cower down, they were already gone, behind him and vanishing round some corner. He didn't react much better the next two times, either.

He told himself that he should be relieved that some aspect of Rubra and the habitat was still functioning, however erratically. It wasn't much reassurance; that the stars had vanished from view had been a profound shock. He'd already decided he wasn't going to share that knowledge with the other residents for a while. What he couldn't understand was, where were they? His panicky mind was constantly filling the blank space outside the windows with dreadful imaginings. It wasn't much of a leap to have whatever skulked outside getting in to glide among the opaque shadows of the empty starscraper. Grouping together and conspiring, flowing after him.

The muscle membrane door at the bottom of the stairwell was partially expanded, its edges trembling slightly. He cautiously stuck the lightstick through the gap, and peered round at the fifth floor vestibule. The high ceilings and broad curving archways that were the mise-en-scène of Valisk's starscrapers had always seemed fairly illustrious before; bitek's inalienable majesty. That was back when they were bathed in light and warmth twenty-four hours a day. Now they clustered threateningly round the small area of illumination he projected, swaying with every slight motion of the lightstick.

Tolton waited for a moment, nerving himself to step out. This floor was mainly taken up by commercial offices. Most of the mechanical doorways had frozen shut. He walked along, reading the plaques on each one. The eighth belonged to an osteopath specialising in sports injuries. There ought to be some kind of medical nanonics inside. The emergency lock panel was on the top of the frame. He broke it open with the blunt end of the axe, exposing the handle inside. Now the power was off, or at least disabled, the electronic bolts had disengaged. A couple of turns on the handle released the lock entirely, and he prised the door open.

Typical waiting room: not quite expensive chairs, soft drinks dispenser, reproduction artwork, and lush potted plants. The large circular window looked out at nothing, a black mirror. Tolton saw his own reflection staring back, with a fat man in a grubby robe standing behind him. He yelped in shock, and dropped the lightstick. Flat planes of light and shadow lurched around him. He turned, raising the axe up ready to swipe down on his adversary. Almost overbalancing from the wild motion.

The fat man was waving his arms frantically, shouting. Tolton could hear nothing more than a gentle murmur of air. He gripped the axe tightly as it wobbled about over his head, ready for the slightest sign of antagonism. None came. In fact, there probably couldn't ever be any. Tolton could just see the door through the fat man. A ghost. That didn't make him any happier.

The ghost had put his hands on his hips, face screwed up

in some exasperation. He was saying something slowly and loudly, an adult talking to an idiot child. Again, there was that bantam ruffling of air. Tolton frowned; it corresponded to the movements of the fat ghost's jaw.

In the end, communication became a derivative of lip reading. There was never quite enough sound (if that's what it truly was) to form whole words, rather the faint syllables clued him in.

"Your axe is the wrong way round."

"Uh." Tolton glanced up. The blade was pointing backwards. He shifted it round, then sheepishly lowered it. "Who are you?"

"My name's Dariat."

"You're wasting your time following me, you can't possess me."

"I don't want to. I'm here to give you a message."

"Oh yeah?"

"Yes. The habitat personality wants you to switch off some zero-tau pods."

"How the hell do you know that?"

"We're in affinity contact."

"But you're a . . ."

"Ghost. Yes, I had noticed. Although I think a revenant is a term more applicable in my case."

"A what?"

"The personality never warned me you were this stupid."

"I am not . . ." Tolton's outrage spluttered to a halt. He started to laugh.

Dariat gave the alleged street poet a mildly annoyed glare. "Now what?"

"I've had some weird shit dumped on me in my time, but I think arguing with a ghost over my IQ has got to be the greatest."

Dariat felt his lips move up in a grin. "Got a point there."

"Thank you, my man."

"So, are you going to help?"

"Of course. Will turning off the pods be of any use?"

"Yeah. That mad bitch Kiera was holding a whole load of my illustrious relatives in stasis. They should be able to get things up and running again."

"Then we can get out of . . ." Tolton took another look at the window. "Where are we, exactly?"

"I'm not sure you can call this a place, more like a different state of being. It exists to be hostile to the possessed. Unfortunately, there are a few unexpected side effects."

"You sound as though you're talking from a position of knowledge; which I frankly find hard to believe."

"I played a part in bringing us here," Dariat admitted. "I'm not completely sure of the details, though."

"I see. Well, we'd better get started, then." He picked up the lightstick. "Ah, wait. I promised a woman I'd try and find some medical nanonic packages for her. She really does need them."

"There's some in the osteopath's storage cabinet, through there." Dariat pointed.

"You really are in touch with Rubra, aren't you."

"He's changed a bit, but, yes."

"Then I'm curious. Why did the two of you choose me for this task?"

"His decision. But most of the other corporeal residents got whacked out when they were de-possessed. You saw them up in the park. They're no good for anything right now. You're the best we've got left."

"Oh, bloody hell."

When they emerged up into the decrepit lobby, Tolton sat down and tried to get a processor block to work. He'd never had a didactic memory imprint covering their operations and program parameters. Never needed one; all he used them for was recording and playing AV fleks, and communications, plus a few simple commands for medical nanonics (mainly concerned with morning-after blood detoxification).

Dariat started to advise on how to alter the operating program format, essentially dumbing down the unit. Even he had to consult with the personality about which subroutines to delete. Between the three of them, it took twenty minutes to get the little unit on line with a reliable performance level.

Another fifteen minutes of running diagnostics (far slower than usual), and they knew what medical nanonics could achieve in such an antagonistic environment. It wasn't good news; the filaments which wove into and manipulated human flesh were sophisticated molecular strings, with correspondingly high-order management routines. They could bond the lips of wounds together, and infuse doses of stored biochemicals. But fighting a tumour by eliminating individual cancer cells was no longer possible.

We can't waste any more time on this, the personality protested.

Tolton was hunched up over the block. Dariat waved a hand under his face—the only way to catch his attention. Out here in the park the poet found it even harder to hear him; though Dariat suspected his "voice" was actually some kind of weak telepathy.

"It'll have to do," Dariat said.

Tolton frowned down once again at the horribly confusing mass of icons eddying across the block's screen. "Will they be able to cure her?"

"No. The tumours can't be reversed, but the packages should be able to contain them until we get back to the real universe."

"All right. I suppose that'll do."

Dariat managed to feel mildly guilty at the sadness in Tolton's voice. The way the street poet could become so anxious and devoted to a stranger he'd only spent five minutes with was touching.

They walked through the moat of decaying shacks and into the surrounding ring of human misery. The loathing directed at Dariat by those that saw him was profound enough to sting. He, a creature now purely of thought, was buffeted by the emanation of raw emotion; his own substance refined against him. It wasn't as strong as the blows inflicted by his fellow ghosts, but the cumulative effect was disturbingly debilitating. When he'd sneaked into the lobby he hadn't attracted such attention, a few glances of sullen resentment at most. But then, he realized, he was still suffering from the effects of the entombment, he'd been weaker, less substantial.

Now, the jeering and catcalls which chased him were building to a crescendo as more and more people realized what the commotion was about and joined in. He started staggering about, groaning at the pain.

"What is it?" Tolton asked.

Dariat shook his head. There was real fear building in him now. If he stumbled and fell here, victim to this wave of hatred, he might never be able to surface from the soil again. At every attempt he would be pressed back by the throng of people above him, dancing on his living grave.

"Going," he grunted. "Got to go." He pressed his hands over his ears (fat lot of good that it did) and tottered as fast as he could out towards the shadowy trees beyond. "I'll wait for you. Come when you've finished."

Tolton watched in dismay as the ghost scurried away; becoming all too aware of the animosity which was now fo-

cusing on him. Head down, he hurried away in the direction
he thought he'd left the woman.

She was still there, propped up against the tree. Dull eyes
looked up at him, suffused with dread, hope denied. It was
the only part of her which betrayed any emotion. Her
stretched-tight face seemed incapable of displaying the
slightest expression. "What was the noise about?" she
mumbled.

"I think there was a ghost around here."

"Did they kill it?"

"I don't know. I don't think you can kill ghosts."

"Holy water. Use holy water." Tolton knelt down, and
gently eased her clutching hands from the blanket. This
time when it parted he was determined not to grimace. It
was hard. He placed the nanonic medical packages on her
breasts and belly the way Dariat had said, and used the
block to activate the pre-loaded programs. The packages
stirred slightly as they started to knit with her skin.

She let out a soft sigh, embodying both relief and happi-
ness.

"It'll be all right," he told her. "They'll stop the cancer
now."

Her eyes had closed. "I don't believe you. But it's nice of
you to say it."

"I mean it."

"Holy water; that'll burn the bastards."

"I'll remember."

Tolton found Dariat skulking among the fringes of the trees.
The ghost couldn't keep still, nervously searching round for
signs of anyone approaching.

"Don't fret, man. The others don't care about you so long
as you stay away from them."

"I intend to," Dariat grumbled. "Come on, we've got a way to go."

He started walking.

Tolton shrugged, and started after him.

"How was the woman?" Dariat asked.

"Perky. She wanted to sprinkle you with Holy water."

"Silly cow," he snorted with derisive amusement. "That's for vampires."

Kiera had decreed that the zero-tau pods should be put in the deep chambers around the base of the northern endcap. The polyp in that section was a honeycomb of caverns and tunnels; the chambers used almost exclusively by the astronautics industry to support the docking ledge infrastructure. Stores, workshops, and fabrication plants all dedicated to supplying Magellanic Itg's blackhawk fleet. It was a logical place to use. The equipment was already close to hand. There wasn't as much danger from Rubra's insurgency in the big, unsophisticated caverns as there was in the starscrapers. And if they wanted them set up anywhere else, they'd be facing a troublesome relocation job.

As soon as Dariat told him where the zero-tau pods were, Tolton tried to use one of the rentcop jeeps abandoned around the starscraper lobby. It crawled along barely at walking pace. Stopped. Started. Crawled some more. Stopped.

They walked the whole way to the base of the northern endcap. Several times during the day Tolton caught Dariat studying the path behind them, and asked what he was trying to see.

"Footprints," the fat ghost replied.

Tolton decided that after what he'd been through, Dariat was entitled to a reasonable degree of neurotic paranoia. The lightstick grew steadily brighter as they ventured into the cavern levels. Indicator lights began winking on some chunks of machinery. After a while, when they were deep inside the habitat shell, the electrophorescent strips were glowing; not as bright as before, but they remained steady.

Tolton switched the lightstick off. "You know, I even feel better down here."

Dariat didn't answer. He was aware of the difference himself. An atmosphere reminiscent of those heady days thirty years ago, endless bright summer days when being alive was such a blessing. The personality was right, the otherworldliness of this continuum hadn't fully penetrated down here. Things worked as they were supposed to.

We might manage to salvage something from this yet.

They found the zero-tau pods in a lengthy cavern. At some time, there had been machinery or shelving pinned to the wall; small metal brackets still protruded from the dark-amber polyp. Deep scratches told of their recent, hurried removal. Now the cavern was empty except for the row of interstellar-black sarcophagi running the length of the floor. Each of them had been taken from a blackhawk, the crudely severed fittings were proof of that. Thick cables had been grafted on to the interface panels, wiring them into clumps of spherical high-density power cells.

"Where do I start?" Tolton asked.

The processor block he was carrying bleeped before Dariat could begin the usual prolonged process of exaggerated enunciation. "It doesn't matter. Pick one."

"Hey," Tolton grinned. "You're back."

"Rumours of my demise have been greatly exaggerated."

Oh, please, Dariat said.

What's the matter with you? We're back on track. Rejoice.

Dariat was abruptly party to a resurgence of optimism, the sense of a hibernating animal approaching winter's end.

Holding his scepticism in check, he watched Tolton go over to the closest zero-tau pod. The personality issued a couple of simple instructions, and Tolton pecked at a keyboard.

Erentz completed her cower as the scene above her switched. One instant a Chinese warlord with a cruel smile, promising that the next thing she would know was the torture leading up to possession, the next a moderately overweight, wide-eyed man with a good ten days' worth of grubby stubble was peering anxiously down at her. The light was dimmer, too. The wail which she'd started before the pod was activated, continued, rising in pitch.

It's all right. Calm yourself.

Erentz paused, gathering her breath. **Rubra?** The mental voice which had chivvied her along since before she could remember felt different slightly.

Almost. But don't worry. The possessed have gone. You're safe.

There was a background emotion which sparked a small doubt. But the obvious apprehension and concern of the man staring down at her was a strange, fast-acting tonic. He definitely wasn't possessed.

"Hello," Tolton said, desperate for some kind of response from the startled young woman.

She nodded slowly, and raised herself gingerly into a sitting position. It didn't help that the first thing she saw was Dariat hanging back by the cavern entrance. She emitted a frightened gasp.

I'm on your side, Dariat told her, earning a twitchy laugh in response.

What is happening here? she demanded.

The personality began to fill her in. Acceptance of her new situation came amid a rush of relief. Erentz, like all the others released from zero-tau, relied on Rubra to provide a substantial part of their confidence. That he was the one who'd beaten the possessed was a heady boost for them. Fifteen minutes saw the last of the zero-tau pods deactivated. Dariat and Tolton were sidelined to slightly peeved observers as the brigade of Rubra's descendants quickly and efficiently set about releasing their cousins. After that, when they'd come down off the hype, the habitat personality began marshalling them into groups and giving them assignments.

First priority was given to igniting the various fusion generators dotted about the spaceport. They made two attempts to initiate fusion, both of which failed. Microfusion generators, they soon found, worked well in the deep caverns; so they began the arduous process of manoeuvring starship auxiliary tokamaks through the spaceport and down the endcap. When the first one came on-line operating at thirty-eight per cent efficiency, they knew they really did stand a chance.

Schedules were drawn up to install another dozen in the caverns, feeding their energy into the habitat's organic conductors. After two days' unstinting effort, the light-tube began to blaze with early-morning intensity. Noonday brightness was beyond them, but the resumption of near-normal light provided a huge psychological kick for every resident (curiously, that also included the ostracised ghosts). In tandem, the habitat's huge organs began to function again, ingesting and revitalising the myriad fluids and gases utilised within the polyp.

Confidence guaranteed, the personality and its team set about investigating their continuum. Equipment was ransacked from physics labs and Magellanic Itg research centres, and taken down to the caverns where it was powered up. Crude space probes were prepared from the MSVs, sprouting simple sensor arrays. Outside that hot hive core of activity, the rest of the residents slowly began to gather themselves together mentally and physically. Although that promised to be possibly the longest journey of all.

But after a week, Valisk had regained a considerable amount of its most desired commodity: hope.

There was a broad grin smeared across Joshua's face during the entire approach manoeuvre; sometimes it came from admiration, sometimes plain affection. He knew he must look utterly dopy. Simply didn't care. *Lady Mac*'s external sensor array was feeding his neural nanonics a panoramic view of Jupiter's snarled pink and white cloudscape. Tranquillity formed a sharp midnight-black silhouette sailing across the storms.

The massive habitat looked completely undamaged; although its counter-rotating spaceport was darker than usual. The docking bays, normally the focus of frantic time-pressure maintenance efforts, were shut down and lightless, leaving the curving ebony hulls of Adamist starships half-hidden in their eclipsed metal craters. Only the navigation and warning strobes were still flashing indomitably around the edges of the big silver-white disc.

"It's really here," Ashly said in a stunned voice from across the bridge. "That's, that's . . ."

"Outrageous?" Beaulieu suggested.

"Damn right it is," Dhabi said. "Nothing that big can be a starship. Nothing."

Sarha laughed quietly. "Face it, people; we're living in interesting times."

Joshua was glad that the Mzu, her compatriots, and the agency operatives were all down in capsule D's lounge. After everything they'd been through, for the crew to show such bewilderment now was almost an admission of weakness, as if they couldn't cope with the rigours of starflight after all.

Jovian flight management authority datavised their final approach vector, and Joshua reduced the fusion drives to a third of a gee as they crossed the invisible boundary where Tranquillity's traffic control centre took over guidance responsibility. Their escort of five voidhawks matched the manoeuvre with consummate elegance; unwilling to show anything other than perfection to Lagrange Calvert, a tribute to the modest debt Edenism owed him for Aethra.

If only they knew, Samuel said. **They'd be flying parabolas of joy.**

The Jovian sub-Consensus which dealt with classified security matters acknowledged the sentiment with an ironic frisson. **Given our culture's fundamental nature, the restriction of knowledge is always a curious paradox to us**, it said. **However, in the case of the Alchemist, it is fully justified. Every Edenist does not need to know specific details, hence the requirement for my existence. And your job.**

Ah yes, my job.

You are tired of it.

Very. As soon as the *Lady Macbeth* had emerged above Jupiter, Samuel had been conversing with the security sub-Consensus. It was the reason there had been relatively little fuss made about their arrival. First Admiral Aleksandrovich's decision had quickly been accepted by Consensus and Tranquillity.

After that, Samuel had immersed his mentality with Consensus, allowing his worries and tension to dissipate among his fellows. Sympathy for Edenists was so much more than a simple expression of compassion; with affinity he could feel it reaching into his mind, warmth and light dispelling the accumulation of icy shadows that were fear's legacy. No longer alone. Floating in a buoyant sea of welcome understanding. His thoughts began to flow in more regular patterns, and with that state achieved his body quietened. A sense of wellbeing claimed him; sharing himself with Consensus, entwined with the billions living contentedly above Jupiter, sporting with the voidhawks, he became whole again.

Yet this is the time we need you most, sub-Consensus replied. You have proved how valuable you are. Your skills are essential to this crisis.

I know. And if I'm needed for another assignment, I'll go. But I think after this, it's time I found a new career. Fifty-eight years of one thing is enough, even for a low-stress job.

We understand. There is no immediate field assignment awaiting you. We would like you to resume the observation of Dr Mzu for the time being.

I think that's a formality now.

Yes. But it will help to have you there in person. You have proved your worth to Monica Foulkes, she trusts you, and it is her report that will influence the Duke more than anything, and through him, the King. In this affair we must reassure the Kingdom we are playing fair.

Of course. Our alliance is a remarkable achievement, even in these circumstances.

Quite.

I'll stay with Mzu.

Thank you.

Samuel used his affinity to stay in communication with the voidhawk escort, so he could borrow the image of Jupiter from their sensor blisters. It was a much more satisfying view than the AV projection of *Lady Macbeth*'s sensor array. He watched their approach to Tranquillity, awed by the giant habitat, and not a little disconcerted by its star-jumping capability. It was so strange seeing it here, a familiar place, in a familiar location; but the two didn't belong together. He smiled at his own discomfort.

"You look happy," Monica said gruffly.

They had taken acceleration couches slightly apart from Mzu and the *Beezling* survivors; the two groups still not quite trusting each other. During the flight they'd been formal and polite, nothing more.

Samuel waved at the lounge's AV pillar with its moiré sparkle, which was also showing the approach. "I rather like the idea of thwarting Capone in such a fashion. A habitat that can perform a swallow manoeuvre! Who'd have thought it? Well, a Saldana did, obviously. I doubt many others would."

"I didn't mean that," Monica said. "You were happy the moment we arrived here, and you've been getting happier ever since. I've been watching you."

"Coming home is always comforting."

"It's more than that, it's like you've mellowed out."

"I have. Communion with my people and Consensus always does that. It's a valuable psychological relief. I don't relish being apart from it for so long."

"Oh God, here we go again, more propaganda."

Samuel laughed. They might not have affinity, but he knew her well enough by now that it almost didn't make any difference. A pleasant revelation when dealing with an Adamist, let alone an ESA operative. "I'm not trying to convert you, I'm just saying it's good for me. As you noticed."

Monica grunted. "You ask me, it's a weakness. You're dependent, and that can't be good in our profession. People should be capable of acting by themselves without any hang ups. If I get wound up, I just run a stim program."

"Ah yes, the natural human method of dealing with stress."

"No worse than yours. Faster and cleaner, too."

"There are many ways of being human."

Monica stole a glance over at Mzu and Adul, still resentful at what they'd all been through. "Inhuman, as well."

"I think she's realized her folly. That's good. It's a sign of maturity to learn from one's mistakes, especially after living with them for so long. She may yet make a positive contribution to our society."

"Maybe. But as far as I'm concerned, she'll need watching till the day she dies. And even then I'd be none too sure, she's that tricky. I still think the First Admiral was wrong, we should have zero-taued the lot of them."

"Well rest easy; I've already told Consensus I'll continue watching over her. I'm too old and jaded for another active assignment. Once this crisis is concluded I'll move on to something else. I always rather fancied wine growing; fine wine, of course. The kind of vintage that would satisfy the real oenophile. After all, I've tasted enough rubbish while I've travelled round the Confederation. Some of our habitats have superb vineyards, you know."

Monica gave him a single surprised look, then snorted in amusement. "Exactly who are you trying to fool?"

It certainly wasn't a hero's welcome. Only Collins bothered to report that the *Lady Macbeth* had docked, and they did it in a tone which suggested Joshua was slinking back home.

Five serjeants greeted Mzu and the *Beezling* survivors, escorting them to their new quarters. They weren't under arrest, Tranquillity explained, speaking through the constructs; but it laid down the guidelines for their residence quite austerely. A few friends were waiting for the crew in the bay's reception compartment. Dahybi and Beaulieu vanished off with them, heading for a bar. Sarha and Ashly took a commuter lift together. Two deputy managers from the Pringle Hotel greeted Shea and Kole, ushering them away to their rooms.

That left Joshua with Liol to take care of. He wasn't entirely sure what to do about that. They were still orbiting round each other, though it was a closer orbit now. A hotel was out, too cold, Liol was family after all. He just wished they'd managed to sort out the problem of *Lady Mac* and Liol's gung-ho claim. Though his brother had definitely become more conciliatory as the flight progressed. A good sign. It looked as though Liol would have to share his apartment. Well, at least he'd understand bachelor mess.

But as soon as Joshua air-swam out from their airlock tube, Ione was in front of him, toes pressed with ballerina grace on the compartment's stikpad. Doubts about Liol vanished. She was wearing a simple maroon polka-dot summer dress, ruffed gold-blond hair floating daintily. It made her seem girlish and elegant all at once. The sight of her like that summoned up memories warmer than any neural nanonics catalogued recollections could ever be.

She grinned knavishly, and held out both hands. Joshua caught hold and let her gently secure him. They kissed, a tingle lost somewhere between just good friends and old lovers. "Well done," she whispered.

"Thanks, I . . ." He frowned when he saw who was waiting behind her. Dominique: dressed in a tight sleeveless black leather T-shirt that was tucked into white sports shorts. All curves and blatant athleticism. As overt as Ione was demure.

"Joshua, darling!" Dominique squealed happily. "My God, you look so divine in a shipsuit. So well packaged. What can those naughty designers have been thinking of?"

"Er, hello, Dominique."

"Hello?" She pouted with tragic disappointment. "Come here, gorgeous."

Arms that were disproportionately strong wrapped round him. Wide lips descended happily, a tongue wriggling into his mouth. Hair and pheromones tickled his nose, making him want to sneeze.

He was too embarrassed to resist. Then she stiffened suddenly. "Oh *wow*, there's two of you."

The embrace was broken. Dominique stared hungrily behind him, long fronds of blond hair writhing about.

"Um, this is my brother," Joshua mumbled.

Liol gave her a languid grin, and bowed. It was a good manoeuvre considering he wasn't anchored to a stikpad. "Liol Calvert, Josh's bigger brother."

"Bigger." Dominique's eyes reflected slivers of light like coquettish diamonds.

In some way he couldn't quite work out, Joshua was no longer between the two of them.

"Welcome to Tranquillity," Dominique purred.

Liol took a hand gently and kissed her knuckles. "Nice to be here. It looks spectacular so far."

A small groan of dismay rumbled up from Joshua's throat.

"There's plenty more to see, and it gets a whole lot better." Dominique's voice became so husky it was almost bass. "If you want to risk it, that is."

"I'm just a simple boy from a provincial asteroid; of course I'm looking forward to the delights of the big bad habitat."

"Oh, we have several bad things you'll never find in your asteroid."

"I can believe it."

She crooked a finger in front of his nose. "This way."

The two of them levitated out of the hatch together.

"Humm." Ione smiled with sly contentment. "Eight seconds total; that's pretty fast even for Dominique."

Joshua looked back from the hatch to her amused blue eyes. He realized they were alone. "Oh, very neat," he remarked admiringly.

"Let's just say, I had a premonition they might hit it off."

"She'll eat him alive. You know that, don't you?"

"You never complained."

"How did you know about him?"

"While you were on your approach flight I was busy assimilating memories from the serjeants. The two that are left, anyway. You had a hell of a time."

"Yeah."

"You'll do all right, you and Liol. Just a bit too similar for comfort at the start, that's all."

"Could be." He squirmed uncomfortably.

She rested a hand on each shoulder, smiling softly. "But not identical."

There was nothing much said while they rode the commuter lift down the spaceport spindle. Just looks and smiles. Shared knowledge of what was to come when they got back to her apartment. Coming from shared relief that they'd both survived, and maybe wanting a return to times past for the reassurance that would bring. It wouldn't be the same, but it would still be familiar. It wasn't until they got into a tube carriage that they kissed properly. Joshua reached up to stroke her cheek.

"Your hand," she exclaimed. A whole rush of noxious memories were bubbling forth: the corridor in Ayacucho, Joshua on all fours in the slush, his hand blackened and charred, the two girls clinging together, whimpering, and the furious arab snarling then horrified as the serjeant opened fire. The roar of bullets and stink of hot blood. Not a sensevise she'd accessed, remote and vaguely unreal; she'd been a genuine witness to the actual event and always would be.

Joshua took his hand away from her face as she gave it a concerned look. A medical nanonic package had formed a thin glove to cover his fingers and palm. "I'm okay. The navy medics matched and grafted some muscle tissue; they've had a lot of practice with this kind of injury. It'll be okay in another week."

"Good." She kissed the tip of his nose.

"You're worried about a couple of fingers; I was scared shitless about Tranquillity. Jesus, Ione, you've no idea what it was like finding you gone. I thought you'd been possessed just like Valisk."

Her broad freckled face crinkled with mild bafflement. "Humm, interesting. I get surprised by other people being surprised. All right, it could have been possession. But you of all people should have worked it out. I as good as told you."

"When?"

"The very first night we met. I said that grandfather Michael believed that we would eventually encounter whatever the Laymil had come up against. Of course, back then everyone thought it was an external threat, which was a reasonable enough assumption. Unfortunately, that also meant that Tranquillity was likely to be the first to confront it. Either we'd find it among the Ruin Ring, or it would return to Mirchusko, the last place it had visited. Grandfather knew we probably wouldn't be able to beat it with conventional weapons, he hoped we'd discover what it was so we could develop some kind of defence in time. But just in case . . ."

"He wanted to be able to run," Joshua concluded.

"Yes. So he ordered a modification to the habitat's genome."

"And nobody realized? Jesus."

"Why should they? There's a ring of energy patterning cells around the shell, at the end of the circumfluous sea. If you look at the habitat from the outside, the ridge containing the water is actually a kilometre wider than the sea itself. But who's going to measure?"

"Hidden in plain view."

"Quite. Michael didn't see any reason to advertise the fact. Our royal cousins know . . . I assume, anyway. The files are stored in the Apollo Palace archives. It gives us the ability to jump away from trouble, a long way away. I chose Jupiter this time, because we considered Jupiter safe. But ultimately Tranquillity could jump across the galaxy in thousand light-year swallows, and the possessed would never be able to follow us. And if the crisis gets that bad, I'll do it."

"Now I get it. That's how you knew the *Udat*'s wormhole vector."

"Yes."

When the tube carriage arrived at Ione's apartment Joshua was feeling comfort as much as excitement. Neither of them took the lead, asking or pressing the other, they simply went to the bedroom because it was what the moment had ordained. They both slipped out of their clothes, admiring each other. Almost dreamily, Joshua tasted her breasts again, regretting how long it had been. Both of them showed off the old skills, knowing precisely what to do to each other's flesh to invigorate and arouse.

Only once, when she knelt in front of him, did Ione speak. "Don't use your nanonics," she whispered. Her tongue licked along his cock, teeth closing delicately on one ball. "Not this time. This should be natural."

He agreed, complying, making the encounter raw, and relishing every second of their performance. It was new. The big jelly-mattress bed was the same, so were the positions they accomplished. This time, though, they had honesty, openly celebrating the physical power they exerted over each other. It was as emotionally satisfying as it was sensually rewarding.

Afterwards they spent the night sleeping in each other's arms, snuggled up like childhood siblings. The loitering contentment made breakfast a civilized meal. They wrapped themselves in huge house robes to sit at a big old oak table in a room mocked up to resemble a conservatory. Palms, ferns, and delecostas grew out of moss-coated clay pots, their multiplying stems interlaced with broad iron trellises to produce verdant walls. The illusion was almost perfect but for the small neon-bright fish swimming past on the other side of the glass.

House chimps served them scrambled parizzat eggs, with English tea and thick-cut toast. While they ate, they accessed various news broadcasts from Earth and the O'Neill Halo, following the Confederation's response to Capone, the build up of forces for the Mortonridge Liberation, rumours of the possessed spreading among the asteroids, appearing in star systems previously thought clean.

"Quarantine busters," Ione said sharply at the item on Koblat being taken out of the universe. "The idiots in those asteroids are still letting them dock. At this rate the Assembly will have to shut down interplanetary flights as well."

Joshua looked away from the AV projection. "It won't make any difference."

"It will! They have to be isolated."

He sighed, regretful at how easily the mood had gone. Forgetting everything for a day had been so comfortable. "You don't understand. It's like saying you'll be safe if Tranquillity jumps across the galaxy where the possessed can't find you. Don't you see, they'll always find you. They are what you become. You, me, everyone."

"Not everyone, Joshua. Laton mentioned some kind of journey through the afterworld, he didn't believe he'd be trapped in the beyond. The Kiint have as good as admitted we don't all wind up there."

"Good, build on that. Find out why."

"How?" She gave him a measured look. "This isn't like you."

"I think it is. I think it took that possessed to make me realize."

"You mean that Arab in Ayacucho?"

"Yeah. No kidding, Ione, I was staring death and what comes after right in the face. Bound to make you stop and wonder. You can't solve everything with direct action. That's what makes this Mortonridge Liberation so ridiculous."

"Don't I know it. That whole miserable campaign is nothing more than a propaganda exercise."

"Yeah. Though I expect the people they do de-possess will be grateful enough."

"Joshua! You can't have it both ways."

He grinned at her over the rim of a huge tea cup. "We're going to have to, though, aren't we? There has to be some solution to satisfy both sides."

"Right," she said cautiously.

5

In any given month, there would be between two and seven armada storms rampaging across Earth's surface, a relentless assault they'd persevered with for over five hundred years. Like so many things, their name had become everyday currency. Few knew or cared about its origin.

It had begun with chaos theory: the soundbite assertion that one butterfly flapping its wings in a South American rain forest would start a hurricane in Hong Kong. Then in the Twenty-first Century came cheap fusion, and mass industrialisation; entire continents elevated themselves to Western-style levels of consumerism within two decades. Billions of people found themselves with the credit to buy a multitude of household appliances, cars, exotic holidays; they moved into new, better, bigger homes, adopting lifestyles which amplified their energy consumption by orders of magnitude. Hungry to service their purchasing power, companies built cities of new factories. Consumer and producer alike pumped out vast quantities of waste heat, agitating the atmosphere beyond the worst-case scenarios of most computer models.

It was after the then largest storm in history raged across

the Eastern Pacific in early 2071 that a tabloid newscable
presenter said it must have taken a whole armada of butter-
flies flapping their wings to start such a brute. The name
stuck.

The storm which had swept up from mid-Atlantic to
swamp New York was ferocious even by the standards of
the Twenty-seventh Century. Its progress had been under
observation for hours by the arcology's anxious weather defence engineers. When it did arrive, their response systems
were already on line. It looked as though a ragged smear of
night was sliding across the sky. The clouds were so thick
and dense no light could boil throughout to illuminate their
underbelly—until the lightning began. Then the rotund
tufts could be sometimes be distinguished, streaked with
leaden grey strata as they undulated overhead at menacing
speed. The energy levels contained within would prove
fatal for any unprotected building. Consequently, the ability
to deflect or withstand the storms was the prime requirement of any design brought before the New York civil engineering review board for a building permit. It was the one
criteria which could never be corroded by backhanders or
political pressure.

The tip of every megatower was crowned with high-
wattage lasers, whose beams were powerful enough to
puncture the heart of the heavy clouds. They etched out
straight channels of ionized air, cajoling the lightning to
discharge directly into the superconductor grids masking
the tower structure. Every tower blazed like a conical solar
flare above the dome residents, spitting out residual glob-
ules of violet plasma.

Amid them fell the rain. Fist-sized drops hurled out by a
furious wind to hammer against the domes. Molecular binding force generators were switched on to reinforce the

transparent hexagons against a kinetic fusillade which had the force to abrade raw steel.

The noise from this barrage of elements drummed through the dome to shake the gridwork of carbotanium struts supporting the metro transit rails. Most above-ground traffic had shut down. Right across the arcology, emergency crews were on full standby. Even the shield of lasers and superconductors were no guarantee against power spikes in such conditions. In such times, sensible people went home or to bars, and waited until sharp slivers of pewter light started to carve up the clouds, signalling the end of the deluge. A time when fear was heightened. When more primitive thoughts were brought to the fore.

A good time. Useful.

Quinn looked up at the old building which was home to the High Magus of New York.

Under cover of the storm, sect members were piling out of the vans behind him. Only ten possessed so far: a manageable number for what he had in mind. The rest, the acolytes and initiates, followed obediently, in awe of the apostles of evil who now commanded them.

Faith, Quinn mused, was a strange power. They had committed their lives to the sect, never questioning its gospels. Yet in all of that time, they had the reassurance of routine, the notion that God's Brother would never actually manifest himself. The bedrock of every religion, that your God is a promise, never to be encountered in this life, this universe.

Now the souls were returning, owning the power to commit dark miracles. The acolytes had fallen into stupefaction rather than terror, the last doubt vanquished. Condemned as the vilest outcasts, they now knew they'd been right all along. That they were going to win. Whatever they were ordered to do, they complied unquestioningly.

Quinn motioned the first team forward. Led by Wener, the three eager acolytes scampered down a set of steps at the base of the wall, and clustered round the disused basement door at the bottom. A codebuster block was applied, then a programmable silicon probe was worked expertly into the crack between the door and the frame. The silicon flexed its way under the ageing manual bolts, then began to reformat its shape, pushing them back. Within thirty seconds, the way in was open. No alarms, and no give away use of energistic power.

Quinn stepped through.

The difference between the headquarters and the dingy centre on Eighty-Thirty street surprised even Quinn. At first he even thought he might have the wrong place, but Dobbie, who now possessed magus Garth's body, reassured him this was indeed where they should be. The corridors and chambers were an inverse mirror of the Vatican's splendour. Rich fittings and extravagant artwork, but sabaritic rather than warmly exquisite, celebrating depravity and pain.

"Fuck, look at this place," Wener muttered as they marched down one of the corridors. Sculptures took bestiality as their theme, featuring both mythical and xenoc creatures, while paintings showed the saintly and revered from history being violated and sacrificed on the altars of the Light Bringer.

"You should take a good look," Quinn said. "It's yours. Those hours ripping off citizens and pushing illegals on the street, that paid for all this. You live in shit, so the High Magus can live like a Christian bishop. Nice, isn't it."

Wener and the other acolytes glowered round at the perverse grandeur, envious and angry. They split up, as arranged. One of the possessed leading each group of acolytes, securing the exits and strategic areas, the weapons cache. Quinn went straight for the High Magus. Three

times, he encountered acolytes and priests scurrying along
the corridors. They were all given the same simple choice:
Follow me, or be possessed.

They took one look at the black robe, listening to the
voice whispering out of the seemingly empty hood, and capitulated. One of them even gave a mad little laugh of relief, a strong sense of vindication flooding his mind.

The High Magus was taking a bath when Quinn strode
into his quarters. It could have been the penthouse of some
multistellar corporation president, certainly there was little
evidence of idolatrous worship amongst the opulence.
Much to Wener's disappointment he didn't even have naked
servant girls to wash him. Slimline domestic mechanoids
stood quietly among the white and blue furnishings. His
one concession to turpitude appeared to be the goblet he
was drinking a seventeen-year-old red wine out of, its vul-
vic influences impossible to ignore. Islands of lime-green
bubbles drifted round his round frame, giving off a scent of
sweet pine.

He was already frowning as Quinn glided over the gold-
flecked marble to the sunken bath, presumably forewarned
by the failure of his neural nanonics. His eyes widened at
the invasion, then narrowed as the eccentric delegation
stared down at him.

"You're a possessed," he said directly to Quinn.

There was no panic in the mind of the High Magus,
which surprised Quinn, if anything the old man appeared
curious. "No, I am the Messiah of our Lord."

"Really?"

The mocking irony of the tone caused the hem of Quinn's
robe to stir. "You will obey me, or I will have your fat shit
body possessed by someone more worthy."

"More compliant, you mean."

"Don't fuck with me."

"I have no intention of fucking with you or anyone else."

Quinn was puzzled by this whole exchange. The original calmness he could sense in the High Magus was slowly replaced by weariness. The High Magus took another sip of the wine.

"I'm here to bring Night to the Earth as Our Lord bids," Quinn said.

"He *bids* nothing of the sort, you pathetic little prick."

Quinn's ashen face materialized to thrust out of his hood.

The High Magus laughed out loud at the shock and anger he saw there, and committed suicide. Without any noise or hysterics, his body froze, then slowly slithered down the side of the bath. It rolled to one side, and floated inertly on the surface, white bloated rims of fat bobbing among the green bubbles. The wine goblet sank, a red stain marking where it had vanished.

"What are you doing?" Quinn shouted at the departing soul. He sensed a final sneer as the retreating wisps of energy evaporated amid dimensional folds. His claw hands shot out of the voluminous sleeves, as if to pull the essence of the High Magus back to face judgement. "Shit!" he gasped. The magus must have been demented. Nobody. No body, went into the beyond, not now they knew for sure what awaited them there.

"Asshole," Wener grunted. Along with the other acolytes, he was perturbed by the death. Trying not to show it.

Quinn knelt down at the side of the bath, searching the corpse with eyes and eldrich senses for the mechanism of its demise. There were the usual weapons implants, he could perceive those all right, hard splinters among the softer grain of organic matter, even the neural nanonics were discernible. But Quinn's energistic power had nullified them. What then? What instrument could effect an in-

stantaneous and painless suicide? And more curiously, why
was the High Magus equipped with it?

He straightened slowly, retracting his head and arms
back within his cloak's veil of night. "It doesn't matter," he
told his agitated followers. "God's Brother knows how to
deal with traitors, the beyond is not a refuge for those who
fail Him."

A dozen heads nodded in eager acceptance before him.
"Now go and bring them to me," he said.

The acolytes scattered to do his bidding. They rounded
up everyone in the headquarters, and herded them into the
temple. It was a vaulting chamber nestled at the core of the
Leicester, a baroque fabrication of gilded pillars and crude
cut stone blocks. Six giant pentagons were etched on the
curving ceiling, emitting a dull crimson glow. The grumble
of the storm was just audible, a bass reverberation sneaking
through the Leicester to give the floor a faint vibration.

Quinn stood beside the altar as the captives were ushered
up to him one at a time. Every time, he repeated the simple
choice of futures: follow me, or be possessed. Merely
claiming you would submit was no use. Quinn interrogated
their innermost beliefs and fears before passing his final de-
cree. He wasn't surprised by how many failed. Inevitably,
this far up the sect hierarchy, they had grown soft. Still evil,
still exploiting the soldiers below them, but not for the right
reasons. Maintaining their own status and comforts had
evolved into their dominant urge, not a willingness to further the cause of the Light Bringer. Traitors.

He made them suffer for their crime. Over thirty were
chained to the altar and vanquished. By now he had become
proficient in opening a fissure back into the beyond; but
more importantly he'd learned how to impose his own presence around the opening, valiantly guarding the gateway
from the unworthy. Even in their utter desperation for es-

cape, many souls turned aside from such a custodian. Those who did emerge conformed to Quinn's ideal. Nearly all of them had been sect members while they were alive.

He gathered them together after the ceremony, explaining what God's Brother had decided for them. "We need more than one arcology to bring Night to this world," he told them. "So I'm leaving you this one for yourselves. Don't piss this opportunity away. I want you to take it over, but carefully, not like the way the possessed do on other planets, even Capone. Those dickheads just rush up and head butt every town they come across. And each time, the cops swoop down and pick them off. This time it's gonna be different. You've got the acolytes worshipping the ground you shit on. Use them. Moving around is what lets those fucking AIs sniff you out. You mess with processors and power cables just by being near them. So don't go near them. Stay in the sect centres and get the acolytes to bring people to you."

"Which people?" Dobbie asked. "I understand how we don't gotta move about. But, shit, Quinn, there's over three hundred million people in New York. The acolytes can't bring them all to us."

"They can bring the ones that count, the police captains and technical guys, the ones gonna cause you grief. Or at least knock them out, stop them from reporting that you've arrived in town. That's all I want from you right now. Get yourselves established. There's a sect centre in every dome, take them over and hole up there for a while. Live like a fucking king, I'm not saying don't enjoy yourself. But I want you ready, I want you to build up a coven of possessed in each dome. Loyal ones, you all know how fucking important discipline is. We're going strategic. Learn where the major fusion generators are, hunt down the fresh water stations, and the sewage plants, see which intersections the transport system depends on, track down critical nodes in the communication net. The acolytes will know all this crap, or they can find out. Then when I give the word, you smash each of those sites into lava. You paralyse the whole fucking arcology with terrorism, bring it to its knees. That way the cops won't be able to organize any resistance when we emerge to claim glory for Him. You come out into the open and start possessing others, and you turn them loose. Nobody can run, there's nowhere to go, no outside. Possessed always win on asteroids, this is no different, just bigger, is all."

"The new possessed, they won't worship God's Brother," someone said. "We can choose a few who will to start with, but if we turn them loose, there's no way millions of them is going to do like we say."

"Of course not," Quinn said. "Not at first, anyway. They have to be forced into this, like I did to Nyvan. Haven't you worked it out yet? What's going to happen to an arcology with three hundred million possessed living in it?"

"Nothing," Dobbie said in puzzlement. "It won't work."

"Right," Quinn purred. "Nothing's going to work. I'm going to visit as many arcologies as I can, and I'm going to seed all of them with possessed. And they're all going to collapse, because energistic power breaks the machinery. The domes won't be able to hold off the weather any more, there isn't going to be any food, or water. Nothing. Not even forty billion possessed wishing at once are going to be able to change that. They'll shift Earth into another realm, but it still won't make any difference. Just being somewhere else isn't going to put food on the table, won't restart the machines. That's when *it* will happen. The revelation that they have nowhere else to turn. Our Lord will have won their minds." He lifted his hands, and allowed a pallid smile to show from his hood. "Forty billion possessors, and

the forty billion they possess. Eighty billion souls screaming into the Night for help. Don't you see? It's a cry so
strong, so full of anguish and fear, that it will bring Him. Finally, He will emerge from the Night, bringing light to
those who have come to love Him." Quinn laughed at the
astonishment on their faces, and dark delight in their minds.

"How long?" Dobbie asked avidly. "How long we gotta
wait?"

"A month, maybe. It'll take me a while to visit all the arcologies. But I'll penetrate them all in the end. Wait for my
word." The silhouette of his robe began to fade. Outlines of
the furniture behind him started to show through. Then he
was gone. A cold breeze drifted across the chamber, per-
turbing the shallow gasps of consternation that echoed from
the dismayed disciples.

The *Mindori* approached Monterey at a steady half gee acceleration. Two hundred kilometres ahead, the asteroid's
features were resolving, crumpled dust-grey rock speared
by metallic spires and panels. It was surrounded by a swarm
of pearl-white specks that flashed and glinted in the tenacious sunlight. The Organization fleet: over six hundred
Adamist warships floating in attendance while small service craft flitted among them. Each one a unique knot in
Rocio Condra's distortion field.

Gliding among them were the more subtle interference
patterns of other distortion fields. Valisk's hellhawks were
here. Rocio called out in welcome. Those who bothered to
acknowledge his arrival were subdued. The emotional content simmering within most of his fellows was one of
grudging acceptance. Rocio accepted it reluctantly. It was
what he'd been expecting.

Glad to see you found your way back to us, Hudson
Proctor said. What have you got?

The affinity link provided Rocio an opening to the man's eyes. He was in one of the docking ledge lounges, overlooking the pedestals where several hellhawks were perched. The room had been altered into an executive-style office. Kiera Salter was sitting at a broad desk, her head coming up to give him a hard, enquiring stare.

Deadnight kids, Rocio said. **I haven't told them Valisk has gone.**

Good, good.

"The Organization hasn't got any real use for that kind of waster trash," Kiera said as Hudson repeated his silent conversation. "Dock here and disembark them. They'll be dealt with appropriately."

And what about us? Rocio asked mildly. **What do the hellhawks do now?**

"I'll have you assigned to fleet support duties," Kiera said impassively. "Capone is preparing another invasion. The hellhawks are becoming essential to ensure viability."

I don't wish to fly combat duties any more, thank you. This starship is proving an excellent host for my soul, I have no intention of endangering it, especially now that you have no reserve body for me to inherit.

Kiera's answering smile portrayed regret. It wasn't an emotion Hudson relayed via affinity, keeping the exchange scrupulously neutral.

"I'm afraid we're effectively on a war footing," Kiera said. "Which means, that wasn't a request."

Are you trying to order me?

"I'm offering you one simple choice. You do as I tell you, or you fuck off back to the Edenists right now. You know why that is? Because we're the only two who can feed you. I am now in full command of the only possessed-owned nutrient supply in this star system. Me, not Capone and the Organization, me. If you want to prevent that excellent host of yours from expiring from malnutrition, you do exactly what I ask, and in return you'll be permitted to dock and ingest as much of that goo as you can hold. No one else can provide you with that, non-possessed asteroids will blow you away with their SD platforms before you get within a hundred kilometres. Only the Edenists can supply you. And they've got their price, too, as I'm sure they've told you. If you cooperate with them, it'll be to help understand the nature of the interface with the beyond. They'll find out how to banish us. You and I will both be zapped back into that infernal oblivion. So decide, Rocio; where your loyalty lies, who you're going to fly for. I'm not asking for you and me to be friends, I want to know if you'll obey, that's all. And you will tell me now."

Rocio opened his affinity to converse with the other hellhawks. **Is this what she holds over us?**

Yes, they answered. **There is no third alternative that we can see.**

This is monstrous. I'm happy with this form. I don't want to risk it in Capone's egotistical conquests.

Then protect it, you pitiful bastard, Etchells said. **Stop whining and fight for what you believe in. Some of you are so pathetic, you don't deserve what you've got.**

Rocio remembered Etchells, always eager to intercept the voidhawks observing Valisk. When Capone had first approached Kiera for help, he'd been excited and anxious to become involved in the conflict.

Piss off, you fascist bigot.

A coward, and a way with words, Etchells retorted. **No wonder you're so insecure.**

Rocio closed his affinity with the offensive hellhawk. **I'll dock at Monterey and offload the passengers.** He told

Hudson and Kiera. **What kind of fleet support are you proposing?**

Kiera's smile lacked grace. "While the fleet is here, all hellhawks are on a rota to interdict the spy globes and stealthed bombs. The voidhawks have just about given up that nonsense, but they're still probing our defences, so we have to remain vigilant. Apart from that, there's also some communication duties, VIP flights and collecting cargo from asteroids. Nothing too demanding."

And when Capone finds a new planet to invade?

"You fly escort for the fleet, and then you help them eliminate the target world's Strategic Defence network."

Very well. I will be docking in another eight minutes, please have a pedestal ready to receive me. Rocio abandoned Hudson Proctor's mind, and analysed what had been said. The situation was almost what he'd been expecting. Controlling the supply of nutrient fluid was the only practical way of binding the hellhawks to the Organization. What he hadn't predicted was Kiera still being in charge. She'd obviously come to the same conclusion about coercion.

A few queries to a couple of friendlier hellhawks, and he found that Etchells had visited most of the asteroid settlements in the New California system, blasting their nutrient production machinery. Kiera had ordered the flight, and Hudson had been on board to make sure everything ran smoothly. Kiera and the Organization were still separate. She was using her control over the hellhawks to maintain her status as a power player. Scheming little bitch. And it would be the hellhawks who paid for that status.

Rocio's ersatz beak parted slightly. Even though he couldn't manage a modestly contented smile any more, the intent was there. Forced obedience always generated discontent. Allies wouldn't be hard to find. He abandoned his favoured bird-image just as he slipped round Monterey's counter-rotating spaceport. The *Mindori* settled its hull on one of the docking ledge pedestals, and gratefully received the hose nozzles probing its underbelly. Muscle membranes contracted round the seal rings, and the thick nutrient fluid pulsed its way up into the nearly-depleted reserve bladders. The whole process served to emphasise just how vulnerable the giant bitek starship was. After such a long flight, Rocio was enduring a strong subconscious pressure to ingest again, and he had absolutely no control over the substance pumped along the pipes. Kiera could be giving him anything, from water to an elaborate poison. It tasted fine, to his limited internal sense and filter glands, but he could never be quite sure. His plight was intolerable. So what? he asked himself, bitterly. Blackmail always was.

The rebellion began at once. Rocio ordered his bitek processor array to open a channel into the asteroid's communication network. Access to any defence-critical system was denied; the Organization had protected its electronic architecture as thoroughly as the New California defence force it had usurped. However, that left a lot of civil memory cores and sensors to access. He began to analyse what information he was permitted, and hooked in to various cameras to look round.

A large bus trundled over the rock ledge, its flaccid elephant-trunk airlock tube snuggling up to the *Mindori*'s life support section. Inside the hellhawk, the Deadnight kids raced through their cabins, snatching up their bags. A long, agitated queue formed outside the main airlock hatch. Choi-Ho and Maxim Payne stood at the end, smiling placidly.

When the hatch swung open amid a hiss of white vapour, the kids let out a collective gasp of delight. Kiera herself was waiting for them. Gorgeous body clad in a small scarlet dress, hair tumbling over her honey-coloured shoulders. And that mesmerising smile every bit as bright in real life as it was in the recording. They filed past her in a numb daze, eyes wide with awe as she said hello to each and every one of them. All she got was a few mumbled words in return.

"That was easy enough," she said to Choi-Ho and Maxim at the end. "We had a couple of flights end in riots when they realized they weren't at Valisk. For no-hopers, they can be vicious little shits. There was a lot of damage, and it's hard getting replacement components for these life support modules."

"So what do we do now?" Maxim asked.

"I always need good officers. Or you can join the Organization if you like. Capone is keen to recruit soldiers to enforce his rule down on the planet. You'll be on the cutting edge of his empire," she said sweetly.

"I'm good at what I do now," Choi-Ho said levelly. Maxim quickly agreed.

Kiera observed their minds. There was a tang of resentment, of course, there always was. But they'd capitulated. "All right, you're in. Now let's get these loser brats into the asteroid. They won't be suspicious if we stay with them."

She was right. Her presence alone was enough to fool the besotted Deadnights, none of them ever questioning why the bus windows were blanked out. It wasn't until they walked through the next set of airlocks that suspicions started to bubble up. They were all from asteroid settlements, and the equipment here was very similar to what they thought they'd left behind. Habitats were supposed to be different, devoid of this many mechanical contrivances. With the elder ones slightly puzzled now, they trooped into the main arrivals hall. The Organization gangsters were waiting. It only took two acts of violence against the

bravest rebels to quell any further resistance. They were
quickly segregated and classified according to the charts
Leroy and Emmet had provided.

Amid a welter of tearful and frightened crying, individuals were hauled off into the corridors. As the Organization
was still very male dominated, the older boys were all taken
down to Patricia Mangano and imminent possession by
new soldiers. With them went the less attractive girls. Pret-
tier girls were dispatched to the brothel where they would
service the Organization's soldiers and non-possessed followers. The children (and definition was difficult, puberty
plus a couple of years appeared to be the deciding factor)
were flown down to the planet, where Leroy paraded them
in front of the rover reporters, claiming their salvation from
Deadnight as more humanitarian charity on Al's behalf. The
distorted image of a weeping seventeen-year-old girl being
shoved along by a machine-gun toting gangster in a brown
pinstripe suit vanished from the processor block's screen in
a hail of static.

"I can't find any further working cameras in that section," Rocio announced. "Would you like me to return to
the arrivals hall?"

Jed had to work hard against his tightening throat muscles. "No. That's enough." When the hellhawk possessor
had shown them the first pictures snatched from cameras,
Jed had wanted to scramble out of their cramped refuge.
Kiera was actually on board! A mere thirty metres away
from him. He'd suddenly wondered what the hell he was
doing, crouched painfully between cold, condensation-
smeared tanks with loops of grimy cable wiping his forehead. The sight of her brought back all the old rapture. And
she was smiling. Kiera would make the angels envious of
her beauty and compassion.

Then he heard bonkers Gerald reciting: "Monster, monster, monster, monster," like it was some kind of freaky spell.

Beth was rubbing the old fart's arm, all full of sympathy, saying, "It's okay, you'll get her back, you will."

Jed wanted to shout out how barmy the pair of them were. But by then the last of the Deadnights were in the bus, and Kiera's smile was gone. In its place was a hideously alien expression of contempt verging on cruelty. The words which came from her lips were cold and harsh. Rocio had been telling the truth.

Despite the evidence, that lost part of Jed's heart had wanted to believe in his divine savour and her promises of a better world. Now he knew that was gone. Worse than that, it had never existed. Even Digger had been right. Bloody Digger, for Christ's sake! He was just a dumb stupid waster kid trying to score the ultimate escape trip from Koblat. If Beth and the girls hadn't been in there with him, he knew he would have burst into tears. For Jed, not even the scenes in the arrivals hall were as horrific than that final moment when Kiera's smile vanished.

By the time Rocio Condra's face reappeared on the block, the girls were sniffling quietly, arms around each other. Beth made no attempt to hide the tears meandering down her cheeks. Gerald had shrunk back into his usual uncommunicative self.

"I'm sorry," Rocio said. "But I did suspect that something like this was going to happen. If it's of any comfort, I am in a similar position."

"Similar?" Beth grunted. "Comfort? I knew some of those girls, damn you. How can you compare what they're going to go through with what you've got to do? That's not patronising, that's sickening."

"They are being forced to prostitute themselves with men in order to survive. I have to risk my life and that of my host in hostile combat conditions if I wish to continue my existence in this universe. Yes, I have to say there is similarity, whether you see it or not."

Beth glared at the processor block through her misery. She'd never felt so low before, not even when those men had grabbed her that time when she met Gerald.

"So now what?" Jed asked dolefully.

"I'm not certain," Rocio answered. "Obviously, we must find a new source of nutrient fluid for myself and those hellhawks that share my beliefs. I shall have to gather a lot more information before that option opens itself."

"Do we have to stay in here the whole time?"

"No, of course not. There is no one inside the life support section, you may come out now."

It took a hot, aggravating five minutes to wriggle free from the confines of the cramped under-floor service ducts. Jed was the first to extricate himself from the hatch in the washroom floor. He quickly helped the others free. They wandered out into the central corridor, glancing about anxiously, not quite believing Rocio when he said they were alone.

They stood in the big forward lounge, looking out of the long window at the docking ledge. The row of pedestals stretched away, gradually curving above them, silver mushrooms sprouting from the grizzled rock, each one bathed in a pool of yellow light. But for three other docked hellhawks suckling their nutrient fluid from the hoses, it could have been a post-industrial wasteland. Some technicians were working on the cargo cradles of one craft, but apart from that, nothing moved.

"So we just wait," Beth said, flopping down into a settee.

Jed pressed his nose to the transparency, trying to see the rock wall at the back of the ledge. "Guess so."

"I'm hungry," Gari complained.

"Then go eat," Jed said. "I'm not going to stop you."

"Come with us."

He turned from the window, seeing his sister's apprehensive expression, and smiled reassuringly. "Sure, kid, no problem."

The galley was one compartment Rocio hadn't tried to modify with his energistic imagination, leaving the contemporary metal and composite surfaces undisturbed. However, they'd plainly been pillaged by some passing barbarian army. A cascade of empty sachets were littering the floor, stuck in place by treacle-like liquids. Storage cabinet doors swung open, revealing empty spaces. The timer on an induction oven bleeped away relentlessly.

A ten minute search turned up five cans of drinking chocolate, a sachet of unhydrated oatmeal cakes, and a serve-3 pizza with extra anchovies.

Jed surveyed the cache with dismay. "Oh Jeeze, there's nothing left to eat." He knew what that meant, one of them would have to sneak into the asteroid to find some supplies. Zero guesses who'd get picked for that doozy.

Jay woke up in a wonderfully soft bed, wrapped inside a smooth cocoon of clean cotton sheets smelling faintly of lavender. It was that warm drowsy state which always followed a really long, deep sleep. She squirmed round a little, enjoying the contentment of being utterly at peace. Some small object had managed to wedge itself under her shoulder, harder than the luxurious pillow. Her hand closed round it, pulling it out. Coarse fur tickled her fingers. Frowning, squinting she held up the . . . doll. Tatty old thing. She smiled cosily, and put Prince Dell down beside her. Snuggling into the mattress.

Her eyes flipped wide open. A fog of hoary light was curving round a pair of plain navy-blue curtains. It illuminated a neat wooden room, with its sloping ceiling supported by a scaffold of naked A-frame beams. The tight-fitting wall boards had all been painted a silky green, bedecked with picture frames that were mainly landscape watercolours, though there were several sepia photos of people in history-text clothes. A glazed pedestal washbasin with brass taps stood in the corner, a towel hanging beside it. There was a wicker chair at the foot of the bed, with a pair of fat cushions crammed into it. The sound of waves rolling gently onto a beach could just be heard in the background.

Jay flung back the sheet and slithered down off the bed. Her feet touched a warm carpet, and she padded over to the window. She lifted a corner of the curtain, then pulled it wide open. The beach was outside; a fringe of grass blending into white sands, followed by gorgeous turquoise water stretching out to a mild horizon haze. A clear azure sky rose from the other side of the haze, cut in half by that incredible curving line of brilliant silver-white planets. She laughed in amazed delight. It was real, really real.

The bedroom's door opened into the chalet's hallway. Jay ran along it, out onto the veranda. The hem of her nightie flapped around bare feet, Prince Dell was clutched in one hand. Outside, the heat and salty humidity gusted over her along with the intense sunlight. She flew down the steps and onto the grass, dancing round and whooping. The sand was hot enough to make her jump up and down before retreating back onto the grass. She gave the glittering water an exasperated look. How lovely it would have been to dive right in. Haile was going to adore this place.

"Good morning to you, young Jay Hilton."

Jay jumped, and turned round. One of the purple globes she remembered from last night was floating half a metre above her head. Her nose wrinkled up in bemusement. It seemed to be the victim of a talented graffiti artist who'd inflicted two black and white cartoon eyes rimmed with black-line eyebrows; more black lines defined a pug nose, while the mouth was a single curve sealed by smile commas. "What are you?" she asked.

"Well, wadda ya'know, my name's Mickey. I'm a universal provider. But I'm a special one, coz I'm all yours." The mouth jerked up and down in time with its voice.

"Oh yeah?" Jay asked suspiciously. That silly face was far too happy for her liking. "What does a universal provider do, then?"

"Why, I provide, of course."

"You're a machine."

"Guess so," it said with goofy pleasure.

"I see. So what do you provide?"

"Whatever you want. Any material object, including food."

"Don't be stupid. You're tiny, what if I wanted a . . . a vac-train carriage."

"Why would you want one of those?"

Jay sneered at it smugly. "I just want one. I'm proving a point."

The face lines squiggled their way into an expression of dozy obedience. "Oh. Okey-dokey, then. It's going to take about quarter of an hour to put it together."

"Sure," Jay sneered.

"Hey! That's got lots of complicated parts inside, you know."

"Right."

"If you'd asked for something simple, I could provide straight away."

"All right. I want the Diana statue from the Paris arcology. That's just a lump of carved rock."

"Easy peasy."

"Uh—" Jay managed to grunt.

Mickey zipped out over the beach, too fast for her to follow. She swivelled, just in time to see it inflating equally fast. At ten metres in diameter, its ridiculous face was suddenly not so pleasant and harmless as it loomed above her. A pair of shoes began to ooze through the bottom. They were as long as Jay was tall. Mickey started to rise up, exposing legs, waist, torso . . .

The full fifteen metre height of the granite statue gazed out serenely across the Kiint ocean. Pigeon droppings scarred its shoulders. Above Diana's head, Mickey shrank back to its usual size and floated back down to Jay. Its mouth line shifted up into feline gratification.

"What have you done?" Jay yelled.

"Provided the statue. Wossamatter, wrong one?"

"No! Yes!" She glanced frantically along the beach. There were figures moving round outside the other chalets and big white clubhouse, but fortunately none of them seemed to have noticed. Yet. "Get rid of it!"

"Oh. Charming." Mickey inflated out again. Its hurt pout ominous on such a scale. The statue was swallowed whole. The only memorial: a pair of giant footprints in the sand.

"You're mad," Jay accused as it shrank once again. "Utterly mad. They should switch you off."

"For what?" it wailed.

"For doing that."

"Just doing what I'm told," it grumbled. "I suppose you want to cancel the vac-train as well, now?"

"Yes!"

"You should make up your mind. No wonder they won't hand over my kind of technology to the Confederation. Think of all the statues you'd leave lying round the place."

"How do you do it," she asked sharply. "How do you

work? I bet you've never even been to Earth, how do you know what Diana's statue looked like?"

Mickey's voice dropped back down to normal. "The Kiint have this whopping great central library, see. There's no end of stuff stored in there, including your art encyclopaedias. All I've gotta do is find the template memory."

"And you make it inside you?"

"Small things, no problem. I'm your man, just shout. The bigger stuff, that's gotta be put together in a place like a high-speed factory. Then when it's done and polished they just ship it in through me. Simplisimo."

"All right. Next question, who decided to give you that silly voice?"

"Whaddya mean, silly? It's magnifico."

"Well, you don't talk like an adult, do you?"

"Ha, hark who's talking. I'll have you know, I'm an appropriate companion personality for a girl your age, young missy. We spent all night ransacking that library to see what I should be like. You got any idea what it's like watching eight million hours of Disney AVs?"

"Thank you for being so considerate, I'm sure."

"What I'm here for. We're partners, you and me." Mickey's smile perked up again.

Jay folded her arms and fixed it with a stare. "Okay, *partner*; I want you to provide me with a starship."

"Is this another of those point thingies?"

"Could be. I don't care what type of starship it is; but I want it to be one I can pilot by myself, and it has to have the range to get me back to the Confederation galaxy."

Mickey's eyes blinked slowly, as if lethargic shutters were coming down. "Sorry, Jay," it said quietly. "No can do. I would if I could, honest, but the boss says no."

"Not much of a companion, are you."

"How about a chocolate and almond ice cream instead? Big yummie time!"

"Instead of a starship. I don't think so."

"Aww, go on. You know you want to."

"Not before breakfast, thank you." She turned her back on it.

"Okay. I know, how about a megalithic strawberry milk-shake, with oodles and oodles of . . ."

"Shut up. And you're not called Mickey, either. So don't pretend you are." Jay smiled at the silence; imagining it must be contorting its sketched face into hurt dismay. Her name was being called from the chalet.

Tracy Dean stood on the veranda, waving hopefully. She was dressed in a pale lemon dress with a lace collar, its design obsolete but still stylish. Jay walked back, aware that the provider machine was following. "The face wasn't a good idea, was it?" Tracy said with dry amusement after Jay climbed the steps to the veranda. "Didn't think so. Not for someone who's seen all you have. But it was worth a try." She sighed. "Program discontinued. There, it's just an ordinary provider, now. And it won't talk stupid anymore, either."

Jay glanced up at the purple sphere, which was now completely featureless. "I don't mean to be awkward."

"I know, sweetie. Now come and sit down. I've got some breakfast for you."

A white linen tablecloth had been spread over a small table beside the weather-worn railings. It had Spanish pottery bowels with cereal and fruit, one jug of milk, and another of orange juice. There was also a teapot with a battered old strainer.

"Twinings Ceylon tea," Tracy said happily as they sat down. "Best you can have for breakfast in my opinion. I became completely addicted to it in the late Nineteenth Century, so I brought some back with me once. Now the providers can synthesise the leaves for me. I'd like to be all snobbish and say that I can tell it's not the same, but I can't. We'll let it brew for a while, shall we?"

"Yes," Jay said earnestly. "If you like." There was something deliciously fascinating about this old woman who had Father Horst's compassion and Powel Manani's determination.

"Have you never brewed tea in a pot before, young Jay?"

"No. Mummy always bought it in sachets."

"Oh dear me. There are some things which the march of progress doesn't improve, you know."

Jay poured some milk over the cereal bowl, deciding not to ask about the strange-shaped flakes. One thing at a time. "Do the Kiint live on all these planets?"

"Ah, yes. I did promise I'd explain things today, didn't I, sweetie?"

"Yes!"

"Such impatience. Where to start, though?" Tracy sprinkled some sugar onto her grapefruit, and sank a silver spoon into the soft fruit. "Yes, the Kiint live on all these planets. They built them, you know. Not all at once, but they have been civilized for a very long time. One planet couldn't possibly accommodate them all any more, just like there are too many humans to live on Earth nowadays. So they learned how to extract matter from their sun and condense it. Quite an achievement, actually, even with their technology. The arc is one of the wonders of this galaxy. Not just physically, culturally, too. All the species who've achieved FTL starflight visit here eventually. Some that haven't, too. It's the greatest information exchange centre we know of. And the Kiint know of a few, believe me."

"The provider said there was a big library here."

"It was being modest. You see, when you've got the technology to take care of your every physical requirement, there's not much else you can do but develop your knowledge base. So that's what they do. And it's a big universe to get to know. It keeps them occupied, and fulfils life's basic requirement."

"What's that?"

"To live is to experience, and experience is living. I had a lovely little chuckle when the first Kiint ambassador from Jobis told the Confederation they had no interest in starflight. Travel broadens the mind, and heavens do they travel. They have this quite magical society, you see, they spend their whole time developing their intellects. The best way I can put it for you, is that wisdom is their equivalent of money, that's what they pursue and hoard. I'm generalising, of course. A population as large as theirs is bound to have dissidents. Nothing like our Edenist Serpents, of course; their disagreements are mostly philosophical. But there are a few Kiint who turn their backs on their own kind. There's even a couple of planets in the arc they can go to where they're free of the central society.

"Whatever faction they come from, they're all very noble by our standards. And I'll admit it leaves them superbly prepared to face transcendence when their bodies die. But to be honest, that kind of existence is rather boring for humans. I don't think we'll ever go quite so far down that road. Different mental wiring, thankfully. We're too impatient and quarrelsome. Bless us."

"So you are really human then?"

"Oh yes, sweetie. I'm human. All of us living here are."

"But why are you here?"

"We work for the Kiint, helping them to record human history. All of us take little unobtrusive jobs where we can get a good view of events. In the old days it was as servants of lords and kings, or joining up with nomads. Then when the industrial age started up we moved into the media companies. We weren't front line investigative reporters, we were the office mundanes; but it meant we had access to an avalanche of information most of which never made it into the official history books. It was perfect for us; and we still mostly work in the information industries today. I'll show you how to use the AV projector later if you want, every broadcast humans make goes into the arc's library. That always tickled me, if those desperate marketing departments only knew just how wide an audience they really have."

"Are the Kiint really that interested in us?"

"Us, the Tyrathca, the Laymil, xenocs you've never heard of. They're fascinated by sentience, you see. They've witnessed so many self-aware races dwindle away to nothing, or self-destruct. That kind of loss is tragic for the races which succeed and prosper. Everybody's different, you see, sweetie. Life alone is precious, but conscious thought is the greatest gift the universe offers. So they try and study any entities they find; that way if they don't survive their knowledge won't be entirely lost to the rest of us."

"How did you end up working for them?"

"The Kiint found Earth when they were exploring that galaxy about two and a half thousand years ago. They took DNA specimens from a few people. We were cloned from that base, with a few alterations."

"Like what?" Jay asked eagerly. This was a wonderful story, so many secrets.

"We don't age so quickly, obviously; and we've got a version of affinity; little things like that."

"Gosh. And you've been on Earth since you were born?"

"Since I grew up, yes. We had to be educated the Kiint way first. Their prime rule in dealing with other species, especially primitive ones, is zero intervention. They were worried that we might become too sympathetic and go native. If we did that, we'd introduce ideas that were wrong for that era; I mean, think what would have happened if the Spanish Armada was equipped with anti-ship missiles. That's why they made us sterile, too; it should help us remain impartial."

"That's horrid!"

Tracy smiled blankly at the horizon. "There are compensations. Oh sweetie, if you'd seen a fraction of what I have. The Imperial Chinese dynasties at their height. Easter Islanders carving their statues. Knights of armour battling for their tiny kingdoms. The Inca cities rising out of jungles. I was a servant girl at Runnymede when King John signed the Magna Carta. Then lived as a grandee noblewoman while Europe was invigorated by the Renaissance. I waved from the harbour when Columbus set sail across the Atlantic; and spat as Nazi tanks rolled into Europe. Then thirty years later I stood on Cocoa Beach and cried when *Apollo 11* took off for the moon, I was so proud of what we'd achieved. And there I was in the spaceplane which brought Richard Saldana down to Kulu. You have no idea how blessed my life has been. I know everything, everything, humans are capable of. We are a good species. Not the best, not by Kiint standards, but so much better than most. And wonderfully unique." She sniffed loudly, and dabbed a handkerchief on her eyes.

"Don't cry," Jay said quietly. "Please."

"I'm sorry. Just having you here, knowing what you could accomplish if you have the chance, makes this hurt so much harder. It's so bloody *unfair.*"

"What do you mean?" Jay asked. Seeing the old woman so upset was making her nervous. "Aren't the Kiint going to let me go home?"

"It's not that." Tracy smiled bravely, and patted Jay's hand. "It's what kind of home that'll be left for you. This shouldn't have happened, you see. Discovering energistic states and what they mean normally comes a lot later in a society's development. It's a huge adjustment for anybody to make. Human-type psychologies need a lot of preparation for that kind of truth, a generation at least. And that's when they're more sociologically advanced than the Confederation. This breakthrough was a complete accident. I'm terrified the human race won't get through this, not intact. We all are, all the Kiint observers want to help, to point the researchers in the right direction if nothing else. Our original conditioning isn't strong enough to restrict those sort of feelings."

"Why don't you?"

"Even if they allowed us, I'd be no use. I've been part of all our history, Jay. I've seen us evolve from dirty savages into a civilization that has spread among the stars. More than anybody I know what we could grow into if we just had the chance. And I have the experience to intervene without anyone ever knowing they'd been guided. But at the most crucial time of our social evolution, when that experience is utterly *vital*, I've got to stay here."

"Why?" Jay pleaded.

Tracy's frail shoulders trembled from repressed emotion. "Oh sweetie, haven't you worked out what this dreadful place is yet? It's a bloody retirement home."

The view arrived suddenly. For over twenty minutes Louise had been sitting in one of the lounge's big chairs, its webbing holding her in the deep hollow of cushioning. Her belly muscles were beginning to strain as they were obliged to hold her in a curving posture. Then she felt a slight trembling in the decking as the lift capsule was shunted onto the tower rail. A tone sounded. Thirty seconds later they flashed out of the Skyhigh Kijabe asteroid. There was a quick impression of soured-white metal mountains, but they quickly shrank from sight overhead. Gentle gravity relieved her muscles, and the webbing slackened.

Earth shone with a mild opalescent light below her. It was midday in Africa, at the base of the tower, and the clouds were charging in from the oceans on either side. There seemed to be a lot more of them than there had been on Norfolk, although the *Far Realm* had been orbiting at a much lower altitude. That might account for it. Louise couldn't be bothered to find the correct meteorology files in her processor block, and run a comparison program. The sight was there to enjoy not analyse. She could actually see the giant white spirals spinning slowly as they battered against each other. It must be a pretty impressive speed for the movement to be visible from such a height.

Genevieve switched her webbing off, and glided over to the lounge window, pressing herself against it. "It's beautiful," she said. Her face was flushed as she smiled back at Louise. "I thought Earth was all rotten."

Louise glanced about, slightly worried by what the other passengers would think of the little girl's remark. With the quarantine, most of them must be from Earth or the Halo. But nobody was even looking at her. In fact, it seemed as though they were deliberately not looking. She went over to stand beside Gen. "I guess that's as wrong as everything else in the school books."

The Halo was visible against the stars, a huge slender thread of stippled light curving behind the planet, like the most tenuous of a gas-giant's rings. For five hundred and sixty-five years, companies and finance consortiums had been knocking asteroids into Earth orbit. The process was standardized now; first the large-scale mining of mineral resources, hollowing out the habitation caverns, then the gradual build up of industrial manufacturing stations as the initial resources were depleted and the population switched to a more sophisticated economy. There were nearly fifteen thousand inhabited asteroids already drifting along in their common cislunar orbit, and new rocks were arriving at the rate of thirty-five a year. Tens of thousands of inter-orbit craft swooped between the spinning rocks, fusion exhausts tangling together in a single scintilating nimbus. Every asteroid formed a tiny bulge in the loop, wrapped behind a delicate haze of industrial stations.

Louise gazed at the ephemeral testament to astroengineering commerce. More fragile than the bridge of heaven in Norfolk's midsummer sky, but at the same time, more imposing. The vista inspired a great deal of confidence. Earth was strong, much stronger than she'd realized; it sprang from a wealth which she knew she would never truly comprehend.

If we're safe anywhere, we're safe here. She put her arm round Genevieve. For once, contented.

Below the majesty of the Halo, Earth was almost quiescent by comparison. Only the coastlines of North and South America hinted at the equal amount of human activity and industry on the ancient planet. They remained in darkness, awaiting the dawn terminator sliding over the Atlantic; but the night didn't prevent her from seeing where people were. Arcologies blazed across the land like volcanoes of sunlight.

"Are they the cities?" Genevieve asked excitedly.

"I think so, yes."

"Gosh! Why is the water that colour?"

Louise switched her attention away from the massive patches of illumination. The ocean was a peculiar shade of grey green, not at all like the balmy turquoise of Norfolk's seas when they were under Duke's stringent white glare.

"I'm not sure. It doesn't look very clean, does it? I suppose that must be the pollution we hear about."

A small contrite cough just behind them made both girls start. It was the first time anyone apart from the stewards had even acknowledged they existed. When they turned round they found themselves facing a small man in a dark purple business suit. He'd already got some thin wrinkles on his cheeks, though he didn't seem particularly old. Louise was surprised by his height, she was actually an inch taller than him, and he had a very broad forehead, as if his hair wouldn't grow properly along the top of it.

"I know this is rude," he said quietly. "But I believe you're from outsystem?"

Louise wondered what had given them away. She'd bought the pair of them new clothes in Skyhigh Kijabe, one-piece garments like shipsuits but more elaborate, with pronounced pockets and cuffs. Other women were wearing the fashion; so she'd hope they would blend in.

"Yes," Louise said. "From Norfolk, actually."

"Ah. I'm afraid I've never tasted Norfolk Tears. Too expensive, even with my salary. I was most sorry to hear about its loss."

"Thank you." Louise kept her face blank, the way she'd learned to do whenever Daddy started shouting.

The man introduced himself as Aubry Earle. "So this is your first visit to Earth?" he asked.

"Yes," Genevieve said. "We want to go to Tranquillity, but we can't find a flight."

"I see. Then this is all new to you?"

"Some of it," Louise said. She wasn't quite sure what Aubry wanted. He didn't seem the type to befriend a pair of young girls. Not from altruism, anyway.

"Then allow me to explain what you are seeing. The oceans aren't polluted, at least not seriously; there was an extensive effort to clean them up at the end of the Twenty-first Century. Their present colouring comes from algae blooms. It's a geneered variety that floats on the top. I think it looks awful, myself."

"But it's everywhere," Genevieve said.

"Alas, yes. That's our carbon sink these days. Earth's lungs, if you like. It performs the job once done by forests and grasslands. The surface vegetation is not what it used to be, so Govcentral introduced the algae to prevent us from suffocating ourselves. Actually, it's a far more successful example of terraforming than Mars. Though I would never be so undiplomatic as to say that to a Lunar citizen. We now have less carbon dioxide in our atmosphere than at any time in the last eight hundred years. You'll be breathing remarkably clean air when you arrive."

"So why do you all live in the arcologies?" Louise asked.

"Heat," Aubry said sadly. "Do you know how much heat a modern industrial civilization of over forty billion people generates?" He gestured down at the globe. "That much. Enough to melt the polar ice and quicken the clouds. We've taken all the preventative measures we can, of course. That was the original spur to build the orbital towers, to prevent spaceplanes aerobraking and shedding even more heat into the air. But however economic we are, we can't dissipate it at a rate that'll turn the clock back. The old ocean currents have shut down, there's no ozone layer at all. And that kind of ecological retro-engineering is beyond even our ability. We're stuck with the current environment, unfortunately."

"Is it very bad?" Genevieve asked. What he'd described sounded worse than the beyond, though she thought the man didn't sound terribly upset by the cataclysm.

He smiled fondly at the planet. "Best damn world in the Confederation. Though I expect everyone says that about their homeworld. Am I right?"

"I like Norfolk," Louise said.

"Of course you do. But if I might make an observation, this is going to be noisier than anything you've experienced before."

"I know that."

"Good. Take care down there. People aren't likely to help you. That's our culture, you see."

Louise gave him a sideways look. "Do you mean they don't like foreigners?"

"Oh no. Nothing like that. It's not racism. Not overtly, anyway. On Earth everybody is a foreigner to their neighbour. It's because we're all squashed up so tight. Privacy is a cherished commodity. In public places, people don't chat to strangers, they avoid eye contact. It's because that's the way they want to be treated. I'm really breaking taboos by talking to you. I doubt any of the other passengers will. But I've been outsystem myself, I know how strange it all is for you."

"Nobody's going to talk to us?" Genevieve asked apprehensively.

"Not as readily as I."

"That's fine with me," Louise said. She couldn't quite bring herself to trust Aubry Earle. At the back of her mind was the worry that he would volunteer to become their guide. It had been bad enough in Norwich when she'd depended on Aunt Celina; Roberto was family. Earle was a stranger, one prepared to drop Earth's customs in public when it suited him. She gave him a detached smile, and led an unprotesting Gen away from the window. The lift capsule had ten decks, and her standard-class ticket allowed her into four of them. They managed to avoid Earle for the rest of the flight. Though she realized he was telling the truth about privacy. Nobody else talked to them.

The isolation might have been safer, but it made the ten

hour trip incredibly boring. They spent a long time watching the view through the window as Earth grew larger, and talking idly. Louise even managed to sleep for the last three hours, curling up in one of the big chairs.

She woke to Gen shaking her shoulder. "They just announced we're about to reach the atmosphere," her sister said.

Louise combed some strands of hair from her face, and sat up. Other passengers who'd been dozing were now stirring themselves. She took the hair clip off as she reorganized her mane, then fastened it up again. First priority when they were down must be to get it washed. The last time she'd managed properly was back on Phobos. Maybe it was time for a cut, a short style that was more manageable. Though the usual arguments still applied: she'd invested so much time keeping it in condition, cutting it was almost a confession of defeat. Of course, back at Cricklade she'd had the time to groom herself every day, and had a maid to help.

Whatever did I do all day back then?

"Louise?" Genevieve asked cautiously.

She raised an eyebrow at the girl's tone. "What?"

"Promise you won't get mad if I ask?"

"I won't get mad."

"It's just that you haven't said yet."

"Said what?"

"Where we're going after we touch down."

"Oh." Louise was completely stumped. She hadn't even thought about their destination. Getting away from High York and Brent Roi had been her absolute priority. What she needed to do was find somewhere to stay so she could think about what to do next. And without consulting her block there was really only one city name from her ethnic history classes which she was certain would still exist. "London," she told Genevieve. "We're going to London."

The African orbital tower had been the first to be built, a technological achievement declared the equal of the FTL drive by the Govcentral committees and politicians who'd authorized it. Typical self-aggrandising hyperbole, but acknowledged to be a reasonable comparison none the less. As Aubry Earle had said, it was intended to replace spaceplanes and the enormously detrimental effect they were having on Earth's distressed atmosphere. By 2180 when the tower was finally commissioned (eight years late), the Great Dispersal was in full swing, and the volume of spaceplane traffic had become so injurious to the atmosphere that meteorologists were worrying about elevating the armada storms to an even greater level of ferocity.

The question became academic. Once the tower was on line, its cargo capacity exceeded thirty per cent of the world's spaceplane fleet. Upgrades were being planned before the first lift capsule ran all the way up to Skyhigh Kijabe. Four hundred and thirty years later, the original slender tower of monocarbon fibre was now nothing more than a support element threading up the centre of the African Tower. A thick grey pillar dwindling off up to infinity, immune to the most punishing winds the armada storms could fling at it. The outer surface was lined with forty-seven magnetic rails, the structure's maximum. It was now cheaper to build new towers than expand it any further.

The lower five kilometres were the fattest section, providing an outer sheath of tunnels to protect the lift capsules from the winds, enabling the tower to remain operational in all but the absolutely worst weather conditions. Exactly where the tower ended and the Mount Kenya station started was no longer certain. With a daily cargo throughput potential of two hundred thousand tonnes, and up to seventy-five thousand passengers, the capsule handling infrastructure had moulded itself tumescently around the base, a mountain in its own right. Eighty vac-train tunnels intersected in the bedrock underneath it, making it the most important transport nucleus on the continent.

To keep the passengers flowing smoothly, there were eighteen separate arrival Halls. All of them followed the same basic layout, a long marble-floored concourse with the exit doors from customs and immigration rooms on one side, and lifts on the other, leading to the subterranean vac-train platforms. Even if an arriving passenger knew exactly which lift cluster they wanted, they first had to negotiate a formidable barricade of retail stalls selling everything from socks to luxury apartments. Keeping track of one individual (or a pair) amid the perpetual scrum occupying the floor wasn't easy, not even with modern equipment.

B7 left nothing to chance. A hundred and twenty GSDI field operatives had been pulled off their current assignments to provide saturation coverage. Fifty were allocated to Hall Nine, where the Kavanagh sisters were due to disembark, their movements coordinated by an AI that was hooked into every security sensor in the building. Another fifty were already on their way to London within minutes of Louise saying that was her intended goal. Twenty had been held in reserve in case of cockups, misdirection, or good old fashioned acts of God.

The arrangements had caused more arguments among B7; all of the supervisors remained extremely proprietorial when it came to their respective territories. Southern Africa, in whose domain the Mount Kenya station fell, disputed Western Europe's claim that he should take personal command of the surveillance. Western Europe counterclaimed that as the tower station was just a brief stopover for the sisters, and the whole operation was his anyway, he should have the necessary authority. The other B7 supervisors knew Southern Africa, renowned for the tedious minutiae of procedure worship, was just going through the motions.

Western Europe was given his way over the tower station, as well as gaining concessions to steer the operation through whichever territory the Kavanaghs roamed in their search for Banneth.

Southern Africa acceded to the decision, and withdrew testily from the sensenviron conference. Smiling quietly at his inevitable victory, Western Europe datavised the AI for a full linkage. With the station layout unfolding in his mind, he began to designate positions to the agents. Tied in with that was the lift capsule's arrival time, and the departure times of each scheduled vac-train. The AI computed every possible travel permutation, plotting the routes which the sisters would have to walk across the concourse. It even took into account the types of stalls which might catch their eye. Satisfied the agents were placed to cover every contingency, Western Europe stoked the logs on his fire, and settled back into a leather armchair with a brandy to wait.

It was probably the ultimate tribute to the fieldcraft of the GSDI agents that after all fifty of them took up position in Hall Nine, Simon Bradshaw didn't notice them, not even with his hyper instinct for the way of things on the concourse. Simon was twenty-three years old, though he could easily pass for fifteen. Selected hormone courses kept him short and skinny, with soft ebony skin. His large eyes were moist brown, which people mistook for mournful. Their endearing appeal had salvaged him from trouble countless times in the twelve years he'd been strutting the concourses of the Mount Kenya station. Local floor patrol cops had his profile loaded in their neural nanonics, along with hundreds of other regular sneak opportunists. Simon used cosmetic packages every fortnight or so, altering his peripheral features, though his size remained constant. It was the act you had to vary to prevent the cops from putting a comparison program into primary mode. Some days dress smart and act little boy lost, dress casual and act street tough, dress neutral act neutral, pay a cousin to lend you their five-year-old daughter and come over as a protective big brother. But never ever dress poor. Poor people had no business in the station, even the stall vendors had neat franchise uniforms below their shiny franchise smiles.

Today Simon was actually in a franchise uniform himself: the scarlet and sapphire tunic of Cuppamaica, the coffee café. Being unobtrusive by being mundane. Nobody was suspicious of station workers. He saw the two girls as soon as they emerged through the customs and immigration archway. It was like they had a hologram advert flashing over their heads saying: EASY. He couldn't ever remember seeing such obvious offworlders before. Both of them gawping round at the cavernous Hall, delighted and amazed by the place. The little one giggled, pointing up at the transit informatives, baubles of light charging about overhead like insane dragonflies, shepherding passengers towards the right channels.

Simon was off immediately, coming away from the noodle stall he'd been slouching against as if powered by a nuclear pulse. Moving at a fast walk, the luggage cab buzzing incessantly at his heels as its small motors strained to keep up. He was desperately trying not to run, the urgency was so hot. His principal worry now was if the others of his profession saw them. It would be like a feeding frenzy.

Louise couldn't bring her legs to move. Her fellow passengers had swept her and Genevieve out of customs, carrying her along for a few yards before her surroundings exerted a grip on her nerves. The arrivals Hall was awe-

some, a stadium of coloured crystal and marble, saturated
with noise and light. There must surely have been more
people thronging across its floor than lived in the whole of
Kesteven island. Like her, they all had luggage cabs chasing after them, adding to the bedlam. The squat oblong box
had been supplied by the line company operating the lift
capsule. Her bags had been dumped inside by the retrieval
clerk, who'd promptly handed her a circular card. The cab,
he promised, would follow her everywhere as long as she
kept the card with her. It was also the key to open it again
when they got down to their vac-train platform. "After that
you're on your own," he said. "Don't try and take it on the
carriage. That's MKS property, that is."

Louise swore she wouldn't. "How do we get to London?" Gen asked in a daunted tone. Louise glanced up at
the mad swarms of photons above them. They were balls of
tightly packed writing, or numbers. Logically, it must be
travel information of some kind. She just didn't know how
to read it.

"Ticket office," she gulped. "They'll tell us. We'll have
to buy a ticket for London anyway."

Genevieve turned a complete circle, trying to scan the
Hall through the melee of bodies and luggage cabs.
"Where's the ticket office?"

Louise pulled the processor block out of her shoulder
purse. "I'll find it," she said with determination. It was just
a question of accessing a local net processor and loading a
search program. An operation she'd practised a hundred
times with the tutorial. Watching the graphics assemble
themselves in the display as she conjured up a welcome
feeling of satisfaction.

I've got a problem and I'm solving it. By myself, and for
myself. I'm not dependent.

She grinned happily at Gen as the search program interrogated the station information processors. "We're actually on Earth." She said it as though she'd only just realized. Which, in a strange way, she had.

"Yes," Genevieve grinned back. Then she scowled as a scrawny youth in a red and blue uniform barged into her. "Hey!"

He mumbled a grudging apology, side-stepped round the luggage cab and walked away.

The block bleeped to announce it had located the vac-train ticket dispensers for Hall Nine. There were seventy-eight of them. Without showing any ire, Louise started to redefine the search parameters.

Easy, easy, *easy*. Simon wanted to yell it out. That jostle with the little kid was the modern equivalent of the shell game. Visually confusing as their respective luggage cabs crossed paths, and allowing his grabber to intercept their tag card code at the same time. He fought the impulse to turn round and check the new luggage cab at his feet. Those girls were in for a hell of a shock when they got to their platform and found only a pile of beefbap wrappers inside it.

Simon headed for the stalls at a brisk pace. There was a staff lift at the middle. Route down to a quieter level, where he could examine his prize. He was ten metres from the front line of stalls when he was aware of two people closing on him. It wasn't an accidental path, either, they were coming at him with all the purpose of combat wasps. Running wasn't going to do any good, he knew that. He pressed the release button on the grabber hidden in his palm. The girls' luggage cab swerved away, no longer following him. Now, if he could just dump the grabber in a waste bin. No proof.

Shit. How could his luck turn like this?

One of the cops (or whoever) went after the luggage cab. Simon hunted round for a bin. Anywhere there was a fast food bar. He ducked round the first stall, making one last check on his pursuers. That was why he never saw the third (or forth and fifth, for that matter) GISD agent until the woman bumped right into him. He did feel, briefly, a small sting on his chest. Exactly the same place she was now taking her hand away from. His guts suddenly turned very cold, then that sensation faded to nothing.

Simon looked down at his chest in puzzlement just as his legs faltered, dropping him to his knees. He'd heard of weapons like this, so slim they never left a mark as they punctured your skin; but inside it was like an EE grenade going off. The world was going quiet and dim around him. High above, the woman watched him with a faint sneer of satisfaction on her lips.

"For a couple of bags?" Simon coughed incredulously. But she'd already turned, walking away with a calm he could almost respect. A real pro. Then he was somehow aware of himself finishing the fall to the floor. Blood rushed out of his gaping mouth. After that, the darkness rushed up to drown him. Darkness, but not total night. The world was only the slightest of distances away. And he wasn't alone in observing it from outside. The lost souls converged upon him to devour the font of keen anguish that was his mind.

"That way," Louise said brightly. The block's little screen was showing a floor layout, which she thought she'd aligned right.

With Genevieve skipping along at her side she negotiated the obstacle course of stalls. They slowed down to window shop the things on display, not really understanding half of them. She also thought there must be a subtle trick to negotiating the crowd which was eluding her. Twice on the way to the dispenser, people banged into her. It wasn't as though she didn't look where she was going.

The block had told her there was neither a ticket office, nor an information desk. A result which made her acknowledge she was still thinking along Norfolk lines. All the information she needed was in the station electronics, it just needed the right questions to extract it.

A vac-train journey to London cost twenty-five fuseodollars (fifteen for Gen); a train left every twelve minutes from platform thirty-two; lifts G to J served that level. Once she knew that, even the transit informatives whirling past overhead began to make a kind of sense.

Western Europe accessed an agent's sensevise to watch the sisters puzzle out the ticket dispenser. Enhanced retinas zoomed in on Genevieve, who had started clapping excitedly when a ticket dropped out of the slot.

"Don't they have ticket dispensers on Norfolk, for heaven's sake?" the Halo supervisor asked querulously. He had maintained executive control over the observation team during the Kavanaghs' trip from High York down to the Mount Kenya station, anxious that nothing should mar the hand over. Now, curiosity had impelled him to tarry. Having initiated a few unorthodox missions in his time, he was nevertheless impressed with Western Europe's chutzpa in dealing with Dexter.

Western Europe smiled at the sensevise overlay of Halo, who appeared to be leaning against the marble fireplace, sipping a brandy. "I doubt it. Some cheery-faced old man in a glass booth would be more their style. Haven't you accessed any recent sensevises of Norfolk? Actually, just any sensevises of the place would do. It hasn't changed much since the founding."

"Damn backward planet. It's like the medieval section of a themepark. Those English-ethnic morons abused the whole Great Dispersal ethos with that folly."

"Not really. The ruling Landowner class introduced a stability we're still striving for, and without one per cent of the bloodshed we employ to keep a lid on things down here. In a way, I envy all those pastoral planets."

"But not enough to emigrate."

"That's a very cheap shot. Quite beneath you. We're as much products of our environment as the Kavanaghs are of theirs. And at least they're free to leave."

"Leave yes. Survive in the real world, no." He indicated the observation operation's status display. It wasn't a pleasing tally. Five people had been eliminated by the guardian blanket of GISD agents—pickpockets, sneak thieves, a scam jockey—as the sisters made their way across the concourse. Extermination was the quick, no arguments, solution. It was also going to cause an uproar with the local police when the bodies were discovered. "At this rate, you're going to wind up slaughtering more people than Dexter has to protect them."

"I always thought station security should be sharper," Western Europe said casually. "What kind of advert is it for Govcentral when visitors get ripped off within ten minutes of their arrival on the good old homeworld?"

"Most don't."

"Those girls aren't *most*. Don't worry, they'll be safer when they reach London and book into a hotel."

Halo studied Western Europe's handsome young face, amused by the mild expression of preoccupation to be found there. "You fancy Louise."

"Don't be absurd."

"I know your taste in women as well as you know my preferences. She's exactly your type."

Western Europe swirled the brandy round his three-hundred-year-old snifter, not looking up at the smug overlay image. "I admit there's something really rather appealing about Louise. Naiveté, one supposes. It does always attract, especially when coupled with youthful physical beauty. Earth girls are so . . . in your face. She has breeding, manners, and dignity. Also something the natives here lack."

"That's not naiveté, it's pure ignorance."

"Don't be so uncharitable. You'd be equally adrift on Norfolk. I doubt you could ride to the hunt in pursuit of the cunning hax."

"Why would anybody, let alone me, want to go to Norfolk?"

Western Europe tilted the snifter back and swallowed the last of the brandy. "Exactly the answer one expects from someone as jaded and decadent as you. I worry that one day this whole planet will think like us. Why do we bother protecting them?"

"We don't," Halo chuckled. "Your memory transfer must have glitched. We protect ourselves. Earth merely is our citadel."

6

It was as if space had succumbed to a bleak midwinter. Monterey was moving into conjunction with New California, sinking deeper through the penumbra towards the eclipse. Looking through the Nixon suite's big windows, Al could see the shadows above him expanding into black pools of nothingness. The asteroid's crumpled rock surface was slowly melting from view. Only the small lights decorating the thermal exchange panels and communication rigs gave him any indication that it hadn't been removed from the universe entirely. Equally, the Organization fleet gathered outside was now invisible save for navigation strobes and the occasional spectral gust of blue ions fired from a thruster.

Beneath his feet, New California slid across the brilliant starscape, a gold-green corona crowning an empty circle. From this altitude, there were no city lights, no delicate web of lustrous freeways gripping the continents. Nothing, in fact, to show that the Organization existed at all.

Jezzibella's arms crept round his chest, while her chin came to rest on his shoulder. A mild forest-morning perfume seeped into the air. "No sign of red clouds," she said encouragingly.

He lifted one hand to his lips, and kissed the knuckles. "No. I guess that means I'm still numero uno about here."

"Of course you are."

"You wouldn't fucking think so the beefs everyone's got. Not just what they say, either. What they think counts for a whole lot."

"They'll be all right once the fleet's in action again."

"Sure," he snorted. "And when's that gonna be, huh? Fucking Luigi, I shoulda popped him properly, screwing up like that. It's gonna take another twenty—thirty days to build up our antimatter stocks to anything like a load we can risk another invasion with. So Emmet says. That means six weeks minimum I know. Goddamn! I'm losing it, Jez. I'm fucking losing it."

Her grip tightened. "Don't be silly. You were bound to have setbacks."

"I can't afford one. Not now. Morale's going to shit out there. You've heard what Leroy said. Possessed crew are going down to the surface for funtime and ain't coming back. They think I'm gonna lose control of the planet and they'll be better off down there when it happens."

"So get Silvano to tighten up."

"Maybe. You can only be so tough, you know?"

"You sure you can't bring the next invasion forward?"

"No."

"Then we need something else to keep the soldiers and lieutenants occupied and committed."

He turned to face her. She was wearing one of those whore's dresses again, just tiny little strips of pale yellow fabric up the front (he had ties wider than that), and a teensy skirt. So much skin tantalisingly revealed; it made him want to tug it off. As if he'd never seen her in the buff before. But then she was always alluring in some new fashion, a mirror hall chameleon.

A sensational piece of ass, no doubt about it. But the way she kept on coming up with ideas for him (just like her never-ending mystique) had become vaguely unnerving of late. It was like he'd become dependent, or something.

"Like what?" he asked flatly.

Jezzibella pouted. "I don't know. Something which doesn't need the whole fleet, but'll still be effective. Not a propaganda exercise like Kursk; we need to hurt the Confederation."

"Kingsley Pryor's gonna do that."

"He might. Although that's a very long shot, remember?"

"Okay, okay." Al wished up one of his prime Havanas, and took a drag. Even they seemed to have lost some of their bite recently. "So how do we use some itsy piece of the fleet to piss the Feds?"

"Dunno. Guess you'd better go call Emmet in; see what he can come up with. That's strictly his field." She gave him a slow wink and sauntered off to the bedroom.

"Where the hell are you going?" he demanded.

A hand waved dismissively. "This dress is for your eyes only, baby. I know how hot you get when other people see what I've got to offer. And you need to have a clear head when you're talking to Emmet."

He sighed as the tall doors closed behind her. Right again.

When Emmet Mordden arrived fifteen minutes later, Al had returned to the window. There was very little light in the big lounge, just some red jewels glimmering high up on the white and gold walls. With Monterey now fully into the umbra, the window was little more than a slate grey rectangle, with Al's ebony silhouette in the middle. His youthful face was illuminated by a diminutive orange glimmer coming from the Havana.

Emmet tried not to show too much annoyance at the cigar smoke clogging the room. The Hilton's conditioners never managed to eliminate the cloying smell, and using energistic power to ward it off was too much like overkill. It might just offend Al, too.

Al raised a hand in acknowledgement, but didn't turn away from the window with its empty view. "Can't see anything out there today," he said quietly. "No planet, no sun."

"They're still there, Al."

"Yeah yeah. And now is when you tell me I got responsibilities to them."

"I'm not going to tell you that, Al. You know the way it is."

"Know what, and don't tell Jez this, I'd trade in the whole shebang for a trip home to Chicago. I used to have a house in Prairie Avenue. You know? Like, for my family. It was a nice street in a decent neighbourhood, full of regular guys, trees, good lighting. There was never any trouble there. That's where I want to be, Emmet, I wanna be able to walk down Prairie Avenue and open my own front door again. That's all. I just wanna go home."

"Earth ain't like it used to be, Al. And it hasn't changed for the best. Take it from me, you wouldn't recognize it now."

"I don't want it now, Emmet. I want to go *home*. Capeesh?"

"Sure, Al."

"That sound crazy to you?"

"I had a girl before. It was a good thing back then, you know."

"Right. See, I had this idea. I remember there was this Limy guy, Wells, I think his name was. I never read any of his books, mind. But he wrote about things that are happening today in this crazy world, about Mars men invading and a time machine. Boy, if he's come back, I bet he's having a ball right now. So . . . I just wondered; he was thinking stuff like that, a time machine, back in the Twentieth Century, and the Confederation eggheads, they can build these starships today. Did they ever try to make a time machine?"

"No, Al. Zero-tau can carry ordinary people into the future, but there's no way back. The big theory guys, they say it can't be done. Not in practice. Sorry."

Al nodded contemplatively. "That's okay, Emmet. Thought I'd ask."

"Was that all, Al?"

"Shit no." Al smiled reluctantly, and turned from the window. "How's it going out there?"

"We're holding our own, especially down on the planet. Haven't had to use an SD strike for three days now. Some of the lieutenants have even caught a couple of AWOL starship crew. They're getting shipped back up here tonight. Patricia's going to deal with. She's talking about setting an example."

"Good. Maybe now those bastards will learn there ain't no get-out clause when you sign up with me."

"The voidhawks have stopped dumping their stealth bombs and spyglobes on the fleet. Kiera's hellhawks have done a good job clearing them out."

"Huh." Al opened the liquor cabinet, and poured himself a shot of bourbon. The stuff was imported from a planet called Nashville. He couldn't believe they'd called a whole goddamn planet after that hick dirt-town. Their booze had a kick, though.

"You remember she moved her people into the rooms along the docking ledge?" Emmet said. "I know why she did it, now. They've knocked out all the machinery which makes the nutrient fluid for the hellhawks. And not just here in Monterey, all over the system, too. The *Stryla* visited all the asteroids we run, and layered their nutrient machinery. Her people are guarding the only one left working. If the hellhawks don't do as they're told, they don't get fed. They don't eat, they die. It's that simple."

"Neat," Al said. "Let me guess, if we try to muscle in on the last machine, it gets zapped."

"Looks like it. They've let slip that it's booby trapped. I'd hate to risk it."

"As long as the hellhawks do what I want, she can stay. Barricading herself in like that is dumb. It makes her even more dependent on me for status. She has to support me, she's not important to anyone else."

"I've put a couple of people on surveying what's left of the machinery she smashed up. We might be able to put a working unit back together eventually, but it'll take time."

"Time is something which is giving me a fucking headache, Emmet. And I ain't talking about Wells's machine here. I need to get the fleet back into action, soonest."

"But, Al—" he stopped as Al held up a hand.

"I know. We can't launch no invasion right now. Not enough antimatter. There's gotta be something else they can do. I'm being honest with you here, Emmet, the boys are so antsy, they'll mutiny if we keep them kicking their heels in port much longer."

"I suppose you could launch some fast strike raids. Let people know we've still got some punch."

"Strike on what? Just blowing things up for the sake of it, ain't my style. We have to give the fleet a purpose."

"There's the Mortonridge Liberation. The Confederation's been beaming propaganda about that to every city on New California, telling us how we're bound to lose eventually. If we hit some of their supply convoys we'd be helping the possessed on Ombey."

"Yeah," Al said. The notion didn't really appeal, too few visible returns. "What I'm looking for is something that'll cause a shitload of trouble for the Confederation each time. Knocking out a couple of ships ain't going to do that."

"Well . . . This is just an idea, Al. I don't know if it's the kind of thing you're looking for. It depends on how many planets you want to rule over."

"The Organization has to keep up its momentum to exist. Ruling planets is only a part of that. So talk to me, Emmet."

Kiera could see eight hellhawks out on the ledge below her. They were all sitting on their pedestals, ingesting nutrient fluid. A rotor had been drawn up so the whole flock could feed on the ten metallic mushrooms which remained functional. Studying the huge creatures, so powerful yet utterly dependant, Kiera couldn't avoid the religious analogy. They were like a devout congregation coming to receive mass from their priestess. Each of them abased themselves before her, and if the correct obeisance was performed, they received her blessing in return, and were allowed to live.

The *Kerachel* swept in above the ledge, appearing so swiftly out of the umbra it might have just swallowed in. A pointed lozenge-shape, a hundred metres long, it hardly hesitated as it found its designated pedestal and sank down. Knowing that even though it couldn't see her expression, it could sense her thoughts, she smiled arrogantly down upon it. "Any problems?" she asked casually.

"Monterey's command centre monitored its patrol flight," Hudson Proctor replied. "No deviations. Eight suspect objects destroyed."

"Well done," she murmured. A hand waved languid permission to start.

Hudson Proctor picked up a handset, and began speaking into it. Two hundred metres below the departure lounge, her loyal little team opened a valve, and the precious fluid surged along a pipe out to the pedestal. A feeling of contentment strummed the air like background music as *Kerachel* began sucking in its food. Kiera could feel the hellhawk's mood, it mellowed her own.

There were eighty-seven hellhawks based at Monterey now. A formidable flotilla by anyone's standards. Securing them for herself had absorbed all her efforts over the last few days. Now it was time to start thinking ahead again. Her position here was actually a lot stronger than it had been at Valisk. If the habitat was a fiefdom, then New California was a kingdom in comparison. One which Capone appeared singularly inept at maintaining. The main reason she'd established herself so easily in the docking ledges was the apathy spreading through Monterey. Nobody thought to question her.

That simply wouldn't do. In building his Organization, Capone had grasped an instinctive truth. People, possessed or otherwise, needed structure and order in their lives. It was one of the reasons they fell into line so easily, familiarity was a welcome comrade. Give them the kind of nirvana which existed (though she had strong suspicions about that) in the realm where planets shifted to, and the population would sink into a wretched, lotus-eating state. The Siamese twin of unending indulgent leisure. If she was honest to herself, she was terrified of the immortality she'd been given. Life would change beyond comprehension, and that was going to be very hard indeed. For an adaptation of that magnitude, she would no longer be herself.

And that, I will not permit.

She enjoyed what she was and what she'd got, the drives and needs. Like this, at least she remained recognizably human. That identity was worth preserving. Worth fighting for.

Capone wouldn't do it. He was weak, controlled by that ingenious trollop Jezzibella, by a non-possessed.

In the Organization, a method of enforcing control over an entire planetary population had been perfected. If she was in charge, it could be used to implement her policies. The possessed would learn to live with their phobia of open skies. In return they would have the normal human existence they craved. There would be no dangerous metamorphosis into an alien state of being. She would remain whole. Herself.

A twitch of motion broke her contemplation. Someone was walking along the docking ledge, someone in a bulky orange and white spacesuit with a globular helmet. Compared to modern SSI suits, the thing was ridiculously old-fashioned. The only reason for wearing one was if you didn't have neural nanonics.

"Are there any engineering crews on the ledge?" Kiera asked. She couldn't see any hellhawks receiving maintenance right now.

"A couple," Hudson Proctor answered. "The *Foica* is being loaded with combat wasps, and *Varrad*'s main fusion generator needs work on its heat dump panels."

"Oh. Where . . ."

"Kiera." Hudson held up the handset in trepidation. "Capone's calling all his senior lieutenants. It's an invite to some kind of glam party this evening."

"Really?" She gave the spacesuited figure one last glance. "And I haven't a thing to wear. But if our Great and Glorious Leader has summoned me, I'd better not disappoint him."

*

Back on Koblat, they called these spacesuits ballcrushers. Jed had worn one before for an emergency evacuation drill, and now he was remembering why. Putting it on was easy enough; when they got it out of the locker it was a flaccid sack three times too large for his frame. He'd wriggled into it, standing with arms outstretched and legs apart so the baggy fabric could hang unobstructed off each limb. Then Beth had activated the wristpad control, and the fabric contracted like an all-over tourniquet. Now every part of his body was being squeezed tight. It was the same principal as an SII suit, preventing any loose bubbles of air becoming trapped between his skin and the suit. If a suit contained any sort of gas, it would inflate like a rigid balloon as soon as he stepped out into a vacuum.

This way, he could move about almost unrestricted. Providing he ignored the sharp pincer sensation besetting his crotch at every motion. Not an entirely easy thing to disregard.

But apart from that, the suit was functioning smoothly. He wished his heart would do the same. According to the hazy purple icons projected onto the inside of his helmet, the suit's integral thermal shunt strips were conducting away a lot of heat. Nerves and an adrenaline high were making the blood pound away in his arteries. His tension wasn't helped by the rank of huge hellhawks he was walking along. He knew they could sense his thoughts and all the guilt cluttering up his skull, which made the torment even worse. A bad case of feedback. Bubbles of plastic and dark metal clung to the underbellies of the bitek starships like mechanical excrescences. Weapons and sensors. He was sure every one of them was tracking him.

"Jed, you're getting worse," Rocio told him.

"How can you tell?"

"Why are you whispering? You are using a legitimate

spacesuit radio frequency. If the Organization is monitoring this, which I doubt, they still have to decrypt the signal, which I also doubt their ability to do. As far as they are concerned you are just one of Kiera's people, while she will think you belong to the Organization. That's the beauty of this in-fighting, nobody knows what anyone else is doing around here."

"Sorry," Jed said contritely into the helmet mike.

"I'm monitoring your body functions, and your heartrate is still climbing."

That brought a shudder which rippled up from Jed's legs to make his chest quiver. "Oh Jeeze. I'll come back."

"No no, you're doing fine. Only another three hundred metres to the airlock."

"But the hellhawks are going to know!"

"Only if you don't take precautions. I think it's time we used a little chemical help here."

"I didn't bring any. We weren't supposed to need that in Valisk."

"I don't mean your underclass narcotics. The suit medical module will provide what you need."

Jed hadn't even known the suit had any medical modules. Following Rocio's instructions, he tapped out a series of orders on the wristpad. The air in the helmet changed slightly, becoming cooler, and smelling of mint. For such a small suffusion, its effect was swift. The cold massaged its way in through Jed's muscles, bringing a nearly-orgasmic sigh from his throat. It was a hit stronger than anything he'd ever scored in Koblat. His mind was being methodically purged of fright by this balmy tide of wellbeing. He held up his arms, expecting to see all his anxiety streaming out of his fingertips like liquid light.

"Not bad," he declared.

"How much did you infuse?" Rocio asked.

The hellhawk's voice came across as brittle and irritating. "What you said," Jed retorted in a fashion which demonstrated quite plainly who was occupying the lead role. A couple of the physiology icons were flashing a rather pleasing pink in front of him. Like pretty little flower buds opening, he thought.

"All right, Jed, let's keep going, shall we?"

"Sure thing, mate."

He started walking forwards again. Even the twinge in his groin was less of an issue now. That medical suffusion was good shit. The hellhawks had stopped radiating their intimidation. With his mind chilling he started to see them in a different context; grounded on their pedestals, sucking desperately at their drink. Not so much different to himself and the girls. He acquired a more confident stride as he passed the last two.

Rocio's voice started issuing directions again, guiding him in towards the airlock. Tall spires of machinery ran up the rock cliff at the back of the ledge, sprouting pipes in a crazed dendritic formation. Several small fountains of thin vapour were jetting out horizontally from junctions and micrometeorite punctures; their presence a testament to Monterey's floundering maintenance programme. Windows were set into the drab, sheered rock; long panoramic rectangles fronting departure lounges and engineering management offices. All but two were dark, reflecting weak outlines of the floodlit hellhawks. The remaining pair revealed nothing but vague shadows moving behind their frosted anti-glare shielding.

Maintenance vehicles, cargo trucks, and crew buses had been left scattered along the base of the cliff. Jed made his way through the maze they formed, thankful of the cover. The airlocks waited for him beyond, unlit tunnels leading into the asteroid. Conduits that would take him directly to the nest of the most feared possessed in the Confederation. His trepidation rose again as he approached them. He stopped on the threshold of a personnel airlock, and used the wristpad again.

"Careful how much of that trauma suppresser you inhale," Rocio said lightly. "It's strong stuff, they designed it to keep you functional after an accident."

"No worries," Jed said earnestly. "I can handle it."

"Very well. There's no one in the area immediately behind the airlock. Time to go in."

"Jed?" Beth's voice sounded loud and high in his helmet. "Jed, can you hear me?"

"Sure, doll."

"Okay. We're watching the screens, too. Rocio is relaying images from the cameras inside, so we'll look out for you, mate. And he's right about the medical module, go easy on it, huh? I want to share some of that suffusion with you when you get back."

Even in his tranquil state, Jed interpreted that right. He went into the airlock feeling majestic.

He took his helmet off, and took a breath of neutral air. It helped to clear his head a bit, not so much euphoria, but none of the fright, either. Good enough. Rocio gave him a whole string of directions to follow, and he started off cautiously down the corridor.

The store room for crew supplies wasn't far from the airlock, naturally enough. Rocio had been keeping a careful watch on things, seeing what happened when other hellhawks came to dock. Several of his bitek comrades still had crew on board. The combat wasps they carried required activation codes, and following standard security procedures, Kiera and Capone had split the codes between loyalists. No one person could fire them. It was a significant point that she hadn't asked Rocio to carry any.

Jed found the door Rocio nominated, and pulled back the clamps. Cold air breezed out, turning his breath to foggy streamers. Inside, the room was split into aisles by long free-standing shelves. Despite the Organization's claim that normalizing food production on New California was a priority, there weren't many packs left. Processing food for the space industry was a specialist business; ideally, everything had to be crumbs-free, taste-strengthened, and packaged in minimum volume. Leroy Octavius had decided that restarting the kitchen facilities of the relevant companies wasn't cost effective. Consequently, fleet crews had been making do with old stocks and standard pre-packed meals.

"What's there?" Beth asked impatiently. There were no cameras actually in the store room, Rocio had to go on what he'd seen being taken in and out.

Jed walked down the aisles, brushing the frost dust off various labels. "Plenty," he muttered. Providing you liked yoghurt, mint potatocakes, cheese and tomato flans (dehydrated in sachets that looked like fat biscuits), blackcurrant and apple mousse concentrate; complemented with hot-frozen cubes of broccoli, spinach, carrot, and sprouts.

"Oh bugger."

"What's the matter?" Rico asked.

"Nothing. The boxes are heavy, that's all. We're going to have a real party when I get this lot back to the ship."

"Are there any chocolate oranges?" Gari piped up.

"I'll have a look, sweetheart," Jed lied. He went back out into the corridor to fetch a trolley which had been abandoned just along from the store room. It ought to fit through the airlock, which meant he could use that to transport everything back to the *Mindori*. Then they'd all have to be carried up the stairs to the life support module's airlock. It was going to be a long hard day.

"Somebody coming," Rocio announced after Jed had got a dozen boxes out of the store room and onto the trolley.

Jed stopped dead, hugging a box of compressed rye chips. "Who?" he hissed.

"Not sure. Camera image isn't too good. Small guy."

"Where is he?" Jed dropped the box, wincing at the sound.

"A hundred metres away. But heading your way."

"Oh Jeeze. Is he possessed?"

"Unknown."

Jed shot across the storage room and closed the door. Nothing he could do about the damning trolley outside, though. His heart began yammering as he flattened himself against the wall beside the door—as if that made a difference.

"Still coming," Rocio announced calmly. "Seventy metres now."

Jed's hand crept down to the utility pocket on his hip. Fingers flicked the seal catch, and he dug inside. His hand closed around the cold, reassuring grip of the laser pistol.

"Thirty metres. He's coming to the junction with your corridor."

Don't look at the bloody trolley, Jed prayed. Christ, please don't.

He drew the laser pistol out, and studied the simple controls for a second. Switched modes to constant beam, full power. Repeater was no good, a possessed would be able to screw with the electrics inside while he was shooting. He was only going to have one chance.

"He's in the corridor. I think he's seen the trolley. Stopping just outside."

Jed closed his eyes, shaking badly. A possessed would be able to sense his thoughts. They would all be hauled off to face Capone. He would be tortured and Beth would get sent to the brothel.

I should have left the door open, that way I could have sprung out and surprised them.

"Hello?" a voice called. It was very high pitched, almost a girl.

"Is that them?" he whispered to his suit mike.

"Yes. He's examined the trolley. Now by the door."

The locking clamp moved, slowly hinging back. Jed stared at it in dread, desperate for one last hit from the suit's medical module.

If the laser doesn't work, I'll kill myself, he decided. Better that . . .

"Hello?" the high voice sounded timid. "Is someone there?"

The door started to open.

"Hello?"

Jed shouted in fury, and jumped from the wall. Holding the laser pistol in a double handed grip, he spun round and fired out into the corridor. Webster Pryor was saved by two things: his own diminutive height, and Jed's quite abysmal aim.

The red strand of laserlight was quite brilliant compared to the corridor lighting. It left Jed squinting against the glare, trying to see what he was shooting at. Blue-white flames and black smoke were squirting out of the corridor wall opposite, tracing a meandering line in the composite. Then the smoke stopped, and a spray of molten metal rained down. He was slicing through a conditioning duct.

He did—just—see a small man dive to the floor at his feet as the laser slashed round in search of a target. There was a yell of panic, and someone was screaming: "Don't shoot me don't shoot me!" in a high pitched voice.

Jed yelled himself. Confused all to hell what was happening. Tentatively, he took his finger off the laser's trigger. Metal creaked alarmingly as the duct sagged around the dripping gap in its side. He looked down at the figure in the white jacket and black trousers grovelling on the floor. "What in Christ's name is going on? Who are you?"

A terrified face was looking up at him. It wasn't a bloke, just a kid. "Please don't kill me," Webster pleaded. "Please. I don't want to be one of them. They're horrible."

"What's happening?" Rocio asked.

"Not sure," Jed mumbled. He took a look down the corridor. All clear.

"Was that a laser?"

"Yeah." He aimed it down at Webster. "Are you possessed?"

"No. Are you?"

"Course bloody not."

"Well I didn't know," Webster wailed.

"How did you get a weapon?" Rocio asked.

"Shut up! Jeeze, give me a break. I just got one, okay?"

Webster was frowning through his tears. "What?"

"Nothing." Jed hesitated, then put the laser pistol back in his utility pocket. The kid looked harmless; though the waiter's jacket with its brass buttons which he wore, along with his oil-slicked hair, was a little odd. But he was more scared than anything else. "Who are you?"

The story came out in broken sentences, punctuated by sobs. How Webster and his mother had been caught up in Capone's take-over. How they'd been held in one of the asteroid's halls with hundreds of other women and children. How some Organization woman came searching them out from the rest. How he'd been separated from his mother and put to work serving drinks and food for the gangster bosses and a peculiar, very pretty, lady. How he kept hearing Capone and the lady mention his father's name, and then glance in his direction.

"What are you doing down here?" Jed asked.

"They sent me for some food," Webster said. "The cook told me to find out if there were any swans left in storage."

"This is the spacecraft section," Jed said. "Didn't you know?"

Webster sniffled loudly. "Yes. But if I look everywhere, I could stay away from them for a while."

"Right." He straightened, and found one of the small camera lenses. "What do we do?" he asked, flustered by the boy's tale.

"Get rid of him," Rocio said curtly.

"What do you mean?"

"He's a complication. You've got the laser pistol, haven't you?"

Webster was looking up at him passively, eyes red-rimmed from the tears. All mournful and beat; the way not so long ago Jed had looked at Digger when the pain was at its worst.

"I can't do that!" Jed exclaimed.

"What do you need, a note from your mother? Listen to me, Jed, the second he steps within range of a possessed, they'll know something's happened to him. Then they'll come looking for you. They'll get you, and Beth, and the girls."

"No way. I can't. I just can't. Not even if I wanted to."

"So what are you going to do instead?"

"I don't know! Beth? Beth, have you been switched on to all this?"

"Yes, Jed," she replied. "You're not to touch that boy. We've got plenty of food, now, so bring him back with you. He can come with us."

"Really?" Rocio enquired disdainfully. "And where's his spacesuit? How's he supposed to get out to me?"

Jed looked at Webster, thoroughly disconcerted. This whole situation was just getting worse and worse. "For Christ's sake, just get me out of this."

"Stop being an arsehole," Beth snapped. "It's bloody obvious, you'll have to steal one of the vehicles. There's plenty of them about. I can see some of them docked to the airlocks close to where you went in. Take one and drive it over to us."

Jed wanted to curl up into a ball and take a decent hit. A vehicle! In full view of this whole nest of possessed.

"Please Jed, come back," Gari entreated. "I don't like it here without you."

"All right, doll," he said, too bushed to kick up an argument. "On my way." He rounded on Webster. "And you'd better not be any trouble."

"You're going to take me away?" the boy asked in wonder.

"Sort of, yeah."

Jed didn't bother about collecting any more food from the shelves. He just started pushing the trolley, making sure Webster was in sight the whole time.

Rocio reviewed the camera images and schematic data available to him, and quickly devised a route to one of the docking ledge vehicles. It meant the two of them taking a lift up to the lounge level, which he didn't like. But previewing enabled him to hurry them past the sections where crews were still working without incident.

The vehicle he'd chosen for them was a small taxi with a five-seater cab. Large enough to take the trolley, and simple enough for Jed to drive. He was back at the *Mindori* three minutes after disengaging from the airlock. It actually took him longer than that to match the taxi's docking tube with the starship's life support module hatch. Once the tube was locked and pressurized, Beth, Gari, and Navar came rushing in to greet the returning hero. Beth put her hands on either side of his face and gave him a long kiss. "I'm proud of you," she said.

That wasn't something she'd ever told him before, and she didn't hand out platitudes, either. Of course, today had been full of not merely the unusual, but the positively weird. However, the words left him warm and uncertain. The moment was only slightly spoilt when the two younger girls started reading labels and found out what he'd brought back.

It had taken the Monterey Hilton's head chef over three hours to prepare the meal. A dozen or so senior lieutenants and their partners had been invited to an evening with Al and Jezzibella. Pasta with a sauce that was at least as good as they used to make on Earth (supervised by Al), swan stuffed with fish, fresh vegetables boosted up from the planet that afternoon, desserts heavy on chocolate and calories, matured cheeses, the finest wines New California could produce, the fanciest liqueurs. As well as the food, there was a five-piece band, and some showgirls for later. Guests would also receive items of twenty-four carat jewellery (genuine, not energistic baubles), personally selected by Al himself. The evening was intended to be memorable. Nobody left Al Capone's party without a smile on their face. His reputation as a wild and exuberant host had to be preserved, after all.

What Al didn't know was that Leroy had to be taken off Organization administration duties in order to make the arrangements. He'd spent over an hour calling senior Organization personnel to facilitate the ingredients and people necessary to make the party work. That bothered the obese manager. The picture he and Emmet were getting from various lieutenants and city bosses down on the surface was a smooth one, things falling neatly into place, people doing as they were told. But not so long ago, when the fleet left for Arnstat, Leroy had put together a grand ball in under a week. A time when the planet and high-orbit asteroids had fought for the privilege of supplying Al with the best of anything they had. This party was a fraction of that scale and a multiple of the effort.

However, despite the grudging donations, the Nixon suite's dining room was an impressive and dramatic example of lavishness when Leroy finally arrived, immaculate tuxedo straining around his huge frame. One of the more lissom girls from the brothel was on his arm; the pair of them a gross example of human glandular divergence. Heads turned to look at him when they arrived together. Silent calculations were quickly performed when a smiling Al greeted them, and handed the girl a diamond necklace which even her cleavage couldn't devour. No snide remarks were ventured, though the mind-tones said it all.

Monterey was out of the umbra again, heading into the light. Outside the broad window, New California's green and blue crescent gleamed warmly. It was a sumptuous atmosphere for the pre-dinner drinks, and the atmosphere was suitably relaxed. Waiters circulated with gold and silver trays of canapés, making sure no glass was ever in danger of heading towards half empty. Conversation flowed, and Al circulated with grace, showing no favouritism.

His mood didn't even falter when Kiera showed up an easy fifteen minutes after everyone else. She wore a provocatively simple sleeveless summer dress of some thin mauve fabric, cut to emphasise her figure. On a girl of her body's age it would have been charmingly guileless, on her it was a declaration of all-out fashion war against the other females in the room. Only Jezzibella in the ever-classic little black cocktail number looked snazzier. And by the bright cherub's smile she used to welcome Kiera, she knew it.

"Al, darling," Kiera's smile was wide and sweltering as she kissed Al's cheek. "Great party, thanks for the invite."

For a second, Al worried her teeth might be going for his jugular. Her thoughts bristled with an icy superiority. "Wouldn't be the same without you," he told her. Jeeze, and to think he'd once considered her a possible lay. His wang would get so cold inside her, it'd snap clean off.

The notion made him shiver. He beckoned to one of the waiters. The guy must have been in his nineties, one of those dignified old coots that were perfect as butlers. Young Webster should have been doing this job, Al thought, it would have made for a cuter image. But he hadn't seen the boy all evening. The old man wobbled forwards obediently, carrying a tray of black velvet with a shimmering sapphire cobweb necklace resting on it.

"For me?" Kiera simpered. "Oh, how lovely."

Al took the necklace off the tray and slowly fastened it round her neck, ignoring her lecherous smirk at his proximity.

"It's so nice to see you here," Jezzibella said, clinging to Al's arm. "We weren't sure if you could spare the time."

"I've always got time for Al."

"That's nice to hear. Keeping the hellhawks in line must take up a big part of your day."

"I don't have any trouble coping. They know I'm in charge of them."

"Yeah, you got some interesting moves, there," Al said. "Emmet was full of praise for what you did. Said it was smart. Coming from him, that's quite a compliment. I'll have to remember them in case I'm ever in a similar situation."

Kiera removed a champagne saucer from one of the waiters, her gaze searched the room like a targeting laser until she found Emmet. "You won't be in a similar situation, Al. I'm covering that flank for you. Very thoroughly."

Jezzibella morphed into her hero-worshipping early-teens persona. "Covering for Al?" her high girlish voice piped.

"Yes. Who else?"

"Come on, Jez," Al grinned in mock-rebuke. "There ain't no one else in the market for hellhawks, you know that."

"I do." Jezzibella looked up adoringly at him, and sighed.

"And without me, there's no reason for New California to keep supporting them," Al said.

Kiera's attention moved back from Emmet. "Believe me, I'm very aware of everyone's position. And their worth."

"That's nice," Jezzibella said blandly.

"Enjoy your drink, babe," Al said, and patted Kiera's arm. "I got a small announcement to make before we sit down to eat." He marched over to Emmet, and signalled the head waiter to bang a gong. The room fell silent, people picking up on the focused excitement in Al's mind. "This ain't the usual kind of speech to make at table. I ain't got no stag jokes, for a start."

Faithful smiles switched on all around. Al took another sip of champagne—damn, but he wanted a shot of decent bourbon. "All right, I ain't gonna bullshit around with you. We got problems with the fleet, on account of it ain't got nowhere to go. You know how it is, we gotta keep momentum going or the boys'll go sour on us. That right, Silvano?"

The brooding lieutenant nodded scrupulously. "Some of

the guys are getting close to the boil, sure, Al. Nothing we can't keep a lid on."

"I don't wanna keep no fucking lid on nothing. We gotta give the bastards something to do while we build up stocks of antimatter. We can't take over no planet again, not for a while. So we're gonna hit the Confederation from another angle. That's what I got for you, something new. This way we cause them one fuck of a lot of damage, and don't get hurt ourselves. And we got Emmet here to thank for that." He put his arm round the Organization's reluctant technology expert, and gave him a friendly hug. "We're gonna launch some raids on other planets, and break through their space fort defences. Once we've done that, we can sling a whole load of our guys down to the surface. Tell them, Emmet."

"I've done some preliminary designs for one-man atmospheric entry pods," Emmet said in a tense voice. "They're based on standard escape boats, but they can descend in under fifteen minutes. That's high gees for whoever's inside, but with our energistic strength it shouldn't be a problem. And they're simple enough, that we shouldn't screw up the guidance electronics. All the fleet has to do is create a window in the SD coverage long enough for them to get down. Once they're on the ground, the good old exponential curve comes into play."

"Without the fleet firepower to back them up, they'll lose," Dwight said bluntly. "The local cops will wipe them out."

"It depends on how together the planet is, and how many soldiers we can shove down there," Al said, untroubled. "Emmet's right about how fast we can expand. That's gonna cause the governments a shitload of grief."

"But, Al, the Organization can't expand as fast as ordinary possessed. We've got to have time to let Harwood and his guys vet the souls that're coming back. Christ, we've had enough trouble with loyalty on New California, let alone Arnstat. If we don't have committed lieutenants, the Organization'll fall apart."

"Who gives a shit?" Al laughed round at the startled expressions. "Come on, you guys! Just how many goddamn planets do you think we can run? Even the King of Kulu's only got half a dozen. If I gave all you dopeheads one apiece to be emperor of, that still leaves hundreds of free ones left out there to screw with us. We gotta start levelling the odds, here. I say shoot possessed down to the surface and let the fuckers run loose. We can use all our hotheads from here, all the crap artists who wanna take New California out of the universe, send them, get rid of the assholes permanently. That way we're solving two problems at once. Fewer traitors here, and planets dropping out of the Confederation. You retards grabbed what that'll mean yet? It means less hassle for us. Every planet we hit is gonna scream to the navy for the same kinda help Mortonridge is getting. That'll cost them plenty to provide. Money they can't spend dicking with us." He looked round the room, knowing he'd won them over. Again. His face reddened with the heat of victory, three tiny white lines proud on his cheek. That reluctant admiration he'd kindled in them proving he was the man with the plan, and the balls to see it through.

Al raised his glass high in triumph. And it was like a room full of krauts doing their knee-jerk fascist salute as the others held their own glasses up, fast. Jezzibella winked impishly at him from behind the back row, while Kiera's face was drawn as she considered the implications.

"A toast. Goodbye to that goddamn pain in the ass Confederation."

*

The *Mindori*'s distortion field expanded outwards in a specific pattern of swirls, generating ripples in the fabric of space-time. They pushed against the hull, lifting it from the pedestal in a simple, smooth motion. Inside the large forward lounge, none of the six passengers noticed even a quiver in the apparent gravity field. They'd just finished their meal of mashed turkey granules, which was the only meat product Beth could hammer into a burger shape. Jed was ignoring the sullen stares that were getting flashed his way. Turkey wasn't so bad after it had been grilled.

Gerald Skibbow looked up at the lounge's big screen as the edge of the docking ledge slipped towards them. "Where are we going?" he asked.

Webster twitched in surprise, it was the first time he'd heard Gerald speak. The others stared at him, slightly nervous of what would follow. Even now, after all this time, he was still nutty Gerald to them. Rocio had privately confided to Jed and Beth he couldn't make any sense of Gerald's thoughts at all.

A small picture of Rocio's face appeared in one corner of the screen. "I've been given a patrol flight vector," he said. "It's not a very demanding one, we'll never be more than three million kilometres from New California. I suspect it's a trial to see if I do as I'm told. I have just filled my reserve bladders with nutrient fluid, if I was going to leave, now would be an obvious time."

"Are you going to?" Beth asked.

"No. The only place to go is the Edenist habitats and the Confederation. The price for their sanctuary would be co-operating with their physicists. And that would ultimately lead to the defeat of the possessed. I told you before, I need to find other options."

"I don't want to leave Monterey," Gerald said. The screen was now showing the asteroid's counter-rotating spaceport receding at a considerable speed. "Please go back and let me disembark."

"Can't do that, Gerald, mate," Beth said. "Them possessed, they'd spot you inside Monterey in a flash. Give the whole game away. We'd all wind up like Marie, that way, and they'd punish Rocio, too."

"I will assist you with Kiera in whatever way I can," Rocio said. "But first, I must establish myself as one of her servile flock."

Beth reached over and gripped Gerald's arm. "We can wait that long, eh?"

Gerald considered her words; although he was sure his thoughts were taking longer to form these days. There was a time when he could give an instant reply to any topic or question. That Gerald existed only in his mind now, a memory that was hard to find and difficult to see. "All right," he said. It was a tough concession to make. To have been so close to *her*. Just a few hundred metres. And now having to leave, to abandon her. It would probably be days until they could return. Days darling Marie would have to spend enduring the torment of that terrible woman's control. The notions of what she would get up to with her captive flesh were horrible. Marie was a lovely little girl, so pretty. Always had lots of boyfriends, which he'd tried not to get upset and protective over. Back on Lalonde, sex seemed the only thing the possessed were interested in. And like every father since the dawn of civilization, Marie's sexuality was the one thing Gerald never dared dwell upon.

It would be that, he admitted in his dark heart. Night after night, Kiera would allow some man to run his hands over her. Would laugh and groan at the abuse. Would demand hot physical violations. Bodies writhing together in the darkness. Beautiful, strong bodies. Gerald whimpered softly.

"You okay?" Beth asked. Beside her, Jed was frowning.

"Fine," Gerald whispered. His hands were rubbing his perspiring forehead, trying to massage the pain inside. "I just want to help her. And if I could just get to her, I know I could. Loren said so, you see."

"We'll be back there in no time, okay, no worries."

He nodded lamely, returning to pick at the food they'd given him. He had to get to Marie soon. He was sorry about everyone else's predicament, but what Marie was suffering was unspeakable. Next time they landed at Monterey, he decided, it would be different. No details, but definitely different.

Rocio was aware of Gerald's ardent, fractured anxiety sinking back under calmer emotions. That man's mind was a complete enigma. Not that Rocio actually wanted to be privy to such tortured thoughts. Shame that he couldn't convince Beth and Jed to stay on board by themselves. This entourage of people were making his position more complicated. Ideally, he'd like to winnow the numbers down again.

Now that he was clear of the asteroid, he began to accelerate. Modifying the distortion field to generate ever-more powerful ripples in space-time. He surfed them at seven gees, a secondary manipulation alleviating the force around the life support section. As the sense of freedom rose in tandem with his speed, he allowed his dreamform to blossom. Dark wings slowly spread wide, sweeping eagerly, sending motes of interplanetary dust swirling in his wake. He shook his neck, blinking huge red eyes, flexing his talons. In this state, he was perfectly at one with himself and life. It reaffirmed the conviction that Kiera's hold over himself and his comrades must be broken.

He began talking to the other hellhawks, probing for emotional nuances. Building a pattern of those who thought as he did. Of the seventy currently in the New California system, he thought there were possibly nineteen he could count on for open support, another ten would probably side with him if things looked favourable. Several were playing it very coy, while eight or nine, led by Etchells and Cameron Leung, revelled in the prospect of following the Organization fleet into glory. Good enough odds.

Eight hours into his patrol, Hudson Proctor delivered new instructions. **There's an interplanetary ship decelerating towards New California,** Kiera's lieutenant said. **Coming straight in along the south pole, one and a half million kilometres out. We think it's come from the Almaden asteroid. Can you sense it?**

Rocio expanded his distortion field, probing where Proctor indicated. The ship slithered into his perception as a tight kink of mass, alive with energy.

Got it, he acknowledged.

Intercept them, and order them to return.

Are they hostile?

I doubt it. Probably just another bunch of idiots who think they can live where they want instead of where the Organization tells them.

Understood. And if they don't want to return?

Blow them to shit. Any questions?

No.

Rocio changed the distortion field again, concentrating it on a small area just ahead of his beak. Power surged through his patterning cells, and the stress he was applying leapt towards infinite. A wormhole interstice opened, and he shot through, emerging from the terminus less than two seconds later. It folded neatly behind his tailfeathers, returning local space-time to its usual consonance.

The interplanetary ship was three kilometres away, a long silk-grey splinter of metal and composite. Standard configuration of barrel-shaped life support module separated from the drive section by a lattice tower. It was decelerating at two thirds of a gee, blue-white fusion flame spearing cleanly from its exhaust. Rocio was also aware of another wormhole terminus opening five thousand kilometres away. A hellhawk slid out, deflating its distortion field immediately, and drifting inert. He resisted the temptation to hail it. Shadowing him in such a fashion to monitor his conduct was very unsubtle.

A radar pulse triggered the ship's transponder: according to the code it was called the *Lucky Logorn*. Rocio matched velocities with it, and opened a short-range channel. "This is the Organization ship *Mindori*," he told them. "You're approaching New California's Strategic Defence network without clearance. Please identify yourself."

"This is Deebank, I guess I'm the captain around here. We haven't been advertising our presence in case we attracted those goddamn voidhawks. Sorry about that, didn't mean to give you a scare. We'd like clearance to rendezvous with a low orbit station."

"Clearance refused. Return to your asteroid."

"Now just a goddamn minute, we're loyal members of the Organization here. What gives you the right to order us about?"

Rocio activated a maser cannon on his lower hull, and targeted one of the thermo-dump panels plumbed into *Lucky Logorn*'s equipment bay. "One. I'm not ordering you, I'm relaying an instruction from the Organization. Two." He fired.

The blast of coherent maser radiation thumped a half-metre hole into the middle of the thermo-dump panel. Fluorescent orange shards spun away, their glimmer slowly fading to black.

"Fuck you," Deebank shouted. "You bastards can't keep us out here forever."

"Realign your drive. Now. My second shot will be through your fusion tube. You'll be left drifting out here. The only thing you'll have to occupy yourselves with is a sweepstake. Is your food going to run out first? Or will it be the air? Then again, a voidhawk might pick you up, and you get used as research lab beasts by the Confederation."

"You piece of shit."

"I'm waiting." Rocio slid closer, picking up the resentment and anger boiling through the eight people in the life support section. There was bitter resignation in there, too.

Sure enough, the fusion drive plume twitched round, sending *Lucky Logorn* on a shallow arc which would ultimately see it heading back to Almaden. Cancelling so much delta-V was a long, energy expensive business. It would take them hours.

"We're going to remember you," Deebank promised. "Time will come when you need to join us. Don't expect it to be easy."

"Join you where?" Rocio asked, genuinely curious.

"On a planet, dick-for-brains."

"Is that what this was all about? Your fear of space?"

"What the hell did you think we were doing? Invading?"

"I wasn't told."

"Okay. So now you understand, will you let us through?"

"I can't."

"Bastard."

Rocio played for the sympathy angle, marshalling his thoughts into contrite concern. "I mean it. There's another hellhawk shadowing me, making sure I do what I'm told. They're not certain about my commitment to the cause, you see."

"Hear that splashing sound? That's my heart bleeding."

"Why doesn't the Organization want you on New California?"

"Because they need the products Almaden makes in its industrial stations. The asteroid has plenty of astroengineering companies who specialise in weapons systems. And we're the poor saps who have to terrorise non-possessed technicians into keeping them running. You got any idea what that's like? It's a crock of shit. I was a soldier when I was alive, I used to fight the kind of fascists who enslaved people like this. I'm telling you, it ain't right. It ain't what I was brought up to do. None of this is."

"Then why stay in the Organization?"

"If you ain't for Capone, you're against him. That's the way it works. He's been real smart the way he's set things up. Those lieutenants of his will do anything to keep their position. They put the screws on us, and we have to put the screws on the non-possessed. If there's any trouble, if we start to object, or get uppity, they just call on the fleet for back up. Don't they? You're the enforcers, you make it all hang together for him."

"We have our own enforcer, she's called Kiera."

"The Deadnight babe? No shit? I wouldn't mind submitting my poor body to some enforcement by her." Laughter rumbled across the gap between the ships.

"You wouldn't say that if you'd ever met her."

"Tough bitch, huh?"

"The worst."

"You don't sound too happy about that."

"You and I are in the same situation."

"Yeah? So listen, maybe we can come to some kind of arrangement? I mean, if we have to go back to Almaden, the lieutenants are going to make us eat shit for pulling this stunt. Why don't you take us back to New California, let us off at a low orbit station, or if you've got a spaceplane we could use that. If we get down there to the surface, we stay. Believe me. There'd be no comeback."

"Fine for you."

"We'll get you a body. A human one, the very best there is. There's millions of non-possessed left on the planet; we'll get one ready for possession and hold it for you. This way you get down there without any of the risk we'll be going through. Listen, you can sense I'm telling the truth. Right?"

"Yes. But it doesn't interest me."

"What? Why not? Come on! It's the greatest deal in town."

"Not for me. You people really hate this empty universe, don't you?"

"Oh, like you don't? You were in the beyond. You can hear the beyond. It's always there, just one step away on the other side from night. We have to get away from that."

"I don't."

"Crap."

"But I don't. Really. Certainly I can still hear the lost souls, but it's not as if they can touch me. All they are is a reminder of that nothingness. They're not a threat themselves. Fear is the only thing that drives you to escape. I've got over that. *Mindori* belongs here in the emptiness, this is its perfect milieu. Having this construct as my host has taught me not to be afraid. Perhaps it should be you who try and find blackhawk and voidhawk bodies? Can you imagine that? It would solve everyone's problem, without all this conflict and violence. If after you die, you were to be given a voidhawk body to possess. Enough could be grown for the lost souls, I'm sure of it, given time and commitment. Then ultimately, space would become filled with billions of us, the entire human race transformed into dark angels flitting between the stars."

"Hey, pal, know what? Possessing that monster didn't cure you, it made you take a swan dive over the edge."

"Perhaps. But which of us is content?"

"You got Kiera to worry about. Remember? How come you don't flap off into the sunset?"

"As you say, Kiera is a problem."

"Right, so don't come over all superior."

"I wasn't. Your offer to deal interests me. It may be possible to come to some arrangement. I have a notion, but it'll take some time to check the requirements. Once you're back on Almaden, I'll look you up."

Coming down to the gym in the Hilton's basement always stirred Kiera's darker animal feelings. She rather enjoyed her new role of laid back vamp, letting her eye wander over the young men being put through their paces by a gruff Malone. Their apprehension was pleasurable as they saw her watching, the nudges and worried glances. It wasn't that she'd never had affairs back on New Munich, she'd taken several lovers during her marriage, both before and after her husband's fall from grace. But they'd all been insipid, cautious encounters. Most of the thrill had come from the concept of having an affair, of cheating and not getting caught. The sex had never been anything special.

Now though, she was free to explore her sexuality to the full, with no one to disapprove or condemn. Part of her allure came from being a woman in power, she was a challenge to any male; the rest came from Marie Skibbow's gorgeous body. It was the second factor which brought her down here to the non-possessed. Possessed lovers, like poor old Stanyon, were so artificial. Men inevitably gave themselves big penises, could stay erect all night, had Greek-god bodies. Strutting clichés, that spoke volumes about their weaknesses and insecurities.

She much preferred the youngsters from the gym for the reality they provided. Unable to hide behind any mental or physical illusion, sex with them was raw and primitive. Dominating them in bed, without a single inhibition, was utterly delicious. And Marie herself had a surprising amount of knowledge which Kiera could extract and experiment with. Despised memories and skill gained during a long river journey spent capitulating to an old man called Len Buchannan. Enduring the nightly humiliation for one reason alone, the freedom which waited at the end of the river. The girl had a single minded determination which Kiera quite admired. It came close to her own. Even now, captive and tragic, inside her mental prison, Marie clung to the notion of deliverance.

But how? Kiera wondered lightly.

Somehow. One day.

Not with me in command of you.

Nothing lasts forever. As *you* know.

Kiera dismissed the impudent girl from her thoughts with a derisory mental sneer. Her gaze found a rather delicious nineteen-year-old hammering his fists into a long leather punch bag. The desperate aggression and sweating muscles were highly arousing. He knew she was standing behind him, but refused to turn. Hoping if he avoided eye contact she would pass by. She crooked at finger at Malone, who came over reluctantly.

"What's his name?" she asked huskily.

"Jamie." The squat trainer's thoughts were full of contempt.

"Are you frightened of me, Jamie?"

He stopped punching, steadying the bag. Gentle grey eyes stared at her levelly. "You, no. What you can do, yeah."

She applauded languidly. "Very good. Don't worry, I'm not going to hurt you." She glanced down at Malone. "I'll bring him back to you in the morning."

Malone took his cap off, and spat on the floor. "Whatever you say, Kiera."

She walked right up to Jamie, enjoying his discomfort at her proximity. "Oh dear, I'm not that bad am I?" she murmured.

He was a head taller than her. When he looked down, his eyes were drawn the rich tanned skin revealed by her mauve summer dress. Embarrassment warred with other, more subtle emotions. Kiera grinned in victory. At least something was going right tonight. Capone and his damn sedition plans! She took his big hand in hers, and began to lead him out of the gym like a giant puppy. Before she reached the double doors, they swung open. Luigi barged through, carrying a pile of towels. He caught sight of Kiera, and glared angrily. Commander of the fleet, now running trivial demeaning errands for the nonentity Malone. The resentment twisting him up was almost strong enough to manifest itself as pernicious violence; he was sure she was here simply to witness his humiliation first hand. The boss's new favourite gloating over her ex-rival's downfall.

"Luigi," Kiera said brightly. "Fancy seeing you here. How wonderful."

"Piss off, bitch." He elbowed past her, scowling.

"After the towels, will you be going down on your knees to tie up their shoes?"

Luigi twisted in mid step, and marched back to her. He thrust his head forward so their noses were touching. "You're a whore. A very cheap whore. With only one thing to sell. When the Organization has used up your hellhawks, you'll be nothing. Best thing is, you know it's coming. Your bullshit ice empress routine doesn't fool anyone. This whole damn asteroid is laughing at you."

"Of course it's coming," she said serenely. "But they wouldn't be used up if the fleet was commanded properly."

Confusion marred his face and his thoughts. "What?"

That uncertainty was enough for Kiera. She patted Jamie's heavily muscled forearm. "Why don't you take those heavy towels from Luigi, darling. It looks like I won't be needing you tonight, after all."

Jamie peered over the pile of towels unexpectedly dumped in his arms, watching the doors close behind Kiera and Luigi. "I don't get it," he complained. Part of him had actually been quite looking forward to the sex, despite what the others kept saying about the Deadnight witch.

Malone patted the big lad's shoulder in a paternal fashion. "Don't worry about it, my boy. You're well off out of that kind of scene."

Given Dr Pierce Gilmore's senior position within the CNIS's scientific staff, weapons analysis division, it was inevitable that a large part of his nature tended towards the bureaucratic. Precise and methodical in his work, he believed strongly in following sanctioned procedures to the letter during his investigations. Such adherence to protocol was something of a joke among his department's junior staff, who accused him of inflexibility and lack of imagination. He endured their behind-his-back humour stoically, while politely and consistently refusing to take short cuts and play up to wild hunches. To his credit, it was exactly the kind of leadership the weapons division needed. Eternal patience is a prime requisite in the dismantling of unknown weapons that have been designed illegally (mostly under government patronage) and tend to incorporate elements that actively discourage close examination. In the seven years he'd held his post, the division's safety record was exemplary.

Also to his credit, he didn't indulge in the usual internal empire building so beloved of government employees, especially those who, like him, were essentially unaccountable. As a result, his office was a modest one, roughly equivalent to the entitlement of a middle manager in some multistellar company. There were few personal items, some ornaments and desktop solid images; a shelf of Stanhopea orchids flourishing under a slim solaris tube. The furniture was formal, a comfortable reproduction of the flared dark-wood Midwest-ethnic style he'd grown up with. Broad holographic windows of Chyenne's heroically rugged countryside did little to disguise the room's actual location, buried deep inside Trafalgar. In its favour, the electronic suite Gilmore had installed was a top-of-the range Edenist processor array verging on AI status. Such a system helped facilitate the twice weekly multi-disciplinary councils he chaired to investigate the capabilities of the possessed.

This was the second time the team heads had met since Jacqueline Couteur had made her bid for freedom in maximum security court three, and the aftermath was still affecting everyone's mood. Professor Nowak, the quantum physicist, was first to arrive, helping himself to some of the coffee from the percolator jug which Gilmore kept going full time. Dr Hemmatu, the energy specialist, and Yusuf, the electronics chief, came in together talking in low tones. They gave Gilmore a perfunctory nod and sat down at the conference desk. Mattox was next, the neurology doctor keeping to himself as usual, choosing a chair one along the desk from Yusuf. Euru completed the group, sitting directly opposite Gilmore. In contrast to the rest of them, the dark-skinned Edenist appeared almost indecently happy.

Gilmore had known his deputy long enough to see it wasn't just the usual contentment which all Edenists shared. "You have something?" he enquired.

"A voidhawk has just arrived from the Sinagra system. It was carrying an interesting recording."

Hemmatu perked up. "From Valisk?" The independent habitat had supplied a large amount of very useful data on the behaviour of the possessed before it vanished.

"Yes, just before Rubra and Dariat took it away," Euru said, smiling broadly. He instructed his bitek processor block to datavise the file to them.

The sensevise they received was a strange one, lacking the resolution normally associated with full nerve channel input. Conversions from Edenist habitat memories to a standard Adamist electronic format were notoriously quirky, but this was something else again. Nesting within its environment of pastel colours, tenuous scents, and mild tactorials, Gilmore tried bravely to avoid using the connotation: spectral. He failed dismally.

The memory was of Dariat, while he bobbed about on the surface of some icy water inside a dark polyp-walled tube. The cold was severe enough to penetrate even his energistic protection, judging by the way it was numbing his appropriated limbs, and making him shiver. A plump black woman clung to him, shaking violently inside her strange waistcoat of cushions.

Did you gain any impression of size? the Kohistan Consensus asked Dariat.

Not really, a universe is a universe. How big is this one?

Consensus received his quick recollection of the beyond. His soul had become a feeble flicker of identity adrift in a nowhere at one remove from reality. Nowhere full of similar souls; all of them with the same craving, the sensations available on the other side.

The memory of someone else's memory: if the sensenviron of the Valisk starscraper waste tube was tenuous, this was as insubstantial as a nearly-forgotten dream. The beyond, as far as Dariat was concerned, lacked any physical sensation, all that betrayed its presence was a transparent tapestry of emotions. Anguish and yearning flooded through the realm Souls clustered round, desperately suckling at his memories for the illusion of physical sensation they contained.

Confusion and fear reigned in Dariat's mind. He wanted to flee. He wanted to plunge into the glorious star of sensation burning so bright as Kiera and Stanyon forced open a path into Horgan's body. The beyond withered behind him as he surged along the tear through the barrier between planes of existence.

And how do you control the energistic power? Consensus asked.

Dariat gave them a visualization (perfectly clear this time) of desire overlaying actuality. More handsome features, thicker hair, brighter clothes. Like a hologram projection, but backed up by energy oozing out of the beyond to shore it up, providing solidity. Also, the destructive power, a mental thunderbolt, aimed and thrown amid boiling passion. The rush of energy from the beyond increasing a thousandfold, sizzling through the possessed body like an electric charge.

What about senses? This ESP faculty you have? The world around him altered, shifting to slippery shadows.

There were several more questions and observations on the nature of Dariat's state, which the rebel possessor did his best to answer. In total, the recording amounted to over fifteen minutes.

"Wealth indeed," Gilmore said when it ended. "This kind of clarification is just what we need to pursue a solution. It seemed to me as though Dariat actually had some freedom of movement in the beyond. To my mind, that implies physical dimensions."

"A strange sort of space," Nowak said. "From the way

the souls were pressed close enough to overlap, there appeared to be very little of it. I won't call it a place, but it's definitely a unified area. It was almost a closed continuum, yet we know it exists in parallel to our own universe, so it must have infinite depth. That's damn close to being paradoxical." He shrugged, disturbed by his own reasoning.

"That perception ability Dariat demonstrated interests me," Euru commented. "The effect is remarkably similar to a voidhawk's mass perception sense."

Gilmore looked across his desk to the tall Edenist, inviting him to continue.

"I'd say the possessed must be interpreting local energy resonances. Whatever type of energy they operate within, we know it pervades our universe, even if we can't distinguish it ourselves yet."

"If you're right," Nowak said. "That's a further indication that our universe is conjunctive with this beyond realm, that there is no single interface point."

"There has to be an identifiable connection," Euru said. "Dariat was clearly aware of the lost souls while he occupied Horgan's body. He could hear them—for want of a better phrase. They were pleading with the possessors the whole time, asking to be given bodies. Somewhere there is a connection, a conduit leading back there."

Gilmore glanced round the desk to see if anyone else wanted to pick up on the point. They were all silent, concentrating on the implications Euru and Nowak raised. "I've been considering that we might need to approach this from a different angle," he said. "After all, we've had a singular lack of success in trying to analyse the quantum signature of the effect, perhaps we should concentrate less on the exact nature of the beast, and more on what it does and implies."

"In order to deal with it, we have to identify it," Yusuf said.

"I'm not advocating a brute force and ignorance approach," Gilmore replied. "But consider; when this crisis started, we believed we were dealing with an outbreak of some energy virus. I maintain that is essentially what we have here. Our souls are self-contained patterns capable of existence and travel outside the matrix of our bodies. Hemmatu, how would you say they are formed?"

The energy expert stroked his cheek with long fingers, pondering the question. "Yes, I think I see what you're driving at. The beyond energy is apparently present in all matter, including cells, although the quantity involved must necessarily be extremely tenuous. Therefore as intelligence arises during life, it imprints itself into this energy somehow."

"Exactly," Gilmore said. "The thought patterns which arise in our neurone structure retain their cohesion once the brain dies. That is our soul. There's nothing spiritual or religious about it, the entire concept is an entirely natural phenomena, given the nature of the universe."

"I'm not sure about denying religion," Nowak said. "Being inescapably plugged into the universe at such a fundamental level seems somewhat spiritually impressive to me. Being at one with the cosmos, literally, makes us all part of God's creation. Surely?"

Gilmore couldn't quite work out if he was joking. A lot of physicists took to religion as they struggled with the unknowable boundaries of cosmology, almost as many as embraced atheism. "If we could just put that aside for the moment, please?"

Nowak grinned, waving a hand generously.

"What I'm getting at is that something is responsible for retaining a soul's cohesion. Something glues those thoughts and memories together. When Syrinx interviewed Malva, she was told: *'Life begets souls.'* That it is *'the pattern which sentience and self awareness exerts on the energy within the biological body.'"*

"So souls accrue from the reaction of thoughts upon this energy," Nowak said. "I'm not disputing the hypothesis. But how can that help us?"

"Because it's only us: humans. Animals don't have souls. Dariat and Laton never mentioned encountering them."

"They never mentioned encountering alien souls either," Mattox said. "But according to the Kiint, they're there."

"It's a big universe," Nowak said.

"No," Gilmore countered. "That can't apply. Only some souls are trapped in the section we know about, the area near the boundary. Laton as good as confirmed that. After death, it's possible to embark on the great journey. Again, his words."

Euru shook his head sadly. "I wish I could believe him."

"In this I agree with him, not that it has much bearing on my principal contention."

"Which is?" Mattox asked.

"I believe I know the glue which holds souls together. It has to be sentience. Consider, an animal like a dog or cat has its individuality as a biological entity, but no soul. Why not? It has a neural structure, it has memories, it has thought processes operating inside that neural structure. Yet when it dies, all that loses coherence. Without a focus, a strong sense of identity, the pattern dissolves. There is no order."

"The formless void," Nowak muttered in amusement.

Gilmore disregarded the jibe. "We know a soul is a coherent entity, and both Couteur and Dariat have confirmed there is a timeflow within the beyond. They suffer entropy just as we do. I am convinced that makes them vulnerable."

"How?" Mattox asked sharply.

"We can introduce change. Energy, the actual substance of souls, cannot be destroyed, but it can certainly be dissipated or broken up, returned to a primordial state."

"Ah yes." Hemmatu smiled in admiration. "Now I follow your logic. Indeed, we have to reintroduce some chaos into their lives."

Euru gave Gilmore a shocked stare. "Kill them?"

"Acquire the ability to kill them," Gilmore responded smoothly. "If they have the ability to leave the part or state of the beyond where they are now, they must clearly be forced to do so. The prospect of death, real *final* death, would provide them with the spur to leave us alone."

"How?" Euru asked. "What would be the method?"

"A virus of the mind," Gilmore said. "A universal anti-memory that would spread through thought processes, fracturing them as it went. The beauty of it is, the possessed are constantly merging their thoughts with one another to fulfil their quest for sensation. En masse, they are a mental superconductor."

"You might just be on to something here," Hemmatu said. "Are there such things as anti-memory?"

"There are several weapons designed to disable a target's mental processes," Mattox said. "Most of them are chemical or biological agents. However, I do know of some that are based upon didactic imprint memories. But so far my colleagues have only produced variants that induce extreme psychotic disorders such as paranoia or schizophrenia."

"That's all we need," Nowak grunted. "Extra demented lost souls. They're quite barmy enough as it is."

Gilmore gave him a disapproving glance. "Would an anti-memory be possible, theoretically?" he asked Mattox.

"I can't think of any immediate show-stoppers."

"Surely it would just self-distruct?" Yusuf said. "If it

eradicates the mechanism of its own conductivity, how can it sustain itself?"

"We'd need something that rides just ahead of its own destruction wave," Mattox said. "Again, it's not a theoretical impossibility."

"Nobody said the concept wouldn't need considerable development work," Gilmore said.

"And trials," Euru said. His handsome face was showing a considerable amount of unease. "Don't forget that phase. We would need a sentient being to experiment on. Probably several."

"We have Couteur," Gilmore muttered. He acknowledged the Edenist's silent censure. "Sorry: natural thought. She caused us more than her fair share of trouble in court three."

"I'm sure there will be bitek neural systems adequate for the purpose," Mattox said hurriedly. "We don't have to use humans at this stage."

"Very well," Gilmore said. "Unless anyone has any objections, I'd like to prioritize this project. The First Admiral has been placing considerable pressure on us for an overall solution for some time. It'll be a relief to report we might be able to finally go on the offensive against the possessed."

Edenist habitats gossiped among themselves. The discovery first surprised, then amused Ione and Tranquillity. But then their multiplicity personalities were made up from millions of people, who like all the elderly were keen to see how their young relatives were doing and spread the word among friends. The personalities were also integral to Edenist culture, so naturally they took an avid interest in human affairs for the reaction it would ultimately have upon themselves. The minutia of political, social, and economic behaviour from the Confederation at large was absorbed, debated, and meditated upon. Knowledge was the right of all Edenists. It was just the method of passing on the more miscellaneous chunks which was delightfully quirky. Manifold sub-groups would form within every personality, with interests as varied as classical literature to xenobiology; early industrial age steam trains to Oort cloud formations. There was nothing formal, nothing ordained about such clusterings of cognate mentalities. It was, simply, the way it was. An informal anarchy.

Observing this, Tranquillity began to consider itself the equivalent of some ageing uncle overseeing a brood of unruly young cousins. Its own decorum generated a mild feeling of alienation from its contemporaries (which Ione also found amusing). Only when the full Jovian Consensus, with all its solemn nobility, arose from the gabbling minds, was there a notion of kinship.

By the time Tranquillity did arrive at Jupiter, there were literally millions of sub-groups convening within the habitat personalities to consider every possible aspect of the possession problem (essentially, Gilmore's committee to the Nth degree). Eager to participate in the search for a solution, Tranquillity contributed its memories and conclusions of the crisis to date; information which was eagerly disseminated and deliberated over. Among the groupings who surveyed all matters religious, the most interesting development was the Kiint's curiosity in the Tyrathca's Sleeping God. The question of what the Sleeping God might actually be was passed to the cosmology groupings. They didn't have much of an idea, so they queried the xenopsychology field. In turn, they wondered if the enigma would be better served by the xenocultural historians . . .

At which point, two very distinct (and in their different ways, very important) mentalities among the collective personalities became aware of the Sleeping God problem. The sub-Consensus for security and Wing-Tsit Chong together decided the matter was best dealt with by themselves and a few of their own specialists. In collaboration with Ione, of course.

Joshua had a bad feeling about Ione calling him to a conference without being told the reason. There were resonances of being asked to go after Mzu coming into play. It got worse when she told him it was to be convened in De Bouvoir Palace. That meant it was going to be formal, official.

When he arrived at the small tube station which served visitors to the Palace, Mzu was climbing the steps ahead of him. He wanted to turn round and go back to supervising *Lady Mac*'s refit. But at least this was as bad as it could possibly get. They made laboured small talk as they walked along the dark-yellow stone path to the classical building. Mzu didn't know why she'd been invited, either.

A horde of servitor chimps were scurrying about on either side of the path, along with specialist agronomy servitors. All of them were busy repairing the once immaculate parkland. Grass had been trampled into mud by thousands of dancing feet, topiary bushes were knocked into odd shapes, with bottles sticking out of unusual crevices. But it was the tomis shrubs which had taken the worst battering; with their blue and gold trumpet-shaped flowers torn from broken branches to form a brown, slippery mat across the path. The servitors were optimistically trying to repair them with adroit pruning and staking; though the smaller ones were simply being replaced. Vandalism on such a scale was unheard of in Tranquillity. Though Joshua did have to smile at the pile of clothes which the chimps had gathered up. It was mostly underwear.

A pair of serjeants were on guard duty outside the basilica's archway entrance. "The Lord of Ruin is expecting you," one intoned. It led them along the nave to the audience chamber.

Ione sat in her accustomed place behind the crescent table in the centre. Long, flat streamers of light from the towering windows intersected around her, giving her an almost saintly portrayal. Joshua was hard pressed not to comment on the theatre of the moment when she smiled a welcome, but he played the game and bowed solemnly. Mzu was given a more punctilious nod of recognition. There were six high-backed chairs set up along the convex side of the table, four of them already occupied. Joshua knew Parker Higgens; Samuel was there as well; but he had to run a search through his neural nanonics to name the Laymil project's chief astronomer, Kempster Getchell. The fourth turned to face him . . .

"You!"

"Hello, Joshua," Syrinx said. The possibility of a smile teased her lips.

"Oh," Ione murmured in a suspiciously sweet tone. "Do you two know each other?"

Joshua gave Ione a punitive look, then went over to Syrinx and gave her a light kiss on the cheek. "I heard what happened on Pernik. I'm glad you came through it all right."

She touched the medical nanonic on his hand. "I'm not the only one who's come through, apparently."

Joshua returned the smile, and sat next to her.

"There's a file I want you and Dr Mzu to review before we start," Ione told him.

The miserable scene of Coastuc-RT swamped Joshua's mind; with Waboto-YAU arguing through its translator, and the two menacing soldier-caste Tyrathca standing close to Reza Malin. He'd avoided accessing most of Kelly's recordings when Collins released them. Lalonde was one planet he didn't want to return to by any method. The close presence of the mercenary leader was a shortcut to emotions he'd rather leave dormant.

When the recording ended, he looked up to see one of the long glass windows behind Ione had darkened. Instead of emitting strong golden light, it now contained the image of an ancient Oriental man sitting in an antique wheelchair.

"Wing-Tsit Chong will speak for the Jovian Consensus today," Ione announced.

"Right," Joshua said. He loaded that name into a search program, ready to run it through his memory files.

Syrinx lent across. "The founder of Edenism," she said softly. "Quite a major historical figure, in fact."

"Name the inventor of the ZTT drive," Joshua retorted.

"Julian Wan normally gets the credit. Although technically he was only the head of the New Kong asteroid's stardrive research team; a bureaucrat, basically."

Joshua frowned in pique.

"Possibly the present would provide us with a more suitable topic for discussion," Wing-Tsit Chong chided gently.

"The Sleeping God throws up a number of questions," Ione said. "Very relevant questions, given the Tyrathca's psychology. They believed it would be able to help them against possessed humans. And they don't lie."

"So far this entity or object has made no appreciable impact upon our situation," Wing-Tsit Chong said. "Implying three options. It is a myth, and the Tyrathca were either fooled or mistaken by their encounter with it. It is not capable of assisting them. Or it does exist, it is capable, and it has simply restrained itself, so far."

"That third implication is the most interesting," Kempster said. "It's an assumption that the Sleeping God is sentient, or at lest self-aware; which rules out a celestial event."

"I always concurred with the artefact possibility myself," Parker Higgens said. "The arkship Tyrathca would surely recognize a celestial event for what it was. And celestial events don't keep watch. Waboto-YAU was quite insistent about that. The Sleeping God dreams of the universe, it knows everything."

"I concur," Wing-Tsit Chong said. "This entity has been assigned extraordinary perceptive powers by the Tyrathca. Although we can assume the memories of Sireth-AFL's family would become open to degradation down the centuries, the major elements must retain their integrity. Something very unusual is out there."

"Have you asked the Kiint direct what it is, and what their interest is?" Joshua asked.

"Yes. They claim a total lack of knowledge on the subject. Ambassador Armira simply repeats Lieria's claim that they are interested in the full record of Kelly Tirrel's sojourn on Lalonde so they might understand the nature of human possession."

"They might be telling the truth."

"No," Parker Higgens said forcefully. "Not them. They've been lying to us since first contact. This is more than coincidence. The Kiint are desperately interested. And I'd love to beat them to it."

"A race that can teleport?" Joshua said light heartedly. The old director's vehemence was out of character here.

"Even if the Kiint aren't interested," Ione said swiftly, "we certainly are. The Tyrathca believe it to be real and able to assist them. That alone justifies sending a mission to it."

"Wait—" Joshua said. He couldn't believe he'd been so slow. "You want me to go after it, don't you?"

"That's why you're here," Ione answered calmly. "I believe you said you wanted to make a contribution?"

"Yes, I did." There was a residue of reluctance in the acknowledgement. Some of the old bravado. *I want to originate the solution. Claim all the glory. Shades of the good old days.*

He grinned at Ione, wondering if she'd guessed what he was thinking. More than likely. But if there was a chance this xenoc God might have an answer, he wanted in. He owed a lot of people the effort. His dead crew. His unborn child. Louise and the rest of Norfolk. Even himself, now he refused to avoid thinking of death and the mysteries that inaugurated. Facing up to fate in such a fashion might be frightening, but it made living a hell of a lot easier. And, to be honest with himself, so did the prospect of flying again.

"And so, I believe, did Syrinx," Ione said. The voidhawk captain nodded admission.

"The Kiint stonewalled you, huh?" Joshua asked.

"Malva was very polite about it, but essentially, yes."

Joshua settled back, gazing up at the domed ceiling. "Let me see. If a Tyrathca arkship encountered this God, then it has to be a long way off, a very long way. Not too much problem for a voidhawk, but . . . ah, now I get it. The antimatter." *Lady Mac*'s inclusion was obvious now. Her delta-V reserve was currently five or six times greater than most Adamist warships, making her an obvious candidate to surmount the problem of galactic orbital mechanics. For starships, there's a lot more than just distance to the gulf between stars. Ultimately, it is velocity which governs their design and finances.

Earth's sun orbits the galactic centre roughly once every two hundred and thirty million years, giving it an approximate velocity of two hundred and twenty kilometres per second relative to the core. Other stars, of course, have different orbital velocities, depending on their distance from the core, so their velocities relative to each other are also different. Voidhawks can cope with the variance by tailoring their wormhole terminus to match a local star's vector. It's a manoeuvre which uses up an inconvenient amount of energy from the patterning cells; however, because they obtain their energy for free it doesn't affect their commercial performance except in terms of recharging time. But for Adamist starship captains, that variance isn't merely inconvenient, it's a positive bane. The ZTT jump might provide a short cut across the interstellar gulf, but it cannot magically change inertia. A starship emerging from a jump has precisely the same vector it had when it started. In order to rendezvous with the planet or asteroid at its destination, its delta-V has to be altered to match. It's a tedious process which uses up plenty of fuel; in other words, it costs money. And the further the stars are away from each other, the greater the velocity difference. For most Adamist starships, a flight right across the longest axis of Confederation space, a distance approaching nine hundred light-years, would use up over ninety per cent of their reaction drive fuel. Several marques would be incapable of the feat anyway. The limit is imposed because they all used fusion drives.

Antimatter, of course, provided a vastly superior delta-V. And the antimatter *Lady Mac* had taken on board from the *Beezling* was still in her confinement chambers. The First Admiral had given Samuel instructions for the secure military facilities at Jupiter to dispose of it. One of the five specialist ships qualified to handle the substance was still en route to Tranquillity.

"There is a high possibility that a long flight will be required to bring this task to a fruitful conclusion," Wing-Tsit Chong said. "I congratulate you on your clarity of thought, young Joshua."

Syrinx and Ione swapped a glance. "You're going to let him use antimatter?" Mzu asked in surprise.

"A voidhawk and Adamist starship are a good pairing for this kind of assignment," Syrinx said. "Both of us have strengths and weaknesses which complement the other. Providing the Adamist ship can manage to keep up with a voidhawk, of course."

"Outperform, or outsmart?" Joshua asked civilly.

"All right," Mzu said. "So why am I here?"

"We believed you might be able to help us analyse the nature of the Sleeping God," Kempster Getchell said. "Especially if it turns out to be a high-technology weapon rather than a natural phenomenon, which is my field."

Alkad glanced round at their faces, depressed when she knew she should have been flattered. "I had one idea," she said. "Once. Thirty years ago."

"One original insight," Wing-Tsit Chong said. "Which is one more than most people have had, or ever will have. You have a mind which is capable of it. An ability which can innovate on such a level is an asset we cannot overlook."

"What about Foulkes?" Alkad asked Samuel.

"If you agree to participate, I'll speak with her. The non-contact prohibition placed upon you does not apply in this situation. You will be permitted to fly on this mission. However, I will accompany you along with Monica."

"I'm flattered."

"Don't be. And please don't interpret our continued presence with approval for what you did. It so happens, that there are sections of this mission which require the kind of ability which Monica and I specialise in."

"How very enigmatic. Very well, if you think I'm the right person for the job, I'd be honoured to take part."

"Good," Ione said.

"But I'll need Peter with me."

"This isn't a honeymoon cruise," Samuel told her, reproachfully.

"We worked as a team putting the Alchemist together. It's a synergistic relationship."

"Somehow, I doubt that," Ione said. "But for argument's sake, I'll permit you to ask him if he wants to accompany you."

"So where were you thinking of sending us?" Joshua asked.

"Regretfully, you will have to go directly to the source," Wing-Tsit Chong said. "Which is one of the reasons this mission is being assembled under the auspices of the Jovian security sub-Consensus. A thorough search of xenology records both at Jupiter and Earth have revealed absolutely no reference to the Sleeping God. The Tyrathca have never mentioned it to us before."

"The source? Oh Jesus, you mean Hesperi-LN, the Tyrathca home planet?"

"Initially, yes. Waboto-YAU told us that it was another arkship which encountered the Sleeping God, not Tanjuntic-RI. Therefore, that arkship must have lasered the information to all the other Tyrathca arkships in the exodus fleet. We must hope that a recording of that message is still aboard Tanjuntic-RI. If you can find it, you may be able to establish the approximate location of the encounter."

"That could be a long way off," Joshua said. His neural nanonics started to access almanac and Tyrathca history files from memory cells, running them through a navigation program. The result rising into his mind in the form of gold and scarlet icons was both fascinating and alarming. "Hesperi-LN isn't their genuine home planet, remember. It's just the last colony world Tanjuntic-RI founded. Look, the original Tyrathca star, Mastrit-PJ, the one they escaped from is on the other side of the Orion Nebula. That puts it *at least* 1,600 light-years away. Now if we get real unlucky, and the arkship which found the Sleeping God was going in the opposite direction to Tanjuntic-RI, you're talking twice as far."

"We are aware of that," Wing-Tsit Chong said.

Joshua sighed with indubitable regret. To take *Lady Mac* on such a voyage would have been awesome. "I'm sorry, there isn't that much antimatter left. I can't take the old girl that far."

"We are aware of your starship's performance capabilities," Wing-Tsit Chong said. "However there is a supply of antimatter which you will be able to use."

"You keep some here at Jupiter?" Joshua asked in what he figured was a casual voice.

"No," Syrinx said. "A CNIS agent called Erick Thakara located a production station which may be supplying Capone."

"Thakara—" Joshua's search program located the appropriate file; he locked eyes with Ione. "Really? That's . . . helpful."

"With the 1st fleet somewhat overstretched, the First Admiral's staff have asked for Jupiter's voidhawks to tackle it," Samuel said.

"Which they are preparing to do," Wing-Tsit Chong said. "However, before the station is finally annihilated, you will be able to take on board as much antimatter as the *Lady Macbeth*'s confinement systems can handle."

"Three thousand light-years," Joshua murmured. "Jesus."

"Meredith Saldana's task force has a large contingent of Confederation Navy marines assigned to it," Ione said. "They'll secure the station for you once the personnel surrender to the voidhawk squadron."

"What if the station operatives just suicide?" Joshua said. "They usually do when the Navy confronts them."

"And take as many of us with them as they can," Syrinx whispered.

"They will be offered a penal planet sentence instead of the usual death penalty," Samuel said. "We can only hope that proves attractive enough to them."

"All right, but even if we load *Lady Mac* with enough antimatter, the Tyrathca have ended communications with the Confederation," Joshua said. "Do you really think they'll allow us to search through Tanjuntic-RI's electronic systems?"

"Probably not," Samuel said. "But as we don't intend to ask their permission, it doesn't really matter, does it?"

7

You didn't have to be attuned to the land like a possessed to know it was about to happen. Most of Ombey's population was aware the time had come.

Day after day the news companies had been broadcasting sensevises from rover reporters covering the build up of Liberation forces. Everybody knew somebody who was connected to somebody who was involved in some way; from hauling equipment out to Fort Forward to serving drinks to Edenists in spaceport bars. Speculation on the current affairs programmes was deliberately vague about specific dates and precise numbers, even the communication net gossips were showing restraint in naming the day. Hearsay aside, the evidence was pretty solid.

The type of cargoes raining down on the planet had changed. Combat gear was slowly being replaced by heavy-duty civil engineering equipment, ready to repair the expected damage to Mortonridge and provide additional support infrastructure for the occupying forces. The personnel arriving at Fort Forward were also subject to a shift in professions. Just under a million serjeants had been sent from Jupiter, along with nearly a quarter of a million marines and mercenaries from across the Confederation. The Liberation army was essentially complete. So now it was the medical teams being ferried down from orbit, civilian volunteers complementing entire mobile military hospitals. Estimated casualty figures (both military and civilian) were strictly classified. But everyone knew the twelve thousand medical staff were going to suffer a heavy workload. Eighty voidhawks had already been assigned evac duties, spreading the wounded around facilities in the Kingdom and its allies.

Throughout the seventh day following Princess Kirsten's visit, Ralph Hiltch and his command staff studied the figures and displays provided by the AI. The neuroiconic image which accumulated in his mind kept expanding as more information was correlated. By late afternoon, his conscious perception point seemed to be hanging below a supergalaxy of multicoloured stars, which threatened to make him giddy as he tried to examine it in all directions at once. Despite its coherence, what he really wanted was more training time, more transport, more supplies, and definitely more intelligence assessments of the terrain ahead. But essentially, his army was as ready as it would ever be. He gave the order for final stage deployment to begin.

Over half of the serjeants and their back-up brigades had already left Fort Forward. The previous two days had been spent mustering at their preliminary positions offshore. Nearly a hundred islands around Mortonridge's coast had been taken over as temporary depots; from reefs which barely showed above the waves to resort atolls dotted with luxury hotels. Where there were no convenient scraps of land, huge cargo ships had been hurriedly converted into floating docks, and anchored thirty kilometres from the shore.

For the first stage of the coastal assault, the army was

scheduled to use boats. They were actually going to storm ashore, wading through the waves and up onto the sand, almost in homage to a great many of the incarnations from the past they were facing. Ralph wasn't prepared to risk flying even the simplest of aircraft into the energistic environment over Mortonridge, not until after they'd dealt with the red cloud at least.

The remainder of the Liberation ground forces emptied out of Fort Forward in massive convoys, spreading out along the firebreak in thousands of multi-terrain vehicles. There was no attempt at secrecy, no hugging the cover behind ridges and hills. The squads drove through the encroaching twilight and into the night; the nimbus of their massed headlight beams creeping like an anaemic dawn along the horizon paralleling the firebreak.

Across Xingu, a civil curfew order was enacted once again, with the police put on full alert. Although they were fairly sure no possessed were left outside Mortonridge, the continent's authorities were taking Annette Ekelund's threat of sabotage very seriously. When dawn arrived, no civilian would be allowed out onto the streets. People grumbled and groaned, and datavised protests to local news shows, remembering what a nuisance the curfew had been last time. It was almost a bravado show of defiance. In the main, they just settled back and accessed the show.

High above the planet, the Strategic Defence centre on Guyana began coordinating the Royal Navy's part of the assault. Thrusters flared on low orbit weapons platforms, refining their new orbits. A flotilla of three hundred voidhawks also began to accelerate, synchronizing their distortion fields to rise away from the planet in a long curve.

The psychic pressure mounting against Mortonridge shifted from faint intimation to blatantly unmistakable.

*

To casual observation, Chainbridge was still a busy town. When Annette Ekelund reached a slight ridge a couple of kilometres from the outskirts, she stopped the sturdy country rover she was driving and looked back over her shoulder. Hundreds of lighted windows shone out across the lame farmland, burning steady against the flickering crimson waves scattered down from the lumbering cloud roof. The buildings were warm, too, warm enough to fool any perfunctory sensor scans into believing they were occupied. But no one was left there, her command group was the last to leave.

"It'll keep the blighters tied up for a while," Delvan assured her. He was sitting in the passenger seat beside her, clad in his old khaki uniform, a discreet row of scarlet and gold ribbons on his chest.

In the back seat, Soi Hon veiled a sneer. He, too, had reverted to type: dark jungle fatigues and a felt bush-ranger hat. "For at least a quarter of an hour."

"Would you like to return to the beyond fifteen minutes early?" Delvan enquired lightly.

"Any time we delay them is good time," Annette told the pair of them. She took the brake off, and accelerated down the secondary road. They were heading for Cold Overton, a small village eighty kilometres away. Their field command centre; picked virtually at random by Soi Hon, central but not strategically so, adequate road links, surrounded by thick forest. It was as good as any, not that they'd be staying long. Fluid tactics was the key to this campaign.

Soi Hon clapped Delvan on the shoulder. "And this is our time, eh? You and I both. Onward to death and glory."

"There is no glory here." Delvan spoke so quietly, the others could only just hear him against the bass grumble of thunder.

"Don't tell me you're having second thoughts?"

"I heard my men wailing at night," the old soldier replied emotionlessly. "The ones left out in No Man's Land, left behind to drown in puddles of their own blood; the ones that weren't vomiting their lungs up from that devilish gas. Screaming for us to help them, more frightened at being alone than they were of being shot."

"You Christians, you always take life so personally. We're here by accident, not design. Nothing is ordained, you are only what you make of yourself. You can never go back, the past doesn't change. Stop thinking about it. The only part of history which matters is the future."

"It broke my heart, not being able to help them. Good, decent men; boys a lot of them. I swore I'd never get involved in such madness again. They called it total war. But it wasn't, it was total bloody murder. Insanity had become a disease, and we all caught it. Twice in my lifetime my nation sent its youth out to die for a just cause, to protect ourselves and our way of life." He smiled frigidly at the eco warrior. "And now here I am once again. Seven bloody centuries later. Seven hundred years, and nothing has changed. Not one damn thing. I'm fighting to preserve myself and my new life. A righteous war with me on the side of the angels, even though they've become fallen angels. And I can already hear the screams, God help me."

"All I hear is our victory song," Soi Hon said. "The voice of the land is louder and stronger than any human cry. This is our place, we are at one with it. We belong here. We have a right to exist in this universe."

Delvan closed his eyes and tipped his head back. "Lord forgive me I am such a fool. Here we all are, embarking on a crusade to storm the very gates of Heaven Itself in our desperation. What a monumental folly. I shall smite at the dark angels massed against us, crying for death, for only in

death will we ever find peace. Yet You have already revealed that death is not our destiny, nor ever can be."

"Wake up, old man. We're not fighting God, we're fighting an unjust universe."

For the first time since his return from the beyond, Delvan smiled. "You think there's a difference?"

The island was enchanting, its botany and geology combining into the kind of synergistic idyll which was the grail of
Edenist habitat designers. Inland, there were craggy rocks
hosting long white waterfalls, and thick lush forests choked
with sweet-scented flowers. The shore comprised cove after
cove, their pale gold sands gleaming under the azure sky;
except for one, where the offshore reef crumbled under the
foaming breakers to give the sands an exquisite fairydust
coating of pink coral. It appealed to humans on a primal
level, urging them to slow down and spend time just soaking in nature. As a reward for their worship, time itself
would expand and become almost meaningless.

Even in his current existence, Sinon wished he was staying longer than their eighteen-hour stopover. Five thousand
serjeants had descended on this tiny jewel of land glinting
in the ocean, along with their equipment and support personnel. Marines were camped ten to a room in the resort hotels; gardens and tennis courts had been requisitioned as
landing pads; and the coves were harbours for a hundred of
the regiment's landing boats. All day, the boats had taken
their turn to nuzzle the shore, extending their forward
ramps so that jeeps and light trucks could drive on board.
Now, in the evening, the serjeants were finally embarking.

Syrinx would like this place, Sinon told Choma. **I
must tell her about it.** He was two thirds of the way along
a line of serjeants who were wading out to their landing
boat. There wasn't enough room on this particular beach to

berth more than three boats at a time, so the other eleven
were anchored a hundred metres offshore. A column of serjeants snaked out to each one, making slow time through
the water. The big constructs were laden with backpacks,
carrying their weapons above their heads to stop them getting wet. Groups of Royal Marines milled about on the
bluff, watching the process. If all went well, they'd be
doing the same thing next morning.

Now there's good healthy optimism, Choma replied.

What do you mean?

**I've been working out our probable casualty rate.
Would you like to know how many of our squad are
likely to survive the entire campaign?**

**Not particularly. I have no intention of becoming a
statistic.**

**Where have I heard that before? In any case, it's
two. Two out of ten.**

Thank you very much. Sinon reached the landing boat.
It was an ugly, rugged affair, one design serving the entire
Liberation armada. A carbosilicon hull mass produced over
on Esparta, with power cells and an engine that could have
come from any of a dozen industrialized star systems allied
to the Kingdom. Hard-pressed navy engineers had plugged
the standard components together, completing several hundred each day. The three on the beach were still being
worked on by technicians.

Honesty is supposed to be our culture's strength,
Choma said, mildly irked by the negative reaction.

We're a long way from Eden now. Sinon slung his rifle
high on his shoulder, and started climbing the ladder up the
side of the boat. When he reached the top of the gunnel he
looked back to shore. The sun was sinking into the sea,
leaving a rosy haze line above the darkening water. Parody-

ing that, on the opposite horizon, the glow of the red cloud was visible, a narrow fracture separating water and air.

Last chance, Sinon told himself. The other serjeants were all climbing down into the boat, their mind-tones subdued but still resolute. Rationally, he was buying the Confederation time to find a genuine answer. And Consensus itself had approved this course of action. He swung his legs over the rail, and put a hand down to help Choma. **Come on, let's go storm the Dark Lord's citadel.**

The Royal Marine ion field flyer was a lone spark of gold shimmering high in the night sky, brighter than any star. It flew across the top of the Mortonridge peninsula, keeping parallel to the firebreak, twenty-five kilometres to the north, and holding a steady fifteen kilometre altitude.

Ralph Hiltch sat in the flyer's cabin as Cathal Fitzgerald piloted them above the northern end of the mountain range which formed the peninsula's spine. Eight hours of neural nanonics enforced sleep had left him feeling fresh, but emotionally dead. His mind had woken immune to the human consequences of the Liberation. Whether it was numb from the torrent of information which had been bullying his brain for weeks, or guilty at the enormity of what he'd organized, he wasn't sure.

It meant that now he was hooked into the flyer's sensor suite, he could view the last stages of the deployment with god-like dispassion. Which was probably for the best, he thought. Accepting personal responsibility for every casualty would drive anyone insane within the first two minutes. Even so, he'd wanted this one last overview. To convince himself it was genuine if nothing else. The last insecurity, that all the data and images he'd handled had been transformed to physical reality.

There could be doubt. The army spread out below him,

his army, was flowing over the black land in streamers of fluid light, bending and curling round hills and valleys. Individual vehicles expressed as twinkles of light, barely different to icons blipping their way across a map. Except here there was no colour, just the white headlight beams contrasting the funeral ground.

It was after midnight, and two-thirds of the ground deployment was complete. Both flanks were established, now there was only the centre to set up, the most difficult aspect. His main spearhead was going to drive right along the M6, allowing the huge supply and back-up convoys an easy ride. Using the motorway was a disturbingly obvious strategy, but essential if they were to complete in a minimum timescale.

Ekelund would have sabotaged the road, but bridges could be repaired, blockades shunted aside, and gorges filled. The combat engineering corps were ready for that. At least the possessed didn't have air power. Though occasionally he had images of propeller biplanes roaring overhead and strafing the jeeps. Victory rolls with the pilot's white silk scarf flapping jauntily in the slipstream. Stupid.

Ralph switched the suite's focus to the red cloud. Its edges were still arched down to the ground, sealing the peninsula away from the rest of the planet. Dusky random wave shadows rolled across the pulpy surface. He thought they might be more restless than usual, though that could well be his imagination. Thankfully, there was no sign of that peculiar oval formation which he'd seen once before. The one he absolutely refused to call an eye. All he really wanted was one glimpse through; to reassure himself the peninsula was still there, if nothing else. They'd had no data of any kind from inside since the day Ekelund had brought the cloud down. No links with the net could be established; no non-possessed had managed to sneak out. A final sweep with the flyer's sensors revealed nothing new.

"Take us back," he told Cathal.

The flyer performed a fast turn, curving round to line up on Fort Forward. Ahead of it, the giant Thunderbirds continued to swoop down out of the western sky, delta heat-shields glowing a dull vermilion against the starfield backdrop. That aspect of the build up, at least, remained unchanged. Cathal landed them inside the secure command complex, along the southern side of the new city. Ralph trotted down the airstair, ignoring the armed Marine escort which fell in around him. The trappings of his position had ceased to register as special some time ago, just another aspect of this extraordinary event.

Brigadier Palmer (the first person Ralph had promoted) was waiting outside the door to the Ops Room. "Well?" she asked, as they walked in.

"I didn't see anyone waving a white flag."

"We'd know if they wanted to." Like a lot of people involved with the Liberation, especially those who'd been on Mortonridge since the start, she considered herself to have a connection with the possessed hidden behind the red cloud, an awareness of attitude. Ralph wasn't convinced, although he acknowledged the possessed exerted some kind of psychic presence.

The Ops Room was a long rectangular chamber with glass walls separating it from innumerable specialist planning offices. Completing electronic systems integration and connecting their architecture with Ombey's military communication circuits was another triumph for the overworked Royal Marine engineering corps, though its rushed nature was evident in the bundled cables hanging between consoles and open ceiling panels, air conditioning which was too chilly, and raw carbon-concrete corner pillars. Its floor-space was taken up by cheap corporate-style desks holding consoles, AV projectors, and communication gear. Right now, it was full to capacity; over fifty officers from the Royal Navy were collaborating with an equal number of Edenists; the next largest contingent was the Confederation Navy with twenty; while the remainder were drawn from various participating allies.

They were going to be the coordinators of the Liberation, the human analysis and liaison between the ground forces and the controlling AI back in Pasto. A failsafe against the maxim: No battle plan survives contact with the enemy. Every one of them stood up as Ralph Hiltch entered. That, he did notice. Together they had spent the past few weeks planning this together, arguing, pleading, contributing ideas, working miracles. They'd learned to cooperate and coordinate their fields of expertise, putting aside old quarrels so they melded into a unified, dedicated team. He was proud of them and what they'd accomplished.

Their show of respect rekindled several of his suppressed emotions. "I'll keep this short," he told the hushed chamber. "We can't pretend this is going to solve the problem possession poses to the Confederation, but it's a damn sight more important than a propaganda war, which is what some reporters have been calling it. We're fighting to free two million people, and we're battling to bring hope into the lives of an awful lot more. To me, that's more than worthwhile, it's essential. So let's make our contribution a good one."

Amid scattered applause, he made his way to his office at the far end. His desk gave him a view down the whole length of the Ops Room, providing he craned his neck over the stack of processor block peripherals connected to his main desktop console. While he was datavising the array for strategic updates, his executive command group joined

him. As well as Janne Palmer who was the Chief of the occupying forces, there was Acacia, the Edenist liaison, an elderly woman who had served as ambassador to Ombey for
five years. He'd also drafted in Diana Tiernan to act as the
army's technical advisor, helping to filter the scientific reports on the possessed which were flooding in from across
the Confederation. Cathal completed the gathering, still
holding his post as Ralph's assistant, but now with the rank
of lieutenant commander.

When the glass door slid shut, isolating them from the
noise from outside, Ralph requested a security level one
sensenviron conference. Princess Kirsten and Admiral Farquar joined them around the white bubble room's table.
"The deployment's going remarkably well," Ralph said.
"All our principal front line divisions will be in place at
zero-hour."

"My occupation troops are effectively ready," Janne said.
"There are a few minor hitches, mostly logistical. But given
the amount of materiel involved, and the different groupings we're attempting to coordinate, I'm happy. We're well
within estimated parameters. The AI should have the bugs
knocked out by morning."

"The serjeants are also ready," Acacia reported. "Again,
there are some hitches, mainly with transport equipment,
but we are committed."

"Admiral Farquar?" Kirsten asked.

"All space based assets are functional. Platform orbits
are synchronized, and the voidhawks are reaching apogee.
It looks good."

"Very well," Kirsten said. "God help me for this, but
they've left us with no alternative. General Hiltch, you now
have full command authority for Ombey's military forces.
Engage the enemy, Ralph, evict them from my planet."

*

Standard military doctrine was, somewhat inevitably, fairly unimaginative. Every kind of tactic and counter-tactic had been attempted, practised, and refined by generals, warlords, and emperors down the centuries until there was little room for mistake. So even though Mortonridge was unique from a philosophical standpoint, it could be defined in military terms as a large scale hostage/siege scenario. Given that assessment, the method of resolving it was clear cut.

Ralph wanted to isolate the possessed in small groups. They were vulnerable like that, capable of being overwhelmed. To achieve it, their communications should be broken, denying them the ability to regroup and mount any kind of counter-attack. Harassment should be constant, wearing them down. And, if possible, he wanted them deprived of the cover provided by their red cloud. In summary: divide and conquer. An ancient principle, but now aided by the kind of firepower which only modern technology could provide.

Ombey had four and a half thousand low orbit Strategic Defence platforms. Their orbital vectors were orchestrated to provide a constant barrier above the surface, similar to the way electrons pirouetted around their nucleus. For the Liberation, all that had changed. Navy starships had taken over the low orbit protection duty, leaving the platforms free for an altogether different task. Their elaborate inclinations had been shifted, ion thrusters firing for hours at a time to clump them into flocks of twenty-five. Now they formed a single chain around the planet, with an inclination tilted at just a couple of degrees to the equator. One flock would pass over Mortonridge every thirty seconds.

Sensor satellites had been manoeuvred into the gaps between the platforms, ready to provide the Liberation Forces with an unparalleled coverage of the peninsula once the red cloud had been broken apart. Admiral Farquar used them to watch the dawn terminator sliding over the ocean towards the lowering band of red cloud. Tactical overlays showed him the positions of the landing boats heading in for the beaches. Far overhead, the flotilla of voidhawks had passed apogee, and were now hurtling downwards, accelerating at eight gees.

In one hour, dawn would reach Mortonridge's eastern seaboard. The Admiral datavised his command authority code to Guyana's SD control centre. "Fire," he ordered.

Though they never knew it, the Liberation forces very nearly won in the first ninety seconds. The initial flock of SD platforms sent seventy-five electron beams slamming down through the upper atmosphere to strike the red cloud. They were aimed along the north/south axis of the peninsula, and defocused, so that at the point of impact they were over fifty metres across. The intention wasn't to pierce the red cloud, just to pump it full of electrical energy, the possessed's one known Achilles Heel. Each beam began scanning from side to side, in gigantic ten second sweeps that took them from coast to coast.

Then the second flock of platforms slid up over the horizon and into range. Another seventy-five beams speared down. There was a ten second overlap before the first flock was out of range.

Annette Ekelund let out a single shriek of agony, and dropped helplessly to her knees. The pain was incredible. A shaft of blue-star sunlight flung down from a height greater than heaven lanced clean through her skull. It didn't just burn her stolen brain, it set fire to her very thoughts. That part of her spirit which communed so gladly with the others on Mortonridge was the treacherous conductor. The part which created the shield of cloud and gave them all a subliminal sense of community. Her belief in whatever humanity has survived the incarceration of the beyond. And now it was killing her.

She abandoned it in its entirety. Her scream twisting from pain to wretchedness. All around her, the other souls were shrinking away from each other, withdrawing into self. The last sob burbled out from her lips, and she flopped limply onto her back. Her body was freezing, shaking in shock. Delvan and Soi Hon were scrabbling in the dirt somewhere nearby, she could hear their whimpers. She couldn't see either of them, the world had gone completely black.

Every possessed across the Confederation was instantly aware of the strike. Pain and shock reverberated through the beyond. Wherever they were, whatever they were doing, they felt it.

Al Capone was underneath Jezzibella when it happened, adopting a complicated position so that her breasts were pushed into his face while he could still bend his knees for the leverage to give her a damn good shafting. Her laugh was halfway between a giggle and a moan when the mental impact knocked him with the force of a wild hockey puck. He convulsed, shouting in pained panic.

Jezzibella cried out as his frantic motion twisted her arm, nearly dislocating her shoulder. "Al! Fuck. That fucking hurts, you fucking dickhead. I told you I don't do that sado shit, fuck you."

Al grunted in confused dismay, shaking his head to clear the weird dizziness foaming inside. He was so disoriented, he fell off the side of the bed.

For the first time, Jezzibella actually caught a glimpse of

Brad Lovegrove's natural features beneath the illusion. Not too different to Al, they could almost be brothers. Her anger faded at the sight of him grimacing, limbs twitching in disarray. "Al?"

"Fuck," he gasped. "What the fuck was that?"

"Al, you okay, baby? What happened?"

"God damn! I don't know." He looked round the bedroom, expecting to see some kind of bomb damage, G-men storming through the door. . . . "I ain't got a clue."

For Jacqueline Couteur the invisible shockwave almost proved fatal. Strapped onto the examination table in the demon trap she couldn't move when her muscles spasmed. Her vital signs monitor alerted the staff to some kind of seizure, at which point her conscious defence against the electric current they were shunting through her body began to crumble. Fortunately, one of the more alert team members shut the power off before she was genuinely electrocuted. It took her five or six minutes to recover her normal antagonism, and prowess.

On patrol a million kilometres above New California, Rocio Condra lost control of the distortion field, letting it flare and contract wildly. The big hellhawk tumbled crazily, its bird-form imploding in a cloud of dark scintillations. Gravity inside the life-support cabin vanished along with the quaint steamship interior. Jed, Beth, Gerald and the three kids suddenly found themselves in freefall. Then gravity returned in a rush, far too strong, and in the wrong direction, making one of the bulkhead walls the floor. The surface swatted them hard, then the gravity failed again to send them flying across the cabin in a tangle of limbs and screams. Stars gyrated savagely beyond the viewport. Another wash of gravity sucked them down onto the ceiling.

In Quinn Dexter's case, it was his first setback on Earth. He had just arrived at Grand Central Station to take a vac-train to Paris. Not the original station building on Manhattan, the island itself was actually abandoned and flooded, but New Yorkers were sentimental about such things. This was the third such edifice to carry the name. Buried nearly a kilometre below the centre of dome five, it formed the hub of the arcology's intercontinental train network.

Once more he had secluded himself within the ghost realm to avoid any risk of detection. That was when he began to notice just how many ghosts haunted the station and other subterranean sections of the vast arcology. Hundreds of them drifted mournfully amid the unseeing streams of commuters. They were drab despondent figures, staring round at the faces that rushed past. There was so much longing and desperation in their expressions, as if every one of them was searching for some long lost child. They were aware of Quinn, gazing at him in bewilderment as he strode through the main concourse on his way to the platforms. In turn, he ignored them, worthless creatures incapable of either aiding or hindering his crusade. They really were as good as dead.

He was twenty metres short of the wave elevator for platform fifty-two when the flashback from the Liberation reached him. The impact wasn't actually too great, he'd withstood far worse at Banneth's hands, it was the suddenness of it all which shocked him. Without warning he was yelling as streaks of pain flared out from the centre of his brain to infect his body. Edmund Rigby's captive thoughts writhed in agony, transfixed by the blast of torment.

Quinn panicked, frightened by the unknown. Until this moment he believed he was virtually omnipotent. Now some witchery was attacking him in a method he couldn't fathom. Souls in the beyond were screaming in terror. The ghosts around him began wailing, clasping their hands together in prayer. His control over the energistic power faltered as his thoughts dissolved into chaos.

Bud Johnson never saw where the guy came from. One second he was hurrying to the wave elevator, on his way to catch a San Antonio connection—the next, some man in a weird black robe was kneeling on all fours on the polished marble floor at his feet. That was almost impossible, everyone who grew up on Earth and lived in the arcologies had an instinctive awareness of crowds, the illogical tides and currents of bodies which flowed through them. He always knew where people were in relation to himself, alert to any possible collision. Nobody could just *appear*.

Bud's momentum kept his torso going forwards, while his legs were completely blocked. He went flying, pivoting over the man's back to crash onto the cool marble. His wrist made a nasty snapping sound, firing hot pain up his arm. And his neural nanonics did nothing. Nothing! There was no axon blocks, no medical display. Bud let out a howl of pain, blinking back tears as he looked up.

Those tears might have accounted for two or three of the curious faces peering down at him. Pale and distressed, wearing extremely odd hats. When he blinked the salty fluid clear, they'd gone. He clutched at his injured wrist. "Sheesh, dear God, that hurts." A murmur of surprise rattled over his head, a strong contrast to the screams breaking out across the rest of the station. No one seemed particularly concerned about him.

"Hey, my neural nanonics have failed. Someone call me a medic. I think my wrist's broken."

The man he'd fallen over was now rising to his feet. Bud was acutely conscious of the silence that had closed around him, of people backing away. When he looked up, any thoughts of shouting curses on the clumsy oaf vanished instantly. There was a face inside the large hood, barely visible. Bud was suddenly very thankful for the robe's shadows. The expression of fury and malice projected by the features he could see was quite bad enough. "Sorry," he whispered.

Fingers closed around his heart. He could actually feel them, individual joints hinging inwards, fingernails digging into his atriums. The hand twisted savagely. Bud choked silently, his arms flapping wildly. He was just aware of people closing in on him again. This time, they registered concern. Too late, he tried to tell them, far too late. The aloof devil turned casually and faded from his sight. Then so did the rest of the world.

Quinn observed Bud's soul snake away from his corpse, vanishing into the beyond, adding his screams to the beseeching myriad. There was a big commotion all around, people shoving and jostling to get a good view of whatever was going down. Only a couple of them had gasped as he returned himself to the ghost realm, fading out right in front of them. At least he'd retained enough composure not to use the white fire. Not that it mattered now. He'd been seen, and not just by people with glitched neural nanonics; the station's security sensors would have captured the event.

Govcentral knew he was here.

Tucked down in the central hold of the landing boat, Sinon couldn't physically see the rest of the squadron closing on the shore. Affinity made it unnecessary; all the Edenist minds on and orbiting Ombey were linked together, providing him with more information than General Hiltch had available. He was aware of his personal position, as well as that of his comrades, even the Liberation's overall situation was available to him. The voidhawk flotilla revealed the red cloud beneath them. Huge lightning bolts were writhing across the upper surface as the SD platforms continued their electron barrage. At the centre, along the spine of hills, the glow was fading, allowing pools of darkness to ripple outward.

Along with all the other serjeants, Sinon craned forwards for a look. The barrier of red cloud had grown steadily through the night as the boats headed in for the beach. From ten kilometres offshore, it stretched right across the water, solid and resolute like the wall at the end of the world.

Small flickers of lightning arose to dance along the bottom, slashing down into the waves. Steam plumes screwed upwards from the discharges. Then the lightning streamers were coming together into massive dazzling rivers, rising up, following the steep curve of the cloud to arch inland. The red glow faded, taking less then five seconds to die completely. Its disappearance startled Sinon and the other serjeants. The victory was too sudden. This was not the epic struggle they'd been preparing for. The crawling webs of lightning more than made up for the absence; blazing bright right across the horizon.

You know, that is actually a very big cloud, Sinon said. The brilliant flashes were near-continuous now, keeping the dark mass illuminated prominently.

You noticed that, Choma retorted.

Yes. Which could be a problem. It was rather nicely contained while the possessed were using it as a shield. As such, we tended to disregard its physical properties; it was, after all, primarily a psychological barrier.

Psychological or not, we can't cruise straight through with all that electrical activity.

Choma wasn't the only one to reach that conclusion. They could already feel the boat slowing as the captain reduced power to the engines. A precaution repeated simultaneously by the entire armada.

*

"Recommendations?" Ralph asked.

"Shut down the SD assault," Acacia said. "The landing boats are already slowing. They can't penetrate that kind of lightning storm."

"Diana?"

"I think so. If the red light is an indication of the possessed's control, then we've already routed them."

"That's a very big if," Admiral Farquar protested.

"We don't have a lot of choice," the elderly technology advisor said. "The landing boats clearly can't get through, nor can the ground vehicles, for that matter. We have to let the energy discharge itself naturally. If the red light returns when they're inside, we can resume the electron beam attack until the cloud itself starts to break up."

"Do it," Ralph ordered. "Acacia, get the serjeants as close as they can to the cloud, then as soon as the lightning's finished, I want them through."

"Yes, General."

"Diana, how long is it going to take to dissipate that electricity?"

"A good question. We're not sure how deep or dense that cloud is."

"Answer me."

"I'm afraid I can't. There are too many variables."

"Oh great. Acacia, is the lightning going to affect the harpoons?"

"No. The cloud's too low for that, and they're going too fast. Even if one took a direct hit from a lightning bolt, the trajectory won't be altered by more than a couple of metres at best."

The voidhawk flotilla was only one and a half thousand kilometres from the surface of Ombey. Mortonridge filled their sensor blister coverage, changing from a red smear to a seething mass of blue-white streamers, more alive than ever before. There was just time for one last query.

We're still go, Acacia assured them.

All three hundred voidhawks reached the apex of their trajectory. Their bone-crushing eight-gee acceleration ended briefly. Each one flung a swarm of five thousand kinetic harpoons from its weapons cradles. Then power surged through their patterning cells again, reversing the previous direction of the distortion field. The punishing intensity was unchanged, still eight gees, pushing them desperately away from the planet with its dangerous gravity field.

Far below, the delicate filigree of shimmering lightning vanished beneath an incandescent corona as the upper atmosphere ignited. The plasma wake left by one and a half million kinetic harpoons had merged together into a single photonic shockwave. It hit the top of the cloud, puncturing the churning grey vapour with such speed there was little reaction. At first. Acacia was quite right, the cloud for all its bulk and animosity could not deflect the harpoons from their programmed targets.

No human could draw up that list, it was the AI in Pasto that ultimately designated their impact points. They descended in clumps of three, giving a ninety-seven per cent probability of a successful hit. Mortonridge's communication net was the main target.

Urban legend dictated that modern communication nets were annihilation proof. With hundreds of thousands of independent switching nodes spread over an entire planet, and millions of cables linking them, backed up by satellite relays, their anarchistic-homogeneous nature made them immune to any kind of cataclysm. No matter how many nodes were taken out, there was always an alternative route for the data. You'd have to physically wipe out a planet before its data exchange was stalled.

But Mortonridge was finite, its net isolated from the redundancy offered by the rest of the planet. The location of every node was known to within half a metre. Unfortunately, ninety per cent of them were proscribed, because they were inside a built up urban area. If kinetic harpoons started dropping amid the buildings, resulting casualties would be horrendous. That left the cables out in the open countryside. A lot of them followed roads, nestled in utility conduits along the side of the carbon concrete, but many more took off across the land, laid by mechanoids tunnelling through forests and under rivers, with nothing on the surface to indicate their existence.

Long-inactive files of their routes had been accessed and analysed by the AI. Strike coordinates were designated, with the proscription that there should be no habitable structure within three quarters of a kilometre. Given the possessed's considerable ability to defend themselves on a physical level, it was considered a reasonable safe distance.

Stephanie Ash lay quivering on the floor even after her mind had recoiled from the communion with other souls. The loss hurt her more than any pain from the electron beam attack against the cloud. That simple act of union had given her hope. As long as people went on supporting each other, she knew, despite everything else, they remained human to some small degree. Now even that fragile aspiration had been wrenched from them.

"Stephanie?" Moyo called. His hand was shaking her shoulder gently. "Stephanie, are you all right?"

The fear and concern in his voice triggered her own guilt. "God, no." She opened her eyes. The bedroom was lit solely by a small bluish flame coming from his thumb. Outside the window, blackness swarmed the whole world. "What did they do?" She could no longer sense the psychic weight pressing against her from the other side of the firebreak. Only the valley was apparent.

"I don't know. But it's not good." He helped her to her feet.

"Are the others all right?" She could sense their minds, spread out through the farmhouse, embers of worry and pain.

"Same as us, I guess." A bright flash from outside silenced him. They both went to the window and peered out. Huge shafts of lightning skidded along the underbelly of the cloud.

Stephanie shivered uncomfortably. What had successfully shielded them from the open sky was now an intimidatingly large mass far too close overhead.

"We're not in charge of it anymore," Moyo said. "We let go."

"What's going to happen to it?"

"It'll rain, I guess." He shot her an anxious look. "And that's a lot of cloud up there. We just kept adding to it, like a baby's security blanket."

"Maybe we should get the animals in."

"Maybe we should get the hell out of here. The Princess's army will be coming."

She smiled sadly. "There's nowhere to go. You know that."

The frequency of the lightning had increased dramatically by the time they rounded up Cochrane, Rana, and Franklin to help chase after the chickens and lambs that normally ambled round inside the farmyard. The first few big drops of water began to patter down.

Moyo stuck his hand out, palm up. As if confirmation was really needed. "Told you," he said smugly.

Stephanie turned her cardigan into a slicker, even though she didn't hold out much hope of staying dry. The drops were larger than any she'd ever known. All the chickens were running through the open gate, the lambs had already vanished into the atrocious night. She was just about to suggest they didn't bother trying to catch them when daylight returned to Mortonridge.

Cochrane gaped up at the sky. The clouds had turned into translucent veils of grey silk, allowing the light to pour through. "Wow! Who switched the sun back on, man?" The bottom of the clouds detonated into incandescent splinters, searing down through the air. Vivid star-tips pulling down a hurricane cone of violet mist after them. Stephanie had to shield her eyes, they were so bright.

"It's the end of the world, kids," Cochrane cried gleefully.

All one and a half million harpoons struck the ground within a five second period. A clump of them were targeted on a cable four kilometres from the farm valley, their terrible velocity translated into a single devastating blast of heat. The radiant orange flash silhouetted the valley rim, lasting just long enough to reveal the debris plume boiling upwards.

"Ho shit," Cochrane grunted. "That Mr Hiltch *really* doesn't like us."

"What were they?" Stephanie asked. It seemed incredible that they were still in their bodies. Surely that kind of violence would wipe them out?

"Some kind of orbital bombardment," Moyo said. "It must have been aimed at Ekelund's troops." He didn't sound too convinced.

"Aimed? It was everywhere."

"Then why didn't it hit us?" Rana asked. Moyo just shrugged. That was when the roar of the impact reached them, a drawn out rumble loud enough to swallow any words.

Stephanie covered her ears, and looked up again. The cloud was in torment, its rumpled underbelly foaming violently. Ghostly billows of luminescent purple air left behind by the harpoons snaked around the tightly packed whorls; the two of them flowing against each other, yet never merging, like liquids with different densities. She frowned, blinking upwards as the light dimmed. A thick slate-grey haze was emerging, oozing out of the cloud to swallow both the lightning and the tattered sheets of ion vapour. It was expanding fast, darkening.

"Inside," she said in a small voice as the last echoes of the explosion reverberated across the valley. They all turned to look at her. The big drops of rain had returned. A breeze arose to stroke their clothes. "Get inside. It's going to rain."

They glanced up at the descending haze, awed and fearful as understanding reached them.

"Nothing!" Annette screamed furiously at the processor block. The primitive schematic displayed on its screen proved it was functioning, yet nobody was answering her calls. "We're cut off."

Soi Hon studied the display on his block. "All the lines are down, from what I can see," he said.

"Don't be absurd, you can't knock out an entire net," Annette protested. Doubt stung. "It's not possible."

"I imagine that was the idea behind the bombardment," Soi Hon replied, unperturbed. "It was rather spectacular, after all. They wouldn't expend that much effort for no reason. And we didn't have the whole net functioning in the first place, only the critical links."

"Damn it, how the hell am I going to organize our resistance now?"

"Everyone has their original orders, and they have no choice but to fight. All this means is that you are no longer in charge of the possessed."

Even his complacency soured at the look she gave him.

"Oh really?" she asked dangerously.

The light began to fade outside. Annette strode across to the big front window. She'd taken over a folksy restaurant called the Black Bull in the middle of Cold Overton, giving her a commanding position at the end of the broad main street. Fifty vehicles were parked on the stone slabs of the market square outside, waiting for the troops who'd taken refuge in the nearby shops and cafés. Milne and a few of his engineers were walking about, inspecting the equipment. There didn't seem to be any damage, though several of the harpoons had fallen just outside the village.

"Soi," she said. "Take a couple of squads and check the roads. I want to know how quickly we can get out of here."

"As you wish." He nodded briskly, and made for the door.

"There's a big group of us in Ketton," she said, almost to herself. "That's only ten kilometres west of here. We'll link up with them. Should be able to convince some civilians to join up, too. After that we can move on to the next group."

"We could use runners to carry messages," Delvan suggested. "That's what we did back in my time. Communications were always pretty damn poor close to the front."

There was very little light left now. Annette saw Milne and the others running. There was no fear in their minds, just urgency. Raindrops splattered against the window. Within seconds the whole of main street was awash. Gutters started to fill up, with small whirlpools forming over the drains.

"I've never seen anything like that before," Soi Hon exclaimed, raising his voice against the noise. He was standing in the open doorway, a waterproof poncho forming round his shoulders. The drumming sound of the huge drops was easily as loud as the red cloud's thunder had been. "And we saw some storms round the Pacific in my day, believe me."

A rivulet of dirty water began to seep in around his feet, trickling round the tables. Annette couldn't see anything outside now, the rain was battering heavily against the glass, producing the kind of spume that normally topped ocean waves. Behind that, there was only blackness.

Delvan moved up beside him to get a better look. "Nobody's going anywhere in this."

"Yes," Annette agreed shakily. "You'd better wait."

"How long, though?" Delvan muttered. "We didn't think about this when we drew the cloud over us."

"Don't worry," Soi Hon said. "Nobody's going to do any fighting for a while. It's just as bad for them. And at least we're inside."

The landing boat surged forwards as soon as the dazzling corona from the kinetic harpoons lit up the sky. Sinon used the voidhawks' vantage point to observe the giant splash of plasma sink into the dark mantle of cloud.

It's expanding, Acacia announced. Confirm that, we're tracking it.

Vast cyclonic spirals of cloud were stirring across the upper surface. Washed by Ombey's pale moonlight, the movement appeared almost majestic. Primeval forces had awoken. Along the edges of the cloud, gargantuan tornadoes began to spin away, careering off over the sea.

The whole damn thing's breaking up, Choma said.

Sinon shared a shiver of consternation with the other serjeants; not just in his boat. All of them were facing the same onslaught. He stared out over the prow, watching mountains of water on the move. A wind had risen from nowhere to blow straight at him.

We can't turn back, Choma said. **It'll catch us on the open water. Best head for shore.**

Sinon's hand patted his lifebelt, seeking reassurance. The massif of cloud seemed to be hurtling towards them, a light-absorbing void distending across the ocean.

Keep going, was the decision concurred by the rest of the Edenists and General Hiltch's command group. Every boat in the Liberation armada rammed its engines to full, and met the stormfront head on.

It wasn't rain they faced, not in the ordinary sense. The deluge crashing down over them was like standing under a waterfall. As the clouds rampaged overhead, so the waves rose, as if seeking to bridge the gap. The landing boats were thrown around pitilessly. Sometimes Sinon had to hold himself against a deck that was lifting over thirty degrees to the vertical. The jeeps secured along the centre of the hold strained against their restraint cables as their weight was flung about in directions the designers had never anticipated. Bilge pumps were wailing plaintively, to little effect. Sinon clung to a guard rail as the cold water mounted steadily against his legs, sloshing between the hull walls. He was worried he'd get tossed overboard. He was worried his newly assembled body would split along surgical lines as he strained muscles and tendons to hold on. He worried that a jeep would break free and crush him. He worried they wouldn't reach the beach before the rain and waves filled the hold and sunk them.

Not even sharing the anxiety in the Edenist fashion did much to alleviate it. There was way too much distress bubbling through the aether as the armada battled for shore.

The Edenists in secondary support roles, safe away from the megastorm, along with the voidhawks and their crews overhead, did their best to offer what reassurance and comfort they could to their beleaguered kinsmen. But they all felt the death toll rising, compounding the alarm. Landing boats collapsed, pitched over, individual serjeants lost their grip to drown amid the monster waves. Voidhawks laboured tirelessly to absorb the fresh memories of the dying serjeant personalities.

A nausea suppression program went primary as an aghast Ralph watched the nightmare unfurling. Neatly tabulated icons blinked up inside his mind, indicating the woeful progress the boats were making. Some were even being driven backwards as the gales howled out from the land. He did what he could. For all it was worth. Ordering the ground forces along the firebreak to stay put and dig in. Putting the medical teams on immediate standby. Designating search patrols for the aircraft, ready for the time when it became feasible to fly.

Diana Tiernan and the AI couldn't give him any estimate when that would be. There was no way of knowing the true weight of water powering the storm. Radar scans from the SD sensor satellites to discover the depth and density were badly distorted by the tremendous electrical discharges still churning madly over Mortonridge. All they could do was wait.

"We couldn't have known," Janne Palmer said. "Dealing with the possessed is one giant unknown."

"We should have guessed," Ralph answered bitterly. "At least considered it."

"Best information we had was that the cloud was a couple of hundred metres thick," Diana said. "That's all it was on Lalonde and every other planet they took over. But this blasted thing, it must be kilometres deep. They must have sucked every gram of water from the air. There may even be some kind of osmotic process involved, siphoning it up out of the sea."

"Damn those bastards," Ralph spat.

"They are afraid," Acacia said calmly. "They built the thickest, highest wall they could to keep us out. It's human nature."

Ralph couldn't bring himself to answer the Edenist. It was Acacia's people who were taking the brunt of the calamity. And it was his plan, his orders, which had put them there. Anything he said would be pathetically inadequate.

Outside, the rain had reached Fort Forward, and was doing its best to wash the city's programmable silicon structures into the nearby river. Fast rivulets were gouging the soil away from their base anchors. Ops Room staff glanced round nervously as banshee winds pummelled away at the walls. Fifty minutes after the kinetic harpoon barrage, the landing boats started to reach the beaches.

"They're coming through," Acacia said. The first strands of confidence were starting to emerge within the combined Edenist psyche as serjeants exported the feeling of sand crunching underfoot. Proof that success was possible, the sense of relief which accompanied it. "It's going to be okay, we're going to make it."

"Right," Ralph croaked. One icon gleamed darkly at the centre of his woeful thoughts: 3129. The number of dead so far. And we're the only ones shooting.

An immense wave smacked the landing craft down on the beach with an almighty crunch. The blow sent Sinon skidding back along the hold on his arse, limbs flailing. Water slowed his momentum quickly. He came to rest in a jumble of other serjeants, all struggling to disentangle themselves. The three at the bottom were completely immersed. Affinity was supremely useful in coordinating their movements, like unpicking a three dimensional puzzle.

They'd just got free when the next wave clobbered the side of the landing boat. It lacked the brutality of the previous one, simply shoving the hull further up the beach, and twisting them at an angle.

Dry land! Choma cried triumphantly.

Well . . . land, anyway, Sinon acknowledged dutifully as he sloshed forwards back up the hold. The rain here was even worse than out at sea. Visibility was down to maybe fifteen metres, and that was with the boat's powerful lights shining down.

Sometimes, I think you have completely the wrong attitude for this.

Sinon sent a smile image at his friend. He carried on searching through the water for pieces of his kit lost during the last portion of the voyage.

The squad began to assess their position. Five had been injured seriously enough to disqualify them from the campaign altogether. Several more had suffered minor cracking in their exoskeletons, which the medical nanonics could cope with. (Surprisingly, the medical nanonics were working reasonably well.) The beach they'd wound up on was three kilometres south of their designated landing point, Billesdon. The truck at the back of the hold was so badly flooded it'd require a complete maintenance overhaul. The landing boat was wedged into the shingle, and would need towing off at high tide before it could return to the resort island for the marines.

On the plus side, the forward ramp worked, allowing the three functional jeeps out. Most of their armament was intact. All the other landing boats containing their regiment had made it ashore, though they were spread out along the coast. After a brief discussion with their Ops Room liaison, they agreed to make their way to Billesdon and regroup there. According to their original plan, the back-up forces and supplies would use the town's harbour as their disembarkation point. But it still had to be secured.

By the time the boat's forward ramp came down it was technically dawn. Hunched down in the almost non-existent shelter provided by the starboard hull, Sinon couldn't notice any difference. The only way he knew the jeeps were lumbering out was by using his affinity to see out through the driver's eyes.

Looks like we're on, Choma said.

They rose to their feet, and checked their kit one last time. Sinon's squad took up position by the second jeep. Intense headlight beams pierced ten metres through the deluge before the grey water defeated them. It was slow going. Their feet sank deep into the saturated shingle. Twice they had to push the jeep when its wide tyres dug themselves into axle-high ruts.

The squad was totally dependant on their guidance blocks. Satellite images taken before the possession provided them with a high-resolution picture of the cove, and the single narrow track leading away from it into the forest at the rear. Inertial guidance designated their position to within ten centimetres. Supposedly. There was no way of checking. Satellite sensors still couldn't penetrate the cloud to give them a verified location reference. They just had to hope the bitek processors hadn't been glitched since they loaded them back on the island.

Shingle gave way to tacky mud. Laggard waves of the yellow slough were creeping down the beach from the land behind. Clumps of grass and small bushes were being trawled along with it.

Great, Sinon said as he waded in. **At this rate, it's going to take a week to get there.** He was aware of other squads encountering similar difficulties all along the coast.

We need to get to higher ground, Choma said. His affinity indicated a point on the guidance block image. **That should give us better terrain to traverse.**

The squad concurred, and changed direction slightly.

Any news on when this rain's going to end? Sinon queried their liaison.

No.

Not even Cochrane could be bothered to maintain the Karmic Crusader's outlandish appearance. The rain was eroding their spirits at the same rate it ate into the valley's soil. Three hours so far, without ever slackening.

Flares of lightning revealed what it was doing to their beautiful circular valley. Water cascaded over the lip, turning the orderly terraces into long curving waterfalls. At each stage it grew muckier and more glutinous as it carried the rich cultivated black soil with it. Avalanches of crops and sturdy young fruit trees were plunging down the ever-steepening slopes to sink without trace into the expanding lake. The lawn at the rear of the farmhouse was slowly submerged, bringing the water up to the ornate iron-framed patio doors.

By that time they were already loading the Karmic Crusader with their cases. Wind had ripped countless slates from the roof, letting the rain in to soak through the ceiling plaster.

"Just bear in mind, there's only one road out of this valley," McPhee said when the first rivulet came churning down the stairs into the living room. "And that runs above the river. If we're going to get out of here, it's got to be soon."

Nobody had argued. They splashed their way upstairs to pack while he and Cochrane brought the bus out of the barn. Moyo was driving, keeping their speed to little more than walking pace. The dirt track along the side of the winding valley was crumbling at an alarming rate as sheets of filthy water poured down out of the trees above them, foaming round trunks and raking out the tangled undergrowth. His mind concentrated on giving the bus broader tyres in an attempt to gain some kind of traction on the quagmire surface. It was difficult; he had to get Franklin and McPhee to collaborate with him, meshing their thoughts together.

A tree crashed onto the track twenty metres ahead of them, uprooted by the relentless water. Moyo stamped down on the breaks, but the bus just kept slithering forwards. Not even the full focus of his energistic ability could affect the motion. An untimely reminder about his acute lack of omnipotence. He just managed to shout: "Hold on to something," before the bus's front collision buffer hit the trunk. The windscreen turned white, bulging inwards to absorb as much of the impact as it could before finally disintegrating into a hail of tiny plastic spheres. A fat bulb of twigs and spiky topaz leaves burst through the rent. Moyo tried to duck, but the seat straps held him fast. Instinct took over, and a stupendous ball of white fire engulfed the twigs. He screeched as his eyebrows smouldered and his hair shrivelled into black frazzled ash. The skin on his face went dead.

Steam belched along the interior as the Karmic Crusader juddered to a halt. Stephanie loosened her grip on the seat back in front of her, leaving deep indentations in the composite. The floor was tilted at quite an incline. What with the rain drumming on the roof, and the water from the slope pouring round them she could only just distinguish the stressed creaking coming from the bodywork. There was no way of telling what was causing it. Even her eldrich sense was cluttered with confusing shadowforms, the rain was equivalent to strong static interference.

Then water came gurgling eagerly along the aisle, pushing a fringe of filthy scum ahead of it. It glided over her shoes. She made an effort to banish the cloying steam, trying to make out the gloomy interior.

"My eyes!" It was just a whisper, but poignant enough to carry the length of the aisle. Everyone swung round towards the front of the bus.

"Oh god, my eyes. My eyes. Help me! My *eyes*!"

Stephanie had to hang on to the overhead racks, swinging one hand in front of the other, to make her way forwards. Moyo was still sitting in the driver's seat, his body rigid. The incinerated remains of the tree's branch cluster loomed centimetres from his face like some fabulously delicate charcoal sculpture. His hands were held close to his cheeks, trembling from the fear of what he'd find if he actually touched himself.

"It's all right," she said automatically. Her mind played traitor, fright and revulsion at what she saw surging to the surface of her thoughts. His skin had roasted away, taking most of his nose and all of his eyelids with it. Blood was dribbling out of the fissures between scabs of crisped corium layers. Both eyes had broiled, turning septic yellow as creamy fluids percolated out in a mockery of tears.

"I can't see," he cried. "Why can't I see?"

She reached out and grasped both his hands. "Shush. Please, darling. It'll be all right. You just got scorched by the flame, that's all."

"I can't see!"

"Of course you can. You've got your sixth sense until your eyes recover. You know I'm here, don't you?"

"Yes. *Don't go.*"

She put her arms round him. "I won't." He began shaking violently. Cold sweat was prickling his undamaged skin.

"He's in shock," Tina said. The others were gathering round, as much as the cramped aisle would permit. Their thoughts tempered by the sight of Moyo's injuries.

"He's all right," Stephanie insisted in a brittle tone.

"It's very common with major burn cases."

Stephanie glared at her.

"Yo, man, give him a drag on this," Cochrane said. He held out a fat reefer, sickly sweet smoke seeping from its glowing tip.

"Not now!" Stephanie hissed.

"Actually, yes, darling," Tina said. "For once the ape man's right. It's a mild sedative, which is just what he needs right now." Stephanie frowned suspiciously at the unaccustomed authority in Tina's voice. "I used to be a nurse," the statuesque woman continued, gathering in her black diamante shawl with a contemptuous dignity. "Actually."

Stephanie took the reefer, and eased it gently into Moyo's lips. He coughed weakly as he inhaled.

The bus groaned loudly. Its rear end shifted a couple of metres, sending them all grabbing for support. McPhee ducked his head to peer through the broken windscreen. "We're not going anywhere in this," he said. "We'd better get out before we get washed away."

"We can't move him," Stephanie protested. "Not for a while."

"The river's nearly up level with this track, and we've got at least another kilometre and a half to go before we're out of the valley."

"Level? It can't be. We were twenty metres above the valley floor."

The Karmic Crusader's headlights were out, so she sent a slender blade of white fire arching over the track. It was as if the land had turned to water. She couldn't actually see any ground, slopes and hollows were all submerged under several centimetres of flowing yellow-brown water. Just below the flattish section which marked the track, a cavalcade of flotsam was sweeping along the valley. Mangled branches, smashed trunks, and snarled up mats of vegetation were all cluttered together; their smooth progress was ominous, nothing stood in their way. As she watched, another of the trees from the slope above slid down past the bus, staying vertical the whole time until it reached the river.

She didn't like to think how many more trees were poised just above them. "You're right," she said. "Let's get out of here."

Cochrane retrieved his reefer. "Feel better?" Moyo simply twitched. "Hey, no need for the downer. Just like grow them back, man. It's easy."

Moyo's answering laugh was hysterical. "Imagine I can see? Oh yes, oh yes. It's easy, it's so fucking easy." He started to sob, tapping his fingertips delicately over his ruined face. "I'm sorry. I'm so sorry."

"You stopped the bus," Stephanie said. "You saved all of us. There's nothing to be sorry for."

"Not *you*!" he screamed. "Him! I'm saying sorry to him. It's his body, not mine. Look what I've done to it. Not you. Oh god. Why did all this happen? Why couldn't we all just die?"

"Get me the first-aid kit," Tina told Rana. "Now!"

Stephanie had her arm round Moyo's shoulder again, wishing there was some aspect of energistic power that could manifest raw comfort. McPhee and Franklin tried opening the door. But it was jammed solid, beyond even their enhanced physical strength's ability to shift. They looked at each other, gripped hands, and closed their eyes. A big circular section of the front bodywork spun off into the bedlam outside. Rain spat down the aisle like a damp shotgun blast. Rana struggled forwards with the first-aid kit case, fiddling with the clips.

"This is no use," Tina wailed. She plucked out a nanonic package, face wrinkled in dismay. The thick green strip dangled from her hand like so much wobbly rubber.

"Come on! There must be something in it you can use," Stephanie said.

Tina rummaged through. The case contained several strips of nanonic package, diagnostic blocks—all useless. Even the phials of biochemicals and drugs used infuser patches, the dosage regulated by a diagnostic block. There was no non-technological method of getting the medication into his bloodstream. She shook her head weakly. "Nothing."

"Damn it—"

The bus groaned, shifting again. "No more time," McPhee said. "This is it. Out. Now."

Cochrane clambered out of the hole, splashing down on the track next to the fallen tree. Keeping his footing was obviously difficult. The water came halfway up his shin. Rana followed him down. Stephanie gripped the seat straps holding Moyo in, and forced them to rot in her palms. She and Franklin hauled him up, and guided him through the hole. Tina followed them through, letting out martyred squeals as she struggled to find footholds.

"Lose those bloody heels, ye moron," McPhee yelled at her.

She glared back at him petulantly, but her scarlet stilettos faded into ordinary pumps with flat soles. "Peasant. A girl has to look her best at all times, you know."

"This is real you stupid cow, not a fucking disaster movie set. You're no' being filmed."

She ignored him, and turned to help Stephanie with Moyo. "Let's try and bandage his face, at the very least," she said. "I'll need some cloth."

Stephanie tore a strip off the bottom of her saturated cardigan. When she passed it over to Tina it had become a dry, clean strip of white linen.

"I suppose that'll be all right," Tina said dubiously. She started to wrap it round Moyo's eyes, making sure the stub remains of his nose were also covered. "Do try and think of your face as being normal, darling. It'll all grow back, then, you'll see."

Stephanie said nothing, she didn't doubt Moyo could re-pair the burns to his cheeks and forehead, but actually growing eyeballs back . . .

Franklin landed with a heavy splash, the last out of the bus. Nobody fancied trying to salvage their luggage. The boot was at the rear, and not even energistic power would help much clambering over the tree. Blasting the trunk to shreds would only send the bus spinning over the edge.

They spent a couple of minutes sorting themselves out. First priority was fending off the rain; their collective imag-ination produced a transparent hemisphere, like a giant glass umbrella floating in the air above them. Once that was established, they set about drying off their clothes. There wasn't anything they could do about the water coursing across the track, so they gave themselves sturdy knee-high wellingtons.

Thus protected, they set off down the track, taking turns to guide and support a shivering Moyo. A bright globe of ball lightning bobbed through the air ahead and slightly to the side of them, hissing as raindrops lashed against it, but lighting the way and hopefully giving them some warning

of any more falling trees. Apart from that, their only worry
was making it out of the valley before the river rose up over
the track. The driving rain and roaring wind meant they
never knew when another tree slithered down the slope into
the dark and battered Karmic Crusader, sending it plunging
into the engorged river.

Billesdon was a cheery little town, tucked into the lee of a
large granite headland on Mortonridge's eastern coast.
Sheltered from the worst of the breakers to come rolling in
off the ocean, it was a natural harbour. District planners
took advantage of that, quarrying the abundant rock to
build a long curving quay opposite the headland, enclosing
a wide deepwater basin with a modest beach at the back.
The majority of boats which used it were trawlers and san-
drakers, their operators earning a good living from
Ombey's plentiful fish and crustacean species. Even the
local seaweed was exported to restaurants across the peninsula.

It also proved a haven for pleasure boats, with several
sport fishing and yachting clubs setting up shop. With so
many boats to service, the marine engineering companies
and supply industries were quick to seize upon the commercial opportunities available and open premises in the
town. Houses, apartment blocks, shops, hotels, entertainment halls, and industrial estates were thrown up all the
way back along the shallow valley behind the headland.
Villas and groves began to blossom along the slopes above,
next to golf courses and holiday complexes.

Billesdon became the sort of town, beautiful and economically successful, that was presented as the Kingdom's
ideal, every citizen's entitlement. Sinon's squad reached the
outskirts around midday. A trivial glimmer of light was pen-

etrating the clouds, giving the world a lacklustre opacity. Visibility had risen to a few hundred yards.

Sinon wished it hadn't bothered. They were poised just outside the town, not far above the sea. Cover was ostensibly provided by a spinney of fallen Fellots. None of the sturdy aboriginal trees remained standing; their dense fan-shaped branches had cushioned the way the trunks fell, leaving them at crazy angles. Rain kept their upper sections clean from the cloying mud, giving the cerise bark a glossy sheen. Choma was pressed up against a fat trunk at the edge of the spinney, waving a sensor block slowly ahead of him. The whole squad hooked in to the block's bitek processor, examining the buildings ahead through a variety of wavelengths.

Not even the money lavished on Billesdon's infrastructure had saved it from the rain. The terraces and groves above had dissolved, sending waves of mud slithering down into the prim streets, clogging the drains within minutes. Water raced along the roads and pavements, submerging tarmac and grass alike before it poured over the quayside wall. There were no boats left in the harbour; every single craft had been used to evacuate the population before Ekelund's invasion reached the coast. In theory, that left the basin clear for the Liberation's landing boats to bring the occupation troops and support materiel ashore.

Seems deserted, Choma said.

Nothing moving, Sinon agreed, **but infrared's useless in all this rain. There could be thousands of them tucked up nice and dry waiting for us.**

Look on the bright side, the water should foul up that white fire of theirs.

Maybe, but that still leaves them with a whole load of options to use against us.

That's good, keep thinking like that. Paranoia keeps you on your toes.

Thank you.

So what do you want to do now?

Simple. We're going to have to go in and check it out one house at a time.

Okay, that's what I signed up for.

They discussed it with the other squads encircling the town. Search areas were designated, tactics coordinated, blockades established on the main roads. Guyana was alerted that they were going in, and readied the low orbit SD platforms to provide groundstrike support if called for.

The outskirts ahead of Sinon were modest houses overlooking the harbour, home to the fishing families. They had large gardens, which had been completely washed away. Long tongues of mud-slimed debris were stretched down the slope, with small streams running down their centres where the water had gauged a channel into the sandy soil. Cover between the spinney and the first house was nonexistent, so the squad moved forwards with long gaps between each member. If the white fire did burst down on them, it would never be able to reach more than one at a time. Hopefully.

Sinon was third in the line. He held his machine gun ready, crouched low to provide the smallest possible target. Ever since they came ashore, he'd been thankful that his serjeant body had an exoskeleton; the rain didn't bother him as much as it would if he had ordinary skin. Body armour had been considered and rejected, it had never been any good against the white fire before. The one concession they all made were shoes, a kind of sandal with deep-tread soles to give them traction.

Even so, it was hard to keep his feet from slipping as he hurried forward through the mud. The first house was ten metres ahead of him: a white box with long silvered windows and a large first floor balcony at the rear. Water poured out of the sagging guttering, diluting the slow-moving sludge that percolated round the base of the walls. He kept sweeping the machine gun nozzle across the facing wall, alert for any sign of motion from inside. Out in the open, wind was driving the rain straight at him. Even his body was aware of how cold it was; not that it was affecting his performance, not yet. Sensor blocks dangled from his belt, unused and redundant as he urged himself on. His training was his one and only defence now.

Choma had already reached the house ahead of him. Ducking down to crawl under the windows. Sinon reached the back wall, and started to follow his friend along the side of the house. It was important to keep moving, not clump together. Palm fronds and limp knots of grass wrapped themselves round his ankles, slowing him. When he reached the largest window, he took one of the sensor blocks from his belt, and gingerly pressed it to the pane. The block relayed a slightly misty image of the room inside. A lounge, cosy, with worn furniture and framed family holograms on the wall. Water was spraying out of the ceiling's central light fitting; the floor was invisible under a layer of mud which had pushed in from the hallway. An infrared scan showed no hot-spots.

Clean downstairs, he said. **And my ELINT block is clear. Looks like nobody's home.**

We need to be sure, Choma replied. **Check out the upper floor. I'll back you.**

Sinon stood up, shouldering the machine gun. He took out a fission blade and sliced through the window frame, cutting out the lock. Raindrops sizzled on the glowing blade. The next two serjeants in his squad had already reached the house when he slipped inside. He pushed out a heavy breath from his lungs, the nearest he could get to a sigh. Actually out of the rain. Its impact was diminished to a dull drum roll on the roof. Choma splashed down into the thin mire beside him.

Hell, that's better.

Affinity made Sinon aware of the rest of the squad; two of them were in the neighbouring houses, while the rest had started to spread out along the street. **My ELINT's still clear,** he said.

Choma looked up at the ceiling, pointing his machine gun at it cautiously. **Yes. I'm pretty sure there's nobody up there, but we've still got to check.**

Sinon made his way out into the hall, machine gun held ready. **How can you be sure? You don't know what's up there.**

Instinct.

Crazy. He put his foot on the first step, sandal sole making a squelching sound against the sodden carpet. **We've barely got imagination operating inside these neural arrays, let alone an intuitive function.**

Then I suggest you work one up fast, you're going to need it.

Sinon turned so he could cover the landing as he ascended. Nothing moved except for the unending water, glistening as it ran down walls, curdling across carpets and tile floors, dripping from furniture. He reached the main bedroom, its door ajar. His foot kicked it hard, dinting the wood. The door slammed back amid a shower of droplets. Choma was right: it was empty. In every room, the signs of panicked departure. Drawers ransacked, clothes scattered about.

Nobody here, Sinon reported to the squad when they cleared the front bedroom. Other house searches across the town were also proving negative as the squads moved in.

Ghost town, Choma said, chortling.

I think you could find a better phrase. He looked

down through the window, seeing squad members scuttling along the road outside. They were going against the flow of mud, their legs churning up deep eddies. Things were trundling along the street, carried along by the relentless current. Bulges in the smooth mud; there was no way of telling if they were stones or crumpled twigs. All of them moved at the same speed.

He held up a sensor block, panning it round in search of anomalous hot-spots. The image was overlapping his actual field of view, which meant he was looking straight at the house on the other side of the street when it exploded.

A serjeant had cut through the lock on a side door and crept cautiously inside, machine gun held ready. The ground floor must have been clear, because a second serjeant followed him in. Thirty seconds later four explosions detonated simultaneously. They were carefully placed, one at each corner of the house. Long flakes of concrete and lumps of stone shot out of the billowing flame. The whole house trembled: then, its crucial support destroyed, it collapsed vertically. Windows all along the street blew out under the impact of the blast wave. Sinon just managed to twist away in time, allowing his backpack to take the brunt of the flying shards.

The affinity bond boiled with hard, frantic thoughts. Both serjeants in the house were hammered by the explosions, their bodies wrecked. But the tough exoskeleton withstood the searing pressure for a few moments, long enough for the controlling personalities to instinctively begin the transfer. One of the orbiting voidhawks accepted their thoughts; then the house descended on their already weakened skulls.

"Shit!" Sinon yelled. He was curled up on the bedroom floor, aware of something being wrong with his left forearm. When he brought it up to his face, the exoskeleton was cracked in a small star pattern. Blood was seeping out of the centre. Rain lashed in through the empty window, washing the crimson stain away.

Are you all right? Choma asked.

Yes . . . Yes, I think so. What happened? He stood up, peering down circumspectly onto the street. The mud and rain had swallowed almost all the immediate signs of the explosion. There was no smoke, no dust cloud. Just a pancake of rubble where the house had stood moments before. The tide of mud was already frothing round it, bubbling eagerly into cracks.

Choma pointed his machine gun along the street, radiating satisfaction that the squad had merged with the scenery. He knew where they were, but they weren't easily visible. **Where are they? Did anyone see where the white fire came from?**

He was answered with a chorus of: No's.

I don't think it was white fire, Sinon said. He ordered his block to replay the memory. The gouts of flame spearing out of each corner were orange, and they came from inside the house.

Sabotage? Choma said.

Could be. They were perfectly placed for demolition. They were on their way down the stairs when the second house exploded. It was on the far side of town, being examined by one of the other squads. One serjeant was killed, another two were injured beyond any field medic's ability to patch up; they needed immediate evacuation. The rest of Sinon's squad stood back as he clambered up over the mound of stone and girders which had been the house. When he was clear of the mud he ran a sensor pad over the exposed rubble close to one of the corners. The rain was washing the mess clean, but the chemical analysis still had enough residual molecules to work with.

Not good, he announced. This wasn't white fire. There's a definite trace of trinitrotoluene here.

Sod it! Choma exclaimed. The bastards have booby trapped the whole town.

Parts of it. I doubt they've got the resources to rig every building.

But you can bet they've done the critical ones, as well as picking on houses at random, he said grudgingly. It's what I would've done.

If you're right, we're going to have to treat each building as potentially hazardous. And we don't even know what the trigger is.

I doubt it'll be electronic. Our sensors would spot active processors, and the possessed wouldn't be able to set them up in the first place. We'll have to get some of the marine engineers in here to find out what kind of mechanism they're employing.

Sinon's response was lost amid a burst of anguish within the communal affinity band. Both of them instinctively turned to the west. The death of another two serjeants was all too clear. A warehouse in a town called Holywell had just exploded.

It's not just here, Choma said. Ekelund's people have been busy.

Confirmation that most major towns around the periphery of Mortonridge were booby trapped came in to the Ops Room throughout the afternoon. Ralph sat in his office accessing the reports in a state of weary disbelief. Progress schematics were being revised on a fifteen minute basis by the AI. Their original timetable was constantly rearranged, targets being pushed further and further back.

"Truly amazing," he told Princess Kirsten during the

evening's briefing. "We're fifteen hours in, and already twenty behind schedule."

"Conditions are pretty foul under there," Admiral Farquar said. "I don't see Ekelund's people having a better time of it."

"How would we know? Fifteen hours, and we haven't had a single encounter with a live possessed. Christ, I mean I know no battle plan survives contact with the enemy, but no one ever said anything about it disintegrating before we even catch sight of them."

"General Hiltch," the Princess said sharply. "I'd like you to give me some positive factors, please. Have all the possessed simply vanished into this other realm they long for?"

"We don't think so, no, ma'am. Pulling back from the coast and the firebreak is a logical move. They obviously worked it out in advance, hence the booby traps."

"There's circumstantial evidence that they're still in the centre of Mortonridge," Diana said. "Our satellite sensor scans are at their worst there. Radar and UV laser is beginning to break through the fringes, but when we try to probe the centre we get the same kind of hazing effect the possessed have always generated. QED, they're still there."

"That's something, I suppose."

"I also think the worst of the rain should be over by midday tomorrow. Results from the sensors we can rely on show us the cloud is thinning out. A lot of it is simply blowing out to sea now they're no longer containing it. And of course, it's falling, bigtime."

"It certainly is," Acacia said. She shuddered at the on-the-ground impressions affinity had delivered to her. "You're going to have real problems with Mortonridge's vegetation when this is all over. I doubt there's a tree standing on the whole peninsula. I didn't know rain like that could exist."

"It can't, normally," Diana said. "This whole meteorology situation is highly artificial. The dispersal will influence the planet's weather patterns for the rest of the year. However, it certainly isn't sustainable; as I said, the heaviest falls will be over by midday tomorrow. After that, the serjeants will be able to make decent progress."

"Over open country, possibly," Ralph said. "But we're going to have to vector in these booby traps."

"Do we know what they are, yet?" the Princess asked.

"The majority so far are good old fashioned TNT," Ralph told her. "Easily produced from the kind of chemicals available in most of our urban zones. We managed to get some marine engineers in to the afflicted towns to examine what they could. There's no standard trigger mechanism, naturally enough. The possessed are using everything from trip wires to wired up door knobs. There's just no quick way to deal with them. The whole point of the front line serjeants is to clear every metre of ground as they advance. Knowing you're in danger just by walking in to a building is going to be very stressful for the entire army, I'm afraid. Doing the job properly is going to slow us down considerably."

"So will the mud," Janne said. "We know where the roads are, but no one's actually seen a solid surface yet."

"Progress down the M6 is slow," Cathal confirmed. "The major bridges are out. We expected that, of course. But the mechanoids are having a lot of trouble erecting the replacements the convoys are carrying, they're just not designed to operate in this kind of environment."

"That situation should ease off tomorrow as well," Diana said.

"The rain, yes; but the mud will still be there."

"We're going to have to learn to live with that, I'm afraid. It's here for the duration."

*

**Did you know, the original ethnic Eskimos on Earth
had several dozen words for snow,** Sinon said.

Really? Choma answered from the other side of the
winding ravine they were following.

Apparently so.

**Excuse me for having my neural array assembled in
too much of a hurry, but I don't quite see the relevance
to our current situation.**

**I just thought, it might be appropriate if we had an
equal number of names for mud.**

**Oh right. Yes. Let's see, we could have real crappy
mud, bloody awful mud, pain in the ass mud,
squeezes inside your exoskeleton and squelches a lot
mud, and then there's always the ultimate: drowning
in mud.**

**You have a much higher emotional context than the
rest of us, don't you? Your jest about neural array assembly might be an unintentional truism.**

You are what you bring to yourself.

Quite. Sinon stepped over yet another fallen branch. It
was mid afternoon of the Liberation's second day. All the
serjeants had received the revised schedule from the Fort
Forward Ops Room, they were expected to move across the
land at about half the speed originally intended. Very opti-
mistic, Sinon thought.

It had taken until four o'clock in the morning to secure
Billesdon. Now they knew they were dealing with TNT, the
sensor blocks had been programmed to sniff it out. Given
TNT's relatively unstable nature, there were usually
enough molecules left floating round inside the building to
provide a positive detection. The damp didn't help, but by
and large, the blocks protected them.

Sinon himself had found two houses that were rigged.
They'd learned to tie the blocks to the end of long poles,
and push them through windows and doors already forced

open by the mud. Each time, he'd designated the buildings, and they were left for the marine engineers to send mechanoids in at some later time. They'd still lost another eight serjeants before the town was cleared.

The landing boats had returned as a feeble dawn broke; carrying their supplies, more jeeps, and the first of the marines troops. The wind had calmed, although the rain was still as intense. And the big harbour basin was now clotting up with mud, hampering their manoeuvring as they docked. But by mid morning, the quayside was thick with activity. A degree of confidence returned to the serjeants. They were getting back on track. With the marines holding Billesdon, the whole battalion began to deploy back out along the coast ready for the push inland.

True to Diana Tiernan's prediction, the rain did start to slacken by midday. Or at least, they convinced themselves it had; the light perforating the clouds was noticeably brighter. It did nothing to alleviate the misery of the mud. There had never been a landscape like it on any terracompatible Confederation world. Rover reporters stood on the edge of town, starkly silent as their enhanced retinas faithfully delivered the devastation back to the millions of citizens accessing the Liberation. Only the contours of the land remained stable, the mud had claimed everything else. There were no fields, or meadows, or scrubland, just a slick piss-brown coating, undulating and gurgling as it crept inexorably along. Mortonridge had become a single quagmire, extending from the sea to the horizon. Sensors in orbit showed the stain around the coast was already ten kilometres wide, and still spreading incursive fingers hungrily into the calm turquoise ocean.

Along with the rest of his squad, Sinon trudged through the forest, scrambling over the fallen trunks and their even more troublesome roots. Nothing had been left standing upright, although the tide of mud lacked the force to carry the trees with it. Superficially, the area resembled a bayou, although here the fractured wood was razor sharp, lacking the worn rottenness of plants growing in genuine swampland. Real bayous didn't have so many dead animals, either.

Like the vegetation, Mortonridge's indigenous creatures had taken a dreadful punishment. Birds and ground animals had drowned in their millions. Their corpses too, were part of the loose detritus carried along by the mud as it slid downwards into the ocean. Except in the forest, where the branches and root webs acted like nets. They were clustered round each tree, anonymous lumps, distending as they started to decompose. Heavy bubbles swelled across them like clumps of inflatable fungus as body gases forced a way out.

His battalion had been arranged in a line eighty kilometres wide, centred around Billesdon and its flanks merging with other battalions. This was the time when the army was stretched to its absolute maximum, completely encircling the entire peninsula. The AI had spaced the serjeants fifty metres apart right along the coast, planning on them yomping forwards together in a giant contracting sweep manoeuvre. If a possessed did try to hide out in the countryside they would never be more than twenty-five metres away from one of the serjeants. A combination of eyesight, infrared, SD satellite observation, and ELINT blocks ought to be able to locate them. Jeeps, trucks and reserve squads trailed behind the front line in columns one kilometre apart, ready to reinforce any section of the line that came under heavy attack. Mustered behind them were the prisoner-handling details.

When the gigantic formation was complete, the serjeants paused, reaffirming their commitment to the Liberation, celebrating the unity and accomplishment. Mortonridge was sealed off ahead of them, and now they were physically in place after all that had befallen, success appeared tangible. Doubt was banished.

"Go," Ralph ordered.

The pattern started to waver as soon as the serjeants left the coast behind. Mountain roads and tracks had vanished altogether. Valley floors were now deep rivers of mud. No vehicles could plough through the broken remains of the forests. The AI began to guide them round obstacles, always keeping the reserves within optimum distance of the front line. Slowing some sections of the advance, directing extra serjeants to expand the line over steep terrain.

They had their first encounter with a possessed seventy-six minutes after they started. Sinon watched through another set of eyes as the serjeant up near the firebreak fired its machine gun at a heat corona coming from behind an upturned car. Sparkling bullets ripped straight through the composite bodywork. Tendrils of enraged white fire curved over the top in retaliation. Another serjeant opened fire. The entire line halted, waiting to see what would happen.

For a moment there was no effect. Then the white fire faded, turning translucent before the rain smothered it, drops steaming as they fell through. A man staggered out from behind the wrecked car, hands waving madly as the bullets thudded into him. Ripples of purple light blazed out from every impact, swathing his body in a wondrous pyrotechnic display. The serjeant upped the fire rate.

"Stop it!" the man screamed. He crashed to his knees, hands batting feebly to ward off the machine gun. "Stop it for fuck's sake. I surrender, goddamn it."

The serjeant eased off the trigger, and walked forwards. "Lie down flat, put your hands behind your head. Do not attempt to move or apply your energistic power."

"Fuck you," the man snarled through clenched teeth. His body was shaking badly.

"Down. Now!"

"All right, all right." He lowered himself into the mud. "Mind if I don't go any further? Even we can't breathe mud."

The serjeant took its holding stick from its belt, a dull silver cylinder half a metre long. It telescoped out to two metres, and a pincer clamp at one end opened wide.

"What the hell . . . ?" the man grunted as the serjeant closed the clamp round his neck.

"This restraint has a dead-man function. If I let go, or I'm made to let go, it will fire ten thousand volts into you. If you resist or refuse to obey any instruction, I will shove a current into you and keep turning it up until your energistic ability is neutralised. Do you understand?"

"You're gonna die one day, you're going to join us."

The serjeant switched on a two hundred volt current.

"Jesus wept," the man squealed.

"Do you understand?"

"Yes. Yes, fuck. Turn it off. Off!"

"Very well. You will now leave this body."

"Or what, asshole? If you zap me too hard we both die. Me and my host."

"If you do not leave of your own violation, you will be placed in zero-tau."

"Fuck. I can't go back there." He started sobbing. "Don't you understand? I can't. Not there. *Please*. Please, if you've got an ounce of humanity in you, don't do this. I'm begging you."

"I'm sorry. That is not an option. Leave now."

"I can't."

The serjeant pulled on the holding stick, forcing the possessed to his feet. "This way."

"What now?"

"Zero-tau."

The cheering in the Ops Room was deafening. Ralph actually grinned out at them from his office, the image of the captured possessed being led away lingering in his mind. It might work, he thought. It just might. He remembered walking out of Exnall, the girl crying limply in his arms, Ekelund's mocking laughter in the air.

"Enjoy your victory with the girl," she'd sneered. His only personal success in that entire frightful night.

"Two down," Ralph whispered. "Two million to go."

The fish were dying. Stephanie thought that the oddest thing. This rain should be their chance to take over the whole world. Instead the ever-thickening mud was clogging up their gills, preventing them from breathing. They lay on the surface, being pushed along by the leisurely waves of water, their bodies flapping madly.

"We should like hollow out some logs, man, use them as canoes. That's what our ancestors used to do, and those cats were like really in tune with nature," Cochrane suggested when they cleared the end of the valley.

They'd only just made it, the sluggish river was leaking over the top of the track. At times it seemed as if the whole surface of the valley was on the move. They stood above the gurgling edge of the flow, and watched the gargantuan outpouring spread out to surge on across the lowlands.

"Fat lot of use that would be," Franklin muttered grimly. "Everything's heading down to the coast, and that's where *they* are. Besides," he gestured round extravagantly at the denuded valley. "What trees?"

"You are such a downer. I want some wheels, man. I have like totally had it with tramping through this shit."

"I thought cars were spawned by the capitalist Establish-

ment to promote our greed and distance us from nature,"
Rana said sweetly. "I'm sure I heard somebody say that recently."

Cochrane kicked at the fish flopping about round his feet.
"Get off my back, prickly sister. Okay? I'm thinking of
Moyo. He can't handle this."

"Just . . . quiet," Stephanie said. Even she was waspish,
fed up with the pettiness they were all displaying. The ordeal of the bus and then the track had stretched everyone's
nerves. "How are you?" she asked Moyo.

His face had returned to normal, the illusion swallowing
his bandage and shielding his scabbed tissue from sight.
Even his eyeballs appeared to dart about naturally. But he'd
taken a lot of cajoling and encouragement to walk along the
track. His thoughts had contracted, gathering round a centre
of sullen self-pity. "I'll be okay," he mumbled. "Just get me
out of this rain. I hate it."

"Amen to that," Cochrane chirped.

Stephanie looked round the shabby landscape. Visibility
was still pretty ropy on the other side of their protective
umbrella, though it was definitely lighter now. It was hard
to believe this eternal featureless mire was the same vigorous green countryside they'd travelled across in the Karmic
Crusader. "Well we can't go that way," she gestured at the
cataract of muddy water rumbling away into the distance.
"So I guess we'll have to stick to this side. Anyone remember roughly where the road is?"

"Along there, I think," McPhee said. Neither voice or
mind-tone suggested much confidence in the claim.
"There's definitely a flat ledge. See? The carbon-concrete
must have held up."

"Till the foundation gets washed out from under it,"
Franklin said.

Stephanie couldn't honestly see any difference in the mud where he was pointing. "All right, we'll go for it."

"How far?" Tina demanded querulously. "And how long will it take to get there?"

"Depends where you're heading, babe," Cochrane said.

"Well I don't know, do I? I wouldn't ask if it did."

"Any kind of building will do," Stephanie said. "We can reinforce it against the weather ourselves. I just want us out of this. We can think what to do next when we're rested up. Come on." Stephanie gripped Moyo's hand and began to walk in the direction the road was supposed to be. Fish tails slapped pitifully at her wellingtons.

"Oh man, it don't make no difference what we decide. We know what's like gonna happen."

"Then stay here and let it," Rana told the miserable hippie. She started off after Stephanie.

"I didn't say I was in a rush." The edge of the invisible shield moved towards Cochrane, and he scrambled after them.

"There was a village called Ketton on this road," McPhee said. "I remember going through it before we turned off up to the farm."

"How far?" Tina asked, her voice rising in hope.

Cochrane smiled happily. "Miles and miles, it'll probably take us like about ten—twenty days."

A ferocious jet of white fire squirted into the wall two metres above Sinon's head. He flattened himself into the mud below as paint ignited and carbon-concrete blistered.

Coming from the shops, seventy metres right. It was hard to see with all the smoke mingling with the rain, but his retinas had a long purple after image scorched across them.

Got it, Kerrial answered.

The white fire expanded into a thin circular sheet, rivulets trickled down, their tips wriggling purposefully towards Sinon. "Shit." If he stayed the fire would get him, if he moved he'd lose the cover which the wall provided. And there must be several of them in the shops; two other serjeants were under attack as well.

Eayres was a nothing village in the guidance block's memory. A cluster of houses clumped round a road junction, its population mostly employed by the local marble quarry. Who would expect the possessed to make a stand here? Expect the unexpected, Choma had chanted happily when the white fireballs burst open amid the squad.

Sinon saw Kerrial swing himself into position, bringing his machine gun to bear on the shops in the middle of the village. Bullet craters slammed across the brickwork in front of him. Then his body was being flung back, nerve channels shutting down. Blackness. Kerrial's memories arose from his neural array to be absorbed by an orbiting voidhawk.

They've got guns! Sinon broadcast.

Yes, Choma said. **I saw.**

Where did they get them from?

This is the countryside, hunting is a sport here. Besides, did you think we had a monopoly?

The white fire rivulets had reached the ground. Steam roared up as they floated sinuously along the top of the mud towards Sinon. He scrambled to his feet, and jumped forward. The white fire behind him vanished. Another, brighter, spear lanced out of a shop's fractured window. He hit the mud, rolling desperately as he brought his grenade launcher to bear.

You'll kill them, Choma warned. Sinon's right leg went dead as the white fire engulfed it. He slamfired the launcher, hand pumping the mechanism with cyborg intent.

Grenades thudded into the upper floor of the shop, detonating instantly. The ceiling split open, hurling down a torrent of rubble as the roof caved in. Three radiant lines of machine gun fire poured through the ground floor windows and into the tumult inside. The white fire evaporated into tiny violet wisps, splattering off Sinon's leg. He scrambled up, and pushed himself hard for the buildings dead ahead, dragging his useless leg along. Crashing through the first door to land in a deserted bar.

Clever, Choma said. *I think that's got them cold.*

The white fire had gone out everywhere. Serjeants converged on the little row of prim shops, walking forwards steadily, firing their machine guns continually. The squad had responded to the possessed like antibodies reacting to an incursive virus. Flowing in towards the village from both sides, the reserve squad racing forward. A miniature version of the noose contracting around Mortonridge. They had it encircled within minutes. Then began their advance.

Seventeen of them walked through the smoke that whirled along main street, impervious to the flames roaring out of the buildings all around. Their gunfire was concentrated on the shops, aiming their vivid bullets through any gap they could find. Weird lights flickered inside, as if someone had activated a nightclub hologram rig. Steam fountained out through windows and cracks in the wall.

"All right. Enough. *Enough*, God damn it. We're through."

The ring of serjeants held their places ten metres from the central shop, feet apart, juddering in time to the roaring guns.

"ENOUGH. We surrender." The machine guns fell silent.

Lumps of stone stirred on the mound of rubble which had been the shop's upper floor, spinning down to splash into the ubiquitous mire. Limbs began to emerge amid a welter

of coughing. Six possessed squirmed free, holding up their
hands and blinking uncomfortably. More serjeants moved
forwards to clamp their necks with holding sticks.

Elana Duncan reached Eayres two hours later. The fires
were out by then, extinguished by the rain. She whistled ap-
preciatively as she climbed out of the truck, a sound violent
enough to make the marines wince. "Must have been a hell
of a fight," she said in envy. The trucks had halted in the
village's main street. Over half of the buildings around her
had been flattened into small hillocks of debris; of those
that remained, few were left with roofs. Naked, heat-
twisted girders skewered up into the gloomy sky. Black
soot stains smeared over entire walls were already dissolving under the rain to reveal deep bullet pocks.

Marines began jumping down from the other trucks in
the convoy. It was a familiar routine by now. Urban zones,
whatever the size, were occupied by a garrison. They
served as emergency reserves and staging post; also a tran-
sitory field hospital a lot of the time. The possessed weren't
giving up without a fight. The marine lieutenant in charge
started shouting orders, and the troops fanned out to secure
the perimeter. Elana and the other mercs began unloading
their truck with the help of five mud-caked mechanoids.

First off was a programmable multipurpose silicon hall.
An oval twenty-five metres long, with open archways along
the sides. It was a standard Kulu Royal Marine corps issue,
designed for tropical climates, with an overhang in anticipation of heavy showers, and allowing a constant breeze to
filter through. Ordinarily ideal for a place like Mortonridge.
Now, they were having to direct the mechanoids to bulldoze
up a base from soil and stone which they then sealed over
with fast-set polymer. It was the only way to keep the hall's
floor above mud level.

Once that was up, they started moving the zero-tau pods in. A double file of serjeants marched down the main street, escorting three possessed. Elana splashed out to greet them. She enjoyed this part of her duty.

One of the possessed had given up, a man in his late sixties. She'd seen that before. Filthy, torn clothes. Not bothering to heal his wounds. Even the rain was allowed to soak him. The other two were more typical. Dignity intact. Clothes immaculate, not a scratch on them. The rain bounced off as if they had a frictionless coating. Elana gave one of them a long look. A woman in a prim antique blue suit, white blouse with a lace collar, and pearl necklace. Her hair was a solid bottle blonde coiffure that could have been carved from rock for all the wind affected it. She gave Elana a single distasteful glance, defiantly arrogant.

Elana nodded affably at the serjeant guarding her, whose leg was wrapped in a medical package tube. "Humm, she's the third one of these today. And I thought that woman was unique."

"Excuse me?" the serjeant asked.

"They enjoy historical figures. I've been accessing my encylopedea's history files ever since this campaign started, trying to place them. Hitlers are quite popular, so's Napoleon and Richard Saldana, then there's Cleopatra. Somebody called Ellen Ripley is a big favourite with the women, too; but none of my search programs have managed to track her down yet."

The blue-suited woman looked dead ahead, and smiled a secret smile.

"Okay," Elana said. "Bring them in."

The mercenaries were hooking the zero-tau pods up to their power cells, datavising diagnostics through the management processors. Elana's ELINT block gave a warning bleep. She rounded on the three prisoners, pulling a high-voltage shockrod from her belt. Her voice boomed out from her facial grille, echoing round the hall.

"Cut that out, shitbrains. You lost, and this is the end of the line. Too late to argue about it now. The serjeants might be too honourable and decent to fry your bodies, but I'm not. And this is my part of the operation. Got that?" The ELINT block quietened. "Good. Then we'll get along just fine in your final minutes in this universe. Any last minute cigarettes, you can indulge yourselves. Otherwise just keep quiet."

"I see you have found an occupation which obviously suits you."

"Huh?" She glanced down at serjeant with the injured leg.

"We met at Fort Forward, just after arriving. I am Sinon."

Her three claws snapped together with a loud *click*. "Oh yes, the cannon fodder guy. Sorry, you all look alike to me."

"We are identical."

"Glad to see you survived. Though God knows how you managed it. Trying to storm ashore through that weather was the dumbest military decision since the Trojans took a shine to that horse."

"I think you're being unduly cynical."

"Don't give me that crap. You must have a decent dose of it too, if you've survived this long. Remember the oldest military rule, my friend."

"Never volunteer for anything?"

"Generals always fuck up bad."

The first zero-tau pod opened. Elana pointed her shock-rod at the blue-suited woman. "Okay, Prime Minister, you first." Sinon kept the holding stick round her neck as she backed in. Metal manacles closed round her limbs, and Elana switched on a mild current. The woman glared out, her face drawn back with the effort of fighting the electricity.

"Just in case," Elana told Sinon. "We had a few try to break free once they finally realize their number's up. You can take the holding stick off now." The clamp sprang open, and Sinon stood clear. "You going to leave all nice and voluntarily?" Elana asked. The front of the zero-tau pod was already swinging shut. The woman spat weakly. "Didn't think so. Not you."

The zero-tau pod turned midnight black. Elana heard a hiss of breath from one of the waiting possessed, but didn't say anything.

"How long do you leave them in there?" Sinon asked.

"Cook them for about fifteen minutes. Then we open up to see if they're done. If not, it's just back in for progressively longer periods. I've had one hold out for about ten hours before, but that was the limit."

"That sounds suspiciously like enjoyment to me."

Elana waved the next possessed into his pod. "Nothing suspicious about it. General Hiltch, God fuck him, says I'm not allowed in the front line. So this is the second best duty as far as I'm concerned. I don't take marine discipline too good. Sitting with a bunch of those pansy-asses in a place like this counting raindrops would have me thrown off-planet inside of a day. So as I'm technologically competent, me and my friends requested this placement. It works out fine. Army's short of skilled techs who can also handle the noise if the possessed start to panic: we fit the bill. And this way I get to see the bastards booted out of their bodies. I *know* it's happening."

The second possessed was put in a zero-tau pod. He didn't resist. Then the third zero-tau pod was activated. Elana aimed the shock rod at the last possessed, the apathetic one. "Hey, cheer up. This is your lucky day, looks like the reserves got called out. You're on, kid." He gave her a broken look and grimaced. His features melted, shrinking back to reveal a wizened face with anaemically pale skin.

"Catch him," Elana yelled. The man's legs buckled. He pitched forward into her arms. "Thought that one might quit," she said in satisfaction.

Choma removed the holding stick's clamp from around his neck. Elana eased him down onto the floor, calling for blankets and some pillows. "Damn it, we haven't had time to unpack the medical gear yet," she said. "And we're going to need it. Those bastards."

"What's the matter?" Sinon asked.

Elana's claw sliced through the man's raggedy shirt, exposing his chest. There were strange ridges swelling out of his skin, mimicking the lines of muscle a healthy twenty-year-old mesomorph might have. When she prodded one with the tip of a claw, it sagged like a sack of jelly.

"They always go for perfection," she explained to Sinon and Choma. "Assholes. I don't know what that energistic power is, but it screws up their flesh real bad under the illusion. Sometimes you get fat deposits building up, that's pretty harmless; but nine times out of ten, it's tumours."

"All of them?" Sinon asked.

"Yep. Never satisfied with what they've got. I'm sure it's a metaphor for something, but I'm buggered if I can figure out what. We're having to ship everyone who gets de-possessed back to Xingu and into one of the major hospitals. They're overflowing already, and they don't have enough nanonic packages to go around. Another week of this, and the entire Ombey system is going to go into medical meltdown. And that's not taking you guys into account; you're not exactly emerging unscathed from the Liberation."

"Can we help?"

"Not a thing you can do, sorry. Now if you could clear

out . . . I've got to try and organize some sort of transport for this batch. Hell, I wish we had hovercraft, they're the only things that can travel properly over this swamp. That dickhead Hiltch won't allow any planes in under the cloud yet."

Sinon and Choma left her and another couple of mercenaries running medical scanners over the unconscious man.

All of them? Sinon repeated gloomily. The prospect kindled a sensation of alarm, in itself a worrying development. He hadn't configured himself to be waylaid by impulsive emotions. **Do you know what that means?**

Trouble, Choma declared. **Real bad trouble.**

THE NAKED GOD

8

The vac-trains were an excellent solution to Earth's transport problem in the age of the arcologies. There were no aircraft any more. The armada storms had finished off air travel in the same way they made people abandon their cars. One of the late Twenty-first Century's most enduring newscable images was of a farmer's pick-up truck rammed through the nineteenth-floor window of the Sears Tower in the wake of a storm. As the planet's population flowed into cities and began strengthening them against the weather, so they turned to trains as the only practical method of transport between urban conglomerations. Heavy and stolid, tornadoes couldn't fling them about so easily. Of course, they still took a battering from the wind if they were caught out in the open. So the next logical stage was to protect the tracks in the same way the domes were going up to shield the city centres. The first real example was the channel tunnel, which was extended to cover the whole journey between London and Paris. Once that proved viable, the global rail network was rapidly expanded. As with any macro-infrastructure project awash with government money, the technology advanced swiftly.

By the time Louise and Genevieve arrived on Earth, the vac-trains were a highly mature system, travelling at considerable speed between stations. Common wisdom had the tunnels drilled kilometres deep in the safety of the bedrock. Not so; a lot of the time they didn't even qualify as tunnels. Giant tubes were laid over the abandoned land, and buried just below the surface. It was much easier to maintain the vacuum inside that kind of factory-manufactured subway than in a rock tunnel. Tectonics played havoc with rigid lava walls that had been melted by a flame of fusion plasma; experience showed they fractured easily, and on a couple of occasions actually sheered. So tunnels were only used to thread the tubes through mountains and plunge deep under arcologies. Even trans-oceanic routes were laid in trenches and anchored in place.

With no air to create friction, the trains were free to accelerate hard; on the longer trans-Pacific runs they touched Mach fifteen. Powered by linear motors, they were quick, smooth, silent, and efficient. The trip from Mount Kenya station to London's Kings Cross took Louise and Genevieve forty-five minutes, with one stop at Gibraltar. Airlocks at both ends of their carriage matched up with platform hatches, and popped open.

"All passengers for London please disembark," the sparkling AV pillars on the carriage ceiling announced. "This train will depart for Oslo in four minutes."

The girls collected their big shoulder bags and hurried out onto the platform. They emerged into a long rectangular chamber, its ornately sculpted walls harking back to long-distant imperial grandeur. The line of twenty hatches connecting to the train appeared to be made of black wrought iron, Victorian-era space technology. On the opposite side, three large archways lead to broad wave escalators that spiralled upwards with impressive curves.

Genevieve stayed close behind her big sister as she negotiated their way across the platform. At least this time they managed to avoid barging in to people. Excitement was powering a smile that would not fade.

An Earth arcology. London! Where we all came from originally. Home—sort of. How utterly utterly stupendous. It was the complete opposite of the nightmare that had been Norfolk by the time they left. This world had massive defences, and its people could do whatever they wanted with lots of fabulous machines to help them. She held Louise's hand tightly as they stepped onto the wave elevator. "Where next?"

"Don't know," Louise said. For some reason she was completely calm. "Let's see what's up there, shall we?"

The wave escalator brought them onto the floor of a huge hemispherical cavern. It was like the arrivals hall of Mount Kenya station, only larger. The base of the wall was pierced by tunnel entrances radiating out to lift shafts and platforms for the local train network, while the floor was broken by concentric rows of wave elevators to the vac-trains. Bright informational spheres formed tightly packed streamers five metres above the heads of the thronging passengers, weaving around each other with serpentine grace. Right in the centre was a single flared spire of rock that rose up to eventually merge into the roof's apex.

"It's just another station," Genevieve said in mild disappointment. "We're still underground."

"Looks like it." Louise squinted up. Black flecks were zipping through the strata of informationals, as if they were suffering from static. She smiled, pointing. "Birds, look."

Genevieve twirled round, following their erratic flight. There were all sorts, from pert brown sparrows to emerald and turquoise parrots.

"We'd better find a hotel, I suppose," Louise said. She

pulled her shoulder bag round to take the processor block out.

Genevieve tugged at her arm. "Oh please, Louise. Can't we go up to the surface first? I just want to look. I'll be good, I promise. Please?"

Louise tucked the shoulder bag back. "I wouldn't mind a peek myself." She studied the informationals, catching sight of one that seemed promising. "Come on." She caught Gen's hand. "This way."

They took a lift up to the surface. It brought them out in a mock-Hellenic temple at the middle of a wide plaza full of statues and fenced in by huge oaks. A small commemorative plaque on a worn pillar marked the passing of the station's old surface structures and iron rail tracks. Louise walked out from the shade of the temple, wandering aimlessly for a few yards until she simply stopped. It was as if the arcology was appearing in segments before her. Slowly. As soon as her mind acknowledged one part, another would flip up behind that, demanding recognition.

Though she didn't know it, Kings Cross was the geographical heart of the tremendous Westminster Dome, which at thirty kilometres in diameter enclosed most of the original city, from Ealing in the west to Woolwich in the east. Ever since the first small protective domes went up over London (a meagre four km wide to start with—the best Twenty-first Century materials technology could manage), preservation orders had been slapped on every building of historical or architectural significance, which the conservationists basically defined as anything not built from concrete. By the time the Westminster Dome was constructed over that initial cluster of ageing weather shields, the outlying districts had undergone significant changes, but any Londoner from the mid Nineteenth Century onwards would have been able to find their way around the central portion without too much trouble. It was essentially one of the largest lived-in museums on the planet.

The nine smaller domes circling round outside the Westminster, however, were a different matter. London didn't have the megatowers of New York, but the arcology still housed a quarter of a billion people beneath its geodesic crystal roofs. The outer domes were purpose built, four hundred square kilometres apiece of thoroughly modern arcology, with only tiny little zones of original buildings left as curios amid the gleaming condos, skyscrapers, and malls.

Louise wasn't aware of them at all. She could see on the other side of the oaks that the plaza was encircled by a wide road jammed with sleek vehicles, all driving so close together you couldn't walk between them. The vehicles merged in and out of the giant roundabout from wide streets that radiated away between the beautiful ancient grey-stone buildings surrounding the plaza. When she raised her gaze above the blue-slate roofs and their elaborate chimney stacks, she could see even grander and taller buildings behind them. Then beyond those . . . It was as though she was standing at the bottom of a mighty crater whose walls were made entirely from buildings. Around the plaza they were elegant and unique, with each one somehow merging cleanly into its neighbours to form compact refined streets; but they grew from that to plainer, larger skyscrapers, spaced further apart. The towers' artistry came from the overall shape rather than detailed embellishments, moulded to suggest Gothic, Roman, Art Deco, and Alpine Bavarian influences among others.

And gathering all those disparate architectural siblings within its sheltering embrace was the external wall. A single redoubtable cliff of windows, a mosaic of panes so dense it blended into a seamless band of glass, blazing gold under the noonday sun. Out of that, rose the dome itself, an artificial sky of crystal.

Louise sat down heavily on the plaza's stone slabs, and let out a whoosh of breath. Gen sat beside her, arms folded protectively round her shoulder bag. London's pedestrians flowed round them, eyes consummately averted.

"It's very big, isn't it?" Gen said quietly.

"Certainly is." All those buildings, so many people. Despite feeling light headed, a weight of worry was threatening to sink her again. *How in heaven's name am I going to find a single person amid this multitude? Especially when they probably don't want to be found.*

"Fletcher would really love this."

Louise looked at her sister. "Yes. I think he would."

"Do you suppose he'd recognize any of it?"

"There may be bits left over from his time. Some of these buildings look quite old. We'll have to look it up in the local library memory." She broke off and smiled. *That's it, everything you ever need to know is in the processor memories. Banneth will be listed somewhere, I just have to program in the right search.* "Come on. Hotel first. Then we'll get something to eat. How does that sound?"

"Jolly nice. What hotel are we going to?"

"Give me a moment." She took her processor block out, and started querying the arcology's general information centre. Category visitors, subsection residential. Central, and civilized. They'd wind up paying more for a classy hotel, but at least they'd be safe. Louise knew there were parts of Earth's arcologies that were terribly crime-ridden. And besides, "Kavanaghs never stay anywhere that doesn't have a four-star rating," Daddy had said once.

Information slid down the screen. They didn't seem to have star ratings here, so she just went by price. Central

London hotels, apparently, cost as much to run as starships.
At least the beds will be a lot more comfortable.

"The Ritz," she said finally.

That just left getting there. With Genevieve getting progressively more impatient, as evidenced by overloud sighs
and shuffling feet, Louise requested surface transport options from Kings Cross to the Ritz. After ten minutes struggling with horribly complicated maps and London Metro
timetables that kept flashing up she realized she wasn't
quite as adept at operating the block as she thought she was.
However, the screen did tell here there were taxies available.

"We'll take a cab."

Under Gen's ungenerously sceptical look, she picked her
shoulder bag up, and started off towards the oaks at the rim
of the plaza. Flocks of parakeets and budgerigars pecking at
the stone slabs stampeded out of her way. Most of the subway entrances had the name of the streets they led to, but a
few had the London Transport symbol on top: blue circle
cut by a red line, with a crown in the middle. Louise went
down one to find herself in a short passage that opened out
into a narrow parking bay. Five identical silver-blue taxi
cars were waiting silently, streamlined bubbles with very
fat tyres.

"Now what?" Genevieve said.

Louise consulted the block. She walked up to the first
taxi, and keyed the Commence Journey icon on the block's
screen. The door hissed out five centimetres, then slid back
along the body. "We get in," she told her sister smugly.

"Oh very clever. What happens if you don't have a block
to do that for you?"

"I don't know." She couldn't see a handle anywhere. "I
suppose everyone on this world is taught how to use things
like this. Most of them have neural nanonics, after all."

There wasn't much room inside, enough for four seats with deep curving backs. Louise shoved her bag in the storage bin underneath, and studied the screen again. The block was interfacing with the taxi's control processor, which made life a lot simpler for her. The whole activation procedure was presented to her as a simple, easy-to-understand menu. She fed in their destination, and the door slid shut. The taxi told the block what their fee was (as much as the vac-train fare from Mount Kenya), and explained how to use the seat straps.

"Ready?" she asked Gen, when they'd fastened themselves in.

"Yes." The little girl couldn't hide her enthusiasm.

Louise held her Jovian Bank disk up to the small panel on the taxi's central column, and transferred the money over. They started to roll forward. The taxi took them up a steep ramp, accelerating fast enough to press the sisters back into their seat cushioning. The reason was simple enough, they emerged right in the middle of the traffic racing round the Kings Cross plaza, slotting in without the slightest fuss.

Genevieve laughed excitedly as they zipped across several lanes, then slowed slightly to turn off down one of the broad streets. "Golly, this is better than the aeroambulance." The little girl grinned.

Louise rolled her eyes. Though once she accepted the fact that the control processor did know how to drive, she began to breathe normally again. The buildings rushing past were old and sombre, which gave them a dignity all of their own. On the other side of the pavement barrier, pedestrians jostled their way along in a permanent scrum.

"I never knew there were so many people," Gen said. "London must have more than live on the whole of Norfolk."

"Probably," Louise agreed.

The taxi took them a third of the way round the expressway, then turned off, heading back down to ground level. There were parks on both sides of the road when they started their descent, then buildings rose up to their left, and they were back on one of the ancient streets again. The pavements here didn't seem so crowded. They slowed drastically, pulling over to the right alongside a large cube of white-grey stone with tall windows lined by iron railings and a steep state roof. An open arcade ran along the front, supported by wide arches. The taxi stopped level with a gate in the roadside barrier, which a doorman opened smartly. He was dressed in a dark blue coat and top hat, a double row of brass buttons gleamed down his chest. At last, Louise felt at home. This was something she could deal with.

If the doorman was surprised at who climbed out of the taxi he never showed it. "Are you staying here, miss?" he asked.

"I hope so, yes."

He nodded politely, and ushered them under the arcade towards the main entrance.

Genevieve eyed the front of the stolid building sceptically. "It looks dreadfully gloomy."

The lobby inside was white and gold, with chandeliers resembling frost-encrusted branches that had dazzling stars at the tip of each twig. Arches along the long central aisle opened into big rooms that were full of prim white tables where people were sitting having tea. Waiters in long black tailcoats bustled about, carrying trays with silver teapots and very tempting cakes.

Louise marched confidently over to the gleaming oak reception desk. "A twin room, please."

The young woman standing behind smiled professionally. "Yes, madam. How long for?"

"Um. A week to start with."

"Of course. I'll need your ident flek, please, to register. And there is a deposit."

"Oh, we haven't got an ident flek."

"We're from Norfolk," Gen said eagerly.

The receptionist's composure flickered. "Really?" She cleared her throat. "If you're from offworld, your passports will be satisfactory."

Louise handed the passports over, thinking briefly of Endron again, and wondering how much trouble the Martian was in right now. The receptionist scanned the passports in a block and took the deposit from Louise. A bellboy came forward and relieved the sisters of their bags before showing them into a lift.

Their room was on the fourth floor, with a large window overlooking the park. The decor was so reminiscent of the kind Norfolk landowners worshiped it gave Louise a sense of déjà vu; regal-purple wallpaper and furniture so old the wood was virtually black beneath the polish. Her feet sank into a carpet well over an inch thick.

"Where are we?" Gen asked the bellboy. She was pressed up against the window, staring out. "I mean, what's that park called?"

"That's Green Park, miss."

"So are we near anywhere famous?"

"Buckingham Palace is on the other side of the park."

"Gosh."

He showed Louise the room's processor block, which was built in to the dresser. "Any information you need on the city for your stay should be in here; it has a comprehensive tourist section," he said. She tipped him a couple of fuseodollars when he left. He'd been holding his own credit disk, casually visible through fingers splayed wide.

Genevieve waited until the door shut. "What's Buckingham Palace?"

The AI was alert to the glitch within a hundredth of a second. Two ticket dispenser processors and an informational projector. It brought additional analysis programs on lines, and ran an immediate verification sweep of every electronic circuit in Grand Central Station.

Half a second. The response to a general acknowledgement datavise from five sets of neural nanonics was incorrect. All of them were within a seven metre zone, which also incorporated the failing ticket dispensers.

Two seconds. Security sensors in Grand Central's concourse focused on the suspect area. The AI datavised to B7's North American supervisor the fact it had located a possessed-type glitch in New York. He had just framed his query in reply when the sensors observed Bud Johnson go cartwheeling over someone in a black robe crouched on the floor.

Three and a half seconds. There was a visual discontinuity. None of the sensor short-term memory buffers had registered the black clad figure before. It was as if he'd just materialized out of nowhere. If he had neural nanonics, then they were not responding to the ident request datavise.

Four seconds. The North American supervisor took direct control of the situation in conjunction with the AI. A datavised warning went out to the rest of the supervisors.

Six seconds. The full B7 complement of supervisors was on line, observing. The AI's visual characteristics program locked on to the shadowed face inside the black robe's hood. Quinn Dexter rose to his feet.

South Pacific: "Nuke him. Now!"

Western Europe: "Don't be absurd."

Halo: "SD platforms armed; do you want groundstrike?"

North America: "No. It's completely impractical. Grand Central Station's concourse is a hundred and fifty metres below ground, and that's spread out below three skyscrapers. There isn't an X-ray laser built that could reach it."

South Pacific: "Then use a real nuke. A combat wasp can be down there in two minutes."

Asian Pacific: "I second that."

Western Europe: "No! Damn it. Will you morons control yourselves."

North America: "Thank you. I'm not going to blast Dome One into oblivion. There are twenty million people living in there. Even Laton didn't kill that many."

North Europe: "You can't let him go. We have to exterminate him."

Western Europe: "How?"

North Europe: "South Pacific's right. Nuke the shit. I'm sorry about the other inhabitants, but it's the only way we can resolve the situation."

Western Europe: "Observe, please."

Eleven seconds. Bud Johnson's face had turned purple. He scrabbled feebly at his chest, then pitched over onto the floor. People clustered round him. Quinn Dexter became translucent and quickly faded from view. The AI reported all the processors had come back on line.

Military Intelligence: "Oh shit."

Western Europe: "Will a nuke kill him now do you think? Wherever he is."

South Pacific: "One way to find out."

Western Europe: "I cannot permit that. We exist primarily to protect Earth. Even with our prerogatives, you cannot exterminate twenty million people in the *hope* that you kill one terrorist."

Halo: "The boy's right, I'm afraid. I'm standing down the SD platforms."

South Pacific: "Terrorist demon, more like."

Western Europe: "I'm not arguing definitions. All this does is confirm I was right the first time. We have got to be extremely careful how we deal with Dexter."

North Pacific: "Well at least shut down New York's vac-trains."

Central America: "Yes. Isolate him in New York. You can creep up on him there."

Western Europe: "I'm going to have to say no again."

North Pacific: "In Allah's name, why? We know where he is, that gives us a tremendous advantage."

Western Europe: "It's psychology. He knows we know he's here. He's not stupid, he'll realize we'll find out about him appearing in Grand Central station. The question is, how long does it take us to find out? If we stop the vac-trains now, it shows him we are right up to speed and deeply worried by him, and also that we'll go all out to stop him. That's not good, that puts him on guard."

Central America: "So, he's on guard? If he's trapped in one place, it won't do him any good. He'll still be on death row. He knows it's coming, and there's nothing he can do about it."

Western Europe: "First thing he'll do is mobilise New York to defend himself. And we'll be back to one option of having to nuke the place. Don't you see? Our arcologies are even more vulnerable than asteroid settlements. They are utterly dependent on technology, not just to protect us from the weather, but to feed us and condition our air. If you confine three hundred million possessed inside one, every single chunk of machinery will break down. The domes will shatter in the first storm that comes along, and the population will either starve or turn cannibal."

Central America: "I'm prepared to sacrifice one arcology to save the rest. If that's what it takes."

Western Europe: "But we don't have to sacrifice one. Certainly not yet. You're being abysmally premature. Right now, Dexter will be skipping round arcologies, establishing small groups of possessed who'll keep their heads down until he gives the word. While he's doing that, we've got a chance. There will only be small groups in each arcology, which *we* really ought to be able to find. If other worlds can track them, so can we. Dexter is our problem, not the ordinary possessed."

Asian Pacific: "Put it to the vote."

Western Europe: "How wonderfully democratic. Very well."

Six supervisors voted for closing down New York's vac-trains right away. Ten voted to keep them open.

Western Europe: "Thank you so much for your confidence."

Southern Africa: "You have the ball for now. But if you haven't dealt with Dexter in another ten days, I shall be voting to isolate him wherever he is. And then we'll see if he can hide from a nuke as well as he can from a sensor."

The conference dissolved. Western Europe asked North America, Military Intelligence, and Halo to remain on line. Natural allies in the eternal warzone of B7's internal politics, they obliged. His sensevise overlay program positioning and dressing them around his drawing room as though they were weekend guests just come in from a stroll round the grounds.

"It'll go against you eventually," Halo warned. "They're happy for you to take responsibility for the chase as long as Dexter hasn't caused any noticeable damage. But the minute he gets noisy, they'll revert."

"That little crap artist, South Pacific," North America complained. "Telling me to nuke New York! Who the hell does she think she is?"

"She always favours the blunt approach," Western Europe said. "We all know that. That's why I like her so much, makes one feel constantly superior."

"Inferior or not, she'll carry the day eventually," Military Intelligence said.

Western Europe walked over to the tall glass-panelled door, and let his two Labradors in. "I know. That's why I found today encouraging."

"Encouraging?" North America asked, astonished. "Are you kidding? I've got that Dexter bastard running round loose in New York."

"Yes, exactly. Something went wrong for him. He was on his knees when he appeared, and he vanished within seconds. *He* was glitched. Another factor in our favour."

"Maybe," Halo said. He sounded very dubious.

"All right," North America said. "So what now?"

"You need to do two things. In forty minutes, I want you to close down all New York's vac-trains."

"Forty minutes? He'll be long gone."

"Yes. As I said, he knows we know he's here. We have to play along with that, but make him think we're lumbering along five steps behind him. So close the vac-trains. He won't be in New York, so it doesn't matter."

"You hope."

"I know. Once he'd been exposed there he had no option but to leave. New York is closed to him now, out of the equation. To do whatever he wants to do, he has to maintain his mobility. He probably took the shortest ride out there is, figuring the police would close down the vac-trains pretty fast; but that's beside the point."

"Okay. How long do you want them shut down for?"

"That's the second thing. We have to work on the assumption he was leaving. Therefore, he's more than likely left a group of possessed behind him. You have to find them, and eliminate them. Keep the arcology sealed up until you do. In fact, keeping the individual domes isolated might be a good idea if you can manage it."

"You really think that's what he's doing?"

"Yes. He wants to inflict maximum devastation on this planet. He'll seed as many arcologies as possible with his followers. And when he gives the word, they'll hit the streets, and we'll be faced with the exponential curve again."

"The AI is monitoring the arcology's electronics anyway."

"Yes. I'm sure that's effective on Kulu and other modern worlds; but you and I know it can never access everything, not here, not in the old areas. There's over five hundred years' worth of electronic junk plugged together out there; we're dealing with millions of old systems, quirky one-offs, and non-standard patch ups. The AI is a good sentry, but don't make the mistake of becoming dependent. The best source we'll have is probably the sects."

"The sects?"

"Certainly. The one set of idiots who'll support the possessed without having to be forced. Dexter knows that, they're the ones he'll go to."

"All right, I'll get on to it."

"So what are you going to be doing?" Halo asked Western Europe.

"Same as before. Engineer an encounter. We have to get our people close to him while he's visible, and therefore vulnerable."

"Vulnerable to what?"

"If he's out in the open, an SD strike. Or if our contact is through an agent, we can try for electrocution or a memory scramble."

"Memory scramble?"

"Yes," said Military Intelligence. "The CNIS believes they can kill souls by firing some kind of mentallic virus at the possessed. It's the opposite of a didactic imprint. They're researching it now."

Western Europe started making a fuss of one of the dogs, scratching its belly as it rolled around on the carpet. "Do try and stay up to date," he chided Halo.

"It won't be available before the end of the week," Military Intelligence warned.

"I know. I doubt I'll manage to arrange an interception by then anyway."

"How's that angle coming along?" Halo asked.

"The Banneth connection is just about covered. I'm not sure about the Kavanagh girls; they're a long shot, and a pretty random one at that. But I'm working on it."

Louise spent an hour using the room's desktop processor block and got nowhere. The directory provided her with enough entries under Banneth (173,364—once she'd removed the deceased), but no matter how she tried to cross reference that with Quinn Dexter the result was always negative. She racked her brains to remember everything Dexter had said back in the hangar at Bennett Field. Banneth was female, she remembered that for certain. And Dexter said she'd hurt him. That was about it, really.

Somewhere, somehow, those facts should link up. She was sure they did. But finding the connection was beyond her woeful programming ability. The idea that had begun back when they got in the taxi was becoming more and more attractive. If she dared.

Why not? she thought. There's nothing dangerous about

neural nanonics, not physically, the rest of the Confederation uses them. Joshua has a set. It's only Norfolk which doesn't allow them. She raised her arm, and looked at the discreet medical nanonic package bracelet. Also banned on Norfolk, yet it was helping her pregnancy. That settled it. She grinned, emboldened by her decision. I have to take responsibility for myself now. If I need neural nanonics to help me on Earth, then I will get myself a set.

They hadn't left the room since arriving at the hotel. Lunch had been a snack delivered by room service. Genevieve had flopped on her bed in weary disgust at the inactivity, and activated her own block. She was smothered by a laser-haze of grid lines and feisty fantasy beasts which leapt about enthusiastically at every excitable shouted command.

"Gen?"

The projection shrank. Genevieve blinked up at her, trying to focus. Louise was sure that being immersed in the projection so much was bad for her little sister's eyesight.

"What?"

"We're going out. I can't get the hang of the desktop block, so I'm going to buy some neural nanonics instead." There, she'd said it out loud. There'd be no backing down now.

Genevieve stared at her in astonishment. "Oh Louise, don't tease so. We're not allowed."

"We *weren't* allowed. We're on Earth, now, remember. You can do anything you want here as long as you've got money."

Genevieve cocked her head to one side. Then the most charming smile graced her face. It didn't fool Louise for a second. "Please, Louise. Can I have one, too? You know I'll never be allowed once we get home."

"I'm sorry. You're not old enough."

"*I am!*"

"Gen, you're not. And you know you're not."

She stamped her foot, little fists clenched in outrage. "That's not fair! It's not. It's not. You always pick on me coz I'm the youngest. You're a bully."

"I'm not picking on you. You just can't have one, your brain is still growing. They can't connect it. I checked. It's not legal, and it'll do a lot of damage to your brain cells. I only just scrape in if you measure my age in Earth years."

"I hate being small."

Louise put her arms round the girl, reflecting on how much she'd done so since leaving home. They never used to hug much before. "You'll be bigger one day," she whispered into her sister's fluffed up hair. "And things are going to be different when we get home."

"You think so?"

"Oh yes."

The receptionist seemed rather amused at being asked, in a lofty sort of way. But she was helpful enough, telling Louise that Oxford Street and New Bond Street were probably their best bet for clothes, while Tottenham Court Road was where they would find any conceivable kind of electronics. The sisters were also assured these areas were safe for girls to walk through by themselves. "And the hotel runs a courtesy collection service for any items that you purchase." She handed over an authorization disk, keyed to Louise's biolectric pattern.

Louise loaded a comprehensive street map into her block, taken from the hotel's memory; and combined it with the guidance program. "Ready?" she asked Gen. "Let's go spend the family fortune."

Aubry Earle had spoken the truth on the lift capsule when he told them arcology dwellers would always respect their privacy. Out on the street, Louise couldn't quite work out how people always slid to one side at the last second. She was constantly scanning bodies all round to try and find a way through the gaps, while locals moved as smoothly as the automated traffic without ever once glancing in her direction. Some of the pedestrians quite literally glided past. People their own age wearing calf-high boots with soles that seemed to flow over the pavement slabs without any resistance. Genevieve watched their effortless progress with admiration and longing. "I want some boots like that," she said.

A subwalk got them under Piccadilly and into New Bond Street. It turned out to be a dainty little pedestrian lane, lined with enchanting boutiques whose marble frontage was embossed with brass lettering saying when they'd been established. None of them were under three centuries old, while some claimed to be over seven. The labels on show meant nothing to either of them, but judging by the prices they must have been admiring the most exclusive designer garments on the planet.

"It's gorgeous," Louise sighed longingly at a shimmering scarlet and turquoise evening gown, sort of like an all-over mermaid's tail—except it wasn't all-over, nowhere near. It was the kind of thing she would love to wear at a summer ball on Norfolk. The planet had never seen its like before.

"Then buy it."

"No. We've got to be sensible. Just everyday clothes that we need to get about in the arcology. Remember, one day I'll have to explain the entire bill to Daddy."

The evening gown was just the start of New Bond Street's provocative temptations. They trailed past window displays she could have bought en masse.

"We'll have to have supper in the hotel dining room,"

Genevieve suggested artfully. "I bet they won't let us in unless we dress up."

It was an insidious suggestion. "Okay. One dress. That's all."

They dashed across the threshold of the boutique in front of them. Privacy didn't apply inside the shop; three assistants swooped eagerly. Louise explained what they wanted, and then spent the next forty-five minutes ricocheting in and out of a changing room. She and Gen would look at each other, comment, and go back for the next trial.

She learned a lot in the process. The assistants were very complimentary about the sisters' hair. Except . . . on Earth, it was fashionable to have actives woven among the strands. Their one-piece suits with big pockets, were current, but not that *à la mode*. Yes, Oxford Street stores were perfect for buying streetfashion clothes, and we recommend these. Louise could have sworn she heard the block's memory creaking under the load of names they entered. She used her Jovian Bank credit disk with only a momentary twinge of guilt.

Out on the street again, they laughed at each other. Gen had wound up with a scarlet dress and deep-purple jacket. While Louise had bought herself a full length gown of deepest blue, that was made from a material crossed between velvet and suede. There was also a short ginger-coloured waistcoat to go with it, which complemented its square cut neck.

"It's true," Louise said happily. "Retail therapy actually works."

They didn't get directly to Oxford Street. There was a stop at a salon at the top of New Bond Street first. The beauticians made an incredible fuss over them, delighted with so much raw material to work on. The owner himself came over to direct the operation (once their credit rating had been verified).

After two hours, several cups of tea, and enthralling the staff with an edited version of their travels, Louise had the wrap taken off. She stared in the mirror, not believing she'd spent her life tolerating unmanaged hair. Norfolk's simplistic regime of washing, conditioners, and sturdy brushing was barbaric ineptitude. Under the salon's professional auspices her hair had become lustrous, individual strands conducting a little starlight shimmer of light along their length. And it flowed. Every day of her life she'd held that thick mane in place with clips and ribbons, sometimes getting the maid to braid fanciful bands. Flexitives made all that irrelevant. Of its own accord, her hair fell back over her shoulders, always keeping itself tidy and together in one large tress. It also rippled subtly, as if she was engulfed in her own permanent private breeze.

"You look beautiful, Louise," Genevieve said, suddenly shy.

"Thank you." Gen's hair had been straightened, darkened, and glossed, its hem curling inwards slightly. Again, it held its shape no matter what.

Stalls were lined up against the road barriers, filled with brassy, cheaper items than those in the shops. Genevieve saw one with pairs of the magical boots hanging from the awning. Slipstream boots, the cheerful owner told her as he found some her size. Popular with the under fifteens because you didn't need neural nanonics to switch the directed frictionless soles on or off.

Louise bought them on the condition Gen waited until they got back to the hotel before she tried them out. She also got a duster bracelet. When Gen clamped the trinket round her wrist and waved it round, it sprayed out a fine powder which emitted a fiery sparkle as it fell to earth.

Holding her arm up and pirouetting, a spiral of twinkling starlight spun around her.

Quinn sat on one of the benches along the banks of the Seine, opening his mind to the demented screeching reverberating through the beyond. It had taken him two and a half hours to reach the Paris arcology since being struck by that inexplicable wave of emotional torment that had swept through the beyond.

The first thing—obviously!—was to get the fuck out of New York. It wouldn't take the cops long to review the memories of sensors covering the concourse and identify him. He'd gone straight down to a platform and taken a vac-train to Washington. A short ride, not quite fifteen minutes. He'd kept within the ghost realm for the whole trip, apprehensive that the vac-train would be halted and returned to New York. But it arrived at Washington on time, and he switched to the first inter-continental ride available: Paris.

Even then, he'd remained invisible as it streaked along the bottom of the North Atlantic. Still anxious that another of those waves would surge up and expose him. If it had done during the journey under the ocean, he knew he'd be finished. He couldn't believe God's Brother would allow that to happen. But the first time was causing all sorts of doubts.

It wasn't until he was out of the Paris terminus and walking through one of the old city's parks that he had allowed himself to fully emerge. He clothed himself in an ordinary shirt and trousers, hating the way his white skin tingled in the bright sun shining through the colossal crystal dome. But it meant he was safe, there were no processors in the middle of the park to glitch at his appearance, nobody near enough to see that he'd appeared from nowhere rather than walked round the ancient tree. He stood there for a minute, scanning the nearby minds for any sign of alarm. Only then did he relax and make his way down to the river.

Parisians strolled along behind him as they had for centuries—lovers, artists, business executives, bureaucrats; none of them paying attention to the solitary downcast youth. Nor did any of them avail themselves to the space left on his bench. Some subliminal warning steered them along past, frowning slightly at the unaccountable chill.

Slowly, Quinn started to gather the strands together, faint images and hoarse wailing voices filling in the story. He saw clouds which surprised even him, an arcology-born. Rain cascaded down on huddled bodies, so thick it was almost solid. Terrifying blasts of lightning ripping through the darkness. The encircling forces, radiating their stern nonhuman determination, closing in.

Mortonridge was not a place where a possessed should be caught outside today; and two million of them had been. Something had struck at them, tearing away their protective covering of cloud. Some technological devilry. The signal for the Liberation to commence. A one-off; a unique act in response to a unique situation. Not some miracle wrought by the Light Bringer's great rival.

Quinn lifted his head, and smiled a contemptuous smile. Such a shock was extremely unlikely to occur again. There was no unknown threat. He was perfectly safe. Night could still dawn.

He stood up, and turned slowly, examining his surroundings properly for the first time. The celebrated Napoleonic heart of the city was encompassed by a range of splendid white, silver, and gold towers. Their burnished surfaces hurt his eyes, as their grandeur hurt his sensibility. But somewhere among all this cleanliness and vitality, the waster kids would be grubbing through dank refuse, hurting each other and unwary civilians for no reason they understood. Finding them would be as easy here as it had been in New York. Just walk in the direction everyone else was coming from. His heartland, where his words would bring its denizens purpose.

He completed his turn. Right ahead of him the Eiffel Tower stood guard at the end of a broad immaculate park, with sightseers wandering round its base. Even in Edmonton, Quinn had heard of this structure. A proud symbol of Gallic forbearance through all the centuries of Govcentral's pallid uniformity. Its very endurance reflecting the strengths and determination of the people who regarded it as their own. Precious to the world. And now, so terribly fragile with age.

Quinn started to chuckle greedily.

Andy Behoo fell in love. It was instantaneous. *She* walked in through the door of Jude's Eworld, kicking off a cascade of datavised alarms, and he was utterly smitten.

Terminal babe. Taller than him by a good ten centimetres, with the most gorgeous cloak of hair. A face with soft features so delicate as to be way beyond anything cosmetic adapter packages could achieve—a natural beauty. She wore a white sleeveless T-shirt that showed off a hot figure without revealing anything, and a scarlet skirt that didn't reach her knees. But it was the way she carried herself that clinched it for him. Perfectly composed, yet she still looked round the shop with child-like curiosity.

The rest of the staff were all giving her clandestine glances as the doorway scanners datavised their findings. Then the smaller girl entered behind her, and the scanners gave out an almost duplicate alert. How weird. They couldn't possibly be a cop grab operation, too obvious. Besides, the manager was pretty regular when it came to slipping the shop's bung to the district station.

Andy told the customer he was dealing with, "Look it over, and have a think about it, you won't find a better deal in London," then left them to scoot over to the girl before any of his so-called colleagues could reach her. If the floor manager had seen, he'd probably lose his job. *Abandoning a customer before the sale is sealed—capital crime.*

"Hi, I'm Andy. I'm your sellrat. Anything you want, it's my job to push the more expensive model on you." He grinned broadly.

"You're my what?" Louise asked, her expression was half puzzlement, half smile.

Her accent did strange things along Andy's spine, making him shiver. The ultimate in class, and foreign-exotic, too. He scanned his enhanced retinas across her face, desperate to capture her image. Even if she walked out of his life now, she would never be entirely lost. Andy had certain male-orientated software packages that could superimpose her into sensenviron recordings. He felt shabby even as he recorded her.

"Sellrat. That's what the public calls Customer Interactivity Officers round these parts."

"Oh," the smaller girl sighed dismissively. "He's just a shopboy, Louise."

Andy's neural nanonics had to reinforce his smile. Why do they always come in pairs? And why always one obnoxious one? He clicked his fingers and pointed both index fingers at the smaller girl. "That's me. Try not to be too disappointed, I really am here to help."

"I'd like to buy some neural nanonics," Louise said. "Is it very difficult?"

The request startled Andy. Her clothes alone must have cost more than twice his weekly pay, why didn't she have a set already? Beautiful and enigmatic. He smiled up at her. "Not at all. What were you looking for?"

She sucked her lower lip. "I'm really not very sure. The best I can afford, I suppose."

"We don't have them on Norfolk," Genevieve said. "That's where we're from."

Louise tried not to frown. "Gen, we don't have to give our history to everyone we meet."

Rich foreigners. Andy's conscience struggled against temptation. Conscience won out, backed up by infatuation. *I can't sell her a pirate set. Not her.* "Okay, your lucky day. We've got some top-of-the-range sets in stock. I can fix a reasonable deal for them, too, so there's no need to get sweaty about the money. This way."

He led them over to his section of the counter, managing to get her name on the way. His neural nanonics faithfully recorded the way she walked, her body movements, even her speech pattern. Like most nineteen-year-olds who'd grown up in London's manky Islington district with its history of low-income employment, Andy Behoo fancied himself as a prospective net don. It combined the goal of fringe-legal work (also his heritage), with very little actual effort. He'd taken didactic memory courses on electronics, nanonics, and software every month since he'd passed his fourteenth birthday. His two-room flat was stocked to the ceiling with ancient processor blocks and every redundant peripheral he'd managed to scrounge or steal. Everyone in his tenement knew Andy was the guy to visit when you had a technical problem.

As to why such an embryonic datasmart prince of darkness was working as a sellrat in Jude's Eworld, he had to get the money to finance his revolutionary schemes from somewhere—or maybe even go to college. And the shop always employed technerd teenagers as their outfront salesforce, they were the only ones who kept up to date on up-grades and new marques that would work on minimum-wage weeks.

The wall behind the counter was made up entirely from boxes of consumer electronics. All of them had colourful logos and names. Louise read a few of the contents labels, not understanding a word. Genevieve was already bored; looking round at other parts of the slightly shabby shop—one of seemingly hundreds of near-identical outlets along Tottenham Court Road. The inside was a maze formed by counters and walls of boxes, with old company posters and holomorph stickers stuck up on every available surface. Holographic screens flashed out enticing pictures of prod-ucts in action. The section opposite Andy Behoo had a big GAMES sign above it. And Louise had promised.

Andy began pulling boxes down and lining them up on the counter. They were rectangular, the size of his hand, wrapped in translucent foil, with the manufacturer's guar-antee seal on the front. "Okay," Andy said with familiar confidence. "What we have here, the Presson050, is a basic neural nanonics set. Everything you need to survive daily arcology life: datavises, mid-rez neuroiconic display, en-hanced memory retrieval, axon block. It's preformatted to NAS2600 standard, which means it can handle just about every software package on the market. There's a company-supplied didactic operations imprint that comes with it, but we do sell alternative operations courses."

"That sounds very . . . comprehensive," Louise said. "How much?"

"How are you paying?"

"Fuseodollars." She showed him her Jovian Bank disk.

"Okay. Good move. I can give you a favourable rate on that. So, we're looking at about three and a half thousand, for which we'll throw in five free Quantumsoft supplement packages from their BCD30 range. Your choice of functions. I can arrange finance for you if you want, better percentage than any Sol-system bank."

"I see."

"Then we've got—" His hand moved on to the next box.

"Andy. What's the top of the range, please?"

"Okay, good question." He disappeared behind the counter for a moment, returning with a fresh box and a suitably awed tone. "Kulu Corporation ANI5000. The King himself uses this model. We've only got three left because of the starflight quarantine. These are most wanted items all over town right now. But I can still give you level retail."

"And that's better than the first one?"

"Yes indeedie. Runs NAS2600, of course, with parallel upgrade potential for when the 2615 comes out."

"Um. What's this NAS number you keep saying?"

"Neural Augmentation Software. It's the operating system for the whole filament network, and the number is the version. 2600 was introduced turn of the century, and boy was it a bugfeist when it came out. But it's a smooth proved system now. And the supplement packages are just about unlimited, every software house in the Confederation publishes compatible products. If you're going serious professional you can add physiological monitors, encyclopaedia galactica, employment waldoing, SII suit control, weapons integration, linguistic translation, news informant, starship astrogration, net search—the full monty. Then there's games applications as well, I can't even list them you have so many." He patted the box with reverence. "No fooling, Louise, this set gives you the full interface range: nerve overrides to control your body, sense amplification, sight-equivalent neuroiconic generation, complete reality sensenviron, implant command, total indexed memory recall."

"I'll take it."

"Got to warn you: not cheap. Seventeen thousand fuseodollars." He held up his hands in placation. "Sorry."

Daddy will kill me, Louise thought, but it has to be done. I promised Fletcher, and that horrid Brent Roi never really believed me. "All right."

Andy smiled in admiration. "Talk about power choosing. That's impressive, Louise. But, hey, I can lighten the burden. For a 5000 set, we'll throw in twenty-five software supplements, and give you twenty per cent discount on the next twenty-five you buy from us."

"That sounds like a jolly good deal," she said inanely, swept along by his enthusiasm. "How long does it take to get a set?"

"For one this complex, ninety minutes. I can give you the operating didactic at the same time."

"What's one of those?"

Andy's breezy ebullience faltered in the face of such an astonishing question. He started to access his encyclopaedia's file on Norfolk, and put a news search in primary mode for good measure. "You don't have them on your planet?"

"No. Our constitution is pastoral, we don't have much technology. Or weapons." Defending Norfolk, yet again.

"No weapons; hey, good policy. Didactic imprints are sort of like the instruction manual, but it gets written directly inside your brain, and you never forget it."

"Well if I'm going to spend this much money, I certainly need to know how to work it, don't I?"

Andy laughed heartily, then stopped quickly when he caught sight of Genevieve's expression. How come nobody ever produced a suavity program he could load? Talking to and impressing girls would be so much easier. The floor supervisor was datavising questions about his oddball customer and the door sensor alert, which he answered briefly. Then the Norfolk information started to emerge.

"We have a preparation room," Andy gestured to the back of the shop.

"Louise, I want to look round," Genevieve said winningly. "There might be something for me."

"All right. But if you see something just ask, don't touch anything. That's all right, isn't it?" she asked Andy.

"Sure thing." Andy winked at Genevieve and gave her a thumbs up. Her sneer could have withered an oak tree.

Louise followed Andy into the small preparation room, a cube-space whose walls were fashioned from dark panelling, with various electronic units poking out. It was furnished with just a glass cubicle, like a shower but without any visible nozzle; and a low padded bench similar to a doctor's examination table.

The attention Andy showed her was somewhat amusing. She thought possibly it wasn't entirely due to her high-spending customer status. Most of the young gentlemen (and others—slightly older) on Norfolk had shown a similar, if less blatant, interest over the last couple of years. Now, of course, she was wearing what amounted to little more than an exhibitionist's costume. Though by Earth's standards it was tame. But the top and skirt had made her look so damn good in the department store's mirror. She could hold her own against London girls in this. For the first time in her life she was *sassy*. And free to enjoy it. And loving it.

The glass door slid shut with a definitive *click* behind her. She shot Andy a suspicious glance.

"Bugger," Western Europe muttered as his linkages with Louise were cut. He switched to Genevieve, which was about as useless; the little girl was investigating a Gothic fantasy, standing in a castle courtyard as a column of priest-ess warriors rode off to battle on their unicorns.

Western Europe had wanted Louise to discover the bugs at some stage. He just hadn't planned on it being quite so early in the operation. But then, buying neural nanonics wasn't what he expected of a girl from Norfolk, either. She was quite a remarkable little thing, really.

Andy Behoo scratched at his arm awkwardly. "You do know you've been stung, don't you?" he asked.

"Stung?" Louise took a guess. "You're not talking about insects, are you?"

"No. The door sensors spotted it as soon as you and your sister came in. There are nanonic bugs in your skin; like miniature radios I guess you'd call them. They transmit all sorts of information about where you are, and what's going on around you. There are four on you, Genevieve has three. That we can detect, anyway."

She drew in a shocked breath. How stupid! Of course Brent Roi wouldn't let her walk round freely. Not someone who'd tried to sneak a possessed down to Earth. He was bound to want to see what she did next. "Oh sweet Jesus."

"I reckon Govcentral must be nervous about foreigners right now, especially as you come from Norfolk," Andy said. "What with the possessed, and all. Don't worry, this room is screened, they can't hear us now."

His sellrat swagger had diminished as he tried to reassure her. In fact, he'd become almost sheepish, which made him actually quite pleasant, she thought. "Thank you for telling me, Andy. Do you scan all your customers?"

"Oh yes. Mainly for dodgy implants. There's quite a few gangs try to siphon our software fleks. Then we do sell bugs ourselves, see, so sometimes we get cops coming in and trying to find who those customers are. Jude's Eworld has a strong neutrality policy, which we enforce. We have to, or we'd never sell anything."

"Can you get them off me?"

"All part of our customer service. I can give you a more detailed scan, too, see if there are any others."

She followed his instructions, standing in the cubicle, which gave her a comprehensive bodyscan down to a sub-cellular level. *So now someone else knows I'm pregnant,* she acknowledged in resignation. *No wonder Earth's population value their privacy so, they don't get very much of it.* The bodyscan located another two bugs. Andy applied a small rectangular patch similar to a medical package (same technology, he said) to her arms and leg; then she pulled up her T-shirt up so he could press it against her back.

"Is there any way of knowing if the police sting me again?" she asked.

"An electronic warfare block should tell you. We had a shipment of front-line equipment in from Valisk a couple of months back. I think there's still some left. Good stuff."

"I think you'd better put one of those removal patches on the list as well." Louise called Genevieve into the room, and explained what'd happened. Thankfully her sister was more curious than outraged. She peered at her skin after Andy took the nanonic package away, fascinated by the removal process. "It doesn't look any different," she complained.

"They're too small to see," Andy said. "Which makes them too small to feel. They shouldn't call it getting stung, really. More like being feathered."

When Genevieve scooted back into the shop to continue her appraisal of consumer goodies, Andy handed over the box of Kulu Corporation neural nanonics to Louise. "You need to check the seal," he said. "Make sure it hasn't been broken, and see that the wrapping hasn't been tampered with as well. You can tell that by the colour. If someone tries to cut or tear it, the stress turns it red."

She turned it over obediently. "Why do I have to do this?"

"Neural nanonics connect directly into your brain, Louise. If someone changes the filaments or subverts the NAS codes they could get into your memories or manipulate your body like a puppet. This guarantees the set hasn't been tampered with since it left the factory; and you have the Kulu Corporation's assurance that their design wouldn't sequestrate you."

Louise gave the box a closer examination. The foil seemed intact and clear.

"Sorry, didn't mean to scare you," he said quickly. "It's a standard speech; we implant fifty of these a day. I mean, think what would happen to the shop or the manufacturer if anything like that did ever happen. We'd be lynched. It's in our interest to make sure everything's kosher for you. Another reason we have sensors at the door."

"Okay, I suppose." She handed the box back. Andy broke the seal in front of her, and took out a small black capsule a couple of centimetres long. He slotted that into the back of a specialist medical implant package. The only other item in the box was a flek.

"This is the operating didactic, which is standard, but it also contains the first time access code specific to this set," he told her. "Basically, it allows you to activate the neural nanonics. After that, you change the code by just thinking of a new one. So even if someone got hold of your flek afterwards it wouldn't do them any good. Don't worry, it's all explained in the didactic."

She lay face down on the cushioned bench, with a pair of collar wings holding her neck steady. Andy pushed her hair to one side, ready to apply the medical package to the nape of her neck. There was already a tiny nearly-healed scar on her skin. He knew exactly what it was, he'd seen it a thousand times before, every time the implant package was taken off.

"Is everything all right?" Louise asked.

"Yes. No problem. It just takes a minute to line this up right." He datavised the bodyscan cubicle's processor. Its memory file of her scan confirmed there was absolutely no foreign matter in her brain.

Andy took the coward's way out and said nothing. Mainly because he didn't want to alarm her. But something here was desperately wrong. Either she was lying to him, which he couldn't believe. Or . . . he couldn't quite decide what the other options were. He was trespassing deep in Govcentral territory. All that did was enhance her mystery up to the level of pure enchantment. A babe in distress right out of the sensevise dramas. In his shop!

"Here we go," he said lightly, and put the package over her existing scar. Now there would never be any proof.

Louise tensed slightly. "It's gone numb."

"That's okay. It's supposed to."

All the medical package did was open a passage through to the base of the skull, and ease the capsule containing the densely pleated neural nanonics into place. Then the filaments began to unwind from each other and porrect forward, their probing tips slowly winding their way round cells as they sought out synapses. There were millions of them, active molecular strings obeying their AI formatted protocol; instructions determined by their own structure of spiralling atoms. They formed a wondrously intricate filigree around the medulla oblongata, branching to connect with the nerve strands inside while the main filaments seeped further into the brain to complete their interface.

With the implant package in place, Andy fetched the didactic imprinter. Louise thought it looked like a pair of burnished stainless steel ski glasses. He put the flek in a small slot at the side, and placed it carefully on her face. "This works in pulses," he said. "You'll get a warning flash of green, then you'll see a violet light for about fifteen seconds. Try not to blink. It should happen eight times."

"That's it?" The edges of the imprinter had stuck to her skin, leaving her in total blackness.

"Yep, not so bad, is it?"

"And this is the way everyone on Earth learns things?"

"Yes. The information is encoded within the light, and your optic nerve passes it straight into your brain. Simple explanation, but that's the principle."

Louise saw a flicker of green, and held her breath. The violet light came on, an otherwise uniform sheen broken by that unique monotone sparkle which a laser leaves on the retina. She managed not to blink until it went off. "Your children don't go to school?" she asked.

"No. Kids go to day clubs, keeps them busy and you make friends there. That's all."

She was silent for some time, considering the implications. The hours—years!—of my life I have sat in classrooms listening to teachers and reading books. And all the time, this way of learning, of discovery, existed. One of the demonic technologies that will ruin our way of life. Banned without question. That's nothing to do with keeping Norfolk pastoral, that's denying people opportunity, stunting their lives. It's worse than cousin Gideon's arm. She clenched her teeth together, suddenly very, very angry.

"Hey, are you all right?" Andy asked timidly.

The violet light came on again. "Yes," she snapped primly. "I'm fine, thank you."

Andy didn't say anything else until the didactic imprinter finished. Too scared he'd say the wrong thing again and annoy her further. He hadn't got a clue why her mood had swung so fast. When the imprinter did come off, it revealed a very pensive expression.

"Could you do me a favour?" Louise said. A knowing smile licked along her lips. "Keep an eye on Genevieve for me. I promised I'd buy her something from here, so if you could steer her to some kind of gadget that's relatively harmless I'd be grateful."

"Sure, my pleasure. Consider her guarded from any possible digital grief." Andy had to use a nerve override impulse to prevent her from seeing how crushing that request was. He'd been counting on using the time it took to implant the neural nanonics to talk to her. Yet again, Andy blows out, he raged silently. Just once, I'd like to score with a major babe. Once!

The games section wasn't nearly as exciting as Genevieve had expected. Jude's Eworld was actively promoting a thousand games through its display screen catalogues, with direct access to ten times that many over encrypted links to publishers; covering the whole genre from interactive roles to strategy general's command. But as she flipped through them she could see they were all variants of each other. Everybody promised newer, hotter graphics, unrivalled worldbuilding, tac-stim activants, ingenious puzzles, more terrifying adversaries, slicker music. Always greater than before, never different. She sampled four or five, standing inside a projection cone beamed out from high-wattage AV lens on the ceiling. Bore-ing. In truth, she'd begun to tire of them back on the *Jamrana*; like spending a whole day eating chocolate cake, really.

There didn't seem to be much else in Jude's Eworld that was interesting. Their main market was neural nanonics and associated software, or else no-fun processor blocks with strange peripherals.

"Hi. How's it going, there? Are you hyping cool yet?"

Genevieve turned to see the gruesomely oiky little shop-boy Andy smiling ingratiatingly at her. One of his front teeth was crooked. She'd never seen that on someone his age before. "I'm having a lovely time, thank you so much for caring." It was the tone that would earn her a sharp slap from her mother or Mrs Charlsworth.

"Uh huh." Andy grunted, fully flustered. "Er, I thought perhaps I could show you what we've got to offer for kids your . . . I mean, the kind of blocks and software you might enjoy."

"Oh whoopee do."

His arms re-arranged themselves chaotically, indicating the section of the shop he wanted her to move towards. "Please?" he asked desperately.

With an overlong sigh and slouched shoulders, Genevieve shuffled along despondently. Why does Louise always attract the wrong type? she wondered. Which sparked an idea. "She's got a fiancé, you know."

"Huh?"

A modest smile at his horror. "Louise. She's engaged to be married. They announced the banns at our estate's chapel."

"Married?" Andy yelped. He flinched, looking round the shop to see if any of his colleagues were paying attention.

This was fun. "Yes. To a starship captain. That's why we're on Earth, we're waiting for him to arrive."

"When's he due, do you know?"

"A couple of weeks, I think. He's very rich, he owns his starship." She glanced round in suspicion, then leaned in towards the boy. "Don't tell anyone I said this, but I think the only reason Daddy gave his permission was because of the money. Our estate is very big, and it takes a lot to keep it running."

"She's marrying for money?"

"Has to be. I mean he's so *old*. Louise said he's thirty years older than she is. I think she was fibbing so it didn't sound so bad. If you ask me, it's more like forty-five."

"Oh my God. That's disgusting."

"It looks so awful when he kisses her, I mean he's virtually bald, and hideously fat. She says she hates him to touch her, but what can she do about it? He's her future husband."

Andy stared down at her, his face stricken. "Why does your father allow this?"

"All marriages are arranged on Norfolk, it's just our way. If it makes you feel any better, I think he really likes Louise." She'd have to stop now. Crying shame, but it getting really difficult to keep a straight face. "He keeps on saying he wants to have a big family with her. He says he expects her to bear him at least seven children." Jackpot! Andy had started trembling with indignation—or worse.

Her day made, Genevieve gently took his hand in hers, and smiled up trustfully. "Can we see the hyper cool electronics now, please?"

Understanding arrived within Louise's mind like a solstice sunrise. Quietly irresistible, bringing with it a fresh perspective on the world. A new season of life begun.

She knew precisely how to utilise the augmented mentality opening up within her brain as the filaments connected with her neurones, controlling the expanded potential with an instinct that could have been a genetic heritage it was so deep seated. Audio discrimination, analysing the murmur of sounds resonating through the door from the shop. Visual memory indexing, saving and storing what she saw. Pattern analysis. A test datavise, requesting an update from the medical package on her wrist. And the neuroiconic display, sight without eyes, moulding raw data into colour. It left her giddy and sweating from excitement. The sense of achievement was extraordinary.

I'm equal to everybody else now. Or I will be when I've learned how to use all the applications properly.

She datavised the implant package on her neck for a status check. A procedural menu sprang up inside her skull, and she ran a comparison. It confirmed the implantation process was complete. She instructed the package to disengage, withdrawing the empty capsule from which the filaments had sprouted, and knitting the cells together behind it.

"Steady on," Andy said. "That's supposed to be my job."

Louise grinned at him as she climbed off the bench, and stretched extravagantly, flexing the stiffness out of limbs held still for too long. "Oh, come on," she teased. "All your clients must do that. It's the first taste of freedom we get. Having neural nanonics must be like being allowed to vote, you've become a full member of society. Aren't they wonderful gadgets?"

"Um. Yeah." He got her to lean forwards, and peeled the implant package from her neck. "You can actually become a full citizen, you know." The strangely hopeful tone earned him an inquisitive look.

"What do you mean?"

"You could apply for residential citizenship. If you wanted. I checked the Govcentral legal memory core. It's no problem; you just need a Govcentral citizen to sponsor you, and a hundred fuseodollars fee. You can datavise them for an application. I've got the eddress."

"That's um . . . very kind, Andy. But I don't really plan on staying here for long." She smiled, trying to let him down gently. "I have a fiancé, you see. He's going to come and take me away."

"But Norfolk laws wouldn't apply to you," Andy blurted

desperately. "Not here. Not if you're an Earth citizen. You'd be safe."

"I'm sure I am anyway. Thank you." She smiled again, slightly more firm this time; and slipped past him out into the shop.

"Louise! I want this," Genevieve shrieked. The little girl was standing in the middle of the shop, arms held rigid at her side as she turned round and round. There was a small block clipped onto her belt with DEMONSTRATOR printed in blue on its top. Louise hadn't seen her smile like that in a long time.

"What have you got, Gen?"

"I gave her a pair of realview lenses to try," Andy said quietly. "Like contact lenses, but they receive a datavise from the block which overlays a fantasyscape on what you're seeing." He datavised a code to her. "That'll let you view direct from the block."

Louise datavised the code, marvelling at how smoothly she did it, and closed her eyes. The world started to spin around her. A very strange world. It had the same dimensions as the inside of Jude's Eworld, but this was a cave of onyx, where every surface corresponded to walls and counters, fat stalagmites had replaced the flek sale bins. People had become hulking black and chrome cyborgs, whose limbs were clusters of yellow pistons.

"Isn't it fabulous?" Gen whooped. "It changes whatever you look at."

"Yes, Gen, it's good." She saw the mouth on one of the cyborgs clank apart to speak her own words, and smiled. The cyborg's mouth froze open. Louise cancelled her reception from the realview block.

"You can get about fifty different imagery programs for it," Andy said. "This one's *Metalpunk Wasteland*. Quite popular. There's an audioplug peripheral to change the voices."

"*Please*, Louise! This one."

"All right, all right."

Andy datavised an off code to the demonstrator block. Genevieve pouted as the cave melted back into the shop. Andy started piling boxes and small flek cases up on the counter. "What supplements do you want?" he asked.

Louise consulted the market menu already included in the NAS2600. "News hound, global eddress directory search, people tracker . . . um, the pregnancy supplement for my physiological monitor, universal message script. I think that's it."

"You're entitled to another twenty."

"I know. Do I have to collect them all today? I'm not really sure what else I'll need."

"Take as much time as you need to choose, and drop in whenever you want. But I'd recommend netA, that'll give you your own eddress, you've got to pay an annual fee to the link company, but nobody will be able to contact you without one. Oh, and streetnav, too, if you're going to stay in London—shows you the short cuts and how to use public transport."

"Okay, fine, put them on." More flek cases began to appear on the counter. "And that electronic warfare block we talked about."

"Sure thing."

When he slapped it down, it didn't look much different to her ordinary processor block, same anonymous oblong of dark grey plastic.

"Who buys bugs and things like that from you?" she asked.

"Could be anyone. Girl wanting to find out if her boyfriend's cheating on her. Manager who needs to know which of his staff are ripping him off. Voyeur perverts. Mostly, though, it's private detectives. Regular spooks convention at times, this place."

Louise didn't approve of that notion that just anybody could come along and spy on their friends and enemies. There ought to be some restrictions on who could buy such items. But then regulation was one thing Earth didn't seem to have much of.

Andy handed over the shop's accounts block with an apologetic smile. Louise tried not to shiver as she transferred the money over from her Jovian Bank disk. She gave the realview block and a packet of disposable lenses to Genevieve, who promptly tore the wrapping off with a gleeful, "Yesss."

"I'll see you when you come back for the rest of your software?" Andy asked. "And if you change your mind about . . . the other thing, I'll be happy to sponsor your application. I'm entitled to do that. I'm an adult citizen."

"Right," she said gingerly. There was something very odd about the way he'd latched onto the idea. She was debating whether to quiz him further when she caught the glint of devilment in Gen's eye. The little girl spun round quickly. "You've been very kind, Andy," Louise said. "Please don't worry about me." She leant over the counter and gave him a light kiss. "Thanks."

Genevieve was already making for the door, giggling wildly. Louise snatched up the carrier bag full of fleks, and chased after her.

Louise lay back on her bed as the brilliant sun finally sank away below Green Park. Genevieve was sleeping on the bed next to her, exhausted by the very long day.

Terrible child, Louise thought fondly. I must make sure she gets a set of neural nanonics when she turns sixteen.

She closed her own eyes and put the news hound program into primary mode. The room's net processor acknowledged her datavise, and she began asking for general items on the possessed. That was when she had her crash course on using news hound's filter program accessories and designating more refined search parameters. It took an hour, but she was eventually able to slot the myriad events reported by Earth's news agencies into an overall picture. The arrival of the *Mount's Delta* was a weird one. The way its crewman had been shredded hinted strongly at Quinn Dexter to her mind.

New York's abrupt isolation was the principal current topic for the agencies, in fact it was just about their only topic. Govcentral's North American Commissioner appeared before the reporters to assure everyone that it was just a precaution, and they were investigating a "possessed-type" incident in Dome One as a matter of procedure. No schedule was given for opening the vac-trains. Police squads, reinforced with riot-control mechanoids, were out in force on the streets as the arcology residents became highly restless.

Then there was the event which caused Louise to jerk upright on the bed, opening her eyes wide in surprise and delight. Tranquillity's arrival at Jupiter. Joshua was *here*! In this star system.

She sank back onto the pillows, shaking with excitement. The universal message script was hurriedly brought into primary mode. She composed a file for him which she really hoped didn't sound too desperate and pathetic, and datavised it triumphantly into the communication net. Her neural nanonics told her that Jupiter was five hundred and fifty million miles away, so the signal would take about forty minutes to reach it. She might have a reply within two hours!

Western Europe, who was monitoring her net connection, instructed the AI to block the message. The last thing he needed right now was some dunderhead boyfriend charging to the rescue, especially one as famous as Lagrange Calvert.

9

The party was a good one, though the guy with only one
arm was kind of weird. Liol knew he was staring, and
loaded a mild protocol reminder into his neural nanonics.
It was just that he'd never seen anything like that before.
Didn't seem to affect the guy's balance out on the dance
floor, and the girl he was with obviously didn't mind. Or
perhaps she enjoyed the novelty value. Knowing the girls in
this habitat, that was a strong option. Come to that, maybe
the missing arm was an obscure fashion statement. Not impossible.

Liol headed for the buffet table, picking his way through
the crowd. Just about everyone smiled and said hello as
they jostled together. He replied to most of them, their
names familiar now without having to access a memory
file. Plutocrat princes and princesses, with media celebri-
ties jumbled in for variety. They tended to work hard during
the day, expanding corporate empires, starting new dynasties, never taking their wealth for granted especially in
these times. Tranquillity's change of location was causing
them unique problems in sustaining their traditional markets, but there were fabulous benefits to be had from being

placed in the Confederation's wealthiest star system. They'd set about exploiting that as ruthlessly and gleefully as only they could. But nights were given over to a single giant funtime: parties, restaurants, shows, clubs; Tranquillity boasted the best of them all in profusion.

He wasn't even sure who his host was. The apartment was as expensively anonymous as all the others he'd been in over the last few days, a hospitality showcase. Everything selected by designers to demonstrate their talent and taste—bitched over by other designers. Just another party. No doubt he and Dominique would grace two or three more before the night was out. The social set he'd belonged to in Ayacucho had never been shy of a good time, and were wealthy enough to indulge themselves. But compared to this mob, they were jejune provincials.

They were fascinated that he was Joshua's brother. Smiled indulgently when he told them he had his own business back in Ayacucho. But he could reveal little about *Lady Mac*'s last flight. So conversation tended to dry up fast after that. He really didn't know much about Confederation politics, or the money shifts in multistellar markets, or hot entertainment items (Jezzibella was Capone's girl—oh, come *on!*); and he certainly didn't relish discussing the possessed, and how the crisis was developing.

He took a plate along the long table of canapés, deliberately picking the more bizarre-looking items. Jupiter was rising across the window behind the table, so he munched and stared, as overwhelmed by the spectacle as any hick farmboy. Not quite the reaction of a sophisticated starship crewman-about-the-galaxy. The aspiration he'd cherished for himself since first hearing *Lady Mac* was supposedly his rightful inheritance. Now he'd flown in *Lady Mac*, actually getting to pilot her. He'd seen new star systems, even fought in an orbital war and (ironically implausible) saved

the Confederation—or at least alleviated some of the
Navy's burden. After the pinnacle, there was always the
journey back down again. He would never, ever be as good
a pilot as Joshua. The manoeuvres his brother had flown
during the *Beezling* encounter had made that quite obvious.
And the Confederation wasn't such a fun place to roam
through any more. Neither was life, now the beyond waited.

A reflection in the window made him turn. Joshua and
Ione were mingling among the guests. Talking with ease,
laughing. A good-looking couple, Josh in a formal black
jacket, her in a flowing green evening dress. He was about
to go over when Joshua led Ione out onto the dance floor.

"Yoo hoo." Dominique waved from across the room.
People struggled to get out of the way as she cut a line
straight for him. Liol was granted the knowledge of what it
must be like for a planet to face an invading fleet. Her hand
grasped his arm, and she rubbed her nose against his. "I
missed you," she murmured with silky reproach.

"I was hungry."

"Me too." The resentment snapped off, replaced with
bountiful mischief. She plucked one of the canapés from his
plate and popped it straight into her mouth. "Eeek. Sung-
wort seaweed, and they coated it in coriander."

"It was interesting," he apologised meekly. She was as
adorable as she was terrifying. By far the most beautiful
girl in the room, Dominique favoured a more natural look
than her contemporaries, a gypsy girl among the glossy
mannequins. Her black evening gown was full-length, but
that somehow didn't stop it from displaying a huge quantity
of strategic flesh. Her broad lips curved up into a delighted
smile. She dabbed her finger on his nose. "I just love your
innocence." A quality of which he had very little left. Sex
with Dominique was narcotic, ruining you with pleasure.

She held his gaze for a moment, face enraptured by devotion. He wanted to turn and flee. "Someone I'd like you to meet," she said neutrally, as if divining his response. A finger beckoned. There was a slim girl standing behind her, completely blocked by Dominique's broad, healthy physique. She had a prim Oriental face with hair several shades fairer than Dominique. "This is Neomone."

"Hi," Neomone darted forward and kissed him. Then swayed back, blushing, looking very pleased with herself.

"Hi." He didn't quite know what to make of her. She was in her late teens, wearing a slinky silk dress that revealed an almost androgynous figure, all ribcage and stringy muscle. Thrilled and nervous at the same time, she kept giving Dominique worshipful glances.

"Neomone is training to be a ballerina," Dominique purred.

"I've never been to a ballet," Liol admitted. "We've had troupes visit Ayacucho, but I didn't think it would be quite me. Sorry."

Neomone giggled. "Ballet is for everyone."

"You should dance with him," Dominique told her. "Let him see there's nothing to be scared of from cultural élitism." She cocked an eye at Liol. "Neomone's quite a fan of yours, you know."

He grinned, slightly awkward. "Oh. Why's that?"

"You flew in the *Lady Mac*," the girl said breathlessly. "Everyone knows Joshua was on a secret mission."

"If you know, then it can't be that secret, can it."

"Told you he was a modest hero," Dominique said. "In public, anyway."

Liol managed to keep smiling valiantly. Maybe he had bragged a little. That was the nature of the starflight business. "You know how it is," he shrugged.

Neomone's giggles were unstoppable. "Not yet," she said. "But I'm going to find out tonight."

*

The beach glowed a pale silver under the light-tube's lunar radiance. Joshua took his shoes off to walk along it, holding Ione's hand. The sand was warm and soft, flowing over his toes like grainy liquid. Tiny fluorescent fish darted about just under the sea's surface, as if a shower of pink and azure sparks were tumbling horizontally through the water. Somebody had made a row of small melted-looking mounds just above the shoreline, meandering away into the distance.

Ione signed contentedly, and leaned into him. "I know it's silly, but I keep coming back. She loved playing on this beach. I suppose I'm expecting to find her here."

"Jay?"

"Yes." She paused. "And Haile. I hope she's all right."

"The Kiint say she is. They wouldn't lie about that. Many things, but not the welfare of a child."

"She must be so lonely." Ione sat down with her back to one of the small dunes. She slid her silk scarf from her neck. "I don't see why they won't let us bring her back from Jobis. Starships are still going there."

"Bloody mystics," Joshua sat beside her. "Probably not in their horoscopes."

"You're starting to sound like dear old Parker Higgens."

Joshua laughed. "I can't believe that old duffer is coming with us. And Getchell as well."

"They're the best I've got."

"Thanks for asking me to go. I need to be flying. I'm no good to anybody just sitting around."

"Joshua." She reached over to trace the stark line of his jaw bone. "I'm pregnant again. You're the father."

His mouth flopped open. She smiled, and kissed him gently. "Sorry. Bad timing. Again. I'm very good at that."

"No," he said with weak defiance. "No, that's, er, not bad timing at all."

"I thought you should know before you left." Even in the twilight she could see the shock and wonder in his eyes. There was something absolutely gorgeous about him when he looked so vulnerable. It means he cares, I suppose. She touched his face again.

"Um. When?" he asked.

"Before you went to Norfolk. Remember?"

He grinned, almost shy. "We'll never know the exact time then. There's an awful lot to chose from."

"If I had a choice, I think I'd make it the one in Adul Nopal's apartment."

"Oh Jesus, yes. The middle of his dinner party." He flopped down onto the sand, and grinned up. "Yeah! That would be fitting."

"And Joshua. It was very deliberate. I'm not in this state by accident."

"Right. Thanks for consulting me. I mean, I thought we'd already established the next Lord of Ruin with Marcus."

"Just say no."

He put his hand round her head, and pulled her down, kissing her. "I think we've already confirmed I can't."

"You're not angry with me?"

"No. Worried, maybe. More about the future than anything. But then the kid won't have it any different to the rest of the human race when he dies. We can't fear for that, or we'd be utterly paralysed. The Kiint found a solution, the Laymil, too—for all it's inapplicable. We damn well can."

"Thank you, Joshua."

"I'd like to know why, though. I mean, we already have the next Lord of Ruin established."

She closed her eyes, shutting out his gentle curiosity.

"Because you're perfect," she whispered. "For me. Great body, good genes."

"Little Miss Romantic."

"And a wonderful lover."

"Yeah, I know that bit. I carry the burden well, though."

She laughed spryly, then she was crying helplessly.

"Hey. No." He cradled her, hugging lightly. "Don't do that."

"Sorry." She wiped a hand across her eyes. "Joshua. Please. I don't love you. I can't love you."

He flinched, but didn't recoil. "I see."

"Oh God damn it. Now I've gone and hurt you. And I didn't want that. I never wanted that."

"What the hell do you want, Ione? I don't understand. Don't tell me this was convenience, that I was the male easily to hand when you happened to make your mind up. You wanted my baby. And now you've told me about it. If you hate me so much, you wouldn't have done that."

"I don't hate you." She gripped him tighter. "I don't."

"Then what?" He made an effort not to shout. Every emotion in his head was freefalling. Thought was almost impossible, only instinct, blind response. "Jesus Christ, do you have any idea what you're doing to me?"

"Well what do you want out of this, Joshua? Do you want to be a part of this child's life?"

"Yes! Jesus, how can you question that?"

"What part?"

"A father!"

"How will you be a father?"

"In the same way you're a mother."

She took both his hands in hers, quelling the trembling. He shook her loose angrily. "You can't be," she said. "I have an affinity bond with the baby. So does Tranquillity."

"Jesus. I can get symbionts, I can be equal to you and this

bloody habitat. Why are you trying to block me out of this?"

"Joshua. Listen to me. What would you do all day? Even if you were my consort, officially my husband. What would you do? You can't run Tranquillity. That's me, that's what I do. And then it'll be the job of our first child."

"I don't know, I'll find something. I'm versatile."

"There is nothing. There can never be anything for you in Tranquillity, not permanently. I keep telling you this, you are a starship captain. This is your port, not your home. If you stay here, you'll become like your father."

"Leave my father out of this."

"No, Joshua, I won't. He was the same as you, a great captain; and he stayed here in Tranquillity, he never flew after you were born. That's what wrecked him."

"Wrong."

"I know he didn't fly again."

Joshua looked at her. For all his instinct, his experience, that beautiful face defeated him every time. What went on inside her head could never be known. "All right," he said abruptly. "I'll tell you. He had it all, and lost it. That's why he never flew again. Staying here didn't break his heart, it was broken before that."

"Had what?"

"Everything. What all us owner captains fly for. The big strike, a flight that kills the banks. And I had it with Norfolk. I was *this* close, Ione, and loving it. That mayope exchange deal could have earned me hundreds of millions, I would have become one of the plutocrats that infest this bloody habitat. Then I would have been your equal. I would have had my empire to run, I could have bought a fleet of ships just like Parris Vasilkovsky. That's what I'd do during the day. And we'd be able to get married, and none of this question about how *worthy* I am would ever arise."

"It's not about being worthy, Joshua. Don't say that, don't ever. You stopped the Alchemist from being used, for heaven's sake. You think I look down on you for that? How could some dusty deskbound company president compare to what you are? Joshua, I am so proud of you it hurts. That's why I wanted you as the baby's father. Because there is nobody better, not just your genes or your intuition, there can be no heritage finer than yours. And if I thought for one second there was a single chance you would be happy staying here with me, as my husband, or my partner, or just fitting me in as one of your harem, then I would have *Lady Mac* flung into a recycling plant to stop you leaving. But you won't be happy, you know that. And you'd end up blaming me, or yourself; or worse, the child, for keeping you here. I couldn't stand that, knowing I was responsible for your misery. Joshua, you're twenty-two, and untamed. And that's beautiful, that's how it should be, that's your destiny as much as ruling Tranquillity is mine. Our lives have touched, and I thank God they have. We've both been rewarded with two children by it. But that's all. That's all we can ever be. Ships that pass in the night."

Joshua searched round for the anger that had blazed so bright just a moment ago. But it had gone. There was mostly numbness, and a little shame. I ought to fight her, make her see I'm necessary. "I hate you for being right."

"I wish I wasn't," she said tenderly. "I just hope you can forgive me for being so selfish. I suppose that's my heritage; Saldanas always get their way, and to hell with the human fall out."

"Do you want me to come back?"

Her shoulders slumped wearily. "Joshua, I'm going to drag you back. I'm not forbidding you anything, I'm not saying you can't be a father. And if you want to stay in Tranquillity and make a go of it, then nobody will help and support that decision more than me. But I don't believe it will work, I'm sorry, but I really don't. It might for years, but eventually you'd look round and see how much you'd lost. And that would creep into our lives, and our child would grow up in an emotional war zone. I couldn't stand that. Haven't you listened to anything I've said? You're going to be the joy of your child's life, he's going to ache for when you visit and bring presents and stories. The times you'll spend together will be magical. It's you and I that cannot be inseparable, one of history's great love affairs. That's the *convention* of fatherhood you'll be missing, nothing more."

"Life never used to be this complicated."

The sympathy she felt for him was close to a physical suffering. "I don't suppose it was before I came along. Fate's a real bitch, isn't she."

"Yeah."

"Cheer up. You get joy without responsibility. The male dream."

"Don't." He held up a warning finger. "Don't make a joke of this. You've altered my life. Fair enough, encounters always result in some kind of change. That's what makes life so wonderful, especially mine with the opportunities I have. You're quite right about my wanderlust. But encounters are chance, natural. You did this quite deliberately. So just don't try and make light of it."

They sat with their backs resting on the dune for some time, saying nothing. Even Tranquillity was silent, sensing Ione's reluctance to discuss what had been said.

Eventually they wound up leaning against each other. Joshua put his arm around her shoulder, and she started crying again. A sharing, if not of sorrow for what had been done, then reluctant acceptance. "Don't leave me alone tonight," Ione said.

"I will never understand you."

*

Preparing to go to bed took on the quality of a religious ceremony. The bedroom's window overlooking the underwater vista was opaqued, and the lights reduced to the smallest glimmer. All they could see was each other. They undressed and walked slowly down the steps into the deep spar hand in hand. Bathing was accomplished with scented sponges, graduating into erotic massage. Their lovemaking which followed was deliberately extreme, ranging from aching tenderness to a passion that bordered brutality. Each body responding perfectly to the demands of the other, an exploitation that only their complete familiarity with one another could achieve.

The one aspect they could never recapture was the emotional connection they'd experienced in the previous few days. This sex was a reversion to their very first time, fun, physically enjoyable, but essentially meaningless. Because they didn't mean the same to each other. The attraction was almost as strong as before, but of the devotion there was little evidence. Joshua finally conceded she was right. They'd come full circle.

He wound up lying across the bed, cushions in disarray around him, and Ione sprawled over his chest. Her cheek stroked his pectoral muscles, rejoicing in the touch.

"I thought the Lords of Ruin sent their children off to be Adamists," he said.

"Father's and grandfather's children became Adamists, yes. I've decided mine won't. Not unless that's what they decide they want to become, anyway. I want to bring them up properly, whatever that is."

"How about that; a revolution from the top."

"Every other part of our lives is changing. This particular little ripple won't be noticed amid the storm. But having a family in whatever form will move me closer to my human heritage. The Lords of Ruin have been terribly isolated figures before."

"Will you marry, then?"

"That really is stuck in your brain, isn't it? I have no idea. If I meet someone special, and we both want to, and we're in a *position* to, then of course I will. But I am going to have a great many lovers, and I'll have even more friends; and the children will have their friends to play with in the parkland. Maybe even Haile will come back and join in the fun."

"That sounds like the kind of neverland I'd want to grow up in. Question is now, will it ever happen? We have to survive this crisis first."

"We will. There's a solution out there somewhere. You said, and I agree."

He ran his fingers along her spine, enjoying the happy sighs it incited. "Yeah. Well let's see if this Tyrathcan God can offer any hints."

"You're really looking forward to the flight, aren't you? I told you, this is what you are." She snuggled up closer, one hand stroking his thigh. "What about you? Will you marry? I'm sure Sarha would be interested."

"No!"

"Okay, strike Sarha. Oh, of course, there's always that farm girl on Norfolk, you know . . . oh what's her name, now?"

Joshua laughed, and rolled her over, pinning her arms above her head. "Her name, as you very well know, is Louise. And you're still jealous, aren't you?"

Ione stuck her tongue out at him. "No."

"If I can't hack it as a consort for you, I hardly think a life tilling the fields is going to enthral me."

"True." She lifted her head, and gave him a fast jocose kiss. He still didn't let go of her arms. "Joshua?"

He groaned in dismay, and collapsed back onto the mattress beside her; which sent out slow waves to flip the cushions. "I hate that tone. I always hear it right before I wind up in deep shit."

"I was only going to ask, what did happen to your father that last flight? *Lady Mac* got back here with a lot of fuselage heat damage and two jump nodes fused. That couldn't be pirates, or a secret mission for the Emperor of Oshanko, or rescuing a lost ship from the Meridian fleet that was caught in a neutron star's gravity well, or any of the other explanations you've come up with over the years."

"Ye of little faith."

She rolled onto her side, and propped her head on one hand. "So what was it?"

"Okay, if you must know. Dad found a xenoc shipwreck with technology inside that was worth a fortune; they had gravity generators, a direct mass energy converter, industrial scale molecular synthesis extruders. Amazing stuff, centuries in advance of Confederation science. He was rich, Ione. He and the crew could have altered the entire Confederation economy with those gadgets."

"Why didn't they?"

"The people who'd hired *Lady Mac* to prospect for gold asteroids turned out to be terrorists, and he had to escape down a timewarp in the centre of the xenoc wreck."

Ione stared at him for a second, then burst out laughing. Her hand slapped his shoulder. "God, you're impossible."

Joshua shifted round to give her a hurt look. "What?"

She put her arms round him and moulded her body contentedly to his, closing her eyes. "Don't forget to tell that one to the children."

Tranquillity observed Joshua's expression sink to mild exasperation. Elaborate thought routines operating within the vast neural strata briefly examined the possibility that he was telling the truth, but in the end decided against.

Harkey's Bar was having a modest resurgence in fortune. Relative to the absolute downtime endured during the quarantine when its space industry clientele were careful with their money, this was a positive boom. Not back up to precrisis levels yet; but the ships were returning to Tranquillity's giant counter-rotating spaceport. Admittedly they were mundane inter-orbit vessels rather than starships, but nonetheless they brought new cargoes, and crews with heavy credit disks, and paid the service companies for maintenance and support. The masters of commerce and finance living in the starscraper penthouses were already making deals with the awesome Edenist industrial establishment in whose midst they had so fortuitously materialized. It wouldn't be long before all the dormitoried starships were powered up and started travelling to Earth, and Saturn, and Mars, and the asteroid settlements. Best of all, the buzz was back among the tables and booths, industry gossip was hot and hectic. Such confidence did wonders for liberating anticipation and credit disks.

Sarha, Ashly, Dahybi, and Beaulieu had claimed their usual booth, as requested by Joshua who'd told them he wanted a meeting. They didn't have any trouble, at quarter to nine in the morning there were only a dozen other people in the place. Dahybi sniffed at his coffee after the waitress had departed. Even their skirts were longer at this time of day. "It's not natural, drinking coffee in here."

"This time isn't natural," Ashly complained. He poured some milk into his cup, and added the tea. Sarha *tsked* at him; she always mixed it the other way round.

"Are we flying?" Dahybi asked.

"Looks like it," Beaulieu said. "The captain authorized

the service engineering crew to remove the hull plates over *Lady Mac*'s damaged node. The only reason to do that is to replace it."

"Not cheap," Ashly muttered. He stirred his tea thoughtfully.

Joshua pulled the spare seat out and sat down. "Who's not cheap?" he asked briskly.

"Replacement nodes," Sarha said.

"Oh, them." Joshua stuck up a finger, and a waitress popped up at his side. "Tea, croissants, and orange juice," he ordered. She gave him a friendly smile, and hurried off. Dahybi frowned. Her skirt was short.

"I'm flying *Lady Mac* tomorrow," Joshua told them. "Just as soon as the *Oenone* returns from the O'Neill Halo with my new nodes."

"Does the First Admiral know?" Sarha inquired lightly.

"No, but Consensus does. This is not a cargo flight, we'll be leaving with Admiral Saldana's squadron."

"We?"

"Yes. That's why you're here. I'm not going to press gang you this time. You get consulted. I can promise a long and very interesting trip. Which means I need a good crew."

"I'm in, Captain," Beaulieu said quickly.

Dahybi sipped some coffee and grinned. "Yes."

Joshua looked at Sarha and Ashly. "Where are we going?" she asked.

"To the Tyrathca Sleeping God, so we can ask it how to solve the possession crisis. Ione and the Consensus believe it's on the other side of the Orion nebula."

Sarha deliberately looked away, studying Ashly's face. The pilot was lost in stupefaction. Joshua's simple words were the perfect bewitchment for a man who'd given up normal life to witness as much of eternity as he could. And Joshua knew that, Sarha thought. "Monkey and a banana,"

she muttered. "All right, Joshua, of course we're with you."
Ashly nodded dumbly.

"Thanks," Joshua told them all. "I appreciate it."

"Who's handling fusion?" Dahybi asked.

"Ah," Joshua produced an uncomfortable expression.
"The not-so-good news is that our friend Dr Alkad Mzu is
coming with us." They started to protest. "Among others,"
he said loudly. "We're carrying quite a few specialists with
us this trip. She's the official exotic physics expert."

"Exotic physics?" Sarha sounded amused.

"Nobody knows what this God thing actually is, so we're
covering all the disciplines. It won't be like the Alchemist
mission. We're not on our own this time."

"Okay, but who do you want as fusion officer?" Dahybi
repeated.

"Well . . . Mzu's specialist field at the Laymil project
was fusion systems. I could ask her. I didn't know how
you'd all feel about that."

"Badly," Beaulieu said. Joshua blinked. He'd never
heard the cosmonik express a definite opinion before, not
about people.

"Joshua," Sarha said firmly. "Just go and ask Liol, all
right? If he says no, fine, we'll get someone else. If he says
yes, it'll be with the understanding that you're the captain.
And you know he's up to the job. He deserves the chance,
and I don't just mean to crew."

Joshua looked round the other three, receiving their encouragement. "Suppose there's no harm in asking," he admitted.

The crews were starting to refer to themselves as the
Deathkiss squadron. On several occasions the phrase had
almost slipped from Rear-Admiral Meredith Saldana's own
mouth as well. Discipline had kept it from being spoken,

rather than neural nanonic prohibitions, but he sympathised with his personnel.

The sol-system news companies were hailing Tranquillity's appearance in Jupiter orbit as a huge victory over the possessed, and Capone in particular. Meredith didn't see it quite that way. It was the second time the squadron had gone up against the possessed, and the second time they'd been forced to retreat. This time they owed their lives entirely to luck . . . and his own rebel ancestor's foresight. He wasn't entirely sure if the universe was being ironic or contemptuous towards him. The only certainty in his life these days was the squadron's morale, which was close to non-existent. His day cabin's processor datavised an admission request, which he granted. Commander Kroeber and Lieutenant Rhoecus air swam through the open hatch. They secured their feet on a stikpad and saluted.

"At ease," Meredith told them. "What have you got for me?"

"Our assignment orders, sir," Rhoecus said. "They're from the Jovian Consensus."

Meredith gave Commander Kroeber a brief glance. They'd been waiting for new orders from the 2nd Fleet headquarters in the O'Neill Halo. "Go ahead, Lieutenant."

"Sir, it's a secure operation. CNIS has located an antimatter production station, they asked Jupiter to eliminate it."

"Could have been worse," Meredith said. For all it was rare, an assault on an antimatter station was a standard procedure. A straightforward mission like this was just what the crews needed to restore confidence in themselves. Then he noticed the reservation in Rhoecus's expression. "Continue."

"A supplementary order has been added by the Jovian

Security sub-Consensus. The station is to be captured intact."

Meredith hardened his expression, knowing Consensus would be observing his disapproval through Rhoecus's eyes. "I really do hope that you're not going to suggest we start arming ourselves with that *abomination*."

If anything, Rhoecus seemed rather relieved. "No, sir, absolutely not."

"Then what are we capturing it for?"

"Sir, it's to be used for fuelling the *Lady Macbeth*'s antimatter drive unit. Consensus is sending a pair of ships beyond the Orion nebula."

The statement was so extraordinary Meredith initially didn't know what to make of it. Though that ship's name . . . Oh yes, of course, Lagrange Calvert; and there was also the matter of a ludicrously ballsy manoeuvre through Lalonde's upper atmosphere. "Why?" he asked mildly.

"It's a contact mission with the non-Confederation Tyrathca. We believe they may have information relevant to possession."

Meredith knew he was being judged by Consensus. An Adamist—a Saldana—being asked by Edenists to break the very law the Confederation was formed to enforce. At the least I should query 2nd Fleet headquarters. But in the end it comes down to trust. Consensus would never initiate such a mission without a good reason. "We live in interesting times, Lieutenant."

"Yes, sir; unfortunately, we do."

"Then let's hope we outlive them. Very well. Commander Kroeber, squadron to stand by for assault duties."

"Consensus has designated fifteen voidhawks to join us, sir," Rhoecus said. "Weapons loading for the frigates has been given full priority."

"When do we leave?"

"The *Lady Macbeth* is undergoing some essential maintenance. She should be ready to join the squadron in another twelve hours."

"I hope this Lagrange Calvert character can stay in formation," Meredith said.

"Consensus has every confidence in Captain Calvert, sir."

The two of them sat at a table by the window in Harkey's Bar. Glittering stars chased a shallow arc behind them as their drinks were delivered. Two slender crystal flutes of Norfolk Tears. The waitress thought that wonderfully romantic. They were both captains, he in crumpled overalls but still with the silver star on his shoulder, she in an immaculate Edenist blue satin ship-tunic. A handsome couple.

Syrinx picked her glass up and smiled. "We really shouldn't be drinking. We're flying in seven hours."

"Absolutely," Joshua agreed. He touched his glass to hers. "Cheers." They both sipped, relishing the drink's delectable impact.

"Norfolk was such a lovely world," Syrinx said. "I was planning on going back next midsummer."

"Me too. I'd got this amazing deal lined up. And . . . there was a girl."

She took another sip. "Now there's a surprise."

"You've changed. Not so uptight."

"And you're not so irresponsible."

"Here's to the sustainable middle ground." They touched glasses again.

"How's the refit coming on?" Syrinx asked.

"On schedule so far. We've got the new reaction mass tanks installed in *Lady Mac*'s cargo holds. I left the engineering team plumbing them in. Dahybi is running integration protocols through the new node; there's some kind of software disparity with the rest of them. But then there always is a problem with new units, the manufacturers can never resist trying to improve something that works perfectly well already. He'll have it debugged ready for departure time."

"Sounds like you have a good crew."

"The best. How's *Oenone*?"

"Fine. The supplement fusion generators are standard items. We already had the attachment points for them in the cargo cradles."

"Looks like we're running out of excuses, then."

"Yeah. But I bet the view from that side of the nebula is quite something."

"It will be." He hesitated for a moment. "Are you all right?"

Syrinx studied him over the top of the flute; her ability to read Adamist emotions was quite adroit these days, so she considered. His genuine concern gladdened her. "I am now. Bit of a basket case for a while, after Pernik, but the doctors and my friends helped put me back together again."

"Good friends."

"The best."

"So why this flight?"

"Mainly *Oenone* and I are flying because we think this is how we can contribute best. If that sounds superior, I apologise, but it's what I feel."

"It's the *only* reason I'm here. You know, you and I are pretty unique. There's not many of us who've come face to face with the possessed and survived. That does tend to focus the mind somewhat."

"I know what you mean."

"I've never been so scared before. Death is always so difficult for us. Most people just ignore it. Then when you start to see your last days drifting away you content yourself that you've had a good life, that it hasn't been for nothing. And, hey, there might be an afterlife after all, which is good because deep down you've convinced yourself you did your best, so the plus column is always going to be in the black when it comes to Judgement day. Only there isn't a Judgement day, the universe doesn't care."

"Laton worked it out; that's what gets me. I've retrieved that last message of his time and again, and he really believed Edenists won't be trapped in the beyond. Not even one in a billion of us, he said. Why, Joshua? We're not that different, not really."

"What does Consensus think?"

"There's no opinion yet. We're trying to ascertain the general nature of the possessed, and compare it to our own psychological profile. Laton said that would provide us with an insight. The Mortonridge Liberation ought to generate a great deal of raw data."

"I'm not sure how helpful that'll be. Every era has a different outlook. What's thoroughly normal behaviour for a Seventeenth Century potter is going to be utterly different from you. I always think Ashly's ridiculously old fashioned on some things; he's horrified by the way kids today can access stim programs."

"So am I."

"But you can't restrict access, not in a universal data culture like ours. You have to educate society about what's acceptable and what isn't. A little adolescent experimentation isn't harmful, in moderation. We have to concentrate on pushing the moderation aspect, help people come to terms with what's out there. The alternative is censorship, which the communication nets will defeat every time."

"That's defeatism. I'm not saying people shouldn't be educated about the problems of stim programs; but if you made the effort, Adamist culture could abolish them."

"Knowledge can't be destroyed, it has to be absorbed and accommodated." He glanced dolefully out at Jupiter. "As I tried to argue with the First Admiral. He wasn't terribly impressed, either."

"I'm not surprised. The fact we're going to use antimatter on this flight is restricted information. Rightly so."

"That's different—" Joshua began, then grunted. "Looks like I'm not going to make it past the beyond. Don't think like an Edenist."

"No, that's not right. This is just a difference in beliefs. We both agree stim addiction is a dreadful blight, we just differ on how to treat it. We still think the same way. I don't understand this! Damnit!"

"Let's hope the Sleeping God can show us the difference." He gave her a tentative look. "Can I ask a personal question?"

She rubbed the tip of her index finger round the rim of the flute, then sucked on it. "Joshua Calvert, I have a devoted lover, thank you."

"Er, actually, I was wondering if you had any children."

"Oh," she said, and promptly blushed. "No, I don't. Not yet anyway. My sister Pomona has three; it makes me wonder what I've been doing with my time."

"When you do have children, how do you raise them? Voidhawk captains, I mean. You don't have them on board, do you?"

"No, we don't. Shipboard life is for adults, even aboard a voidhawk."

"So how do they grow up?"

"What do you mean?" It was a strange question, especially from him. But she could see it was important.

"They haven't got you there as a mother."

"Oh, I see. It doesn't matter, for them anyway. Voidhawk captains tend to have fairly large extended families. I must take you to see my mother some time, then you'll see first-hand. Any children I have while I'm still flying with *Oenone* will be taken care of by my army of relatives, and the habitat as well. I'm not propagandising, but Edenism is one giant family. There's no such thing as an orphan among us. Of course, it's hard on us captains, having to kiss good-bye to our babies for months at a time. But that's been the fate of sailors for millennia now. And of course, we do get to make up for it at the end. When *Oenone*'s eggs are birthed, I wind up at ninety years old in a house with a dozen screaming infants. Imagine that."

"Are they happy, those other children? The ones you have to leave behind."

"Yes. They're happy. I know you think we're terribly formal and mannered, but we're not mechanoids, Joshua, we love our children." She reached over and squeezed his hand. "You okay?"

"Oh yeah. I'm okay." He concentrated on his flute. "Syrinx. You can count on me during the flight."

"I know that, Joshua. I reviewed the Murora memory a few times, and I've spoken to Samuel, too."

He gestured out at the starfield. "The real answer lies out there, somewhere."

"Consensus has known that all along. And as the Kiint wouldn't tell me . . ."

"And I'm not smart enough to help the research professors . . ."

They smiled. "Here's to the flight," Syrinx said.

"Soaring where angels fear to fly."

They downed the remainder of their Norfolk Tears. Syrinx blew heavily, and blinked the moisture away from her eyes. Then she frowned at the figure standing at the bar. "Jesus, Joshua, I didn't know there was two of you."

The enjoyable surprise of hearing an Edenist swear in

such a fashion was quelled with pique when he saw who
she was talking about. He stuck his hand up and waved Liol
over.

"Delighted to meet you," Liol said when Joshua introduced them. He polished up the Calvert grin for her benefit,
and kissed her hand.

Syrinx laughed, and stood up. "Sorry Liol, I'm afraid I
had my inoculation some time ago." Joshua was chuckling.

"I'll leave the pair of you to it," she said, and gave
Joshua a light kiss. "Don't be late."

"Got her eddress?" Liol asked from the side of his mouth
as he watched her walk away.

"Liol, that's a voidhawk ship-tunic. Syrinx doesn't have
an eddress. So how are you?"

"Absolutely fine." Liol reversed a chair, and straddled it,
arms resting on the back. "This is party city for me all right.
I think I'll move Quantum Serendipity here after the crisis."

"Right. Haven't seen much of you since we docked."

"Well hey, no surprise there. That Dominique, hell of a
girl." He lowered his voice to a throaty gloating growl.
"Game on, five, six times a night. Every position I know,
then some that's got to be just for xenocs."

"Wow."

"Last night, you know what? Threesome. Neomone
joined in."

"No shit? You record a sensevise?"

Liol put both hands down on the table, and stared at his
brother. "Josh."

"Yep."

"For Christ's sake take me with you."

Kerry was the first planet, the test. Catholic Irish-ethnic to
the bedrock, its inhabitants gave the priests of the Unified
Church a very hard time. Stubbornly suspicious of technol-

ogy, it took them a half a century longer than the development company projected to reach full technoindustrial independence. When they did achieve it, their economic index never matched the acceleration curve of the more driven Western-Christian work-ethic planets. They were comfortably off, favoured large families, traded modestly with nearby star systems, contributed grudgingly to the Confederation Assembly and Navy, and went to Church regularly. There were no aspirations to become a galactic player like Kulu, Oshanko, and Edenism. Quiet people getting on with their lives. Until the possession crisis arrived.

The planet was seven light-years from New California, and worried. Their Strategic Defence network was the absolute minimum for a developed world; and combat wasp stocks were never kept very high; maintenance budgets were also subject to political trimming. Since the crisis began, and especially post-Arnstat, Kerry had been desperately trying to upgrade. Unfortunately their industrial stations weren't geared towards churning out military hardware. Nor were they closely allied to Kulu or Earth who did produce an abundance of such items. The Edenists of the Kerry system, orbiting Rathdrum, leant what support they could; but they had their own defences to enhance first.

Still, went the hope and reasoning, that's the benefit of being galactic small fry, Capone isn't going to bother with us. When it came to the effort of mounting a full scale invasion along the lines of Arnstat they were absolutely right. Which is why Al's sudden change of policy caught them woefully unprepared.

Twelve hellhawks emerged five and a half thousand kilometres above Kerry's atmosphere, and fired a salvo of ten (fusion powered) combat wasps each. The bitek craft immediately started accelerating at six gees, flying away from each other in an expanding globe formation. Their combat wasps raced on ahead of them, ejecting multiple submunitions. Space was infected by electronic warfare impulses and thermal decoys, a rapidly growing blind spot in Kerry's sensor coverage. Submunitions began to target sensor satellites, inter-orbit ships, spaceplanes, and low orbit SD platforms. A volley of fusion bombs detonated, creating a further maelstrom of electromagnetic chaos.

Kerry's SD network controllers, surprised by the vehemence of the attack, and fearing an Arnstat-style assault, did their best to counter. Platforms launched counter salvos of combat wasps; electron beams and X-ray lasers stabbed out, slashing across the vacuum to punch submunitions into bloating haze-balls of ions. Electronic warfare generators on the platforms began pumping out their own disruption. After four seconds spent analysing the attack mode, the network's coordinating AI determined the hellhawks were engaged in a safe-clearance operation. It was right.

Ten front-line Organization frigates emerged into the calm centre of the combat wasp deluge. Fusion drives ignited, driving them down towards the planet at eight gees. Combat wasps slid out of their launch tubes, and their drives came on.

The AI had switched all available sensor satellites to scanning the frigates. Radars and laser radars were essentially useless in the face of New California's superior electronic warfare technology. The network's visual pattern sensors were being pummelled by the nuclear explosions and deception impulse lasers, but they did manage to distinguish the unique superhot energy output of antimatter drives. The ultimate horror unchained above Kerry's beautiful, vulnerable atmosphere.

Unlike ordinary combat wasps, a killstrike didn't eliminate the problem. Hit a fusion bomb with a laser or kinetic bullet, and there is no nuclear explosion, it simply disintegrates into its component molecules. But knock out an antimatter combat wasp, and the drive's confinement spheres will detonate into multi-megaton fury, as will as the warheads.

As soon as the launch was verified, the AI's total priority was preventing the antimatter combat wasps from getting within a thousand kilometres of the stratosphere. Starships, communication platforms, port stations, and industrial stations were reclassified expendable, and left to take their chances. Every SD resource was concentrated on eliminating the antimatter drones. Weapons were realigned away from the hellhawks and frigates, and brought to bear solely on the searing lightpoints racing over the delicate continents. Defending combat wasps performed drastic realignment manoeuvres; platform-mounted rail guns pumped out a cascade of inert kinetic missiles along projected vectors. Patrolling starships accelerated down at high-gees, bringing their combat wasps and energy beam weapons in range.

The hellhawks fired another barrage of combat wasps, sending them streaking away from the nebulous clot of plasma which the initial drone battle had smeared across the sky. They were aimed at the remaining low orbit SD platforms shielding the continent below. Apart from activating the platforms' close-defence weapons, there was little the network controllers could do. Hurtling towards the planet, the frigates began to diverge, curving away from each other. Nothing challenged their approach. The continent was completely open to whatever they chose to throw at it.

As the antimatter exploded overhead in a pattern that created an umbrella of solid incandescent radiation three thousand kilometres across, they made a strange selection. Two hundred kilometres above the atmosphere, each warship flung out a batch of inactive ovoids, measuring a mere three metres high. Their task complete, the frigates curved up, striving for altitude with an eight-gee acceleration. A second, smaller salvo of antimatter combat wasps was fired, providing the same kind of diversionary cover as they'd enjoyed during their descent.

This time, the invaders didn't have it all their own way. The number of weapons focused on, and active within, the small zone where the frigates and hellhawks were concentrated began to take effect. Even Kerry's second-rate hardware had the odds tilting in its favour. A nuclear tipped submunition exploded against one of the frigates. Its entire stock of antimatter detonated instantaneously. The radiation blaze wiped out every chunk of hardware within a five hundred kilometre radius. Outside the killzone, ships and drones spun away inertly, moulting charred flakes of null-foam. Exposed fuselages shone like small suns under the equally intense photonic energy release. To those on the planet unlucky enough to be looking up at the silent, glorious blossoms of light during the first stage of the battle, it was as though the noon sun had suddenly quadrupled in vigour. Then their optic nerves burnt out.

Two of the hellhawks were crippled in the explosion, their polyp penetrated by lethal quantities of gamma radiation. One of the frigates was unable to handle the massive energy impact. The dissipation web beneath its hexagonal fuselage plates turned crimson and melted. The patterning nodes facing the massive explosion flash suffered catastrophic failures as the radiation smashed delicate molecular junctions into slag. The fusion drives failed. Plumes of hot vapour squirted angrily out of emergency vent nozzles. Inside, the crew charged through their contingency procedures, desperate to sustain the integrity of the antimatter confinement spheres in their remaining combat wasps.

None of their Organization colleagues went back for them. As soon as the eight remaining frigates reached a five thousand kilometre altitude, they jumped outsystem. The hellhawks followed within seconds, leaving Kerry's population wondering what the hell had happened. Behind the shrinking wormhole interstices, the black eggs thundered earthwards with total impunity. SD sensors never found them amid the electronic disorder. People on the planet couldn't see their laser-like contrails against the dazzling aftermath of the orbital explosions.

They fell fast before decelerating at excruciatingly high gees in the lower atmosphere. Sonic booms rocked across the sleepy farmland, the first indication that anything was wrong. When the rural folk started to scan the sky in mild alarm, all that was to be seen were chunks of flaming debris streaking down from the battle—to be expected, claimed those who knew something of such things. The eggs reached subsonic speed a kilometre above the land. Petals flipped out from the lower half, presenting a wider surface area to the air, doubling the drag coefficient. At four hundred metres, the drogue chute shot up. Two hundred metres saw the main chute deployment.

Two hundred and fifty of the black eggs thudded to ground at random across an area measuring over three hundred thousand square kilometres. The petals failed on eign., while a further nine suffered chute failure. The remaining two hundred and thirty three produced a bone-rattler landing for their passengers, bouncing and rolling for several metres before they came to a halt. Their sides slit open with a loud *crack*, and the possessed stepped forth to admire the verdant green land they had volunteered to infiltrate.

The hellhawks arrived back at New California thirty hours later. They didn't even get a hero's welcome. The Organization already knew the seeding flight had been a success; information from the infiltrators had already squirmed its way back through the beyond.

Al was jubilant. He ordered Emmet and Leroy to put together another five seeding flights immediately. The fleet crews and asteroids cooperated enthusiastically. The success was nothing like as momentous as the Arnstat victory, but it kicked in a resurgence of confidence throughout the Organization. We're a power again, was the shared opinion. Beefs and recalcitrance sloped away.

The *Varrad* discarded its fantasy starship image as it approached Monterey. It slid over the docking ledge pedestal and slowly sank down, radiating a desultory relief.

You did well, Hudson Proctor told Pran Soo, the hellhawk's resident soul. **Kiera says she's pleased with you.**

Commence nutrient fluid pumping, Pran Soo said flatly.

Sure thing. Here it comes. Enjoy.

Hudson Proctor gave a short command, and the fluid surged along the pipes and into the hellhawk's internal reserve bladders.

Two of us were exterminated, Pran Soo announced to the other hellhawks. **Linsky and Maranthis. They were irradiated when Kerry's SD network took out the Dorbane. It was awful. I felt their structure withering.**

Price we pay for victory, Etchells said swiftly. **Two of us, against an entire Confederation planet taken out.**

Yeah, said Felix, who possessed the *Kerachel.* **Kerry had me real worried. When it comes to drinking contests and pub brawls, they'd got us beat every time.**

Keep your Goddamn pinko looser opinions to yourself, Etchells sneered back. **This was a concept-proving mission. What the fuck do you know about overall strategy? We're the hard edge of operations, the cosmic shock troops.**

Give it a rest, you boring little prat. And don't pretend you were ever in an army. Even armies have a minimum IQ requirement.

Oh yeah? What you know. I killed fifteen men when I was in combat.

Yeah, he was a nurse. Couldn't read the label on the medicine bottle.

Careful, shit-for-brains.

Or what?

I'm sure Kiera would be interested to know about this sedition you're spreading. See what a little fasting does to your attitude.

SHUT THE FUCK UP, YOU BOLLOCKBRAINED NAZI REDNECK MORON.

The general affinity band fell silent for quite some time.

Were you listening to all that? Pran Soo asked Rocio on singular engagement.

I heard, the *Mindori*'s possessor replied. I think things might be starting to slide our way.

Could be. I'm sure each of us can do simple maths. Two of us per soft-target planet. When we start hitting hard targets, Kiera's going to have a full scale strike on her hands.

Which she'll win unless we can provide everyone with an alternative food source.

Yeah. How's it going?

I have been tracking the *Lucky Logorn,* they're almost back at Almaden.

You think this Deebank guy will go for our pitch?

He was the first to offer us a deal. At least he'll listen to what I suggest.

The First Admiral had stayed away from the CNIS secure laboratory ever since the incident in court three. Maynard Khanna had been a damn fine officer, not to mention young and personable. The boy would have gone a long way in the Confederation Navy, so Samual Aleksandrovich had always told himself. With or without my patronage. Now he was dead.

The funeral ceremony in Trafalgar's multi-denominational church had been short and simple. Dignified, as was fitting. A flag draped coffin, the enduring image of military service for centuries, placed reverently on a pedestal before the alter by the Marine dress guard. It was intended as a focus for their honour. But Samual had thought it looked more like a sacrificial offering.

Standing in the front pew, mouthing the words of a hymn, he suddenly wondered if Khanna was actually watching them. Information gleaned from captured possessed indicated those ensnared in the beyond were aware of events inside the real universe. It was a moment of profound spookiness; he even lowered his hymn book to stare at the coffin in suspicion. Was this why the whole funeral ritual had started back in pre-history times? It was one of the most common cross-cultural events, a ceremony to mark the passing of life. The deceased's friends and relatives coming to pay homage, to wish them well on their way. It would be reassuring for a soul, otherwise so naked and alone, to gain the knowledge that so many considered their life to be worthwhile.

The remnants of Maynard Khanna's body mocked the notion of a fulfilled existence. Young, tortured to death, his ending had been neither swift nor noble.

Samual Aleksandrovich had raised his hymn book again and sung with a vigour which surprised the other officers. Perhaps Khanna would witness the mark of devotion from his superior officer, and draw some comfort from the fact. If it made a difference, the effort should be made. Now Samual Aleksandrovich was having to confront the cause of his regret. Jacqueline Couteur was still possessing her stolen body, immune from the usual laws that would deliver justice upon such a treacherous multiple murderess.

He was accompanied by Mae Ortlieb and Jeeta Anwar from the Assembly President's staff, as well as admiral Lalwani and Maynard Khanna's replacement, Captain Amr al-Sahhaf. The presence of the two presidential aides he found mildly annoying; an indication of how his decisions and prerogatives were increasingly coming under political scrutiny. Olton Haaker had that right, Samual acknowledged, but it was being wielded with less subtlety as the crisis drew out.

For the first time he was actually thankful for the Mortonridge Liberation. Positive physical action on such a massive scale had diverted the attention of both the Assembly and the media companies from Navy activities. The politicians, he conceded grimly, might have been right about the psychological impact such a campaign would create. He'd even accessed a few rover reporter sensevises himself to see how the serjeants were doing. My God, the mud!

Dr Gilmore and Euru greeted the small elite delegation with little sign of nerves. A good omen, Samual thought. His spirits lifted further when Gilmore started to lead them along to the physics and electronics laboratory section, away from the demon trap.

Bitek Laboratory Thirteen was almost the same as any standard electronic research facility. A long room lined with benches, several morgue-like slabs arranged up down the centre, and glass-walled clean rooms at one end. Tall stacks of experimental equipment were standing like modern megaliths on every surface, alongside ultra-high-resolution scanners and powerful desktop blocks. The only distinguishing items the First Admiral could see were the clone vats. Those you normally wouldn't find outside an Edenist establishment.

"Exactly what are you demonstrating for us?" Jeeta Anwar asked.

"The prototype anti-memory," Euru said. "It was surprisingly easy to assemble. Of course, we do have a great many thoughtware weapons on file, which we've studied. And the neural mechanisms behind memory retention are well understood."

"If that's the case, I'm surprised no one has ever designed one before."

"It's a question of application," Gilmore said. "As the First Admiral pointed out once, the more complex a weapon is, the more impractical it becomes, especially in the field. In order for the anti-memory to work, the brain must be subjected to quite a long sequence of imprint pulses. You couldn't just fire it at your opponent the same way you do a bullet. They have to be looking straight into the beam, and a sharp movement, or even an inappropriately timed blink will nullify the whole process. And if it was known to be in use, retinal implants could be programmed to recognize it, and block it out. However, once you hold a captive, application becomes extremely simple."

Mattox was waiting for them by the last clean room, looking through the glass with the air of a proud parent. "Testing has been our greatest stalling point," he explained. "Ordinary bitek processors are completely useless in this respect. We had to design a system which duplicates a typical human neurone structure in its entirety."

"You mean you cloned a brain?" Mae Ortlieb asked, a blatant note of disapproval in her voice.

"The structural array is copied from a brain," Mattox said defensively. "But the construct itself is made purely from bitek. There was no cloning involved." He indicated the clean room.

The delegation moved closer. The room was almost empty, containing a single table which held a burnished metal cylinder. Slim tubes of nutrient fluid snaked out of the base to link it with a squat protein cycler mechanism. A small box protruded from the side of the cylinder, half-way up. Made of translucent amber plastic, it contained a solitary dark sphere of some denser material, set near the surface. The First Admiral upped the magnification on his enhanced retinas. "That's an eye," he said.

"Yes, sir," Mattox said. "We're trying to make this as realistic as possible. Genuine application will require the anti-memory to be conducted down an optic nerve."

A black electronic module was suspended centimetres from the bitek eye, held in place by a crude metal clamp. Fibre optic cables trailed away from it, to plug into the clean room's utility data sockets.

"What sort of routines are you running inside the construct?" Mae Ortlieb asked.

"Mine," Euru said. "We connected the cortex to an affinity capable processor, and I transferred a copy of my personality and memories into it."

She flinched, looking from the Edenist to the metal cylinder. "It's that somewhat unusual?"

"Not relative to this situation," he replied with a smile. "We are attempting to create the most realistic environment we can. For that we need a human mind. If you would care to give it a simple Turing test." He touched a processor block on the wall beside the clean room. Its AV lens sparkled.

"Who are you?" Mae Ortlieb asked, with some self-consciousness.

"I suppose I ought to call myself Euru-two," the AV lens

replied. "But then Euru has transferred his personality into a neural simulacrum twelve times already to assist with the anti-memory evaluation."

"Then you should be Euru-thirteen."

"Just call me junior, it's simpler."

"And do you believe you've retained your human faculties?"

"I don't have affinity, of course, which I regard as distressing. However, as I won't be in existence for very long, it's absence is tolerable. Apart from that, I am fully human."

"Volunteering for a suicide isn't a very healthy human trait, and certainly not for an Edenist."

"None the less, it's what I committed myself to."

"Your original self did. What about you, have you no independence?"

"Possibly if you left me to develop by myself for several months, I would become reluctant. At the moment, I am Euru senior's mind twin, and as such this experiment is quite acceptable to me."

The First Admiral frowned, troubled by what he was witnessing. He hadn't known Gilmore's team had reached quite this level. He gave Euru a sidelong glance. "I'm given to understand that a soul is formed by impressing coherent sentient thought on the beyond-type energy which is present in this universe. Therefore, as you are a sentient entity, you will now have your own soul."

"I would assume so, admiral," Euru junior replied. "It is logical."

"Which means you have the potential to become an immortal entity in your own right. Yet this trial will eliminate you forever. This is an alarming prospect, for me if not for you. I'm not sure we have the moral right to continue."

"I understand what you're saying, Admiral. However,

my identity is more important to me than my soul, or souls. I know that when I am erased from this construct, I, Euru, will continue to exist. The sum of whatever I am goes on. This is the knowledge which rewards all Edenists throughout their lives. Whereas I now exist for one reason, to protect that continuity for my culture. Human beings have died to protect their homes and ideals for all of history, even though they never knew for certain they had souls. I am no different to any of them. I quite plainly choose to undergo the anti-memory so that our race can overcome this crisis."

"Quite a Turing test," Mae Ortlieb said sardonically. "I bet the old man never envisaged this kind of conversation with a machine trying to prove its own intelligence."

"If there's nothing else," Gilmore said quickly.

The First Admiral looked in at the cylinder again, contemplating a refusal. He knew such an instruction would never be allowed to stand by the President. *And I don't need that kind of interventionism in Navy affairs right now.* "Very well," he said reluctantly.

Gilmore and Mattox exchanged a mildly guilty look. Mattox datavised an instruction to the clean room's control processor, and the glass turned opaque. "Just to protect you from any possible spillback," he said. "If you'd like to access the internal camera you can observe the process in full. Not that there will be anything much to see. I assure you the spectrum we're using to transmit the anti-memory has been blocked from the sensor."

True to his word, the image the delegation received when they accessed the sensor was pallid, the colour almost nonexistent. All they saw was a small blank disc slide out of the electronic module, positioning itself over the encapsulated eye. Some iconic overlay digits twisted past, meaningless.

"That's it," Mattox announced.

The First Admiral cancelled his channel with the processor. The clean room's window turned transparent again, in time to catch the disc retract back into the electronic module.

Gilmore faced the AV lens. "Junior, can you hear me?" The lens's diminutive sparkle remained constant.

Mattox received a datavise from the construct's monitoring probes. "Brainwave functions have collapsed," he said. "And the synaptic discharges are completely randomized."

"What about memory retention?" Gilmore queried.

"Probably around thirty to thirty-five per cent. I'll run a complete neurological capacity scan once it's stabilized." The CNIS science team members smiled round at each other.

"That's good," Gilmore said. "That's damn good. Best percentage yet."

"Meaning?" the First Admiral asked.

"There are no operative thought patterns left in there. Junior has stopped thinking. The bitek is just a store for memory fragments."

"Impressive," Mae Ortlieb said reflectively. "So what's your next stage?"

"We're not sure," Gilmore said. "I have to admit, the potential for this thing is frightening. Our idea is to use it as a threat to force the souls away from their interface with this universe."

"If it works on souls themselves," Jeeta Anwar pointed out.

"That prospect is bringing about a whole range of new problems," Gilmore conceded cheerlessly.

"Let me guess," Samual said. "If anti-memory is used on a possessed, you will also erase the host's memories, and destroy their soul."

"It seems likely," Euru said. "We know a host's mind is still contained within their brain while the possessing soul retains control of the body. The host's reappearance after zero-tau immersion forces the possessor out proves that."

"So, anti-memory cannot be used on an individual basis?"

"Not without killing the host's soul as well, no sir."

"Will this version work in the beyond?" Samual asked sharply.

"I doubt it would ever get through to the beyond," Mattox said. "At present, it's too slow and inefficient. It managed to dissipate Junior's thought processes; but as you saw, it didn't get all the memories. The areas of the mind which are not employed when the anti-memory strikes are likely to be insulated from it as the thought channels which would ordinarily connect them are nullified. If you analogise the mind with a city, you're destroying the roads and leaving the buildings intact. Given that the connection a possessing soul has with the beyond is tenuous at best, there is no guarantee the anti-memory would manage to pass through in its current form. We must develop a much faster version."

"But you don't know for sure?"

"No sir. These are estimations and theories. We won't know if a version works until after it's proved successful."

"The trouble with that is, a successful anti-memory would exterminate every soul in the beyond," Euru said quietly.

"Is that true?"

"Yes, sir," Gilmore said. "That's our dilemma. There can be no small scale test or demonstration. Anti-memory is effectively a doomsday weapon."

"You'll never get the souls to believe that," Lalwani said. "In fact, given what we know of conditions in the beyond, you wouldn't even get many of them to pay attention to the warning."

"I cannot conceivably permit the use of a weapon which will exterminate billions of human entities," the First Admiral said. "You have to provide me with alternative options."

"But Admiral—"

"No. I'm sorry, Doctor. I know you've worked hard on this, and I appreciate the effort you and your team have made. Nobody is more aware than myself of just how extreme the threat which the possessed present. But even that cannot justify such a response."

"Admiral! We've explored every option we can think of. Every theorist I've got in every scientific discipline there is has been working on ideas and wild theories. We even tried an exorcism after that priest on Lalonde claimed his worked. Nothing. *Nothing* else has come close to being viable. This is the only progress we have made."

"Doctor, I'm not denigrating your work or your commitment. But surely you can see this is completely unacceptable. Morally, ethically, it is wrong. It cannot be anything other than wrong. What you are suggesting is racial genocide. I will tell you this, the authorization to use such a monstrosity will never come from my lips. Nor I suspect, and hope, would any other Navy officer issue it. Now find me another solution. This project is terminated."

The First Admiral's staff ran a quiet sweepstake to see how long it would be before President Haaker datavised for a conference, the winner called it in at ninety-seven minutes. They sat facing each other across the oval table in a security-level-one sensenviron bubble room. Both kept their generated faces neutral and intonations level.

"Samual, you can't cancel the anti-memory project," the President opened with. "It's all we've got."

In his office, Samual Aleksandrovich smiled at the way

Haaker used his first name, the man always did that when he was going to adopt a totally intransigent line. "Apart from the Mortonridge Liberation, you mean?" He could imagine the tight lips drawn at that jibe.

"As you so kindly pointed out earlier, the Liberation is not a solution to the overall problem. Anti-memory is."

"Undoubtedly. Too final. Look, I don't know if Mae and Jeeta explained this fully to you, but the research team believe it would exterminate every soul in the beyond. You can't seriously consider that."

"Samual, those souls you're so concerned about are attempting to enslave every one of us. I have to say I'm surprised by your attitude. You're a military man, you know that war is the result of total irrationality combined with conflict of interest. This crisis is the supreme example of both. The souls desperately want to return, and we cannot allow them to. They will extinguish the human race if they succeed."

"They will ruin almost everything we have accomplished. But total life extinction, no. I don't even believe they can possess all of us. The Edenists have proved remarkably resistant; and the spread has all but stopped."

"Yes, thanks to your quarantine. It's been a successful policy, I won't deny that. But so far we've been unable to offer anything that can reverse what's happened. And that's what the vast majority of the Confederation population want. Actually, that's what they insist upon. The spread might have slowed, but it hasn't stopped. You know that as well as I do. And the quarantine is difficult to enforce."

"You really don't understand what you're proposing, do you. There are billions of souls there. Billions."

"And they are living in torment. For whatever reason, they cannot move on as this Laton character claimed is possible. Don't you think they'd welcome true death?"

"Some of them might. I probably would. But neither you nor I have the right to decide that for them."

"They forced us into this position. They're the ones invading us."

"That does not give us the right to exterminate them. We have to find a way to help them; by doing that we help ourselves. Can you not see that?"

The President abandoned his image's impartiality and leant forwards, his voice becoming earnest. "Of course I can see that. Don't try to portray me as some kind of intransigent villain here. I've supported you, Samual, because I know nobody can command the Navy better than you. And I've been rewarded by that support. So far we've kept on top of the political situation, kept the hotheads in line. But it can't last forever. Sometime, somehow, a solution is going to have to be presented to the Confederation as a whole. And all we've got so far is one solitary possible answer: the anti-memory. I cannot permit you to abandon that, Samual. These are very desperate times; we have to consider everything, however horrific it appears."

"I will never permit such a thing to be used. For all they are different, the souls are human. I am sworn to protect life throughout the Confederation."

"The order to use it would not be yours to give. A weapon like that never falls within the prerogative of the military. It belongs to us, the politicians you despise."

"Disapprove of. Occasionally." The First Admiral permitted a slight smile to show.

"Keep on searching, Samual. Bully Gilmore and his people into finding a decent solution, a humanitarian one. I want that as much as you do. But they are to continue to develop the anti-memory in parallel."

There was a pause. Samual knew that to refuse now would mean Haaker issuing an official request through his office. Which in turn would make his position as First Admiral untenable. That was the stark choice on offer.

"Of course, Mr President."

President Haaker gave a tight smile, and datavised his processor to cancel the meeting, safe in the knowledge that their oh-so diplomatic clash would be known to no one.

The encryption techniques which provided a security-level-one conference were, after all, known to be unbreakable. The most common statistic quoted by security experts was that every AI in the Confederation running in parallel would be unable to crack the code in less than five times the life of the universe. It would, therefore, have proved quite distressing to the CNIS secure communications division (as well as their ESA and B7 equivalents, among others) to know that a perfect replica of a 27-inch 1980's Sony Trinitron colour television was currently showing the image of the First Admiral and the Assembly President to an audience of fifteen attentive duomillenarians and one highly inattentive ten-year-old girl.

Tracy Dean sighed in frustration as the picture vanished to a tiny phosphor dot in the middle of the screen. "Well, that's gone and put the cat amongst the pigeons, and no mistake."

Jay was swinging her feet about while she sat on a too-high stool. As well as being their main social centre, the clubhouse catered for the retired Kiint observers who weren't quite up to living by themselves in a chalet anymore. A huge airy building, with wide corridors and broad archways opening into sunlit rooms that all seemed to resemble hotel lounges. The walls were white plaster, with dark-red tile floors laid everywhere. Big clay pots growing tall palms were a favourite. Tiny birds with bright gold and scarlet bodies and turquoise membrane wings flittered in and out through the open windows, dodging the purple provider globes. The whole theme of the clubhouse was based around comfort. There were no stairs or steps, only ramps; chairs were deeply cushioned; even the food extruded by the universal providers, no matter what type, was soft, requiring little effort to chew.

The first five minutes walking through the building had been interesting. Tracy showed her round, introducing her to the other residents, all of whom were quite spry despite their frail appearance. Of course they were all very happy to see her, making a fuss, patting her head, winking fondly, telling her how nice her new dress was, suggesting strangely named biscuits, sweets and ice creams they though she'd enjoy. They didn't move much from their lounge chairs; contenting themselves with watching events around the Confederation and nostalgic programmes from centuries past.

Jay and Tracy wound up in the lounge with the big TV for half the afternoon, while the residents argued over what channel to watch. They flipped through real-time secret governmental and military conferences, alternating those with a show called "Happy Days," which they all cackled along to in synchronisation with the brash laughter track. Even the original commercial breaks were showing. Jay smiled in confusion at the archaic unfunny characters, and kept sneaking glances out of the window. For the last three days she'd played on the beach with the games the universal providers had extruded; swam, gone for long walks along the sand and through the peaceful jungle behind the beach. The meals had easily been as good as the ones in Tranquillity. Tracy had even got her a processor block with an AV lens that was able to pick up Confederation entertainment shows, which she watched for a few hours every evening. And Richard Keaton had popped in a couple of times to see how she was getting on. But, basically, she was fed-up. Those planets hanging so invitingly in the sky above were a permanent temptation, a reminder that things in the Kiint home system were a bit more active than the human beach.

Tracy caught her wistful gaze once and patted her hand. "Cultural differences," she said confidentially as the mortified Fonz received his army draft papers. "You have to understand the decade before you understand the humour."

Jay nodded wisely, and wondered just when she'd be allowed to see Haile again. Haile was a lot more fun than the Fonz. Then they'd flicked stations to the First Admiral and the President.

"Corpus will have to intervene now," one of the other residents said, a lady called Saska. "That anti-memory could seep outside the human spectrum. Then there'd be trouble."

"Corpus won't," Tracy replied. "It never does. What is, is. Remember?"

"Check your references," another woman said. "Plenty of races considered deploying similar weapons when they encountered the beyond. We've got records of eighteen being used."

"That's awful. What happened?"

"They didn't work very well. Only a moderate percentage of the inverse transcendent population were eliminated. There's too much pattern distortion among the inverses to conduct an anti-memory properly. No species has ever developed one that operates fast enough to be effective. Such things cannot be considered a final solution by any means."

"Yes but that idiot Haaker won't know that until after it's been tried," Galic, one of the men, complained. "We can't possibly allow a human to die, not even an inverse. No human has ever died."

"We've suffered a lot though," a resentful voice muttered.

"And they'll start dying on the removed worlds soon enough."

"I tell you, Corpus won't intervene."

"We could appeal," Tracy said. "At the very least we could ask for an insertion at the anti-memory project to monitor its development. After all, if anyone's going to come up with an anti-memory fast enough to devastate the beyond, it'll be our weapons-mad race."

"All right," Saska said. "But we'll need a quorum before we can even get the appeal up to an executive level."

"As if that'll be a problem," Galic said.

Tracy smiled mischievously. "And I know of someone who's perfectly suited to this particular insertion." Several groans were issued across the lounge.

"Him?"

"Far too smart for his own good, if you ask me."

"No discipline."

"We never ran observer operations like that."

"Cocky little bugger."

"Nonsense," Tracy said briskly. She put her arm round Jay. "Jay likes him, don't you, Jay?"

"Who?"

"Richard."

"Oh." Jay held up Prince Dell; for some unexplainable reason she hadn't managed to abandon the bear in her room. "He gave me this," she announced to the lounge at large.

Tracy laughed. "There you go then. Arnie, you prepare the appeal, you're best acquainted with the minutia of Corpus protocol procedures."

"All right." One of the men raised his hands in gruff submission. "I suppose I can spare the time."

The TV was switched back on, playing the signature tune for "I Love Lucy." Tracy pulled a face, and took Jay's hand. "Come on, poppet, I think you're quite bored enough already."

"Who's the Corpus?" Jay asked as they walked through the front entrance and into the sharp sunlight. There was a black iron penny-farthing bicycle mounted on a stone pedestal just outside. The first time Jay had seen it, she'd taken an age to work out how people were supposed to ride it.

"Corpus isn't a who, exactly," Tracy said. "It's more like the Kiint version of an Edenist Consensus. Except, it's sort of a philosophy as well as a government. I'm sorry, that's not a very good explanation, is it?"

"It's in charge, you mean?"

Tracy's hesitation was barely noticeable. "Yes, that's right. We have to obey its laws. And the strongest of all is non-intervention. The one which Haile broke to bring you here."

"And you're worried about this anti-memory weapon thing?"

"Badly worried, though everyone is trying not to show it. That thing could cause havoc if it gets released into the beyond. We really can't allow that to happen, poppet. Which is why I want Richard sent to Trafalgar."

"Why?"

"You heard what they were saying. He lacks discipline." She winked.

Tracy led her back to the circle of ebony marble above the beach. Jay had seen several of them dotted around the cluster of chalets, including a couple in the clubhouse itself. A few times she'd even seen the black spheres blink into existence and deposit somebody. Once she'd actually scampered on to a circle herself, closing her eyes and holding her breath. But nothing had happened. She guessed you needed to datavise whatever control processor they used.

Tracy stopped at the edge of the circle, and held up a finger to Jay. "Someone to see you," she said.

A black sphere materialized. Then Haile was standing there, half-formed arms waving uncertainly.

Friend Jay! Much gladness.

Jay squealed excitedly, and rushed forward to throw her arms around her friend's neck. "Where've you been? I missed you." There was plenty of hurt in the voice.

I have had time learning much.

"Like what?"

A tractamorphic arm curled round Jay's waist. **How things work.**

"What things?"

The Corpus. Haile's tone was slightly awed.

Jay rubbed the top of the baby Kiint's head. "Oh that. Everyone here's really annoyed with it."

With Corpus? That cannot be.

"It won't help humans with possession, not big help like we need, anyway. Don't worry, Tracy's going to lodge an appeal. Everything will be all right eventually."

This is goodness. Corpus is most wise.

"Yeah?" She patted Haile's front leg, and the Kiint obediently bent her knee. Jay scrambled up quickly to sit astride Haile's neck. "Does it know any good sandcastle designs?"

Haile lumbered off the ebony circle. **Corpus has no knowledge concerning the building of castles from sand.** Jay grinned smugly.

"Now you two be good," Tracy said sternly. "You can swim, but you're not to go out of your depth in the water. I know the providers will help if you get into trouble, but that's not the point. You have to learn to take responsibility for yourselves. Understood?"

"Yes, Tracy."

I have comprehension.

"All right, go on then, have fun. And Jay, you're not to stuff yourself with sweets. I'm cooking supper for us tonight, and I shall be very cross if you don't eat anything."

"Yes, Tracy." She squeezed her knees into Haile's flanks, and the Kiint started moving forwards, taking them quickly away from the old woman.

"Did you get into lots of trouble for rescuing me?" Jay asked anxiously after they'd left Tracy behind.

Corpus has much understanding and provides forgiveness.

"Oh good."

But I am not to do it again.

Jay scratched her friend's shoulders fondly as they hurried down towards the water. "Hey, you're getting lots better at walking."

The rest of the afternoon was a delight. Like old times back in Tranquillity's cove. They swam, and the attendant universal provider extruded a sponge and a brush so Haile could be scrubbed, they built some sandcastles, though this fine loose sand wasn't terribly good for it, Jay risked asking for a couple of chocolate almond ice creams—was pretty sure the provider would tell Tracy if she had any more—they swatted an inflated beach ball to and fro, and once they'd tired themselves out they talked about the Kiint home system. Haile didn't know much more than Tracy had already explained, but whatever new question Jay asked, the Kiint just consulted Corpus for an answer.

The information was rather intriguing. For a start, the cluster of retirement chalets were one of three such human establishments on an otherwise uninhabited island fifty kilometres across. It was called The Village.

"The island's called The Village?" Jay asked in puzzlement.

Yes. The retired human observers insisted this be so. Corpus suggests there is much irony in the naming. I know not about irony.

"Cultural difference," Jay said loftily.

The Village was one of a vast archipelago of islands, home to the observers of eight hundred different sentient xenoc races. Jay looked longingly at the yacht anchored offshore. How fabulous it would be to sail this sea, where every port would be home to a new species.

"Are there any Tyrathca here?"

Some. It is difficult for Corpus to insert into their society. They occupy many worlds, more than your Confederation. Corpus says they are insular. This has troubled Corpus recently.

Haile told her of the world she was living on now, called Riynine. Nang and Lieria had selected a home in one of the big cities, a parkland continent studded with domes and towers and other colossi. There were hundreds of millions of Kiint living there, and Haile had met lots of youngsters her own age.

I have many new friends now.

"That's nice." She tried not to feel jealous.

Riynine was invisible from The Village; it was a long way around the Arc, almost behind the dazzling sun. One of the capital planets, where flocks of xenoc starships arrived from worlds clear across the galaxy, forming a spiralling silver nebula above the atmosphere.

"Take me there," Jay pleaded. She ached to see such a wonder. "I want to meet your new friends and see the city."

Corpus does not want you alarmed. There is strangeness to be had there.

"Oh please, please. I'll simply die if I don't. It's so unfair to come all this way and not see the best bit. Please, Haile, ask Corpus for me. Please!"

Friend Jay. Please have calmness. I will appeal. I promise.

"Thank you, thank you, thank you." She jumped up and danced around Haile, who snaked out slender tractamorphic arms to try and catch her.

"Hey there," a voice called. "Looks like the two of you're having a good time."

Jay stopped, breathless and flushed. She squinted at the figure walking across the glaring sand. "Richard?"

He smiled. "I came to say goodbye."

"Oh." She let out a heavy breath. Everything in her life was so temporary these days. People, places . . . She tilted her head. "You look different."

He was wearing a deep-blue uniform, clean and creased; with shining black boots. A peaked cap was tucked under his arm. And the ponytail was gone; his hair trimmed down to a centimetre high crop. "Senior Lieutenant, Keaton, Confederation Navy, reporting for duty, ma'am." He saluted.

Jay giggled. "This is my friend, Haile."

Hello, Haile.

Greetings Richard Keaton.

Richard tugged at his jacket, shifting his shoulders. "So what do you think? How do I look?"

"It's very smart."

"Ah, I knew it. It's true. All the girls love a uniform."

"Do you really have to go?"

"Yep. Got drafted by our friend Tracy. I'm off to Trafalgar to save the universe from the wicked Doctor Gilmore. Not that he knows he's being wicked. That's part of the problem, I'm afraid. Ignorance is a tragic part of life."

"How long for?" She hadn't quite realized things would move so fast. Tracy had only talked about the insertion a few hours ago. And now here it was, about to happen.

"Not sure. That's why I wanted to make sure I saw you before I left. Tell you not to worry. Tracy and all her cronies mean well, but they get panicked too easily. I want you to know the human race is a lot smarter and resilient than those wonderful old coots think we are. They've seen too much of us at the wrong end of history. I know what we are now. And this is the time that counts. We stand a damn good chance, Jay. I promise you that."

She put her arms round him. "I'll look after Prince Dell for you."

"Thanks." He looked about with theatrical slyness, and lowered his voice. "When you get the chance . . . ask the provider for a surfboard and a jetski. And that was your idea. Okay?"

She nodded extravagantly. "Okay."

This refit hadn't been on quite the scale as the last two she'd undergone; but there was no doubt about it, the *Lady Macbeth* was an honoured source of income to the service and engineering companies that operated in Tranquillity's counter-rotating spaceport. Several of her life support capsule fittings had collapsed under the incredible acceleration of the antimatter drive. Then there were the additional reaction mass tanks to install in the cargo bays. A whole new specialist sensor suite wired in for Kempster Getchell, as well as loading a fleet of small survey satellites. Hull plates had been removed to allow the replacement energy patterning node to be installed.

When Ione floated into the docking bay's control centre, the nullfoam spray nozzles were folding back against the sides of the bay. *Lady Mac* glistened a pristine silver-grey under the ring of lights at the top of the steep metal crater.

Joshua was talking to some of the staff operating the consoles in front of the windows, discussing colour and style for the name and registration A spindly waldo arm was already sliding out under the direction of one operator, its ion-jet painter head rotating into position.

"You're supposed to be launching in twenty-eight minutes," Ione said.

Joshua glanced across and smiled. He left the control centre staff, and glided over to her. They kissed. "Plenty of time. And you can't fly without a name on the fuselage. Besides, the C.A.B. inspectors have already cleared us for flight."

"Did Dahybi sort out the new node?"

"Yeah. Eventually. We had to get him some help. A voidhawk actually went and collected two of the manufacturer's software team from the Halo for us. They solved the synchronization glitch. Jesus, I love ultra priority projects."

"Good."

"We just have to load the combat wasps, and Ashly's flying our new MSV over from the Dassault service bay. Your science team is already on board. We got Kempster and Renato along with Mzu and the agents. Parker Higgens insisted on travelling in the *Oenone* with Oski Katsura and her assistants."

"Don't be offended," Ione said. "Poor Parker gets dreadfully spacesick."

Joshua gave her a blank look, as if she'd come out with a non sequitur. "And we've got the serjeants in zero-tau as well. *Lady Mac*'s hauling a much bigger load than *Oenone*."

"It's not a contest, Joshua."

He grinned lopsidedly and pulled her close. "I know."

Liol erupted through the hatchway. "Josh! There you are. Look, we can't—oh."

"Hello, Liol," Ione said sweetly. "So have you been enjoying yourself in Tranquillity?"

"Er, yeah. It's great. Thanks."

"You made a big impression on Dominique. She can't stop talking about you."

Liol grimaced, appealing silently to Joshua.

"I don't think you've said goodbye to her yet, have you?" Ione asked.

Liol's blush was beyond the ability of any neural nanonic override to control. "I've been very busy helping Josh. Er, hey, perhaps you could do it for me?"

"Yes, Liol." She struggled against a laugh. "I'll let her know you've gone."

"Thanks, Ione, I owe you one. Er, Josh, we really need you on board now."

Ione and Joshua both started chuckling after he vanished back out of the hatch. "You take care," she told him after a while.

"Always do."

The ride back to her apartment took a long time. Or perhaps it was because she suddenly felt so lonely.

He took it all very well, Tranquillity said.

You think so? He hurts a lot inside. There's a lot to be said for ignorance being bliss. But then again, he would've guessed eventually. I wouldn't have been doing either of us any favours, not in the long run.

I am proud of your integrity.

Not much compensation for a broken heart . . . Sorry, that was bitchy of me. Hormones again.

Do you love him?

You're always asking that.

And each time you give me a different answer.

I have very strong feelings for him. You know that.

God, having two children with a man shows something. He's absolutely adorable. But love ... love I
don't know. I think I love what he is, not him. If I truly
loved him, I would've tried to make him stay. We
could've found something worthwhile for him to do
here. Then again, maybe it's me. Maybe I can never
love anyone that way, not when I have you. She closed
her eyes on the empty tube carriage, and watched the docking cradle slide *Lady Mac* up out of the bay. The starship's
thermo-dump panels unfolded, and the umbilicals jacked
into sockets around her lower hull section disengaged. A
cloud of gas and silver dust blew away. Bright blue ion
flames burned around the starship's equator, and she lifted
smoothly.

Ten thousand kilometres away, Meredith Saldana's
squadron was coming together in formation. The *Oenone*
lifted cleanly from its pedestal, and swept out to join *Lady
Mac*. The two very different starships matched velocities,
and headed towards the squadron.

I am no substitute for a human, Tranquillity said gently. I would never claim you.

I know. But you're my first love, and you always will
be my love. That's strong competition for a man.

Voidhawk captains succeed.

You're thinking of Syrinx.

And all her kind.

But they're Edenists. They have it different.

Perhaps you should get to know some while we're
here. They at least would not be intimidated by me.

Good idea. But ... I don't know if it's because I'm a
Saldana, but I just don't feel right about embracing
Edenism as the solution to all my problems. It's a wonderful culture. But if we stayed here, if I had an Edenist
for a partner, we'd wind up becoming absorbed.

We have no future returning to Mirchusko. The Laymil are no longer a mystery.

I know. But I'm still not converting to Edenism. We're unique, you and I. We might have been created for one purpose, but we've evolved beyond that now. We have our own lives to live; we have the right to chose our own future.

If the possessed don't do that for us.

They won't. Joshua's flight is only one of a hundred different explorations into this problem. The human race will surmount this.

Not without change. Edenism will change, they will surely have to rethink their attitude to religion.

I doubt it. They'll see the beyond as justifying their stance that spirituality is a null concept, everything has a natural explanation however bizarre. Laton telling them they won't be caught in the beyond will simply reinforce their position.

Then what do you propose?

I'm not sure. Perhaps nothing except for a clean start in a new star system. After that we'll see what happens.

Ah. Now I think I understand the urge for you to have and keep this child. You intend to found a new culture. A people who have affinity, but outside the context of Edenism.

That's very grand: founding a culture. I'm not sure my ambition extends to that.

You are a Saldana. Your family has done this once already.

Yes, but I've only got one womb. I can hardly birth an entire race.

There are ways. Exowombs. People who might like to try something new. Look how many youngsters flocked to Kiera Salter's call—false though it was. And new habitats can be germinated.

Ione smiled. This excites you, doesn't it? I've never known you quite so enthusiastic before.

I am intrigued, yes. I had never given the future much consideration. My life has been spent running human affairs and dealing with the Laymil project.

Well, we'll have to wait until the immediate crisis is over before we consider our options. But it would be something, wouldn't it? Creating the first post-possession culture, one that overthrows this ridiculous Adamist prejudice against bitek. We could incorporate the best of both cultures.

Now you talk like a true Saldana.

Luca Comar reined in his horse at the end of the drive, and dismounted to wait. It was near to midday, and people were drifting in from the fields to take a break. He didn't begrudge them that, the sticky heat was quite something. Bloody unnatural for Norfolk.

But it was the community's choice. Every day's weather was a constant summer optimum, with bright light and warm breezes; while the nightly rains doused the land. Such a combination produced a vicious humidity. He was worried it might start to affect the aboriginal plants; late summer was normally a period of gradually increasing rain and reducing heat. There was also the question of how they'd react to missing Duchess's crimson light. So far there was no visible malaise, but he felt uneasy about it.

But these conditions seemed to be doing wonders for the new cereal crops. He'd never seen them so advanced. It was going to be a great harvest. Things are getting back to normal.

You could tell the world was at rights just from the general mood. There was a heartiness that'd been missing before. Individual homes were being taken care of, kept properly clean and tidy, not just *wished* presentable. People paid attention to their clothes and general appearance.

And there'd been no sign of Bruce Spanton and his motley crew for awhile now. Though Luca had heard from other community leaders he was down at the southern end of Kesteven, giving decent folk a hard time. Apart from the odd problem like that, this was becoming a good life, gentle and unhurried. Satisfying.

Oh really, you'll live it for a quintillion years, will you?

Luca shook his head, clearing it to open his perception wide. He'd sensed her approaching early this morning. A solitary figure making her way across the wolds, a knot in the uniformity of thought enveloping the county. Unhurried, untroubled. Not a threat like Spanton. But certainly a curiosity. Something about her was slightly out of kilter. He didn't have a clue what.

So just before Cricklade's lunch bell was rung, Luca had told Johan he would go and investigate the stranger. They still had newcomers drift in. Anyone prepared to work was given a place in the community.

The stranger was half a mile away now, dawdling along the main road in some kind of vehicle. Luca frowned. That's a Romany caravan. The sight was a pleasing one, bringing up the old memories. Young girls pleased with his attentions, the coquettish and blatant. Their bodies yielding willingly, in fields of tall corn, secluded glades, darkened caravans. Year after year I proved my sexuality with them.

I?

He wrapped his horse's reins around one of the spikes on the huge wrought iron gate, feet shuffling impatiently. The caravan's driver must have been aware of his mood, yet her horse's plodding gait never altered. It was a big sturdy horse, Luca saw while it was on the last couple of hundred yards, its piebald coat muddied and a wild mane in long tangles. He got the impression that it could have hauled the caravan right round the world without pausing.

It kept on coming, and Luca twitched slightly, knowing his nerve was being tested. He refused to give ground as the huge beast lumbered inexorably towards him. At the last minute, the woman sitting on the driver's bench *clucked* softly, and pulled back on her slender reins. The caravan halted, rocking slightly on its lightweight spoke-sprung wheels. Carmitha applied the brake, and hopped down. She studied the man edging cautiously round Olivier. The horse whinnied at him.

"Greetings," he said. Then gave a sudden start as he found himself staring into the twin barrels of her shotgun. Not for the first time, she regretted giving Louise Kavanagh her pump-action weapon.

"My name is Carmitha. I am not one of you. I am not a possessor. Is that a problem?"

"None!"

"Good. Believe me, I will know if it becomes one. I do have some of your powers." She concentrated, and the seat of Luca's trousers became very hot indeed.

He twisted about, frantically slapping at the fabric with his hands before it started smouldering. "Bloody hell."

Carmitha smiled artfully. His thoughts were equally agitated, pastel whorls of colour that hung just outside her physical sight. I can read them, she told herself happily. Along with the rest of the magic.

The heat gone, Luca squared himself, recovering some dignity. "How did you . . ." His jaw moved silently. "Carmitha? Carmitha!"

She shouldered the shotgun, and brushed some loose strands of hair from her face. "I see part of you remembers. Then, no man would ever forget an afternoon in my bed."

"Eh." Luca blushed. The memories were certainly strong and colourful, with her vital flesh hot beneath his hands, the smell of her sweat, rapturous grunting. He felt the stirrings of an erection.

"Down boy," she murmured laconically. "What do you call yourself these days?"

"Luca Comar."

"I see. At the town they said you were the one in charge up here. Nice irony, that. But then you're all reverting."

"I am not reverting!" he said indignantly.

"Of course not."

"How have you got our powers?"

"I've no idea. It must be something to do with this place you've taken us to. After all, you don't have any contact with the beyond any more, do you?"

"No. Thank God."

"So it must be the way everybody's thoughts impinge on reality here. Congratulations, you made us all equal in the end. Grant must be real pissed about that."

"If you say so," he said disdainfully.

Carmitha had a throaty chuckle at the umbrage on show. "Never mind. Just as long as you lot realize you can't turn me into a host for one of your own anymore, we'll get along okay."

"What do you mean, get along?"

"It's very simple. I hate what you've done to these people, don't be under any illusion about that. But there's nothing I can do about it; nor you, now. So I might as well try and live with it, especially as you're reverting and re-establishing everything that's gone before."

"We are not reverting," he insisted. Yet there was the nagging worry about just how much of Grant Kavanagh's personality he was employing these days. *I must stop being* so dependent on him, treat him as encyclopaedia, nothing more.

"Okay, you're not reverting, you're mellowing out. Call it whatever you want to salvage your dignity. I don't care. Now, I've spent the last few weeks hiding out in the woods, and I'm getting very sick of cold rabbit for breakfast. I also haven't had a hot bath for a while either. As you're probably aware. So I'm looking for a place to stay over for a while. I'll pull my weight, cooking, cleaning, pruning; whatever you like. It's what I always do."

Luca pulled thoughtfully at his lower lip. "You shouldn't have been able to hide from us before. We're aware of the whole world."

"My people still have the earthlore your kind—both of you—have forgotten. When you brought magic back into the world, you made the old enchantments strong again, no longer just words mumbled by crazed old women."

"Interesting. Are there any more of you?"

"You know how many caravans are here for the midsummer collection. You tell me."

"I don't suppose it matters. Even if all the Romanies survived, you don't have the power to take us back to the universe we escaped from."

"That idea really frightens you, doesn't it?"

"Terrifies, actually. But then you can see that if you have got our ability."

"Hummm. So, do I get to stay?"

He deliberately let his gaze meander over her leather jerkin, remembering the full breasts and flat belly which lay beneath. "Oh, I think I can find room for you."

"Ha! Well don't even think about that!"

"Who, me? I'm not Grant anymore." He walked back to his horse, and took the reins off the gate.

Carmitha slid her shotgun into the leather holster beside

the seat, and started to lead Olivier along the drive with Luca. The caravan wheels crunched loudly on the gravel. "Damn this humidity." She wiped a hand across her brow, mussing her hair again. "We are going to have a winter, aren't we?"

"I expect so. I'll certainly make sure we have it on Kesteven, anyway. The land needs a winter."

"Make sure! My God. What arrogance."

"I prefer to call it practicality. We know what we need, and we make it happen. That's one of the joys of this new life. There's no fate any more. We control destiny now."

"Right." She looked round the grounds of the big stone manor house as they approached it. Surprised by how little had changed. But then the possessed tendency to establish glorious facades over everything they occupied was nullified here. When you already live in what was essentially a palace, you don't need gaudy energistic trinkets to enhance your status. For some reason, the sight of the well maintained fields was comforting. The normality, I suppose. What we all crave.

Luca led her into the courtyard at the side of the house. The solid stone walls of the manor and the stable wings magnified the clatter which the hooves and caravan wheels made on the cobblestones. It was hotter in the confines of the courtyard, too. Something Carmitha's small energistic ability could do little about. She took off her jerkin, ignoring the way Luca openly looked at the way her thin dress stuck to her skin.

One of the stables was a burnt-out hulk, with long soot-marks lashing up over the stone above each empty window. The centre of its slate roof had collapsed inwards. Carmitha whistled silently. Louise hadn't been lying. Several groups of field labourers were sheltering from the radiant sky in open doorways. They were munching on big sandwiches and baguettes, passing bottles round. Carmitha could feel every pair of eyes on her as Luca took her over to the remaining stable.

"You can put Olivier in here," he said. "I think the stalls are big enough. And there's oats in the sacks at the far end. The hose is working as well, if you want to wash him down first." It was something of which he seemed quite proud.

Carmitha could well imagine Grant's Kavanagh's reaction if the hose hadn't been working. "Thank you, I'll do that."

"Okay. Are you going to sleep in the caravan?"

"I think that's for the best, don't you?"

"Sure. When you're ready, go into the kitchen and ask for Susannah. She'll find something for you to do." He started to walk away.

"Grant . . . I mean Luca."

"Yeah."

Carmitha held her hand out. Light sparked sharply off the diamond ring. "She gave it to me."

Luca stared at it in shocked recognition, and took a couple of fast paces towards her. He grabbed her hand and brought it up in front of his face. "Where are they?" he demanded hotly. "Damnit, where did they go? Are they safe?"

"Louise told me about the last time she saw you," Carmitha said coolly. She glanced pointedly at the burnt out stable.

Luca clenched his fists, his face contorted in anguish. Every thought in his head was suffused with shame. "I didn't . . . I wasn't . . . Oh, shit! Goddamn it. Where are they? I promise you, I swear, I am not going to hurt them. Just tell me."

"I know. It was a crazy time. You're ashamed and sorry, now. And you'd never harm a hair on their heads."

"Yes." He made an effort to regain control. "Look, we

did terrible things. Brutal, inhuman things. To people, women, children. I know it was wrong. I knew the whole time I was doing it, and I still kept on doing them. But you don't understand what was driving me. Driving all of us." He shook an accusing finger, shouting. "You've never died. You've never been that insanely fucking *desperate*. Lucifer's deal would have been the most blessed relief from that place we were imprisoned. I would have done that. I would have walked right through the gates of hell and begged to be let in if I'd just been given the chance. But we never were." He crumpled, energy withering from his body. "Damnit. Please? I just want to know if they're all right. Look, we've got some other non-possessed here, kids; and there's more in the town. We look after them. We're not total monsters."

Carmitha looked round the courtyard, almost embarrassed. "Are you letting Grant know all this?"

"Yes. Yes, I am. I promise."

"Okay. I don't know exactly where they are. I left the pair of them at Bytham, they took the aeroambulance. I saw it fly away."

"Aeroambulance?"

"Yes. It was Genevieve's idea. They were trying to reach Norwich. They thought they'd be safe there."

"Oh." He held his horse tightly, almost as though he would fall without its support. His face brimmed with regret. "It would take me months to reach the city. That's if there's a ship that'll take me. Damn!"

She put a tentative hand on his arm. "Sorry I'm not much more help. But that Louise is one tough girl. If anyone is going to avoid possession, it'll be her."

He stared at her incredulously, then gave a bitter laugh. "My Louise? Tough? She can't even sugar her own grapefruit for breakfast. God, what a stupid bloody way to bring up children. Why did you do that? Why don't you let them see the world for what it really is? Because they're born to be ladies, our society protects them. I protect them, as every father should. I give them everything that's right and decent in the world. Your society is *shit*, worthless, irrelevant; it doesn't even qualify as a society; you're playing out a medieval pageant, not living. Being pathetic and insignificant isn't a way of defending yourself and everyone you love. People have to face up to what's outside their own horizon. Nothing was outside, not until you demon freaks came and ruined the universe. We have lived here for centuries and made ourselves a good respectable home. And you scum ruined that. Ruined! You stole it from us, and now you're trying to rebuild everything you say you hate. You're not even bloody savages, you're below that. No wonder hell didn't want you."

"Hey!" Carmitha shook him hard. "Hey, snap out of it."

"*Don't touch me!*" he screamed. His whole body was trembling violently. "Oh God." He sank to his knees, hands pressed into his face. A wretched voice burbled out between clawed fingers. "I'm him, I'm him. There's no difference any more. This isn't what we wanted. Don't you understand? This isn't how life's supposed to be here. This was meant to be paradise."

"No such place." She rubbed the top of his spine, trying to ease some of the badly knotted muscles. "You've just got to make the best of it. Like everybody else."

His head bobbed weakly in what Carmitha supposed was acknowledgement. She decided this probably wasn't the best time to tell him his dear precious Louise was pregnant.

10

Mortonridge was bleeding away into the ocean, a prolonged and arduous death. It was as though all the pain, the torment, the misery from a conflict that that could never be anything other than excruciatingly bitter had manifested itself as mud. Slimy, insidious, limitless, it rotted the resolve of both sides in the same way it ravaged their physical environment. The peninsula's living skin of topsoil had torn along the spine of the central mountain range to slither relentlessly down-slope into the coastal shallows. All the rich black loam built up over millennia as the rainforests regenerated themselves upon the decayed trunks of timelost past generations was sluiced away within two days by the unnatural rain. Reduced to supersaturated sludge, the precious upper few metres containing abundant nitrates, bacteria, and aboriginal earthworm-analogues had become an unstoppable landslip. Hill-sized moraines of mire were pushed along valleys, bulldozed by the intolerable pressure exerted by cubic kilometres of more ooze behind.

The mud tides scoured every valley, incline, and hollow; exposing the denser substrata. A compacted mix of gravel and clay, as sterile as asteroid regolith. There were no seeds or spores or eggs hidden tenaciously in its clefts to sprout anew. And precious few nutrients to succour and support them even if there had been.

Ralph used the SD sensors to watch the thick black stain expanding out across the sea. The mouth of the Juliffe had produced a similar discoloration in Lalonde's sea, he remembered. But that was just one small blemish. This was an ecological blight unmatched since the worst of Earth's dystopic Twenty-first Century. Marine creatures were dying in the plague of unnatural dark waters, choking beneath the uncountable corpses of their mammalian cousins.

"She was right, you know," he told Cathal at the end of the Liberation's first week.

"Who?"

"Annette Ekelund. Remember when we met her at the Firebreak roadblock? She said we'd have to destroy the village in order to save it. And I stood there and told her that I'd do whatever I had to, whatever it took. Dear God." He slumped back in the thickly cushioned chair behind his desk. If it hadn't been for the staff in the Ops Room on the other side of the glass wall he would probably have put his head in his hands.

Cathal glanced into the sparkling light of the desktop AV pillar. The unhealthy smear around Mortonridge's coast had grown almost as a counterbalance to the shrinking cloud. It was still raining over the peninsula, of course, but not constantly. The cloud had almost reverted to a natural weather formation, there were actual gaps amid the thick dark swirls now. "Chief, they did it to themselves. You've got to stop punishing yourself over this. No one who's been de-possessed in zero-tau is blaming you for anything. They're gonna give you a fucking medal once this is over."

Medals, ennoblement, promotions; they'd all been mentioned. Ralph hadn't paid a lot of attention. Such things were the trappings of state, government trinkets of no practical value whatsoever. Saving people was what really counted; everything else was just an acknowledgement, a method of reinforcing memory. He wasn't entirely sure he wanted that. Mortonridge would never recover, would never grow back to what it was. Maybe that was the best memorial, a decimated land was something that could never be overlooked and ignored by future generations. A truth that remained unsusceptible to the historical revisionists. The Liberation, he had decided some while ago, wasn't a victory over Ekelund, at best he'd scored a few points off her. She'd be back for the next match.

Acacia rapped lightly on the open door, and walked in, followed by Janne Palmer. Ralph waved at them to sit, and datavised a codelock at the door. The sensenviron bubble room closed about them. Princess Kirsten and Admiral Farquar were waiting around the oval table for the daily progress review. Mortonridge itself formed a three dimensional relief map on the tabletop, small blinking symbols sketching in the state of the campaign. The number of purple triangles, indicating clusters of possessed, had increased dramatically over the last ten days as the cloud attenuated allowing the SD sensors to scan the ground. Invading forces were green hexagons, an unbroken line mimicking the coastline, sixty-five kilometres inland.

Admiral Farquar leant forwards, studying the situation with a despondent expression. "Less than ten kilometres a day," he said sombrely. "I'd hoped we would be a little further along by now."

"You wouldn't say that if you'd tried walking through that devilsome mud," Acacia said. "The serjeants are making excellent progress."

"It wasn't a criticism," the admiral said hastily. "Given the circumstances, they've performed marvellously. I simply wish we could have one piece of luck on our side, everything about these conditions seems to swing in Ekelund's favour."

"It's starting to swing back," Cathal said. "The rain and the mud have triggered just about every booby trap they left in wait for us. And we've got their locations locked down now. They can't escape."

"I can see the actual campaign is advancing well on the ground," Princess Kirsten said. "I have no complaint about the way you're handling that. However, I do have a problem with the number of casualties we're incurring, on both sides."

The relevant figures stood in gold columns at the top of the table. Ralph had done his best to ignore them. Not that he could forget. "The suicide rate among the possessed is increasing at an alarming rate," he conceded. "Today saw it reaching eight per cent; and there's very little we can do about it. They're doing it quite deliberately. It's an inhibiting tactic. After all, what have they got to lose? The whole purpose of the campaign is to free the bodies they've captured; if they can deny us that opportunity then they will weaken our resolve, both on the ground and in the political arena."

"If that's their reasoning, then they're badly mistaken," Princess Kirsten said. "One of the main reasons for the Kingdom's strength is because my family can take tough decisions when the need arises. This Liberation continues until the serjeants meet up on Mortonridge's central mountain. However, I would like some options on how to reduce casualties."

"There's only one," Ralph said. "And it's by no means perfect. We slow the front line's advance and use the time to concentrate our forces around the possessed. At the moment we're using almost the minimum number of serjeants against each nest of them we encounter. That means the serjeants have to use a lot of gunfire to subdue them. When the possessed realize they've lost, they stop resisting the bullets. Bang, we lose. Another of our people dies, and the lost souls in the beyond have another recruit."

"If we increase the number of serjeants for each encounter, what sort of reduction do you expect us to be looking at?"

"At the moment, we try to have at least thirty per cent more serjeants than possessed. If we could reach double, then we think we can hold the suicide rate down to a maximum of fifteen per cent each time."

"Of course, the ratio will improve naturally as the length of the front line contracts and the numbers of possessed decreases," Admiral Farquar said. "It's just that right now we're about at maximum stretch. The serjeants haven't got far enough inland to decrease the length of the front line appreciably, yet they're encountering a lot of possessed."

"That entire situation is going to change over then next three to four days," Cathal said. "Almost all the possessed are on the move. They're retreating from the front line as fast as they can wade. The advance is going to speed up considerably, so the length will reduce anyway."

"They're running for now," Janne Palmer said. "But there's a lot of heavy concentrations of them fifty kilometres in from the front line. If they've got any sense, they'll regroup."

"The more of them there are, the stronger they get, and the more difficult they'll be to subdue. Especially in light of the suicides," Acacia said. "I've had the AI drawing up an SD strike pattern to halt their movements. I don't think they should be allowed to retreat any further. We're worried that we'll wind up with a solid core at the centre which will be just about impossible to crack without large scale casualties."

"I really don't want to wait three to four days for an improvement," Princess Kirsten said. "Ralph, what do you think?"

"Denying them the ability to congregate is my primary concern, ma'am. They've already got a lot of people in Schallton, Ketton, and Cauley, I do not want to see that increase any further. But if we prevent them from moving from their present locations, and then switch our tactics to a slower advance, you're looking at almost doubling the estimated time of the campaign."

"But with significantly reduced casualties?" the Princess asked.

Ralph looked over at Acacia. "Only among the people who've been possessed. Trying to subdue them with a larger number of serjeants using less firepower will significantly increase the risk to the serjeants."

"We volunteered for this knowing the risks would be great," Acacia said. "And we are prepared for that. However, I feel I should tell you that a significant number of serjeants are suffering from what I can only describe as low morale. It's not something we were expecting, the animating personalities were supposed to be fairly simple thought routines with basic personalities. It would appear they are evolving into quite high-order mentalities. Unfortunately, they lack the kind of sophistication which would allow them to appreciate their full Edenist heritage. Normally we can mitigate one person's burden by sharing and sympathising. However, here the number of suffering is far in excess of the rest of us, which actually places quite a strain on us. We haven't known a scale of suffering like this since Jantrit."

"You mean they're becoming real people?" Janne Palmer asked.

"Not yet. Nor do we believe they ever will do. Ultimately they are limited by the capacity of the serjeant processor array, after all. What I am telling you is that they're progressing slightly beyond simplistic bitek servitors. Do not expect machine levels of efficiency in future. There are human factors involved which will now need to be taken into account."

"Such as?" the Princess asked.

"They will probably need time to recuperate between assaults. Duties will have to be rotated between platoons. I'm sorry," she said to Ralph. "It adds considerable complications to the planning. Especially if you want them to prevent the possessed suicides."

"I'm sure the AI can cope," he said.

"It looks like the campaign is going to take a lot longer whatever option we go for," Admiral Farquar said.

"That does have one small benefit," Janne Palmer said.

"I'd love to hear it," the Princess told her.

"Reducing the flow of de-possessed is going to alleviate some of the pressure on our medical facilities."

Back in her private office, Kirsten shuddered, a movement not reproduced inside the bubble room. That, out of all the other horrors revealed by the Liberation, had upset her the most. Cancers were such a rarity in this day and age, that to see several bulging from a person's skin like inflated blisters was a profound shock. And there were very few de-possessed who didn't suffer from them. To inflict such a incapacitating disease for what was apparently little more than vanity was hubris at an obscene level. That it might also be simple blind ignorance was almost as bad. "I have requested aid from the Kingdom and our allies as a matter of urgency," she said. "We should start to receive shipments of medical nanonic packages over the next few days. Every hospital and clinic on the planet is being used, and civilian ships are being deployed to fly people out to asteroid settlements in the system—not that they have many beds or staff, but every little helps. I just wish we could ferry people out-system, but at the moment I can't break the quarantine for that. In any event, my Foreign Minister has cautioned me that there would be some reservation from other star systems about accepting our medical cases. They're worried about infiltration by the possessed, and I can't say I blame them."

"Capone's new lunacy doesn't help ease the paranoia," Admiral Farquar grunted. "Damn that bastard."

"So you would prefer the slow down scenario?" Kirsten asked.

"Very much so, ma'am," Janne Palmer said. "It's not just a question of providing medical support, there are transport bottlenecks as well. It's improved slightly now we can land aircraft at the coastal ports, but we have to get the de-possessed there first, and they need care which my occupation forces really aren't geared up to provide."

"General Hiltch, what do you favour?"

"I don't like slowing down the advance, ma'am. With all respect to Admiral Farquar's SD officers, I don't think they'll be able to prevent the possessed from congregating. Slow their movements, maybe, but halt them no. And once that happens, we'll be in a real mess. The kind of firepower we're going to need to break open Ketton at the moment is way in excess of any assault so far. We have to prevent it from turning into a runaway situation. At the moment we're dictating the pace of events to them, I'd hate to abandon that level of control. It's our one big advantage."

"I see. Very well, you'll have my decision before dawn local time."

The sensenviron ended with its usual abruptness, and Kirsten blinked irritably, allowing her eyes to register the familiar office. Touching base with normality. Necessary, now. These nightly reviews were becoming a considerable drain. Not even the Privy Council Grand Policy Conclaves back in the Apollo Palace had quite the same impact, they implemented policies that would take decades to mature. The Liberation was all so *now*. Something the Saldanas were not accustomed to. In any modern crisis, the major decision would be whether or not to dispatch a fleet. After that, everything was down to the admiral in charge.

I make political decisions, not military ones.

But the Liberation had changed all that, blurring the distinction badly. Military decisions were political ones.

She stood up, stretching, then went over to Allie's bust. Her hand touched his familiar, reassuringly sober features. "What would you do?" she murmured. Not that she would ever be accused of making the wrong choice. Whatever it was, the family would support her. Her equerry, Sylvester Geray, scrambled to his feet in the reception room, the chair legs scraping loudly on the tushkwood floor as Kirsten came out of her office.

"Tired?" she asked lightly.

"No ma'am."

"Yes you are. I'm going back to my quarters for a few hours. I won't need you before seven o'clock. Have a sleep, or at least a rest."

"Thank you, ma'am." He bowed deeply as she walked out.

There were few staff about in the private apartments, which was how she liked them. With the rooms all dark and quiet, it was almost how she imagined a normal home would be late in the evening. An assistant nanny and a maid were on duty, sitting up chatting quietly in the lounge next to the children's bedrooms. Kirsten stood outside for a moment, listening; the nanny's fiancé was in the Royal Navy, and hadn't called her for a couple of days. The maid was sympathising.

Everyone, Kirsten thought, this has touched and involved every one of us. And the Liberation is only the beginning. So far the Church had been noticeably unsuccessful in quelling people's fears of the beyond. Though Atherstone's Bishop reported that attendance was high in every parish on the planet, greater than Christmas Eve, he'd said almost in indignation.

She opened the door to Edward's study without knocking, only realising her mistake once she was well inside. There was a girl with him on the leather settee; his current mistress. Kirsten remembered the security file Jannike Dermot had provided: minor nobility, her father owned an estate and some kind of transport company. Pretty young thing, in her early twenties, with classic delicate bonework. Tall with very long legs; as they all invariably were with Edward. She stared at Kirsten in utter consternation, then frantically tried to adjust her evening dress to a more modest position. Not that she could achieve much modesty with so little fabric, Kirsten thought in amusement. The girl's wine glass went flying from trembling fingers.

Kirsten frowned at that. The antique carpet was Turkish, a beautiful red and blue weave; she'd given it to Edward as a birthday present fifteen years ago.

"Ma'am," the girl squeaked. "I . . . We . . ."

Kirsten merely gave her a mildly enquiring glance.

"Come along, my dear," Edward said calmly. He took her arm and escorted her to the door. "Affairs of state. I'll call you in the morning." She managed a strangled whimper in response. A butler, responding to Edward's datavise, appeared and gestured politely to the by-now thoroughly frightened and bewildered girl. Edward shut the study door behind her, and sighed.

Kirsten started laughing, then put her hand over her mouth. "Oh Edward, I'm sorry. I should have let you know I was coming."

He spread his hands wide. *"C'est la vie."*

"Poor thing looked terrified." She knelt down and picked the wine glass up, dabbing at the carpet. "Look what she did. I'd better get a valet mechanoid, or it'll stain." She datavised the study's processor.

"It's a rather good Chablis, actually." He picked the bottle out of its walnut cooler jacket. "Shame to waste it, would you like some?"

"Lovely, thank you. It has been a very bad day at the office."

"Ah." He went over to the cabinet and brought her a fresh glass.

Kirsten sniffed at the bouquet after he'd poured. "She was jolly gorgeous. Slightly young, though. Wicked of you." She brushed at imaginary dust on his lapel. "Then again, I can see why she's so obliging. You always did look rather splendid in uniform."

Edward glanced down at his Royal Navy tunic. There were no Royal crests, just three discreet medal ribbons—earned long ago. "I'm just doing my bit. Though they are all depressingly young at the base. I think they regard me as some kind of mascot."

"Oh poor Edward, the indignity. But not to worry, Zandra and Emmeline are terribly impressed."

He sat on the leather settee and patted the cushion. "Come on, sit down and tell me what's wrong."

"Thank you." She stepped round the small mechanoid that was sniffing at the wine stain, and sat beside him, welcoming his arm around her shoulders. The secret of a successful royal marriage: don't have secrets. They were both intelligent people, which had allowed them to work out the grounds of a sustainable domestic arrangement a long time ago. In public and in private he was the perfect companion, a friend and confident. All she required was loyalty, which he supplied admirably. In return he was free to gather whatever perks his position presented—and it wasn't just girls; he was an avid art collector and bon viveur. They even still slept together occasionally.

"The Liberation is not progressing as well as could be," he said. "That much is obvious. And the net is overloading with speculation."

Kirsten sipped some of the chablis. "Progress is the key word, yes." She told him about the decision she was faced with.

After she'd finished, he poured some more wine for himself before answering. "The serjeants developing advanced personalities? Humm. How intriguing. I wonder if they'll refuse to go back into their habitat multiplicities when the campaign is over."

"I have no idea; Acacia never ventured an opinion. And to be honest, that part is not my problem."

"It might be if they all start applying for citizenship afterwards."

"Oh God." She snuggled up closer. "No. I'm not even going to consider that right now."

"Wise lady. You want my opinion?"

"That's why I'm here."

"You can't ignore the serjeant situation. We are utterly dependent on them to liberate Mortonridge, and there's a hell of a way to go yet."

"A hundred and eighty thousand people de-possessed, seventeen thousand dead, so far; that leaves us with one-point-eight-million left to save."

"Exactly. And we're about to enter the phase which will see the heaviest fighting. If they keep advancing at their current rate, the front line will reach the first areas where the possessed are concentrated the day after tomorrow. If you slow them now, the serjeants are going to start taking heavy losses just before that. Not good. I'd say, keep things as they are until the front line hits those concentrations, then shift to General Hiltch's outnumbering tactics."

"That's a very logical solution." She stared at the wine. "If only all I had to consider were numbers. But they're depending on me, Edward."

"Who?"

"The people who've been possessed. Even locked away in their own bodies, they know the Liberation is coming now; a practical salvation from this obscenity. They have faith in me, they trust me to deliver them from this evil. And I have a duty to them. That duty is one of the few true burdens placed on the family by our people. Now I know there is a way of reducing the number of my subjects killed, I cannot in all conscience ignore it for tactical convenience. That would be a betrayal of trust, not to mention an abdication of duty."

"The two impossibles for a Saldana."

"Yes. We have had it easy for an awful long time, haven't we?"

"Shall we say: moderately difficult."

"Yet if I want to reduce the death rate, I'm going to have to ask the Edenists to take it on the chin for us. You know what bothers me most about that? People will expect it. I'm a Saldana, they're Edenists. What could be simpler?"

"The serjeants aren't quite Edenists."

"We don't know what the hell they are, not any more. Acacia was hedging her bets very thoroughly. If they're worried enough to bring the problem to me, then it has to be a substantial factor. One I cannot discount from the humanist equation. Damn it, they were supposed to be automatons."

"The Liberation is a very rushed venture. I'm sure if Jupiter's geneticists had been given enough time to design a dedicated soldier construct then this would never have arisen. But we had to borrow from the Lord of Ruin. Look, General Hiltch was given overall command of the Liberation. Let him make the decision, it's what he's paid for."

"Get thee behind me," she muttered. "No, Edward, not this time. I'm the one who insisted on reducing the fatalities. It is my responsibility."

"You'll be setting a precedent."

"Hardly one that's likely to be repeated. All of us are sailing into new, and very stormy territory; that requires proper leadership. If I cannot provide that now, then the family will ultimately have failed. We have spent four hundred years engineering ourselves into this position of statesmanship, and I will not duck the issue when it really counts. It stinks of cowardice, and that is one thing I will never allow the Saldanas to stand accused of."

He kissed her on the side of her head. "Well you know you have my support. If I could make one final observation. The personalities in the serjeants are all volunteers. They came here knowing what their probable fate would be. That purpose remains at their core. In that, they are like every pre-Twenty-first Century army; reluctant, frightened even, but committed. So give them the time they need to gather their nerve and resolution, and then use them for the purpose for which they were created: saving genuine human lives. If they are truly capable of emotion, then their only hope of gaining satisfaction will come from achieving that."

*

Ralph was eating a cold snack in Fort Forward's command complex canteen when he received the datavise.

"Slow the assault," Princess Kirsten told him. "I want that suicide figure reduced as low as you can practically achieve."

"Yes ma'am. I'll see to it. And thank you."

"This is what you wanted?"

"We're not here to recapture land, ma'am. The Liberation is about people."

"I know that. I hope Acacia will forgive us."

"I'm sure she will, ma'am. The Edenists understand us pretty well."

"Good. Because I also want the serjeant platoons given as much breathing space between assaults as they require."

"That will reduce the rate of advance even further."

"I know, but it can't be helped. Don't worry about political and technical support, General, I'll ensure you get that right to the bitter end."

"Yes ma'am." The datavise ended. He looked round at the senior staff eating with him, and gave a slow smile. "We got it."

High above the air, cold technological eyes stared downwards, unblinking. Their multi-spectrum vision could penetrate clean through Mortonridge's thinning strands of puffy white cloud to reveal the small group of warm figures trekking across the mud. But that was where the observation failed. Objects around them were perfectly clear, the dendritic tangle of roots flaring from fallen trees, a pulverised four-wheel-drive rover almost devoured by the blue-grey mud, even the shape of large stones ploughed up and rolled along by thick runnels of sludge. In contrast, the figures were hazed by shimmering air; infrared blobs no more substantial than candle flames. No matter which combination of discrimination filters it applied to the sensor image, the AI was unable to determine their exact number. Best estimate, taken from the width of the distortion and measuring the thermal imprint of the disturbed mud they left behind, was between four and nine.

Stephanie could feel the necklace of prying satellites as they slid relentlessly along their arc from horizon to horizon. Not so much their physical existence; that kind of knowledge had vanished along with the cloud and the possessed's mental unity. But their avaricious intent was forever there, intruding upon the world's intrinsic harmonies. It acted as a reminder for her to keep her guard up. The others were the same. Messing with the sight on a level which equated to waving a hand at persistent flies. Not that satellites were their problem. A far larger note of discord resonated from the serjeants, now just a couple of miles away. And coming closer, always closer. Machine-like in their determination.

At first Stephanie had ignored them, employing a kind of bravado what was almost entirely alien to her. Everybody had, once they'd reached the shelter (and *dryness!*) of the barn. The building didn't amount to much, set on a gentle hillock, with a low wall of stone acting as a base for composite panelling walls and a shallow roof. They'd stumbled across it five horrendous hours after setting out from the end of the valley. McPhee claimed that proved they were following the road. By then, nobody was arguing with him. In fact, nobody was speaking at all. Their limbs were trembling from exertion, not even reinforcing them with energistic strength helped much. They'd long since discovered such augmentation had to be paid for by the body in the long run.

The barn had come pretty much at the end of their endurance. There'd been no discussion about using it. As soon as they saw its dark, bleak outline through the pounding rain they'd trudged grimly towards it. Inside there was little respite from the weather at first. The wind had torn innumerable panels off the carbotanium frame, and the concrete floor was lost beneath a foot of mud. That didn't matter, in their state, it was pure salvation.

Their energistic power renovated it. Mud flowed up the walls, sealing over the lost panels and turning to stone. The rain was repelled, and the howl of the wind muted. Relief united them again, banishing the misery of the retreat from the valley. It was an emotion which produced an overreaction of confidence and defiance. Now, they found it possible to ignore the occasional mind-scream of anguish as another soul was wrenched from its possessed body by the peril of zero-tau. They cooperated gamely in searching round outside for food, adopting a campfire jollity as they cleaned and cooked the dead fish and mud-smeared vegetables.

Then the rain eased off, and the serjeants crunched forwards remorselessly. Food became very scarce. A week after the Liberation began, they left the barn, tramping along the melted contour line which McPhee still insisted was the road. Even living through the deluge under a flimsy roof hadn't prepared them for the scale of devastation wrought by the water. Valleys were completely impassable. Huge rivers of mud slithered along, murmuring and burbling incessantly as they sucked down and devoured anything that protruded into their course.

Progress was slow, even though they'd now fashioned themselves sturdy hiking attire (even Tina wore strong leather boots). Two days spent trying to navigate through the buckled, decrepit landscape. They kept to the high ground, where swathes of dark-green aboriginal grass were the only relief from the overlapping shades of brown. Even they were sliced by deep flash gorges where the water had found a weak seam of soil. There was no map, and no recognizable features to apply one against. So many promising ridges ended in sharp dips down into the mud, forcing them to backtrack, losing hours. But they always knew which way to travel. It was simple: away from the serjeants. It was also becoming very difficult to stay ahead. The front line seemed to move at a constant pace, unfazed by the valleys and impossible terrain, while Stephanie and her group spent their whole time zigzagging about. What had begun forty-eight hours ago as a nine mile gap was down to about two, and closing steadily.

"Oh, hey, you cats," Cochrane called. "You like want the good news or the bad news first?" He had taken point duty, striding out ahead of the others. Now he stood atop a dune of battered reeds, looking down the other side in excitement.

"The bad," Stephanie said automatically.

"The legion of the black hats is speeding up, and there's like this stupendously *huge* amount of them."

"What's the good?" Tina squealed.

"They're speeding up because there's like a road down here. A real one, with tarmac and stuff."

The others didn't exactly increase their pace to reach the bedraggled hippie, but there was a certain eagerness in their stride that'd been missing for some time. They clambered up the incline of the dune, and halted level with him.

"What's there?" Moyo asked. His face was perfect, the scars and blisters gone; eyes solid and bright. He was even able to smile again, doing so frequently during the last few days they'd spent in the barn. That he could smile, yet still refuse to let them see what lay underneath the illusory eyeballs worried Stephanie enormously. A bad form of denial.

He was acting the role of himself; and it was a very thin performance.

"It's a valley," she told him.

He groaned. "Oh hell, not again."

"No, this is different."

The dune was actually the top of a steepish slope which swept down several hundred yards to the floor of Catmos Vale, a valley that was at least twenty miles wide. Drizzle and mist made the far side difficult to see. The floor below was a broad flat expanse whose size had actually managed to defeat the massive discharges of mud. Its width had absorbed the surges that coursed out of the narrower ravines along either side; spreading them wide and robbing them of their destructive power. The wide, boggy river channel which meandered along the centre had siphoned the bulk of the tide away, without giving it a chance to amass in dangerously unstable colloidal waves.

Vast low-lying sections of the floor had turned directly into quagmire from the rain and overspill. Entire forests had subsided, their trunks keeling over to lean against each other. Now they were slowly sinking deeper and deeper as the rapidly expanding subsurface water level gnawed away at the stability of the loam. Watched over the period of a day or two, it was almost as if they were melting away.

Small hillocks and knolls formed a vast archipelago of olive-green islands amid the ochre sea. Hundreds of distressed and emaciated aboriginal animals scurried about over each of them, herds of kolfrans (a deer-analogue) and packs of the small canine ferrangs were trampling the surviving blades of grass into a sticky pulp. Birds scuttled among them, their feathers too slick with mud for them to fly.

Many of the islands just below the foot of the slope had sections of road threaded across them. The eye could stitch them together into a single strand leading along the valley. It led towards a small town, just visible through the drizzle. Most of it had been built on raised land, leaving its buildings clear of the mud; as if the entire valley had become its moat. There was a church near the centre, its classic grey stone spire standing defiantly proud. Some kind of scarlet symbols had been painted around the middle.

"That's got to be Ketton," Franklin said. "Can you sense them?"

"Yes," Stephanie said uncomfortably. "There's a lot of us down there." It would explain the condition of the buildings. There wasn't a tile missing from the neat houses, no sign of damage. Even the little park was devoid of puddles.

"I guess that's why these guys are like so anxious to reach it." Cochrane jerked a thumb back down the valley.

It was the first time they'd actually seen the Liberation army. Twenty jeeps formed a convoy along the road. Whenever the carbon-concrete surface left the islands to dip under the mud, they slowed slightly, cautiously testing the way. The mud couldn't have been very deep or thick, barely coming over the wheels. A V-shaped phalanx of serjeants followed on behind the jeeps, big dark figures lumbering along quite quickly considering none of them was on the road. On one side of the carbon-concrete strip, their line stretched out almost to the central river of mud; on the other it extended up the side of Catmos Vale's wall. A second train of vehicles, larger than the jeeps, was turning into the valley several miles behind the front line.

"Ho-lee shit," Franklin groaned. "We can't make that sort of speed, not over this terrain."

McPhee was studying the rugged land behind them. "I cannot see them up here."

"They'll be there," Rana said. "They're on the other side

of the river as well, look. That line is kept level. There's no break in it. They're scooping us up like horse shit."

"If we stay up here we'll be nailed before sunset."

"If we go down, we can keep ahead of them on the road," Stephanie said. "But we'll have to go through the town. I have a bad feeling about that. The possessed there know the serjeants are coming, yet they're staying put. And there's a lot of them."

"They're going to make a stand," Moyo said.

Stephanie glanced back at the ominous line moving towards them. "They'll lose," she said, morosely. "Nothing can resist that."

"We've no food left," McPhee said.

Cochrane used an index finger to prod his purple sunglasses up along the bridge of his nose. "Plenty of water, though, man."

"There's nothing to eat up here," Rana said. "We have to go down."

"The town will hold them off for a while at least," Stephanie said. She resisted glancing at Moyo, though he was now her principal concern. "We could use the time to take a break, rest up."

"Then what?" Moyo grunted.

"Then we move on. We keep ahead of them."

"Why bother?"

"Don't," she said softly. "We try and live life as we always wanted to, remember? Well I don't want to live like this; and there might be something different up ahead, because there certainly isn't anything behind. As long as we keep going, there's hope."

His face compressed to a melancholic expression. He held one arm out, moving his hand round to try and find her. She gripped his fingers tightly, and he hugged her against him. "Sorry. I'm sorry."

"It's all right," she murmured. "Hey, you know what? The way we're heading, it takes us right up to the central mountain range. You can show me what mountain gliding is like."

Moyo laughed gruffly, his shoulders trembling. "Look, guys, I hate to fuck up my karma any more by breaking up your major love-in scene here, but we have to decide where we're like going. Like *now*. This is one army that doesn't take time out, you dig?"

"It has to be down to Ketton," Stephanie said briskly. She eyed the long slope below. It would be slippery, but with their energistic power they ought to cope. "We can get there ahead of the army."

"Only just ahead," Franklin said. "We'll be trapped in the town. If we stay up here, we can still keep ahead of them."

"Not by much," McPhee said.

"And you'll not have time to gather any food," Rana said. "I don't know about you, but I know I can't keep this pace up for much longer without eating a full meal. We must consider the practicalities of the situation. My calorie intake has been very low over the last couple of days."

"It's a permanent downer," Cochrane said. "Your practical problem is that you don't eat properly anyway."

She glared at him. "I really hope you aren't going to suggest I should eat dead flesh."

"Oh brother," he raised his arms heavenwards. "Here we go again. Check it out: no meat, no smoking, no gambling, no sex, no loud music, no bright lights, no dancing, no fucking fun."

"I'm going down to Ketton," Stephanie said, overriding the pair of them. She started to walk down the slope, her hand holding on to Moyo's fingers. "If anyone else wants to come, you'd better do it now."

"I'm with you," Moyo said. He moved his feet along cau-

tiously. Rana shrugged lightly, and started to follow. A
reefer slid up out of Cochrane's fist and the tip ignited. He
stuck it in his mouth and went after Rana.

"Sod it!" Franklin said wretchedly. "All right. But we're
giving up by going down there. There'll be no way out of
that town."

"You can't keep ahead of them up here," McPhee said.
"Look at the bastards. It's like they can walk on mud."

"All right, all right."

Tina gave Rana a desperate look. "Darling, those *things*
will simply demolish the town. And we'll be in it."

"Maybe. Who knows? The military always makes ludicrously extravagant propaganda claims about their macho
prowess. Reality invariably lags behind."

"Yo, Tina." Cochrane proffered the reefer. "Come with
us, babe. You and me, we could like have our last night on
this world together. Fucking-A way to go, huh?"

Tina shuddered at the grinning hippie. "I'd rather be captured by those beastly things."

"That's a no, is it?"

"No it is not. I don't want us to split up. You're my
friends."

Stephanie had turned to watch the little scene. "Tina,
make up your mind." She started off down the slope again,
leading Moyo.

"Oh *heavens*," Tina said. "You simply never give me
time to decide anything. It's so unfair."

"Bye, doll," Cochrane said.

"Don't go so fast. I can't keep up."

Stephanie made a deliberate effort to expel the woman's
whining from her mind. Concentrating solely on navigating
her way down the slope. She had to take quite a shallow
angle, constantly reinforcing the slippery soil below her

boot soles with energistic power. Even then her progress was marked by long skid marks.

"I can sense a lot of possessed below us," Moyo said when they were a hundred yards above the quagmires of the valley floor.

"Where?" Stephanie asked without thinking. She hadn't been paying attention to what waited below, traversing the tricky slope required her complete attention. Now she looked up, she could see the convoy of jeeps was barely a mile behind them. The sight gave her heart a cold squeeze.

"Not far." His free hand pointed out across the valley. "Over there."

Stephanie couldn't see anyone. But now she scrutinized the mental whispers around the edge of her perception she was aware of rising anticipation in many minds.

"Hey, Moyo, man, good call." Cochrane was scanning the valley. "Those cats are like *low* in the mud. I can't see anyone."

"Come on," Stephanie said. "Lets find out what's happening."

The last section of the slope started to flatten out, allowing them to increase their speed. Stephanie was tempted just to keep to the undulating foothills that ran along the valley wall. They could certainly make good time on the reasonably dry ground. Except it curved gradually away from Ketton. One of the visible sections of road was about three hundred yards away across a perfectly flat expanse of slough. Stephanie stood on the edge, mud oozing round her ankles. Her boots kept her feet dry, but as a precaution she made the leather creep up her shins towards her knees. The silence down here was unnerving, it was as if the mud had some kind of anti-sound property. "I don't think it's very deep," she ventured.

"One way to find out," McPhee said vigorously. He

struck out for the road with confident strides. Mud sloshed away slowly from his legs as he ploughed across. "Come on, ye great bunch of woofters. It's not like *we* can drown." Cochrane and Rana gave each other a reluctant glance, then started in.

"It's going to be all right," Stephanie said. She kept a tight grip on Moyo's hand, and they waded in together. Tina held on to Franklin's hand as they went in. The action drew a lecherous grin from Cochrane.

Stephanie was right about it not being particularly deep, but the mud was soon up to her knees. After a couple of attempts to clear a trench through it with her energistic power, she gave up. The mud responded so sluggishly it would have taken at least an hour for them to reach the road by such a method. This had to be crossed the hard way, and the level of exertion needed to keep going placed a terrible strain on already fatigued muscles. All of them diverted their energistic power to force recalcitrant legs forward against mud that seemed to exert an equal pressure against them. Their efforts were given an extra edge by the onward march of the army. They were travelling almost at right angles to the front line, losing precious separation distance with every minute.

Stephanie kept telling herself that as soon as they made the road they'd be able to build it back up again. But even using the road, there was a lot of mud to surmount before Ketton, and her body was already approaching its physical limit. She could hear Cochrane wheezing loudly, a sound which carried a long way over the quagmire.

"They're right ahead of us now," Moyo said. He'd opened the front of his oilskin jacket in an attempt to cool himself. The drizzle was seeping through his energistic barrier, combining with sweat to soak his shirt. "Two of them. And they're not happy with us."

Stephanie glanced up, trying to distinguish the source of the animus thoughts. The slight rise carrying the road was seventy yards in front. Badly mangled grass and a few straggly bushes gleaming dully in the grizzly skin of rainwater. Dozens of ferrangs were pelting about excitedly, running together in packs of six or seven. Their cohesive motion reminded her of fish schools, every movement enacted in unison.

"I can't see anyone," McPhee grunted. "Hey, shitheads," he shouted. "What the fuck is wrong with you?"

"Oh groovy," Cochrane said. "Way to go, dude. That'll make them real friendly. I mean it's not like we're in cosmically deep shit at this point and need help, or anything."

Tina let out a miserable gasp as she slipped. "I hate this fucking mud!"

"You tell it as it is, babe." Franklin helped her up, and the two of them leant against each other as they forced their way onwards. Stephanie glanced back down the length of Catmos Vale, and sucked in a fast breath. The jeeps were barely half a mile away. Fifty yards to solid ground.

"We're not going to make it."

"What?" Moyo asked.

"We're not going to make it." She was panting heavily now. Not bothering with clothes, appearance, any energistic frippery—even the satellites would be able to see her now. She didn't care. All that mattered was maintaining the integrity of her boots and shoving near-useless legs one in front of the other. Muscle spasms were shaking her calves and thighs.

Rana stumbled, falling to her knees. Mud squelched obscenely as it closed over her legs. She blew heavily, her face radiant, glistening with sweat. Cochrane sloshed over and put his arm under her shoulders, dragging her up. The glutinous mud was reluctant to let go. "Hey, man, give me a hand here," he yelled at the land ahead. "Come on, you guys, quit fooling around. This is like bigtime serious."

The ferrang packs dodged round each other as they wheeled about aimlessly. Whoever the people were up ahead, they chose not to reveal themselves. A slight single-tone mechanical whine was becoming audible. The jeep engines.

"Get me to her," Moyo hissed.

He and Stephanie staggered over to the faltering couple. McPhee had come to a halt twenty yards from the land, staring back at them. "Keep going," Stephanie yelled at him. "Go on. Somebody's got to get out of this."

With her help, Moyo took some of Rana's weight from Cochrane. They slung her between them, and kicked their way forward again. "My legs," Rana groaned miserably. "I can't keep them going. They're like fire. God damn it, this shouldn't happen, I can move mountains with my mind."

"No matter," Cochrane said through gritted teeth. "We got you now, sister." The three of them stumbled forwards. McPhee had reached the land, standing just above the mud to urge them on. Tina and Franklin was almost there. The pair of them were plainly exhausted. Only the big Scot seemed to have any stamina left.

Stephanie brought up the rear. The jeeps were seven hundred yards away now, on a stretch of dry road. Picking up speed. "Shit," she whispered. "Oh shit oh shit." Even if McPhee started sprinting right now, he'd never make it to Ketton; they'd overhaul him easily. Perhaps if the rest of them started flinging white fire at the serjeants . . . What a ridiculous thought, she told herself. And I don't have any to spare. I must focus on channelling my energistic power.

Ten yards to go.

I won't put up a fight. It wouldn't be the slightest good, and it might damage the body. I owe her that much.

At the heart of her mind she could feel the captive host stirring in anticipation. All four of them staggered up out of the mud, and simply collapsed on the soggy ground next to Tina and Franklin. And she still couldn't see the owners of the two minds impinging so strongly on her perception.

"Stephanie Ash," a woman's voice said from the empty air. "I see your timing is as fucking atrocious as always."

"Any second now," an unseen man announced.

Both of their minds were hot with eagerness. Somewhere nearby, the slow-motion wheeze of bagpipes started up, swirling to a level piercing tone. Stephanie raised her head. Halfway between her and the jeeps, a lone Scottish piper stood facing the vehicles. Dressed in a kilt of Douglas tartan, black leather boots shining, he seemed totally oblivious the mortal foe riding towards him. His fingers moved sedately as he played "Amazing Grace." One of the serjeants in the front vehicle was standing up to get a clear look in over the mud-caked windscreen.

"I like it," McPhee hooted.

"Our call to arms," the concealed man replied. "It has a certain *je ne sais quoi*, no?"

Stephanie glanced round urgently, trying to pin down the voice. "Call to arms?"

An explosion sounded in the distance, rumbling fast over the quagmires and stagnant pools smothering Catmos Vale. A mine had detonated under the leading jeep, punching the front of the chassis into the air. It crashed down, spilling serjeants across the road. Blue white smoke billowed out from the crater in the concrete. Lumps of debris rained down. The other jeeps braked sharply. Serjeants froze all along the front line, crouching down.

The piper finished, and bowed solemnly at his enemies. There was a dull, potent *thock*, loud enough to quiver Stephanie's gullet. Then another. A whole barrage started up, the individual thumps merging into a single soundwave. Tina squealed in fright.

"Ho shit," Cochrane growled. "Those are mortars."

"Well done," said the woman. "Now keep down."

It was, the Liberation's coordinating AI acknowledged, a classic ambush, and executed perfectly. The jeeps were confined to one of the narrowest strips of land in the valley, unable to veer away. A sleet of mortar shells fell upon them, ranged precisely. High explosives detonated in a near con-stant bombardment, pulverizing the stalled vehicles, and shredding the serjeants riding them. Smoke, flame, and spumes of superfine mud belched out, obliterating the car-nage from view.

The AI could do absolutely nothing to prevent it. Radar pulses from the SD sensor satellites swept the length of the valley, but they required several seconds to acquire lock on. The first bombardment lasted for ninety seconds, then the mortar operators switched to airburst shells, and changed elevation. Dense black clouds burst open above the line of serjeants as they toiled desperately through the quagmire. Broad circles of mud erupted into cyclones of beige foam as the shrapnel slashed down, obliterating the struggling figures.

Only then did the SD radars finish backtracking the mor-tar trajectories. The AI launched its counterstrike. Incandes-cent scarlet beams stabbed down in retaliation, vaporising the possessed and their weapons in micro-seconds. Over a dozen patches of dry land were targeted. Supersonic tor-rents of steam flared out from the base of each impact. When they gusted away, the mortar sites had been reduced to shallow craters of hardbaked clay, their centres still radi-ant. They chittered softly as the drizzle fell, prizing open millions of tiny heat stress fractures.

The empty silence returned. Swirls of smoke drifted over

the valley floor, dissipating slowly to reveal the burning wrecks of the jeeps. Spread out across the quagmire, the ruptured bodies of the serjeants were gradually claimed by the mud's tireless embrace. Within an hour, there would be little left to hint at the conflict.

Stephanie found herself clawing into the soft soil, every muscle locked solid to resist the laser pulse. It never came. She let out a wretched sob, surrendering to the severe shaking that claimed her limbs. Two of the ferrang packs crept towards Stephanie and her friends. They dissolved into a pair of human figures dressed in dark grey and green combat fatigues. Annette Ekelund and Soi Hon looked down at them with anger and contempt.

"You idiots could have got us blown back into the beyond by blundering about like that," Annette said. "What if dear Ralph considered you to be part of this operation? They would have zeroed this patch of ground for sure."

Cochrane lifted his head, mud dribbling down his face to saturate his wild beard. His dead reefer was squashed against his lips. He spat it out. "Well like fuck me gently with a chainsaw, sister. I'm real sorry to cause you any inconvenience."

Not even Lalonde's oppressive climate prepared Ralph for the awesome humidity when he stepped out of the Royal Marine hypersonic transport plane. It prickled his skin at the same time as it siphoned away vital body energies. Just breathing it in was exhausting.

With the last strands of cloud at last gusting out to sea, the tropical sun could finally exert its full strength against poor malaised Mortonridge. Thousands of square kilometres of mud began to effervesce, thickening the air with hot cloying vapour. Looking round from the top of the airstair, Ralph could see long ribbons of tenuous white cloud flow-

ing with oily tenacity around the hummocks and foothills of
the broad valley. More mist was percolating up from the
highlands on either side, with long snow-white streamers
spilling out through clefts in the valley walls to slither
down the slope like slow-motion waterfalls.

He sniffed at the air. Threaded through the blanket of
clean moisture were the traces of corruption. The peninsula's dead biomass was starting to rot and ferment. In another few days the stench would be formidable, and no
doubt extremely unhealthy. One more factor to consider.
Though it was a long way down on the priority list.

Ralph hurried down the aluminium stairs, with Brigadier
Palmer and Cathal just behind him. For once there was no
Marine detail waiting to guard him. They'd landed outside
the staging camp established in the mouth of Catmos Vale.
Hundreds of programmable silicon igloos had sprung up in
rows like giant powder-blue mushrooms, a miniature re-
creation of Fort Forward. The only people here were serjeants, occupation troops, and medical case de-possessed.
Plus a handful of rover reporters; all officially authorized
Liberation correspondents, with a pair of Royal Marine information officers shepherding them.

When he looked up the valley, the loose smears of mist
blurred into a single featureless white sheet carpeting the
floor. His enhanced retinas zoomed in on the only visible
feature, the slim greyish spire of Ketton's church rising out
of the mist. Just by looking at it, Ralph could sense the possessed mustering in the town, a replay of the gentle mental
pressure they'd all known in the days of the red cloud.

"She's here," he murmured. "The Ekelund woman. She's
in Ketton."

"Are you sure?" Cathal asked.

"I can feel her, just like before. In any case, she's one of their leaders, and this bunch are well organized." Cathal gave the distant spire a dubious glance.

The camp's commander, Colonel Anton Longhurst, was waiting at the bottom of the airstairs. He saluted Ralph. "Welcome to Catmos Vale, sir."

"Thank you, Colonel. Looks like you've got yourself an interesting command here."

"Yes, sir. I'll show you round. That's after . . ." he indicated the reporters.

"Ah yes." Ralph kept his ire under control. They'd probably all be using audio discrimination programs, the bastards never missed a trick.

The information officers signalled the all clear, and the rover reporters closed in. "General Hiltch, Hugh Rosler with DataAxis; can you please tell us why the front line has stalled?"

Ralph gave a wan, knowing smile to the plain-looking man in a check shirt and sleeveless jacket who'd asked the question. An in-your-face transmission of the cordial public persona he'd developed and deployed for the last few weeks. "Oh come on, guys. We're consolidating the ground we've already recovered. There's a lot more to the Liberation than just rushing forward at breakneck pace. We have to be sure, and I mean absolutely sure, that none of the possessed has managed to sneak through. Don't forget, it was just one possessed who got into Mortonridge that was responsible for this in the first place. You don't want a repeat of that, do you?"

"General, Tim Beard, Collins; is it true the serjeants simply can't hack it anymore now that the possessed have started to put up real resistance?"

"No, it is categorically not true. And if you show me the person who said that, I'll give them a personal and private demonstration of my contempt for such a remark. I flew in here today, and you people drove in from the coast." He waved a hand back at the mud-covered land. "They walked the whole way from the beaches, engaged in tens of thousands of separate combat incidents. And on the way they've rescued nearly three hundred thousand people from possession. Now does that really sound as though they can't hack it to you, because it doesn't to me."

"So why isn't the front line continuing its advance?"

"Because we've reached a new stage of the campaign. Forgive me for not broadcasting our gameplan before, but this kind of reinforcement manoeuvre was inevitable. As you can see, we've reached Ketton, which has a large number of well organized and hostile possessed in residence—and this is just one of several such assemblies around Mortonridge. The army is simply redeploying accordingly. When we have sufficient resources assembled, then the serjeants will take the town. But I have no intention of committing them until I'm convinced such an operation can be achieved with the minimum of loss on both sides. Thank you." He started to walk forwards.

"General, Elizabeth Mitchell, Time Warner; one final question, please." Her voice was authoritative and insistent, impossible to ignore. "Have you got any comment about the defeat in the valley?"

Trust the owner of that voice to ask something he'd really rather avoid, Ralph thought. "Yes, I have. In hindsight advancing down Catmos Vale so fast was a tactical error, a very bad one; and I take full responsibility for that. Although we knew the possessed are equipped with hunting rifles we weren't expecting them to have artillery. Mortars are about the crudest kind of artillery it's possible to build; but even so, very effective given certain situations. This was one of them. Now we know what the possessed are capable of, it won't happen again. Every time they use a new weapon or tactic against us, we can analyse it and guard against it in future. And there are only a very limited number of these moves they can play." He moved on again, more determined this time. A fast datavise to the two information officers, and there were no more shouted questions.

"Sorry about them," Colonel Longhurst said.

"Not a problem for me," Ralph replied.

"You shouldn't play up to scenes like that," Cathal said in annoyance as they made their way to the camp's headquarters. "It's undignified. At least you could hold a proper press conference with vetted questions."

"This is as much propaganda as it is physical war, Cathal," Ralph said. "Besides, you're still thinking like an ESA officer: tell nobody, and tell them nothing. The public wants to see authority in action on this campaign. We have to provide that."

Convoys of supply trucks were still arriving at the camp, Colonel Longford explained as he took them on an inspection tour. The Royal Marine engineering squads had little trouble securing the programmable silicon igloos; this section of land was several metres above the mud of the valley floor. But there were logistics problems with supplying the troops.

"It's taking the trucks fifteen hours to get here from the coast," he said. "The engineers have virtually had to rebuild the damn road as they went along. Even now there are some sections that are just lines of marker beacons in the mud."

"I can't do anything about the mud," Ralph said. "Believe me, we've tried. Solidifying chemicals, SD lasers to bake it; they're no good on the kind of scale we're dealing with here."

"What we really need is air support. You flew out here."

"This was the first inland flight," Janne Palmer said.

"And your landing field could barely accommodate the hypersonic. You'll never be able to handle cargo planes."

"There's plenty of clear high ground nearby, we can build a link road."

"I'll look into authorizing it," Ralph said. "We should certainly consider flying in the serjeants ready for the assault on the town."

"Appreciate that," the colonel said. "Things out here are a little different than the AI says they should be."

"That's one of the reasons I'm here, to see how you're coping."

"We are now. It was bedlam the first day. Could certainly have done with the planes to evac the injured and the depossessed out. That ride back to the coast isn't doing them any good."

They came to the big oval hall where Elana Duncan and her team had set up shop. The massive boosted mercenary greeted Ralph with a casual salute of her arm, *clicking* her claws together. "Not much ceremony in here, General," she said. "We're rather too crowded for that right now. Go see whatever you want, but don't bother my people, please, they're kind of busy right now."

Ten zero-tau pods were lined up down the centre of the hall, all of them active. The big machines with their thick power cables and compact mosaic of components looked strangely out of place. Or it could be out of era, Ralph acknowledged. The rest of the hall was given over to cots for the serjeants, a field hospital whose primitiveness dismayed him. Elana's mercenaries were carrying large plastic bottles and rolls of disposable paper towels, doing their rounds along the dark bitek constructs. There was a strong chemical smell in the air which Ralph couldn't place. He had some distant memory of it, but certainly not one indexed by his neural nanonics, nor a didactic memory—although they were notoriously inaccurate when it came to imparting smells.

Ralph went over to the first serjeant. The construct was sucking quietly at the tube of a clear polythene bag containing its nutrient syrup, a liquid like thin honey. "Did you get hit by the mortars?"

"No, General," Sinon said. "I wasn't here for the Catmos Vale incident. I am, I believe, one of the lucky ones. I have participated in six assaults which resulted in a possessed being captured, and received only minor injuries during the course of those actions. Unfortunately, that means I have walked the whole way here from the coast."

"So what happened?"

"Moisture exposure, General. Impossible to avoid, I'm afraid. As I said, I was slightly injured previously, resulting in small cracks within my exoskeleton. Although they are not in themselves dangerous, such hairline fissures are ideal anchorages for several varieties of aboriginal fungal spores." He indicated his legs.

Now that he knew what he was looking for, Ralph could see the long lead-grey blotches crisscrossing round the serjeant's lower limbs; they were slightly fuzzy, like thin velvet. When he glanced along the row of cots, he could see some serjeants where the fungus was full grown, smothering their legs in a thick furry carpet, like soggy coral.

"My God. Does that . . ."

"Hurt?" Sinon enquired. "Oh no. Please don't be concerned, General. I don't feel pain, as such. I am aware of the fungus's presence, of course. It does itch rather unpleasantly. The major problem is derived from its effect on my blood chemistry. If left unchecked the fungus would extrude a quantity of toxins that my organs will be unable to filter out."

"Is there a treatment?"

"Funnily enough, yes. An alcohol rub to eradicate the bulk of the fungus, followed with iodine, appears to be effective in eliminating the growth. Of course, further exposure to these conditions will probably reintroduce the spores, especially as they appear to thrive in this current humidity."

"Iodine," Ralph said. "I thought I knew that smell. Some of the Church clinics on Lalonde used the stuff." The incongruity of the situation was starting to nag at him. He could hardly be playing the role of older officer giving comfort to a young trooper. If Sinon followed usual Edenist lines, he must have been at least a hundred and fifty when he died. Older than Ralph's grandfather.

"Ah, Lalonde. I never visited. I used to be a voidhawk crew member."

"You were lucky; I was posted there for years."

Somebody started wailing, a piteous gasping cry of bitterness. Ralph looked up to see a couple of the boosted mercenaries helping a man out of a zero-tau pod. He was wrapped in tattered grey clothes, almost indistinguishable from the folds of pale vein-laced flesh drooping from his frame. It was as if his skin had started to melt off him.

"Aww shit," Elana Duncan snapped. "Excuse me, General, looks like we've got another crash course anorexic." She hurried over to help her colleagues. "Okay, let's gets some protein infusers on him pronto." The de-possessed man was puking a thin greenish liquid on the floor, an action which was almost choking him.

"Come on," Ralph said. "We're just in the way here." He led the others out of the hall; ashamed that the most helpful thing he personally could do was run away.

Stephanie went out on to the narrow balcony and sat in one of the cushioned deck chairs next to Moyo. From there she

could look both ways along Ketton's high street where
squads of Ekelund's guerrilla army marched about. All
signs of the mud deluge had been ruthlessly eradicated
from the town, producing a pristine vision of urban pros-
perity. Even the tall scarlet trees lining the streets and central park were in good health, sprouting a thick frost of
topaz flowers.

They had been billeted in a lovely mock-Georgian town
house, with orange brick walls and carved white stone window lintels. The iron-railed balcony ran along the front,
woven with branches of blue and white wisteria. It was one
of a whole terrace of beautiful buildings just outside the
central retail sector. They shared it with a couple of army
squads. Not quite house arrest, but they were certainly discouraged from wandering round and *interfering*. Much to
Cochrane's disgust.

But Ekelund and her ultra-loyalists controlled the town's
diminishing food supply, and with that came the power to
write the rules.

"I hate it here," Moyo said. He was slumped down almost horizontally in his chair, sipping a margarita. Four
empty glasses were already lined up on the low table beside
him, their salt rims melting in the condensation. "The
whole place is wrong, a phoney. Can't you sense the atmosphere?"

"I know what you mean." She watched the men and
women thronging the road below. It was the same story all
over Ketton. The army gearing up to defend the town from
the serjeants massing outside. Fortifications were first con-
ceived as ghostly sketches in the air, and then made real by
an application of energistic strength. Small factories around
the outskirts had been placed under Delvan's command. He
had his engineers working round the clock to churn out
weapons. Everybody here moved with a purpose. And by

doing so, they gave each other confidence in their joint cause.

"This is fascist efficiency," she said. "Everybody beavering away as they're told for her benefit, not their own. There's going to be so much destruction here when the serjeants come in. And it's all so pointless."

His hand wavered in the air until he found her arm. Then he gripped tight. "It's human nature, darling. They're afraid, and she's tapped into that. The alternative to putting up a fight is total surrender. They're not going to go for that. *We* didn't go for that."

"But the only reason they're in this position is because of her. And we weren't going to fight. I wasn't."

He took a large drink. "Ah, forget about it. Another twenty-four hours, and it won't matter any more."

Stephanie plucked the margarita from his hand and set it down on the table. "Enough of that. We've rested here quite long enough. Time we were moving on."

"Ha! You must be drunker than me. We're surrounded. I know that, and I'm fucking blind. There's no way out."

"Come on." She took his hand and pulled him up from the chair.

Muttering and complaining, Moyo allowed himself to be led inside. McPhee and Rana were in the lounge, sitting round a circular walnut table with a chess game in front of them. Cochrane was sprawled along a settee, surrounded by a haze of smoke from his reefer. A set of bulky black and gold headphones were clamped over his ears, buzzing loudly as he listened to a Grateful Dead album. Tina and Franklin came in from one of the bedrooms when they were called. Cochrane chortled delightedly at the sight of Franklin tucking his shirt in. He only stopped at that because Stephanie caught his eye.

"I'm going to try and get out," Stephanie told them.

"Interesting objective," Rana said. "Unfortunately, la Ekelund is holding all the cards, not to mention the food. She's hardly given us enough to live on, let alone build our strength back to a level where we can contemplate hiking through the mud again."

"I know that. But if we stay in the town we're going to get captured by the serjeants for sure. That's if we survive the assault. Both sides are upping their weapons hardware by an alarming degree."

"I told you this would happen," Tina said. "I said we should have stayed above the valley. But none of you listened."

"So what's the plan?" Franklin asked.

"I haven't got one," Stephanie said. "I just want to change the odds, that's all. The serjeants are about five miles away from the outskirts. That leaves a lot of land between us and them."

"So?" McPhee asked.

"We can use that space. It certainly improves our chances from staying here. Maybe we can sneak through the line in all the confusion when they advance. We could try disguising ourselves as kolfrans; or we could hide out somewhere until they pass by us. It's got to be worth a try."

"A non-aggressive evasion policy," Rana said thoughtfully. "I'm certainly with you on that."

"No way," McPhee said. "Look, I'm sorry Stephanie, but we've seen the way the serjeants move forwards. You couldn't slide a gnat between them. And that was before the mortar attack. They're wise to us using the ferrangs as camouflage now. If we go out there, we're just going to be the first to be de-possessed."

"No, no, wait a minute," Cochrane said. He swung his feet off the settee and walked over to the table. "Our funky sister might be on to something here."

"Thanks," Stephanie grunted sarcastically.

"Listen, you cats. The black hats and their UFOs are like scoping the ground out with microscopes, right? So if we like cooperate with each other and dig ourselves a nice cozy bunker out in the wilderness, we could sit tight down there until they've invaded the town and moved off."

Several surprised looks were passed round. "It could work," Franklin said. "Hot damn!"

"Hey, am I like *the man*, or what?"

Tina sneered. "Definitely a what."

"I keep expecting to be asked for my ident disk," Rana said as the seven of them walked down Ketton's main street.

They were the only people not wearing military fatigues. Ekelund's army gave them suspicious glances as they passed by. Cochrane's tinkling bells and cheery, insulting waves didn't contribute to making them inconspicuous. When they walked out of the house, Stephanie considered junking her dress and adopting the same jungle combat gear style. Then she thought to hell with that. I'm not hiding my true self anymore. Not after what I've been through. I have a right to be me.

Near the outskirts, the road lead between two rows of houses. Nothing as elaborate as the Georgian town house, but comfortably middle-class. The barrier between town and country was drawn by a deep vertical-walled ditch, with thick iron spikes driven into the soil along the top. Some kind of sludge trickled along the bottom of the trench, stinking of petrol. The arrangement wasn't terribly practical, it was more a statement than a physical danger.

Annette Ekelund was waiting for them, lounging casually against one of the big spikes. Several dozen of her army were ranged beside her. Stephanie was quite sure the hulking guns they had slung over their shoulders would be impossible to lift without energistic power fortifying their muscles. Three-day stubble seemed compulsory for the men, and everyone wore ragged sweatbands.

"You know, I'm getting a bad case of déjà vu here," Annette said with ersatz pleasantry. "Except this time you haven't got a good cause to tug my heartstrings. In fact, this is pretty close to treachery."

"You're not a government," Stephanie said. "We don't have loyalties."

"Wrong. I am the authority here. And you do have obligations. I saved your pathetic little arse, and all these sad bunch of losers you have trailing round with you. I took you in, protected you, and fed you. Now I think that entitles me to a little loyalty, don't you?"

"I'm not going to argue this with you. We don't want to fight. We won't fight. That gives you three choices, you either kill us here on the spot, imprison us which will take up valuable manpower, or let us go free. That's the only issue, here."

"Well that's actually only two choices then, isn't it? Because I'm not diverting anybody from their assigned duty to watch over ingrate shits like you."

"Fine, then make your choice."

Annette shook her head, genuinely puzzled. "I don't get you, Stephanie, I really don't. I mean, where the fuck do you think you're going to go? They do have us surrounded, you know. An hour walking down that road, and you're straight into zero-tau. Do not pass go, do not collect two hundred dollars. And you will never ever get out of jail again for the rest of time."

"We might be able to dodge them in open ground."

"That's it? That's your whole game plan? Stephanie, that's pitiful even for you."

Stephanie pressed closer to Moyo, unnerved by the level

of animosity running free in Annette's thoughts. "So what's your alternative?"

"We fight for our right to exist. It's what people have been doing for a very long time. If you weren't such a small-town imbecile you'd see that nothing easy ever comes free; life is cash on delivery."

"I'm sure it is, but you haven't answered my question. You know you're going to lose, what's the point in fighting?"

"Let me explain," Soi Hon said. Annette flashed him a look of pure anger, then nodded permission.

"The purpose of our action is to inflict unacceptable losses on the enemy," Soi Hon said. "The serjeants are almost unstoppable here on the ground, but the political structure behind them is susceptible to a great many forces. We might not win this battle, but our cause will ultimately triumph. That triumph will come sooner once the Confederation leadership is forced to retreat from ventures like this absurd Liberation. Their victory must be as costly as we can make it. I ask you to reconsider your decision to leave us. With your help, the time we have to spend in the beyond will be reduced by a considerable margin. Just think, the serjeant you exterminate today may well be the one that breaks the camel's back."

"You lived before Edenism matured, didn't you?" Moyo asked.

"The habitat Eden was germinated while I was alive. I didn't survive long after that."

"Then I have to tell you, what you're talking is total bullshit. The political ideologies you're basing your justifications on are centuries out of date—just like all of us. Edenism has a resolution which is frightening in its totality."

"All human resolve can be broken in the end."

Moyo turned his perfect, unseeing eyes to Stephanie, and twisted his lips in a humble grimace. "We're doomed. You can't reason with a psychopath and a demented ideologue."

"You should tell your boyfriend to watch his lip," Annette said.

"Or what?" Moyo laughed. "You said it, psycho mamma, you told Ralph Hiltch all those weeks ago: the possessed don't lose. It doesn't matter how many bodies of mine you blast away. I will always be back. Learn to live with me, because you can never escape. For all of eternity you have to listen to me whining on and on and on and on . . . How do you like that, you dumb motherfucker?"

"Enough." Stephanie patted his shoulder in warning. He couldn't see Annette's expression, but he'd be able to sense her darkening thoughts. "Look, we're just going to go, all right."

Annette turned and spat into the trench. "You know what's down there? Its something called napalm. Soi Hon told us about it, and Milne made up the formula. There's tons of the stuff; lying down there, in squirt bombs, loaded into flame throwers. So when the serjeants come over, it's going to be barbecue time. And that's just this section. We've got a shitload of grief rigged up for them around this town. Every street they walk down is going to cost them in bodies. Hell, we're even running a sweepstake, see how many we can take with us."

"I hope you win."

"The point is, Stephanie, if you leave now, you don't come back. I mean that. If you desert us, your own kind, then you're our enemy just as much as the non-possessed are. You're going to be trapped out there between the serjeants and me. They'll shove you into zero-tau, I'll have you strung up on a crucifix and fried. So you see, it's not me that makes the choices. In the end, it's down to you."

Stephanie gave her a sad smile. "I choose to leave."

"You stupid bitch." For a moment, Stephanie thought the woman was going to launch a bolt of white fire straight at her. Annette was fighting very hard to control her fury.

"Okay," she snapped. "Get out. Now."

Praying that Cochrane would keep his mouth shut, Stephanie tugged Moyo gently. "Use one of the spikes," she murmured to McPhee and Rana. They both began to concentrate. The nearest spike started to droop, lowering itself like a drawbridge across a moat. When its tip touched the other side, the metal flattened out, producing a narrow walkway.

Tina was over first; shaking and subdued at the naked hostility radiating from Ekelund and imitated by her troops. Franklin guided Moyo over. Stephanie waited until the other three were on the far side before using it herself. When she turned round, Annette was already marching back down the road into Ketton. Soi Hon and a couple of others walked behind her, taking care not to come too close. The remaining troops stared hard over the trench. Several of them primed the pump action mechanism on their guns.

"Yo, nooo problem, dudes," Cochrane crooned anxiously. "We're outta here. Like yesterday."

It was midday, the sun blazed down on them like a visible X-ray laser, and the mist had gone long ago. Three miles ahead, the rumpled foothills of the valley wall rose up out of the sluggish quagmires. The serjeants were strung out across the slopes, forming a solid line of dark blobs standing almost shoulder to shoulder. Larger groups were arranged at intervals behind the front line, reserves ready to assist with any sign of resistance.

A couple of miles behind, the air shimmered silver, twisting lightbeams giddily around Ketton. Dry mud creaked and crumbled under their feet as they tramped along the gently undulating road. They weren't going particularly fast. It wasn't just hunger draining their bodies. Apathy was coming on strong.

"Oh hell," Stephanie said abruptly. "Look, I'm sorry."

"What for?" McPhee asked. There was bravado in his voice, but not his thoughts.

"Oh come on!" She stopped and flung her arms out, turning full circle on a heel. "I was wrong. Look at this place. We're snowflakes heading straight for hell."

McPhee gave a grudging look around the flat, featureless valley floor. During the few days they'd rested in Ketton the mud had claimed just about every fallen tree and bush. Even the long pools between the quagmires were evaporating away. "Not much in the way of ground cover, granted."

She gave the big Scot an admonitory stare. "You're very sweet, and I'm really glad that you're with me. But I goofed. There's no way we can avoid the serjeants out here. And I do think Ekelund was serious when she said we wouldn't be allowed back in."

"Yeah," Cochrane said. "That's the impression I got, too. You know, that bug is shoved so far up, it's going to be flapping its way out of her mouth any day now."

"I don't understand," Tina said miserably. "Why don't we just stick to Cochrane's original idea, and dig in?"

"The satellites can see us, lass," McPhee said. "Aye, they don't know how many of us there are, exactly, or what we're doing. But they know where we are. If we stop moving and suddenly vanish, then the serjeants will come and investigate. They'll realize what we've done and excavate us."

"We could split up," Franklin said. "If we walk about at random and keep crossing each other's tracks, then one or two of us could vanish without them realizing. It'd be like a giant-sized version of the shell game."

"But I don't want us to split up," Tina said.

"We're not splitting up," Stephanie told her. "We've been through too much together for that. I say we face them together with dignity and pride. We have nothing to be ashamed of. They're the ones who have failed. That huge, wonderful society with all its resources, and all it can do is fall back on violence instead of trying to find an equitable solution for all of us. They've lost, not us."

Tina sniffed, and dabbed at her eyes with a small handkerchief. "You say the most beautiful things."

"Certainly do, sister."

"I'll face the serjeants with you, Stephanie," McPhee said. "But it might be a good idea to get off this road first. I'll give you good odds our friends behind have got it in their mortar sights."

Ralph waited until there were twenty-three thousand serjeants deployed at Catmos Vale before giving the go ahead to take the town. The AI estimated at least eight thousand possessed were trapped inside Ketton. He wasn't going to be responsible for unleashing a massacre. There would be enough serjeants to overcome whatever lay ahead.

As soon as the first mortar attack had finished, the AI had pulled the front line back. Then the flanks, up in the high ground above the valley, had been directed forwards again. By the time the sun fell, Ketton was surrounded. To start with, the circle was simply there to prevent individual possessed from trying to sneak out. Any large group that tried their luck would be warned off with SD lasers in a repeat of the firebreak protocol across the neck of the peninsula.

Very few did attempt to run the gauntlet. Whatever method of discipline Ekelund was using to keep her people in check, it was impressive. The perimeter was progressively reinforced as planes and trucks brought in fresh squads. Occupation forces were also assembled and dispatched around the front line, ready to handle the captured possessed. Medical facilities were organized to cope with the predicted influx of new, unhealthy bodies (though shortages of equipment and qualified personnel were still acute). The AI had exhaustively analysed every possible weapon from history which the possessed could have constructed, and computed appropriate counter-measures.

Ralph was quietly pleased to see that the simplest policy was amongst the oldest: the best defence is a good offence. He might not be able to employ saturation bombardment against the town, or melt it down into the bedrock. But he could certainly rattle the doors of Ekelund's precious sanctum, a quite severe rattling, in fact. "Quake them," he datavised.

Two thousand kilometres above Ombey, a lone voidhawk began its deployment swoop.

Ralph waited beside the rectangular headquarters building with Acacia and Janne Palmer standing beside him. They all stared along Catmos Vale at the sliver of dense mangled air at the far end which marked the town. Maybe he should have been back at the Fort Forward Ops Room, but after visiting the camp he realized how restricted and isolated he was sitting in his office. Out here, at least he had the illusion of being involved.

It was one of the larger patches of land above the lagoons and mires that cluttered the valley floor. Plenty of aboriginal grass poked up through the solidifying cloak of mud, as yet untrampled by animals. There were even some trees surviving near the centre; they'd fallen down, their lower branches stabbing into the soft ground; but the trunks were held off the ground, and their battered leaves were slowly twisting to face the sky.

Stephanie made her way over to them, putting the road quarter of a mile behind her. The ground around the sagging boughs was deeply wrinkled, producing dozens of small meandering pools of brackish water. She threaded her way through them, into the small dapple of shade thrown by the leaves, and sank down with a heavy sigh. The others sat down around her, equally relieved to be off their feet.

"I'm amazed we didn't step on a mine," Moyo said. "Ekelund must have rigged that road. It's too tempting not to."

"Hey guys, let's like turn her into an unperson, please," Cochrane said. "I don't want to spend my last remaining hours in this body talking about that bitch."

Rana lent back against a tree trunk, closed her eyes and smiled. "Well well, we finally agree on something."

"I wonder if we get a chance to talk to the reporters," McPhee said. "There's bound to be some covering the attack."

"Peculiar last wish," Rana said. "Any particular reason?"

"I still have some family left alive on Orkney. Three kids. I'd like to . . . I don't know. Tell them I'm all right I suppose. What I'd really like to do is see them again."

"Nice thought," Franklin said. "Maybe the serjeants will let you record a message, especially if we cooperate with them."

"What about you?" Stephanie asked.

"I'd go traditional," Franklin said. "A meal. You see, I used to like eating, trying new stuff, but I never really had much money. So, I've done most everything else I want to. I'd have the best delicacies the universe can offer, cooked by the finest chef in the Confederation, and Norfolk Tears to go with it."

"Mine's easy," Cochrane said. "That's like apart from the obvious. I wanna re-live Woodstock. Only this time I'd listen to the music more. Man, I can like only remember about five hours of it. Can you dig that? What a bummer."

"I want to be on the stage," Tina said breathlessly. "A classical actress, in my early twenties, while I'm so beautiful that poets swoon at the sight of me. And when my new play opens, it would be The event of the year, and all the Society people in the world are fighting to buy tickets."

"I'd like to walk through Elisea woods again," Rana said. She gave Cochrane a suspect look, but he was listening politely. "It was on the edge of my town when I was growing up, and the Slandau flowers grew there. They had chromatactile petals; if you touched one, it would change colour. When the breeze blew through the trees it was like standing inside a kaleidoscope. I used to spend hours walking along the paths. Then the developers came, and cleared the site to make room for a factory park. It didn't matter what I said to anyone, how many petitions I organized; the mayor, the local senator, they didn't care how beautiful the woods were and how much people enjoyed them. Money and industry won every time."

"I think I'd just say sorry to my parents," Moyo said. "My life was such a waste."

"The children," Stephanie said. She grinned knowingly at McPhee. "I want to see my children again."

They fell silent then, content to daydream what could never be.

The sky suddenly brightened. Everyone apart from Moyo looked up, and he caught their agitation. Ten kinetic harpoons were descending, drawing their distinctive dazzling plasma contrails behind them. It was a conical formation, gradually expanding. A second batch of ten harpoons ap-

peared above the first. Sunglasses automatically materialized on Stephanie's face.

"Oh shit," McPhee groaned. "It's yon kinetic harpoons,
again."

"They're coming down all around Ketton."

"Strange pattern," Franklin said. "Why not fire them
down all at once?"

"Does it matter?" Rana said. "It's obviously the signal to
start the attack."

McPhee was eyeing the harpoons dubiously. The first
formation was still expanding, while the blazing, ruptured
air around their nose cones was growing in intensity.

"I think we'd better get down." Stephanie said. She
rolled over, and imagined a sheet of air hardening protectively above her. The others followed her example.

The harpoons Ralph had chosen to deploy against Ketton
were different to the marque he'd used to smash Mortonridge's communication net at the start of the Liberation.
These were considerably heavier and longer, a design
which helped focus their inertia forwards. On impact, they
penetrated clean through the damp, unresisting soil. Only
when they struck the bedrock below did their tremendous
kinetic energy release its full destructive potential. The explosive blast slammed out through the soft soil. Directly
above the impact point, the whole area heaved upwards as
if a new volcano was trying to tear its way skywards. But
the major impetus of the shockwaves radiated outwards.
Then the second formation of harpoons hit. They formed a
ring outside the first, with exactly the same devastating effect.

Seen from above, the twenty separate shockwaves spread
out like ripples in a pond. But it was the one very specific
interference pattern they formed as they intersected which
was the goal of the bombardment. Colossal energies

clashed and merged in peaks and troughs that mimicked the surface of a choppy sea, channelling the direction in which the force was expended. Outside the two strike rings, the newly formatted shockwaves rushed off across the valley floor, becoming progressively weaker until they sank away to nothing more than a tremble which lapped against the foothills. Inside the rings, they merged into a single contracting undulation, which swept in towards Ketton, building in height and vigour.

Annette Ekelund and the troops manning the town's perimeter defences watched in stupefaction as the newborn hill thundered towards them from all directions. The surviving network of local roads leading away from the outskirts were ripped to shreds as the swelling slope flung them aside. Boulders went spinning through the air in long lazy arks. Mud foamed turbulently at the crest while mires and pools avalanched down the sides, engulfing the frenzied herds of kolfrans and ferrangs.

It grew higher and higher, a tsunami of soil. The leading edge reached Ketton's outlying buildings, trawling them up its precarious ever-shifting slope. Defence trenches either slammed shut or split wide as though they were geological fault lines, their napalm igniting in third-rate imitation of lava streams. People diverted every fraction of their energistic strength to reinforcing their bodies, leaving them to bounce and roll about like human tumbleweed as the demented ground trampolined beneath them. Without the possessed to maintain them, the prim, restored houses and shops burst apart in scattergun showers of debris. Bricks, fragments of glass, vehicles, and shattered timbers took flight to clot the air above the devastation.

And still the quake raced on, hurtling into the centre of the town. Its contraction climaxed underneath the charming little church, culminating in a solid conical geyser of ground fifty metres high. A grinding vortex of soil erupted from its pinnacle, propelling the entire church into the sky. The elegant structure hung poised above the cataclysm for several seconds before gravity and sanity returned to claim it. It broke open like a ship on a reef, scattering pews and hymn books over the blitzed land below. Then as the quake's pinnacle ebbed, shrinking down, the church tumbled over, walls disintegrating into a deluge of powdered bricks. Yet still, somehow, the spire remained almost intact. Twisting through a hundred and eighty degrees, with its bell clanging madly, it plunged down to puncture the tormented crater of raw soil that now marked the quake's epicentre. Only then, did its structural girders crumple, reducing it to a pile of ruined metal and fractured carbon-concrete.

Secondary tremors withdrew from the focal point, weaker than the incoming quake, but still resulting in substantial quivers amid the pulverised ruins. The quake's accompanying ultrasound retreated, only to echo back off the valley walls. In ninety seconds, Ketton had been abolished from Mortonridge; leaving a two-mile-wide smear of treacherously loose soil as its sole memorial. Spears made from building rafters jabbed up out of the rumpled black ground, ragged lumps of concrete were interspersed with the mashed up remnants of furniture, every fragment embedded deep into the loam. Rivulets of flaming napalm oozed along winding furrows, belching out black smoke. A curtain of dust thick enough to blot out the sun swirled overhead.

Annette raised herself to her elbows, fighting the mud's suction; and swung her head slowly from side to side, examining the remains of her proud little empire. Her energistic strength had protected her body from broken bones and torn skin, though she knew that there was going to be heavy bruising just about everywhere. She remembered being about ten metres in the air at one point, cartwheeling slowly as a single storey café did a neat summersault beside her to land on its flat roof, power cables and plastic water pipes trailing from a wall to lash about like bullwhips.

Strangely enough, through her numbness, she could admire the quake; there was a beautiful precision to it. Strong enough to wreck the town, yet pitched at a level that enabled the possessed to protect themselves from its effects. As dear Ralph had known they would. Self preservation is the strongest human instinct; Ketton's buildings and fortifications would be discarded instantly in the face of such a lethal threat.

She laughed hysterically, choking on the filthy dust. "Ralph? I told you, Ralph, you had to destroy the village first. There was no need to take it so fucking literally, you shit!" There was nothing left now to defend, no banner or cause around which she could rally her army. The serjeants were coming. Unopposed. Unstoppable.

Annette flopped onto her back, expelling grit from her eyes and mouth. Her mouth puffed away, eager for much needed oxygen. She had never been so utterly terrified before. It was an emotion shining at the core of every mind littered around her in the decimated town. Thousands of them. The one aspect they had left in common.

The trees had stood up and danced during the quake. They left the cloying mud behind with loud sucking sounds and pirouetted about while the ground rearranged itself. It was probably an impressive sight. But only from a distance.

Stephanie had screamed constantly as she wriggled frantically underneath the carouselling boughs, ducking the smaller branches that raked the ground. She'd been struck several times, slapped through the air as if by a giant bat.

Only the energistic power binding her body's cells together had saved her from being snapped in two.

Tina hadn't been so fortunate. As the ground started to calm, one of the trees had fallen straight on top of her. It pushed her deep into the soaking loam, leaving only her head and an arm sticking out. She was whimpering softly as the others gathered round. "I can't feel anything," she whispered. "I can't make myself feel."

"Just melt the wood away," McPhee said quickly, and pointed. "Here to here. Come on, concentrate."

They held hands, imagining the scarlet bark parting, the hard dark wood of the trunk flowing like water. A big chunk of the trunk turned to liquid and splattered down on the mud. Franklin and McPhee hurried forward and pulled Tina out from the mud. Her hips and legs were badly crushed, blood was running out of several deep wounds, splintered bones protruded through the skin.

She looked down at her injuries and wailed in fear. "I'm going to die! I'm going to go back to the beyond."

"Nonsense, babe," Cochrane said. He knelt down beside her and passed his hand over one of the abdominal cuts. The torn flesh sealed over, melding together. "See? Don't give me none of this loser shit."

"There's too much damage."

"Come on, guys," Cochrane looked up at the rest of the group. "Together we can do it. Each take a wound."

Stephanie nodded quickly and sank down beside him. "It'll be all right," she promised Tina. The woman had lost an awful lot of blood, though.

They circled her, and laid on their hands. Power was exerted, transmuted by the wish to heal and cleanse. That was how Sinon's squad found them, kneeling as if in prayer around one of their own. Tina was smiling up placidly, her pale hand gripping Rana, their fingers entwined.

Sinon and Choma approached cautiously through the jumbled trees, and levelled their machine guns at the devout-seeming group. "I want all of you to lie down flat, and put your hands behind your head, now," Sinon said. "Do not attempt to move or apply your energistic power."

Stephanie turned to face him. "Tina's hurt, she can't move."

"I will accept that claim for the moment, providing you do not try to resist. Now, the rest of you lie down."

Moving slowly, they backed away from Tina and lowered themselves onto the mushy loam.

You can come forward, Sinon told the rest of the squad. **They appear to be compliant.**

Thirty serjeants emerged from the tangle of branches and twigs, making remarkably little sound. Their machine guns were all trained on the prone figures.

"You will now leave your captured bodies," Sinon said.

"We can't," Stephanie said. She could feel the misery and fear in her friends, the same as that found in her own mind. It was turning her voice to a piteous croak. "You should know by now not to ask that of us."

"Very well." Sinon took his holding stick out.

"You don't have to use those things, either," Stephanie said. "We'll go quietly."

"Sorry, procedure."

"Look, I'm Stephanie Ash. I'm the one that brought the children out. That must count for something. Check with Lieutenant Anver of the Royal Kulu marines, he'll confirm who I am."

Sinon paused, and used his processor block to query Fort Forward's memory core. The image of the woman certainly appeared to match, and the man with flamboyant clothes and a mass of hair was unmistakable.

We can't rely on what they look like, Choma said.
They can forge any appearance they want.

Providing they cooperate, there is no reason to use
unnecessary force. So far they have obeyed, and they
know they cannot escape.

You're far too trusting.

"You will get up one at a time when instructed," Sinon
told them. "We will escort you back to our field camp
where you will be placed in zero-tau. Three machine guns
will be trained upon you at all times. If any order is refused,
we use the holding sticks to neutralize your energistic ability. Do you understand?"

"That's very clear," Stephanie said. "Thank you."

"Very well. You first."

Stephanie climbed cautiously to her feet, making sure
every motion was a slow one. Choma flicked the nozzle of
his machine gun, indicating the small track through the collapsed trees. "Let's go." She started walking. Behind her,
Sinon was telling Franklin to get up.

"Tina will need a stretcher," Stephanie said. "And someone will have to guide Moyo, he's damaged his eyes."

"Don't worry," Choma said gruffly. "We'll make sure
you all get to the camp okay."

They emerged from the trees. Stephanie looked at where
Ketton had been. A dense cloud of dark-grey dust churned
over the annihilated town. Small fires burned underneath it,
muted orange coronas shining weakly. Twenty slender purple lines glowed faintly in the air above, linking the cloud
with the top of the atmosphere. Streaks of lightning dis-
charged along them intermittently.

"Bloody hell," she murmured. Thousands of serjeants
were walking along the valley floor towards the silent,
murky ruins. The possessed cowering within knew they
were coming. Raw fear was spilling out of the dust cloud

like gaseous adrenaline. Stephanie's heart started to beat faster. Cold shivers ran along her legs and up her chest. She faltered.

Choma nudged her with his machine gun. "Keep going."

"Can't you feel it? They're frightened."

"Good."

"No, I mean really frightened. Look."

Glimmers of burgundy light were escaping through gaps in the dust cloud. Billowing tendril-like wisps around the edges were flattening out, becoming smooth and controlled. The shield against the open sky was returning.

"I didn't think you were stupid enough to try that again," Choma said. "General Hiltch won't permit you to hide."

Even as he spoke an SD electron beam stabbed down through the clear air. A blue-white pillar two hundred metres wide that struck the apex of the seething roof of dust. It sprayed apart with a plangent boom, sending out broad lightning forks that roamed across the boiling surface to skewer into the mud. This time, the possessed resisted. Ten thousand minds concentrated within a couple of square miles, all striving for the same effect. To be free.

The random discharges of the SD beam were slowly tamed. Jagged forks compressing into garish rivers of electrons that formed a writhing cage above the dust. Carmine light brightened underneath. Fear turned to rapture, followed swiftly by determination. Stephanie stared across at the clamorous spectacle, her mouth open in astonishment, and pride. Their old unity was back. And with it came a formidable sense of purpose: to achieve the safety that so many other possessed had obtained. To be gone.

The red light in the cloud strengthened to a lambent glare, then began to stain the ground of the valley floor. A bright circular wave spreading out through the mud and sluggish water.

"Run," Stephanie told the confounded serjeants. "Get clear. Please. Go!" She braced herself as the redness charged towards her. There was no physical sensation other than a near-psychosomatic tingle. Then her body was glowing along with the ground, the air, her friends, and the hulking bodies of the serjeants.

"All right!" Cochrane whooped. He punched the air. "Let's go for it, you crazyass mothers."

The earth trembled, dispatching all of them to their knees again. Sinon tried to keep his machine gun lined up on the nearest captive, but the ground shook again, more violently this time. He abandoned that procedure, and flattened himself. All the serjeants in the Ketton assault linked their minds through general affinity, clinging to each other mentally with a determination that matched their grip on the ground.

"What is happening?" he bellowed.

"We're like outta here, man," Cochrane shouted back. "You're on the last bus out of this universe."

Ralph watched the red light inflate out of the dust cloud. Datavises from SD sensors and local occupation forces spread around Catmos Vale relayed the image from multiple angles, granting him complete three hundred and sixty degree coverage. He knew what it looked like from the air, from the ground, even (briefly) as it engulfed marines who were following close behind the serjeants. But most of all, he just stared ahead as it poured out across the valley.

"Oh my God," he breathed. It was going to be bad. He knew that. Very bad.

"Do you want a full SD strike?" Admiral Farquar asked.

"I don't know. It looks like it's slowing."

"Confirmed. Roughly circular, twelve kilometres across. And they've got two thirds of the serjeants in there."

"Are they still alive?" Ralph asked Acacia.

"Yes, General. Their electronics have collapsed completely, but they're alive and able to use affinity."

"Then what—" The ground shifted abruptly below his feet. He landed painfully on his side. The programmable silicon buildings of the camp were jittering about. Everywhere, people were on their knees or spread-eagled.

"Shit!" Acacia shouted.

A sheer cliff was rising up vertically right across the valley floor, corresponding to the edge of the red light. Huge cascades of mud and boulders were tumbling down its face. The red light followed them down, pervading the rock, and growing brighter.

Ralph refuted his instinct. What he was seeing was just too much, even though he knew they'd done this to entire planets. "They can't," he cried.

"But they are, General," Acacia replied. "They're leaving."

The cliff was still ascending. Two hundred metres now, lifting with increasing confidence and speed. It was becoming difficult to look at as the light turned scarlet, casting long shadows across the valley. Three hundred metres high, and Ralph's neural nanonics had crashed in the backwash of the blossoming reality dysfunction. On the ground around him, the battered blades of grass were wriggling their way back upwards again, shedding their cloak of mud to turn the camp into a verdant parkland. Fallen trees bent their trunks like the spine of an old man rising from his chair, cranking themselves upright again.

The vivid red light began to diminish. When Ralph squinted against it, he could see the cliff retreating from him. It was five hundred metres high, moving away with the majestic serenity of an iceberg. Except it wasn't moving, he realized. It was shrinking, the red light contracting in on itself, enveloping the island of rock which the possessed had uprooted from Mortonridge to sail away into another universe. As it left he could see its entire shape, a flat-topped inverted cone wrapped with massive curving stress ridges that spiralled down to its base, as if it had unscrewed itself from the peninsula.

Air was roaring hard overhead, sucked into the space the island was vacating. It still hovered in the centre of the valley, but now it was becoming insubstantial as well as small. The light around it turned a dazzling monochrome white, obliterating details. Within minutes it had evaporated down to a tiny star. Then it winked out. Ralph's neural nanonics came back on line.

"Cancel the other two assaults," he datavised to the AI. "And halt the front line. Now."

He scrambled cautiously to his feet. The reinvigorated grass was withering all around him, shrivelling back to dry brown flakes that crumbled away in the howling wind. Images from the SD sensors showed him the full extent of the massive crater. Its edges had already begun to subside, mountain-sized landslides were skidding downwards, taking a very long time to reach the bottom. Waiting for them five kilometres down was a medieval orange glow that fluctuated in no comprehensible rhythm. He frowned at that, not understanding what it could be. Then the vivid area ruptured, and a vast fountain of radiant lava soared upwards.

"Whoever's left, get them back," he shouted desperately at Acacia. "Get them as far away from the lip as possible."

"They're already retreating," she said.

"What about the others? The ones on the island? Can your affinity still reach them?"

Her forlorn look was all the answer he needed.

Stephanie and her friends looked at the serjeants, who stared back with equal uncertainty. For the first time in what her dazed thoughts insisted must have been hours, the ground had stopped oscillating beneath her. When she looked up, the sky was a starless ultradeep blue. White light flooded down from nowhere she could see—but felt right, what she wanted. Her gaze tracked round to where the other side of the valley had been. The blank sky came right down to the ground, and the true size of their island became apparent. A tiny circle of land edged with a crinkled line of hillocks, adrift in its own eternal universe.

"Oh no," she murmured in despair. "I think we screwed up."

"Are we free?" Moyo asked.

"For now." She started describing their new home to him.

Sinon and the other serjeants used the general affinity band to call to each other. There were over twelve thousand of them spread out around the island. Their guns worked, their electronics and medical nanonics didn't (several had been injured in the waves of quakes), affinity was unaffected, and there were new senses available. Almost a derivative of affinity, allowing him to sense the minds of the possessed. And there was also the energistic power. He picked a stone from the mud and held it in his palm. It slowly turned transparent, and began to sparkle. Not that a kilogram of diamond was a lot of use here.

"Could you dudes like give this heavy military scene a break now?" Cochrane asked.

It would appear our original purpose is invalid in this environment, Sinon told his comrades. He shouldered his machine gun. "Very well. What do you propose we do next?" he asked the hippie.

"Wow, man, don't look at me. Stephanie's in charge around here."

"I'm not. And anyway, I haven't got a clue what happens now."

"Then why did you bring us here?" Choma asked.

"Because it's not Mortonridge," Moyo said. "That's all. Stephanie told you, we were frightened."

"And this is the result," Rana said. "You must now face the consequences of your physical aggression."

We should regroup and pool our physical resources, Choma said. **It may even be possible for us to use the energistic power to return to the universe.**

Their minds flashed together into a mini-consensus and agreed to the proposal. An assembly area was designated.

"We are going to join up with our comrades," Sinon told Stephanie. "You would be very welcome to come with us. I expect your views on the situation could prove valuable."

That last image of Ekelund popped up annoyingly in Stephanie's mind. The woman had banished them from Ketton. But Ketton no longer existed. Surely they wouldn't be excluded now? Somehow she couldn't convince herself. And the only other alternative was staying by themselves. Without food. "Thank you," she said.

"Wait wait," Cochrane said. "You guys have like got to be kidding. Look, the end of the world is maybe half a mile away. Aren't you even curious what's out there?"

Sinon looked to where the island's crumpled surface ended. "That's a good suggestion."

Cochrane grinned brightly. "You cats'll have to get used to them if you're going to hang with me."

The breeze picked up considerably as they approached the edge of the island. Blowing outward, which troubled the serjeants. Air had become a finite commodity. Long rivulets of mud were sliding gently to the edge and spilling over, dribbling down the cliff like ribbons of candle wax. There was nothing else to see. No break in the uniformity of the midnight blue boundary of the universe that might indicate another object, micro or macro. The realization they were on their own percolated through all of them, growing stronger as they approached the rim.

It was only Cochrane who inched his way cautiously right up to the edge and peered down into the murky void of infinity which buoyed them along. He spread his arms wide and threw his head back, letting the breeze flowing over the island blow his hair around. "WAAAAAHOOOO." His feet jigged about crazily as he cried out ecstatically: "I'm on a fucking flying island. Can you believe this? Here be dragons, mom! And they're GROOVY."

11

For some reason, the tangled strands of black mist which
filled this dark continuum would always slide apart to allow
Valisk through. Not one wisp had ever touched the polyp.
The habitat personality still hadn't managed to determine
the nature of movement outside its shell. Without valid reference points, there was no way of knowing if it was sailing
along on some unknowable voyage, or the veils of darkness
were simply gusting past. The identity, structure, and quantum signature of their new continuum remained a complete
mystery. They didn't even know if the ebony nebula was
made from matter. All they did know for certain was that a
hard vacuum lay outside the shell.

Rubra's uncorked brigade of descendants had devoted
considerable effort into modifying spaceport MSVs into automated sensor platforms. Five of the vehicles had already
been launched, their chemical rockets burning steadily as
they raced off into the void. Combustion, at least, remained
an inter-universal constant. The same could not be said for
their electronic components. Only the most basic of systems would function outside the protection of the shell, and
even those decayed in proportion to the distance travelled.

The power circuits themselves failed at about a hundred kilometres, by which time the amount of information transmitted had fallen to near zero. Which was information in itself. The continuum had an intrinsic damping effect on electromagnetic radiation; presumably accounting for the funereal nature of the nebula. Physicists and the personality speculated that such an effect might be influencing electron orbits, which in turn would explain some of the electrical and biochemical problems they were encountering.

The gigantic web of ebony vapour wouldn't touch the probes, either, denying them a sample/return mission. Radar was utterly useless. Even laser radar could only just track the modified MSVs. Ten days after the axial light tube was powered up, they were floundering badly. No experiment or observation they'd run had resulted in the acquisition of hard data. Without that, they couldn't even start to theorize how to get back.

By contrast, life inside the habitat was becoming more ordered, though not necessarily pleasant. Everybody who'd been possessed required medical treatment of some kind. Worst hit were the elderly, whose possessors had quite relentlessly twisted and moulded their flesh into the more vigorous contours sported by youthful bodies. Anyone who'd been overweight was also suffering. As were the thin, the short; anyone with different skin colour to their possessor, different hair. And without exception, everyone's features had been morphed—that came as naturally as breathing to the possessed.

Valisk didn't have anything like the number of medical nanonic packages required to treat the population. Those packages that were available operated at a very low efficiency level. Medical staff who could program them correctly shared the same psychologically fragile demeanour as all the recently de-possessed. And Rubra's descendants were tremendously busy just trying to keep the habitat supplied with power to give much assistance to the sick. Besides, the numbers were stacked hard and high against them.

After the initial burst of optimism at the return of light, a grim resignation settled among the refugees as more and more of their circumstances were revealed to them. An exodus began. They started walking towards the caverns of the northern endcap. Long caravans of people wound their way out from the starscraper lobby parks, trampling down the dainty parkland paths as they set off down the interior. In many cases, it took several days to walk the twenty kilometre length across the scrub desert. They were searching for a haven where the medical packages would work properly, where there was some kind of organized authority, a decent meal, a place where the ghosts didn't lurk around the boundaries. That grail wasn't to be found amid the decrepit slums encircling the starscraper lobbies.

I don't know what the hell they expect me to do for them, the habitat personality complained to Dariat (among others) as the first groups set out. **There's not enough food in the caverns, for a start.**

Then you'd better work out how to get hold of some, Dariat replied. **Because they've got the right idea. The starscrapers can't support them any more.**

Power within the towers was as erratic as it had been ever since they arrived in the dark continuum. The lifts didn't work. Food secretion organs extruded inedible sludge. Digestion organs were unable to process and flush the waste. Air circulation tubules spluttered and wheezed.

If the starscrapers can't sustain them, then the caverns certainly won't be able to, the personality replied.

Nonsense. Half the trees in your interior are fruiting varieties.

Barely a quarter. In any case, all the orchards are down at the southern end.

Then get teams organized to pick the fruit, and strip the remaining supplies from the starscrapers. You'd have to do this, anyway. You are the government here, remember. They'll do as you tell them; they always have. It'll be a comfort having the old authority figure take charge again.

All right, all right. I don't need the psychology lectures.

Order, of a kind, was established. The caverns came to resemble a blend of nomad camps and field hospital triage wards. People slumped where they found a spare patch of ground, waiting to be told what to do next. The personality resumed its accustomed role, and started issuing orders. Cancers and aggravated anorexias were assessed and prioritized, the medical packages distributed accordingly. Like the fusion generators and physics lab equipment, they worked best in the deeper caverns. Teams were formed from the healthiest, and assigned to food procurement duties. There were also teams to strip the starscrapers of equipment, clothes, blankets—a broad range of essentials. Transport had to be organized.

The ghosts followed faithfully after their old hosts, of course, flittering across the desert during the twilight hours to skulk about in the hollows and crevices decorating the base of the northern endcap during the day. Naked hostility continued to act as an intangible buffer, preventing them from entering any of the subterranean passages.

It also expelled Dariat. The refugees didn't distinguish between ghosts. In any case, had they discovered he was the architect of their current status, their antipathy would probably have wiped him out altogether. His one consolation was that the personality was now part self. It wouldn't disregard him and his needs as an annoying irritation.

In part he was right, though the assumption of privilege was an arrogant one—the pure Dariat of old. However, in these strange, dire times, there were even useful jobs to be had for cooperative ghosts. The personality gave him Tolton as a partner, and detailed the pair of them to take an inventory of the starscrapers.

"Him!" Tolton had exclaimed in dismay when Erentz explained his new duties.

She looked from the shocked and indignant street poet to the fat ghost with his mocking smile. "You worked well together before," she ventured. "I'm proof of that."

"Yeah, but—"

"Okay. Most of that row need seeing to." She gestured at the long line of beds along the polyp wall. It was one of eight similar rows in the vaulting cavern; made up from mattresses or clustered pillows hurriedly shoved into a loose kind of order. The ailing occupants were wrapped in dirty blankets like big shivering pupas. They moaned and drooled and soiled themselves as the nanonic packages sluggishly repaired their damaged cells. Their helpless state meant they needed constant nursing. And there were few enough people left over from the teams prospecting the habitat able to do that.

"Which starscraper do we start with?" Tolton asked.

Each starscraper took at least three days to inventory properly. They'd adopted a comfortable routine by the time they started on their third, the Djerba. The tower had survived Valisk's recent calamities with minimal damage. Kiera's wrecking teams hadn't got round to "reclaiming" it from Rubra's control. There had been few clashes between possessed and servitors inside before it was abandoned. That meant it should contain plenty of useful items. They just needed cataloguing.

To send the work teams down on a see/grab brief was inefficient, especially as there were so few of them. And the personality's thought routines had almost been banished from the habitat's extremities; its memories of room contents were unreliable at best.

"Mostly offices," Tolton decided as he waved a lightstick around. He was holding one in his hand, with another two slung across his chest on improvised straps. Together, the three units provided almost as much illumination as one working at full efficiency.

"Looks like it," Dariat said. They were on the twenty-third floor vestibule, where the walls were broken by anonymously identical doors. Tall potted plants in big troughs were wilting, deprived of light their leaves were turning yellow-brown and falling onto the blue and white carpet.

They moved down the vestibule, reading names on the doors. So far offices had resulted in very few worthwhile finds; they'd learned that unless the company was a hardware or medical supplier there was little point in going in and searching. Occasionally the personality's localized memory would recall a useful item, but the neural strata was becoming more incapable with each floor they descended.

"Thirty years," Tolton mused. "That's a long time to hate." There hadn't been much else to do except swap life stories.

Dariat smiled in recollection. "You'd understand if you'd ever seen Anastasia. She was the most perfect girl ever to be born."

"Sounds like I'll have to write about her some time. But I think your story is more interesting. Man, there's a lot of suffering in you. You died for her, you actually did it. Actually went and killed yourself. I thought that kind of thing really did only happen in poems and Russian novels."

"Don't be too impressed. I only did it after I knew for sure souls existed. Besides—" He gestured down at his huge frame and grubby toga. "I wasn't losing a lot."

"Yeah? Well I'm no sensevise star, but I'm hanging on to what I've got for as long as I can. *Especially* now I know there are souls."

"Don't worry about the beyond. You can leave it behind if you really want to."

"Tell that to the ghosts upstairs. In fact, I'm even keener to hang on to my body while we're in this continuum."

Tolton stopped outside a sensevise recording studio, and gave Dariat a shrewd look. "You're in touch with the personality, is there any chance of us getting out of here?"

"Too early to say. We really don't know very much about the dark continuum yet."

"Hey, this is me you're talking to. I survived the whole occupation, you know. Quit with the company line and level with me."

"I wasn't going to hold anything back. The one conjecture all my illustrious relatives are worried about is the lobster pot."

"Lobster pot?"

"Once you get in, you can't get out. It's the energy levels, you see. Judging by the way our energy is being absorbed by this continuum's fabric it doesn't have the same active energy state. We're louder and stronger than normal conditions here. And that strength is slowly being drained away, just by being here. Its an entropy equilibrium effect. Everything levels out in the end. So if we take height as a metaphor, we're at the bottom of a very deep hole with our universe at the top; which means it's going to take a hell of an effort to lift ourselves out again. Logically, we need to escape through some kind of wormhole. But even if we knew how to align its terminus coordinates so that it opens inside our own universe, it's going to be incredibly difficult to generate one. Back in our universe, they took a lot of very precisely focused energy to open, and the nature of this continuum works against that. With this constant debilitation effect, it may not be possible to concentrate enough energy, it'll dissipate before it reaches critical distortion point."

"Shit. There's got to be something we can do."

"If those rules do apply, our best bet is to try and send a message out. That's what the personality and my relatives are working towards. If they know where we are, the Confederation might be able to open a wormhole to us from their side."

"*Might* be able?"

"All new suggestions welcome. But as it stands, getting them to lower us a rope is the best we can come up with."

"Some rescue plan. The Confederation has its own problems right now."

"If they can learn how to grab us back, they'll be half way to solving them."

"Sure."

They reached the end of the vestibule and automatically turned round.

Nothing here, Dariat reported. **We're moving down to the twenty-fourth floor.**

All right, the personality replied. **There's a hotel, the Bringnal, a couple of floors down from where you are now. Check its main linen store, we need more blankets.**

You're going to ask one of the teams to lug blankets up twenty-five floors?

All the large hoards above that level have been used. And right now it's easier to find new ones than wash the old; nobody's got enough energy for that.

All right. Dariat faced Tolton, taking care to exaggerate his speech. "They want us to find blankets."

"Sounds like a real priority job we got ourselves here." Tolton slithered through a partly open muscle membrane and into the stairwell. The quivering lips didn't bother him nearly so much now.

Dariat followed him, taking care to use the gap. He could slip through solid surfaces, he'd found, if he really wanted to. It was like sinking through ice.

One of the random power surges flowered around them. Electrophorescent cells shone brightly again, illuminating the stairs in stark blue-tinged light. A jet of foggy air streamed out of a tubule vent, sounding like a sorrowful sigh. A thin film of grey water was slicking every surface. Tolton could see the breath in front of his face. He gripped the handrail tighter, fearful of slipping.

"We're not going to be able to salvage stuff from the starscrapers for much longer," Tolton said, wiping his hand against his leather jacket. "They're getting worse."

"You should see what kind of state the ducts and tubules are in."

The street poet grunted in resentment. He was actually eating a lot better than most of the population. Inventory duties had a great many perks. The private apartments with their small stocks of quality food and fashionable clothes were his to pick over as he wished. The salvage teams were only interested in the larger stores that were in restaurants and bars. And now the endless succession of lightless floors no longer bothered him, he was glad to be away from the caverns with all their suffering—and smell.

Dariat.

The startled tone made him halt. **What?**

There's something outside.

Affinity made him aware of the consternation spreading

through his relatives, most of whom were in the counter-rotating spaceport and the caverns.

Show me.

One of the slow flares of red and blue phosphorescence was shimmering through the ebony nebula, sixty kilometres away from the southern endcap. As it dwindled, several more began to bloom in the distance, sending pastel waves of light washing across the gigantic habitat's shell. The personality didn't believe the sudden increase in frequency was a coincidence. It was busy concentrating on collecting the images from its external sensitive cells. Once again, Dariat was uncomfortably aware of the effort expended in what should be a simple observation routine.

A speck of hoary-grey flitted among the strands of blackness, snapping in and out of view. Following the smooth curving motions put Dariat in mind of a skier, the thing's course was very much like a slalom run. Every turn brought it closer to Valisk.

The nebula doesn't get out of its way, the personality remarked. **It's dodging the braids.**

That implies a controlling intelligence, or at least animal-level instinct.

Absolutely.

The initial consternation of Rubra's descendants had given way to a slick buzz of activity. Those out in the spaceport were activating systems, aligning them on the visitor. An MSV was powered up, ready for an inspection/interception flight.

An MSV can't match that kind of manoeuvrability, Dariat said. The visitor performed a fast looping spiral around a grainy black curlicue, shooting off in a new direction parallel to Valisk's shell, fifteen kilometres distant. Visual resolution was improving. The visitor was about a hundred metres across, appearing like a disk of ragged petals. **Even a voidhawk would have trouble making rendezvous.**

The visitor darted behind another frayed column of blackness. When it re-emerged it was soaring almost at right angles to its original course. Its petals were bending and flexing.

They look like sails to me, Dariat said.

Or wings. Although I don't understand what it could be pushing against.

If this continuum has such a low energy state, how come it can move so fast?

Beats me.

Several spaceport dishes started tracking the visitor. They began transmitting the standard CAB xenoc interface communication protocol on a multi-spectrum sweep. Dariat allowed his affinity bond to decline to a background whisper. "Come on," he told a frowning Tolton. "We've got to find a window."

The visitor didn't respond to the interface protocol. Nor did it show any awareness of the radar pulses fired at it. That was perhaps understandable, given that they produced no return signal. The only noticeable change as it spun and danced ever-closer was the way shadows congealed around it. Visually it actually appeared to grow smaller, as though it were flying away from the habitat.

That's like the optical distortion effect which the possessed use to protect themselves with, Dariat said. He and Tolton had found a snug bar called Horner's on the twenty-fifth floor. The two big oval windows were misted over inside, forcing Tolton to wipe them clean with one of the coarse table cloths. His breath kept splashing against the icy glass, condensing immediately.

Well we did choose a realm suitable for ghosts, the personality said.

I've never heard of a ghost that looked like that.

The visitor was within five kilometres of the shell now, about where the filigree of nebula stands began. There was only empty space between it and the habitat now.

Maybe it's scared to come any closer, the personality said. **I am considerably larger.**

Have you tried an affinity call?

Yes. It didn't respond.

Oh. Well. Just a thought.

The visitor left the convoluted weave of the nebula and flashed towards the vast bulk of the habitat. By now its deceptive *glamour* had reduced it to a rosette of oyster ribbons twirling gracelessly in the wake of a fluctuating warp point. The image of the nebula and its strange borealis storms fluxed and bent as the visitor traversed them; oscillating between iridescent scintillations and a black boundary deeper than an event horizon. Nothing about it remained stable.

It streaked over to within fifty metres of the shell then veered round to follow the curve, wriggling wildly from side to side. The quick serpentine orbit allowed it to cover a considerable portion of the habitat's exterior.

It's searching, the personality said. **That implies a degree of organisation. It has to be sentient.**

Searching for what?

A way in, I imagine. Or something it can recognize, some method of establishing communication.

Do any of the spaceport defences still work? Dariat asked.

You have to be bloody joking. We need all the allies we can get.

Before we fused, you used to be the mother of all suspicious neurotic bastards. I think that would be a preferable attitude for you right now.

Well that's the effect of your mature calming influ-

ence for you. So you've only got yourself to blame.
But don't worry, I'm not going to send the MSV after it.

Thank Tarrug for that.

Our visitor should be coming over your horizon any
second now. Perhaps your eyes will do better than my
sensitive cells.

"Wipe the glass again," Dariat told Tolton.

The soaking table cloth smeared the moisture in long
streaks. Tiny flecks of frost were glistening dull white over
the rest of the big oval. Tolton switched off two of his light-
sticks. Both of them peered forward. The visitor arched
over the rim of the shell, lensing thin spires of vermilion
and indigo light as it came. They wavered in the runnels of
water, wobbling insubstantially before sinking back down
into the visitor's core. Now all that remained was a black
knot in the continuum's fabric racing over the dark rust-
coloured polyp.

Tolton's weak grin was bloated with uncertainly. "Am I
being paranoid, or is that heading towards us?"

In the earlier time and place, long ago and far away, they
had called themselves the Orgathé. Now, names had lost all
meaning and relevance, or perhaps they themselves had de-
volved into something else, such was the way of this atrocious existence. There were many others adrift in the dark
continuum, sharing their fate. Identity was no longer singular. A myriad of racial traits had blended and faded into a
singleton over the aeons.

Purpose, though, purpose remained steadfast. The quest
for light and strength, a return to the sweet heights from
whence they had all fallen. A dream sustained even within
the mélange. Few forms existed now outside of the
mélange. The process of diminution claimed every life to
fall into these depths. But this one had risen yet again,
buoyed up by the tides of chaotic chance that rioted within

the mélange, spat out to roam the murk for as long as it had strength. The freeflying state of such escapees was still that of the Orgathé, though the essence of many others rode upon its wings. Its chimerical shape was a tortured mockery of the once glorious avian lords who ruled the swift air currents of their homeworld.

Ahead of it now drifted the exotic object. It was composed of a substance to be found only in the oldest of the Orgathé's memories, those that pre-dated the dark continuum. How strange that it could barely recognize the antecedent of its own salvation.

Matter. Solid organized matter. Alive with a heat so fierce it took the Orgathé some time to acclimatise to the radiance; elevating itself to a near ecstatic level of warmth. Incredibly, just within the scorching surface, a sheet of life energy burned bright and vigorous. The entire object was a single mighty entity. Yet passive. Vulnerable. This was a feast which would sustain a huge proportion of the mélange for a long time. It might even trigger a total dispersal.

The Orgathé slithered close to the object's surface, feeling the mind within follow its flight. Vast swirls of rich thought flowed underneath it as it basked in the warmth. But there was no way to reach the abundant life-energy through the hard surface. If the Orgathé attempted to claw its way through, it would surely incinerate itself. Contact with so much heat for so long could probably not be sustained. But the craving within itself from proximity to so much vital life-energy was overwhelming.

There must be some way in. Some orifice or chink. The Orgathé coasted along over the object, heading for the spikes radiating out from the centre. They were smaller, weaker than the rest of it. Long hollow minarets leaking their energy away into the dark continuum. The life-energy was shallower here, the heat not so intense. Each of the structures was broken by thousands of dark ovals, curtained by cooler sheets of transparent matter. Light twinkled briefly through some of them, never lasting long. Except one. A single oval burning steadily.

The Orgathé glided eagerly towards it. Two flames of life-energy gleamed behind the transparent sheet. One naked, the other clad in hot matter; both enraging the Orgathé's craving. It surged forward.

"FUCK!" Tolton screamed. He dived to one side, scattering tables and chairs. Dariat jumped the other way just as the Orgathé hit the window. Frost blossomed like a living thing, strands of long delicate crystals multiplying across the glass, then reaching out through the air. Shapes moved on the other side of the hoary fur, dark indistinct serpents, thicker than a human torso, that could be tentacles or tongues scrabbling furiously at the outer surface. The unmistakable grinding shriek of deep score lines being ripped into the material penetrated the bar, drowning out Tolton's terrified cries.

Do something! Dariat wailed.

You name it, I'll do it.

Tolton was scuttling backwards on his hands and legs, unable to take his eyes from the window. The serpent shapes were writhing with rabid aggression as they clawed their way through. A badly stressed *snap* sounded above the vicious squealing; corresponding to a thin dark shadow materializing across the frosted window. Furniture was rattling, shaking its way erratically across the floor. Glasses and bottles abandoned on top of the marble bar juddered vigorously and tumbled off.

It's coming through! Dariat cried. When he tried to clamber to his feet, he discovered he didn't have the strength. Fatigue was numbing every limb.

"Kill it!" Tolton bellowed.

We can try and zap it, the personality said, **like we did the possessed.**

Just bloody do it!

It might kill you as well; we don't know.

You're part me. Do you seriously think I want *that* to catch me?

Very well.

The personality began to re-route its patched-up power supply. Diverting current away from the axial light tube and the caverns, pumping the precarious fusion generators up to their maximum output. Electricity poured back into the Djerba starscraper's organic conductor grid. The first-floor windows blazed with golden light; mechanical and electronic systems came alive in frantic chitters of movement and data emissions. Milliseconds later the second floor sprang back to life. The third, fourth . . .

Dazzling shafts of light sliced out from the Djerba's windows, piercing the gloom outside. They snapped downward storey by storey towards the beleaguered twenty-fourth floor. The personality gathered its major thought routines and plunged them down into the starscraper, a sensation like diving into a pitch-black well shaft. Bitek networks were swiftly resurrected around its descending mentality.

A dead zone was concentrated around Horner's window. The external polyp was so cold the personality could no longer calibrate it. Living cells deeper in had frozen solid. The personality could feel vibrations running through the floor as the Orgathé pounded and scraped against the window.

Junctions within the organic conductor web switched polarity, high order sub-routines cancelled the safety limiters. Every erg of power from the fusion generators was channelled into Horner's. Ceiling strips of electrophorescent cells ignited, flooding the bar with searing white light. Organic conductors behind the walls fused, burning out long lines of polyp in a cascade of amber sparks. Incandescent arcs stormed through the air as a lethal charge of electrons was fired into the external wall.

Coming on top of the heat and life-energy, the electron hammer blow was just too much. The Orgathé recoiled from the window, appendages flailing madly as the streams of alien energy churned within its body. There was a brief glimpse of sinuous chrome-black tendrils bristling with curving blades coiling back protectively around a bulbous midsection. Ragged wing petals began to flex. Then the distortion smeared it with refracted scintillations from the gleaming starscraper, and it shot away at a bruising acceleration. Within seconds it was lost inside the nebula.

Dariat took his arm away from his face. The tremendous barrage of noise and light saturating the bar had faded. A few sparks were still popping out from the deep scorch marks in the walls. The glossy electrophorescent cells had shattered and shrivelled to rain across the floor, their fragments curling up, puffing out licks of smoke.

You all right, my boy? the personality enquired.

Dariat looked down at himself. The feeble yellow glow from Tolton's remaining lightstick showed his spectral body unchanged. Though possibly more translucent than usual. He still felt terribly weak. **I think so. I'm bloody cold, though.**

Could have been worse.

Yeah. Dariat felt the personality's major routines withdrawing from the starscraper. The lights were going off again in the upper floors, autonomic bitek functions shutting down.

He struggled to his knees, shivering intensely. When he looked round he could see ice encrusted on every surface, turning the bar into an arctic grotto. The electrical discharge had melted very little of it. That was probably what had saved them; it was several centimetres thick over the window. And the fracture pattern in the glass underneath was unnervingly pronounced.

Tolton was spasming on the floor, spittle flecking his lips. His hair was rimed with frost. Each shallow panted breath was revealed in a cloud of white vapour.

"Shit." Dariat staggered over to him. Just in time he remembered not to try and touch the tormented body. *Get a medical team down here.*

Oh yeah. I'll get right on it. They should be with you in about three hours.

Shit. He knelt down next to Tolton, and leaned right over, staring into delirious eyes. "Hey." Limpid fingers clicked right in front of Tolton's nose. "Hey. Tolton. Can you hear me? Try and steady your breathing. Take a deep breath. Come on! You've got to calm your body down. Breathe."

Tolton's teeth chittered. He gurgled, cheeks bulging.

"That's it. Come on. Breathe. Deep. Suck that air down. Please."

The street poet's lips compressed slightly, making a whistling sound.

"Good. Good. And again. Come on."

It took several minutes for Tolton's bucking to subside. His erratic breathing reduced to sharp gasps. "Cold," he grunted.

Dariat smiled down at him. "Ho boy. You had me worried there. We really don't need any more ghosts floating around in here right now."

"Heart. My heart. God! I thought . . ."

"It's okay. It's over."

Tolton nodded roughly, and tried to lever himself up.

"Stop! You just lie there for another minute longer. There's no paramedic service any more, remember? First thing we need is some proper food for you. I think there's a restaurant on this floor."

"No way. As soon as I can get up, we're leaving. No more starscrapers." Tolton coughed, and started to glance round. "Jesus." He scowled. "Are we safe?"

"Sure. For now, anyway."

"Did we kill it?"

Dariat grimaced. "Not exactly, no. But we gave it a hell of a fright."

"That lightning bolt didn't kill it?"

"No. It flew off, though."

"Shit. I nearly died."

"Yeah. But you didn't. Concentrate on that."

Tolton slowly eased himself into a sitting position, wincing at each tiny movement. Once he was propped up against a table leg, he reached out and caressed the ice which was engulfing a chair, fingers stroking curiously. He gave Dariat a grim look with badly bloodshot eyes. "This isn't going to have a happy ending, is it?"

The seven hellhawks glided in towards Monterey, acknowledging the query from the SD network defence as the sensors locked on.

The Sevilla SD network was a hell of a lot stronger than anything we were briefed about, they told Jull von Holger, when he asked how the mission had gone. Seven frigates were lost, and we're all that's left of our squadron.

Did the infiltration succeed?

We think over a hundred got through.

Excellent.

Neither side said anything more. Jull von Holger could

sense the quiet rage of the surviving hellhawks. He chose not to mention the fact to Emmet Mordden; the hellhawks were all Kiera's problem.

Go straight to the docking ledges, Hudson Proctor told the hellhawks. **We've already cleared the pedestals. You'll be fed as soon as you land.** He focused on Kiera's face. She smiled her brightest ingénue smile, pouring as much gratitude into her thoughts as possible for her deputy to relay. "Well done. I know it's not easy, but believe me there won't be many more of these ridiculous seeding missions." She arched an eyebrow in query to Hudson. "Was there a reply?"

He coloured slightly at the emotional backlash to her little speech that flooded the affinity band. "No. They're pretty tired."

"I understand." Her sweet expression hardened. "End your contact."

Hudson Proctor nodded curtly, signalling it had been done.

"You hope there ain't going to be many more seeding flights, you mean," Luigi said indolently.

The three of them were sitting in one of the smaller, more private lounges above the asteroid's docking ledges, waiting for the last member of their group to arrive. Kiera's small revolution had picked up a respectable degree of momentum over the last ten days. The success of the seeding flights had bolstered Al's popularity and authority considerably. But that triumph came with a high price in terms of starships, and quite a few people were starting to acknowledge that the infiltration campaign was short-termism. Slowly, quietly, Kiera had exploited that. Being able to see the dissatisfaction and worry in people's minds gave her a handy advantage when it came to spotting potential recruits.

Silvano Richmann came in and took his seat around the coffee table. There was a cluster of bottles in the centre, he poured himself a shot of whisky.

"The Sevilla flotilla is back," Kiera told him. "Seven frigates and five hellhawks got zapped."

"Fuck." Silvano shook his head in dismay. "Al's putting together another fifteen of these missions. He just doesn't see it."

"He sees it the way he wants to see it," Kiera said. "They're successful in that they're landing infiltrators each time. The Confederation is going apeshit. We're knocking off five of their planets a day. It buys him complete respect and loyalty with the Organization down on the planet."

"While my fleet gets chopped to shit," Luigi snapped. "That goddamn whore Jezzibella. She's got him by the balls."

"Not just your fleet," Kiera said. "I'm losing hellhawks fast. Much more of this, and they'll leave."

"Where to?" Silvano asked. "They've got to stick with you. That was a neat sting you pulled on them with the food."

"The Edenists keep making offers to try and lure them away," Hudson said. "Etchells keeps us informed. The latest offer is that they'll actually accept the blackhawk host personality into their habitat neural strata, leaving our guys as the only soul in there. In exchange they get all the food they want, providing they just cooperate with the Edenists, help them find out about our powers."

"Shit," Silvano muttered. "We gotta stop this. I'd be mighty tempted by any offer that got rid of this body's host soul."

"Wouldn't we all," Kiera said. She sat back and sipped at her wine. "Okay, the question is, how far are you prepared to go?"

"Pretty goddamn obvious for me," Luigi said. "I'll waste that shit Capone myself. Busting me down to a fucking errand boy. Nobody could have handled Tranquillity any different."

"Silvano?"

"He's got to go. But there's one condition for me signing up with you. And it ain't negotiable."

"What's that?" Kiera asked, though she was fairly sure she knew. Silvano was feared as Al's chief enforcer, but he did have one major difference with his boss.

"After we do this, there are no more non-possessed in the Organization. We take them all out. Understood?"

"Suits me," Kiera said.

"No way!" Luigi shouted. "I can't run my fucking fleet with just possessed crews. You know that. You're shitting on me here, man."

"Yeah? Who says there's going to be a fucking fleet after this. Right, Kiera? We're doing this for our own safety. We're going to take New California out of here; out of this universe. Just like all the other possessed have done. And for that, we can't afford no non-possessed to be around. Come on, Luigi, you know that. As long as there's one of them left, they're going to be plotting and scheming how to get rid of us. For Christ's sake. We steal their bodies from them. If you was alive right now, you wouldn't give jack shit about anything else other than getting them back from us." He slammed his tumbler back down on the table. "We eliminate all the non-possessed, or there's no deal."

"Then there's no fucking deal," Luigi stormed.

Kiera held up her hands. "Boys, boys, this is how Al wins. You ever heard of divide and rule? All of us have different interests, and the only way we can hang on to them is if we're part of the Organization. Only the Organization needs a fleet, and hellhawks, and lieutenants that have to be kept in line." She shot Silvano a significant look. "He's made it complicated so that we have to support him to keep our own places. What we've got to do is dismantle the Organization, but rig whatever's next so that we three come out on top."

"Like what?" Luigi asked suspiciously.

"Okay, you want the fleet back, right? Tell me why?"

"Because it's fucking mine, you dumb broad. I built that fleet up from nothing. I was here right from the start, the day Al walked into San Angeles City Hall."

"Fair enough. But all the fleet did was make you a player. Do you really want to risk flying to Confederation planets and going up against their SD networks? They're getting wise to us now. These seeding flights are pissing them off bad. They're killing us out there, Luigi."

"So? Like I should care. I'm the admiral. I don't have to go with them every time."

"The whole fleet doesn't have to go anywhere, Luigi; that's the point. What you need is to exchange the fleet for something else that will keep you in the game, right?"

Luigi eyed her cautiously. "Maybe."

"That's what we've got to work out between the three of us. Right now, we can carry the Organization if we eliminate Capone. But the Organization's a dead end. Dishing out tokens instead of money, for Christ's sake. If we take it over, we've got to use it to establish a new type of government. One that has us at the top."

"Like what?" Silvano asked. "The second New California leaves this universe then nobody needs any kind of government."

"Says who?" Kiera sneered. "You've seen the cities down there. Unless the Organization keeps putting the squeeze on the farmers to supply food, they'd collapse overnight. If New California escapes this universe, everyone on it is going to have to turn into some kind of medieval peasant just to stay alive. And that's such bullshit. Five per cent of the population working in the fields can sustain the rest of us. Now I don't know what kind of society we can build on the other side, but I'm damned if I'm going to live in a mud hut and spend my days walking behind a horse's arse to plough a field. Especially when someone else can be made to do it for me."

"So what are you saying here?" Silvano asked. "That we keep the farmers working while the rest of us live it up?"

"Basically, yeah. It's just like what I've done with the hellhawks, but on a much bigger scale. We have to keep the farmers farming, and we have to be in charge of distributing the food to the urban areas. Convert the Organization into a giant supplier; and the only people who get supplied, are the ones who we say."

"You'd need a fucking army for that!" Luigi exclaimed.

Kiera gestured magnanimously. "There you are then. That's what you turn the fleet into. Find a portable weapon that's effective against the possessed: something like those bastard serjeants use on Mortonridge, manufacture it up here, and equip our supporters with it. Use the same chain of command network that's already in place, but with a land army to back it up instead of the SD platforms."

"That might work," Silvano said. "So if Luigi's got himself an army, what do I get?"

"Communications are vital, otherwise this whole thing will just collapse. And we'd need to be more subtle with the farmers than forcing them at gunpoint. That's an enforcer's job."

He poured himself another whisky. "Okay. Let's talk about it."

*

Western Europe always took his dogs for a walk himself. Dog ownership was a healthy reminder of responsibility; you either do it properly or not at all. There weren't many crises which could make him skip a day. Though he suspected one of his staff was going to have to start substituting fairly soon.

The formal lawns extended for over three hundred metres from the back of the house (they were yards back in the days when he bought the estate, but even he had fallen to using that appalling modern French metric system now). A hedge of ancient yews marked the end, ten metres high, laden with their squishy dull-red berries. He pushed through the gap marked by crumbling stone pillars that used to be gateposts, making a mental note to get a gardening construct to prune the twigs. The carpet of dry needles compressed beneath his brogues as the Labradors scampered round him. It was meadowland beyond, the shaggy grass thick with daisies and buttercups. A gentle slope led down to a long still lake eight hundred metres away. He whistled softly, and threw his stick.

"Found them," North America datavised.

"Who?"

"The possessed Quinn Dexter left behind in New York. Just to make you more insufferable, you were right. He went for the Light Bringer sect."

"Ah." The Labradors found the stick, one of them clamped it in his jaw. Western Europe slapped his hands on his thighs, and the dogs stared to bound back to him. "How bad is it?"

"Not too bad, I believe. I lost the High Magus, of course. I guess he suicided. But there are several actives left. Two of them called me before the energistic effect glitched their neural nanonics. They're taking over the covens one at a time. Eight down already, including the arcology headquarters in the Leicester skyscraper."

"Numbers?"

"That's the good news. About ten possessed to each coven. The moron acolytes are actually welcoming them, and doing as they're told. Their new masters are just sitting tight, and holding some pretty gross orgies. They've made sure each coven's electronics are switched off, not that many of their units were ever interfaced with the net anyway."

"I knew it. They're moving with a purpose."

"Definite infiltration tactics. They've got their foothold, now they're waiting."

"If they're spreading to each dome, then some of them must be on the move."

"Yes, I know. And they've had it easy in all the confusion. With all those riots resulting from the vac-train shutdown there's been a lot of vandalism; that makes it tough for the AI to locate glitches."

"So when are you going to hit the covens?"

"Good question. I wanted your opinion on that. If I hit them now, then whoever's moving about will be warned and go to ground. That'll leave New York vulnerable."

Western Europe took the stick from the Labrador, and paused. "Yes, but if you wait until every coven is taken over, you'll have a lot of the bastards to deal with. Someone will inevitably get through the police cordons, and you'll be back in the same leaky boat. How many covens can you monitor in real time?"

"All of them. That's already being done. Those I have no direct access to are being watched by agents."

"Then you've got it covered. Wait until a group of possessed shows up at a new coven, then take them all out together."

"And if there's more than one group moving round?"

"I'm paranoid, but am I paranoid enough. What sort of assault were you planning?"

"GISD tactical team, with shoot to kill orders. Wipe each coven out, I don't want prisoners to interrogate. Fletcher is still cooperating with Halo's science teams."

"Given the stakes, here, I'd suggest using a gamma pulse against them first. You'll get peripheral casualties, but it'll be nothing like as bad as an SD strike. Send the tactical teams in to secure and mop up afterwards."

"All right. I can live with that."

"We might even get a vote of confidence from our illustrious colleagues."

"Not even this century's geneering can make pigs fly yet. I'll get the assault organized for three hundred hours EST."

"If you need any help, just whistle." Western Europe smiled happily, and slung the stick high into the air.

Not even B7 could block news of events inside New York from spilling out across the global net. Speculation had been hot and intense ever since the arcology's vac-trains had been shut down after the Dome One "incident." Several riots had been captured by rover reporters; two of whom had been badly injured during the coverage, adding extra spice to the sensevise. Then eleven hours later, the North American Commissioner had appeared before the press once more to announce the investigation had been completed, and confirm the incident was not caused by the possessed. It was in fact a professional assassination carried out in Grand Central Station involving a sophisticated weapons implant and a chameleon suit. Business rivals of the deceased Bud Johnson were currently being sought for questioning.

The vac-trains had been re-opened. The rioters and looters had cleared the streets. The police reinforcements had been stood down. Celebrity news presenters were given extended programmes to cover the paranoia raging across the planet. The arrival of the *Mount's Delta* appeared to have acted as the trigger for a multitude of small events that were blamed on the possessed, culminating in the Grand Central Station disturbance. And Capone's recent switch in tactics to flying infiltration attacks against Confederation planets served to exacerbate people's fears. The Confederation Navy and local SD networks seemed unable to prevent the Organization's strike flotillas. After the quarantine appeared to be preventing the spread, worlds were starting to fall again. Everyone, ran the feeling, was vulnerable.

But the lifting of the vac-train restrictions eased the tension a little, right up until 2:50 EST when they were abruptly shut again. Frustrated commuters datavised the information to the news agencies within ten seconds. New York's rover reporters, who had descended en masse into the arcology's bars after a hard day's sensationalising, were hauled back out onto the concrete canyons by their editors. Agencies which datavised information requests to the arcology's civic authority were met with blank puzzlement. Nobody had told the graveyard shift about the vac-trains. The police precinct houses were equally baffled. Even the urgent requests to in-house sources produced a blank, at least in the ten minutes that counted.

With all of the B7 supervisors on-line and observing, North America gave the order to launch the assault.

The Internal Security Directorate tactical teams had been arriving in New York ever since the vac-trains started running again. By the time the assault was launched, there were over eight hundred personnel deployed around the various sect covens. They were all armed with projectile weapons loaded with chemical or electric rounds. Complementing them were the gamma lasers. Intended for anti-terrorist interception situations, they were powerful enough to penetrate at least five metres of carbon-concrete. Such a range would allow the teams to strike at targets holed up deep inside skyscrapers and megatowers. One would usually be sufficient to eliminate an entire room full of hostiles instantaneously.

North America had ringed each coven with nine, while the Leicester skyscraper had fifteen ranged against it. The supervisor's deepest worry was that the possessed with their extended senses would discover the preparations. To try and deny them any hint, engineering mechanoids had been used throughout the day to unpack and install the gamma lasers in surrounding buildings. Give-away human supervision had been kept to an absolute minimum. As well as the gamma lasers, North America had the exits and service tunnels rigged to electrify anyone who scuttled down them. That was the most dangerous aspect of the work, but again mechanoids with New York's civic service emblem on their sides trundled along modifying wires and cables without drawing questions or interest.

The tactical teams had assembled several blocks away to avoid attention. North America started to move them forward simultaneously with closing down the vac-trains. He also closed down all road traffic and metro transit carriages inside the arcology, and sealed the domes from each other; an aspect the news agencies didn't realize until a lot later. According to every asset and functional bug infiltrated into the covens, neither the possessed nor the acolytes were aware of the preparations. They didn't even know the tactical teams were advancing.

The gamma ray lasers fired at 2:55 EST. The fifteen beams transfixing the Leicester skyscraper swept through the lower eight stories which made up the sect's headquarters. They used a scan pattern, switching between vertical and horizontal to cover every cubic centimetre. When the beams were aimed right through the core of the skyscraper, the energy was absorbed by the structure, while furnishings and composite walls ignited instantly under the intense radiation barrage. Thick, radiant orange lines were scratched across the carbon-concrete support pillars and floors as the beams traversed the building. The air was superheated, dissolving into its component atoms. Windows detonated outward from the appalling pressure, showering the street below with daggers of glass.

Fire sprinklers burst into life, only for their water to vaporise first into steam then clouds of ions. Glaring blue and violet streamers jetted out of the smashed windows, and fountained up the skyscraper's elevator shafts. Ruptured air-conditioning ducts provided secondary routes for the heatstorm to pervade the building. The entire lower floors were engulfed in a dazzling fireball.

Human bodies caught within the flexing three-dimensional mesh of beams burst apart from the terrible energy input. Their water content exploded into steam as the carbon combusted. When the beams reached the outer sections of the skyscraper, they were powerful enough to pierce clean though the walls. Surrounding skyscrapers were strafed with the radiation, resulting in vast tracts of damage. Then the sharp spires of ions exhaled by the Leicester played across their outer walls, igniting dozens of ordinary fires.

The gamma ray lasers switched off. The night was filled with the roar of flames and the screams of those being burnt alive. There was enough light thrown out from the fires to light the entire district. Unharmed residents of the nearby buildings lucky enough to live on the lower floors rushed onto the street; while those higher up could only stare out helplessly as the flames took hold. The images they relayed to the news agencies, which were distributed across the planet in real-time, showed the GISD tactical teams marching down every approach road to the Leicester. Against the raging orange flames, their heat-proof flexarmour suits appeared as matt-black silhouettes. Weapons with long snouts were cradled casually on their arms as they walked into the conflagration with astounding nonchalance.

Three times, figures rushed out of the skyscraper's main entrance doors, making their bid for freedom. They were like fire monsters, flames shooting from every part of their bloated figures. The tactical team guns spat short pulses of turquoise flame with quiet efficiency, and the fiery creatures crumpled to burn unhindered on the wide sidewalk.

It was those scenes of perfunctory extermination which finally convinced the world that the possessed had somehow penetrated the titanic defences of the Halo. The political fallout was considerable. A motion of impeachment was put before the Govcentral Grand Senate, condemning the President for not informing the senatorial defence committee in advance. The President, who could hardly publicly admit to knowing nothing about the situation, fired the chiefs of GISD Bureaus 1 through 4, for gross insubordination and overreaching their authority. The GISD's New York chief was charged with reckless homicide, and put under immediate arrest. Such machinations went almost unnoticed by the public, who were fed a continual stream of updates of the on-the-ground aftermath by the news agencies.

Once the tactical teams had confirmed that there were no possessed left alive in any of the sect covens, they withdrew. Only then were the emergency services allowed in. It took ten hours for the fire department mechanoids to extinguish the last fires. Paramedic crews followed them through the burnt out floors. The arcology hospitals were swamped by casualties. Preliminary insurance damage estimates ran into hundred of millions of G-dollars. Dome One's mayor, in conjunction with the other fourteen mayors of the arcology, instigated an official day of mourning, and opened a bereavement fund.

Officially, one thousand two hundred and thirty-three people died in the assault against the New York possessed; nearly half as a result of being hit by gamma radiation. The rest were either burned or asphyxiated. Over nine thousand needed hospital treatment for minor burns, shock, and other injuries. Double that number lost their homes; with several hundred businesses forced to try and relocate. The vac-trains in and out of New York remained closed.

"Well?" North Pacific asked. It was five hours after the tactical teams had finished their sweep of the covens, and B7 had reconvened to hear the genuine results.

"We got a hundred and eight possessed, that's the best estimate I can provide. There wasn't a hell of a lot left for the forensic crew to analyse after the gamma lasers finished."

"I'm more interested in the ones you didn't eliminate."

"Eight of the electrocution traps we rigged along possible escape routes were triggered. The teams pulled eleven corpses out of various ducts and service tunnels."

"Quit stalling!" South America said. "Did any of them get out?"

"Probably, yes. Forensics thinks maybe three or four people got past the electrocution traps. There's no way of telling if they were possessed or not, but it would take one inhumanly tough mother to survive what we threw at them."

"Shit! We're right back where we started. You're going to have to initiate this kind of slaughter operation each time

they regroup. Only now they don't have any convenient
sects to flee back to."

"Well this time, I'm going to insist on keeping New
York's vac-trains shut," North Pacific said. "We can't let
them get out of New York."

"I quite agree," Western Europe said.

"Only because you can't risk another vote."

"There's no need to get personal. We remain on top of the
situation."

"Really? Where's Dexter, then?"

"When the time comes, I will eliminate him."

"You're so full of shit."

The K5 star had a catalogue number, but that was all. Only
three planets were in orbit around it, two of them smaller
than Mars, and a gas giant fifty-thousand kilometres in diameter. Undistinguished in astronomical terms, it lay forty-
one light-years outside the loose boundary of space claimed
by the Confederation. There had been a single scoutship
visit in 2530, which quickly established its worthlessness.
As far as official records were concerned, that was the first
and last time humans had visited the barren system. Certainly the Navy never bothered with it; their patrols were
stretched thinly enough as it was searching for illegal activity within the Confederation and through the stars fringing
the boundary. Although the surrounding wreath of stars was
an obvious locations for illegal operations (and several
highly dubious independent colony ventures), forty-one
light-years was just too far away to justify the expense of
regular inspection flights.

Such a safeguard made it ideal for the black cartel. Their
antimatter station orbited five million kilometres from the
star's surface, a closeness which stretched human materials
science to its limit. The radiation, heat, particle, and mag-

netic forces it encountered were appalling. An approaching
ship would see it as a simple black disk sailing across the
incandescent solar glare. Sixty kilometres in diameter, it
cast a significant cone-shaped umbra behind it; a zone insulated from the star's heat, the one place where hell's proverbial snowflake might just have survived. The surface facing
the star was a radial concertina array of solid state cells ab-
sorbing the incredible blast of heat and converting it directly into electricity. At the back they glowed a gentle
pink, utilizing their own shade to radiate the immense thermal load away into space. In total, the array was capable of
generating over one and a half terawatts of electricity.

The antimatter production system itself was housed in a
cluster of boxy silver-white industrial modules right in the
centre of the array. The mundane method of churning out
antimatter was essentially unchanged since the late Twentieth Century; although the levels of scale and efficiency had
risen considerably since the first few experimental antiprotons had been manufactured in high-energy physics labora-
tories. Production requires individual protons to be
accelerated until their energy becomes greater than a giga-
electron-volt, at which point each one has more energy in
its motion than its mass. Once that state has been achieved,
they are collided with heavy nuclei, resulting in a spray of
elementary particles that includes antiprotons, antielec-
trons, and antineutrons. These are then separated, collected,
cooled, and merged into antihydrogen. But it is that initial
proton acceleration stage which absorbs the phenomenal
amount of electricity produced by the solar array in its entirety.

The whole operation was overseen by a crew of twenty-
five technicians, stationed in a large, heavily-shielded rotating carbotanium wheel that floated deep inside the array's
umbra. They had now been joined by eight members of the

Organization to keep them in line. Taking over the station had been absurdly easy.

Because the black cartel took the elementary precaution of installing its own modified neural nanonics in everyone who knew of the station's location, there could only ever be two kinds of visitor: the Confederation Navy on a search and destroy mission, or a legitimate buyer. The arrival of Capone's lieutenants came as a severe shock to the crew. The few hand weapons available were utterly useless against the possessed; their only other option was to kamikaze. Once the Organization's terms and conditions had been laid on the line, that was postponed indefinitely. The same kind of uneasy stand-off balance between need and fear that had claimed New California settled across the station.

After supplying the first Organization convoy with every gram of antimatter held in storage, the station had been operating a full production schedule ever since, attempting to cope with Capone's desperate demands for more. Starships came from New California every five or six days for new supplies.

Admiral Saldana's squadron made no attempt at stealth or subtlety when it jumped into the system, emerging twenty-five million kilometres from the star. Navy starships always had a tremendous advantage against the stations they hunted. Deep inside the star's gravity field, there could be no quick escape for the station's crew. Defensive weapons were almost useless. Not even antimatter propulsion and warheads could produce their usual overwhelming advantage; in such proximity to the star, combat wasp sensors were almost blind.

Standard procedure for the Navy starships was to launch a volley of kinetic projectiles in a retrograde orbit. It was a tactic that would quickly exhaust the station's stock of drones, leaving them with beam weapons alone. Against a swarm of ten thousand harpoons, their chances of vaporizing every one before it hit was effectively nil. That was assuming the station sensors were even capable of locating the incoming missiles to begin with. In most cases the hellish solar environment completely masked their approach. And the Navy vessels would never issue a warning, the station might never know of their presence until the first missile struck.

All the attackers needed was a single strike against the production system. Any large explosion would inevitably set off a chain reaction within the antimatter storage chambers. The resulting blast could at times be five or six times the size of a planet-buster, depending on how much of the substance was in store.

This time it was going to have to be a little different. Meredith Saldana waited impatiently on the *Arikara*'s bridge while the voidhawks deployed around the star in small swallow manoeuvres. Each of them launched a pack of small sensor satellites to scan the huge magnetosphere in which they were all immersed.

Locating the station was easy enough, though the sheer volume of space they were searching through made it a lengthy task. The *Arikara*'s tactical situation computer started to receive datavises from the satellites, blending them into a harmonized picture of the whole near-solar environment. When the information was complete, it showed the star as a dark sphere surrounded with graded shells of pale gold translucence. The innermost seethed like a restless sea as the magnetic forces fluxed and coiled, above that they smoothed out considerably.

A tiny knot of twisted copper light was sliding along a circular, five million kilometre orbit. The squadron's comparative position was fed in, and Meredith began issuing orders. Because of their vulnerability to the star's heat and radiation, the voidhawks maintained their orbits, enabling them to keep watch for any emerging starships. The Adamist starships flew inward. Eight frigates were vectored into high inclination orbits, a location from which they could launch a kinetic assault on the station. The remaining starships, including *Lady Macbeth*, aligned themselves on an interception course and accelerated along it at three gees.

When they were three million kilometres away, the *Arikara* pointed her main communication dish on the station, and boosted the signal to full strength.

"This communiqué is directed to the station commander," Meredith datavised. "This is the Confederation Navy ship *Arikara*. Your illegal operation is now terminated. Ordinarily, you would be executed for your actions in producing antimatter, but I have been authorized to offer you transport to a Confederation penal colony planet if you cooperate with us. This offer is also applicable to any possessed who are resident at the station. I will require your answer within one hour. Failure to respond will be taken as a refusal to cooperate, and you will be destroyed." He datavised the flight computer to repeat the message, and the squadron waited.

It took ten minutes for a static-heavy signal to emerge from the station. "This is Renko, I'm the guy Al left in charge around here. And I'm telling you to get the fuck out of here before we smear your pansy asses across the sun. You got that clear, pal?"

Meredith glanced across the bridge's acceleration couches to where Lieutenant Grese was lying. The intelligence officer managed to grin, despite the gee force.

"That's a break," he said. "We got Capone's source, no matter what the outcome."

"I believe the Navy is due a break," Meredith said. "Especially our section of it."

"He'll have to stop those bloody infiltration flights now. His fleet will need all the antimatter they've got left to defend New California."

"Indeed." Meredith was almost cheerful when he ordered the computer to datavise a reply to the station. "Consult your crew, Renko. You're in the losing position here. All we have to do is launch a single missile once an hour. You have to fire five each time just to make sure it doesn't get through. And we're in no hurry, we can keep shooting at you for a couple of weeks if we have to. There's just no way you can win. Now are you going to accept my offer, or do you want to go back to the beyond?"

"Nice try, but you don't mean it. Not for us, leastways. I know you guys, you'll slam us into zero-tau the second we put our hands up."

"For what it's worth, I am Rear Admiral Meredith Saldana, and you have my word that you will be given passage to an uninhabited world capable of supporting human life. Consider your alternatives. If we attack the station, you go back to the beyond, if I'm lying about transporting you to a planet you go back. But there is the very strong possibility that I'm not lying. Can you really reject that hope?"

Along with the rest of the squadron, Joshua had to wait another twenty minutes for the answer. Eventually, Renko agreed to surrender. "Looks like we're on," Joshua said. They were accelerating hard again, preventing him from smiling. But there was no hiding the rise of excitement in his labouring voice.

"Christ, the other side of the nebula," Liol marvelled. "What's the furthest anyone's ever been before?"

"A voidhawk scout group travelled six hundred and eighty light years from Earth in 2570," Samuel replied. "Their course took them directly galactic north, not in this direction."

"I missed that," Ashly complained. "Was there anything interesting out there?"

Samuel closed his eyes, questioning the voidhawks racing along their orbits millions of kilometres away. "Nothing unusual, or dramatic. Stars with possible terracompatible planets, stars without. No sentient xenoc species."

"The Meridian fleet went further," Beaulieu said.

"Only according to legend," Dahybi countered. "Nobody knows where they vanished to. In any case, that was centuries ago."

"Logically then, they must have gone a long way if no one's ever found them."

"Found the wreckage, more like."

"Such pessimism is bad for you."

"Really? Hey, Monica." Dahybi lifted one hand to make an appeal before the acceleration made him lower it fast again. "Do your lot know where they went? It could be important if they're waiting out there for us."

Monica stared stubbornly at the compartment's ceiling, a headache building behind her compressed eyeballs that no program could rid her of. She really hated high gees. "No," she datavised (her throat was suffering along with the rest of her), irritated she couldn't put any emphasis into her digitalized speech. Not that snapping at the crew would endear her to them, but their relentless discussions of utter trivia were starting to chafe. And she'd possibly got a month or more to go. "The ESA was in its infancy back when the Meridian fleet was launched. Even today I doubt we'd bother planting assets in with a bunch of paradise seeking fools."

"I don't want to know what's there," Joshua said. "The whole point of this mission is discovery. We're real explorers going out on a limb, first for at least a century."

"Amen to that," Ashly said.

"Where we are now is new for most people," Liol said. "Just look at that station."

"Standard industrial modules," Dahybi said. "Hardly exotic or inspiring." Liol sighed sadly.

"Okay, we're getting close to injection point," Joshua announced. "Systems review, please. How's our fuselage holding out?" The flight computer was datavising images from the localized sensors into his neural nanonics. *Lady Mac*'s thermo dump panels were fully extended, constantly rotating to present their narrow edges towards the raging star. Their flat surfaces were glowing radiant pink as they expelled the ship's accumulated heat. He'd programmed a permanent spin into their vector, a fifteen minute cycle to ensure the immense thermal input was distributed evenly across the fuselage. Fine manoeuvring was slow, given the additional reaction mass they were carrying, but the balance compensation programs were handling it providing he kept tweaking them.

"No hot spots yet," Sarha reported. "That extra layer of nulltherm foam is doing its job quite well. But it is picking up a lot of particle radiation, far more than we're used to. We'll have to watch that."

"Should lose it when we get behind the shield," Liol said. "Won't be long now."

"See?" Beaulieu told Dahybi. "You are surrounded by optimists."

The squadron's interception ships were sliding into an orbital slot three thousand kilometres behind the antimatter station. If Renko did decide to switch off the storage confinement chambers, the radiation impact from the blast would tax the shielding on the starships to an uncomfortable degree. But they should be safe. So far, he appeared to be cooperating.

Commander Kroeber was handling the negotiation on how the hand over was to be accomplished. The civil starship already docked at the station was to depart with everyone on board. It would rendezvous with one of the squadron's marine cruisers. The possessed would disembark and proceed directly to the brig under heavily armed guard where they would stay for the duration of the flight. Any indication of them using their energistic power, for whatever reason, would result in a forty-thousand-volt current being run through the brig. The cruiser, accompanied by two frigates, would fly directly to an uninhabited terra-compatible world (currently in the middle of an ice age) where the possessed would be shot down to the tropical-zone surface in one-way descent capsules, with a supply of survival equipment. There would be no further contact with that planet by the Confederation, apart from delivering any further possessed with whom similar exceptional deals had been made.

Kroeber's other offer, that they help the CNIS with its research into energistic power until such time as a solution was found for possession, was summarily rejected.

Once the possessed were safely incarcerated, another marine cruiser would rendezvous with the starship and take off the station's regular crew ready to transport them to a penal planet. Complete control of the station systems was to be handed over to the Navy technical crew, who would remote test their new domain. If total access was confirmed, a third marine cruiser would dock with the station itself, and perform a boarding and securement manoeuvre.

After some haggling, mainly over the contents of the survival equipment they could take with them down to the icy planet, Renko agreed to the arrangement. *Lady Macbeth*'s crew watched the proceedings through the sensors. The hand-over went remarkably smoothly, taking just less than a day. A datavise from the first marine cruiser showed the possessed, dressed defiantly in double-breasted suits, laughing brashly as they were led into the brig. The station crew looked frankly relieved that they'd escaped with exile. They datavised over their access codes without a qualm.

"You may proceed to docking, Captain Calvert," Admiral Saldana datavised. "Lieutenant Grese informs me we are now in full command of the station. There is enough anti-matter in storage for your requirements."

"Thank you, sir," Joshua replied. He triggered the fusion drives. The simple course over to the station had been plotted for hours. Accelerate, flip, and decelerate. They were already inside the station's umbra and commencing final rendezvous manoeuvres when the Organization's convoy arrived.

"Eleven of them, sir," Lieutenant Rhoecus said. "Confirmed emergence twenty-three million miles out from the star, eighty-nine million miles from the station."

"Threat assessment?" the admiral enquired. How typical, he thought, that something should come along to thwart the squadron's mission once again.

"Minimal." The Edenist liaison officer appeared almost happy. "*Ilex* and *Oenone* report there are five hellhawks and six frigates in the enemy formation. Their hellhawks can't swallow down to us, not at this altitude. And even if we assume the frigates are armed with antimatter combat wasps, they would take hours to reach us accelerating continually. I've never heard of a combat wasp that has an hour's fuel in it."

"They'd have to be custom built," Grese said. "Which is

unlikely for Capone. And even if they do exist, we can
evade them easily at this distance."

"Then Calvert can carry on?" the admiral asked.

"Yes, sir."

"Very well. Kroeber, inform the *Lady Macbeth* to proceed as planned. I'd appreciate it if the good captain didn't
dawdle."

"Aye, sir."

Meredith reviewed the tactical display. The *Oenone* was
barely five million kilometres from the cluster of Organization ships. "Lieutenant Rhoecus, voidhawks to group together twenty-five million kilometres directly above the
antimatter station. I don't want them isolated, it might give
the hellhawks ideas. Commander Kroeber, move the rest of
the squadron up to rendezvous with the voidhawks, the
frigates in high inclination orbits to meet us there. Two of
our frigates to remain with the station until *Lady Macbeth*
has completed her fuelling. Once they're at a safe distance,
the station is to be destroyed."

"Aye, sir."

Meredith instructed the tactical computer to compile options. The resulting assessment just about matched his own
opinion. The two sides were evenly matched. He had more
ships, but the Organization was expected to be armed with
antimatter combat wasps. And if he did order the squadron
up to intercept, it would take hours to reach them. The Organization ships could simply jump away, leaving only the
voidhawks to pursue them—who would then be outgunned.

Effectively, it was a stand-off. Neither side could do
much to affect the other.

Yet I cannot allow them to go unchallenged, Meredith
thought, it sets a bad precedent. "Lieutenant Grese? What
do we know about the non-possessed crews on board Orga-

nization ships? Just how much of a hold does Capone have on them?"

"According to the debriefings we've conducted; they all have family being held captive on Monterey. Capone is very careful about who is given command authority over antimatter. So far it's a strategy that's worked for him. A number of crews on ordinary Organization starships have managed to eliminate their possessed officers and desert. But we've never had any indication of attempted mutiny on ships equipped with antimatter."

"Pity," Meredith grunted as the *Arikara* started to accelerate up to the rendezvous with the voidhawks. "Nevertheless, I'll issue them with the same ultimatum as the station was given. Who knows, the opportunity to capitulate might be enough to spark a small rebellion."

Etchells listened to the admiral's message as it was beamed out to the convoy. Slippery, vague promises of pardons and safe passage. None of it was relevant to him.

We repeat Edenism's offer to you, the voidhawks added. *You may transfer your host's personality over to us, and we will provide your nutrient fluid. All we ask in return is your help in finding a satisfactory resolution.*

Don't any of you bastards even answer, Etchells warned his fellow hellhawks. *They're running scared. They wouldn't make that kind of offer unless they were absolutely desperate.*

He could sense the uncertainty rumbling through their affinity bond. But none of them were brave enough to challenge him directly. Satisfied he'd kept them in line for now, Etchells asked the convoy's commander what he intended to do. *Withdraw,* came the answer, *there's nothing else we can do.*

Etchells wasn't so sure. The Navy hadn't destroyed the station. And that went against everything the Confederation stood for. There had to be a phenomenal reason for such a change of policy. We should stay, he told the convoy commander. They cannot engage us for hours yet. That gives us a chance to discover what they are doing here. If they're going to start using antimatter against us, Capone should be told. Reluctantly, the commander agreed. However, he did order the Adamist ships to accelerate towards a new jump coordinate that would take them back to New California, leaving the hellhawks to observe the station.

It was difficult to look directly into that dangerous glare. Etchells's sensor blisters began to suffer from glare spots, similar to purple after-images which plagued human eyes. He started to roll lazily, flicking his ebony wingtips to bank against the gusts of solar particles, switching the view between the blisters. Even then, concentrating on that tiny speck millions of kilometres away was inordinately stressful. A headache began to pound away inside his stolen neurone structure.

None of the electronic sensors loaded into his cargo cradles were any use, they were mostly military systems, intended for close defence work. And his distortion field couldn't reach that far. The visual spectrum provided him with the greatest coverage. He could see the Navy's Adamist ships accelerating up out of the star's enormous gravity field, little sparks of light, actually brighter than the photosphere.

After half an hour, three more fusion drives ignited around the station. Two of them started to follow the Navy squadron. The last one took a different course altogether; curving round the star's southern hemisphere on a very high inclination trajectory.

Etchells opened his beak wide to let out an imaginary

warble of success. Whatever it was doing, the lone starship had to be the reason behind the Navy's strange action. He issued a flurry of instructions to the other hellhawks. Despite his brute-boy attitude, Etchells had actually absorbed a great deal of information from his host's mentality. The facade of toughness was a deliberate ploy—always let your opponents believe you're dumber than you are. Becoming Kiera's most dependable and trusted hellhawk made sure she wouldn't risk him on those mad seeding flights, or any other dangerous actions. Convoy escort was about the safest duty to pull.

Wasted decades spent bumming round pointless mercenary actions across the Confederation, had taught him to disguise his true potential. Survival was dependant on intelligence and the lowest cunning, not worthy courage. And he knew for sure that surviving his current situation was going to take a great deal of ingenuity. Like Rocio in the *Mindori*, he had come to admire his new bitek form, finding it utterly superior to a human body. Quite how he could hang on to it was a question he'd been unable to resolve. There would be no place for hellhawks in the place where possessed took their planets to escape the universe, he was sure. And the Confederation would never rest until they'd solved the problem of how to evict souls back into the beyond permanently.

So he bided his time, keeping a giant yellowing eye open for some opportunity to save his own ass, and to hell with his comrades.

The Navy's unconventional behaviour might just be the break he'd been looking for.

When the last three starships were thirty thousand kilometres from the antimatter station, it exploded with a violence which outshone the prominence arching through the chromosphere below. As if in acknowledgement of their defeat, the hellhawks swallowed away.

The voidhawks analysed the way their distortion fields applied energy against space-time to open a wormhole interstice. All five hellhawks appeared to be heading back to New California.

They have left the remaining frigates extremely vulnerable, Auster, *Ilex*'s captain, reported to Rhoecus. *What are the admiral's orders?*

Hold your position. If you attack they will just jump clear. We could harass them all the way home, but there is no tactical advantage to be gained from that. Our objective has been accomplished.

Very well.

Syrinx.

Yes, Rhoecus.

Oenone is cleared to rendezvous with the Lady Macbeth. The admiral wishes you both bon voyage.

Thank you.

Etchells didn't believe the voidhawks would follow, certainly not instantaneously. The hellhawks all swallowed ten light-years clear of the star, then swallowed again three seconds later. Unless a voidhawk had been with them to observe the second swallow, there was no way of knowing where they'd gone.

Four of them carried on back to New California. Etchells returned directly to the star, emerging twenty-two million kilometres above its south pole. With the voidhawks all clustered together in their twenty-five million kilometre equatorial orbit, there was no way they could detect his wormhole terminus opening and closing. His position was ideal to observe the Navy starships flying out from their low orbit. His sensor blisters didn't have to focus against the overwhelming white blaze. Even his headache started to fade.

He did keep a cursory watch on the Navy ships as they rose out of the gravity field, but it was the lone ship heading south that interested him. When it was twenty million kilometres from the star its drive cut out. Etchells projected its course, and started to check his captured spatial memories. Given its jump alignment there were twenty possible Confederation systems it could be heading for. And one other. Hesperi-LN. The Tyrathca planet.

12

Fifteen minutes Courtney sat up at the bar waiting. Four men offered to buy her a drink. Not as many as usual, but then there were very few civilians abroad these days. Even the Blue Orchid was suffering from the scare stories flashing across the net, its numbers well down. Normally it would be jammed at this time of night; the kind of not-quite-sleazy club where lower-middle management could hang out after work and not have to worry if someone else from the company saw them. Courtney had been in a lot worse than this. The doormen didn't give her any hassle even though her ass was virtually hanging out of her cocktail dress. Courtney liked the dress, cool black fabric with straps on the front to hold her titties up high, and more cross straps down the cut out back. It made her look hot, without being too cheap.

Banneth said she looked good wearing it. Best thing the sect had ever done putting her in this dress; she'd never been so fem before. And it worked. There hadn't been a night she didn't deliver for them. Sometimes twice. It was a good gig, taking the men back to one of the student rent hotels where the sect had squeezed the manager. Then as soon as the mark's pants were off, Billy-Joe, Rav, and Julie would storm in and kick the shit out of him. Then when he was unconscious Billy-Joe took a recording of his biolectric pattern and emptied his credit disk.

She'd done much the same thing for all of the last three years since her brother introduced her to the Light Bringer. Except to start with she'd attracted paedopervs, who mostly had their own dens to take her to, or just hauled her into the dark end of a downtown alley. Those days, it had been Quinn Dexter who pimped her. In a strange way, she'd always been safer with him in charge. No matter how big a sicko the man was, Quinn had always arrived in time.

Now she was fifteen, and too big to pass for a juvenile any more. Banneth had switched the hormones she took. This new batch didn't prevent her breasts from growing; quite the opposite, they promoted development. She'd still got a skinny frame, but now she was huge with it. In the last nine months her targets had changed completely. It wasn't the pervs who wanted her now, just the losers. Courtney reckoned she'd come out of the alteration okay. Big tits was one of the mildest modifications Banneth made to sect members.

The fifth man to ask if she was all right and did her glass need freshening had what it took. Overweight, round face with perspiration on his brow, hair slicked back with gel, a good suit cleaned too often. His expression was hesitant, ready for a slapdown. Courtney drained her glass, and held it out to him, smiling. "Thanks."

He was too fat to dance. That was a shame, she liked to dance. So that meant having to sit and listen to about an hour of bitching—his boss, his family, his apartment; how none of it was going right for him. The drone was so she'd see he was a real genuine guy who'd had a couple of bad breaks lately, hoping for the sympathy fuck.

She made all the right sounds at the right places. After this time working the arcology's clubs she could probably have

filled in his life story just by looking at him. Proof of that:
she never chose wrong. They always had a loaded disk. After
the hour and three drinks he had enough nerve to make his
innocent suggestion. To his utter surprise the answer was a
demure smile and a hurried nod.

It wasn't far to the student hall, which was good. Courtney
didn't like getting into a cab with them; there was too much
chance Billy-Joe might lose her. She didn't look to see if the
three sect members were trailing after her down the street.
They'd be there. This was a real smooth routine now.

Twice though, she thought she heard footsteps following.
Real distinctive, regular thuds of someone using a lot of
metal in their heels. Dumb idea, there was a whole bunch of
people walking along the street. When she did snatch a look,
there was no one she could see that looked like a cop. Just a
bunch of civilians scurrying around, making out their stupid
lives meant something.

The cops were her only worry. Even given the fact less
than a quarter of the targets reported the assault and theft, it
wouldn't take an AI to spot the pattern. But Banneth would
know if there was any sort of operation being mounted. Banneth knew fucking everything going down in Edmonton. It
was scary, sometimes. Courtney knew some of the sect's
acolytes didn't really believe in God's Brother, they were just
too shit-scared of Banneth to step out of line.

"This is it," she told the man. They'd stopped outside the
worn entrance of a two-century-old skyscraper. A couple of
genuine students were sitting on the steps, taking charges
from a power inhaler. They looked at Courtney with glazed
uncaring eyes. She pulled the man past and into the foyer.

In the elevator he made his first tentative move. Going for
a kiss, which she let him have. Tongue straight down her
throat. He didn't have time for anything more; the room
they'd hijacked for the night was on the third floor. Its real

owner lost somewhere in the arcology as the black stimulant program shorted out her neurones.

"What are you studying?" he asked once they were inside.

That caught her short. She didn't have a story in place for that—he wasn't supposed to care. Nothing to help here, either. The room was a usual student's jumble, badly lit with fleks and clothes everywhere, a decades-old desktop block on the one shabby table. Courtney didn't read too good, so she couldn't tell what the tiny print on the flek cases said.

Easy way out. She shoved the shoulder straps down, and let her tits bobble free. That shut him up. It took him about thirty seconds to push her down on the bed, then one hand was up her skirt while the other was squeezing a tit crudely. She groaned like it was good, hoping Billy-Joe and the others got a fucking move on. Sometimes the shits waited and let the man fuck her. Watching the show through some sensor or peep hole, getting off on the scene and laughing quietly. They always claimed it looked less like a set-up if they came in afterwards. Banneth laughed too if she complained.

The man's hand was tugging at her panties. Mouth all hot and slobbering over a nipple. Courtney tried not to grimace. Then she was shivering, as if the conditioning duct had suddenly dumped a shitload of ice into the air.

He gave out a single puzzled grunt, pulling his head back. They looked at each other for an instant, both equally bewildered. Then a white hand clamped over his gelled hair, yanking his head away from her. He yelled in shock and pain as he was pulled off her and flung over the room. His flabby body hit the opposite wall with a loud crash, and crumpled to the floor. A figure in a black robe was standing at the side of the bed, blank hood tipped down towards Courtney. She drew in a breath to shriek, knowing fucking well this wasn't Billy-Joe or any of the others.

"Don't," the figure warned. The darkness inside the hood withered to reveal the face.

"Quinn!" Courtney squeaked. A smile flicked her lips. "Quinn? God's Brother, where the fuck did you come from? I thought you got transported."

"Long story. Tell you in a minute." He turned and went over to the quivering man, grabbed his head and pulled back viciously. The man's throat was exposed along its entire length, skin stretched tight.

"Quinn, what are you . . . Urrgh!" Courtney watched in a kind of interested shock as a couple of sharp fangs slid out of Quinn's mouth. He winked at her as he lowered his head to bite the man's neck. She could see Quinn's Adam's apple bobbing as he sucked down the blood, several drops dribbled past his lips. The man was whimpering in high-pitched terror. "Oh fuck, Quinn, that's disgusting."

Quinn stood up, grinning, and wiped the back of his hand across his mouth, smearing the blood. "No it's not. It's the final conquest. Blood is the best food a human can have. Think on it; every nutrient you need all nicely refined and cooked ready for you. It's your right to take it from the followers of the false lord you defeat. Use them to make you strong, Courtney, replenish your body." He looked down at the fat man who was clutching the neck wound desperately. Blood was pouring through his fingers.

Courtney giggled at the feeble gurgling sounds the man was making. "You've changed."

"So have you."

"Yeah!" She cupped her tits and lifted them. "Grew these for a start. Good, aren't they?"

"God's Brother, Courtney, you are a total slut."

She straightened a leg and dangled her shoe from one toe. "I like what I am, Quinn. That's my serpent beast, remember? Dignity is a weakness, along with all the other crap on the middle-class wish list."

"You did listen to the sermons."

"Sure did."

"So how's Banneth?"

"Same, I guess."

"Not for long. I'm back now." He held out his hands, making simple gestures. The room began to change; the walls darkening, furniture turning to matt black cast iron. Manacles appeared on the metal railings at the head of the bed.

Courtney looked round wildly at the manifestations, and scrambled backwards over the crumpled duvet, cramming herself into a corner away from Quinn. "Shit, you're a possessed!"

"Not me," he said softly. "I possess. I am the one God's Brother has chosen as his Messiah. This power the returning souls have depends on the force of their will. And nobody believes in themselves more than me. That's how I regained control of my body, through the belief He gave me in myself. Now I'm stronger than a hundred of those snivelling lost dickheads."

Courtney unfolded her legs and peered forward. "It is you, isn't it. I mean, like really you. You've got your own body and everything."

"You never were very quick, were you? But then, it was never your brain the sect wanted."

"Were you in New York?" she asked in quiet admiration. "I saw all the fighting on the AV. The police killed skyscrapers full of people they were so scared."

"I was there a while back. I was also in Paris, Bombay, and Johannesburg, which the police don't know about yet. Then I gave in to myself, and came home."

"I'm glad you did." Courtney bounded off the bed, and

flung her arms round him, licking from his ear to his mouth. "Welcome back."

"You will follow me now, not Banneth."

"Yes." She slid her tongue over the tacky blood congealing on his chin, tasting its salt.

"You will obey."

"Of course."

Quinn focused on the thought currents in her brain, and knew she was telling the truth. Not that he'd expected anything else from Courtney. He opened the door and let the other three in. Billy-Joe and Rav he knew from before; it hadn't taken much to cow them. Five people standing made the little student room badly cramped, their breath helping to heat it up. Fast breathing which came from nerves and excitement. They were all eager to see what Quinn would do next.

"I came back to Earth so I could bring down the Night," he told them. "You'll play a big part in that, and so will the possessed. I'm going to leave a nest of you in every arcology. But Edmonton is special for me, because Banneth's here."

"What you going to do to her?" Billy-Joe asked.

Quinn patted the slender youth's wire-like arm. "The worst I can imagine," he said. "And I've spent a lot of time imagining."

Billy-Joe's mouth split into an oafish grin. "All right!"

Quinn looked down at the fat man. He was gasping like a fish. Blood had formed an enormous puddle on the scuffed tile floor. "You're dying," Quinn said cheerfully. "Only one way to save you now." Fields of energy shifted at his command, exterting a specific pressure against reality. The cries of the souls began to filter out of the beyond. "Courtney, hurt him."

She shrugged to the others, and kicked the man hard in the crotch. He shivered, eyes bugging before the lids began to flutter uncontrollably. An extra squirt of blood pumped out of the wound.

"And again," Quinn directed mildly. In his mind, he was dictating terms to the lost souls who clustered round the weak rent between universes. Hearing the pleas of those who claimed they were worthy. Making his judgement.

Courtney did as she was told, watching in fascination as a soul (a real dead person!) took control of the wretched man. The wound closed up. He started hissing in consternation. Tiny rivulets of lightning slithered along the creases of his blood-soaked suit fabric.

"Give him something to drink," Quinn said.

Billy-Joe and Julie ransacked the cupboards for cans of soda, popping them and handing them down to the grateful possessed.

"It'll take you a while to replace that much blood," Quinn said. "Just lie there and take it easy for a while. Enjoy the show."

"Yes, Quinn," the possessed muttered weakly. He managed to roll onto his back, the effort coming close to making him faint.

The iron manacles snapped open loudly. Courtney took one look at them, and glanced back enquiringly at Quinn. His robe was already dissolving. "You know how to use them," he told her.

She wriggled out of her dress and bent over the bed, placing her wrists in the manacles. They hinged shut, and locked.

Ilex emerged above Avon, radiating profound satisfaction (and considerable hunger). Every Edenist within Trafalgar picked up the emotional emission, and smiled simultaneously at the results Auster was declaring. Lalwani immediately declassified the strike mission against the antimatter station, and the navy press office started relaying the information to the system's news companies. Everything happened so fast that the First Admiral's staff only just managed to officially brief Jeeta Anwar before the Presidential office staff received it off the communication net.

The voidhawk's easy two-gee flight to the naval base's docking ledges was considerably more relaxed than the last time it had burst out of wormhole close to Trafalgar. General affinity hummed with a great many ironic comments pointing this out to its triumphant crew.

Two hours after *Ilex*'s arrival, Captain Auster was escorted into the First Admiral's office by Lieutenant Keaton, the newest member of the admiral's staff. Samual Aleksandrovich greeted the Edenist captain warmly, and gestured to the sunken reception area. Lalwani and Kolhammer joined them on the leather couches, while the lieutenant served tea and coffee. As he was moving round with their china cups, the bulky AV cylinder at the apex of the ceiling shimmered brightly, and the images of President Haaker and Jeeta Anwar materialized in the reception area.

"My congratulations to the Navy, Admirals, Captain," Haaker said. "The destruction of an antimatter station at this time is particularly satisfying."

"Capone's antimatter station, Mr President," Kolhammer said significantly. "That's a considerable bonus."

"Essentially he will be unable to mount any more of these damnable infiltration missions against Confederation planets, let alone attempt another full scale invasion along the lines of Arnstat," Samual said. "That means he's been neutered. We shall now resume our harassment campaign, and enhance it considerably this time around. That should wear down the hellhawks, and deplete his stock of antimatter in defence. Given its unstable social base, we expect the Organization to collapse within a few weeks, two months at the most."

"Unless he pulls another rabbit out of his capacious fedora," Haaker said. "I don't mean to disparage your action against the antimatter station, Samual, but in Allah's name, it was a long time coming. Possibly too long. According the latest report I have, nearly a third of Kerry's population is now possessed, and it's only a question of time until the remainder are taken over. On top of that, we know of eleven other worlds Capone has successfully managed to infiltrate. That means we'll lose them, too, you know that as well as I do. And there will no doubt be starships currently en route, telling us of more infiltrations launched before the station was destroyed. Your pardon, but this success rings hollow indeed."

"What else would you have us do?"

"You know very well. How is Dr Gilmore's project progressing?"

"Slowly, as Mae Ortlieb has been telling you."

"Yes, yes." Haaker waved an irritable hand. "Well keep me informed of any further developments. Preferably ahead of the media."

"Yes, Mr President."

The image of the President and his aide vanished.

"Ungrateful old git," Kolhammer muttered.

"It's understandable," Lalwani said. "The Assembly is beginning to resemble a zoo these days. The ambassadors have realized that for once their magnificent speeches alone aren't going to solve this crisis. They're shouting for action, though of course they don't name a specific."

"The antimatter ought to relieve a lot of pressure on the Navy," Kolhammer said. "We should be able to press individual governments to maintain the civil starflight quarantine."

"There's still a lot of reticence there," Lalwani said. "The smaller, more distant asteroids are suffering badly from the economic situation. To them, the conflict is a remote one. That justifies their clandestine flights."

"It's only remote until their selfish idiocy allows a possessed into their settlement," Kolhammer snapped.

"We're making progress on identifying the principal offenders," Lalwani said. "I'm getting a lot of cooperation from other intelligence agencies. Once we've confirmed the offence, the problem then becomes a diplomatic one."

"And everything goes pear-shaped," Kolhammer said. "Bloody lawyers."

Samual put his tea cup down on the central rosewood table, and turned directly to Auster. "You were with Meredith's squadron at Jupiter, I believe?"

"Yes, Admiral," Auster said.

"Good. I accessed all of your report on the antimatter station mission while the *Ilex* was docking; and I'd like you to tell me directly why Consensus is sending two ships to the other side of the Orion nebula. *Specifically* why one of them is the *Lady Macbeth*. I simply could not make it plainer that I expected Captain Calvert and that despicable Mzu woman to remain in Tranquillity, and incommunicado."

The voidhawk captain gave a slight bow, his face respectfully grave. Despite all the mental bolstering which came from unity with other Edenists, and his link with *Ilex*, facing the displeased First Admiral was quite an ordeal. "I assure you, Consensus regards the Alchemist problem with the utmost seriousness. However, there was some on-the-ground information available which required reassessing your proscription."

Samual Aleksandrovich settled back in the leather upholstery, knowing he shouldn't enjoy playing the inflexible tyrant. Sometimes it was hard to resist. "Go on."

"The Lord of Ruin has discovered that the Tyrathca religion may have some physical basis."

"I didn't know they had a religion," Kolhammer said. His neural nanonics was running a search through various encyclopaedia files.

"That was also something of a revelation," Auster said. "But they do, and their God would appear to be some kind of powerful artefact. They believe it capable of saving them from human possessed."

"So Consensus sent a pair of starships to investigate," Samual said.

"Yes. Given the distance involved, the only kind of Adamist ship that can get there is one that has an antimatter drive."

"And such a flight also removes Calvert and Mzu from any possible contact with the possessed. How very convenient."

"Consensus considered it so, Admiral."

Samual laughed dryly. "Lagrange Calvert meeting a real live god. What a spectacle. We should be able to see that clash of egos from this side of the nebula." Lalwani and Auster grinned in unison.

"Well, there are slimmer straws to grasp, I suppose," Samual said. "Thank you, Captain, and my congratulations to *Ilex* on a successful mission."

The Edenist stood, and bowed formally. "Admiral." Lieutenant Keaton went with him to the door.

Although he considered it faintly ridiculous, if not rude, Samual waited until Auster was outside before speaking to the other two admirals. Privacy was a hard concept for him to abandon; and he knew Lalwani kept their secure sessions confidential as a matter of courtesy. "A god?" he asked Lalwani.

"I don't know anything about it," she said. "But Consensus wouldn't embark on such a course unless it had a degree of confidence in the result."

"Very well," Samual said. "I'd like to receive a complete briefing from the Jovian Consensus, please."

"I'll see that we're updated."

"Until we are, we won't be including biblical salvation in our strategic planning sessions."

"Yes, Admiral."

"That just leaves us with our last current problem," Samual said. "Mortonridge."

"Could have told you that was a waste of time," Kolhammer retorted.

"You did. Frequently. As did I. But it is first and foremost a politically motivated campaign. However, we cannot ignore the fact it isn't going quite to plan. This latest development is unnerving to say the least. It also looks as though our marine battalions are going to be tied up there for a longer than we originally estimated."

"Longer! Ha," Kolhammer said in disgust. "Have you accessed any of those sensevises? God, that mud. The whole bloody Liberation is completely stalled."

"It hasn't stalled, they're just encountering more problems than they anticipated," Lalwani said.

Kolhammer chuckled, and raised his coffee cup in salute. "I've always been a massive admirer of the Edenist ability to understate. But I think defining a chunk of land fifteen kilometres across that suddenly takes flight and wanders off into another dimension as a little problem is possibly the best example yet."

"I never said *little*."

"Ketton's disappearance isn't my main concern," Samual said. He received the surprised look which the others gave him with calm humour. "I was thinking about the medical difficulties de-possession is leaving us with. So far we've been fortunate the news companies have been playing it down, but that won't last. People will eventually wake up to the implications if we're ever successful in returning planets like Lalonde and Norfolk to this universe. There's been a commendable effort by the Kingdom's allies to assist with fresh medical supplies, but the number of cancer-related deaths is still rising." He clicked his fingers at Keaton, who was hovering near the samovar.

"Sir." The lieutenant stepped forward. "Trafalgar's medical office have been examining the consequences of de-possession. Frankly, we're lucky Mortonridge doesn't have a larger population. The Kingdom and its allies should just manage to provide enough nanonic packages to cope with two million cancer patients. Though we're dubious about correct application; the number of experienced doctors is a critical factor. However, we estimate that an entire planet of de-possessed, with an average population of three quarters of a billion, would essentially exhaust the entire Confederation's medical facilities. To our knowledge, the possessed have so far taken over eighteen planets, with several hundred additional asteroid settlements. And we expect the planets Capone has infiltrated will soon join them. Ultimately, we could be dealing with as many as thirty planetary populations, possibly more than that."

"Shit," Kolhammer exclaimed. He gave the youngish lieutenant a very worried frown. "So what's going to happen if we get them all back?"

"Given the development level of cancers we've seen on the de-possessed so far, there will be a rapid and extremely high mortality rate among their respective populations if they remain untreated."

"That's a very clinical way of putting it, lieutenant."

"Yes, sir. You should also consider, the possessing souls are either unaware of the damage they're inflicting on their hosts, or are unable to cure it. Their energistic power is capa-

ble of repairing physical injury, but we haven't seen them
deal with this kind of illness yet. It may be they can't."

"What are you getting at?" Lalwani asked.

"Unless the biochemical environment on the planets
they've removed from this universe is radically different in
some way, then the possessed will all be suffering like this no
matter where they are. In which case, if they don't start to effect some kind of treatment, their host bodies might die."

Lalwani's shock was so vehement she couldn't prevent
some of it from leaking into the general affinity band.
Edenists in the asteroid automatically opened their minds,
proffering emotional support.

Reluctantly, Lalwani refused. "Thirty planetary populations?" she demanded, incredulous. She glanced from the
lieutenant to the First Admiral. "You knew?"

"I accessed the report this morning," Samual admitted.
"And I haven't informed the President, yet. Let him get on
top of the Assembly again before we break news like this."

"Dear God," Kolhammer muttered. "If we pull them back
from wherever they've gone, we won't be able to save them.
And if we leave them alone, they won't survive either." He
gave Keaton a look that was almost a plea. "Did the medical
office come up with *any* ideas?"

"Yes sir, they had two."

"Finally! Someone with some bloody initiative. What are
they?"

"The first is fairly simple. We broadcast a warning to the
possessed groups we know are still remaining in this universe. Ask them to stop trying to change the appearance of
their host bodies. It should appeal to their own self interest."

"If they don't just ignore it as propaganda," Lalwani said.
"By the time a tumour actually becomes noticeable, it's usually too late for primitive medical treatments."

"Nonetheless, we will definitely proceed with that option," Samual said.

"And the second?" Kolhammer asked.

"We formally request the Kiint ambassador for help."

Kolhammer let out a disgusted breath. "Ha! Those bastards won't help us. They've already made that clear enough."

"Um, sir?" Keaton said. He gave the First Admiral a glance, and received a nod of permission. "They said they wouldn't provide us with a solution to possession. In this case, we're just asking them for material aid. We know they have a more sophisticated technology than ours; human companies have been buying upgrades and improvements for a variety of products ever since we made contact with them. And now with the Tranquillity incident we know they haven't abandoned their manufacturing base as thoroughly as they claimed. They may well be able to produce the kind of medical systems we require in the quantities we'll need. After all, we'll only have a use for them if we solve the possession problem for ourselves. If the Kiint are as sympathetic as they assure us they are, then there is a good chance they'll say yes."

"Excellent analysis," Lalwani said. "We can't possibly ignore the option."

"I wasn't planning to," Samual said. "In fact, I've already requested a personal meeting with Ambassador Roulor. I'll sound him out about the prospect."

"Good move," Kolhammer said. "That's a commendable advisory team your medical office put together, Samual."

It felt strange to be back. Quinn stalked through the ghost realm, observing the sect's Edmonton headquarters. His peculiar, hazy perception of the real world from this shadowed existence might account for his new interpretation of the familiar rooms and corridors. Or it could just be time and a very different attitude to when he was last here.

This had been home for many years. A place of refuge and of terror. Now it was just a cluster of gloomy chambers, devoid of any appeal or memories. The routine of the place hadn't changed, though it was slowing down, much to the fury of the senior acolytes. He smiled as they shouted and brutalized the juniors. His fault. His word was spreading.

All of Edmonton would soon be aware of his arrival. So far he'd taken over eight covens, and was ready to visit the remainder. Those that had fallen under his thrall were now actively pursuing the will of God's Brother. Over the last few days he'd been dispatching several small groups to attack strategic sections of the arcology's infrastructure. Generators, water stations, transport junctions; they'd all been damaged to some degree. It was primitive stuff, chemical explosives concocted from formulae loaded into public databanks centuries ago by freethink anarchists, the files replicated so many times they were impossible to erase. On Quinn's orders, the possessed would only supervise the missions, never actually venturing to the target themselves. That was left to the faithful: useful, disposable, imbeciles. He couldn't risk the authorities discovering a possessed in Edmonton, not yet. So for now such destruction would appear to be the work of a breakaway sect faction, fanatics who had split away from their High Magus. That way they would appear as sympathisers to the anarchist groups in Paris, Bombay, and Johannesburg that were also bombing and terrorizing their fellow citizens.

The authorities would discover who was behind it eventually. But by then he would have established enough cells of possessed to bring about the Night.

Quinn arrived at the temple, and surveyed it slowly. A tall chamber, more elaborate than the smaller covens. Pictures of

violent depravity alternated with runes and pentagons along
the walls. A wreath of small yellow flames flickered weakly
around the tarnished inverted cross on the altar. He was
drawn to the big slab as the memories of this place finally returned. There was the pain of his initiation, then more pain as
he was used for further ceremonies. Each time, Banneth had
smiled down serenely; a dark angel ministering to his body.
Drugs and packages were applied, and an obscene variety of
pleasure would be combined with his agony. Banneth's laugh
would wrap around him, taking on the power of an indecent
caress. She/he/it, that terrible androgynous multi-sexed monster, conditioned him to respond to the torment in the way
that generated the most enjoyment—for it. Eventually the
two extremes of sensation merged, becoming one.

A triumph, Banneth had declared. The creation of the perfect sect mentality. Birthing the serpent beast.

Quinn gave the altar a curious look, seeing himself bound
to it, skin glistening with sweat and blood as he screamed.
The pain and the images were real enough, but he couldn't
recall anything before then. It was as if Banneth had created
his flesh at the same time as his mind.

"Quinn? Is that you, Quinn?"

Quinn turned slowly, squinting at the ghostly figure sitting
on the front pew. A face he was sure he knew, belonging to
this place but from a long time ago. The figure stood, a
hunched up adolescent in a torn leather jacket and dirty jeans.
He was pitifully insubstantial. "It is you, isn't it? You remember me, Quinn. It's me. It's Erhard."

"Erhard?" He wasn't sure.

"Damn, we shovelled shit together for long enough. You
must remember."

"Yes. Yes, I do." A novice acolyte who'd joined the sect
around the same time as Quinn. One who lacked the strength
to survive such a brotherhood. The same relentless battery of

ordeals and punishments which had fortified Quinn had crushed Erhard. It had culminated in a ritual in the temple, one which Banneth had never intended Erhard to live through. There was rape and torture and drugs and burrowing parasites of Banneth's devising; atrocities performed to the hot chants and wild laughter of the entire headquarters coven. Erhard's final pleas had risen above their chorus, a thin wail of ultimate terror. Then Banneth had brought the jewelled sacrificial knife down in a fast slash.

The joy Quinn had experienced that day was almost orgasmic. He'd been the one tasked to carry the knife for Banneth.

"It's not fair, Quinn. I don't belong here. I hate this place. I hate the sect."

"You never did feed your serpent beast," Quinn said contemptuously. "Now look at you. You're as much a loser now as you ever were."

"It's not fair!" Erhard cried. "I didn't know what the sect was like, not really. And then they killed me. You killed me, Quinn. You were one of them."

"You deserved it."

"Fuck you. I was nineteen. I had my life, and you took it away, you and that psycho fruit Banneth. I want to kill Banneth. I swore I would."

"No!" Quinn stormed. Erhard quailed, cowering back from the command. "Banneth does not die," Quinn said. "Not ever. Banneth belongs to me."

The ghost edged forward, holding out a hand as though feeling the warmth thrown out by a fire. "What are you?"

Quinn giggled quietly. "I don't know. But God's Brother has shown me what I've got to do." He walked out of the temple, leaving the ghost behind.

Three figures were marching along the corridor, one of them with desperate reluctance. Quinn recognized him.

Acolyte Kilian. They'd met a few days ago. All three frowned as they passed their invisible watcher, puzzled by why they suddenly felt so chilly.

Quinn followed them. He knew where they were going, he'd taken this route himself enough times. Soon he would see it again: Banneth. That's all it would be, this time. Just a look, a reminder of that face. Nothing fast would happen to Banneth. It had taught Quinn well, in that respect. The most delectable punishments were the slowest ones. And when Night came, it would be in tandem with eternity.

Darkness has arrived. Even when the acolytes didn't whisper it, the phrase hung in the smoky air of the sect's Edmonton headquarters. A threat more menacing than any sadism the sergeant acolytes could bestow.

Banneth knew what that meant. The AV projectors were broadcasting a constant coverage of the New York situation, which the entire headquarters coven was obsessed by. The arcology's continuing isolation. Rumours of free possessed. Portents wherever you looked. And many of the coven looked very hard indeed.

Their work suffered as a consequence. Income from the scams and hustling were well down in every coven across town. Even she, the High Magus, couldn't rack up much enthusiasm. What chance did the lesser maguses have?

When she did rage at the sergeant acolytes, they just shuffled their feet and muttered dourly that there was little point continuing their old activities. Our time has come, they said, God's Brother is returning to Earth. Who cares about knocking off dumb-ass civilians. Given the creed of the Light Bringer sect, it wasn't an attitude she could effectively argue against. The irony of the situation didn't escape her.

All she could do was keep listening to the rap from the street, hunting out clues. It was a thin source of information,

especially now. Like a great many of Earth's arcologies, Edmonton was slowly shutting down as it spewed out its own
fear. Commercial districts were reporting increasing absen-
teeism. People were calling in sick, taking holidays. Parks
and arcades were nearly deserted. Football, baseball, ice
hockey, and other game fixtures were played to small
crowds. Parents kept their kids away from day clubs. For the
first time in living memory it was always possible to get a
seat on metro buses and tube carriages.

The vac-trains weren't shut. Keeping the routes open was
a bravado example of Govcentral confidence, intended to reassure people that Earth was still safe. Passenger numbers
were under thirty per cent. Nobody wanted to do anything
that brought them into contact with other people, especially
strangers. Civic utility companies had to threaten employees
with lawsuits to keep essential services going. Government
workers were intimidated with the prospect of disciplinary
proceedings if they didn't perform their duties as normal, especially the police. The mayors were desperate to provide the
image of normality in the hope the public would follow their
cue. A desperation that was taking on increasingly surreal dimensions in the face of such stubborn public reticence.

Banneth kept dispatching sect members to wander through
the eternal half light gullies that were downtown streets,
hunting any sign of a score. The usual broken inhabitants
shuffling along the sidewalks would huddle away from them
in sealed-up doorways, sniffing suspiciously as they strutted
past. Cop cars swished along silently, creating whirlpools of
silvery wrapping foils; the only vehicles moving at ground
level. They slowed as they drew level with the sect gangs,
examining the sullen faces through misty armoured glass before tooting the siren and accelerating away. Forcing them to
go out was a mostly futile exercise. But she had persevered

while the world slowly choked on its own paranoia. And now it seemed as though she'd got lucky.

Acolyte Kilian was doing his level best not to shake as the sergeant acolytes hurriedly left him alone in Banneth's inner sanctum. The chamber was buried at the centre of the skyscraper which the sect used as its headquarters. As with the Light Bringer covens the world over, the original layout of rooms and corridors had been corroded and corrupted as acolytes burrowed their way through walls and ducts like human maggots. Haphazard partitions were hammered and cemented up behind them, creating a bizarre onion-layer topology of chambers and cells that protected the core. Banneth had dwelt there for nearly three and a half decades without once ever venturing out. There was no need now, everything necessary to make her life enjoyable was brought to her.

Unlike several High Maguses she was aware of, Banneth didn't go in for ostentation. Her senior acolytes were permitted whatever decadent luxuries they could steal and bribe for themselves. But they lived several floors above her, decorating their apartments with expensive hedonistic amenities, and harems of beautiful youths and freakish supplicants. She indulged herself on somewhat different levels.

When Kilian started to look round, he found he was in a place that was way beyond the worst-case scenarios that acolytes whispered among themselves. Banneth's sanctum was an experimental surgery. Its mainstay was a broad bench desk with high-capacity processor blocks and shiny new medical equipment. Three stainless steel tables were lined up in the middle of the floor, with discreet leather restraint straps placed strategically round the edges. Life support canisters were arranged around the walls, like huge glass pillars. Aquarium-style lighting caps shone brightly on their contents. Kilian really wished they didn't, the things inside were enough to make him shit his pants. People, in a few of them. Suspended by a white silk web in some thick clear fluid, tubes going into their mouths and noses (those that still had mouths and noses). Always with their eyes open, looking about. Acolytes he remembered from not so long back; with new appendages grafted on; others with parts removed, their incisions raw and open to reveal the missing organs. Then there were the less than human creatures, made worse by having very human pieces attached. Clusters of organs bound together by a plexus of naked pumping veins. Animals, game cats and gorillas with the tops of their skull removed, and no brain left inside. Pride of place on the wall above the work desk was taken by an ancient oil painting of a young woman in a dress with a stiff bodice and long skirt.

Although Kilian had never been in the sanctum before, it was the place where everyone came eventually, either for boosting or punishment. Banneth performed both types of operation herself. Now he stood as still as his trembling limbs would allow as the High Magus walked briskly across the floor to him.

Banneth's face had a male jawline, a blunt protuberant blade of bone. But that was the only masculine feature, the eyes and mouth were soft, very feminine. A shaggy pelt of straw-blonde hair completed the enigma. Kilian glanced nervously at the white shirt Banneth wore. Everyone said the High Magus got aroused at the sight of fear. If her nips were jutting, then she was in the feminine stage of her cycle.

Dark circles of skin were definitely tenting the cotton. Kilian wondered if it really made a difference. Banneth was a hermaphrodite—by design, so rumour said. She looked as if she was about twenty, either as a male or a female; though age was an easy enough cosmetic adaptation. Nobody knew how old she really was, nor even how long she had been

High Magus. In fact, legend and rumour were all that existed about her past. Questions were discouraged.

"Thank you for coming to see me," Banneth said. Her hand stroked Kilian's cheek, the cool skin of her knuckles drifting gently along his cheekbone. An appraisal by a gifted sculptor, finding his exact form. He quivered at the touch. Pink eyes with feline irises blinked in amusement at his reaction.

"Nervous, Kilian?"

"I don't know what I've done, High Magus."

"That's true. But then a barely human grunt like you doesn't know much of anything. Do you? Well don't worry yourself too much. Actually, you've been quite useful to me."

"I have?"

"Amazingly, yes. And as you know, I always reward the devout."

"Yes, High Magus."

"What can I do for you now, I wonder?" She began to circle the apprehensive acolyte, grinning boyishly. "You're how old now? Twenty-five, isn't it? So I ask myself what does a nice young boy your age always want. And the answer's a much bigger cock, of course. That's pretty standard. I can do that, you know. I can snip off that pitiful rat-sized cock you've got now, and replace it with something much better. A cock that's as long as your forearm and as hard as steel. You would like me to do that, wouldn't you?"

"Please, High Magus," Kilian whimpered.

"Was that a 'yes please,' Kilian?"

"I . . . I just want to help you. However I can."

She blew him a kiss, still prowling her circuit around him. "Good boy. I asked to see you because I'd like to know something. Do you believe in the teachings of the Light Bringer?"

Trick question, Kilian screamed silently. If I say no, she'll do whatever she wants as punishment; if I say yes she'll ask me to prove it through endurance. "All of it High Magus, every word. I've found my serpent beast."

"An excellent answer, Kilian. Now tell me this: do you welcome the coming darkness?"

"Yes, High Magus."

"Really? And how do you know it's coming?"

Kilian risked a glance over his shoulder, trying to follow the High Magus as she circled round him. But she was directly behind him now, and the only thing he really noticed was the way the eyes of the acolytes in the life support containers were tracking her movements. "The possessed are here. He sent them, our Lord. They're going to bring His Night to the whole world."

"So everyone says. The whole arcology is talking about nothing else. Indeed the whole planet has little else to say. But how do you know? You, Kilian?"

Banneth stopped in front of him, lips curved in a sympathetic, expectant smile.

I'll have to tell the truth, Kilian realized in horror. But I don't know if that's what she wants to hear. Fuck! Oh God's Brother, what'll she do to me if it's wrong? What will she turn me into?

"Cat got your tongue?" Banneth asked coyly. The smile hardened slightly, becoming less playful. Her glance flicked to one of the life support canisters containing a puma. "Of course, I can give the cat your tongue, Kilian. But what would I fit in its place? What would be appropriate do you think? I have so much material I don't really need any more. Some of it is long past its sell-by date. Ever felt flesh that's started to decay, Kilian? Necromorphology is a somewhat acquired taste. You never know, though, you might get to like it in time."

"I saw one!" Kilian shouted. "Oh fuck, I saw one. I'm sorry High Magus, I didn't tell my sergeant acolyte, I . . ."

She kissed his ear lobe, shocking him into silence. "I understand," she whispered. "Really I do. To understand the way people think, you must first understand the way they work. And I've made the workings of the human body my special area of study for a long time. Physiology begets psychology, you might say. Mightn't you, Kilian?"

Kilian *hated* it when the High Magus talked all this weird big-word shit. He never knew how to answer. None of the acolytes did, not even the seniors.

"It—I saw him in the Vegreville dome coven's chapel," Kilian said. He knew for sure now that the High Magus wanted to hear about the possessed. Maybe this would get him off the hook.

Banneth stopped her pacing, standing directly in front of the woeful acolyte. There were no more smiles left on her androgynous face. "You didn't tell your sergeant acolyte because you thought you'd wind up in deep shit. Because if the possessed are real, then the sect hierarchy that you've so devoutly been kissing ass to for the last six years will be replaced by them. By telling everyone what you'd seen you would in effect be spreading sedition; though I doubt you would be able to rationalize it quite like that. To you it was simple instinct. Your serpent beast looks after you, it puts you first. As indeed it should, in that respect you've been loyal to yourself and God's Brother. Of course, you couldn't resist telling a few people, could you? You should have known better, Kilian. You know I reward acolytes who betray their friends to me."

"Yes, High Magus," Kilian mumbled.

"Well I'm glad that's settled then. Unfortunately the golden rule of the sect is that I am to be told everything. I and I alone decide what is important, and what is not." Banneth walked over to one of the stainless steel tables, and tapped a finger on it. "Come over here, Kilian. Lie down for me."

"*Please,* High Magus."

"Now."

If he'd thought running would have done him the slightest good, he would have run. Actually, he even had the wild thought that he could attack Banneth. The High Magus was physically weaker. But that idea was resolved in a second by a simple clash of wills. He was foolish enough to glance at her pink eyes.

"That's a very bad thought," Banneth said. "I don't like that at all."

Kilian walked over to the table, taking the smallest steps possible. In the faintly violet light thrown out by the life support containers, he could see the scuffed silvery surface was sprinkled with small black flecks of dried blood.

"Remove your clothes first," Banneth told him. "They get in the way of what I want to do."

The initiation ceremonies, the punishments, the degradations he'd undergone for the sect—none of them prepared him for this. Simple pain he could endure. It was soon over, making him all the meaner, stronger for it. Each time his serpent beast would come away slightly larger, more dominant. None of that helped him now. Each garment he took off was another portion of himself sacrificed to her.

"In times gone by, they used to say the punishment should fit the crime," Banneth said. Kilian removed his jeans, and she smiled thinly at his flabby legs. "An appropriate sentiment, I always thought. But now I believe it's more fitting that the body part should fit the crime."

"Yes," Kilian said thickly. That, he needed no explanation for. He had spent hour after hour mucking out the pigs as part of his duty. All the acolytes had to do it. All of them detested the filthy squealing animals. It was an insidious reminder of what fate ultimately greeted Edmonton sect members, no matter you were being disciplined or rewarded.

Banneth's herd were special; developed centuries ago when geneering was in its infancy. They were originally designed to provide organs for human transplants. A worthy project, to help people with worn out hearts or failed kidneys. Pig organs were the same size as human ones, and it was the first practical success of the geneticists to modify porcine cells so they didn't trigger a rejection by their new host's immune system. For a few brief years at the start of the Twenty-first Century the concept had flourished. Then medical science, genetics, and prosthetic technology had raced on ahead. Humanized pigs were abandoned and forgotten by everyone except medical historians and a few curious zoologists. Then Banneth had come across the obscure file in some long-outdated medical text.

She had identified and traced descendants of the original pigs, and began breeding them anew. Modern genetic improvements had been sequenced in, strengthening the bloodline. It was the raw primitiveness of the concept which appealed to her. The sect's use of modern technology was so much at odds with its basic gospel. Pigs and old fashioned surgery were an ideal alternative.

When an acolyte needed boosting, it wasn't AT muscle she implanted to enhance the original human ones. Like the rest of the porcine organs, the muscles wouldn't cause rejection. Pig skin, too, was thicker, sturdier, than its human counterpart. Lately, she had begun to experiment with other animals. Grafted monkey feet turned an acolyte into an efficient acrobat, useful for gaining entry to upper-storey floors. Lighter leg bones allowed them to outrun police mechanoids. Given time and research subjects, she knew she could match any modification used by cosmoniks and the combat boosted mercenaries so prevalent out there among the Confederation worlds.

The surgical techniques could also be used to rectify behaviour. For example, an attempt to run away from the sect would be easily curtailed by replacing legs with trotters. In Kilian's case, Banneth hadn't finalized on an effective lesson. Though she did favour extending and re-routing his colon into the back of his throat, so that every time he wanted to shit, he'd have to do it through his mouth. The extra tubing would give him a very thick neck. A nice irony, that. It would match his thick head.

When he was naked, she made him lie face down on the table, then used the straps to secure him in place. Creative punishment would have to wait. Since he blurted confirmation about a possessed, only one thing had mattered to her. She smeared a big dollop of depilatory cream on the back of his neck, and squirted it off with a cold water hose. It left his skin clean and bare, ready to receive the nanonic implant package.

Kilian wasn't permitted an anaesthetic or sedative. He groaned and whimpered continually as the personality debrief filaments pierced his brain; their brutal intrusion sparking cascades of aberrant nerve impulses that sent spasms rippling along his limbs. Banneth sat on one of the desk bench stools, sipping a chilled, hand-mixed martini as she supervised the procedure, occasionally datavising new instructions into the package. After nearly two hours, the first erratic impulses started to flood back along the invading filaments. Banneth brought her AI on-line to analyse and interpret the confusing deluge of impulses. Visualizations that were nothing more than randomized detonations of colour slowly calmed as the AI began to marshal Kilian's synaptic discharges into ordered patterns. Once his thought patterns had been catalogued and correlated with his neural structure, his entire consciousness became controllable. The filaments could simply inject new impulses into the synaptic clefts they'd penetrated, superseding any natural thoughts he had.

Kilian was thinking about his family, such as it was. Mother and two younger half-brothers, living in a couple of dingy rooms in a downtown skyscraper over in the Edson dome. Years ago, now. Mother surviving on a Govcentral parent work-pay scheme; never there during the day. All he had was the constant noise, the shouted arguments, fights, music, footsteps, metroline traffic. At the time he'd wanted nothing more than to escape. A bad decision.

"Why?" Banneth asked.

Kilian flinched. He was sprawled on the sagging bed-settee by the window, looking fondly at all the familiar old objects that had occupied his brief childhood.

Now Banneth stood by the doorway, regarding him contemptuously. She was brighter than anything else in the room, more colourful.

"Why?" she repeated.

A spherical wave of pressure contracted through Kilian's skull, squeezing his thoughts out through his mouth in an unstoppable stream. "Because I left this to join the sect. And I wish I hadn't. I hate my life, I fucking hate it. And now I'm on your table and you're gonna turn me into a dog, or chop my dick off and give it to someone else to fuck me with. Some kind of crap like that. And it's not fair. I didn't do anything wrong. I've always done whatever the sect asked. You can't do this to me. You can't, please God. You're not human. Everybody knows that. You're a fucking weirdo freak cannibal."

"Now there's gratitude. But who gives a fuck about this pathetic little comfort regression you're in. I want when you saw the possessed."

The pressure wave found another part of Kilian's mind to

crush. He screamed out loud as memories erupted like fountains of acid behind his eyes. Home was coldly scorched out of existence, huge great sections of it peeling away like rotten flesh to reveal the Vegreville chapel's temple. Kilian had been there three days back, sent by his sergeant acolyte to pick up some package. He didn't know what was in it, just that: "Banneth wants it fast."

The coven was different than before. There was a new atmosphere percolating through the dark nest of rooms. They regarded him as a joke. His urgency to complete the assignment, to get the package and leave, made them snigger and scoff. Every time he asked them to be quicker they delighted in delaying. They were like frisky kids at a day club who'd found a new boy to taunt and bully.

Eventually he'd been taken to the temple where the senior acolyte told him the package was waiting. The chamber walls were made from thousands of slim metal reinforcement rods welded together, the inside of a bird's nest woven out of iron twigs. Its altar was a tight-packed mound of rusty spikes, their tips all shaved down to the same length. Twin flames rose out of the bristling metal at each end, long yellow tongues dancing in the gloom. Pews were composite roof planks nailed to a variety of pedestals. The sect's usual runes were still on the walls, but they were barely visible now. A single new slogan had been sprayed everywhere: Night is coming. On the walls, on the ceiling, even on the floor.

Kilian was made to enter alone, his little escort clustering round the thick doors behind him, giggling wildly. His annoyance dropped away as he walked quietly towards the altar, replaced by growing nervousness. Three figures waited silently for him behind the altar, clad in black robes. These garments had none of the embellishments or pentagons usually favoured by senior sect members. If anything it made them appear even more menacing than usual. Their faces were almost lost inside the large hoods. Flickering yellow beams from the candles would occasionally reveal a feature within two of the hoods: bloodshot eyes, hooked nose, wide mouth. The third hood could have been empty for all that Kilian saw. Even when he reached the altar, he could see nothing inside that night-like cavity of fabric.

"The High Magus sent me," he stammered. "You've got a package for me, yeah?"

"We certainly have," a voice said from somewhere inside that veiled hood.

Alert now, Banneth ran the voice through an analysis program, though ordinary memories of voices were a notoriously unreliable source for such verification programs. Nonetheless, it showed remarkable similarities to recordings of Dexter's voice. Kilian trembled as the hidden figure slowly held out an arm. He was almost expecting a pistol nozzle to poke out at him. But it was just a snow-white hand that emerged from the voluminous sleeve. A small plastic container was dropped carelessly on the altar.

"Our gift to Banneth. I hope it is useful."

Kilian scooped it up hurriedly. "Right. Thanks." All he wanted now was to get the fuck out of here. These guys were almost as creepy as Banneth.

"I am interested that the High Magus is carrying on as though nothing is happening."

Kilian didn't know how to answer. He cast a glance over his shoulder, wondering if he should make a dash for it. Not that he could ever get out of the chapel unless he was allowed to. "Well, you know how it is." He shrugged lamely.

"I certainly do."

"Sure. I'd better get this back to her, then."

"The Night will fall."

"I know."

"Excellent. Then you will join us when the time comes."

"My serpent beast is strong."

A head emerged from the hood, the darkness slowly washing backwards to expose more and more features. "You'll need to be," Quinn said.

Banneth froze the image. No doubt about it. Skin as white as snow, eyes infinite pools of black—though that could have just been emotion-aggravated exaggeration. But it was Quinn.

The High Magus smiled thinly as the image hung in her mind. The fierceness which had once so animated him, and fascinated her, was gone. If anything, he looked rather stressed out. Crinkled lines radiated away from the corner of his eyes, while those sweet cheeks were rather sadly sunken.

She concentrated her thoughts, focusing on the personality traits of one individual. **Dexter's in Edmonton. One of my acolytes encountered him three days ago.**

Ah. Thank you, Western Europe replied.

The ten ships in the convoy emerged above New California, immediately confirming who they were to Monterey's SD command. For once the hellhawks accompanying the frigates hadn't raced on ahead. They were quite content to let the convoy commander break the bad news they were carrying.

Where's Etchells? Hudson Proctor asked once the four remaining hellhawks had checked in.

We don't know, Pran Soo said. **He left us to scout round the antimatter station. He will probably emerge soon.**

You're sure the Confederation destroyed it?

The frigates were still there. They saw it explode.

A fact which the convoy commander was very reluctantly confirming to Monterey. The news was all around the asteroid within thirty minutes, and down to New California's cities in roughly the same timescale. Word spread across the countryside within a couple of days. The more remote Organization asteroid settlements lagged behind by anything up to a week. The last ones actually got to hear about it from Confederation propaganda broadcasts—who damn well weren't going to miss that opportunity.

This time Emmet Mordden refused point blank to be the one who had to tell Al. So the senior lieutenants decided that Leroy Octavius should be awarded the honour. Their unspoken thought as they watched him waddle out of the asteroid's command centre was that he too would chicken out and simply tell Jezzibella.

A lifetime juggling temperamental personalities in the entertainment industry had left Leroy wise to that option. Knowing that Jezzibella was the only guarantee his own precious body and soul remained intact, he simply couldn't permit her position to be weakened. Leroy gathered his courage and went down to the Nixon Suite. Walking along the last few metres to the doors his legs had more than a little wobble of apprehension. The two gangsters on guard outside picked up on his emotions, and studiously avoided eye contact as they opened the big doors for him.

Al and Jezzibella were having breakfast in the conservatory, a long, narrow room with one wall made entirely of curving enhanced sapphire, which gave a slightly bluish tint to the view of the planet and stars outside. The opposite wall had vanished beneath a trelliswork of flowering vines. Pillars running the length of the conservatory were transparent tubes, aquariums filled with the strange and beautiful fish from a dozen worlds.

There was only one table, a broad wrought iron oval, with a vase of orange lilies in the middle. Al and Jezzibella sat next to each other, dressed in identical aquamarine bathrobes, and casually munching toast. Libby was limping round the table, pouring coffee.

Al looked up as Leroy came in. His welcoming smile faded when he caught the anxiety in the obese manager's mind. "You don't look too happy, Leroy, my boy. What's eating you?" Jezzibella glanced up from her history book.

Leroy took a breath and plunged in. "I have some news. It's not good."

"Okay, Leroy, I ain't gonna bite you because those wiseasses dumped a shitty job on you. What the fuck's happened?"

"That last convoy we sent to the antimatter station just made it back. Thing is, the Navy was there waiting for them. They blew it up, Al. We're not going to get any more antimatter, not ever."

"Jesus H Christ!" Al's fist thumped the table, bouncing the crockery. Three slim scars throbbed white on his cheek. "How the hell did they find out? Ain't *nothing* we do more careful than sending the convoy to the station. Did the last lot get followed?"

"I don't know, Al. The frigates'll dock in another ninety minutes; maybe the captains'll tell us more."

"They'd fucking better." Al's fists clenched. He stared at the starfield outside the conservatory.

Leroy hesitated, glancing at Jezzibella. She inclined her head silently to the door. It was all the permission Leroy needed; he ducked his head at Al, and shifted himself the hell out of there as fast as his thick legs would allow. Jezzibella waited patiently, not saying anything. By now she was well used to the cycle of Al's moods.

After a minute in which he could have been frozen, Al roared: "Fuck it!" and smashed a fist down on the table again. This time it had his energistic power behind the blow. The iron bent alarmingly. Plates, jam pots, cups, and the vase went sliding down the new valley to crash together along the fold. He stood up fast as the boiling coffee splashed onto the floor with the lilies. His chair legs caught on the tiling. "FUCK!" Al spun round and kicked the chair, sending it flying into the curving sapphire window. Libby whimpered in fright, cradling the milk jug as if it alone could protect her. Jezzibella sat back, holding on to the coffee cup she'd saved. Her expression was strictly neutral.

"Goddamn motherfucking shit-eating bastards! That was *my* goddamn station. *Mine*." He put both hands under the buckled table and shoved it upwards. The entire thing went somersaulting along the conservatory. Crockery tumbled away to smash against the floor. Libby cowered as one of the heavy metal legs flashed centimetres above the bun of her grey hair. "Nobody takes my property away from me. No Body! Don't they know who the fuck they're dealing with here? I'm not some chickenshit small-time loser pirate! I am Al goddamn Capone. I've got a fleet that kicks the shit out of whole planets, for Christ's sake. Are they fucking insane? I'll blow that whole stinking pennyass navy of theirs out of the goddamn water. That knucklehead Ruski admiral is gonna get a baseball rammed so far up his ass he'll be pitching it out of his mouth."

"Space," Jezzibella said firmly.

"What?" Al whirled round and bellowed at her. "What did you fucking say to me?"

"You'll blow them out of space. Not water. We're not on Earth now, Al."

He pulled a fist back. It shook violently as he held it over her. Then he swung round and punched one of the tall aquariums. The glass shattered. Water and a shoal of long purple fish poured out of the big hole, splattering the hem of his robe.

"Shit. Goddamn." He danced backwards, trying to keep his house slippers out of the water.

Jezzibella calmly lifted her feet off the tiles as the tide swirled round her chair. Fish started wriggling frantically over the mosaic, their movements skidding them against the planters. "Did you have antimatter when you started?"

Al was watching the fish in mild perplexity; as if he couldn't quite understand where they'd come from. "What?" he demanded.

"You heard." She deliberately looked away from him, and gave Libby a gracious smile. "Go and fetch a bucket, or something, there's a dear."

"Yes, poppet," Libby said nervously. She scurried away.

"You frightened her," Jezzibella accused.

"Fuck her," Al said irritably. "What did you say about antimatter?"

"First off, we've still got tonnes of the stuff. Think how many convoys got through."

"Tonnes?"

"Alright, not tonnes, but certainly kilograms. Work it out if you don't believe me: one kilogram equals two and a fifth pounds. So the fleet and the SD network still has more than enough to wipe the floor with any Confederation Navy task force stupid enough to try its luck against New California. Then there's Kingsley Pryor. You haven't forgotten him, have you?"

Al stopped his mental arithmetic. He was actually very good at it, a hangover from the days when he was working as an accountant in Baltimore. Jez was right again, they had got a healthy stash of the superbomb material. And no he hadn't forgotten Kingsley, exactly, it was just a long time since they set him loose on his clandestine assignment. "That flaky asshole? I've written him off. Christsake, it's been too long."

"No it hasn't. He's a courier, not a missile. He'll get there eventually."

"Could be."

"Will be, and then you've won. Once the Confederation's been broken, you don't have to worry about New California being hauled back here."

"Could be," he sighed. "But we ain't going to get any more antimatter. Hell, Jez, if they send two task forces, we're up shit creek."

"They won't. Believe me. It's a political impossibility. So we're back to my original question. You didn't have antimatter when you started out, and you still managed to take over this planet. Antimatter was a beautiful bonus, Al. And you used it perfectly. You've not only got the Confederation public terrified of you, but with those infiltration flights you've weakened them physically. Twenty-five planets seeded. That's *crippled* their economies and leadership. They can't challenge you on your home ground. No way. And that's what really counts." She extended her legs, and rested her heels on one of the two remaining chairs. "We're never going to see Navy warships outside this window. Not now. You're secure, Al. You've made it clean. You've dug the moat to keep those bastards out, now concentrate on cementing what you've conquered. Don't let those moaning weaklings who claim to be your friends chip away at the Organization."

"God damn, you're beautiful." He splashed through the thin runnels of water to kiss her. She smiled up at him, and used a forefinger to tickle under his chin.

"The guys are going to go apeshit about losing the station."

"They're going to be frightened, that's all," she said. "Just show them they don't have to be, that you're in charge of the situation. They need that reassurance. They need you, Al, no one else can hold things together."

"You're right. I'll call the senior lieutenants in. Spin them some bullshit, and kick ass."

Her hand curled round the back of his neck. "It can wait an hour."

Al buckled down on his disapproval when he arrived at the Chiefs of Staff office. No point in biting people's balls off before they'd even started the meeting. It was just—he couldn't help remembering what the plush office had looked like the first time they'd used it. Tidy and gleaming, with coffee served from a silver pot into elegant china. Now, it was suffering from the general tide of crap washing through Monterey. Without mechanoids, nothing was being cleaned, let alone polished. There were plates and crumpled sachets on the table, dating back three or four meetings; cups with mould growing in the bottom. No one could be bothered to take them back to the nearest canteen.

It wasn't good. Not at all. Jez was right. He had to consolidate what he'd got. Make things function smoothly again. Like it all had at the start.

Kiera was last to arrive. That was getting to be a habit. Al couldn't work out if she was doing it to annoy him, or to make everyone take notice of her. She took her place halfway down the side of the table, between Patricia and Leroy. Al performed his own theatre by getting up again and refilling his coffee cup from the wheezing espresso machine.

"Hey, Leroy, where's Webster?" Al asked suddenly. "He should be dishing this stuff out."

The manager broke off his murmured conversation with Patricia and glanced round the office in surprise. "Kid's probably skiving off."

"Yeah? I ain't seen him about for a while. How come?" Now he thought about it, Al couldn't remember the last time the boy had been in attendance. It was goddamn typical of the sloppy way things were being run these days. No hostage was more important than Webster Pryor; he was the only person who could make Kingsley Pryor go through with the assignment.

Leroy took out his pocket block and typed quickly, summoning up staff rotas. The results made him uneasy, which everyone was very aware of. "He's down in the kitchens, I think. That was his last assignment, helping the chef. His supervisor hasn't reported back since."

Al sat down and stirred his coffee. "Silvano, where's the kid?"

The morose lieutenant's scowl deepened. "I don't fucking know."

"It's your job to fucking know. Je-zus, I put you in charge of keeping people in order, and you can't even look after a brat. You know what's riding on keeping Webster in line. He's more important than all the other hostages put together."

"Sure, Al. I'll find him."

"You'd better. Fuck me, this is goddamn typical of how slack things are getting up here." He took a sip of coffee, making sure his temper sank back. "Okay, are you guys all up to speed on what's happened with the antimatter station?" By the way everyone mumbled and avoided his eye he guessed they had. "Well don't all make out like it's the end of the world. It ain't. We just about achieved what we set out to do. Dwight, how many planets have we screwed now?"

The fleet commander flushed as everyone concentrated on him. "Seventeen confirmed infiltrations, Al. We're waiting for another two flights to get back."

"Nineteen planets." Al grinned round the lieutenants. "Plus Arnstat. Not bad. Not bad at all. We've kicked so much shit into the Navy's face they can't even see us now. And if they do try a raid . . . What'll happen, Emmet? We still got what it takes to see them off?"

"No problem, Al. The SD platforms are all armed with antimatter, along with half the fleet. The only Navy ships that'll visit New California for a rumble are the ones on a suicide mission."

"Glad to hear it. You all hear that, too?" He searched round, trying to spot any major-league dissenters with his ethereal senses as they all swore they heard and approved. There was the obvious ones; Kiera with her cool contempt, the rest were just jittery, or, like Silvano, sullen and resentful. But so far he was carrying it. "Okay, so we've done what we set out to when we walked into City Hall. We got us an entire planet, along with a haul of space factories. And the important thing is, we took out the nearest opposition. This planet is a fucking fortress now. That means we can ease up on watching our backs, and get on with running this shebang properly. Leroy, how's the food situation down on the surface?"

"Nobody's starving, Al. The farms aren't producing as much as they did before. But they are producing. I think we can get them back up to the old levels if the lieutenants on the ground applied some pressure. We need to motivate them."

"Okay. So food is something we can improve if we had the time. Mickey, your boys jiving you, or are they marching round like a bunch of krauts whenever you give the word?"

Mickey Pileggi licked at the beads of sweat that had suddenly erupted on his upper lip. "I got them under control, Al. Yeah. Sure thing."

"Mickey, you're full of crap. This whole fucking joint is going down the pan. We've been humping away at the Confederation so bad, we ain't noticed the rain coming in."

"That's what you wanted."

Al stopped in full flow, hauling back on his anger. He'd

just been getting nicely into his spiel. "Kiera, stop being such a ballbuster. I did what I had to to protect us. Ain't nobody here gonna argue with that."

"I'm not arguing, Al. I'm saying the same thing as you. We are where we are, because this is where you've brought us."

"You want to be somewhere else right now?"

"No."

"Then shut the fuck up. I'm telling you, all of you; now is when we start getting things working properly again. You gotta start keeping tabs on the soldiers under your command, else everyone's gonna finish up going AWOL like Webster. And that way, we wind up in deep shit. We gotta have things working smoothly around here again. If you don't start exerting some proper discipline then the whole Organization's gonna fall apart. And if it goes down, then we go down with it."

"Al, the Organization is set up to keep the fleet working," Kiera said.

"Hey, fucking lady Einstein, you just worked that out for yourself, or did one of the kids from the gym explain it when he was banging you?" Al chuckled loudly, encouraging the others to join in.

"I've always known it. I just wondered if you did."

Al's humour faded out. "What are you getting at?"

"The only reason we need the fleet is if New California remains in this universe."

"Aw shit, not this crap again. Don't you get it? If we leave, then the Confederation longhairs are going to be free to dream up some way of snatching us back. We have to stay here, it's the only way we can see what's coming."

"And if you see something like that coming at you, Al, what are you going to do about it? A technology powerful enough to pull a planet back from the other side of the beyond. Launch a combat wasp at it? Believe me, if the Confederation ever gets to be that powerful, then we don't stand a chance. But I don't think they'll ever learn how to do anything like that. We can do it because we've got the devil's own power charging us up. No chunk of machinery can challenge that. If we leave, then I say we're going to be a hell of a lot safer there than we are here."

There was an itch in Al's palm, running across his skin exactly where he gripped the handle of his baseball bat. He held off from making it real. Her talk about the devil being behind them made him uncomfortable. A Catholic by birth, he didn't like examining the implications of what he was now, nor why. "We ain't pinning our future on what you *think* might be right, sister," he growled. "If we want a certainty, then we stay right here."

"The Organization can be transported down to the planet," Kiera said, as if Al hadn't even spoken. "We can use the SD network to keep our power base secure until we assume control of the cities. After that, we use ground troops to enforce order. Al was right about that. There's been too much slippage allowed recently. We know we have to keep the farms and a lot of the industries going if we want any kind of decent life on the other side. It'll take a strong, positive government to achieve that. And that's us."

"We can do all that crap, and still stay here," Al said. His voice had become little more than a whisper. That worried those who had been with him the longest, though Kiera didn't seem to notice the barely concealed danger. "When I want someone else to tell me how to run my Organization, I'll let you know. Got that, baby doll? Or do I need to make it real plain for you?"

"I hear what you say, Al." The tone was amused indolence.

"That's smart of you. Now I want the rest of you guys to start doing like I've said. We need a crackdown like God's foot is stomping through the clouds. I want things up and jumping around here. Put the word out to your soldiers, as of now you shape up or ship out. And out is where you don't want to be."

Al told Emmet and Silvano to stay behind after the others trooped out. He flicked a switch to turn the wall clear, and waited impatiently as transparent waves skidded about in front of him. With his mind all het up, it was hard to cool down his energistic power. Eventually, the wall stabilized, giving him a view across the SD Tactical Operations Centre. Five people were sitting behind the long ranks of consoles; two of them playing cards.

"The bitch is good," Al said. He was surprised more than anything.

"She used to be married to a politician," Silvano said. "Knows how to sound plausible."

"Certainly convinced me scooting our asses out of here is a good idea," Al muttered. He turned back to his two senior lieutenants. "Emmet, is what she said right? Can we take the planet out of their reach? I mean, right away?"

Emmet wiped a hand across his forehead. "Al, I can make the machines we've got work for you. Do a few repairs, make sure everything's plugged in where it oughta be. But, shit, questions like that . . . That's out of my league, Al, way out. You need a theoretical physicist, or a priest. But even if they can learn how to do that, it's not gonna be tomorrow. We'd be safe there a long time. And could be we'd learn how to keep ourselves there. Shit, I just don't know, Al."

"Ha." Al sat himself down, annoyed by how badly he'd come out of the clash. "And we don't get to find out, neither. God damn that bitch. Now she's declared for the running away option, I've gotta make my stand to stay here. And you can be certain she'll start shouting her idea about."

"Leaving this universe has a strong appeal to the possessed," Silvano said. "It's intrinsic. Perhaps you should bow to the inevitable, boss."

"You think I'm gonna knuckle under to that whore?"

"Not to her, no. But she's backing a winning idea."

"I still need the hellhawks a while," Al said. "Emmet, you done anything more about building another feeding trough for them?"

"Sorry, Al, haven't had time."

"You've got it now."

Banneth was making her preliminary preparations to Kilian when one of the senior acolytes pounded on the door of her sanctum. Kilian gurgled weakly as she eased the slim tube deeper inside him.

"I'll be back in a minute," Banneth promised him cheerfully, and fastened a clamp around the incision to stop the bleeding. She stripped the thin isolation gloves from her hands as she walked over to the door.

"A body, High Magus," the acolyte panted. "There's a body in the temple."

She frowned. "Who?"

"Acolyte Tilkea, High Magus. He was butchered. We didn't authorize it. Tilkea is one of the better ones."

"I see." Banneth datavised a codelock at her sanctum door, and strode off towards the temple. "How awful, a corpse we didn't authorize."

"Yes, High Magus," the acolyte agreed nervously. Like everyone in the headquarters, he never knew if she was joking or not.

Even by the standards of the sect, the killing was fairly extreme. The remains of acolyte Tilkea were suspended from strands of carbon wire above the altar, arms and legs extended wide. Large hooks punctured the skin above his shoulder blades, as well as his buttocks, wrists, and ankles, fastening him to the wires. His chest had been split open from throat to crotch, ribs levered apart to allow the internal organs to spill out. They'd splattered down on the altar, along with a small lake of blood. Banneth circled the corpse carefully, while a gaggle of acolytes stood at a respectful distance. It was ironic, she thought, that a death in the temple where they themselves had killed hundreds over the last few decades should invoke such trepidation. A sign of the times.

The blood was still warm. Banneth took a small medical block from her pocket, and pressed its sensor pad against Tilkea's glistening liver. "This happened within the last half hour," she announced. "Was he on duty in here?"

"Yes, High Magus."

She datavised the headquarters network processor, and instructed it to review the security systems. Nobody had left the building within the last hour. "I want every door guarded by a team of five acolytes. You can issue the hand weapons, chemical projectiles only."

The senior acolytes hurried to obey. When she stood up, Banneth saw the writing on the wall behind the altar. Someone had used Tilkea's heart as a sponge, scrawling in blood: **Darkness has arrived.** Her gaze switched from that to the wires disappearing into the shadows cloaking the ceiling. "Who fixed them up there?" she asked quietly. Not a difficult job, but hardly one that could be done unnoticed. The acolytes simply shrugged helplessly.

This is a very elaborate death, Banneth told Western Europe. **It obviously took some time to prepare. And getting in and out of the building would be hard even for the possessed. My AI is running a constant glitch scan.**

It wouldn't be difficult for Dexter, Western Europe replied. **From what we've seen so far he can circumvent all your electronics. I'd suggest he's starting a war of nerves. If he's as fixated on you as we believe, then a quick death will hardly suffice.**

I expect you're right.

Cheer up, it confirms that he's still in Edmonton. And if Tilkea was killed only half an hour ago, he can't have left yet. I'll have the vac-trains shut down immediately.

If Dexter can make himself invisible, he's probably still inside this temple right now. Banneth resisted the urge to stare round into the many dark recesses. I imagine he'll want to see my reaction.

You could make him happy. Scream, faint; that kind of thing.

I'll consider it for the future.

Perhaps you ought to trigger your gender cycle early, Western Europe suggested. Shift into a man.

I fail to see the relevance.

A male's aggression would probably be a more appropriate response to this situation. Dexter is a raging psychotic, after all.

Banneth dispatched a dry laugh down the affinity bond. That's one of my more treasured privileges, an intimate knowledge of both psychological profiles owned by the human race. I can exploit the relevant weaknesses to perfection. Men have less of a conscience, I'll grant you; but your claim that you're rougher and tougher is a rather sad ego-enhancing lie you tell yourselves.

Charmed, I'm sure. Well if you don't want to do that, is there anything else you need?

I can't think of anything. This place is so heavily booby trapped I'm more worried about one of these bumpkin acolytes setting off a charge than I am an invasion of possessed.

Very well.

Are you watching the other sects?

Yes. North America and I have them all covered. Eight of Edmonton's chapels have been taken over by possessed. It's only a matter of time until the remainder follow. Quinn has also started to sabotage Edmonton's infrastructure. The acolytes have been sent out several times to damage fusion generators and water pumping stations. They actually got through in three or four instances.

I haven't noticed any reduction in services.

Because there haven't been any. Not yet. But the margins are being cut; which raises an considerable question mark over Dexter's ultimate goal. However, it's proved an interesting footprint for us. There have been similar acts in Paris and Bombay.

You think that's where he's been?

Yes. I'm investigating Paris myself, of course. The East Asian supervisor is giving the Bombay sect his personal attention.

Your observers here should keep watch for Courtney and Billy-Joe. Banneth concentrated on their images. They've been missing for a couple of days now. Dexter used to pimp Courtney for me when he was an acolyte. You couldn't classify her as a friend, but she'll be loyal to him. If he keeps anyone close, it'll be her.

Thank you. We'll keep an eye out.

The program's visualization took the form of a three dimensional spider web that filled the entire universe. Strands were all primary colours, crossing and recrossing against each other, a weave that stretched away to an infinity where they blurred into null-grey uniformity. Louise's mind hung in the centre, looking in every direction at once.

What her neural nanonics were showing her was Earth's communication net. Or at least, part of London's informational structure. Then again, it might have been just the Ritz's internal house network. She wasn't entirely sure, only that this was what surrounded her room's net processor . . . when she ran this particular symbology protocol, anyway. There were some interpretations which were like cybernetic coral, others that had cartoon roads, looping gas-giant rings, even one that was an intertexture of glowing liquids. But this, she felt, was the most real.

Information taxis were flooding back towards her, silent sparkles of light riding the strands down to the centre, condensing around her like a new galaxy. A response to the latest questor she'd fired into the digital aether; the fiftieth variant on that one basic inquiry: find a connection between Quinn Dexter and Banneth, any category. She'd tried multiple combinations of the most preposterous phonetic spellings, removed time restrictions so that the questors could search centuries-old memories, allowed fictional works (every media type from books onwards) to be incorporated. If she could just get that first connection, discover a single positive reference, then the questors and news hounds and directory extractors and credit profilers and a hundred other search programs installed in her neural nanonics could be unleashed on Banneth like dogs after a hax.

The information taxis loaded their passenger files into the analysis program she was running in primary mode. "Oh hell," she groaned. The neuroiconic display vanished, and she propped herself up on her elbows.

Genevieve was sitting at the room's desk, running an English geo-historical tutorial through her processor block. She gave her big sister a sympathetic look. "Zeroed out again?"

"Yep." Louise leaned over the side of the bed, and hunted round for her shoes. "Not a single file entry, not that combines them."

"You've just got to keep asking." Genevieve indicated the pile of flek cases on the desk. "Computers aren't smart, just fast. Garbage in, garbage out."

"Is that so?" Louise wasn't going to quibble about Gen's new-found interest of boning up on educational texts. It was better than games. Trouble was, the knowledge was superficial.

Like mine.

"I don't know enough," she confessed. "Even with the program tutors to help me format the questor." It wasn't just her inability to get a lead on Banneth that bothered her. There was still no response from Joshua. She'd sent half a dozen messages now without so much as an acknowledgement from Tranquillity. "I need professional help."

She was back. Andy Behoo sighed helplessly as soon as he saw her walk in. The magic was only slightly soiled by Genevieve trailing after her. This time he didn't even bother to say anything to the customer he was serving before he abandoned them. Louise was standing in the middle of the shop, looking round with that same slightly befuddled expression as the first time. She smiled lightly when she saw him approaching (not too fast, don't run—you'll look pathetic).

"Back for some more?" he asked. God, what a stupid thing to say. Why not just yell out: I don't have a life.

"I'd like to choose some programs, yes," Louise said.

"Excellent." His eyes tracked up and down in a fast sweep, feeding the image into a memory cell. Today she wore a lemon-yellow dress made from a sparkly fabric that was tight around her bottom; and a pair of antique wire rimmed sunglasses. An odd combination, but very stylish. You just had to have considerable poise to carry off the effect. "What can we get you?"

"I need a very powerful questor. You see. I'm trying to find someone, and I've got very little information about them. The NAS2600 questor can't locate them for me."

Interest in what she was saying actually diverted Andy's eyes from her cleavage. "Really? It's usually pretty good.

Your friend must be very well hidden." And pray it's her loathsome fiancé.

"Could be. Can you help?"

"What I'm here for." Andy walked back to his counter, working out in his mind what he could do to use the situation. He plain didn't have the nerve to ask her outright if she'd like to come for a drink with him after work. Especially not with Genevieve at her side. But there had to be some way he could get to see her again, outside Jude's Eworld.

He was very conscious of Liscard, the general manager, tracking his progress. Liscard had been on edge ever since a couple of Special Branch cops had paid Jude's Eworld a visit. They'd taken the manager back into her office, and spoken to her for over an hour. Whatever they said, her suppresser programs couldn't get a grip on her subsequent nerves. She'd certainly given Andy a hard time all day, snarling at him for little or no reason.

Andy had a horrible feeling it might all be connected with Louise. Specifically de-stinging her and Genevieve. If they had been Govcentral bugs, then Jude's Eworld had probably broken the law removing them. But there'd been no real reprimand. The sellrats had been nibbling on curiosity and rumour ever since. Each of them bragged about their own special shady customer who was the probable cause.

The shop's inventory flashed up in Andy's head, and he ran through the specs for questors. "I expect half of your trouble is that the 2600 questor only reviews current file indexes," he told Louise. "What we need to do is get you one that'll review entire files and disregard data status, that should help with obscure references." Andy ducked down below the counter top, and looked at the clutter of fleks stacked up on the shelves below. "Here we go." He surfaced, holding up a flek case. "Killabyte. It's almost an AI in its own right. A one shot request that operates on fuzzy breeder intuition, which means it can utilise whatever references it finds to build new associations which you haven't loaded in, and search through them. It won't taxi back until it's found the answer, no matter how long it takes. Tenacious little bugger."

"That's good. Thank you, Andy."

"What I'd really like to give you is the Hyperpeadia, but we haven't got any fleks of it in stock right now. If it's used in tandem with Killabyte I'd guarantee you'll find your friend. They're the two market leaders right now."

"I'm sure Killabyte will be fine."

"I'll put in an order for Hyperpeadia. The software collective won't datavise it to us, they're worried about bootlegs." He put his elbows on the counter and leaned towards her in a confidential fashion. "Course, the encryption has already been cracked. You can get a pirate clone at any stall in Chelsea market, but it'll probably have transcription degradation. Best you have an original. It'll be here tomorrow morning. I can have it delivered straight to wherever you're staying."

"I'm at the Ritz." Louise fished round in her shoulder bag and produced the hotel's courtesy collection disk.

"Ah." Andy held up the counter's delivery log block to accept the Ritz's code. "Your fiancé hasn't arrived yet, then?" Genevieve had to bend over and hide her face in her hands to stop the giggles.

"No, not yet," Louise answered levelly. "But I'm expecting him any day now. He's already in the solar system. I was wondering if you could help me with something else?"

"Sure. Anything!"

Louise smiled demurely at his enthusiasm. *I ought to be firmer with him. But somehow being firm with Andy Behoo would be like drowning kittens.* "It's just in case the questors

can't find what I want. You said some private detectives use
the store. Could you recommend one?"

"I can ask," he said thoughtfully. "Hang on a minute."

Liscard gave him an alarmed look as he walked over to
her. "A private dick?" she mumbled when Andy asked which
one he should recommend.

"Yeah," Andy said. "One that's good at finding people. Do
you know if any of them are?"

"I think so," Liscard stammered. She waited apprehensively. As soon as the Kavanagh girls had come back into the
store, she'd established a sensevise link to the eddress which
the Special Branch officers had given her. Her retinas and
audio discrimination program had been capturing the scene
for whoever was at the other end of the link. She didn't have
the nerve to load any of the tracer programs available to employees of Jude's Eworld. The software houses who produced them guaranteed they would be completely
undetectable, but she wasn't about to take the risk. Not with
the people who claimed they were from Special Branch.
When she asked her fixer in the local police about them he'd
abruptly told her never to contact him again, and cut the
datavise.

"What do you want me to say?" she datavised to the
anonymous receiver.

"There's someone I know who can help the girl," came the
answer.

Liscard datavised the information directly into Andy's
neural nanonics. He took his time walking back across the
shop, a measured approach allowed him to savour her shape.
The images he'd snatched before were fine as far as they
went, but they amounted to little more than photonic dolls in
his sensenviron. After conjuring them up he was left craving
for more substantial replicants. Now, with his retinas
switched to infrared, and feeding through discrimination pro-

gram, he could trace her abdominal muscle pattern and rib cage through the fabric of her dress. A scan grid overlay revealed the precise three-dimensional measurements of those wonderful breasts. And her skin tone spectrum was already on file; that would be a simple continuation for the sculptor program, extending up from the legs, and down from her bare shoulders. That just left the taste of her as he ran his tongue along her belly and down between her thighs. The correct pitch as she cried out in gratitude, the praise she would moan to him, her greatest ever lover.

Andy hated himself for resorting to senseniron sprites. It was the final humiliating proof that he was a complete loser. But she was so fantastic. Better to have loved and lost, than never loved at all. Even if that love was purely digital.

"What's the matter with him?" Genevieve asked loudly. "Why's he looking at you all funny?"

Andy's smile was a thin mask over his horror as her piping voice broke through his distracted thoughts. Cool sweat was beading across his flushed skin. His neural nanonics couldn't help dispel the blush, they were too busy fighting down his erection.

Louise gave him a vaguely suspicious look. "Are you all right?"

"Fine," Andy mumbled. He scurried back behind the counter, ignoring Genevieve's frown. "I think the person you want is Ivanov Robson. He specializes in missing persons, both kinds."

"Both kinds?"

"Yeah. Some people are genuinely missing; they drop out of life, or haven't updated their directory entries—like your friend. Then there's the kind who're deliberately trying to vanish; debtors, unfaithful partners, criminals. You know."

"I see. Well thank you, this Mr Robson sounds about right."

Andy datavised the detective's address and eddress over. Louise smiled and gave him an uncertain wave as she walked out. Breath whistled out between Andy's crooked teeth. His hands were shaking again, forcing him to grip the edge of the counter. Idiot. Idiot. *Idiot!* But she hadn't stormed out, or made an issue of his stupid erotic daydreaming. There was still a chance.

Yeah, about the same as me getting crowned King of Kulu.

He looked down to double check. The counter's middle shelf held a stack of fifteen Hyperpeadia fleks, all with their wrapping intact. His one and only excuse to see her again.

The taxi pulled up at the end of Fernshaw Road, where it intersected with Edith Terrace. Louise and Genevieve stepped out, and the door slid shut behind them. The vehicle accelerated away silently down the road. It had deposited them in a quiet residential street, where the pavements were actually made from slabs of stone rather than a simple band of carbon-concrete. Silver birch and sycamore trees that must have been a couple of centuries old lined both sides of the road, their giant boughs merging together to provide a gentle emerald shield against the fierce sunlight. The houses were all ancient two or three storey affairs, painted white or cream. Bricks and slate roofs were betraying their age by sagging and bulging; centuries of subsidence and environmental decline had distorted every wall and support timber. Window frames were tilted at the oddest angles. There wasn't a straight line to be seen anywhere in the street. Each house had a tiny front garden, though they'd all been paved over; the massive trees absorbed so much light they prevented any shrubs or vines from growing underneath.

"This must be it," Louise said dubiously. She faced a high wall with a single golden oak door in it, heavily tarnished with age. There was a brass panel with a grill on one side. It looked far too primitive to datavise at. She pressed the ivory button on top.

"Yes?" the grille squealed.

"I'm here to see Mr Robson," she said. "I called before. I'm Louise Kavanagh."

The door buzzed loudly, and she pushed it open. There was a rectangular patio beyond, running along the front of the building; home to a set of wrought iron furniture and a couple of dead conifer bushes in cracked pots. The front door, a duplicate of the one behind, was open. Louise peered cautiously into the small hallway. A blonde girl, barely older than she, was standing behind a reception desk whose surface was smothered with folders, flek cases, and china coffee mugs. She was staring into a small AV pillar that protruded from the top of a very expensive-looking stack of processor blocks. Pale turquoise light from the sparkling pillar was reflected in her narrow, brown eyes. Her frozen posture was one of shock.

Her only acknowledgement of the sisters' entry was to ask: "Have you accessed it?" in a hoarse voice.

"What?" Genevieve asked.

The receptionist gestured at the pillar. "The news."

Both sisters stared straight into the pillar's haze of light. They were looking out across a broad park under a typical arcology dome. Right across the centre of their view, a big tapering tower of metal girders had collapsed to lie in a lengthy sprawl of contorted wreckage across the immaculate emerald grass. Several of the tall, cheerfully shaggy trees that surrounded it had been smashed and buried beneath the splinters of rusty metal. A vast crowd encircled the wreckage, with thousands more making their way along the paths to swell their numbers. They were people in profound mourning, as if the tower had been some precious relative. Louise could see they all had their heads bowed, most were weeping. Thin cries of grief wove together through the air.

"Bastards," the receptionist said. "Those utter bastards."

"What is that thing?" Genevieve asked. The receptionist gave her a startled look.

"We're from Norfolk," Louise explained.

"That's the Eiffel Tower," the receptionist said. "In Paris. And the Nightfall anarchists blew it up. They're a bunch of crazies who're going round wrecking things over there. It's their mission, they say, preparing the world for the fall of Night. But everyone knows they're just a front for the possessed. Bastards."

"Was the tower really important?" Genevieve asked.

"The Eiffel Tower was over seven hundred years old. What do you think?"

The little girl looked back into the projection. "How horrid of them."

"Yes. I think that's why there is a beyond. So that people who do things like that can suffer in it until the end of time."

A glassed-in spiral stair took Louise up to the first floor. Ivanov Robson was waiting for the sisters on the landing. Travelling in the *Far Realm* had accustomed Louise to people who didn't share the bodyform template she'd grown up with. And of course, London had an astonishing variety of people. Even so, she nearly jumped when she first saw Robson. He was the biggest man she'd ever seen. Easily over seven feet tall, and a body that seemed bulky even for that height. Not that any of it was fat, she noticed. He was frighteningly powerful, with arms thicker than her legs. His skin was the deepest ebony, glossy from a health club's spar treatment. With thick gold-tinted auburn hair twirled into a tiny pony tail, and wearing a stylish yellow silk business suit, he looked amazingly dapper.

"Miss Kavanagh, welcome." From the confident humour

in his smooth voice, it was obvious he knew the effect he had on people.

Floorboards creaked under his feet as showed them into his office. The bookcases reminded Louise of her father's study, although there were very few leather-bound volumes here. Ivanov Robson eased himself into a wide chair behind a smoked-glass desk. The surface was empty apart from a slimline processor block and a peculiar chrome-topped glass tube, eighteen inches high, that was full of clear liquid and illuminated from underneath. Orange blobs glided slowly up and down inside it, oscillating as they went.

"Are they xenoc fish?" Genevieve asked. It was the first time she'd spoken. The huge man had even managed to quash her usual bravado. She'd kept well behind Louise the whole time.

"Nothing as spectacular," Ivanov said. "It's an antique, a genuine Twentieth Century lava lamp. Cost me a fortune, but I love it. Now, what can I do for you?" he tented his fingers, and looked directly at Louise.

"I have to find somebody," she said. "Um, if you don't want to take the case when I've told you who, I'll understand. I think she's called Banneth." Louise launched into a recital of her journey since leaving Cricklade, not quite as heavily edited as usual.

"I'm impressed," Ivanov said softly when she'd finished. "You've come face to face with the possessed, and survived. That's quite a feat. If you ever need money, I know a few people in the news media."

"I don't want money, Mr Robson. I just want to find Banneth. None of the questors seem to be able to do that for me."

"I'm almost embarrassed to take your money, but I will, of course." He grinned broadly, revealing teeth that had been plated entirely in gold. "My retainer will be two thousand fuseodollars, payable in advance. If I locate Banneth, that will be another five thousand. Plus any expenses. I will provide receipts where possible."

"Very well." Louise held out her Jovian Bank credit disk.

"A couple of questions first," Ivanov said after the money had been transferred. He tilted his chair back, and closed his eyes in thought. "The only thing you know for certain about Banneth is that she hurt Quinn Dexter. Correct?"

"Yes. He said so."

"And Banneth definitely lives on Earth? Interesting. Whatever happened between the two of them sounds very ugly, which implies they were involved in some kind of criminal activity. I think that should provide my investigation with an adequate starting point."

"Oh." Louise didn't quite look at him. It was so obvious, laid out like that. She should have sent a questor into criminal archives.

"I am a professional, Louise," he said kindly. "You do know the possessed have reached Earth, don't you?"

"Yes. I accessed the news from New York. The mayor said they'd been eliminated, though."

"He would. But Govcentral still hasn't opened the vactrain lines to New York. That should tell you something. And now we've had the Eiffel Tower blown up for no reason other than to demoralize and anger people. That probably means they're in Paris as well. A feat like that is beyond the ability of some stimbrained street gang. What I'm trying to say, Louise, in my dear bumbling way, is that if Quinn Dexter is here, then he'll be heading for Banneth as well. Now do you really want to bump into him again?"

"No!" Genevieve squeaked.

"Then bear in mind that's where your current path is taking you."

"All I need is Banneth's eddress," Louise said. "Nothing else."

"Then I will do my best to ensure you receive it. I'll be in touch."

Ivanov waited until the sisters were circling down the spiral stair before asking: Do you want me to give her Banneth's eddress?

I'm afraid it's a bit pointless right now, Western Europe answered. Edmonton has been sealed up, with Quinn inside. I can't get her in to meet him; so she'll just have to sit this out on the substitute's bench for a while.

13

The prospect of interstellar flight had been real to certain sections of the human race for a long time before *Sputnik One* thundered into orbit. A notion which began with visionaries like Tsiolkovskii, Goddard, and somewhat more whimsical science fiction writers of that age, was quickly taken up and promoted by obsessive space activists when the first microgee factories came on line, proving that orbital manufacturing was a profitable venture. With the development of the O'Neill Halo and the Jupiter mining operation in the Twenty-first Century the concept finally began to seem practical. Asteroids were already being hollowed out and made habitable. Now it was only an engineering and finance problem to propel them out of Earth orbit and across the gulf to Proxima Centauri. There were no theoretical show stoppers; fusion or antimatter engines could be built to accelerate the giant rocks up to speeds of anything between five and twenty per cent of lightspeed, depending on which physicist you asked. Generations of crew would live, tend their machinery, and die within the rock as they crawled across the emptiness, with the anticipation that their descendants would inherit a fresh world.

Sadly, human nature being what it is, century-duration flights were just too long, the ideal of colonization too abstract to motivate the governments and large institutions of the time into building these proposed space arks. The real clincher, inevitably, was cost. There could never be any return on the investment. So it seemed as though the fresh start idealists would just have to go on dreaming.

One such thwarted dreamer was Julian Wan, who, more resourceful than his colleagues, persuaded the board of the New Kong corporation to research faster than light travel. His pitch was that it would be a small, cheap project testing the more dubious equations of Quantum Unification Theory, essentially a few wild theoretical physicists with plenty of computer time. But if it could be made to work, the commercial opportunities would be phenomenal. Noble concern for human destiny and the search for pure knowledge never got a look in.

New Kong successfully tested the ZTT drive in 2115, and the arkship concept was quickly and quietly discarded. Beautifully detailed plans and proposals drawn up by a multitude of starflight societies and associations were downloaded into university library memories to join the ranks of other never-made-it technologies like the nuclear powered bomber, the English Channel bridge, geostationary solar power stations, and continent birthing (the so-called Raising Atlantis project, where fusion bombs were proposed to modify tectonic activity). Then the Tyrathca world of Hesperi-LN was discovered in 2395, along with the news that it was actually a colony founded by an arkship. The old human plans were briefly revisited by history of engineering students, interested to see how they stood up to comparison with a proven arkship. That academic interest faded away inside of a decade.

Joshua, who fancied himself as something of a spaceflight buff, was fascinated by the dull blip of light which *Lady*

Mac's sensors were focused on. It was in a wildly elliptical orbit around Hesperi-LN, with a twelve thousand kilometre perigee and four hundred thousand kilometre apogee. Fortunately for their mission, it was just under three hundred thousand kilometres away from the Tyrathca planet, and climbing.

They'd emerged two million kilometres out from Hesperi-LN; a distance which put them safely beyond the planet's known SD sensor coverage. The Tyrathca world was not a cradle for the kind of space activity found above industrialized human worlds. There were a few low-orbit docking stations, industrial module clusters, communication and sensor satellite networks, and twenty-five SD platforms supplied and operated by the Confederation Navy. Not that there was a lot of worry about pirate activity, the Tyrathca simply didn't manufacture the kind of goods which could be sold on any human market let alone the underground one. The Confederation was far more concerned by the prospect of blackmail by a rogue starship captain armed with ground-assault weapons. Although they didn't have consumer products, the Tyrathca did mine gold, platinum, and diamonds among other precious commodities for their indigenous industries. And the colony had been established in AD 1300; rumours of vast stockpiles accumulated over millennia persisted on every human world. Any bar or dinner party would have someone who knew somebody else who had been told of a first-hand witness who'd walked through the endless underground caverns filled with their glittering dragon hoards.

So the Navy maintained a small cost-ineffective outpost to guard against the possibility of any inter-species *incident*. It had been abandoned, along with all the other human-maintained systems, when the Tyrathca broke off contact. According to the briefing Monica and Samuel had given to the *Lady Mac*'s crew, the Tyrathca would find it difficult to keep the SD systems functional for very long.

"But we have to expect them to try," Monica said. "Their ambassador was pretty damn insistent that we don't intrude on them again."

Joshua and Syrinx assumed the SD network was on-line and fully functional, and planned their tactics accordingly. The goal was to land an explorer team on Tanjuntic-RI, who would attempt to locate a reference to the Sleeping God in the arkship's ancient electronics. Getting them inside unnoticed was the big problem.

Both craft were in full stealth mode when they emerged. Jumping into the system, Joshua had aligned *Lady Mac* so that her vector would carry her in a rough trajectory from the emergence coordinate towards the arkship. As long as he didn't have to use either the fusion or antimatter drives, the starship would probably remain undetected. At this stage, they were back up; there to rush in and provide covering fire in case things got noisy and *Oenone* had to rescue their team. They were using passive sensors only, with just the chemical verniers firing occasionally to hold them stable; every non-essential system was in stand-by mode, reducing the power consumption and with it their thermal emission. Internal heat stores were soaking up the fusion generator output, although they could only last for a couple of days before the thermodump panels would have to be extended to dissipate the heat. Even that wasn't too much of a problem, the radiation could be directed away from the SD network sensors. They'd have to be extremely unlucky to be discovered by anything that guarded Hesperi-LN.

"Picking up some radar pulses from the SD network," Beaulieu reported. "But it's very weak. They're not scanning for us. Our hull coating can absorb this level easily."

"Good," Joshua said. "Liol, what about spacecraft activity?"

"Infrared's showing twenty-three ships using their drives above the planet. The majority are travelling between low orbit and the SD platforms. Four seem to be heading up for high polar orbits. I'd say they're complementing the platforms. But none of them are moving very fast, half a gee maximum. They are big ships, though."

"That's how the Tyrathca like them," Ashly said. "Plenty of room to move round in the life support sections. It's like being inside a bloody cathedral."

"Offensive potential?"

"If they're armed with human-made combat wasps, considerable," Liol said. "With that drive signature I'm assuming they're Tyrathca inter-planetary ships; they have a dozen asteroid settlements to provide the planetary industries with several kinds of bulk microgee compounds. Which means their payload is considerably larger than ours. They're like highly manoeuvrable weapons platforms."

"Wonderful." Joshua datavised the new bitek processor array they'd installed during the last refit. "*Oenone*, what's your situation?"

"I remain on schedule, Joshua. We should be rendezvousing with Tanjuntic-RI in another forty-two minutes. The exploration team is suiting up now."

Unlike the *Lady Macbeth*, *Oenone* had been able to accelerate and manoeuvre after emerging above the planet. By reducing its distortion field to a minimum, the voidhawk could accelerate at half a gee towards the arkship. Given the distance involved, the network satellites were unable to pick up such a small ripple in space-time. The disadvantage was, with such a reduced field the voidhawk couldn't perceive a fraction of the local environment it usually did. If for some unaccountable reason, the Tyrathca had surrounded Tanjuntic-

RI with proximity mines, they wouldn't know until they were very close indeed.

Syrinx always hated being dependant on just the sensor blisters and passive electronic arrays. The voidhawks' ability to pervade a huge spherical volume of space around the hull was intrinsic to their flight.

We managed like this in our Navy days, *Oenone* said, unperturbed.

Syrinx grinned in the half-light of the bridge. The crew toroid's internal power consumption was minimal as well. **You mean back when we were young and foolish?**

This is not a foolish venture, the voidhawk chided. **Wing-Tsit Chong considers it of the utmost importance.**

Me too. But this part just brings back memories. Of Thetis, though she didn't mention him. Lately she'd started to wonder if her brother had managed to elude the beyond as that ever-damned Laton had promised. Mild feelings of guilt had kept her away from his strange stunted existence within the Romulus multiplicity before they left. Really, what was the point in preserving him when his soul was free?

What is our best landing point, do you think? *Oenone* asked.

As always, the voidhawk knew when she needed distracting. **I'm not sure. Show me what we can see.** She accessed the all-too scant files on Tanjuntic-RI stored in the on-board processors, and attempted to match them up with the image the voidhawk was seeing.

Tanjuntic-RI had been completely abandoned less than fifty years after it arrived in the Hesperi-LN star system. An unduly harsh treatment by human standards, but it had fulfilled every duty its long-dead builders had required of it, and the Tyrathca were not a sentimental species. Fifteen thousand years old, it had travelled one thousand six hundred light-years to ensure the Tyrathca race didn't die along with their exploding home star. Five separate, successful colonies had been established along its route. Each time the arkship had stopped inside a star system to create a new colony, the Tyrathca had virtually rebuilt it, refuelled it, then carried on with their crusade of racial survival. Even so, there are limits to the most sturdy machinery. After Hesperi-LN was founded, Tanjuntic-RI was left to circle ceaselessly above the planet.

Borrowing *Oenone*'s sensor blisters, Syrinx could see the details becoming clear as they glided in for a rendezvous. Tanjuntic-RI was a dark cylindrical rock six kilometres long, two and a half in diameter. Its surface was a gentle mottle of flattened craters, resembling a wind-sculpted ice field. Remnants of vast machines sketched out a random topology of tarnished metal lines along the floors of the meandering valleys. These appurtenances had succumbed to millennia of particle impacts and vacuum ablation. What had once been a surface bristling with elaborate towers and radiator panels the size of lakes was left with little more than their stubby mounting fixtures as a reminder of past grandeur. The forward end was the most heavily speckled, due mainly to the extensive remnants of a coppery hexagonal grid.

With Tanjuntic-RI capable of travelling at over fifteen per cent lightspeed, a collision with a single pebble at that speed could result in catastrophic damage. So in flight the arkship was protected by a plasma buffer, a cloud of electrically charged gas that broke up and absorbed any mass smaller than a boulder. It rode ahead of the arkship, a luminous mushroom-shape held in place by a magnetic field generated by the superconductor grid.

Right in the centre of the grid, aligned along the rotation axis, was the arkship's spaceport. Although the concept was the same as the counter-rotating spaceports on Edenist habitats, the Tyrathca had fashioned an elaborate conical structure made up from tiers of disks. Its peak disappeared below the surface of the rock, as if it were a kind of giant arrow tip which had impaled itself in some forgotten era. The larger disks at the top end had broken off centuries ago, probably when the magnetic bearing seized up. Those that remained were vacuum ablating, their edges fraying like worn cloth, while their flat surfaces slowly dissolved, reducing their overall thickness. With the last maintenance crew departing thirteen centuries previously, the vast sheets of metal were down to a few centimetres thickness, and perforated by thousands of micrometeorite holes.

Oenone was also relaying the image of the arkship to the little exploration team suiting up in the crew toroid's airlock prep chamber. Given the clandestine nature of their mission, Monica Foulkes and Samuel were leading the team. There were only two technical staff coming with them; Renato Vella, who was Kempster Getchell's chief assistant, and Oski Katsura, head of the Laymil project's electronics division. Their job would be to reactivate Tanjuntic-RI's electronic library and extract whatever files concerning the Sleeping God that they could locate. Tactical support was supplied by four serjeants, loaded with Ione's personality.

Kempster Getchell and Parker Higgens were also in the prep chamber; helping with the suits when they were asked, but mainly rehearsing mission goals with Renato and Oski. The formless black silicon of the SII suits had enveloped each of the team, now they were busy clipping their rigid exoskeleton suits on top. They were using standard issue Confederation Navy Marine armour, generator reinforced monobonded carbon with power augmentation. As sleek and featureless as the SII suits, they were designed for both asteroid and ship assault roles, capable of supporting and keeping the wearer active in high gee environments, and with built in manoeuvring packs.

The team started to run integration diagnostics. Arm joints bent and twisted, sensor inputs flicked through the spectrum. Monica, Samuel, and the serjeants ran their weapons interface programs, and stowed the various items of lethal hardware on their belts and racks once the suit processor confirmed the connection. Oski and Renato started picking up their blocks and equipment kits; there were too many to hang on their belts, so they were both using small chestpacks.

Kempster held Renato's pack steady as it adhered to the armour suit. "I can't feel the weight," the young astronomer datavised. "I just have to balance right. And I've even got a program for that."

"The wonders of science," Kempster muttered. "Mind you, I ought to be flattered. Commando raids to acquire astronomical data. I suppose that's a sign of how important my profession has become."

"The Sleeping God isn't an astronomical event," Parker chided irritably. "We're sure of that now."

Kempster smiled at the blank neutral-grey back of his assistant. Now he was ready, Renato datavised *Oenone*'s processor array for an update on their approach. Tanjuntic-RI's dilapidated spaceport was a hundred and fifty kilometres away, and the voidhawk's sensor blisters had it in perfect focus. The large disks were separated by a single central column that appeared to be made up from hundreds of braided pipes. They were spaced far enough apart, a hundred metres at least, to admit ships between them. Tyrathca craft had used them as hangar floors, anchoring themselves to docking pins and plugging into the utility sockets. Now, the disks were essentially flat sheets of decaying metal; their thin lattice of ancillary systems had evaporated away along with the rim.

"We're not going to land on those, are we?" Renato Vella asked. "They don't look very reliable."

Samuel used his suit's bitek processor to datavise a reply.

"*Oenone* will take us in under the bottom disk. We'll go EVA and try and find a way in along the spaceport's support column."

"It shouldn't be a problem," Monica datavised. "The archaeology team from the O'Neill Halo got in easily."

"A hundred and thirty years ago," Kempster said. "The decay rate Tanjuntic-RI is suffering from could well make things difficult for you. The original route may be blocked."

"This isn't an archaeology project, doc," Monica datavised. "We'll just cut our way in if we have to. Decay should help us there. The structure won't put up much resistance."

Kempster caught Parker's eye, the two of them registering their disapproval in unison. Cut it open, indeed!

"At least we have a basic layout file of the internal chambers," Oski datavised. "If we really did have to explore, I doubt we'd achieve anything."

"Yeah," Monica agreed. "How come the Tyrathca allowed that university team in?"

"Wrong question," Parker said. "Why shouldn't they? The Tyrathca couldn't understand our interest in the arkship at all. You know they seal up and abandon a house once the breeders have died? Well Tanjuntic-RI is a similar case. Once something of theirs has ended its natural life, it becomes . . . *invalid*, is about the nearest definition we have. They just don't use it, or visit it again. And it's not due to the kind of respect we have for graves; they don't consider their relics or burial houses to be sacred."

"Weird species," Monica datavised.

"That's what they think of us, too," Parker said. "The various Lords of Ruin have asked them on several occasions if they would join the Laymil research project, another viewpoint would always be valuable. It was the same answer each time. They're simply not interested in examining obsolete artefacts."

Oenone folded its distortion field to almost nothing as it crept across the last kilometre to Tanjuntic-RI. The arkship was rotating around its long axis once every four minutes, with only a small wobble picked up over the centuries. Which said a lot for how well they'd managed the internal mass distribution, Syrinx thought. As a result of the minute instability, the spaceport was pursuing a small loop which the voidhawk could match easily.

They slid in under the bottom disk, which was only seventy metres in diameter. The short length of the support column which emerged from the disk's centre to burrow into the rock was twenty-five metres wide.

That lower disk must have been used to dock the Tyrathca analogue of our MSV's, Syrinx suggested. With the big inter-planetary ships on the top deck.

That would be logical, *Oenone* agreed. I wonder what they looked like?

Very similar to those the Tyrathca use today, Ruben said. They don't innovate much. Once a system is finalized they never change it.

That doesn't make a lot of sense, Serina said. How can you know when something is as good as possible unless you keep analyzing and tinkering with the design? A bicycle is a good, efficient method of getting from one place to another, but the car came along because we weren't satisfied with it.

I hadn't really thought about it, Ruben admitted. Now you mention it, thirteen hundred years is a long time to stick with one design, an awful lot more if you add their voyage time to that. We're still improving our fusion drives, and we've only had them six hundred years.

And they're a lot better than Tyrathca fusion drives,

Oxley said. **We've been selling them improvements ever since we made contact.**

You're applying human psychology to them, Ruben said. **It's a mistake. They don't have our intuition or imagination. If it works, they really don't try to fix it.**

They must have some imagination, Cacus protested. **You can hardly design an arkship without it.**

Ask Parker Higgens, Ruben said. A slight tinge of defensiveness was leaking into his affinity voice. **Maybe he can explain it. I guess being slow and methodical gets you there in the end.**

Syrinx examined the twisted braid of pipes and girders that made up the spaceport's support column. Following her silent urging, *Oenone* expanded its distortion field enough to pervade the dilapidated structure. A picture of entwined translucent tubes filled her mind. The number of black-crack flaws in the metal and composite was alarming, as was the thinness of individual tubes. **That really is very fragile,** she declared. **Samuel, please be careful when you egress. It won't take much to snap the spaceport clean off.**

Thanks for the warning.

Oenone rotated gently, turning its crew toroid airlock towards the lead-grey shaft. Standing in the open hatch, Samuel's suit sensors showed him the stars slip past until he was facing the wrinkled mesh of metal. Even though it was basically just a frayed mechanical structure, it had a quality that told him it wasn't human. Neatness, he decided, it lacked neatness, the kind of confident elegance that was the signature of human astroengineering. Where humans would use failsofts and multiple redundancy, the Tyrathca built tough simple devices in tandem. If one was taken out of service for repair or maintenance they trusted the second to remain functional. And it was obviously a philosophy which worked.

Tanjuntic-RI's existence and triumph was evidence of that. It was just . . . reality at one degree from human sensibilities.

The voidhawk's movement halted. Shadows plagued the hull, turning the marbled polyp a dingy walnut. Gravity in the airlock faded away as the distortion field flowed away from it.

This is as close as we can get, Syrinx said. **The archaeology team went in just above the bearing ring.**

The spaceport support column appeared to be holding steady just past the lip of the hull. Stars waved about behind it. Samuel triggered the cold gas jets in his armour, and drifted out from the airlock. Gaps in the column were easy enough to find. The original close weave of pipes and structural girders had been loosened when the bearings seized up, opening a multitude of chinks, though it was impossible to guess which one had been used by the archaeology team all those years ago. He selected one ten metres above the huge bearing ring set in the rock.

Nitrogen puffed out from tiny nozzles around his slimline manoeuvring backpack, edging him closer to the gap. It was lined with a buckled pipe on one side, and a tattered conduit casing on the other. He reached out with his left gauntlet, and made a tentative grab for one of the flaky cables inside the conduit. Dust squirted out around his fingers, and tactile receptors in his palm told him the cable had compressed slightly in his grip. But it held. His main worry had been that everything they touched along the column would disintegrate like so much brittle porcelain.

"Okay, there's a degree of integrity left in the material," he datavised back to the rest of the team. "You can come over. I'm going in."

Helmet and wrist lights came on, and he shone the beams into the black cavity ahead. When the column bearings seized up, the torque stress exerted by the spaceport's inertia had splintered hundreds of structural girders, ripping apart the multitude of pipes and cables they carried. The result was to fill the inside of the column with a forbidding tangle of wreckage. Samuel activated his inertial guidance block. Bright green directional graphics flicked up over the monochrome sensor image, and he eased himself forward. According to his suit sensors, the spaces between the interlocking struts contained a thin molecular haze from the slowly ablating metal.

The chinks were becoming smaller, with fragments scraping against his armour as he hauled himself in the direction the graphics indicated. He pulled a ten centimetre fission knife from his belt. The blade's yellow light shone brightly, shimmering off the strands of ash-grey metal. It cut through without the slightest resistance.

I feel like some kind of Victorian soldier aristocrat hacking through a jungle, he confided to the *Oenone*'s crew.

Scraps of crumbling metal were whirling round him, bouncing and twirling off the corners and angles of the shambolic maze. The second armour-suited figure had reached the gap: Renato Vella, who was quickly wriggling along after him. One of the serjeants was next, followed by Monica, another serjeant, then Oski Katsura. Syrinx and the crew used the sensor blisters to watch them vanish inside one after the other.

Looking good, she said, sharing a quiet confidence with her crew.

Parker Higgens and Kempster Getchell walked into the bridge, and took the chairs Syrinx indicated. "They're making progress," Edwin told the two elderly science advisors. "At this rate, Samuel will have reached the main airlock chamber in another ten minutes. They could be at their target level in a couple of hours."

"I hope so," Tyla said. "The quicker we're away from here, the better. This place gives me the creeps. Do you suppose the Tyrathca souls are watching us?"

"An interesting point," Parker said. "We've not had any reports of our returning souls encountering a xenoc soul in the beyond."

"So where do they go?" Oxley asked.

"We'll put that on the list of questions for the Sleeping God," Kempster said jovially. "I'm sure that's quite trivial compared to—" he broke off as all the Edenists froze, closing their eyes in unison. "What?"

"A starship," Syrinx hissed. "*Oenone* can sense its distortion field. Which means the Tyrathca detectors will pick it up, too. Oh . . . bloody hell."

I see you, the *Stryla* gloated.

Etchells hadn't realized that there was a voidhawk accompanying the rogue Adamist starship. Not until he swallowed in above Hesperi-LN, and started scanning round for the ship he'd pursued from the antimatter station. There was plenty of activity above the xenoc planet, big sedate ships powering their way into high inclination orbits, complementing the protective sphere thrown up by the SD platforms. The twin moons were sending out constant gravitational perturbations as they orbited round each other, half a million kilometres above Hesperi-LN itself. A network of sensor satellites. An unusually thick band of dust slithering above the upper Van-Allen belt. He had to move around cislunar space in small swallows so that his distortion field could complete a clean sweep above the planet. The Adamist starship was easy to locate, a tight curve in the uniformity of space-time. He focused on it, prying and probing at its composition by creating a multitude of tiny ripples within his distortion field, seeing how they reacted to the encounter, the defraction pattern created as they washed across the hull and internal machinery. One thing was clear, it wasn't a Navy ship. The layout was all wrong for that. And Navy ships didn't have an antimatter drive. Its main fusion generators were shut down, leaving just a couple of ancillary tokamaks to power the life support capsules; and the biggest give-away of all: its thermo-dump panels were retracted. It was in stealth mode.

A Confederation Navy sanctioned starship on a clandestine mission in the Tyrathca system. It would have to be a very important mission to risk an inter-species clash at this delicate time. Etchells knew damn well it had to be connected to the issue of possession somehow. Nothing else would warrant approval. When he extrapolated its trajectory, he saw it was going to fly past a moonlet. He ran through a batch of his stolen almanac memories, discovering that the moonlet was actually an arkship, abandoned over a thousand years ago after a flight from an exploding star. His knowledge of Tyrathca history was almost zero, although the fundamentals were there. But he certainly couldn't imagine any connection with their ancient ship and the possession crisis.

A quick swallow manoeuvre put him a thousand kilometres from Tanjuntic-RI, hours ahead of the Adamist starship, and he began to examine it. That was when he found the stealthed voidhawk lurking so close to the surface it was almost touching.

His flush of achievement was tempered by continuing worry. What the hell were they doing here? It had to be important. Critical, even. Which meant it was a threat to him. Among all his possible options, one thing was very clear. They had to be prevented from achieving their goal, whatever it was.

This is captain Syrinx of the voidhawk *Oenone*. **Who am I addressing?**

The name's Etchells, and I'm one of Capone's hell-hawks.

Leave this star system immediately. We will not hesitate to use force to make you comply.

Tough bitch, huh? Well, give me a reason to leave. In fact, I'd like you to tell me what you two are doing here.

Our task is not your concern. Leave, now.

Wrong. I think it has a lot to do with me. Etchells launched a combat wasp at the arkship, then immediately swallowed away. The wormhole terminus opened a hundred kilometres from the Adamist starship. He loaded a hunter program into another combat wasp, and launched it as he emerged into real space.

As soon as Syrinx warned him a hellhawk had arrived, Joshua initiated combat status. He knew damn well their cover either had been, or was about to be, blown. *Lady Mac*'s main fusion generators powered up, the full suite of combat sensors rose out of their recesses, combat wasp launch tubes opened. Alkad Mzu and Peter Adul hurriedly secured themselves on the large, zero-tau capable acceleration couches in the lounge. Up in the bridge, webbing tightened around the crew.

"Wormhole terminus opening," Beaulieu warned. "One hundred kilometres."

Joshua triggered the *Lady Mac*'s triple fusion drives. That close wasn't an accident, the hellhawk had their exact coordinate. "Liol, maser the bastard."

"On it, Josh." A targeting program went primary in his neural nanonics. Three of the starship's eight maser cannons aligned themselves on the terminus and fired. The beams caught the hellhawk as it slid out, and tracked it perfectly. At a hundred kilometres, the inverse square law meant they couldn't kill the hellhawk immediately. Joshua didn't care about that. He just wanted to force it away. *Lady Mac* could take a lot more radiation punishment than any bitek construct if the hellhawk wanted an energy beam duel.

It didn't. A single combat wasp shot out of its launch cradle, curving round to intercept *Lady Mac*. The hellhawk's harpy shape wavered and imploded into a narrow polyp ovoid pimpled by steel-grey mechanical modules. It rolled frantically, trying to dodge the beams. After three seconds of futile manoeuvring, its distortion field applied a near-infinite force against space, and an interstice blossomed open. Joshua fired four combat wasps to intercept the incoming drone, and changed course again. His crew groaned in dismay as they accelerated at ten gees. Space behind *Lady Mac*'s triad of dazzling fusion drive plumes ruptured into a gale of plasma as the combat wasps ejected their submunitions. A curtain of nuclear explosions erected an impenetrable barrier while particle beams and X-ray lasers lashed out.

"I think we're clear," Beaulieu datavised. "Our combat wasps knocked out their combat wasp."

Joshua reviewed the sensor data, which was calming as the expanding plasma wreathes from the explosions turned to purple then began to decay through the spectrum. Stars began to shine through the squall of enraged ions again. He reduced their acceleration to four gees, and switched course once more.

"We just ditched our softly softly policy," Sarha grunted.

"Yeah," Dahybi said. "Whoever possesses that hellhawk knows their tactics. One combat wasp was never going to hurt us. But it made us expose ourselves to the SD network."

"Not just us," Beaulieu said.

The sensors were showing them another combat wasp clash developing several hundred kilometres away from Tanjuntic-RI. "Syrinx, where the hell did it go?" Joshua datavised. "Could you get a fix?"

"It swallowed over to the moons," Syrinx said.

Joshua already had the star system's almanac file open. He reviewed the data on the twin moons. Airless rocks, three thousand kilometres in diameter. If they hadn't been orbiting Hesperi-LN they'd be categorised as exceptionally large asteroids. "There's nothing there for it," he protested. "The Tyrathca don't even bother mining them the ore's so poor."

"I know. We think it's just a good location for a tactical withdrawal at this point in time. And it'll be at least partially shielded from the SD sensors. The Tyrathca probably don't know it's here."

"Great. Did you manage to get the team in?"

"Yes, they're in. But *Oenone* is now holding station a hundred kilometres out from Tanjuntic-RI in case the hellhawk tries to swallow in and launch some more combat wasps. The arkship is very fragile, Joshua, it couldn't withstand a nuclear assault. That leaves us totally exposed. The Tyrathca's sensors have already locked on to us."

The flight computer reported that three radars were already focused on *Lady Mac*'s hull. "Shit." Joshua shut down the fusion drives and let the starship coast along. Their trajectory wasn't taking them anywhere near Tanjuntic-RI anymore. "They're watching us, too," he told Syrinx. "Now what?"

"It's their move. We wait."

The message came eight minutes later, beamed at both *Lady Macbeth* and *Oenone* from one of the low orbit docking stations. "Human craft, you are not permitted here. You have fired weapons above our planet. This is an act of war. Leave now. Do not return."

"Brief, but not open to much misinterpretation," Ashly said as the message began to repeat. "I'm surprised they didn't put in an *or else*."

"They just have," Beaulieu said. "Three ships on their way to intercept us. One-point-two-gee acceleration."

"For them, that's really racing along," Liol said. "The Tyrathca hate high gees."

"Another three fusion drive ignitions," Beaulieu said. "One heading for us. Two aligning on Tanjuntic-RI."

"At least we're out of range from the platforms' combat wasps," Liol said. "That could have been nasty."

"What's your assessment?" Joshua asked Syrinx. He started to run the Tyrathca ship trajectories through some tactical analysis programs. While he was doing it, another two ships ignited their fusion drives and started to fly up on a course for the arkship.

"I think the situation's still manageable," she replied. "Providing it doesn't escalate any further."

"Yeah. I'm working on that aspect. We've got to make sure the team can continue. You're going to have to stop that hellhawk from coming back to Tanjuntic-RI."

"We can swallow out to the moons and keep it very busy. But that leaves the team without protection. One of those Tyrathca ships is bound to investigate the arkship. Even with their phlegmatism, they'll want to know what we're doing here."

"Leave it to me. I'll divert them. You get over to the moons."

"Acknowledged." Joshua lifted his head, and smiled round at his crew.

"Oh God," Sarha moaned with unfeigned consternation. "I hate it when you smile like that!"

"Cheer up. We're going to invade Hesperi-LN."

The rotating airlock chamber had survived the spaceport bearing seizure almost intact. Samuel cut through the wall and floated into the big empty space. His helmet lights automatically defocused, throwing their radiance all around him. It was a cylindrical chamber, fifteen metres in diameter, and fifty long; stark even by Tyrathca standards. The walls were lined with a petrified sponge material resembling pumice

stone, with thousands of regularly spaced indentations. Each
one was just big enough to accept a Tyrathca breeder's hoof.

There were three airlock hatches at each end, large circular affairs with chunky electromechanical locking rims. Precisely halfway down the chamber was a bulging hoop; the
rotating seal to provide the Tyrathca with a pressurized transfer from the arkship to the spaceport. Now, its working fluid
had evacuated, internal components were reduced to granular
sculptures of their former selves; a technological cave etch-
ing.

Renato Vella squirmed into the chamber with jerky motions, knocking large chips of the wall material from the edge
of the hole Samuel had cut. "Oh great, late era gloomy," he
pronounced. "They didn't exactly go in for frills, did they?"

"I doubt a translator could even find an equivalent word,"
Samuel datavised back.

The first serjeant was emerging from the hole, fracturing
even more wall material as it came. There was an almost
identical hole a third of the way round the wall, slightly
larger. A matching opening had been made next to one of the
airlocks at the ship end of the chamber. Samuel's gauntlets
gripped the indentations in the desiccated sponge fabric, and
he moved cautiously hand over hand towards it.

"This must be where the archaeology team cut their way
in," he datavised. "Wait. Yes." The suit sensors showed him
a small plastic box fixed close to the jagged rim by a blob of
epoxy, narrow lines of red human lettering covered a third of
its dark blue surface. "Some kind of communication block.
There are several cables running through the hole." He ordered his suit communicator to transmit a standard interroga-
tion signal. "No response. I guess the power's drained by
now."

"Shame," Renato datavised. "It would have been convenient to have some kind of communication net in there."

"We could probably power it up again," Oski replied. "It's only a century old, the processors will be fully functional."

"Forget it," Monica told them. "The bitek processors can keep us in touch with each other and *Oenone*. We're not going to be inside long enough to justify getting cosy."

"We hope," Samuel said. With the whole team now in the airlock chamber, his helmet lights refocused into wide beams. He grasped the edge of the old hole and pulled himself through.

The archaeology team had cut their way into a broad corridor that served one of the large jammed-up airlocks. It was a simple, square section shaft sliced straight through the rock, with the spongy hoof-grab fabric along the floor, and pipes fastened to both walls. He barely did more than look round, when Syrinx announced the presence of a hellhawk. She gave them a running commentary as the other team members emerged into the corridor.

"The *Oenone* is swallowing over to the moons to tag the hellhawk," Syrinx told them. "*Lady Macbeth* will distract the Tyrathca."

"For how long?" Monica asked.

"As long as possible," Joshua replied. "Worst case, we fail completely. Their first ship should reach Tanjuntic-RI in fifty-three minutes—mark."

"That's no good. We won't even have reached the second level by then."

"I'll swap with you any time."

"Sorry, Joshua; that wasn't a complaint. How did that hellhawk know we were here?"

"Probably followed us from the antimatter station," Syrinx said. "It wouldn't be too difficult."

"Thank you, Captains," Samuel datavised. "We'll try to be as quick as we can."

"If things get too hot, let us know," Joshua replied.

"We'd better get on," Samuel told the team. "Every minute of lead time could be indispensable later." He ordered his backpack to fire the cold gas jets, and slid easily along the corridor to the first big airlock. Monica triggered her own backpack, and glided after him.

The corridor flared out around the airlock, which was a typical example of Tyrathca engineering: a square of titanium four metres in diameter with rounded corners, edged with locking seals, thick, sturdy, and reliable. And vacuum welded into place. The archaeology team had solved the egress problem by cutting out a metre-wide circle of metal from the Tyrathca slab and installing their own airlock. It was a simple mechanical hatch with frictionless hinges and seals. A chrome handle was half-recessed in the middle, with standard operating instructions stencilled beside it.

Samuel secured himself and pulled the handle. His armour's power augmentation barely kicked in to help. The handle slid up, and rotated ninety degrees.

"One up to human engineering," Renato datavised as Samuel pushed the hatch inwards.

"Not really," Oski datavised. "It's our materials science that makes the difference. The hatch was designed for long-term vacuum exposure. Their airlock was built with regular maintenance services in mind."

There was another corridor identical to the first on the far side of the airlock. One of the serjeants shut the small hatch after them. This corridor also ended in a big titanium airlock, with an identical human hatch inserted. Samuel pulled the lever up. Before he could attempt to push the hatch open, his suit sensors advised him of an environment change. "It's venting," he datavised. "Very small nitrogen release, minute contamination. Pressure must be equalising."

"Open it," Monica datavised. "There can't be any real atmosphere in there. We're wasting time."

Samuel gripped one of the titanium spars with one gauntlet, and pushed with the other. The suit's power augmentation whined on the threshold of audibility. A whirl of silvery dust scooted around Samuel's armour as the hatch flipped back.

"Just how many of these corridors are there?" Renato asked as he air-swam through, only to be faced with yet another blank rock shaft. His inertial guidance display showed him it was inclined slightly, heading away from the rotation axis. Though there was still no appreciable gravity.

"This is the last one, according to our file," Samuel said.

The airlock at the far end had a human hatch in it; there was also a small plaque.

HIGH YORK UNIVERSITY
ARCHAEOLOGY EXPEDITION OF 2487

**We respectfully offer our tribute to the
generations of Tyrathca who ventured
forth in this vessel.**

**In this place we have stumbled through
the remnants of greatness, eternally thankful
for the glimpse of nobility they reveal.**

**Though the Tyrathca have no god, they
are clearly not devoid of miracles.**

Renato floated over to the silvered plaque after Monica moved aside. "Well that's a nice way to start," he datavised. "The arcology expedition never found any reference to a Tyrathca god."

"We knew that already," Oski datavised. "Besides, I doubt they were looking. The only memory files they accessed were in the systems management architecture. We've got to go a lot deeper than that to find anything useful."

Samuel shifted his sensors from the plaque to the hatch. "I don't think I've ever felt more like a grave robber."

"There have been worse assignments," Monica datavised. "For you as well as me, I suspect."

Samuel didn't reply. He grasped the hatch's handle and pulled up. This time there was a significant gas vent.

"This is it," Oski datavised. "We're in. Terracompatible nitrogen oxygen mix, several trace gases. Three per cent standard atmospheric pressure. No water vapour content. Guess it's too cold. Registering thirty degrees below zero."

"Checks with the file," Monica confirmed. Samuel pushed the hatch open and glided through.

The archaeology expedition had spent six weeks exploring the interior of Tanjuntic-RI. Given the timescale, it could hardly be thorough. But the main sections were all mapped, allowing the nature of the arkship's engines and environmental maintenance mechanisms to be inspected. Tanjuntic-RI was arranged in three principal levels. Along the rotation axis were three long cylindrical chambers six hundred metres wide. Each contained a shallow lake which served as the principal biological recycling system. The water was a combination fish-tank/ algal air regenerator, powered by a thermal lighting array strung along the axis. Surrounding that was an extensive warren of hemispherical caverns linked by kilometre after kilometre of broad corridors. This level was devoted to engineering and flight maintenance; the caverns filled with machinery, everything from fusion generators to chemical filtration plants, cybernetic factories to mineral storage silos. The rear quarter of the caverns were all used to house support systems and fuel for the fusion engines.

Encircling the second level were the eight principal life support rings. Tunnelled out of the rock and lined with metal, like giant binding bands; they had a rectangular cross section, five hundred metres wide, a hundred metres high. Their floor was a single looped strip of Tyrathca tower houses threaded by narrow roads of greenery, a computer design program's notion of urban pleasantries.

"We need the third level, ring five," Oski datavised as soon as they were through the last airlock. "That's where the archaeologists found the control offices." A three dimensional map of the interior expanded into her mind. Her guidance block extended a glowing green line through the tunnels, linking her present location to ring five.

The last airlock had brought the team into a standard-sized corridor that circled the forward end of the arkship. Over a hundred other corridors branched off from it. Gravity was barely noticeable, taking several minutes to pull objects towards the floor. Monica used her gas jets to take her over to a clump of human crates stacked against the wall. The thin, freezing atmosphere had turned the white plastic a faint cream. She read some of their labels. "Nothing we can use," she datavised. "It's their camp equipment. Programmable silicon shelters, life support units, microfusion generators; that kind of thing."

"What about lighting?" a serjeant asked.

"Good question." Monica shifted position, scanning more labels. "Yes, here we go. Monochrome projectors, three hundred metre illumination radius. I don't think they're self powered, though."

"Leave it," Samuel datavised. "We don't have the time." He fired his manoeuvring pack and started drifting along the corridor. The wall opposite the airlocks had archways leading away into the interior, their depth defeating his suit sensors and lights. "There should be a lift here somewhere. Ah." The fifth archway had a palm-sized plastic disk stuck on the wall beside it, a small lifelong beacon light in the centre.

Samuel couldn't resist flicking it with a gauntlet finger as he went past. There was no spark of light from the beacon, its tritium-decay power source had been exhausted decades ago.

His gas jets squirted strongly, steering him through the archway. Fifteen metres down the corridor was a lift door: a single panel of metal ten metres long and three high. The team didn't even pause by it. There was a smaller door on either side, each heading a ramp that spiralled, DNA-fashion, around the entire length of the lift shaft. One of them was open; it had a dead light beacon just inside.

"This should take us nearly a kilometre straight down," Samuel datavised.

"At least it'll be a smooth ride once the gravity kicks in," Renato datavised. "Thank god the Tyrathca don't use steps. Can you image the size and spacing?"

Monica halted in mid-air beside the doorway and focused her suit beams through the gap. The downward slope was barely noticeable, though the curve was pronounced. She took a tube dispenser from her belt, and thumbed out the first disk. Jupiter had supplied the little bitek sensors, completely transparent disks a centimetre wide. Their affinity range was only a few kilometres—enough for this mission. She pressed it against on the door rim. It stuck instantly. When she requested an affinity bond with it from her suit's bitek processor, the disk revealed a fish-eye view of the corridor, with the suits floating before the ramp doorway.

"Pity we don't have a swarm of bitek insects covering the interior," she datavised. Samuel didn't rise to the jibe. "But this'll give us plenty of warning. There's a motion trigger if anything starts moving around behind us."

"Onward, then," Samuel datavised. His gas jets flared, pushing him along the ramp.

Everyone's bitek processor received Joshua's troubled

hail. "I'm afraid you're going to have company," he announced.

Lady Mac was accelerating at six gees, a quarter of a million kilometres above Hesperi-LN and heading in a shallow curve around the planet's north pole. Two five-strong formations of Tyrathca ships were heading out to intercept, rising from their hundred thousand kilometre orbits at one and a half gees. He wasn't worried about them, nor the three ships that were on course for the twin moons to investigate the antics of the two bitek starships. Another group of four ships were flying straight for Tanjuntic-RI, seventy-five thousand kilometres from *Lady Mac*.

"Definite interception course," Beaulieu confirmed. "Looks like they want to know what was going on there."

"Wonderful," Joshua grunted. "The only way to stop them is if they think we're hostile."

"I think they know that already," Sarha said with as much irony as five gees allowed.

As soon as they'd accelerated along their present course, Joshua had launched three combat wasps. There was no real target designation, just the planet; and they were programmed to detonate ten thousand kilometres above the atmosphere if they managed to get that far. But the Tyrathca didn't know that. All they'd seen was three nuclear missiles charging in towards their planet at twenty-seven gees: an unprovoked attack from a human starship that was continuing to manoeuvre in a hostile manner.

Joshua changed course again, flying along a vector which would take him below the ships heading for Tanjuntic-RI—logically, a position he could bombard the planet from. Another two combat wasps flew out of their tubes, searing fusion drives thrusting them towards the four ships.

It was a good tactical move, which almost paid off. Three

of the Tyrathca ships changed course to defend themselves against the combat wasps and pursue *Lady Mac*. The fourth remained on course for the arkship.

"Thirteen ships heading right at us," Beaulieu confirmed. "Twelve SD platforms have also acquired lock on. No combat wasp launch yet."

Joshua reviewed the tactical situation display again, purple and orange vector lines flipping round inside his skull. *Lady Mac* was now heading in almost the opposite direction to the last Tyrathca ship. There was nothing left he could do to distract it. The only option left was an attack, which wasn't an option at all. First he would have to reverse his current vector which would take up a vast amount of time and delta-V, then he would have to fight his way past the three other ships with their potentially large stock of combat wasps. And even if he achieved that, he'd have to kill the ship to stop it rendezvousing.

It was a bad deal. The Tyrathca crewing the ship were innocent—just trying to defend themselves and their world against aggressive xenocs. Although, if you looked at it in an abstract way, they could well be all that stood between the exploration team and salvation from the possessed. Can you really allow a dozen Tyrathca to bring about the end of an entire race because of what was essentially a communication breakdown on a multitude of levels?

Joshua used the bitek array to call the exploration team and warn them of the approaching ship. "We estimate it'll dock in another forty minutes," he said. "Just how long do you need?"

"If everything goes without a hitch, a couple of hours," Oski said. "But I would think a day would be more realistic."

"A day is out of the question," Joshua said. "If I get seriously noisy out here I might be able to buy you an hour or so."

"That's not necessary, Joshua," a serjeant said. "This is a very big ship. If they do come on board, they'll have to find us."

"Not too difficult with infrared sensors."

"That's assuming a straightforward pursuit scenario. Now we know the Tyrathca are coming, we can make that pursuit extremely difficult for them. And there is also the Horatius option to consider. We four are expendable, after all."

"Our weapons are superior, as well," Monica said. "Now we haven't got to worry about the hardware glitching on us, we can deploy some real firepower."

"What about getting out afterwards?" Dahybi asked.

"Advance planning for a situation this fluid is a waste of time," Samuel said. "Let's wait until we have the relevant data before we consider how to achieve extraction."

"Okay," Joshua said reluctantly. "Your call. But we're here if you need us." He returned to the tactical situation. *Lady Mac* wasn't in any real danger from the planet's defences. She was too far away from the Tyrathca ships and SD platforms. At this separation distance, any combat wasp would take a minimum of fifteen minutes to reach them. The starship could jump out of trouble long before that.

"Right, let's keep these bastards busy," Joshua said. He instructed the flight computer to fire another combat wasp at the planet.

Halfway down the giant spiral ramp, the easiest way to descend was to sit and slide. Black frost had coated the floor, sending broad tendrils scurrying up the wall like frigid creepers. Along with the others Monica was bumping along on her bum as if she was on an après ski glissade, gradually picking up speed, and ignoring the total lack of dignity. Clouds of filthy ice motes were spraying up from where the suit was making its grinding contact with the ramp. Every now and then she'd hit an uneven patch and glide through the air for a metre.

"Getting near the bottom," Samuel datavised.

He was two people down the line from Monica, nearly obscured by the black particle haze. Suit beams were jouncing about chaotically, throwing discordant shadows across the walls.

Monica put her gauntlets down to try and brake her speed. They just skipped and skidded about. "Just how do we slow down?" she asked.

"Manoeuvring pack." Samuel triggered the jets at full throttle, feeling the gentle thrust slow him. The serjeant directly behind bumped into his back. "Everybody at once, please."

The ramp shaft was suddenly full of whirling pearly-white fog as ice granules and nitrogen blended together, boosting the air pressure. Suit lights fluoresced it to a uniform opacity.

Monica shifted to micro-radar as her speed slowed drastically. This time when she put her hands down she pressed hard enough to activate the augmentation. It allowed her to dig her fingertips into the sheet of ice, producing a loud wince-inducing screech as they gouged out ten straight furrows. She halted on a relatively flat section. Radar showed her the end of the ramp fifteen metres ahead and the other armour suits skating elegantly to a halt around her. The white fog vanished as quickly as it'd emerged, sucked away back up the ramp, and out through the archway ahead.

They picked themselves up and scanned round. The ramp had come out at an intersection of eight corridors. Beacons had been stuck on each archway. The ice along the floor of every corridor was slightly rumpled, like stone paving slabs worn by centuries of feet. Nothing else showed the archaeology expedition had once passed this way.

"This is where we should split up," one of the serjeants

datavised. "Two of us will lay heat trails, while you head for ring five."

Monica accessed the archaeology expedition's map file, and integrated it with her inertial guidance block. Orange graphics overlaid her sensor vision, indicating the corridor they should take. She took another sensor disk from the tube and stuck it on the wall. "Okay. You two take care, they'll be here in another twenty minutes. Oski, Renato, let's go." The four humans and two remaining serjeants started off down the corridor, bouncing along in low glides in the one-third gravity field.

Ione's quad mind started to melt away into four more individual, independent identities as the serjeants separated from each other. One of her chose a corridor which the map file showed would lead towards a chemical plant of some kind. She drew a laser pistol and datavised it to a very low power setting, with an intermittent discharge varying over three seconds. As she walked forwards in long loping steps she began sweeping it in a short arc, keeping the muzzle pointed at the ground. Speckle points of warmth blossomed around her feet—never enough to thaw the ice, just to make an imprint. To an infrared sensor it would appear as if several people had walked along beside her.

The darkness which contracted around the bubble of light from her suit lights was absolute, isolating her to an unnerving degree, a fact only slightly alleviated by affinity contact with her other three selves and Samuel.

My third experience of life outside Tranquillity, and it's just rock tunnels not much different from Ayacucho. But a lot more oppressive, and that's without the possessed after me.

The others in the team were feeling the same low harmonic of unease. Monica was leading now, a locomotion auto-balance program keeping her movements smooth and steady in the low gravity. Despite the depressing surroundings, their easy progress was confidence enhancing. She'd had a lot of misgivings about the whole mission, and this part most of all. In her mind during the flight here, Tanjuntic-RI had taken on the appearance of a large chunk of debris, just like the fragments that made up the Ruin Ring. Reality was considerably better. Nothing was broken inside the arkship, merely neglected and cold. She could even imagine revitalizing the old wanderer. If the fusion generators could be started up again, and power fed through the distribution net, it would be a simple matter for light and heat to return.

"How come they abandoned this?" she asked. "Why not rendezvous with an asteroid and use it as a ready-made base for their microgee industry?"

"Because of the upkeep," Oski datavised back. "The whole thing is interdependent, you can't just keep a life support ring going and dump the rest. And it's big. Keeping it functioning would take too much effort for the level of return. They were much better off building smaller-scale asteroid habitation caverns from scratch."

"Shame. At the very least the Tyrathca could have made a fortune selling it as a human tourist destination."

"That'll be that famous phlegmatism of theirs. They just don't care about it."

After five minutes they came to the first second-level cavern. A hemisphere two hundred metres high, the walls ribbed by bands of tubes. There was a single huge machine in the centre, supported by ten three-metre-thick pipes that rose out of the ground to act as its legs. Another ten pipes emerged from the top of the machine to vanish into the chamber's apex. The team stood just inside the entrance, playing their suit beams over the metal beast. Its sides were fluted with long glass columns, tarnished on the inside with heat-blackened chrome. Valves, coils, relays, motors, intake grids, high-voltage transformers, and pumps protruded from the rest of the edifice like metallic warts.

"What in Christ's name is that?" Renato asked.

"Access your file," Oski told him. "It's some kind of biological reactor. They bred a lot of organic compounds inside it."

Renato walked over to one of the big pipes and took a look directly underneath the reactor's formidable bulk. The casing had cracked as the arkship lost its heat, allowing ragged strings of some blue green compound to ooze out all over the base. They'd clotted in hanging webs before freezing solid. Smears and stains of other liquids were splattered across the floor.

"There's something wrong with all of this," Renato datavised.

"What do you mean?" Samuel asked.

"Just look at this thing." The young astronomer slapped his hand against the pipe. Even in the rarefied atmosphere, the suit audio sensors could pick up a faint clang. "It's, like ... immortal. I can't imagine anything else occupying this chamber since the day they left their star. I know they'll have rebuilt it a hundred times during the voyage. And I know they go for the brute strength engineering solutions. But I don't understand how nothing can have changed in fifteen thousand years. Nothing, for Christ's sake. How can you draw a line across your technology and say we will never develop anything that goes beyond this?"

"You'll be able to ask them soon," Monica datavised. "Their ship will reach us in another ten minutes. Look, Renato, I know this is all fascinating, but we really don't have the time. Okay?"

"Sure, I'm sorry. I just hate unsolved puzzles."

"That's what makes you a good scientist. And I'm glad you're here to help us. Now, this is the corridor we want."

Monica left another sensor disk on one of the stolid pipes and started walking again. Renato took a last glance at the ancient reactor and followed her. The two serjeants brought up the rear.

"The Tyrathca ship is definitely docking," Beaulieu said. "They've matched velocities with Tanjuntic-RI."

"Bugger," Joshua grunted. They were enjoying a slight lull in the three-dimensional chess game that was the high-orbit diversion. *Lady Mac* was accelerating at one gee, sliding over Hesperi-LN's pole at a hundred and seventy-five thousand kilometres altitude. Eighteen combat wasps were arrowing in towards her from every direction, a classic englobing manoeuvre. The closest one would reach them in another four minutes. At least the hellhawk wasn't a current factor. Syrinx confirmed they were still chasing the *Stryla* round the two moons.

"Liol, break the bad news to the team, will you?" Joshua concentrated on the starship's systems schematic, ordering the flight computer to configure the hull for a jump. Somewhere near the back of his mind, almost in the subconscious, was a smiling astonishment that he could now be so confident about taking part in a space battle. Contrast his, and the crew's, calm responses and performance today to the frantic shouting and adrenaline powered high-gee desperation above Lalonde, and it was as though they used to belong in an alternative universe. The major difference, of course, was that he'd initiated this, he was calling the shots.

"Dahybi?"

"Nodes charged and on line. Ready to jump, Captain."

"Great. Let's see how accurate we can be." He cut the fusion drives and initiated the jump.

The watching Tyrathca saw the dangerous invader vanish from the middle of their combat wasp swarm. SD sensors picked up its emergence point simultaneously, fifty thousand kilometres from where it had jumped. Its fusion drive came on again, powering it back down towards the planet, presenting fresh danger to the population. The pursuing craft all changed course to resume their chase.

A crackling smog of hot ions splashed across the front of Tanjuntic-RI as the Tyrathca ship finished its approach manoeuvre. Electrical discharges flashed along the remnants of the superconductor grid, burning off the fragile surface molecules in scintilating spectral fountains. The pilot hadn't bothered to rendezvous at a distance and nudge in towards the spaceport cone using secondary drives. Their flight vector was projected to bring them to a halt less than a kilometre from the arkship, completely disregarding the damage the fusion drives would inflict on the ancient vessel.

The ship was a typical Tyrathca inter-planetary craft, a simple cylinder a hundred and fifty metres wide, three hundred long. Unlike human designs which were built round a load-carrying gantry to which modules and capsules were attached as required, this had everything encased inside an aluminium hull. A basic, ugly workhorse of a ship, discoloured by years of exposure to the thermal and ultraviolet emissions of Hesperi-LN's star. Four big rectangular hatches were spaced equidistantly round its front end, while five stumpy fusion rocket nozzles protruded from the rear.

When it finished its deceleration burn it was floating parallel to Tanjuntic-RI's spaceport, two kilometres out. Small chemical rockets flared around its edges, brilliant sulphur yellow flames pushing the ship in towards the rotation axis. It started to turn at the same time, aligning its base towards the spaceport. The chemical rockets around its front end throttled up to maximum, and two fusion rockets ignited briefly. Their plasma plumes stabbed out, twin incandescent spears transfixing the centre of the spaceport. The burn didn't last for more than a couple of seconds, nor was it particularly powerful. But the damage caused was immense. Metal and composite detonated into vapour, roaring out from the impact point.

It was too much for the enfeebled spaceport structure to withstand. The entire cone of stacked disks snapped off close to the base, tumbling away. Individual disks tore loose, spinning off in every direction, spewing fragments as they went. One disk actually collided with Tanjuntic-RI, crumpling as if it were made from paper before it started to rebound. All that was left of the spaceport's support column was a shattered ten metre stub sticking out from the rock. It was rapidly eclipsed as the massive Tyrathca ship positioned itself directly overhead. Two hatches hinged open, and several dozen pale ovoid shapes were ejected. At first they drifted as aimlessly as thistledown in a zephyr, then puffs of gas erupted from small spouts around their crests, and they started to fly in towards the broken end of the support column.

Hesperi-LN's twin moons were not a hospitable location for spacecraft. Their clashing gravity fields had drawn in a great deal of cosmic debris since their formation, and continued to do so. Dust, sand, and smaller motes were eventually liberated by the solar wind, light-pressure and high energy elementary particles blowing them back out towards the stars. But the larger chunks remained. Pebbles, boulders, entire asteroids; once they'd fallen into a looping orbit, they were slowly hauled in over the millennia as the ever-changing gravity perturbed their new orbit. Ultimately, they wound up at the central Lagrange point, poised equidistantly between the moons. It was a cluttered zone over a hundred kilometres across, visible from the surface of Hesperi-LN as a fuzzy grey patch. In composition, it mimicked a galaxy, with the largest asteroids clumped together at the centre, surrounded by a whirl of smaller boulders and stony nuggets.

A place, then, where the use of combat wasps and energy beams was essentially impossible. You could stay within its fringes and observe your enemy waiting outside with impunity. Providing you could ward off the clouds of dark, high-velocity gravel swirling endlessly around the periphery of the Lagrange cluster.

Oenone's attempts to pursue the hellhawk inside the cluster had come to nothing. After twenty minutes of dangerous slaloming and weaving, during which it gained barely a hundred metres on the contemptuous hellhawk, Syrinx had decided enough was enough. They were draining the energy cells at an alarming rate to maintain the distortion field, essential to deflect the hail of stone from the hull. And they would need that power later, no matter what the outcome at Tanjuntic-RI. She told *Oenone* to halt and match the orbital vector of the surrounding particles.

Once Etchells realized he was no longer being actively pursued, he also eased back, and simply held his position. They were no more than fifteen kilometres apart. Though the only way they knew that was by sensing each other with their distortion fields, visual or radar observation was impossible.

This is not a valid status quo, Syrinx told the hellhawk. *There are three Tyrathca ships on their way to us. You cannot stay inside the cluster forever. Leave this system.*

Not a chance, Etchells said. *You've got to stay here with me, now. That means I've won. You can't achieve whatever the fuck you came here to do. And your Adamist pals are in deep shit. They're neutered, too.*

With reservations, I will accept that observation, she told him, careful not to let any emotional context slip into the affinity contact. He obviously wasn't aware they'd landed the team in Tanjuntic-RI. All they had to do was keep him here until Oski and Renato had accessed the files.

String him along, she told the crew. **I want to monitor the spacecraft situation. We may have to move in a hurry.**

Of course, Cacus said.

Ruben, get our new fusion generators on line. I'd like *Oenone*'s **energy cells recharged as fast as possible. When we leave here, I want to be able to leave this hellhawk far behind.**

Understood. Ruben ordered the processor array to begin the generator power up sequence.

The links between the second and third levels on Tanjuntic-RI were mainly cargo lifts. Again, each of them was wrapped by the ubiquitous spiralling ramps. The exploration team had to engage their boot spikes as they made their way down one which led to ring five. Icy floors combined with the strengthening gravity provided a treacherous environment.

There was a large airlock chamber at the bottom, with doors more suited to bank vaults than spaceships. But this had been the Tyrathca's first line of defence against a breech in the upper levels, their design philosophy had come into its own here. As tribute to that efficiency, Tanjuntic-RI's caverns and rings still retained a tiny atmosphere after thirteen centuries of disuse.

A cache of human machinery was spread out before the door at the end of the ramp: a couple of microfusion generators, mobile cherry-picker platforms, industrial thermal inducer plates, hydraulic rams, and electromechanical actuators; all hooked together with loosely bundled cables and flexible hoses. The archaeology expedition had used them to reactivate the massive airlock. It was a quarter open, allowing them access to ring five. Four small jeeps were parked just inside, standard airless-planet mobility vehicles, with large low-pressure tyres and a composite latticework chassis. Ridiculously dainty in comparison to the engineering on display around them.

Samuel went over and inspected them, flicking switches on the dashboard. "I'm getting a response from the control processor," he datavised. "There's some power left in the standby circuits, but that's about all. The main energy cells are dead."

"Irrelevant," Monica datavised. She ordered her suit lamps to emit a high-wattage pulse, and readied the sensors. Her neural nanonics memory froze the image when the lights flared. Buffer programs isolated the image for her to examine.

Not even the suit's lights could penetrate the gloom right across the ring. As a result, the curvature effect was completely lost. She was standing in a metal cave, walls, floor, and ceiling made up from millions of aluminium alloy panels, heat sealed to the naked rock underneath and welded together. Plants had been grown up the walls while the arkship was occupied, vigorous creepers clawing their way along metal trellises. Their leaves were black and wizened now, dead from lack of water and light long before the heat seeped away into space. But the cold had arrived before they'd fallen in their final autumn, sprinkling them with frost then freezing them into place against the dull metal tiling.

The ring's ceiling had an analogue in human warehouse roofs; criss crossed with thick pipes and sturdy gantry crane rails, giving the vast chamber an overtly industrial feel. Its illumination had been provided by thousands of large circular disks of smoked glass, which peered out of the gaps.

"A winter wonderland palace," Monica datavised. "Even if it was built by the devil's own elves."

"How could they live in this, for Christ's sake?" Renato

asked. "It's just a machine. There's no attempt to make it pleasing or hospitable. You couldn't stay inside all of your life, it would drive you insane."

"Us," Oski datavised. "Not them. They don't have our psychological profile."

"I expect they would find one of our habitats to be equally disenchanting," Samuel said.

"The Tyrathca have arrived," one of the serjeants datavised.

Everyone saw it through the sensor disk Monica had left up in level one. A flash of light from the airlock which led up to the spaceport support column. Large jagged sections of the square titanium hatch flew into the corridor, rebounding from the walls amid cascades of ice chips to twirl away in both directions. The Tyrathca emerged, and began moving in a slow canter towards the entrance to the spiral ramp. They were in spacesuits, which made it hard to tell between breeders and soldiers. Although the SII had tried many times to sell them programmable silicon suits modified to their physiology, they'd resolutely stuck to their own original design.

The body of Tyrathca spacesuits was made from a tough flexible plastic, a silvery blue in colour, like metallic silk. They formed overalls that were loose and baggy enough for the big creatures to slip into easily, with concertina-like tubes for legs and arms. After that, instead of inflating them with oxygen, they were pumped full with a thick gel, expelling all the air. Given how many limbs (and therefore joints) a Tyrathca body had, such a concept neatly did away with the problem of providing multiple pressurized joints on every suit. In order to breathe, they wore simple tight-fitting masks inside the suits. Oxygen tanks, a regulator mechanism, and a heat exchanger were worn in a pack along their backs, with two black radiator fins running along their spine. Additional equipment was carried on a harness around their necks.

"Looks like subtlety is another trait we don't share," Monica datavised. "They must have blown out every airlock along that first corridor to get inside. The sensor disk is registering a lot of gas motion in that corridor. They just don't care that Tanjuntic-RI is going to vent its remaining atmosphere."

"If they don't, we shouldn't," Renato datavised. "It won't affect our mission."

"They're all armed," Samuel datavised. "Even the breeders."

The Tyrathca were each carrying a pair of long matt-black rifles, with coiled leads plugged into power packs on their harnesses. Monica put an armaments library file into primary mode, and let it run through the catalogue for a match. "Masers," she datavised. "Fairly basic medium-output projectors. Our armour should withstand an energy strike from them. But if we get caught in a saturation situation we'll be in trouble. And they're carrying other ordnance as well. I think I can make out some guided rockets, and EE grenades on those harnesses. Human-built."

"I wonder who sold those to them," Oski datavised. "I thought the Confederation didn't permit armaments sales to the Tyrathca."

"Not relevant," Samuel datavised. "Come on, let's locate that control office the archaeology expedition found."

Monica bled in her suit sensor's infrared visualization as they moved off. The Tyrathca buildings materialized around her, tapering towers of a pale blue luminescence, like flame frozen against the empty blackness which stretched out along the ring. It was a cold necropolis, with every street and building identical, as if each section had been stamped from the same die and laid out end to end. Gardens of tangled plants besieged each of the towers, their entwined stalks caught in the act of sagging. Unrelenting cold had turned the vegetation as hard and black as cast iron. Fanciful leaves, strangely shaped flowers and bloated seed pods had all been reduced to the same sombre shade of charcoal.

"Damn, those Tyrathca can move fast in low-gee," Samuel datavised. They hadn't been walking ten minutes, and already the Tyrathca had reached the bottom of the first spiral ramp. A sensor disk showed one of them sweeping a portable electronic scanner over the floor while the others waited behind. The group split into three, following the various thermal trails.

"I make that eighteen coming our way," Monica datavised. "I think we've got four breeders. They're slightly larger."

"I will return to the entrance," one of the serjeants datavised. "I will have time to lay several false heat trails before they reach this ring. That should split them again. And I may manage to close the airlock door. Either way, it will reduce the force that will ultimately pursue you."

"Thank you," Monica datavised.

The serjeant turned round, and walked back down the road.

"And then there were five," Renato muttered uneasily round his respirator tube.

Ione wanted to know as soon as possible what the Tyrathca intended. The knowledge would certainly help her plan the kind of tactics needed to keep them away from the team. The two diversion serjeants had busily laid their heat trails, meandering between several of the big machinery chambers on the second level. That was when she found that the map made by the archaeologists was not perfect. Several times, she'd had to use her inertial guidance to work out where she was when corridors didn't correspond to the indicated layout. It was a factor to consider when she sketched in her possible escape routes. The Tyrathca wouldn't suffer from such misinformation. Tanjuntic-RI's exact topology would be known to them; passed down from generation to generation via their chemical program glands.

One of the diversion serjeants was now hanging back from the archway that opened into a hemispherical chamber. It was a big space, occupied by what appeared to be a refinery constructed entirely out of glass. Colonnades, spheres, bulbs, and minarets formed their own miniature city, bound together with a tangled lattice of tubes. Individual containers were full of coloured liquids that had turned to ice. Cracks were visible everywhere. If heat ever did return to this chamber, the whole edifice would probably collapse.

There were three other entrances to the glass refinery, the one opposite the serjeant was where the heat trail from the ramp led. Sensor disks on the corridor wall showed Ione the Tyrathca advancing steadily along it. Ione waited. She knew her suit's heat signature would be visible to the Tyrathca as soon as they entered the refinery chamber, shining with the tenacity of a red dwarf star against the arctic corridor.

The first Tyrathca came in. Stopped. Raised the scanner it was holding, pointing it directly at her. Her suit communication block picked up a burst of encrypted data. The whole column of Tyrathca came to a halt. Then two of them moved up to support the first. They immediately fanned out on either side of the chamber, reducing her target opportunity.

Damn, she said. **I think we can kiss the entrapment goodbye. The rest are waiting to see what happens.**

It was to be expected, Samuel replied. **They are soldier-caste, after all. Bred for conflict. The breeders don't need to impart chemical programs of tactics among them; such knowledge is instinctive.**

The serjeant moved out of the shallow alcove which had been masking it. Ione was ordering the communication block to open a channel on the frequency the Tyrathca were using when both the soldiers fired their maser rifles. The beams struck the serjeant's armour, almost overloading its energy dissipation web. She jumped, a movement enhanced considerably by low gravity and the suit's augmentation. At the same time she triggered the EE charges she'd placed above each of the chamber's entrances. Tonnes of rock descended in four separate avalanches, sealing the three Tyrathca in.

Ione climbed to her feet, and focused the suit sensors back. The jump had sent her soaring fifty metres down the corridor, barely avoiding hitting the roof. Small lumps of rock were spinning and bouncing towards her in lazy motions. The sensor disks in the refinery chamber showed nothing but a swirling cloud of dust, while the others showed the remaining Tyrathca retreating swiftly. They started to split up, vanishing down side corridors where there were no sensors to follow them.

The bad news is they're operating a shoot-to-kill policy, she said. **I guess they're not curious why we're here.**

That's to be expected, Samuel said. **You don't evolve an entire caste devoted to aggression unless you have a great need for them. The Tyrathca social structure is based around a clan hierarchy, they are extremely territorial. And we're violating their oldest piece of territory in defiance of their explicit instructions.**

Yes. Well at least you know what to expect when they reach ring five. Now I'd better get out of here before they pop up from some secret passage and shoot me.

The control offices were a series of rooms bored into the wall of ring five, fourteen hundred metres from the spiral ramp. Simple open rectangles, plated in aluminium alloy, with the floor covered in composite. Each room was lined by bulky computer terminals, with twin rosette keyboards for Tyrathca fingers. The walls above them were covered by long display screens to project the arkship's engineering schematics and navigational plot. To all intents and purposes, this was Tanjuntic-RI's bridge.

According to the archaeology expedition there was less frost and ice inside, which had permitted them to reactivate several of the electronic systems without much trouble. The control offices were on an independent environmental circuit with a much reduced humidity level; and the airlocks were shut prior to the arkship's final evacuation so there was no contamination from ring five's damper atmosphere.

The archaeology expedition had known the sealed rooms were important; they'd traced the arkship's internal communication network, and discovered the principal node was inside. With due respect, they'd installed their own hatches in the Tyrathca airlocks, as they had up in level one. There was no worry about atmospheric contamination any more, not with all the water frozen out. But they wanted to maintain the environmental integrity. This was the first human exploration through an artefact belonging to a sentient xenoc species; ethics was a paramount concern—even though the Tyrathca were indifferent to such matters.

So, Monica and the others discovered, was someone else.

The large titanium rectangles leading to the control offices had been reactivated and opened, swinging back against the chamber wall. Not only that, the safety interlocks had somehow been circumvented, allowing all three to be opened at once. The five suited figures stood in front of the opening, scanning round with their sensors.

"This has got to be it," Monica datavised. "The human hatches are still here. The archaeologists didn't install them anywhere else."

"Has there been another expedition since the first?" Renato asked.

"If there was, then neither Earth, Jupiter, nor Kulu knew

anything about it," Samuel datavised. "I have to say that's extremely unlikely."

"In any case, why not just use the archaeology team's hatches?" Renato asked. "We know they work. It must have taken a lot of effort to get these brutes open again."

Oski stepped forward gingerly, using a hand-held sensor pad to scan around the airlock rim. "I can't pick up any electrical impulses. But this was opened very recently. There's still some very faint thermal traces in the surrounding structure. They probably had to warm the airlocks back up to their operating temperature to get them to function again."

Monica resisted the instinct to whirl round and check the streets of the necropolis behind. Her suit's micro radar was scanning constantly for any sign of local movement. But the arkship's chill had somehow managed to stroke her skin through the armour. "How recent?" she asked.

"Within the last five days."

"And not human," Renato datavised.

"Why do you say that?"

"Obvious. If it was our species, they would have used the hatches the archaeologists installed. Whoever it was, they were too big to fit through them."

"It has to be the Kiint," Samuel datavised. "After all, they are partly the reason we're here. Ione and Kelly were right, Lieria was interested in the Sleeping God. And this is the obvious place where information on it would be stored. They must have teleported in here not long after they left Tranquillity. And simply opening the original airlock is the kind of elegance I'd expect from them. We've seen what the Tyrathca do to doors that won't budge for them."

"Why not just teleport directly inside the control offices?" Monica asked.

"They're extremely small on a cosmic scale. I'm guessing

such an action would require impossible accuracy, especially over three hundred light years from Jobis."

"Could be. Do you think they're still here?"

Oski pointed her sensor pad along the short airlock tunnel. "It's inert as far as I can tell."

"And our time is running out," Monica datavised. "Let's get in there."

The control offices were noticeably warmer. Suit sensors detected thermal concentrations around three of the computer terminals in the second room. "This is the astrogration centre," Oski datavised. "One of our information targets. If we're to get a fix on the Sleeping God's location, we ought to find it stored in here."

"Get started," Monica datavised. The sensor disks were showing her the Tyrathca moving through the second level chamber with the biological reactor. They'd slowed their advance slightly since the diversion serjeant's attempted entrapment, treating each chamber with suspicion, never allowing more than three soldiers inside together. Even so, they'd be at the spiral ramp leading to ring five in another fifteen minutes.

Oski and Renato knelt down beside one of the terminals, and spread out their equipment. Monica, Samuel, and the last serjeant quickly searched the remaining rooms, then went back out into ring five.

"We should backtrack a bit and lay some false heat trails," Monica datavised. "That will give us a few minutes more."

"I don't think it will," Samuel replied. "By the time they get here, it will be obvious to them that we came for the control offices. Diversions won't work. We shall have to defend our position."

"Shit, I hope not, because this is a tactical lost cause. They can come at us from all sides, and we don't have a way out."

"But we do have superior weaponry. Let's just hope we don't have to use it."

"Fine. And now we've actually reached the mission target, why don't we start thinking of a way out of here."

The second diversion serjeant had rigged a hundred-and-fifty-metre length of corridor. A simple enough entrapment: wait until the lead Tyrathca reached the EE charge, then trigger both of them. The length of corridor should trap all twelve of the pursuing xenocs between the rockfalls. But when the lead Tyrathca approached the first EE charge, it slowed, and the others stopped. Ione cursed as it moved forwards carefully, waving its scanner round. She must have left an abnormal thermal trace in the corridor when she was placing the EE charges.

The Tyrathca consulted the scanner display a final time, and pointed its maser rifle at the corridor roof. If the beam did wash over the EE charge's trigger electronics, the radiation would destroy them.

Annoyed, Ione set off the EE charge, bringing down a five metre section of roof. It didn't harm any of the Tyrathca. They cantered back down the corridor and split up, presumably to bypass the blockage and pick up the diversion serjeant's heat trail again. Although without any sensor disk coverage, she couldn't be sure where they were. She started to move again, heading deeper into the arkship's interior, certain they weren't ahead of her, at least.

Oski was in her element. Worry about her physical predicament had vanished completely as she and Renato removed the computer terminal panels, exposing the circuitry inside. Tyrathca electronics lagged behind current human systems by several generations—if not centuries. She hadn't dealt with anything this crude since her compulsory History of Electronics semester while she was studying for her degree.

Renato followed her datavised instructions efficiently, tracing the terminal's main power cable and splicing in one of the energy matrices they'd brought with them. Small coloured symbols ringing the rosette keyboard lit up.

"Thank heavens they don't have any imagination," Oski datavised. "I'd hate to try and do this kind of thing on non-standard systems in the timescale we've got. But that's a null concept for the Tyrathca."

"Which I still think is a paradox," Renato datavised. "Imagination is the root cause of all fresh ideas. You can't design a starship without it. It's the Siamese twin of curiosity."

"Which they also don't seem to have much of."

"But probing your environment is a basic survival trait. You have to know if there's any kind of threat out there if you want to keep on living. Then you have to work out how to overcome it."

"I'm not arguing. Let's just save it for another time, okay?" Oski began attaching the processor blocks she'd brought to the databuses inside the terminus; unspooling long ribbons of fibre optic cable with custom built interface plugs on the end. The Laymil project had the specifications of known Tyrathca electronic systems on file in Tranquillity, of course; but she'd referenced the archaeology expedition's records to be sure. Tanjuntic-RI's systems were identical to those used today, even down to the size and configuration of the sockets. Fifteen thousand years of standardisation! Renato was right: that wasn't merely odd, it was downright eerie.

The interface plugs clicked smoothly into their sockets, and the block datavised that the high density photonic link had been established. Which was ridiculous. She'd been waiting to apply a chemical spray that would have eased the plugs into place. It had been invented by her division to clean up optical contacts that had been exposed to the vacuum, dust, and general degradation of the Ruin Ring; they used a lot of it on the scant remnants of Laymil electronics they acquired.

She put the spray canister down and picked up a micro scanner. "I can accept that their electronics are in a much better condition than the Laymil modules we have," she datavised. "The environment here is so much more benign, and they haven't been abandoned as long. But *this* lucky is absolutely impossible." The blocks finished assembling an iconographic display of the terminal's architecture. "The entire terminal is on-line, there isn't a single element not functioning. The Kiint didn't just access this, they repaired the damn thing to full operational status. Some of these components are brand new, for heaven's sake."

"How much of it is new?"

"According to my scanner, it's just processors and some support circuitry. The memory crystals are original. Which makes sense. They want the data stored inside them, just like us."

"Can you get it?"

"No problem." They already knew the Tyrathca program language, and there was certainly no such thing as security protocols or codes to guard against unauthorised access. Before leaving Tranquillity, the division's software experts had written customised questors that could examine all the information contained within Tyrathca memory crystals. Oski datavised the first batch of pre-formatted programs into the terminus architecture. Some of them were hunting for distinct references, while the others were classifying the information according to file type. The pair of them accessed the questor results as they returned.

"Well, it would have been too much to expect a direct reference to the Sleeping God," Renato datavised.

"No mention of an unusual cosmological event, either," Oski observed. She studied the file index, seeing what kind of database they'd activated, and shaping the next batch of questors accordingly. "We have plenty of navigational fixes."

"I'm going to see if the questors can find a list of star fixes they used to align their communication laser during the flight. At least that'll give us an idea of their contact protocol with the other arkships."

"Good idea. I'll see if any other arkship flight paths are stored in here. That should tell us what kind of spatial volume we're dealing with."

The questors revealed several tens of thousands of star fixes performed to align the interstellar communication laser. Eighty-five per cent of them were performed during the first six thousand years of the flight, after that the number of communiqués transmitted and received by the arkship dropped off considerably. During the latter stages of the flight, the star fixes were performed almost exclusively to align the laser on the five colony planets which Tanjuntic-RI had established.

With the fixes established, Oski began to search for associated files. "The messages aren't stored in here," she datavised eventually. "I keep getting a link code with all the laser alignment files. But it's to a different system altogether."

"Do you know where it is?" Renato asked.

"Not yet." She composed a new batch of questors, and sent them probing through the terminal's basic management routines. "How are you doing?"

"Unpleasantly successful. The Tyrathca built over a thousand arkships."

"Good god."

"Yeah, quite. If they all travelled as far as this one, that gives us a phenomenal area to search through for their Sleeping God. We're talking about a percentage of the entire galaxy. Small, admittedly. But everything is relative. Parker and Kempster will love this."

The questors started to display their answers to Oski. "Ah, here we go. The files we want are stored in some kind of principal archive. I've got the identification code."

"But it could be anywhere. We can't access anything from here."

"Yes. Come on. We want the office which dealt with the arkship's general systems. We'll see if we can activate one of the terminals in there, and call up a general schematic."

The maser beam caught the diversion serjeant on its thigh as it was crossing one of the hemispherical chambers. Ione's response was automatic, a fast powered dive behind a huge clump of machinery. The beam cut off as she fell behind it. Her armour's electronic warfare block had pinpointed the origin. The Tyrathca was shooting from just inside one of the corridors.

She loaded the coordinate into her weapons hardware. A homing grenade shot out of her belt dispenser, curving over the top of the sheltering machinery. An EE explosion obliterated the corridor entrance. Another maser slashed across the serjeant's armour. Ione rolled quickly, swinging the launcher round. A second homing grenade eliminated the corridor the Tyrathca soldier was charging out of.

They're moving bloody fast, she told her other selves and Samuel. **It was a good pincer manoeuvre.** She used the suit's sensors to scan down the corridor ahead. No motion or anomalous infrared source was detectable.

You can't go back, the serjeant with Monica and Samuel down in ring five told her. **You know they're behind you.**

Yes. She unclipped a magazine from her belt and slotted it into her multi-barrelled launcher as she walked over to the one remaining corridor entrance. Three slender missiles were fired at two second intervals, streaking away down the lightless tunnel. The serjeant flattened itself against the wall.

Each of the three missiles was tipped with a neutron pulse warhead. They detonated simultaneously, soaking a five hundred metre length of the corridor with a lethal cascade of radiation. If there had been any Tyrathca lurking down there, the neutron bombardment would have killed them almost instantaneously. Holding the fat missile launcher in one hand, and an X-ray laser in the other, the diversion serjeant started to creep down the radioactive corridor.

"Oski, progress report, please," Monica datavised. A sensor disk showed her the Tyrathca massing at the top of the spiral ramp which led down to ring five. "We're getting a little critical out here."

"I'm in the general systems layout. Should have the archive location any second now. This is another terminal the Kiint have refurbished. That must mean we're on the right track."

"Oski," Samuel datavised. "Please store as much of the layout as possible. It might help us to get out of here."

"To get out?" Monica queried.

"Yes. I have an idea."

"I'd love to hear it."

"One moment." *Syrinx?*

Yes Samuel. Are you making progress?

Not as much as I'd like, but yes. Oski will start to datavise the information we have acquired so far to you and the Lady Macbeth *in case we do not get out.*

There's still only one Tyrathca ship at Tanjuntic-RI. They'll be no match for Oenone. *As long as you can get back up to what's left of the spaceport support column, you'll be fine.*

That may prove difficult. The Tyrathca soldier-caste are very capable, as the serjeants are discovering. And they know where we have to return to. An ambush would be easy for them.

What do you propose?

Monica and I were both present when Dr Mzu escaped from Tranquillity.

Now wait a minute—Syrinx protested.

I could do that, *Oenone* said. If the *Udat* can, I can. There was considerable eagerness in the voidhawk's mental tone.

No, Syrinx said, instinctively protective. Tanjuntic-RI is a hell of a lot smaller than Tranquillity. You'd never fit into one of the rings.

But I would fit into the level-one chambers.

That was what I was going to suggest, Samuel said. We ought to be able to reach one of them. And I doubt the hellhawk could swallow in to harass you. Whereas if you came back here to fight your way past the Tyrathca ship, it could certainly complicate the situation for you.

I can do it, *Oenone* insisted.

Are you sure? This isn't just bravado, is it?

You know I can. And we would honour *Udat*'s memory by doing so.

All right. Syrinx couldn't hide the pride and simmering excitement in her mind. Samuel, we'll attempt to pick you out from one of the axial chambers.

Thank you, Samuel said emphatically.

Oski and Renato were almost running as they emerged from the control office airlock. Their suit programs were having to limit the augmentation to stop them from hitting their heads on the airlock chamber ceiling. "I've found the archive." Renato datavised the layout file over to Monica, Samuel, and the serjeants. "It's on the other side of the ring, a kilometre away."

"Move out," Monica datavised. Her guidance block was analysing the new data, incorporating it into existing files.

"According to this file, there's a ramp up to the second level just past the archive," Samuel datavised. "I'll blow the airlock hatch, and we'll evacuate through there as soon as you've got the information."

"Sounds good," Renato datavised.

The five of them were skating along the lightless streets in long low bounds, utterly reliant on their guidance programs. Nothing changed around them. At every turn, the wintered towers were the same ahead and behind, their infrared signatures identical.

"The Tyrathca are on their way down the ramp to this ring," datavised the serjeant who was guarding the entrance. "I've rigged the airlock. Do you want me to blow it?"

"No," Monica datavised. "Wait until they're all inside the ring, then blow it."

"You want to trap them in here?" Renato datavised. "With us?"

"Good tactics," Samuel confirmed. "If we block them now, we won't know where they are, nor how they gain entry. But once they're in, they can't get out easily, and we can monitor them via the sensor disks. It gives us the strategic high ground."

A glimmer of infrared started to shine down the corridor ahead of the diversion serjeant, like an autumnal dawn. Ione stopped and slapped a magazine of smart-seeker missiles in the launcher, datavising the Tyrathca profile into their processors. Suit sensors showed a similar infrared glow expanding behind her.

Surrounded, she informed her other selves. **Be warned. They really are making good use of their knowledge.**

A couple of neutron pulse tipped missiles were fired at the group behind her. She dropped a grenade, and started to run forwards. Smart-seeker missiles sliced out of the big launcher ahead of her. The neutron pulses went off. She triggered the grenade, bringing down the corridor roof. Small EE detonations were flaring up ahead as the missiles punctured the Tyrathca spacesuit fabric, burying themselves deep in the xenoc bodies before detonating.

Infrared vision was wiped out in splashes of brilliant crimson. Still firing missiles. Something like a medium-sized cannonball hit her right leg. Exploding. She was flung violently against the ceiling, bouncing down against the floor. Internal bones snapped. Cracks multiplied across her exoskeleton. But the armour held, reinforced by the molecular binding generators.

The diversion serjeant raised its head, dislodging various rocks which were lodged on its helmet. It moved its arms, actuators pushing hard against the weight of rocks holding its torso down. More rocks slithered off the armour. Two soldier-caste Tyrathca were bounding towards it. Ione waited until they were fifteen metres away, and fired a couple of homing grenades.

The sensor disk by the spiral ramp up in level one noted a rise in the thermal environment beyond its pre-set parameters, and broadcast an alert. Visual observation showed twenty new Tyrathca marching into the interior.

"Oh God," Monica datavised. "Just what we need."

"It will take them forty minutes to reach ring five," Samuel datavised. "If Oski hasn't retrieved what we need by then I doubt it will matter."

They were fifty metres short of the ring wall, passing the last of the towers. Five sets of suit lights slithered erratically over the wall, kindling small refractive auras from the curtain of frosted creeper leaves.

"There," Renato datavised. Rather uselessly, he raised an arm and pointed. But the others saw where his suit lights had come to rest, and focused their own beams on the spot. The airlock door to the archive was very similar to those of the control offices. And like them, open.

"It's recent," Oski datavised. "Several faint infrared footprints, very similar to those at the control offices."

"Monica, you go in with them," Samuel datavised. "I'll set the charges ready to open that ramp for us."

Monica drew an X-ray laser rifle from her belt, and switched her homing grenades to active mode. Feeling slightly more confident, she stepped through the open airlock. Oski and Renato had been issued with the same weapons suite as she, but not even full field combat programs could turn a pair of academics into decent troops. She didn't have surprise on her side. Instead she went for speed, flashing through the final doorway with sensor gain on maximum. Radar and infrared covered the whole interior of the archive chamber in milliseconds. The results filtered through her tactical location program, which declared there was nothing active inside.

"You can come in," she datavised.

The archive was substantially different to the control offices. A lot larger, a long hall tunnelled out of naked rock, with an arching ceiling thirty metres high. Despite having Tyratha-sized computer terminals and display cases, it was the most human place they'd seen in Tanjuntic-RI.

Principally, Monica decided, because it was instantly recognisable: a museum. Five-metre glass cube display cabinets were standing in regimented rows the whole length of the hall. The glass was fogged by grime and ice. When they shone their suit beams on the cabinets, the contents were visible only as intriguing dark shadows. From what they could discern, it was machinery inside; the outlines had too many flat sides and regular angles to be anything biological.

Each line of cubes was divided into sections by broad areas given over to computer terminals clustered round a central hexagonal pedestal of giant display screens. Oski walked over to the nearest one. "These zones must be the archive's operating stations," she datavised. Her light beams fanned up and down the casings, then settled on the screens. "There's a plaque here." Neural nanonics put her Tyratcha translation program into primary mode. "Atmospheric engineering," she read out. "They must cover different disciplines at each station. Try and find anything relating to navigation or communications."

"Can you see if the Kiint repaired any of the terminals?" Renato asked. "That would save a minute or two."

"Nothing like that showing yet," Monica datavised.

Renato walked along a row of the big cubes, annoyed they were all so opaque. The first station of terminals was mineral distillation, followed by thermal maintenance, then distillation mining. On impulse he wiped a gauntlet against the ice on one cube, upping the brightness on his suit lights. It was a chunk of machinery inside. "These gizmos look like they're brand new," he datavised. "I'm not sure this is a museum. Could be they archived actual physical components, the ultimate template back-up in case something screwed up their electronics."

"Any kind of disaster big enough to eradicate their crystal memories would wreck these machines first," Oski datavised. "Besides, think how many different components there are to make Tanjuntic-RI work. A hell of a lot more than we can see in here."

"Okay, so it's just the really critical ones."

"I think I've found it," Monica datavised. "This terminal has been spruced up, and it's still a couple of degrees warmer than the rest."

Oski scanned her suit sensors round to locate the ESA operative. "What's the station?"

"Planetary habitation."

"That doesn't sound quite right." She hurried over to where Monica was standing, suit lights converging on one of the terminals.

"The Tyrathca are now in ring five," the serjeant guarding the ramp entrance datavised. "I am blowing the airlock behind them."

Despite her high suit sensor resolution, Monica could receive no indication of the explosion. "Oski, we really don't have any more time to hunt round," she datavised. "Just get what you can from this terminal, and pray the Kiint knew what they were doing."

"Confirmed." The electronics specialist knelt down beside the terminal, and started working on the front panel.

Ione was tracking the Tyrathca through multiple observation points as they spread out through the streets of ring five. As soon as the airlock detonated and collapsed behind them, trapping the last two in the rubble, they had deployed in a wide sweep formation. The sensor disks were picking up microwave radar pulses from several of the soldiers. Their emissions helped to target the first batch of homing grenades which she launched, eliminating a further three. Then they wised up to that and switched the radars off. She launched a swarm of smart seeker missiles, programming them to flit above the tops of the towers. Arrowing down as soon as they located a suit.

The launch betrayed her general direction. Ultimately, an-

other plus point. She was on the other side of the airlock from
the control offices and archive, drawing them away from the
exploration team.

One of the sensor disks showed a soldier raise a rifle the
size of a small human cannon. Ione started running, not caring about the lack of cover. A tower disintegrated behind her;
the blast strong enough to create a rumble in the ring's near-
non-existent atmosphere. Big nodules of debris crashed into
neighbouring towers, shattering the brittle concrete. Three of
them toppled over, throwing up thick clouds of black dust
which surged along the streets in every direction, blocking
vision in all spectrums.

Monica followed what she could of the fight via the sensor
disks. Nervous energy created a nasty itch along her spine
and ribs. It was impossible to scratch through the suit. Even
twisting round inside the armour was useless. There was
nothing she could do to assist Oski and Renato. The pair of
them had exposed the terminal's electronics, and were busy
attaching their own blocks to the primitive components inside. Their fluid motions were bringing effective results. Little lights were flashing around the rosette keyboard, and the
monitor screen was producing a snowstorm of green and
scarlet graphics.

She started walking round the outlying display cubes, alert
for any other signs of Kiint activity. It was the one contribution she could still make. Not that it would be a lot of use at
this point. It wasn't until after she'd started on her second circuit of the planetary habitation station that her subconscious
alarm grew strong enough to make her stop and take a proper
look at what she was seeing. The shapes inside the opaque
cubes were no longer nice and regular.

With real unease replacing her anxiety now, Monica
swiped her gauntlet over the crinkled, sparkling ice, rubbing

a patch clear. Her suit lights brightened, converging on the cube. Visual sensors altered their focus. Monica took a half step back, breath catching in her throat. Her medical monitor program warned her of a sudden fast heart rhythm. "Samuel?" she datavised.

"What is it?"

"They've got xenocs in here. Xenocs I've never seen before." She scanned her sensors across the creature inside the cube, building up a pixel file image for the Edenist. It was bipedal, shorter than a human, with four symmetrically arranged arms emerging from mid-torso. No elbow or knee joints were apparent, the limbs moved as a single unit. Bulbous shoulder/hip joints hinted at a considerable articulation. All four arms ended in stumpy hands with four claw-fingers; while the legs finished in rounded pads. The head was a fat cone, with deep folds of skin ringing a thick neck, which would permit a great deal of rotation. There was a vertical gash, which could be either a nose or mouth, and deep sockets that could have held eyes.

"My God, Samuel, it's sentient. It's wearing things, look." She focused on an arm, where a silver bracelet was wrapped around the wizened caramel skin. "That could be a watch, I think. It's certainly technological. They caught a sentient xenoc and stuffed the poor bastard for their kids to look at in this freak show. Oh for Christ's sake, what are we dealing with here?"

"You're jumping to some very wild assumptions, Monica."

"Then you explain what the fucking hell it's doing in here. I'm telling you, they put it on show. It must have come from one of the planets they stopped at."

"You're in an archive, not a circus zoo."

"Is that supposed to make me happy? So this is scientific

not entertainment. What were they doing studying it? It's sentient. It's not a laboratory creature."

"Monica, I know it's shocking, but it isn't relevant to our current situation. I'm sorry, but you'll just have to ignore it for the moment."

"Jesus fucking wept." She spun round, and marched back towards the terminal where Oski and Renato were working. Heat and anger kept her going for several paces. Then she stopped and scanned the cube again. Her suit lights refracted off the gritty ice with its dark adumbrate core of sorrow and suffering.

When they'd come on board, she'd wondered about Tyrathca souls watching them. Now all she could think about was the soul of the unknown xenoc; lost and alone, crying out desperately for others of its kind. Could it see her now? Was it shouting its pleas for salvation from some obscure corner of the dreadful beyond? Unheard even by its own deities?

The medical monitor warned Monica she wasn't breathing properly. She made an effort to inhale in a regular motion. "Oski? How are you doing?"

"I'm not sure. There are some files in here that look like communiqués. I've just reverted to our fall-back option. We're copying every memory to analyse later."

"How long?"

"Programming is almost complete. It'll take half an hour to datavise all their files over to our processors."

"We can't afford that."

"I know. The bitek processors can shunt the information directly over to *Oenone* and *Lady Mac* in real time. We just have to hope the Tyrathca don't come in here and find out what we're doing until it's finished."

"That's a safe enough bet. I expect they'll be too busy chasing us."

*

How the hell did they get up there? Ione asked.

At least three Tyrathca soldiers were cantering along ring five's ceiling gantries. The narrow metal walkways threaded amongst the crane rails and irrigation pipes were shaking alarmingly as the heavy bodies thundered down them. But they were holding. And they provided the Tyrathca with a dangerously effective vantage point.

There were now six separate smears of billowing dust blotting out entire sections of the ring, evidence of shattered towers caught in the increasingly brutal crossfire. Tyrathca bodies lay everywhere, bleeding fluid and heat onto the cold alloy floor. One of the two remaining serjeants was limping badly, its suit leg crushed almost flat around the knee. Caught by a huge chunk of debris whose inertia defeated the binding generators. Several processors and hardware units on its belt were dead, ruined by maser fire.

Worse, from a tactical viewpoint, only one Tyrathca was currently stalking it. The remainder had moved away from the mayhem it'd unleashed to chase down the remaining heat trails. Four of them, including one breeder, were congregating round the open airlock into the control offices.

"They know we went in there now," Samuel datavised.

"The ones on the gantries will be looking for us," Ione datavised. "And they'll see us soon enough."

"We've finished programming the file extraction," Oski said. "The data is being received by the starships."

"Excellent. Get out of the archive, I'm about to blow the airlock. Ione, can you take out the soldiers on the gantries?"

"I'll try."

"At this point, you're not expendable to us, okay? We're going to need back-up to get out of here."

"Understood. But only one of me will be able to keep up with you on the ramp."

The injured serjeant raised its missile launcher, and fired the two remaining smart seeker missiles. They soared off into the gloom, twin spikes of intense amber light, seemingly rising out of sight around the ring's curvature. It began to limp into the seething dust, heading back towards the archive. Searching round on its belt, Ione found a magazine containing neutron pulse missiles. Only four of the twelve responded to a datavise. She slipped the magazine into the launcher anyway.

When the others made it to the shelter of the ramp, she could then make life seriously unpleasant for the Tyrathca left in ring five.

Samuel and the last serjeant were waiting for Monica, Oski, and Renato right outside the archive. Monica's thoughts were still in such turmoil after finding the xenoc that she didn't trust herself to say anything to him.

"There's still one soldier-caste left up on the gantry," Samuel datavised. "Not that it matters much now." He triggered the charges he'd laid around the airlock.

They were close enough to see the flash: a dazzling ripple of pure white light that burst across the ring, fading fast.

Samuel started running straight at it. They only had a hundred and fifty metres to go. He datavised instructions to the others, who activated their rocket launchers. A semicircle of towers fell in unison as the missiles pulverised their ground floors. Dust strangled the thin plumes of potent flame, sending out a curtain of impenetrable darkness that fountained straight upwards.

The airlock leading to the ramp had been wrenched to one side by the charges Samuel had laid around its rim, buckling the thick slab of titanium like so much plastic sheeting. A tide of rock had spewed out of the gap, narrowing it still further. His boots dislodged small loose fragments as he scrambled up. There was enough space to pass through, providing he turned sideways. As soon as he was on the other side, he started slapping EE charges on the walls. Monica and the others wriggled through the gap, with the serjeant bringing up the rear.

Eighteen combat wasps were closing on *Lady Mac*, the third time in an hour Hesperi-LN's defences had launched such a salvo at them. Each time, *Lady Mac* had simply jumped away before any of them were in range, leaving the drones to search round helplessly for their target.

"Good job the Tyrathca never met anything hostile when they were on their voyage here," Joshua remarked. "I mean, Jesus, they are absolutely crap at space warfare. Why do they keep firing salvos when we're far enough above the planet to jump?"

"They're lulling us into complacency," Ashly said cheerfully. "They've worked out roughly where we've got to emerge next time, and they've flown their superweapon there ready to zap us."

"Nope. Keeping the jump emergence coordinate as a random variable is file-one in the combat manual."

"They wouldn't have a superweapon anyway," Liol said. "Building stuff like that takes inventive flair. And they just ain't got it."

"They do seem to be very dogmatic," Dahybi said. "As they haven't got a combat capable starship to field against us, their options are limited."

"Limited, yes," Joshua agreed. "But not to one." He studied the tactical display. The nearest combat wasp would be close enough to start deploying submunitions in another two minutes. "Stand by for jump. Sarha, how's the memory dump coming on?"

"No problems, Joshua. The bitek array is accepting the load."

"Great, let's hope there's something useful in there." He cut the fusion drives, holding the starship stable with ion thrusters. The flight computer showed him the energy patterning node status as the combat sensors retracted. "Here we go." They emerged forty thousand kilometres from the combat wasp swarm. Hesperi-LN's SD network took nearly three minutes to acquire lock on.

"Are you launching another combat wasp?" Liol asked.

"Not yet," Joshua said. He datavised the bitek array for a link to the exploration team. "Where are you?"

"Coming up to level two," Monica replied. "The ramp is sealed behind us, so if we don't get ambushed, we'll be at level one in another twelve minutes."

"Okay, thanks, Monica. Syrinx, we'd better start finalizing our next move."

"Agreed. We must assume the blackhawk will try and follow us again."

"I can throw it off with multiple consecutive jumps. Can you do something similar?"

"No problem. Designate a rendezvous coordinate."

"That's trickier. This bloody diversionary battle has screwed around with our vector. I can get a rough alignment on the second planet with a small burn. We'll slingshot around it, and re-align on the Orion nebula. After that, we can lose the hellhawk."

"Very well. *Oenone* will swallow out to the second planet as soon as we've picked the team up. See you there."

The second level cavern housed a gigantic fusion generator, three pale metal spheres standing one on top of the other, eighty metres high. Arching buttresses of pipes and cables were wrapped around the main section like mechanized viaducts, sinking away into the walls and floor. A quintet of heat exchangers surrounded it. Fluids had leaked from their valves and feed tube junctions, dribbling down the casings to solidify in colourful multi-layered ribbons. The cavern's irradiated rock kicked off datavised Geiger warnings as soon as the exploration team bounded in from one of the corridors.

"This is it," Samuel datavised. "Our shortcut."

"It will be very short with this radiation level if we're not careful," Monica datavised. "This is as bad as a fission core meltdown. What kind of fuel did they use?"

"Heaven only knows." Samuel scanned his sensors across the pipes that disappeared into the curving apex overhead. "Any of those three." His suit's tactical program datavised the designation icon to the others, highlighting the pipe he'd chosen. "According to the file Oski pulled from the control offices it's a thermal gas duct. The exchangers transferred some of their heat along it to keep the level-one lakes warm. It's an express route straight there. All we have to do is slice it open."

Monica didn't argue with him, despite the sudden doubts. She'd stayed with Oski and Renato in the archive, leaving details of their withdrawal to Samuel. That was teamwork. And it was as though he'd been her partner forever. They knew they could rely on each other now. She took the stumpy laser rifle from her belt, datavised its control processor for a continual burn, and lined it up on the pipe he'd designated.

Five ruby red beams stabbed out, puncturing the pipe. Bright molten metal droplets drizzled down slowly, losing their radiance before they reached the ground. Monica's radar caught the movement just before the maser beam hit her suit. A couple of homing grenades fired immediately from her dispenser, looping through the three dimensional maze of pipes to smash the corridor entrance where the Tyrathca soldier was lurking.

Backwash from the EE blast rolled her across the ground to clang against the base of a heat exchanger. Her infrared sensor caught a blur of motion away on the other side of the chamber. Radar was useless, there was too much machinery in the way.

"They're in," she warned.

"Oski, Renato, finish cutting the pipe open," Samuel ordered. "We'll take care of them."

One of the Tyrathca cannon fired, blowing a hole in the side of the fusion generator. Monica grabbed her missile launcher, and fired off a pair of smart seekers. Samuel was kangaroo jumping up the side of a heat exchanger. Homing grenades spat out of his dispenser, zipping away to pummel the corridor entrances. Maser beams slashed at him. Monica's sensors triangulated their origin, and she launched more smart seekers in retaliation. Explosions ripped round the chamber as the corridor entrances were closed.

"Pipe's open," Oski datavised.

"Go straight in," Samuel datavised. "We'll cover you."

Monica dived under a buttress, scanning at ground level. The lower section of four hot Tyrathca spacesuit legs were visible ahead of her, below a coil-wound beam. She chopped them with the laser, slashing straight through the fabric. Large globs of weird purple gel burped out, oscillating wildly as they bounced off the floor and machinery. The Tyrathca stumbled and fell. Monica slid the laser along its flank. A tidal wave of gel blobs erupted. Then the body went into explosive decompression.

Oski's manoeuvring pack fired at full power, lifting her towards the apex of the cavern. Every suppresser program she had that could squash down on her fear was in primary mode. They must have worked, she was quietly delighted at how calmly she was reacting to being shot at. Guidance programs bent her flight around the clutter of arching pipes as she rose higher and higher. She actually passed a two metre section of the pipe on her way up, its edges still glowing pink as it tumbled end over end.

A maser beam struck her legs. The suit's tactical program shot a homing grenade down in response. Then she was concentrating solely on her flight, arrowing for the gaping hole they'd sliced in the pipe. Its rim flashed past her, catching her shoulder, and scraping along her arms. Then she was completely inside. Radar was the only sense which functioned in here, showing a rigid, featureless tube stretching out above her for nearly three hundred metres. Her manoeuvring pack thrusters throttled down, slowing her to a less reckless speed as the gravity dropped off. A second armour suit slid into the pipe below her.

"Hell of an escape route," Renato datavised.

Etchells had no warning that the *Oenone* was going to swallow away from the twin moons. The crew were still boring him crazy with their promises and propaganda when it happened. But he felt it go, a massive tear in the uniformity of his distortion field.

What are you doing? he asked. The Tyrathca ships were still hours away.

We're leaving now, Ruben said. **Why don't you go home? Think about what we've been saying.**

There was a momentary lapse in the affinity contact. Etchells observed the amount of energy *Oenone* applied to open the wormhole interstice, determining the terminus location. They had returned to that damn arkship!

Why are you here? he demanded. **What's so special about that ship?**

If you join our efforts to solve this crisis, then such questions will be answered for you, Syrinx said.

Fuck your psychobabble bullshit. He sent the energy

flashing through his patterning cells, uncomfortably aware of how much he had expended in warding off impacts from the Lagrange point particles. A wormhole opened, and he dived down it, emerging into real space again, barely twenty kilometres from the arkship.

The *Oenone* was probing the ancient vessel very thoroughly with its distortion field (an act which Etchells didn't understand). And the large Tyrathca ship was firing its secondary drive, moving up from its holding position at the front of Tanjuntic-RI. Etchells didn't really want to go into combat against the xenocs at this point, especially not with uncertain allies like the Edenists.

Oenone was performing another swallow manoeuvre.

You can't elude me, Etchells said.

Fine, Syrinx replied with icy superiority. **Follow us in, then.**

Etchells derived the voidhawk's wormhole terminus. Which was impossible. They were swallowing *inside* the arkship. There were cavities in there, he could feel them. Tenuous bubbles within the hard rock. So very small.

He didn't dare. That kind of accuracy was staggering.

The Tyrathca ship had risen above the arkship's horizon. It launched fifteen combat wasps straight at him. He swallowed away fast.

The level-one cavern was quickly and silently saturated with light, revealing the cyclorama of frozen water. Ripples and waves were caught in mid-swell, drained of colour as they had been of heat. The endocarps were different. Flat cliffs of rock, rimmed with ledges of metal just above the ice. One of them boasted a tiny pinprick of warmth. Five armour-suited figures hovered in front of it, watching the light source expand; twisted fragments of starlight threaded through length of the wormhole to spray out at random. There was no other indication of the terminus opening.

As the light dimmed it shone across *Oenone*'s marbled blue hull, glinting off the crew toroid. The huge voidhawk swept round the lake's curvature towards the exploration team, skirting the rickety old axial gantry with simple grace.

You've no idea how good it is to see you, Samuel said, accompanying the statement with a wash of gratitude and relief.

You too, *Oenone* replied. **I knew I could do this.**

Etchells conceded defeat. He wasn't going to find out why the two starships had come here, not now. *Oenone* was inside the arkship for less than five minutes before swallowing away again. Its wormhole terminus opened out above the star system's second planet. The Adamist ship jumped there as well.

Etchells joined them, at a non-threatening distance, observing the Adamist ship fly round the planet on a tight slingshot trajectory. When it jumped, Etchells tried to follow. But it must have used multiple consecutive jumps, because he couldn't find it anywhere near the emergence coordinate. With his energy patterning cells badly depleted, and his nutrient reserve getting low, he began the long, lonely trip back to New California. It was time to hand the whole problem over to Kiera and Capone.

14

Candles shaped like dark lily pads bobbed about over the bath water, never managing to touch the two bodies resting in the middle. Several of them had become mired in the burgs of apple-scented bubbles, their wicks sizzling as the flames struggled to stay alight. More candles were flickering gamely along the bath's marbled rim, half a metre tall; they were cemented into place by thick rivulets of wax. As the only source of light in the suite's dilapidated bathroom, their weak yellow flickers bestowed an appropriately dingy appearance.

For years the Chatsworth had been one of central Edmonton's most renowned five-star hotels, attracting the wealthy and the famous. But successive changes of management and ownership had seen it decay badly over the last two decades as too much of its cash flow had been diverted from maintaining standards to inflating shareholder dividends. Eventually it was trading solely on its name, and that could never last. Now it was closed for a much needed refurbishment and re-launch. But the work crews and their mechanoids hadn't even started stripping the old fittings out when New York's problems with the possessed hit the

AV news. After that, most of Earth's long-term commercial investment projects were put on hold while the financiers and entrepreneurs waited to see what the outcome would be. The Chatsworth included.

Quinn had taken it over with quiet efficiency to use as his home base in the arcology. The three-man caretaker team left inside were possessed, and every last connection to the outside world was severed: power, water, data, air conditioning. He knew that police and government security forces tracked the possessed by the glitches they caused, but they could only do that when there was working processor-governed machinery nearby. So he and his loyal followers made do with the water left in the hotel tanks, cooked on camping gear in one of the ritzy function rooms, and used candles. Bath water was heated purely by energistic power. The soaps and oils were stolen from a local mall. Along with booze.

Quinn reached for the bottle of Norfolk Tears chilling in an ice bucket among the candles, and poured the pale liquid over Courtney's glistening breasts. She giggled as her nipples hardened from the cold, and arched herself further out of the water. There were bruises and teeth marks on her gold-tanned skin, evidence of Quinn's recent predilections. She didn't mind the kind of sex he wanted; it was kind of interesting, the physical things he could do with his new black magic. That kind of misused power really turned her on, further proof of his omnipotence. He didn't have to worry about censure, or being caught. He wrote the rules now. And there was never much pain, nor did it last long. He didn't have to hurt her to confirm their relationship; he knew she had submitted herself completely to him and the cause. Joyfully, too. By embracing the serpent beast in its dark lair, Courtney's life had changed, becoming so much better. Hotter. Brighter. She got all the stuff like clothes and

AV fleks she wanted now; and she didn't have to take shit from anyone anymore, either. Not bad going for a sect whore.

Quinn threw away the bottle, and started to lick the luxurious drink off her skin. "This is the fucking max," he said. "You know, it really is true; the bad guys get the best of everything. Best clothes. Best drugs. Best babes. Best parties. Best sex. It's fucking *great*."

"We're the bad guys?" Courtney asked, puzzled. "I thought we were doing the right thing smashing up the world?"

Quinn stood up, sending the floating candles surfing into the bubbles. His erection grew to a thick flesh sword hanging over Courtney's upturned face. "We're both; we're bad and we're right. Believe it."

Her confusion vanished, and she was smiling with simple contentment again. "I believe in you." She cupped his balls, squeezing like he'd taught, and started to lick the length of his dick.

"After I've finished fucking you, I'm going to go over and kill another one of Banneth's people," Quinn said. "This time, I'm going to do it right in front of her. Force her to see how impotent she is."

"I don't get it." Courtney sat back, glancing up inquiringly. "Why don't you just march in there and start torturing her? It's not like she can stop you, or anything."

"Because this is exactly what she did to me. To us. All of us. She frightens people. It's her bang. What she can do to you up in that sanctum of hers is so fucking freaky and scary it hammers into your brain like some monster prick. All you can think of is how to stop her doing anything bad to you. Everybody in the coven knows they're gonna be strapped down on one of her tables some day. All you can do is ask God's Brother that when it's your turn, she does something that boosts you. Nothing you can do about the pain. That's fucking standard issue with Banneth."

"I see what you're doing," Courtney said, pleased with herself. "You're stalking her."

"That's a part of it, yeah. Each time I go over there and kill one of her people, it ruins a little more of what she is. The Banneth they all fear is growing smaller and smaller every day. Even dickheads that dumb are going to realize that the one person who can defeat anything is utterly helpless against the coming Night. I want her sitting there while the entire headquarter's coven freaks out and deserts her. I'm going to make that he-bitch feel what we all did. That she's a total nothing; all that power she's spent fuck-knows how many decades building up isn't worth shit any more. She used to make people piss themselves just by being sarcastic. *Sarcastic,* for shit's sake! Can you believe that? But that's how strong she was. Well now she's going to *know* what I'll do to her, and she's going to *know* there's no way out when I come for her. That puts me in control, and me on top. It switches her whole life around; screws with the way her brain's wired. I love that almost as much as I love the pain I'm going to inflict."

Courtney rubbed her cheek along his dick, eyes closed in dreamy admiration. "I want to watch."

"You can." He beckoned. She was taken up against the wall, hands pinned above her head. A loutish violation of hard thrusts, energistically strengthened muscles overcoming any hindrance to pummel his body against hers. In his mind he let it be Banneth, enhancing the pleasure.

Halfway through, when Quinn's orgasm was building, Billy-Joe knocked tentatively on the door. "Get in here, you little shit," Quinn yelled. "Wait. Watch us."

Billy-Joe did as he was told. Standing well out of the way. Keeping still, but with inflamed eyes following every aspect of Courtney's contortions. Quinn finished with her, and let go. She sank to the floor, propped up clumsily against the wall, shivering heavily. Her hands stroked gingerly over her body, touching the fresh bruises.

"What do you want?" Quinn asked.

"It's one of the possessed come to see you," Billy-Joe said. "He's one of the new ones. Come from the Lacombe sect. Says he's got to see you. It's like real urgent, he says."

"Shit." Quinn's skin dried; his robe materialized around him. "Hey! You want any of those healed up?"

"It's all right, Quinn," Courtney said thickly. "I've got some cream and stuff to rub on. I'm fine."

"This better be fucking important," Quinn said. "I told you dickheads not to move around the arcology. The police are going to be watching for you."

"I was careful," the possessed man said. His name was Duffy. He'd taken over the Lacombe coven's magus. Unlike the magus, Quinn judged him devout enough to God's Brother. Duffy had been left in charge of the coven, organizing several successful strikes against Edmonton's infrastructure.

Quinn sat down in one of the lounge's fraying leather armchairs, and let his mind wander through the Chatsworth and its neighbouring buildings. They were only a couple of blocks away from Banneth's headquarters, a location perfect in every respect.

There were no suspicious minds anywhere near. If Duffy had been spotted and followed, then the police were keeping well back. Quinn resisted the impulse to go over to the window and pull back one of the tatty curtains to peer down onto the street. "Okay, you haven't completely fucked up. What is it?"

"This magus, Vientus, I been squeezing him. He ain't a magus, not a real one. Doesn't believe in God's Brother."

"Big deal. None of those shits ever did, not really."

Duffy played with his hands, wretchedly nervous. Nobody liked the idea of telling Quinn what to do—like shut up and *listen*—but this was vital.

"All right," Quinn grunted. "Go on."

"He's some kind of secret police informer. Has been for years. Every night he makes a report to some kind of supervisor about what the coven's been doing and what's going down on the street."

"That's impossible," Quinn said automatically. "If the police had that kind of information they would have raided the coven."

"I don't think the supervisor's that kind of police, Quinn. Not like you get in the local precinct house. Vientus never met them, he just datavised the information to some eddress each night. There was other stuff going on, too. Vientus sometimes got told to target people for this supervisor, local business people, buildings that needed to be firebombed. And they'd talk about what other gangs were doing, and if they needed to be chopped back. Real detailed shit like that. It was almost like the supervisor was running the coven, not Vientus."

"Anything else?" Quinn was listening, but not really paying attention. He was too involved thinking through the implication, and with that came a growing sense of alarm.

"This supervisor must have had some influence with the cops. Quite a bit, I guess. There were times when Vientus got useful sect members released from custody. All he had to do was ask the supervisor for them, and the cops would let them go. Easy bail, or community work sentence, some shit like that."

"Yeah," Quinn said quietly. That recollection was one of

the most bitter he owned. Waiting in Edmonton's Justice
Hall for days with the dwindling prospect that Banneth
would get him released. Banneth could make the whole
legal system do tricks for her, like every judge owed her a
favour. Murder suspects out on parole within an hour. Stim
suppliers given house arrest sentences.

"Er." Duffy was sweating badly now. "And, er . . . the
supervisor had told Vientus to look out for you."

"Me? The supervisor used my name?"

"Yes. There was a visual file on you and everything. The
supervisor said you were using the possessed to take over
sect covens, and they thought you'd try to kill Banneth."

"Shit!" Quinn stood up, and sprinted for the door. Halfway across the lounge he shifted into the ghost realm, running through the closed door without breaking stride.

Half past two Edmonton local time, and the arcology was at
its quietest. Solaris tubes suspended underneath the elevated roads between the uptown skyscrapers shone down
on deserted streets. Hologram adverts swarmed up the
frontage of the ground level shops, bright fantasy worlds
and beautiful people shining enticingly. An army of munic-
ipal mechanoids crawled along the pavements in front of
them, spraying their solvents on tacky patches and guzzling
down fast food wrappers. The only pedestrians left to avoid
were a few late night stimheads thrown out of clubs by the
bouncers, and romantic youthful couples slowly strolling
the long route home.

Quinn adopted Erhard's image as he hustled along the
street. Not an exact replicant, but a reasonable facsimile of
the pathetic ghost. Good enough to deceive any characteristics recognition program scanning pedestrian faces through
the street monitor sensors for a glimpse of Quinn Dexter.
He stopped by the taxi rank a full block from the

Chatsworth, and the barrier slid down. One of the sleek silver Perseus cabs glided up out of the subway garage, opening its door for him.

Quinn pulled the seatbelt on with one hand, keying in his destination on the central control column with the other. He transferred the displayed fee from his bank disk and the little vehicle sped off along the street.

It all made a frightening amount of sense. He remembered the High Magus in New York; who obviously knew too much to risk being possessed. And back in Edmonton when he'd been a junior acolyte; the way everyone on a sect gig had to tell their sergeant acolyte all the crap that was going down on the street. It happened every single day. The sergeants would report to the senior acolytes, who in turn reported to Banneth. An uncompromising routine, drilled in to Quinn along with all the others right from their initiation. Information is the weapon which wins all wars. We need to know what the gangs are doing, what the police patrols are doing, what the locals are doing. Every coven was the same, in every arcology. The sect knew the moves of every downtown illegal on the whole planet.

"Perfect!" Quinn shouted. He thumped his fist into the seat cushion. "Fucking perfect." The taxi was starting to rise up a ramp to the elevated express-road. Vertical lines of blanked windows zipped past as they increased speed, then curved round to a horizontal blur. Thousands of slumbering minds slipstreamed through his consciousness. Restful and content. Just as they were supposed to be. As they had to be.

Arcologies were the social equivalents of nukes. Half a billion people crammed into a couple of hundred square kilometres; an impossibility of human nature. The only society which could conceivably hang together in those circumstances was a total-control dictatorship. Everything licensed and regulated with no tolerance of dissent or rebellion. Anarchy and libertarian freedoms didn't work here, because arcologies were machines. They had to keep working smoothly, and the same way. Everything interlocked. If one unit fucked up, then every other unit would suffer. That couldn't be allowed. Which was a paradox, because you couldn't keep the jackboot stamping down forever. However benign a dictatorship, some generation down the line will rebel. So somebody, centuries ago, had worked out how to keep the lid screwed down tight. An old enough idea, never quite managed in practice. Until now. A government department that quietly and secretly takes control of society's lowest strata. Criminals and radical insurgents actually working for the very people whose existence they threaten.

Quinn could feel his energistic power starting to boil up. His thoughts were so hot with fury he could barely contain the power. "Gotta keep it in," he spat through clenched teeth. One mistake now, and they'd have him. "Got to." He pummelled his hands against his head, the shock of the craziness helping to bring himself back under control. Deep breath, and he glanced out of the cab's window. Uptown's layout was second nature, though he'd rarely experienced it from an elevated road before, much less a cab. They'd be taking the down ramp soon, angling in to Macmillan Station. Minutes only.

His breathing evened out, though he was still outraged. The sect, the awesome gospel he'd given his very life to, was being used as the front of some ultra-spook department. No wonder Banneth and Vientus could fix for an acolyte's bail with the cops; they *were* the fucking cops. Anyone with the slightest potential for danger was sucked in by the sect. And if they couldn't be cowed into dumb obedience and neutralized that way, then they were thrown to the cops and given an Involuntary Transportee sentence.

"That was me," he whispered in pride. "Banneth couldn't subdue me. Not even with all that shit she can do to bodies. Not me!" So the cops had been told about the persona-sequestrator nanonics he was bringing into the arcology. He'd always wondered who'd tipped them off, who the traitor was amongst his fellow devout. There probably had never even been any in the carton.

Banneth. Always fucking Banneth.

The taxi drew up in front of one of the hundreds of vehicle entrance bays to Macmillan Station. Quinn knew there and then that he was in the deepest shit imaginable. He climbed out of the cab and walked slowly into the main concourse.

The giant arena of corporate urban architecture was almost as empty as the streets outside. There were no arrivals. No streams of frantic passengers racing away from the tops of the escalators. Icons had evaporated from the informationals, which were hanging motionless in the air. Stalls had been folded up and abandoned by their sellrats. A few clumps of listless people stood under holoscreens, cases clutched tightly, staring up at the single red message that was repeated like a parallel mirror image everywhere you looked across the station: ALL VAC-TRAIN SERVICES TEMPORARILY SUSPENDED. Even the scattering of ghosts Quinn could see were wandering aimlessly about their haunt, their expressions even more glum and bewildered than usual.

A group of cops were standing together outside a closed BurrowBurger outlet, drinking from plastic cups, talking quietly among themselves. The loud echo of his footsteps as he walked towards them stirred way too many memories inside Quinn's skull. It was the same concourse, same dark cop uniform. Then, there had been pounding feet, heart thudding hard in his chest. Screams as people dived out of his way, shouted warnings. Alarms blaring. Brilliant light-bursts. The pain of the nervejam shot.

"Excuse me, officer; could you tell me what's happening here? I have a connection to San Antonio in half an hour." Quinn smiled Erhard's twitchy smile at the cops. It must have been a good copy; most of them sneered. Finally, the failed acolyte had performed a useful service for God's Brother.

"Check the station bulletin," one of them said. "Christ's sake."

"I, a ha, I don't have a set of neural nanonics. I qualify for the company loan scheme next year."

"Okay . . . sir; what we have here is a vacuum breach. The tunnels were pressurizing, so the transit company had to activate the emergency seals. There's a repair crew down there now. Should be fixed in a day or so. Nothing to worry about."

"Thank you." Quinn walked back to the taxis.

I can't get out, he realized. God's Brother! The bastards have snared me here. Unless I can get to the other arcologies, His work will remain incomplete. The Night may be held off. And that cannot be allowed. They are thwarting the Light Bringer Himself!

It was frightening, the way he'd been lulled into a false sense of security. He, of all people. Ever suspicious, ever mistrustful. And he'd fallen into their trap. Yet they must be frightened of *him* to go to such elaborate lengths. Whoever they were.

He stood outside a taxi for a long time, working out where he should go. In the end, there wasn't a lot of choice. He was in Edmonton for one person. And only one person would be able to tell him who his real enemy was.

*

This was the part Billy-Joe didn't like. He was holding a laser pistol in one hand, there was a heavy-calibre magnetic carbine hanging on a strap round his left shoulder, fitted with a magazine of EE-tipped projectiles, a bag full of EE demolition charges on his right shoulder, codebuster and ELINT blocks on his belt, and a slim omniview band worn like a tiara on his forehead to boost his sight. It was enough hardware to start a war. Kicking the shit out of Courtney's punters was Billy-Joe's usual gig. Fast, nasty, and personal. None of this commando shit, where security systems would shoot back at him if anybody in the group screwed up.

But Quinn had wanted to stir things up in Edmonton, keep the cops busy and away from uptown. So Billy-Joe was sneaking down a lightless alley at half past four in the morning with ten other acolytes from Duffy's coven.

"This is the place," said the possessed man who was leading them, and stopped at a blank section of the alley wall.

He gave Billy-Joe the creeps, maybe even more than Quinn. One of the five possessed which Duffy had let into the bodies of snatched civilians. They all lived at the coven headquarters, treating the acolytes like shit and lording it up: the core of what Quinn promised was to be the army of the Night. Billy-Joe wasn't so sure about all that dark destiny stuff now, despite all he'd seen Quinn do. From where he was, it was just replacing one bunch of turds for another. The sect never changed; he always got dumped on no matter who was in charge.

The possessed rested his hands on the wall, tensing as if he was trying to push it over. He probably could, Billy-Joe acknowledged. And that was without energistic power. He was at least thirty centimetres taller than Billy-Joe, and must have weighed half as much again.

A door materialized in the wall, made of wooden planks

with big black iron bolts and with a sturdy circular handle.
It opened silently, letting a wedge of bright light spill out
into the fetid alley. There was a long hall of machinery on
the other side; bulky turbine casings half-submerged in the
carbon-concrete floor. Billy-Joe was looking down on them
from at least sixty metres; the door had opened onto a high
metal gantry running round the inside.

"In you go," the possessed man ordered. His bass voice
rumbled along the alley, agitating the rats.

"I thought you weren't supposed to use your power,"
Billy-Joe said. "The cops know how to look for it now."

"They can only detect those fireballs we use," the possessed said glibly. "Listen, kid; Quinn wants you to bugger
up this water station, he was real keen for you to do that.
That's why I'm here with you, so I can let you guys in quietly. Now, unless you'd like to go in by the front gate, this
is the way to do it."

Three of the sensors perched along the top of the alley
wall picked up the blasé assurance, relaying it to the intrigued supervisors of North America and Western Europe.
The big possessed man had been leaving a trail of glitched
processors ever since the little sabotage group emerged
from the coven headquarters.

The ever-vigilant AI had datavised North America as
soon as the first two were confirmed. A GISD covert tactical team had been dispatched to shadow them within seconds. But the trail had been so ridiculously blatant that
North America had alerted Western Europe, and kept the
tactical team a block away. Both of the B7 supervisors
waited to see exactly where Billy-Joe and the others were
heading.

"I can't let them damage the water station," North America said. "Edmonton's operating margins are becoming critical as it is, thanks to Quinn's vandalism."

"I know," Western Europe said. "And our big friend has to know that as well. Use the snipers to target the waster scum, but don't let them shoot this new possessed. I've become very curious about his attitude."

"Haven't we all." North America issued his orders to the tactical team, who started to take up position inside the water station hall.

Internal sensors showed the sabotage group sneaking in through the new door, glancing from side to side to make sure no one was watching them, then stalking along the catwalk in an almost theatrical mime of caution. Nine of them went inside. Then the possessed man grabbed Billy-Joe's shoulder with a meaty hand and pulled him back just as he was about to slip through. White fire spat from the fingertips of his free hand, soaring into the hall. A couple of balls struck an electrical junction panel, detonating loudly.

"What the fuck?" Billy-Joe gasped. He struggled uselessly in that implacable grip as his colleagues shouted in panic. The door slammed shut with a vociferous *bang*, and vanished. "You bastard!" Billy-Joe screamed. He swung his laser pistol round, and fired at the chuckling possessed at point blank range. Nothing happened. The weapon's electronics had crashed.

Several explosions sounded inside the hall, reverberating through the solid wall. Both supervisors watched with little interest as the tactical team eliminated the saboteurs. Their attention was focused almost entirely on the small, intense drama unravelling outside in the alley.

"Traitor!" Billy-Joe yelled recklessly. "You killed them, they're dying in there."

The possessed man's grip tightened, lifting Billy-Joe off the floor, and bringing their faces close together. "Quinn's gonna chop you into rat bait," Billy-Joe hissed in defiance.

"I spared you so you can deliver a message to him."

"What? What . . . I—"

A palm slapped into Billy-Joe's cheek. It was hard enough to make bones rattle. A red veil flashed up over Billy-Joe's vision, like someone had shot the omniview band with a targeting laser. He groaned, tasting blood. "Are you listening to me?" the possessed purred.

"Yeah," Billy-Joe whimpered miserably.

"You tell Quinn Dexter that the friends of Carter McBride are coming for him. We're going to piss all over his crazy little schemes, then we're going to make him pay for what he's done. Understand? The friends of Carter McBride."

"Who are you?"

"I just told you, dickhead."

Billy-Joe was dropped to stumble among the slippery bags of trash and fleeing rats. A boot kicked his ass with terrible force, sending him flying. He hit the wall and rebounded, crying out at the pain stabbing through his buttocks.

"Now start running," the possessed said. "I want you out of here before the cops start hunting us."

"Keep the tactical team away from them," Western Europe said. A shout had almost escaped from his lips, the revelation was so astounding.

"Thank you for your insight," North America said caustically. "They'll stay clear."

"My God, we've got an ally. A bona fide ally. A possessed at war with Quinn Dexter."

"We won't have him for very long, I suspect."

The big possessed man was almost chasing a terrified Billy-Joe along the alley. They emerged onto a broad patch of wasteland, cracked sheets of carbon-concrete with rows of severed metal support pillars sticking up all along the edges. Typical of that area on the edge of dome, dominated by warehouses and shabby industrial buildings.

"What are you talking about?" Western Europe demanded.

"Smart boy, this friend of Carter McBride. He's heading for the utility labyrinth." North America datavised the file over.

Neural icons flowed together, producing a horrendously complex three dimensional maze for Western Europe to examine. Pipes, tunnels, subway tracks, underground cargo roads, power conduits, they all seemed to interlock under that one section of the dome. It was a nexus where utility providers and transport industries joined together to supply Edmonton with the essentials its inhabitants expected; the busy powerhouse behind the public stations, efficient suppliers, and immaculate malls. The ground for kilometres around the water station was riddled with concrete warrens and bunkers, with a thousand entrances and ten thousand junctions.

"And those are just the ones marked on the file," North America said bitterly. "Christ knows what's actually down there."

The possessed man and Billy-Joe stopped beside a giant metal trapdoor whose rectangular rim was marked out by thin lines of thistles. It hinged upwards, tearing the tangle of yellow tap roots with a loud ripping sound. Crumbs of soil dribbled down into the chasm revealed underneath. The top rungs of a rusty ladder were just visible. Bill-Joe started to climb down. The possessed man followed. As soon as his head was level with the ground, the trapdoor closed over him. For a second, the rim glowed purple, as if it had been haloed by neon tubes.

"I bet he just sealed it up," North America said.

"Get the tactical team over there fast," Western Europe

said. "Welding the edges isn't going to stop them cutting it open, not with their firepower."

"They're on their way."

"Can the AI track him down there?"

"It's already accessed all sensors and processors in the labyrinth. But that shaft they went down was an inspection and maintenance access for an old industrial heat exchange coolant fluid pipe. There's no active electronics in there, it hasn't been used for fifty years. They could come out anywhere."

"Damnit. Flood the place with your bitek insects. Use every operative you have to physically cover the exits. We cannot let him escape."

"Please. Don't tell me how to manage my assets. I have some experience in these matters."

"I apologise," Western Europe said. "Damn, this is so frustrating. That possessed could be the real break we're looking for. He might manage to neutralize Dexter for us. We have to make contact."

The tactical team reached the metal trap door and promptly carved a circle out of it. One by one they hurried down the ladder.

"Billy-Joe would probably lead us direct to Dexter," Western Europe said. "If we could just find him when he comes out."

"Maybe," North America said. "I'm not making any promises."

Searching the labyrinth was a huge operation, though subtle enough to avoid the attention of the media. Police were diverted from their usual patrol routes to cover every entrance. Swarms of bitek spiders, bees, earwigs, and roaches were released into the maze of tunnels and passageways, their examination coordinated by North America's subsentient bitek processor array. Every employee working in the labyrinth was stopped and questioned as they came on and off shift. The AI assumed direct control of every mechanoid the labyrinth companies used, reassigning them to assist the search.

North America discovered several stim dens, enough deadbeats to populate a couple of condos, caches of weapons dating back decades, and enough illegally dumped toxic waste canisters to warrant urgent official attention. There were also a large number of bodies, ranging from the freshly dumped to skeletons picked clean by the rats.

Of Billy-Joe and the friend of Carter McBride there was no sign.

"Carter McBride?" Incredulity swept all Quinn's anger away as the name finally registered. "God's Brother! This possessed definitely said Carter McBride? You're sure?" Quinn could barely remember Carter's face, just one of the little brats running loose round Aberdale. Then, as he found out later, Laton had the boy murdered, making it look as though the Ivets had done it. The villagers had systematically set out to kill Quinn and his colleagues in revenge.

"Yes," Billy-Joe said. His limbs wouldn't stop trembling. He expected Quinn to blast him into a lump of smoking meat when he returned to the Chatsworth. In fact, he'd been wondering if he should even bother returning to the old hotel at all. Five hours of shitting himself about the consequences as he slunk round diseased tunnels full of those fucking rats and worse. Expecting the cops to burst out of the walls any second. Getting mugged. Fucking mugged! Some bunch of deadbeats clubbing him over the head and making off with most of his gear. Not daring to shoot them in case the cops detected his weapon.

It had taken a long time before he trudged back to the

Chatsworth. In the end he did it because he believed Quinn would ultimately win. Edmonton would fall into a state of demonic anarchy, ruled over by sect possessed. And when that happened, the dark messiah would catch up with Billy-Joe. Explanations would have to be made. Punishment would follow that. So he came back. This way only one failure had to be accounted for.

"Shit," Quinn breathed. "Him! It's got to be him again."

"Who?" Courtney asked.

"I don't know. He keeps . . . pissing me off. He's appeared a few times now, screwing with what I do. What else did he say?" he asked Billy-Joe.

"That he was going to wreck whatever you were doing."

"Figures. Anything else?" The tone was unnervingly mild.

"You'll pay for what you've done. He said it, Quinn, not me. I swear."

"I believe you, Billy-Joe. You've been obedient to Our Lord. I don't punish loyalty. So he said he'd make me pay, did he? How?"

"Just that he'd catch up with you. Didn't say nothing else."

Quinn's robe changed, the fabric hardening around his limbs. "I shall enjoy that encounter."

"What are you going to do, Quinn?" Courtney asked.

"Shut up." He stalked over to the window and peered down through a gap in the heavy curtains. Cars and trucks flashed along the ramp five stories below, curving down to street level. Fewer vehicles than usual, and the crowds on the sidewalk were noticeably thinner. But then Edmonton had been in a mild panic for most of the day since the early morning commuters discovered the vac-trains were closed. Every Govcentral spokesperson in the arcology assured the reporters that there were no possessed loose. Nobody believed them. Things were falling apart across the domes. But not in the way Quinn intended.

I don't fucking believe this, he raged silently. Some kind of supercops know I'm here. I can't bring about the fall of true Night without the vac-trains. And now heaven's own bastard vigilante is gunning for me. God's Brother, how could everything go so *wrong*? Even Banneth is diminished.

It was another of His tests. It must be. He is showing me the true path to Armageddon lies elsewhere. That as His messiah I must not rest, not even to gorge my own serpent beast. But who the fuck is Carter's friend? If he knew Carter, then he must be someone from Lalonde, Aberdale itself. One of the men.

Although that conclusion hardly reduced the field of suspects. All the men at that sewer of a village hated him. He forced himself to be calm, to remember the few words the bastard had spoken back on Jesup asteroid when he fucked up the sacrifice ceremony.

"Remember this part?" Quinn's own mimicked face had taunted. So whoever it was had witnessed the sect ceremony before, then. And was from Aberdale.

The realization was so pleasurable it blessed Quinn's face with the kind of smile usually bought by orgasm. He turned from the window. "Call everyone," he told one of the nervous acolytes. "We're going to tool up and march against Banneth. I want every one of my followers to accompany me."

"Shit, we're going for her?" Courtney's eyes were shining with greed.

"Of course."

"You promised I could watch."

"You will." It was the only way. The cops would only

allow the vac-trains to run again if they thought they'd eliminated all the possessed in the arcology.

Quinn would bring them together, and do to them what Carter McBride's friend had done to the sabotage group. After that, time would become his most powerful weapon. Not even the supercops could keep the vac-trains closed for months when there were no further signs of possession.

"But first, I have something else which needs taking care of."

Courtney did as she was told and switched on a processor block, establishing a link with Edmonton's net. Quinn stood a couple of metres away, watching the little screen over her shoulder as the questor was launched into Govcentral's main citizens directory. It took eight minutes before the requested file expanded into the block's memory. He read down the information, and smiled victoriously. "Her!" he said, and thrust the block towards Courtney and Billy-Joe, showing them the picture he'd found. "I want her. You two go down to the vac-train station and wait. I don't give a fuck how long you have to stay there for, but the first vac-train out of here, you take it and you get over to Frankfurt. Find her, and bring her to me. Understand? I want her alive."

A call from reception informed Louise that she had a delivery to accept. The house telephone was almost identical to the chunky black instruments back on Norfolk, except it had a bell rather than a shrill chime. Now she had neural nanonics, the whole thing seemed absurdly primitive. Presumably, for people who didn't have them as their sole planetary communication system, they were endearingly quaint. Part of the Ritz's old-world elegance.

Louise looked around the lobby as soon as the lift doors opened, curious about what could have been sent to her. She was sure all the department stores had delivered. Andy

Behoo was slouching against the reception desk under the suspicious gaze of the concierge. He jerked to attention when he saw Louise, his elbow nearly knocking over a vase of white freesia. She smiled politely. "Hello, Andy."

"Uh." He stuck his hand out, holding a flek case. "The Hyperpeadia questor's arrived. I thought I'd better bring it round myself to make sure you got it okay. I know it was important to you."

The concierge was watching with considerable interest. He didn't get to see such naked adoration very often. Louise gestured towards the other end of the vaulting chamber. "Thank you," she said when Andy pressed the flek into her hand. "That's very kind."

"Part of the service." He smiled broadly, crooked teeth on show.

Louise was rather stuck for what to say after that. "How are you?"

"You know. The usual. Overworked underpaid."

"Well you do a very good job at the shop. I'm grateful for the way you looked after me."

"Ah." Andy's world was suddenly very short on oxygen. But she'd come down by herself. That must mean her fiancé hadn't arrived yet. "Um, Louise."

"Yes?"

Her soft smile was wired directly into his brain's pleasure centre, shorting out his coordination. He knew he was making a right old balls up of this. "I was wondering. If you haven't got anything planned, that is. I mean, I'll understand if you have and all that. But I thought, you know, you haven't been in London long and had a chance to see much of it. So if you like, I could take you out to dinner. This evening. Please."

"Oh. That's really sweet of you. Where?"

She hadn't said no. Andy stared, his smile numbed into

place. The most beautiful, classy, sexy girl in existence hadn't said no when he asked her for a date. "Huh?"

"Where do you want to go for dinner?"

"Um, I thought the Lake Isle. It's not far, over in Covent Garden." He'd asked Liscard for a two week advance on his pay, just in case Louise said yes; Liscard granted it on a four per cent interest rate. That way he could actually afford the Lake Isle. Probably. It had cost a lot more than he'd expected to reserve the table; and that deposit was non-refundable. But the other sellrats all said it was the right kind of place to take a girl like Louise.

"That sounds nice," Louise said. "What time?"

"Seven o'clock. If that's okay?"

"That's fine." She gave him a light kiss on his cheek. "I'll be here."

Andy walked back with her to the waiting lift. There had been something about a dress code in the datavise when he reserved the table. He now had two and a quarter hours to find a dinner jacket. A clean one, that fitted. It didn't matter. A man who'd got himself a date with Louise Kavanagh could do anything. Louise pressed the button for her floor. "You don't mind if I bring Genevieve, do you? I really can't leave her here by herself, I'm afraid."

"Uh." From nirvana to hell in half a second. "No. That'll be lovely."

"I don't want to spend an evening with *him*," Genevieve whinnied. "He's all peculiar. And he fancies you. It's creepy."

"Of course he fancies me," Louise said with a grin. "He wouldn't have asked me out otherwise."

"You don't fancy him, do you?" a thoroughly shocked Genevieve asked. "That would just be too hideous, Louise."

Louise opened the wardrobe and started to rifle through the dresses they'd managed to acquire on their shopping trips. "No, I don't fancy him. And he's not peculiar. He's quite harmless."

"I don't understand. If you don't fancy him, why did you say yes? We can go out by ourselves. Please, Louise. London isn't nearly as dangerous as Daddy thinks it is. I like it here. There's so much to do. We could go to one of the West End shows. They sell tickets at reception. I checked."

Louise sighed and sat down on the bed. She patted the mattress, and Gen made a show of being reluctant to sit beside her. "If you really, really don't want to go out with Andy for the evening, I'll cancel."

"You're not going to kiss him or anything, are you?"

"No!" Louise laughed. "Devil child. What a dreadful thing to say."

"Then why?"

Louise stroked the dark hair from Gen's face, letting the flexitives ripple it over her ears. "Because," she said softly. "I've never been asked out to dinner with a boy before. Not to a fancy restaurant where I can dress to kill. I don't suppose it'll ever happen again. Not even Joshua asked me out. Not that he could, of course. Not when we were at Cricklade."

"Is he the baby's father?"

"Yes. Joshua's the father."

Gen brightened. "That means he's going to be my brother-in-law."

"Yes. I suppose it does."

"I like Joshua. It'll be stupendous having him living at Cricklade. He's such jolly fun."

"Oh yeah. He's fun all right." She closed her eyes, remembering the way his hands had caressed. Warm and skilful. It had been so long since she'd seen him. But he did promise . . . "So, what do I tell Andy Behoo, then? Do we go, or do we stay here all night?"

"Can I wear my party dress, too?" Gen asked.

*

The scene playing out above the B7 sensenviron conference room table was the one involving the failed sabotage attempt against Edmonton's water station. It wasn't a particularly good image, the station's perimeter sensors were hardly commercial-quality; but the two humanoid figures shouting at each other had enough colour and resolution to sketch in their individual features. Billy-Joe was being suspended several centimetres off the floor of the alley by the large possessed man. Their noses were almost touching. Then Billy-Joe was slapped hard, more words were exchanged. The two of them ran off down the squalid alley.

"We think we know who Carter McBride is," Western Europe told the other supervisors as the recording ended. "The AI found several references. He was the child of a colonist family on the same starship that took Quinn Dexter to Lalonde. According to the Lalonde Development Company files I accessed, the McBrides were also in the same village that Dexter was assigned to for his work-time."

"A friend of Carter McBride," Southern Africa mused. "You mean this new possessed was on Lalonde?"

"Yes," Western Europe said. "And the whole Quallheim Counties trouble was originally thought to be an Ivet rebellion over the killing of some boy. The obvious conclusion is that it was Carter. That implies the possessed who blew the sabotage group in Edmonton has to be someone killed on Lalonde at around the same time."

"So you're saying that this possessed person is out for revenge against Quinn Dexter?"

"Exactly," North America said. "We have a new ally."

"Bullshit," South Pacific said sharply. "Just because the possessed have internal disputes, that doesn't make one faction friendly towards us. Suppose this new possessed does manage to eliminate Dexter? Do you really think he'll just conveniently vanish for us afterwards? I certainly don't. In any case, we're not exactly communicating with him, are we? You lost him and this waster boy. What kind of amateurism is that?"

"I'd like to see you do better in that goddamn labyrinth," North America snapped.

"Given the speed at which this new development broke, I think the situation was handled as adroitly as possible," Western Europe said. "However, it does introduce some new factors which I believe warrant our consideration."

"Such as?" North Pacific asked suspiciously.

"I believe it will force Dexter to abandon all his activities for a while. Unfortunately, this wretched little oik Billy-Joe couldn't be intercepted, so we must assume he returned to Dexter and passed on the message he was given. As a consequence, Dexter will know he has a possessed stalking him; and that after the sabotage mission was exposed, the authorities have confirmed there are possessed in Edmonton. If we're right about his reasons for being here—to wreck as much of the planet as possible—he'll have no choice but to ignore Banneth and either abandon or betray the remaining possessed in the arcology. Then he'll lay low until political pressure forces the North American senate to reopen the vac-train lines. Face it, we can't keep them shut for months unless there is a visible threat to rattle the public with. Time is on his side. We're already compromising ourselves with the actions we've taken to date."

"Not a chance," South Pacific blurted. She pointed a hostile finger at Western Europe. "Very smooth. But I can see what you're angling for, and I say no. No way."

"Angling for what?" Central America asked.

"He wants us to open Edmonton's vac-train routes."

"Count me out," Asian Pacific said quickly.

"Absolutely not," East Asia agreed. "We've got Dexter

bottled up in one place. Keep him there. You'll just have to improve your surveillance techniques and track him down."

"He's goddamn invisible!" North America stormed. "You saw what happened in Grand Central Station. There aren't any techniques to improve that can catch up with that kind of ability."

"If we don't re-open the vac-train routes, then we'll be condemning Edmonton and everyone in it to possession," Western Europe said. "And very probably removal from this universe. Remember what happened to Ketton on Morton-ridge. That's what they'll do to it. They can't survive here."

"That outcome is certainly acceptable to me," North Pacific said. "We've discussed this through before. Better to lose one arcology if that means saving the rest."

"But we don't have to," Western Europe insisted. "Dexter becomes visible to us when he's moving. That's when he's vulnerable."

"He's not visible," South Pacific said. "We know he's moved simply by the destruction he leaves behind. I mean, shit, blowing up the Eiffel Tower! Face it, we can't catch him."

"We have to make the attempt. It's the reason we exist, the only reason. If we cannot protect Earth from a single possessed when we have the opportunity, especially because of political cowardice, then we have failed."

"I'm not buying into any of this noblesse oblige crap, I never did. That might be your heritage, but it certainly isn't mine. We formed B7 out of sheer bloody minded self inter-est. And you were a big part of that, don't forget. We exist to protect our own interests. Ninety-nine times out of a hun-dred, that means protecting Earth and looking out for its citi-zens. Well bravo us. I don't begrudge them that expenditure. But this is not one of those benevolent times. This time we safeguard ourselves against possession, and especially against Quinn bloody Dexter. I'm sorry about the inhabitants, but Edmonton falls to this Night of his. Probably Paris and the others as well. Tough. We'll be safe, though."

"I was wrong," Western Europe said coldly. "It's not political cowardice. You're frightened of him."

"That's beneath contempt," South Pacific sneered. "I'm not going to open the vac-trains simply because you insult me."

"I know that. I was just insulting you anyway. You deserve it."

"Big deal. Don't tell me you're not making preparations to desert the sinking ship."

"All of us are, as we all know. It would be foolish not to. But for me it's a last resort. To be perfectly honest, starting afresh on some new world holds little appeal. I suspect the same applies to the rest of you."

The representations around the table remained silent.

"Exactly," Western Europe said. "We have to defeat Dexter on the ground. Our ground."

"By letting Edmonton fall, we are defeating him," Central America said. "He'll vanish from the whole planet along with the arcology."

"He won't. He's too smart to fall into that trap, and his agenda is different to the ordinary possessed. The vac-trains will be opened again no matter how determined you all are. It's only a matter of time. I say we should lure him out into a target ground of our own choosing."

"He's already exterminated four of Banneth's acolytes in her own headquarters," Military Intelligence said. "We know he keeps going back there, yet we still haven't managed to kill the little bastard. I don't see how taking him to another arcology helps."

"We can't change Banneth's environment now, that would

be too blatant. Dexter would be warned off. But we can take her to a more suitable location for a strike."

"You just said he'll sacrifice his vendetta against Banneth to achieve his greater objective," Asian Pacific said. "Do try to present a consistent argument, please."

"I can get him out of Edmonton," Western Europe insisted. "The Kavanagh girls appearing at this stage will be an irresistible enigma to him. He'll have to follow them to find out what's happening. And they will be manoeuvred wherever I choose."

"Well you needn't try choosing my territory," South Pacific said.

"I wouldn't dream of it. This requires efficiency and total cooperation. Qualities apparently beyond your ability to provide."

"Lead him into your territory then."

"I intend to."

"Then what are you whining about?"

"I don't want any interference. This requires finesse. If I initiate this operation, you stay out of it. No surprise Presidential decrees wrecking my preparations. No media novas. We all know what we're capable of if we want to screw each other over. We've been at it long enough in our other arenas, but this is not the time for those sort of games."

South Pacific looked from Western Europe to North America. "You two do whatever you like. But you do it between yourselves. Your territories are now embargoed, along with Bombay and Johannesburg. Would you like to put a counter motion to the vote?"

"No," Western Europe said. "I have what I want."

In the end Andy had to go back to Liscard and ask for a further advance. Four week's pay at seven and a half per cent interest! He deliberately didn't put a calculator program in primary mode, didn't want to know how long he was going to be shackled to Jude's Eworld to finance one date. But he could hardly ask Louise to pay for Genevieve. That would be cheap.

This time when he walked into the lobby of the Ritz, the concierge smiled pleasantly. Andy's dinner jacket had been loaned from someone he'd done repair work for a couple of months back; midnight black with a reasonably fashionable cut. The white dress shirt he'd borrowed from a fellow sell-rat, along with the scarlet bow tie. His black shoes came from a neighbour. Even the silk handkerchief in his top pocket was his mother's. In fact the only thing he wore of his own were his boxer shorts. He could risk that, somehow he was pretty sure Louise wouldn't get to see them tonight.

Seven o'clock and she wasn't there. Six minutes past and he was debating if he should ask reception to call her room. Eight minutes, and he knew he'd been stood up. Hardly surprising.

The lift doors opened. Louise was wearing a full length gown of deep-blue fabric, accessorised by a small rust-coloured waistcoat. No longer the breezy teenager who'd sauntered into Jude's Eworld needing assistance, her demeanour had gained twenty years. Andy didn't bother recording her image into a memory cell. No program could ever capture that combination of beauty and sophistication. His own recollection of this moment would stay with him throughout his entire life, he knew.

When he smiled at her, it was almost in sadness. "Thank you for coming."

Her answering expression was uncertain, sensing somehow just how important this had become for him. "I'm flattered to be asked, Andy." She prodded Genevieve.

"Thank you very much for letting me come along," the little girl said. There was nothing in the voice that gave hint of duplicity.

"That's okay," Andy said. "Hey, you look great. Give us a twirl."

Genevieve smiled in appreciation, and put her arms out to turn a complete circle. Her scarlet dress flapped about. A slim chain was fastened round her throat, its tarnished pendant bobbing against her neckline. Andy looked straight at Louise. "Another five years and the boys won't know what hit them."

"What do you mean?" Genevieve asked.

"He means you're very pretty," Louise told her.

"Oh." Genevieve blushed, but still managed to grin up at Andy.

Having her along wasn't so bad, after all, Andy found. In fact, she removed a lot of the tension that would probably have come from being alone with Louise for the whole evening. It wasn't boy-girl, one on one; with him desperate to impress with every word. That, he acknowledged, would have been an utter disaster.

He paid for the short taxi ride to Covent Garden. The Lake Isle was one of a hundred restaurants in the area. It had an antique frontage enclosing a small bar, with a seating area at the back which was inexplicably large given the size of the neighbouring buildings, and too shiny to be genuinely old. As they stepped inside, Louise tapped Andy's shoulder. "We're going Dutch tonight. No arguments. I brought Gen along after all. It wouldn't be fair."

The head waiter handed them over to an assistant waiter, who showed them to a table. Glancing round, Louise thought that they were possibly overdressed. But she couldn't turn down the chance to wear the blue dress, and Andy certainly didn't complain. If eyes had been hands, he would've crushed her.

"Did you find your friend?" he asked once they were seated.

"Not yet. That detective you recommended seemed quite good, though. Thank you."

The wine list appeared. Louise looked wistfully at the Norfolk Tears, not quite believing the price. She let Andy choose; a dry white wine from the Jovian habitats, and sparkling mineral water for Gen.

"You can have one glass of wine," Louise said when her sister started to look mutinous.

"Yes, Louise. Thank you, Louise."

She stared the little girl down. Gen had been threatened with dire retribution if she stepped out of line during the meal.

It was a strange evening. Louise enjoyed it for the knowledge it gave her. What it would really be like to live in a vibrant arcology, and be asked out by boys. Dressing up. The taste of exotic food. Conversation that wasn't just about crops, relatives, and local events; but of the momentous things facing the Confederation, and how the Navy was coping, and the latest news from the Mortonridge Liberation campaign. She had the freedom to say what she thought, based on her personal experience. To have an astonishing tale to tell, and be listened to.

While it was happening, she could actually forget how phony it all was. That she could never actually be that girl about town, because she was due to be a mother. That Joshua had never seen her dressed like this. How life could never be lived without a care anymore now that the human race knew the beyond awaited. And Quinn Dexter, who stalked Earth's beautiful, awesome arcologies, ready to smash them into a trillion pieces.

Over dessert she found herself looking at Andy in what was near to envy. He could still have that life; chase girls, go out partying with his friends, attend university, earn his degree, write his programs, travel. Possibly. If the possessed didn't win.

"Are you okay?" Andy asked. He'd been in the middle of telling her about his plans to set up his own software house when he'd raised enough money. This month's dream.

"I'm sorry." She put her hand on top of his, and squeezed softly. "You probably won't believe the cliché, but this has been one of the nicest evenings of my whole life. I'm very grateful you asked me out." The look of utter longing he gave her in reply nearly made her cry for what could never be. She caught their waiter's attention. "Three glasses of Norfolk Tears, please."

Genevieve stopped attacking her dessert bowl with a spoon in an attempt to scrape out the very last morsels of chocolate orange soufflé. She smiled in hopeful astonishment.

"Yes, you, too," Louise laughed. To Andy she said: "My treat. If you've never had it, you should. It's the only way to end an evening as perfect as this."

The drinks arrived in slim crystal glasses on a silver tray. Louise sniffed gently at the bouquet. "Wessex County, probably the Clayton estate."

"Yes miss," the startled waiter said. "That's right."

The three of them raised their glasses. "To living life, not wasting it," Louise said.

They drank to that.

Louise received the datavise when they were in the taxi heading back to the Ritz; a purple telephone handset icon blinking silently at the corner of her vision (NAS2600 had thousands of symbols and sounds to choose from—but this was the most familiar). The sense of cosiness which the evening had engendered immediately shrank away. It couldn't be anything other than business.

Her neural nanonics acknowledged the call, and Ivanov Robson's icon tag replaced the purple telephone.

"I've got some good news for you," the detective datavised. "I've found Banneth."

"Where?" Louise datavised back.

"She's currently in Edmonton."

"Thank you." That was one of the arcologies which the news had said was isolated. "Do you have an eddress for her?"

"Certainly." He datavised the file over. "Louise, you may have a problem selling this story of yours to her. If that happens, please call me. I might be able to help."

"Of course, and thank you again."

The doorman gave Andy a dubious stare when they got back to the hotel. Louise saw him hesitate, full of his old uncertainties, and felt an uncomfortably strong stab of sympathy. "Wait for me inside the lobby," she told Genevieve.

Her sister smiled mischievously up at Andy, winked, then skipped inside.

Thankful no giggles had been audible, Louise took a deep breath. "I have to go now, Andy."

"Can I see you again?"

The amount of hope in his voice was awful. I should never have agreed to come out tonight, she thought, he was always going to misinterpret it. Yet for all his faults, he has a good heart. "No, Andy, I'm sorry. I have this person I need to find, and I also have my fiancé. I shall be leaving Earth as soon as I can. It wouldn't be right, not for either of us. I don't want you to think this is something it isn't."

"I see." His head drooped down.

"You can kiss me goodnight, though," she said shyly.

More in fear than joy, he pressed himself against her,

touching his lips to hers. When they parted, her mouth crinkled up in compassion. "I really did enjoy tonight, Andy. Thank you."

"If it doesn't work with your fiancé, and you come back . . ." he began optimistically.

"You'll be top of my list. Promise."

He watched her disappear through the doors, standing with his arms hanging limply at his side. The finality of it was appalling. For one mad moment he wanted to rush after her.

"You'll get over it, son," the doorman said. "Plenty more of them out there."

"Not like her!" Andy shouted back.

The doorman shrugged, and smiled with infuriating smugness.

Andy turned fast, and walked away through the night-time crowds that were clogging the pavement. "I kissed her, though," he whispered. "I really did." He gave an incredulous little guffaw as the enormity of the contact finally registered. "I kissed Louise Kavanagh." Laughing broadly he set off towards Islington; he was far too broke to pay for a metro trip.

Louise waited until Genevieve was tucked up in bed before she called Banneth.

"Hello. You don't know me, but I'm Louise Kavanagh. I'm calling to warn you about someone called Quinn Dexter. Do you know him?"

"Fuck off." The contact was cancelled.

Louise datavised Banneth's eddress to the room's net processor again. "Look, this is important. I met Quinn Dexter on Norfolk, and he's going to . . ."

A red cross icon flashed persistently as the contact was cancelled again. The next time Louise datavised Banneth's eddress she got a filter program which requested her icon tag.

She loaded it in, only to be told she wasn't on the receiver's approved reception list. "Damnation!"

"What's the matter?" Genevieve peered over at her from the bed, duvet clutched round her shoulders.

"Banneth won't talk to me. I don't believe this, after everything we've been through to warn her. How . . . How *stupid.*"

"What are you going to do now?"

"Call Robson, I suppose." She datavised the detective's eddress into the processor, wondering if the man was psychic. Not a bad thing for a private eye.

"Don't worry," he told her. "I'll come right over."

The cocktail lounge was a mistake. Louise sat at a table by herself and ordered an orange juice while she waited for Ivanov Robson to arrive. The decor was as polished as the rest of the hotel, with honey-brown wooden panels and gold-framed mirrors covering the walls. Chandeliers kept it well lit, although it seemed shady, like a woodland glade. There were enough different bottles behind the rosewood bar to make the shelving look like an art exhibition.

Whether it was the wine and Norfolk Tears finally catching up with her, or just the superb cushioning of the deep leather chair, Louise suddenly started to feel warm and drowsy. It didn't help that she had to deflect seemingly dozens of offers from young (and not-so-young) men to buy her a drink and keep her company. She was worried that she was being too sharp when she turned them down. Whatever would mother say?

One of the tailcoated waiters eventually came over, an ancient man with large white sideburns who put her in mind of Mr Butterworth. "Are you sure you want to stay here, miss?" he asked kindly. "There are quieter rooms available for residents."

"I'll take care of her," Ivanov Robson said.

"Of course, sir." The waiter bowed, and backed away.

The giant detective's gaze slid along the line of men sitting up at the bar. All of them suddenly found something else of interest.

"No offence, Louise, but if you're going to wear that kind of dress, you really shouldn't be in a bar by yourself. Not even here. It sends out some seriously strong signals." He sat down in the chair beside her, his bulk making the leather creak.

"Oh." She looked down, only just realizing she was still in the blue dress she'd worn as a treat for Andy. "I think I may have had too much to drink. I went out for a meal with a friend earlier on."

"Indeed? I didn't think you were wearing it for my benefit. Though I would have been highly flattered. You look quite gorgeous."

Louise blushed. "Um . . . thank you."

"You do know your neural nanonics have a suppression program to deal with a wee bit too much mouth-alcohol interaction, don't you?"

"No."

"Well they do. Perhaps if you were to put it into primary mode, this would be a more productive meeting."

"Right." She called up the control architecture, and hunted round for the suppresser program. It took a couple of minutes, but eventually the bar wasn't so warm. Deep breaths conjured up the kind of alertness she employed during difficult school exams.

A cut-crystal tumbler of whisky had appeared on the small table at Ivanov's side. He took a sip, watching her intently. "Better now?"

"Yes. Thank you." Though she was unhappy about the

dress; people were still giving her the kind of looks Andy had, but without his endearing reticence.

"What happened with Banneth?" Ivanov asked.

"She cut me off. I couldn't tell her anything."

"Humm. Not entirely surprising. I accessed several facts about her during my investigation that indicate she's not an average citizen. The Edmonton police have amassed a rather large file on her activities. They believe she's involved with some kind of criminal organization; supplying illegal hormones and bitek products. Any mention of her former colleagues is bound to make her prickly. And you were right about this Dexter character, he was deported; the charge was aggravated resistance of arrest. The cops suspected he was a courier for Banneth."

"Now what do I do?"

"You have two options. One, you can forget it and stay in London. We're safe for now. I keep my ear close to the ground, the possessed haven't appeared here yet."

"I can't. Please don't ask why, but I have to give Banneth a proper warning. I didn't come all this way to be thwarted by the last mile."

"I understand. In that case, I reluctantly advise you to visit Edmonton. If you meet Banneth face to face she'll see you are neither a police entrapment agent, nor a nutcase. She'll take your warning seriously."

"But Edmonton has been isolated."

"Not any more." He took a sip of whisky, watching her closely. "The vac-trains have started running again. I guess the authorities have eliminated the possessed, or think they have."

"Quinn Dexter will be there," she said softly.

"I know. That's why I advised you to stay away before. However, if you're set on this, I'll accompany you and provide what protection I can. If he's as bad as you say he is, it won't amount to much. But it's better than nothing."

"You'd do that?"

"You'll have to pay for it. But I include bodyguard services in my job description."

It still wasn't over. Louise fought to hold back the fear she felt at the prospect of walking into an arcology where she was sure Quinn would visit. But dear Fletcher had been so adamant, and she'd promised. "Do you know where Banneth is?"

"Yes. I have a contact in the Edmonton police who's keeping me informed. If you decide you want to do this, we can go straight to her. You deliver your message, and we walk out. I doubt that'll take more than ten minutes. We could be back here in London in less than five hours."

"I can't leave Gen. Not even for that."

"I'm sure the hotel can arrange for someone to look after her tonight."

"You don't understand. She's my responsibility; Gen and I are all that's left of our home, our family, maybe even our whole planet. I can't put her in any more danger. She's only twelve years old."

"The danger is the same here as it is in Edmonton," he said levelly.

"No it isn't. Just being in the same arcology as Banneth is dangerous. Govcentral should never have opened the vac-trains to Edmonton again."

"I can get my hands on the kind of weapon which the Liberation army is using on Mortonridge. They're proven against the possessed. That puts the odds back in our favour."

She gave him a long look, puzzled by his attitude. "It's like you want me to go."

"All I'm doing is explaining the options to you, Louise. We agreed before that I know most of the ground rules in this arena, didn't we. This kind of mission is well inside my expertise."

Maybe it was his sheer presence, or just his intimidating size, but Louise certainly felt a lot safer with the detective around. And everything he said did sound plausible.

She propped her forehead up against a hand, surprised to find she was perspiring. "If we go, and I don't like what we find at Banneth's home, then I'm not going in to meet her."

Ivanov smiled gently. "If it's so bad that even you can see it's wrong, I won't let you go in."

Louise nodded slowly. "All right. I'll go and fetch Gen. Can you book us some tickets?"

"Sure. There's a vac-train in thirty minutes. We can be at Kings Cross by then."

She climbed to her feet, dismayed at how tired she'd become.

"Oh, and Louise? Appropriate clothing please."

The AI picked up the deluge of telltale glitches a few seconds before frantic citizens started to bombard Edmonton's police with emergency datavises about the army of the dead that had risen to march through the centre of the dome. It was mid-afternoon, and the sun shone down brightly from an admirable storm-free sky, illuminating the scene perfectly. Cars and metro buses performed emergency braking manoeuvres as their motors jammed and power cells failed. Their occupants spilled out, sprinting away from the advancing possessed and sect acolytes. Pedestrians hammered against closed doors, desperate for admission.

Quinn had spent most of the afternoon carefully positioning his minions along the four main roads leading to the sect's headquarters. Ordinary acolytes were easy: dividing them into pairs or threes, designating cafes and shops where they should wait, keeping their weapons out of sight in bags or backpacks. The possessed were more difficult; he had to identify deserted offices or empty ground-floor apartments for them. A couple of non-possessed acolytes who'd been given basic didactic electronics courses would break in and deactivate any processors they found, leaving it safe for the possessed to wait inside. It had taken two hours to get everyone into position. None of them complained, at least not to his face. They all accepted that it was part of some grand strategy to bring about his Night. The only thing standing in their way, he told them, was the sect headquarters and the traitors inside.

With every possessed in Edmonton assembled (except one, Quinn thought glumly), Quinn had given the order to advance. If the supercops were as good as he suspected, then the response would be swift and effective. None of the possessed, and few acolytes, would survive.

Quinn walked the first few paces with his small doomed army as they flooded out into the streets, pulling out their weapons and taking on a variety of gruesome appearances. Once everyone was committed, he discreetly slipped away into the ghost realm.

Those civilians lucky enough to be behind the possessed when they emerged slowed their retreat and glanced nervously over their shoulders. The more commercially minded among them contacted local media offices and began to relay sensevises. Anyone receiving the show was presented with an astonishing display of defiance; the deliberate flaunting of a prowess which even the possessed could never truly own. A magnificent final charade, blowing their cover in a single grand *fuck you* gesture. Entire offices of editorial staff froze in slack-jawed amazement at what they were witnessing.

The marchers closed swiftly on the unexceptional fifty-storey skyscraper. There were over a hundred in each of the groups, spearheaded by the possessed. Elaborate, archaic warrior costumes sparked and flashed, ripe with energistic power. Whenever they passed the pillars which supported elevated roads, the air would seethe with wrestling coils of miniature lightning bolts, grounding out through the metal amid jitteriness spumes of molten droplets. Following close behind their silent deadly leaders, the bulk of each group was made up by the non-possessed acolytes; striding along blithely, weighed down by the largest pieces of weapons hardware the covens had stashed away in their secret armouries.

None of them paid any attention to the whimpering civilians scampering out of their way, they were focused on the skyscraper alone. Vehicles littering the street ahead of them flared electric-blue before bursting apart into a sleet of black granules. The army of the damned walked through the smouldering wreckage. Again, it was all panache. Showtime.

To the majority of Edmonton's citizens, the skyscraper that was the centre of their wrath was just a modest, ordinary building divided into standard commercial and residential sections. The police knew different, as did most of the locals. Rumours of the sect presence inside began to filter back to the media anchors. But by then professional rover reporters were on the scene, watching the police seal off the area and armed squads take up position.

Sixty per cent of Earth's population was now on-line, waiting for the shoot out. The greatest audience in history.

Inside the sect headquarters, the senior acolytes broke open the armoury and began handing out heavy-calibre chemical projectile rifles and machine guns to the acolytes. There was little panic; the beleaguered sect members were almost glad they had a tangible enemy at last. Banneth herself supervised setting up their defences. First she established a ring of snipers peeking through the skyscraper's windows, then consolidated their heavier firepower around the convoluted barriers inside.

She hurried round all of them, issuing orders and offering encouragement—never threats, not now. Quinn and the possessed had become the new fear-figures. It was interesting that they had now returned to her. After all Quinn had done to fill them with doubt and mistrust, the random tortures and deaths he had silently enacted throughout the headquarters had come to nothing in the end. They still believed that she was the stronger of the two.

You realize this is probably a diversion, don't you? she asked. **He's most likely planning to snatch me or kill me in the battle.**

Possibly, Western Europe replied equitably. **Personally, I believe this pathetic conflict he's staging is purely a case of collateral slaughter while he achieves his real goal: escaping from our grasp.**

Thanks. That makes me feel a lot better.

Frightened? You?

Wouldn't you be?

If I was physically in your position, no doubt I would, yes. But I'm not, am I?

Don't give me that natural superiority crap.

I apologise.

Very magnanimous. Does that mean you've got the SD platforms zeroed in on me?

I'm afraid so, yes. Again, I doubt if we'll have to use them. Quinn won't reveal himself, not today.

Banneth took a look along the familiar darkened corridors of the headquarters as she made her way back to her own rooms. On her orders, they were lit with candles and crude chemical batteries powering low-voltage halogen bulbs—technology the possessed would be unable to glitch without considerable effort. Not that it particularly mattered, she thought, we're not protecting anything we can salvage. After this, the headquarters would be no more. All her acolytes were doing was fighting a delaying action until the police and B7 eliminated Quinn's ersatz invasion. But then, the sect was nothing more than a B7 creation anyway. A convenient umbrella for them and her.

She walked through the temple giving it a nostalgic look. The first rocket hit the skyscraper; a light EE tipped anti-armour missile. Duffy fired it; Quinn had given him the honour of opening the fighting as a reward for unswerving loyalty to the cause of Night. The explosion sent shockwaves yammering through the skyscraper's structure, blowing out a huge crater on the northern corner and shattering hundreds of surrounding windows. Huge lumps of rubble cascaded down onto the street to smash apart in front of the possessed. The surviving snipers inside picked themselves up and opened fire.

The vac-train carriage had seating for a hundred. Louise, Genevieve, and Ivanov Robson were the only people using it. In fact, Louise had only seen a dozen or so people milling about on the platform at King's Cross when they got on. She wasn't sure if they were passengers or station staff.

Despite her growing uncertainty, and Gen's sulky resentment, she'd followed the private detective in through the airlock door. Even now there was something about him that reassured her. Even beyond physical size, he had a self-confidence greater than Joshua. Which was saying a lot. She settled back with dreamy thoughts of her fiancé filling her mind. Although the seats were worn, they were comfortable; and her alcohol suppresser program was off. Joshua had such a warm smile, she remembered. It would be so nice to have it shine on her again.

"I love you, and I'm coming back for you." His words.

Spoken to her when they were naked and alone, their bodies clinging together. A promise that could be nothing but totally honest.

I *will* find him again, despite all this horrid mess.

Her news hound program alerted her to the situation developing in Edmonton. She went through Time Universe to access a sensevise of the fight. And there she was, crouched behind one of the abandoned buses, peering cautiously round the front at the crazy army marching along the street. Dazzling white fireballs were pumping up from a dozen upstretched hands, smacking into the skyscraper. Flames were roaring out of windows and missile craters all the way up the first eight or nine stories. Heavy-calibre guns were firing down in retaliation, pummelling the carbon-concrete sidewalk with small intense topaz explosions. Several bodies were scattered along the street, clothes still smouldering from beam weapon scorches.

Figures began to race past the bus. Police in dark-grey armour suits, hauling even larger automatic guns than those in use up ahead. Their movements were arachnid, scuttling from cover to cover. They began to fire; the discharge from their weapons a continuous howl ripping into the delicate tissue of her inner ear. She started, hands halfway to her ears before the reporter's audio limiter program cut in. Then she was ducking down as multiple explosions ploughed up the street. White fireballs flew directly overhead.

Louise reduced the sensevise to monitor function, bundling it away until it became a vivid real-time memory. She looked at Ivanov. "Now what?" she asked. "They won't let this train into Edmonton now, will they? Surely?"

"They ought to. Access the overview commentary. The possessed are concentrated in one area, and the police have them contained. They've got enough firepower concentrated on them to exterminate ten times as many as there are on the ground. Besides, if we were being diverted, the train company would have told us immediately."

Louise accessed the carriage's processor, and requested a schedule update. It reported that they were going to arrive in Edmonton in forty-one minutes. "That doesn't make any sense. The authorities were paranoid about outbreaks before."

"It's politics. Edmonton is trying to prove they don't have a problem with the possessed; that they're on top of the situation."

"But—"

"I know. They should have waited until after this fight is over before any grand announcements. Being premature with the good news is hardly new for Govcentral. As soon as the Edmonton isolation was announced, a lot of highly connected lobbyists will have been called in to pressure the president's office and sympathetic senators to have the vac-train lines re-opened. If Edmonton is taken out of the global economic loop, all the companies in the arcology will start to fall behind their competitors; and an entire arcology is a huge market for outside companies to sell into; that's a factor, too."

"They're endangering people because of money?" Louise asked in astonishment. "That's awful."

"Welcome to Earth."

"Don't they understand what'll happen if the possessed get into other arcologies?"

"Of course they do. Now the possessed have been exposed in Edmonton, there'll be an equal amount of pressure applied to close the vac-trains down again. Action and reaction, Louise."

"You mean we might not get out after we arrive?"

"We will. There'll be enough time. I promised you: back home again in five hours. Remember?"

She glanced over at Gen, who was sleeping, curled up in the seat, her small face scowling even as she dreamed. "I remember." Not that there was much she could do about her worries now. The train was going to stop in the arcology. She hadn't felt this out of control since that first mad horse ride away from Cricklade the day Quinn Dexter appeared.

That the fight around the skyscraper would be uneven was never in doubt. Even so, the effectiveness of the police tactical team was impressive. Heavy-calibre portable weapons deployed by the front line were backed up by X-ray lasers from the rear support groups, far enough back to resist glitching by the possessed. As a consequence, very few possessed actually made it in to the skyscraper; and judging by the amount of gunfire coming from inside, the sect members weren't exactly a pushover. That was where the commercial sensevise coverage ended. B7 immediately switched to the surviving sensors in the headquarters, watching nervous, indistinct figures creeping along dark smoke-filled corridors. One of them walked over a grid with twenty thousand volts running through it. The body ignited into a pillar of flame hot enough to melt the concrete corridor around it.

"Well, that's a neat trick," Northern Europe said. "What kind of energy level is that, do you think?"

"Could be total chemical conversion," Central America suggested. "It can't be a direct mass energy reaction. That would eliminate the entire arcology."

"Hardly relevant," South Pacific said.

"On the contrary," Central America said. "The more we learn of their ability, the closer we come to defeating them."

"You can hardly classify their death throes as part of their ability."

"All information is useful," Western Europe said, deliberately bleeding a note of snobbery in to his representation's voice. "We wouldn't have had this kind of success without it."

"Success?" South Pacific pointed at the image above the conference table. The possessed had burnt out, leaving a human sculpture of ash standing amid the drizzle of molten carbon-concrete. It pitched over, disintegrating into a slush of grey flakes. "That's a success; Edmonton under siege from the possessed? May we please be preserved from your failures."

"By studying the data on Dexter we determined his likely course of action. I told you he'd betray the remaining possessed to us. This merely proves I was right all along."

"And Edmonton is not under siege," North America said. "The police tactical teams have the possessed surrounded."

"Wrong," South Pacific said. "That friend of Carter McBride won't be among this group. You haven't got him surrounded."

"He is not a threat to anyone other than Dexter," Western Europe said.

"Only in your book. As far as I'm concerned, nothing has changed. One invisible possessed and one elusive possessed are running round loose. Your territories remain embargoed."

"Thank heavens for that. We all know what would happen to Edmonton if you had any say in events over here."

"At least with my way only one arcology suffers. I can't believe you're willing to expose another to Dexter."

"You can't win at this level without taking risks. And I do intend to win. Dexter is the epitome of all we have fought against these last five hundred years. He is the yobbish anarchy that B7 has successfully banished from this world. I'll not have him return. The investment in blood and money it has cost us must be honoured."

"You sound like a third-rate Shakespearean king the night before battle. Damn, and you accuse me of arrogance."

*

Banneth walked back into her sanctum as the police tactical team searched through the rest of the sect headquarters for any possessed that might have survived the assault. She knew none had, but it wasn't her place to interfere. The North American supervisor had given the police commissioner instructions that she was to be left alone, along with her suite of rooms. Senior officers had taken up position outside the doors to enforce the order in case any of the tactical team turned bolshie. People hyped high on adrenaline after a fight were liable to have a healthy disregard for authority, especially where the possessed were concerned.

The rest of the sect, those that had survived, weren't so fortunate. Police officers, while sympathetic to their erstwhile allies, were disarming and cuffing them. The temple was proving a popular viewing point for awed, angry officers. Quinn's last two victims were still in there on show. And when the forensic crew got to work they'd find an awful lot of DNA samples around the altar and in the drains. It was going to be a busy night down at Edmonton's justice hall.

The sanctum was a wreck. A couple of lights had survived when the ceiling cracked open, hanging on their cables, spinning slowly round and round. Clear fluid from the life support canisters sloshed over Banneth's shoes, several centimetres deep and tinged with blood. Most of the canisters had been smashed, spilling their bizarre occupants on to the floor. Their tubules had invariably torn out, depriving them of the vital chemicals she was feeding into them, leaving the poor creatures to flop their limbs (those that had any) feebly until death overcame them. The organs and appendages that were simply being suspended until she found a use for them were ruined.

Banneth picked up the oil painting of Mary Shelley and tipped the broken glass out of its frame. Life-support fluid had discoloured the canvas quite badly. She stared at the author's drawn face for a moment, then sighed and cast the painting aside. "How poetic," she said quietly. Her suspicions about the sanctum were strengthening. There was an awful lot of damage considering it hadn't taken a direct hit. If the structural quakes and blastwaves from the explosions had been this powerful they ought to have brought down the entire skyscraper.

Louise Kavanagh has arrived, Western Europe said. **Please stick to the scenario we worked out.**

Sure. She knew her rebelliousness was coming through. Not that it mattered. She certainly couldn't evade the supervisors. That was the bargain she'd shaken on all those years ago. Not that she'd ever suspected it would come to this: a suicide bait. But when you sign in blood, you must expect the devil to write the small print in his favour.

Go down to one of the lower floors, Western Europe said. **I don't want Louise to see your little dungeon of horrors. It's important she isn't upset by you.**

Banneth hesitated. Her legs quivered, a pointed reminder of what this particular affinity bond was capable of. If she refused, they would simply take her over and puppet her body.

Okay, God's Brother I'm doing it. Just don't expect me to smile and say thanks. She turned slowly, gazing carefully round the ruins. One last nostalgic look. A cool breeze drifted against her cheek, causing the dangling lights to sway as they spun. The door was shut.

Is something the matter? North America asked.

No, she said, then relented. They could pick up on her emotional state easily enough through affinity. **Possibly. I think he might be in here with me right now. I have the feeling I'm being watched. It's the spookiest thing.** She projected a starched ironic smile.

Call out, Western Europe said excitedly. **Challenge him.**

**Provoke him. Something. See if you can get him to ma-
terialize. We only need a second.**

"Quinn? Is that you, my little darling? Are you here at
last?" Banneth put out a hand and stroked the central table,
fingers lingering on the straps. "Have you come home to me?
You're not afraid are you, my darling? I made you better than
that. Remember that beautiful pain that birthed you. I
cleansed you of fear amid that pain so you could serve God's
Brother properly. And you have, haven't you. How you've
grown since I banished you. The very messiah of darkness,
now. That's what you claim, isn't it. But can you do what you
claim, or have you become flawed? I can correct that, Quinn,
I can make you whole again. Submit to me. Return to me,
and I'll love you in that very special way. Our way. Just like
before." She held up the strap invitingly.

Quinn trembled in fury. He wanted to take her there and
then. Every word she spoke, each mocking syllable teased
out the memories of what she'd done to him. This room had
been the place where the real violations had been performed.
His screaming and her silken laughter mingling long into the
nights. The urge to reverse those acts made his serpent beast
howl in torment as he denied himself. *She* should be the one
bound by those straps. He should be the one standing over
the table.

His hands reached out to her, ready to caress and crush.

An annoyed frown creased her face, verging on petulance.
"It's no good," she muttered. "The little prick can't hear me."

Quinn leaned closer, puzzled. It was as though she was
talking to someone.

Banneth came to a decision, and strode out of the door,
anger evident in every tense muscle and furious grimace. Her
mind-tone was sullen and extremely fearful. It was similar to
those Quinn had perceived in his sacrificial victims. He followed her as she stomped through the headquarters. Two police officers fell in beside her, escorting her down the stairs.

More proof of the treachery she had indulged in at the expense of God's Brother. As if he needed more.

They came to an office below the headquarters edifice itself. The place belonged to an alcohol wholesaler, one of the sect's commercial fronts. And Quinn received the biggest shock of all since he'd returned to Earth. The Kavanagh sisters were there, waiting for Banneth.

Louise was amazed to find they'd arrived at the skyscraper featured on the news sensevise. It did make her wonder about Ivanov Robson, though. For a start, there was something very odd about the way he was always right about things. And then there was this "contact" he had inside the Edmonton police division. She could believe that he'd worked with police departments before, and no doubt a few favours were owed on both sides. But to pass so effortlessly through the cordon of armed police around the skyscraper was hard to credit.

Nonetheless, the major in charge of the tactical squad had been waiting to greet them when their taxi pulled up fifty metres short from the rear of the buzzing crowd. Now it was safe, thousands of Edmonton's ordinary citizens had flocked in to soak up whatever was left of the drama. Rover reporters and several district councillors formed the inner wall, pressing against the barriers, shouting and datavising the line of implacable police for snatches of information, or pleading to be allowed just that fraction closer than their rivals.

Six tactical team officers fell in around Louise's party and cleared their way through the tightly packed crowd. Inside the barriers, the fire department was doing most of the work. Hoses snaked away from large tenders, trailing down from mechanoids that were scampering across the vertical walls of the skyscraper, extinguishing the last of the fires. The police were concerned only in bundling the surviving combatants from both sides into secure trucks so they could be driven away to the justice hall. One of them, a girl younger than Louise, was sobbing hysterically, kicking and bucking violently as four officers carried her to a waiting truck. She screamed: "The messiah lives! His Night will claim you all!" as they flung her unceremoniously inside.

Just as they were going in through the main entrance, three fully grown pigs rampaged out, squealing and grunting as they raced down the broken stairs towards the street. Sweating, angry officers chased after them. Louise simply stood aside and let them go past; it was one of today's milder insanities.

The major led them inside. Fire and explosions had wrecked the lobby. Water and foam from the fire mechanoids was pooling underfoot. Lighting came from temporary rigs set up at strategic corners. None of the lifts or escalators were working. They went up four flights of stairs before being shown into some kind of office that had escaped any serious damage. Despite the fires, Louise felt chilly. The major left them, and a strange-looking woman walked in.

At first Louise wasn't entirely sure she was a woman. Her jaw was strong enough to be male, although her feminine figure countered the argument. And the way she walked, straightforward easy strides, that was masculine, too. The oddest feature was her eyes with their pink irises. When she looked at Louise, there was no hint of what she was thinking.

"I don't know who you people are," Banneth said. "But you must have a lot of clout to get in here right now." She stared at Genevieve. For the first time her face betrayed an emotion. "Very strange," she muttered in puzzlement.

"I have contacts," Ivanov said modestly.

"I'm sure you do."

"My name is Louise Kavanagh. I called you earlier, about Quinn Dexter. Do you remember?"

"Yes. I remember."

"I think he may have done all this; or at least sent people to do it. He told me he was coming back to Earth to get you. I did try and warn you."

Banneth's gaze remained on Genevieve, who was fingering her pendant. "So you did. My mistake for not listening. Although as you can imagine, I have good reason to be sceptical. Quinn was deported. I didn't expect to see him again."

"He really hated you. What did you do to him?"

"We had several disagreements. As you might have guessed, my occupation is outside the mainstream. I earn a living by supplying certain items to people, which cannot be bought through normal commercial channels. It's an activity which has brought me into conflict with the police on several occasions. Dear Quinn was one of my couriers. And he rather stupidly got caught. That was the reason he was deported, in fact. I expect he blames me for his sentence. I didn't contribute to his defence; at the time I was using my contacts to protect myself. His incompetence landed me in a very difficult legal situation. So you see, the antipathy is mutual."

"I'm sure it is," Louise said. "But he's a possessed now, one of the strongest. That makes him very dangerous, especially to you."

Banneth gestured round. "I'm beginning to appreciate that. Though I'm curious, why are you, someone I've never met before, interested in saving me? I guarantee, I really am someone a nice girl like you wouldn't want to meet."

Louise was beginning to ask herself the same thing. Banneth was nothing like the image in her mind; she'd been expecting a slightly older version of herself: innocent and bewildered. Not this cold, criminal woman, whose every gesture and syllable was rich with disdain. "He was obsessed with you, and people need to be warned what he's capable of.

I'm frightened that once he's murdered you, he'll do to Earth what he did to Norfolk. That was my home planet, you see."

"How very noble and unselfish of you, Louise. Behaviour no one on this planet is remotely accustomed to. Not in this day and age." She arched an eyebrow at Ivanov. "So what do you suggest I do now?"

"I'm not sure," Louise said. "I just had to deliver the warning, I promised myself that. I didn't really think about afterwards. Can you convince the police to give you a twenty-four hour guard?"

"I expect that if I told them a possessed was hunting me, they'd probably show Quinn where I was, and laugh at lot while they were doing it. I've used up every contact and legal resource I had merely to avoid getting arrested for the crime of being in the same building he attacked."

"Then you'll have to leave."

"I can see this means a lot to you. But the police have killed every possessed involved in the attack. I wouldn't worry. Quinn Dexter's soul is back where it belongs, suffering badly in the beyond."

"You don't know that," Louise insisted. "If any of them survived, it'll be him. At least leave here until the police confirm there are no more possessed left in Edmonton. If they didn't get him, he'll come after you again. I know he will. He told me. Killing you is a filthy obsession with him."

Banneth nodded. Reluctantly, Louise considered, as if there was something demeaning in taking advice from her. What horrible snobbery. To think of everything I risked in coming to her aid, not to mention the money it's cost. Not even Fletcher would have bothered if he'd known how awful she is.

"I suppose there's no harm in playing it safe," Banneth said. "Unfortunately, Quinn knows all my associates and safe houses here in the arcology." She paused. "The vac-trains are open to half of Europe and most of North America; though the rest of the world seems more sceptical about Edmonton's assurances. Good for them."

"We're going back to London this evening," Ivanov Robson said. "Do you know anyone there you can stay with?"

"Like you, I have contacts."

"Okay, I can arrange for a police tactical team to escort us back to the station. But once we get to London, you're on your own."

Banneth gave an indifferent shrug.

Quinn watched the entire scene play out, resisting the impulse to interfere at Banneth's petty lies. He was captivated, not just by what was said, but the emotional content behind the words. Louise backed every word she spoke with intense fervour. Banneth was her usual serene, egotistical self, a state she shared with the husky private detective (which made Quinn highly suspicious of him). It was pure theatre. It had to be. Yet it must be a paradox. Louise Kavanagh had no script, no coaching; she believed what she was saying, that she had some higher mission to save Banneth from him. That couldn't be forged. The entire thing must have been orchestrated by the supercops.

For whose benefit? That was the really unnerving part.

There was no possible way Louise could have found Banneth unless the High Magus wanted her to. The girl must have been steered here by the supercops for one reason, to get Banneth out of Edmonton. Yet Banneth was part of the supercop set-up, she didn't need Louise to tell her where to go. It didn't make any sense.

One thing he couldn't ignore, the vac-trains were running again. Though that might be the trap, the reason for this charade. To snare him on the ocean bed halfway between continents; even he couldn't get out of that. But how would they know if he was on board a specific train?

He followed the group out of the office and down the stairs, not really paying much attention. His mind was savaging the possibilities. If they could detect me when I'm in this realm, they would have done everything they could to destroy me. That means they can't. So this must be a ploy to lure me out. The supercops know I want Banneth, so they're using her as bait. The vac-train isn't the trap; wherever she goes in London is their kill arena. And that's where they'll be: this planet's strongest, most subtle line of defence against His Night.

Quinn smiled lustily and increased the speed of his gliding walk through the ghost realm, determined not to let Louise and her party out of his sight. After so many false starts, the true Armageddon was beginning.

TIMELINE

2020 . . . Cavius base established. Mining of Lunar sub-crustal resources starts.

2037 . . . Beginning of large-scale geneering on humans; improvement to immunology system, eradication of appendix, organ efficiency increased.

2041 . . . First deuterium-fuelled fusion stations built; inefficient and expensive.

2044 . . . Christian reunification.

2047 . . . First asteroid capture mission. Beginning of Earth's O'Neill Halo.

2049 . . . Quasi-sentient bitek animals employed as servitors.

2055 . . . Jupiter mission.

2055 . . . Lunar cities granted independence from founding companies.

2057 . . . Ceres asteroid settlement founded.

2058 . . . Affinity symbiont neurons developed by Wing-Tsit Chong, providing control over animals and bitek constructs.

2064 . . . Multinational industrial consortium (Jovian Sky Power Corporation) begins mining Jupiter's atmosphere for He_3 using aerostat factories.

2064 . . . Islamic secular unification.

2067 . . . Fusian stations begin to use He$_3$ as fuel.

2069 . . . Affinity bond gene spliced into human DNA.

2075 . . . JSKP germinates Eden, a bitek habitat in orbit around Jupiter, with UN Protectorate status.

2077 . . . New Kong asteroid begins FTL stardrive research project.

2085 . . . Eden opened for habitation.

2086 . . . Habitat Pallas germinated in Jupiter orbit.

2090 . . . Wing-Tsit Chong dies, and transfers memories to Eden's neural strata. Start of Edenist culture. Eden and Pallas declare independence from UN. Launch buyout of JSKP shares. Pope Eleanor excommunicates all Christians with affinity gene. Exodus of affinity capable humans to Eden. Effective end of bitek industry on Earth.

2091 . . . Lunar referendum to terraform Mars.

2094 . . . Edenists begin exowomb breeding programme coupled with extensive geneering improvement to embroyos, tripling their population over a decade.

2103 . . . Earth's national governments consolidate into Govcentral.

2103 . . . Thoth base established on Mars.

2107 . . . Govcentral jurisdiction extended to cover O'Neill Halo.

2115 . . . First instantaneous translation by New Kong spaceship, Earth to Mars.

2118 . . . Mission to Proxima Centauri.

2123 . . . Terracompatible planet found at Ross 154.

2125 . . . Ross 154 planet named Felicity, first multiethnic colonists arrive.

2125–2130 . . . Four new terracompatible planets discovered. Multiethnic colonies founded.

2131 . . . Edenists germinate Perseus in orbit around Ross 154 gas giant, begin He$_3$ mining.

2131–2205 . . . One hundred and thirty terracompatible planets discovered. Massive starship building programme initiated in O'Neill Halo. Govcentral begins large-scale enforced outshipment of surplus population, rising to 2 million a week in 2160: Great Dispersal. Civil conflict on some early multiethnic colonies. Individual Govcentral states sponsor ethnic-streaming colonies. Edenists expand their He$_3$ mining enterprise to every inhabited star system with a gas giant.

2139 . . . Asteroid Braun impacts on Mars.

2180 . . . First orbital tower built on Earth.

2205 . . . Antimatter production station built in orbit around sun by Govcentral in an attempt to break the Edenist energy monopoly.

2208 . . . First antimatter-drive starships operational.

2210 . . . Richard Saldana transports all of New Kong's industrial facilities from the O'Neill Halo to an asteroid orbiting Kulu. He claims independence for the Kulu star system, founds Christian-only colony, and begins to mine He$_3$ from the system's gas giant.

2218 . . . First voidhawk gestated, a bitek starship designed by Edenists.

2225 . . . Establishment of a hundred voidhawk families. Habitats Romulus and Remus germinated in Saturn orbit to serve as voidhawk bases.

2232 . . . Conflict at Jupiter's trailing Trojan asteroid cluster between belt alliance ships and an O'Neill Halo company hydrocarbon refinery. Antimatter used as a weapon; twenty-seven thousand people killed.

2238 . . . Treaty of Deimos; outlaws production and use of antimatter in the Sol system; signed by Govcentral, Lunar nation, asteroid alliance, and Edenists. Antimatter stations abandoned and dismantled.

2240 . . . Coronation of Gerrald Saldana as King of Kulu. Foundation of Saldana dynasty.

2267–2270 . . . Eight separate skirmishes involving use of antimatter among colony worlds. Thirteen million killed.

2271 ... Avon summit between all planetary leaders. Treaty of Avon, banning the manufacture and use of antimatter throughout inhabited space. Formation of Human Confederation to police agreement. Construction of Confederation Navy begins.

2300 ... Confederation expanded to include Edenists.

2301 ... First Contact. Jiciro race discovered, a pre-technology civilization. System quarantined by Confederation to avoid cultural contamination.

2310 ... First ice asteroid impact on Mars.

2330 ... First blackhawks gestated at Valisk, independent habitat.

2350 ... War between Novska and Hilversum. Novska bombed with antimatter. Confederation Navy prevents retaliatory strike against Hilversum.

2356 ... Kiint homeworld discovered.

2357 ... Kiint join Confederation as "observers."

2360 ... A voidhawk scout discovers Atlantis.

2371 ... Edenists colonize Atlantis.

2395 ... Tyrathca colony world discovered.

2402 ... Tyrathca join Confederation.

2420 ... Kulu scoutship discovers Ruin Ring.

2428 ... Bitek habitat Tranquillity germinated by Crown Prince Michael Saldana, orbiting above Ruin Ring.

2432 ... Prince Michael's son, Maurice, geneered with affinity. Kulu abdication crisis. Coronation of Lukas Saldana. Prince Michael exiled.

2550 ... Mars declared habitable by Terraforming office.

2580 ... Dorado asteroids discovered around Tunja, claimed by both Garissa and Omuta.

2581 ... Omuta mercenary fleet drops twelve antimatter planet-busters on Garissa, planet rendered uninhabitable. Confederation imposes thirty-year sanction against Omuta, prohibiting any interstellar trade or transport. Blockade enforced by Confederation Navy.

2582 ... Colony established on Lalonde.

THE NIGHT'S DAWN SERIES CONCLUDES IN

THE NAKED GOD

PART 2: FAITH

On Earth, satanist Quinn Dexter possesses a new army of the damned, using them to initiate The Night's Dawn, the entropic annihilation of all Creation. At the same time Joshua Calvert, master of the Lady Macbeth, seeks a miracle in a haystack: the truth behind a legend that 15,000 years ago the alien Tyrathca intercepted a single message from unexplored space beyond Orion: "IT SEES THE UNIVERSE. IT CONTROLS EVERYTHING. OUR ARRIVAL WOKE IT."

Could a God be sleeping somewhere between the stars? And can Joshua possibly find this unknown Deity before The Night's Dawn devours the cosmos?

coming in December 2000
from Warner Aspect

(0-446-60518-2, $6.99 U.S./$9.99 Can.)

1151